THE DIAMOND CHARIOT

By the same author

The Winter Queen
Leviathan
Turkish Gambit
The Death of Achilles
Special Assignments
The State Counsellor
The Coronation
She Lover of Death
He Lover of Death

Pelagia and the White Bulldog
Pelagia and the Black Monk
Pelagia and the Red Rooster

THE DIAMOND CHARIOT

*The Further Adventures
of Erast Fandorin*

BORIS AKUNIN

Translated by Andrew Bromfield

Weidenfeld & Nicolson

LONDON

First published in Great Britain in 2011
by Weidenfeld & Nicolson.
An imprint of the Orion Publishing Group
Orion House, 5 Upper St Martin's Lane, London WC2H 9EA

An Hachette UK Company

First published in Russian by Zakharov Publications,
Moscow, Russia and Edizioni Frassinelli, Milan, Italy.

Published by arrangement with Linda Michaels Limited,
International Literary Agents

A CIP catalogue record for this book is available
from the British Library

ISBN 978 0 297 86067 9 (cased)

Typeset by Input Data Services Ltd, Bridgwater, Somerset

Printed in Great Britain by Clays Ltd, St Ives Plc

The Orion Publishing Group's policy is to use papers that
are natural, renewable and recyclable products and made
from wood grown in sustainable forests. The logging and
manufacturing processes are expected to conform to
the environmental regulations of the country of origin.

www.orionbooks.co.uk

CONTENTS

Dragonfly-Catcher

KAMI-NO-KU

NAKA-NO-KU

SHIMO-NO-KU

THE DIAMOND CHARIOT

In Two Books

Book 1: Dragonfly-Catcher

Book 2: Between the Lines

BOOK 1

DRAGONFLY-CATCHER

Russia, 1905

KAMI-NO-KU

**The first syllable,
which has a certain
connection with the East**

On the very day when the appalling rout and destruction of the Russian fleet near the island of Tsushima was approaching its end and the first vague and alarming rumours of this bloody Japanese triumph were sweeping across Europe – on that very day, Staff Captain Vasilii Alexandrovich Rybnikov, who lived on a small street with no name in the St Petersburg district of Peski, received the following telegram from Irkutsk: 'Dispatch sheets immediately watch over patient pay expenses'.

Thereupon Staff Captain Rybnikov informed the landlady of his apartment that business would take him to St Petersburg for a day or two and she should not, therefore, be alarmed by his absence. Then he dressed, left the house and never went back there again.

Initially Vasilii Alexandrovich's day proceeded entirely as usual – that is, in a bustle of ceaseless activity. After first riding to the centre of the city in a horse cab, he continued his peregrinations exclusively on foot and, despite his limp (the staff captain dragged one foot quite noticeably), he managed to visit an incredible number of places.

He started with the Major General Commandant's Office, where he sought out a clerk from the transport accounts section and returned with a solemn air one rouble, borrowed from the clerk two days previously. Then he called into the Cossack Forces Directorate on Simeonovskaya Square, to enquire about a petition he had submitted two months ago, which had got bogged down in red tape. From there he moved on to the Military Department of Railways – he had been trying for a long time to obtain a position as an archivist in the drafting office there. On that day his small, fidgety figure was also seen in the Office of the Inspector General of Artillery on Zakharievskaya Street, and the Office of Repairs on Morskaya Street, and even at the Committee for the Wounded on Kirochnaya Street (Rybnikov had been attempting without any success to obtain an official note concerning a concussion suffered at Luoyang).

The agile army man managed to show his face everywhere. Clerks in offices nodded offhandedly to their old acquaintance and quickly turned away, immersing themselves, with an emphatically preoccupied air, in their documents and conversations about work. They knew from experience that once the staff captain latched on to someone, he could worry the life out of them.

Vasilii Alexandrovich turned his short-cropped head this way and that for a while, sniffing with his plum-shaped nose as he selected his victim. Having chosen, he seated himself unceremoniously right there on the victim's desk and started swaying one foot in a shabby boot, waving his arms around and spouting all sorts of drivel: about the imminent victory over the Japanese macaques, his own heroic war exploits, the high cost of living in the capital. They couldn't just tell him to go to hell – after all, he was an officer, and he'd been wounded at Mukden. They poured Rybnikov tea, regaled him with *papiroses*, answered his gormless questions and dispatched him with all possible haste to some other section, where the whole business was repeated all over again.

Between two and three o'clock in the afternoon, the staff captain, who had called into the office of the St Petersburg Arsenal on a procurement matter, suddenly glanced at his wristwatch with the mirror bright glass (everyone had heard the story of this chronometer at least a thousand times – it had supposedly been presented to him by a captured Japanese marquis) and became terribly agitated. Blinking his yellowish-brown eyes at the two shipping clerks, who by now were completely exhausted by his gabbling, he told them:

'Well, that was a great chat. I'm sorry, but I have to leave you now. *Entre nous*, an assignation with a lovely lady. The fever-heat of passion and all that. As the Jappos say, strike while the iron's hot.'

He gave a brief snort of laughter and took his leave.

'What a character,' said the first shipping clerk, a young warrant officer. 'But even he's managed to find himself some woman or other.'

'He's lying, just talking big,' the second clerk said reassuringly – he held the same rank, but was much older. 'Who could ever be seduced by an old Marlborough like that?'

The worldly-wise shipping clerk was right. In the apartment on Nad-ezhdinskaya Square, to which Rybnikov made his way via a long, roundabout route through connecting courtyards, the staff captain was not met by a lovely lady, but a young man in a speckled jacket.

'What on earth took you so long?' the young man exclaimed nervously when he opened the door at the prearranged knock (twice, then three times, then a pause and twice again). 'You're Rybnikov, right? I've been waiting forty minutes for you!'

'I had to weave around a bit. Thought I saw something ...' replied Vasilii Alexandrovich, sauntering round the tiny apartment and even looking into the toilet and outside the back door. 'Did you bring it? Let me have it.'

'Here, from Paris. You know, I was ordered not to come straight to Petersburg, but go via Moscow, so that . . .'

'I know,' the staff captain interrupted before he could finish, taking the two envelopes – one quite thick, the other very slim.

'Crossing the border was really easy, incredibly easy, in fact. They didn't even glance at my suitcase, never mind tap it for secret compartments. But the reception I got in Moscow was strange. That Thrush person wasn't exactly polite,' declared the speckled young man, who obviously wanted very much to have a chat. 'After all, I am risking my own head, and I have a right to expect . . .'

'Goodbye,' Vasilii Alexandrovich interrupted him again after examining both envelopes and even feeling along their seams with his fingers. 'Don't leave straight after me. Stay here for at least an hour, then you can go.'

Stepping out of the entrance, the staff captain turned his head left and right, lit up a *papirosa* and set off along the street with his usual gait – jerky, yet surprisingly brisk. An electric tram went rattling past. Rybnikov suddenly stepped off the pavement into the road, broke into a run and leapt nimbly up on to the platform.

'Now then, sir,' the conductor said with a reproachful shake of his head. 'Only the young shavers do that sort of thing. What if you'd come a cropper there? With that gammy leg of yours.'

'Never mind,' Rybnikov replied brightly. 'What's that the Russian soldiers say? A chestful of medals or your head in the bushes. And if I get killed, that's all right. I'm an orphan, there's no one to cry over me . . . No thanks, friend, I just hopped on for a minute,' he continued, waving aside the ticket, and a minute later he jumped down on to the road in the same boyish fashion.

He dodged a horse cab, darted in front of the radiator of an automobile that started bellowing hysterically with its horn, and limped nimbly into a side street.

It was completely deserted there – no carriages, no pedestrians. The staff captain opened both envelopes. He glanced briefly into the thick one, saw the respectful form of address and regular rows of neatly inscribed hiero-glyphs and put off reading it all until later – he slipped it into his pocket. But the second letter, written in a hasty cursive hand, engrossed Rybnikov's attention completely.

The letter said this:

My dear son! I am pleased with you, but now the time has come to strike a decisive blow – this time not at the Russian rear line, and not even at the Russian army, but at Russia itself. Our forces have accomplished all that they can, but they are bled dry and the might of our industry is waning. Alas, Time is not on our side. Your task is to ensure that Time will no longer be an ally of the Russians. The tsar's throne must be made to totter beneath him. Our friend Colonel A. has completed his preparatory work. Your task is to deliver the shipment, which he has dispatched to Moscow, to the consignee, whom you already know. Tell him to hurry. We cannot hold out for longer than three or four months.

One more thing. We badly need an act of sabotage on the main railway line. Any interruption in supplies to Linevich's army will help stave off imminent disaster. You wrote that you had been thinking about this and you had some ideas. Put them into action, the time has come.

I know that what I ask of you is almost impossible. But were you not taught: 'The almost impossible is possible'?

Your mother asked me to tell you she is praying for you.

After he had read the letter, Rybnikov's high-cheekboned face betrayed no sign of emotion. He struck a match, lit the sheet of paper and the envelope, dropped them on the ground and pulverised the ashes with his heel. He walked on.

The second missive was from Colonel Akashi, a military agent in Europe, and consisted almost entirely of numbers and dates. The staff captain ran his eyes over it and didn't bother to read it again – Vasilii Alexandrovich had an exceptionally good memory.

He lit another match and, while the paper was burning, glanced at his watch, lifting it almost right up to his nose.

There was an unpleasant surprise waiting for Rybnikov. The mirror-bright glass of the Japanese chronometer reflected the image of a man in a bowler hat with a walking cane. This gentleman was squatting down, inspecting something on the pavement, at the very spot where one minute earlier the staff captain had burned the letter from his father.

The letter didn't matter at all, it had been completely incinerated. What alarmed Vasilii Alexandrovich was something else. This wasn't the first time he had glanced into his cunning little piece of glass, and he hadn't seen anyone behind him before. Where had the man in the bowler hat come from? That was what concerned him.

Rybnikov walked on as if nothing had happened, glancing at his watch more frequently than before. However, once again there was no one behind him. The staff captain's black eyebrows arched up uneasily. The curious gentleman's disappearance concerned him even more than his sudden appearance.

Yawning, Rybnikov turned into a gated passage that led him into a deserted stone courtyard. He cast a glance at the windows (they were dead, untenanted) and then suddenly, no longer limping, he ran across to the wall separating this yard from the next one. The barrier was immensely high, but Vasilii Alexandrovich demonstrated quite fantastic springiness – vaulting almost seven feet into the air, he grabbed hold of the edge and pulled himself up. He could have jumped across the wall with no effort, but the staff captain contented himself with glancing over the top.

The next yard was residential. A skinny little girl was hopping over chalk marks scrawled across the asphalt. Another, even smaller, was standing nearby, watching.

Rybnikov did not climb over. He jumped down, ran back to the passage, unbuttoned his fly and started urinating.

He was surprised in this intimate act by the man with the bowler hat and cane, who came jogging into the passage.

The man stopped dead, frozen to the spot.

Vasilii Alexandrovich was embarrassed.

'Beg your pardon, I was desperate,' he said, shaking himself off and gesticulating at the same time with his free hand. 'It's all our swinish Russian ignorance, not enough public latrines. They say there are toilets on every corner in Japan. That's why we can't beat the damn monkeys.'

The expression on the hasty gentleman's face was wary but, seeing the staff captain smile, he also extended his lips slightly beneath his thick moustache.

'Take your samurai now, how does he fight?' said Rybnikov, continuing with his buffoonery, buttoning up his trousers and moving closer. 'Our soldier boys will fill the trench right up to the top with shit, but your samurai, that slanty-eyed freak, he stuffs himself full of rice, so he's got natural constipation. That way he can go a week without a crap. But then, when he's posted back to the rear, he's stuck on the crapper for two whole days.'

Delighted at his own wittiness, the staff captain broke into shrill laughter and, as if he was inviting the other man to share his merriment, prodded him lightly in the side with one finger.

The man with the moustache didn't laugh; instead he gave a strange kind of hiccup, clutched the left side of his chest and sat down on the ground.

'Oh, mother,' he said in a surprisingly thin little voice. And then again, quietly, 'Oh, mother . . .'

'What's wrong?' Rybnikov asked in sudden alarm, looking around. 'Heart spasm, is it? Oi-oi, that's really terrible! I'll be straight back. With a doctor! In just a jiffy!'

He ran out into the side street but, once there, decided not to hurry after all.

The staff captain's face assumed an intent expression. He swayed to and fro on his heels, thinking something through or trying to reach a decision, and turned back towards Nadezhdinskaya Street.

The second syllable,
in which two earthly vales
terminate abruptly

Evstratii Pavlovich Mylnikov, head of the surveillance service at the Department of Police, sketched a hammer and sickle inside a roundel, drew a bee on each side of it, a peaked cap above and a Latin motto below, on a ribbon: 'Zeal and Service'. He tilted his balding head sideways and admired his own handiwork.

He had composed the crest of the House of Mylnikov himself, investing it with profound meaning. As if to say: I'm not trying to sneak into the aristocracy, I'm not ashamed of my common origins: my father was a simple blacksmith (the hammer), my grandfather was a son of the soil (the sickle), but thanks to zeal (the bees) in the sovereign's service (the cap), I have risen high in accordance with my deserts.

Evstratii Mylnikov had been awarded the rights and privileges of the hereditary nobility the previous year, along with an Order of Vladimir, Third Class, but the College of Arms was still smothering the approval of the crest in red tape, still nitpicking. It had approved the hammer and sickle, and the bees, but baulked at the peaked cap – supposedly it looked too much like the coronet that was reserved for titled individuals.

In recent times Mylnikov had got into the habit, when he was in a thoughtful mood, of drawing this emblem so dear to his heart on a piece of paper. At first he couldn't get the bees right at all, but in time Evstratii Pavlovich got the hang of it so well that they were a real delight to look at. And now here he was again, diligently shading in the stripes on the toilers' abdomens, glancing every now and again at the pile of papers lying to the left of his elbow. The document that had plunged the court counsellor into a brown study was titled: 'Log of the surveillance of honorary citizen Andron Semyonov Komarovsky (alias 'Twitchy') in the city of St Petersburg on 15 May 1905'. The individual who called himself Komarovsky (there were compelling reasons to believe that his passport was false) had been handed on from the Moscow Department for the Defence of Public Security and Order (the Moscow Okhrana) 'with a view to establishing contact and communications'.

And now this.

The mark was taken over from an agent of the Moscow Flying Squad at 7.25 at the railway station. The accompanying agent (Detective Gnatiuk) stated that on the way Twitchy had not spoken with anyone and had only left his compartment to answer calls of nature.

Having taken over the mark, we followed him in two cabs to the Bunting Building on Nadezhdinskaya Street, where Twitchy walked up to the fourth floor, to apartment No. 7, from which he never emerged again. Apartment No. 7 is rented by a certain Zwilling, a resident of Helsingfors, who only appears here very rarely (according to the yard keeper the last time was at the beginning of winter).

At 12.38 the mark summoned the yard keeper with the bell. Agent Maximenko went up to him, disguised as the yard keeper. Twitchy gave him a rouble and told him to buy bread, salami and two bottles of beer. There was apparently no one in the flat apart from him.

When he brought the order, Maximenko was given the change (17 kop.) as a tip. He observed that the mark was extremely nervous. As if he was waiting for someone or something.

At 3.15 an army officer who has been given the code name 'Kalmyk' appeared.

(A staff captain with the collar tabs of the Supply Department, a limp on his right leg, short, high cheekbones, black hair.)

He went up to apartment No. 7, but came down 4 minutes later and set off in the direction of Basseinaya Street. Agent Maximenko was dispatched to follow him.

Twitchy did not emerge from the entrance of the building. At 3.31 he walked over to the window and stood there, looking into the yard, then walked away.

At this moment Maximenko has still not returned.

I am presently (8 o'clock in the evening) handing over the surveillance detail to Senior Agent Goltz.

Sen. Agent Smurov

Short and clear, apparently.

Short enough, certainly, but damn all about it was clear.

An hour and a half ago Evstratii Pavlovich, having only just received the report cited above, also received a phone call from the police station on Basseinaya Street. He was informed that a man had been found dead in the courtyard of a building on Mitavsky Lane, with documents that identified him as Flying Squad agent Vasilii Maximenko. In less than ten minutes the court counsellor himself had arrived at the scene of the incident and ascertained that it really was Maximenko. There were absolutely no signs of violent death, nor any traces of a struggle or of any disorder in the agent's clothing. The highly experienced medical expert, Karl Stepanovich, had said immediately that all the signs indicated heart failure.

Well, of course, Mylnikov was upset for a while, he even shed a tear for the old comrade with whom he had served shoulder to shoulder for ten years – the number of scrapes they'd been through together! And, as a matter of fact, Vasilii had even been involved in the winning of the Order of Vladimir that had led to the genesis of a new noble line.

In May the previous year, a secret message had been received from the consul in Hong Kong, saying that four Japanese disguised as businessmen were making their way towards the Suez Canal – that is, to the city of Aden. Only they were not businessmen at all, but naval officers: two minelayers and two divers. They intended to place underwater bombs along the route of cruisers from the Black Sea Squadron that had been dispatched to the Far East.

Evstratii Pavlovich had taken six of his best agents, all of them genuine wolfhounds (including the now-deceased Maximenko), skipped across to Aden and there, in the bazaar, disguised as sailors on a spree, they had started a knife fight: they carved the Jappos to shreds and dumped their luggage in the bay. The cruisers had got through without a single hitch. True, those lousy macaques had smashed them to pieces afterwards anyway but, like they say, that wasn't down to us, was it?

This was the kind of colleague the state counsellor had lost. And not even in some rollicking adventure, but from a heart attack.

After giving instructions concerning the mortal remains, Mylnikov went back to his office on Fontanka Street and reread the report about Twitchy, and something started bothering him. He dispatched Lenka Zyablikov, a very bright young lad, to Nadezhdinskaya Street, to check Apartment No. 7.

And then what came up? Well, the old wolfhound's nose hadn't led him astray.

Zyablikov had phoned just ten minutes ago, talked about this and that, said how he'd dressed up as a plumber, and started ringing and knocking at No. 7 – no answer. Then he opened the door with a picklock.

Twitchy was dangling in a noose, by the window, from the curtain rail. All the signs indicated suicide: no bruises or abrasions, paper and a pencil on a chair, as if the man had been going to write a farewell note, but changed his mind.

Evstratii Pavlovich had listened to the agent's agitated jabbering and ordered him to wait for the group of experts to arrive, then sat down at the desk and started drawing the crest – to clear his mind and, even more importantly, to calm his nerves.

Just recently the court counsellor's nerves hadn't been worth a rotten damn. The medical diagnosis read: 'General neurasthenia resulting from excessive fatigue; enlargement of the pericardium; congestion of the lungs and partial damage to the spinal cord that might pose the threat of paralysis'. Paralysis! You had to pay for everything in this life, and the price was usually much higher than you expected.

So here he was, a hereditary nobleman, the head of a supremely important section in the Department of Police, with an annual salary of six thousand roubles – and never mind the salary, he had a budget of thirty thousand to use entirely at his own discretion, every functionary's dream. But without his health, what good was all the gold in the world to him now? Evstratii Pavlovich was tormented by insomnia every night, and if he ever did fall asleep, that was even worse: bad dreams, ghoulish visions, with the devil's work in them. He woke in a cold sweat, with his teeth chattering wildly. He kept thinking he could see something stirring repulsively in the corners and hear someone chuckling indistinctly, but derisively, or that 'someone' might suddenly start howling. In his sixth decade Mylnikov, the scourge of terrorists and foreign spies, had started sleeping with a lighted icon lamp. For the sanctity of it, and to keep away the darkness in the nooks and crannies. All those steep hills had nigh on knackered the old horse . . .

The previous year he had applied to retire – and why not, he had a bit of money put by, and a little homestead bought, in a fine area for mushrooms, out on the Gulf of Finland. And then this war happened. The head of the Special Section, the director of the Department and the minister himself had implored him: Don't betray us, Evstratii Pavlovich, don't abandon us in dangerous times like these. You can't refuse!

The court counsellor forced himself to focus his thoughts on more pressing matters. He tugged on his long Zaporozhian Cossack moustache, then drew two circles on the paper, a wavy line between them and a question mark up above.

Two little facts, each on its own more or less clear.

So, Maximenko had died, his overworked heart had given out under the stresses and strains of the service. It happened.

Honorary citizen Komarovsky, whoever the hell he was (the Moscow lads had picked up his trail the day before yesterday at a secret Socialist Revolutionary meeting place), had hanged himself. That happened with some neurasthenic revolutionaries too.

But for two existences that were to some degree interconnected, two, so to speak, intersecting earthly vales, both to be broken off abruptly and simultaneously? That was too queer by half. Evstratii Pavlovich had only the vaguest idea of what an earthly vale was, but he liked the sound of the words – he had often imagined himself wandering through life as just such a vale, narrow and tortuous, squeezed in between bleak, rocky cliffs.

Who was this Kalmyk? Why did he go to see Twitchy – on business or, perhaps, by mistake (he was only there for four minutes)? And what took Maximenko into a dead-end courtyard?

Oh, Mylnikov didn't like this Kalmyk at all. He was more like the Angel of Death than a plain staff captain (the court counsellor crossed himself at the thought); he left one man, and he promptly hanged himself; another man followed the Kalmyk, and he died a dog's death in a filthy passageway.

Mylnikov tried to draw a slant-eyed Kalmyk face beside the crest, but the likeness turned out poorly – he didn't have the knack of it.

Ah, Kalmyk-Kalmyk, where are you now?

And Staff Captain Rybnikov, so accurately nicknamed by the agents (his face really was rather Kalmykish), was spending the evening of this troublesome day hurrying and scurrying more intensely than ever.

After the incident on Mitavsky Lane, he dropped into a telegraph office and sent off two messages: one was local, to the Kolpino railway station, the other was long-distance, to Irkutsk, and he quarrelled with the telegraph clerk over the rate – he was outraged that they took ten kopecks a word for telegrams to Irkutsk. The clerk explained that telegraphic communications to the Asiatic part of the empire were charged at a double rate, and he even showed Rybnikov the price list, but the staff captain simply wouldn't listen.

'What do you mean, it's Asia?' he howled, gazing around plaintively. 'Gentlemen, did you hear what he said about Irkutsk? Why, it's a magnificent city, Europe, the genuine article! Oh, yes! You haven't been there, so don't you talk, but I served three unforgettable years there! What do you make of this, gents? It's daylight robbery!'

After raising a ruckus, Vasilii Alexandrovich moved to the queue for the international window and sent a telegram to Paris, at the urgent rate, that is to say, all of thirty kopecks for a word, but he behaved quietly here, without waxing indignant.

After that the irrepressible staff captain hobbled off to the Nicholas station, where he arrived just in time for the departure of the nine o'clock express.

He tried to buy a second-class ticket, but the ticket office didn't have any.

'Sorry, it's not my fault,' Rybnikov informed the queue with obvious satisfaction. 'I'll have to travel in third, even though I am an officer. Government business, I've no right not to go. Here's six roubles. My ticket, please.'

'There's no more places in third class,' the booking clerk replied. 'There are places in first, for fifteen roubles.'

'How much?' Vasilii Alexandrovich gasped. 'My father's not called Rothschild, you know! If you're really interested, I happen to be an orphan!'

They started explaining to him that there weren't enough places, that the number of passenger trains to Moscow had been reduced because of the military traffic. And even that one ticket in first class had only become free by sheer chance, just two minutes ago. A lady had wanted to travel in a compartment alone, but this was forbidden by decree of the director of the line, and the passenger had been forced to return the extra ticket.

'Well, are you taking it or not?' the booking clerk asked impatiently.

Cursing plaintively, the staff captain bought the hugely expensive ticket, but he demanded 'a paper with a seal' stating that there hadn't been any cheaper tickets available. They barely managed to get rid of him by sending him off to the duty station supervisor for a 'paper', but the staff captain didn't go to him, instead he called into the left luggage office.

There he retrieved a cheap-looking suitcase and a long, narrow tube, the kind used for carrying blueprints.

And then it was already time to go to the platform, because they were ringing the first bell.

The third syllable,
in which Vasilii Alexandrovich
visits the WC

There was a lady passenger sitting in the first-class compartment – presumably the one who had been prevented from travelling in solitude by the rules of the railway.

The staff captain greeted her glumly, evidently still smarting over his fifteen roubles. He hardly even glanced at his travelling companion, although the lady was good-looking – in fact more than merely good-looking, she was quite exceptionally attractive: a delicate watercolour face, huge moist eyes behind a misty veil, an elegant travelling suit in a mother-of-pearl hue.

The lovely stranger took no interest in Rybnikov either. In reply to his 'hello' she nodded coldly, cast a single brief glance over her companion's common features, his baggy uniform tunic and gingerish scuffed boots and turned away towards the window.

The second bell pealed out.

The female passenger's delicately defined nostrils started fluttering. Her lips whispered:

'Ah, get a move on, do!' but the exclamation was clearly not addressed to her companion in the compartment.

Newspaper boys dashed, gabbling, along the corridor – one from the respectable *Evening Russia*, the other from the sleazy *Russian Assembly*. They were both howling at the tops of their voices, trying to out-yell each other.

'Woeful news of the drama in the Sea of Japan!' called the first one, straining his lungs to bursting point. 'Russian fleet burned and sunk!'

The second one yelled: 'Famous "Moscow Daredevils" gang strikes in Petersburg! High society lady undressed!'

'First lists of the dead. Numerous names dear to all hearts! The whole country will be weeping!'

'Countess N. put out of a carriage in the costume of Eve! The bandits knew she had jewels hidden under her dress!'

The staff captain bought *Evening Russia* with its huge black border of mourning and the lady bought *Russian Assembly*, but before they could start reading, the door burst open, and in charged a huge bouquet of roses that wouldn't fit through the frame, immediately filling the compartment with unctuous fragrance.

Protruding above the rosebuds was a handsome man's face with a well-groomed imperial and a curled moustache. A diamond pin glinted and sparkled on his necktie.

'Anddd who is thissss!' the new arrival exclaimed, eyeing Rybnikov intently, and his black eyebrows slid upwards menacingly, but after only a second the handsome fellow had had his fill of observing the staff captain's unprepossessing appearance and lost all interest in him, after which he did not deign to notice him again.

'Lycia!' he exclaimed, falling to his knees and throwing the bouquet at the lady's feet. 'I love only you, with all my heart and soul! Forgive me, I implore you! You know my temperament! I am a man of sudden enthusiasms, I am an artiste.'

It was easy to see that he was an artiste. The owner of the imperial was not at all embarrassed by his audience – in addition to the staff captain glancing out from behind his *Evening Russia*, this interesting scene was also being observed by spectators in the corridor, attracted by the mind-numbing scent of the roses and the sonorous lamentations.

Nor did the lovely lady's nerve fail her in front of an audience.

'It's over, Astralov!' she declared wrathfully, throwing back her veil to reveal her glittering eyes. 'And don't you dare show up in Moscow!' She waved aside the hands extended in supplication. 'No, no, I won't even listen!'

Then the penitent did something rather strange: without rising from his knees, he folded his hands together on his chest and started singing in a deep, truly magical baritone:

'*Una furtive lacrima negli occhi suoi spunto . . .*'

The lady turned pale and put her hands over her ears, but the divine voice filled the entire compartment and flowed far beyond – the entire carriage fell silent, listening.

Donizetti's entrancing melody was cut short by the particularly long and insistent trilling of the third bell.

The conductor glanced in at the door:

'All those seeing off passengers please alight immediately, we are departing. Sir, it's time!' he said, touching the singer's elbow.

The singer dashed over to Rybnikov:

'Let me have the ticket! I'll give you a hundred roubles! This is a drama of a broken heart! Five hundred!'

'Don't you dare let him have the ticket!' the lady shouted.

'I can't do it,' the staff captain replied firmly to the artiste. 'I would gladly, but it's urgent government business.'

The conductor dragged Astralov, in floods of tears, out into the corridor.

The train set off. There was a despairing shout from the platform:

'Lycia! I'll do away with myself! Forgive me!'

'Never!' the flushed lady passenger shouted, and flung the magnificent bouquet out of the window, showering the little table with scarlet petals.

She fell back limply on to the seat, covered her face with her fingers and burst into sobs.

'You are a noble man,' she said through her sobbing. 'You refused his money! I'm so grateful to you! I would have jumped out of the window, I swear I would!'

Rybnikov muttered:

'Five hundred roubles is huge money. I don't earn a third of that, not even with mess and travelling allowances. But I've got my job to do. The top brass won't excuse lateness . . .'

'Five hundred roubles he offered, the buffoon!' the lady exclaimed, not listening to him. 'Preening his feathers for his audience! But he's really so mean, such an *economiser*!' She pronounced the final word with boundless contempt and even stopped sobbing, then added: 'Refuses to live according to his means.'

Intrigued by the logical introduction inherent in this statement, Vasilii Alexandrovich asked:

'Begging your pardon, but I don't quite understand. Is he thrifty or does he lives beyond his means?'

'His means are huge, but he lives too far within them!' his travelling companion explained, no longer crying, but anxiously examining her slightly reddened nose in a little mirror. She dabbed at it with a powder puff and adjusted a lock of golden hair beside her forehead. 'Last year he earned almost a hundred thousand, but he barely spent even half of it. He puts it all away "for a rainy day"!'

At this point she finally calmed down completely, turned her gaze on her companion and introduced herself punctiliously.

'Glyceria Romanovna Lidina.'

The staff captain told her his name too.

'Pleased to meet you,' the lady told him with a smile. 'I must explain, since you have witnessed this monstrous spectacle. *Georges* simply adores histrionic scenes, especially in front of an audience!'

'Is he really an artiste, then?'

Glyceria Romanovna fluttered her almost inch-long eyelashes incredulously.

'What? You don't know Astralov? The tenor Astralov. His name is on all the show bills!'

'I'm not much for theatres,' Rybnikov replied with an indifferent shrug. 'I don't have any time to go strutting about at operas, you know. And it's beyond my pocket, anyway. My pay's miserly, they're delaying the pension, and life in Petersburg is too pricey by half. The cabbies take seventy kopecks for every piddling little ride . . .'

Lidina was not listening, she wasn't even looking at him any more.

'We've been married for two years!' she said, as if she were not addressing her prosaic companion, but a more worthy audience, which was listening to her with sympathetic attention. 'Ah, I was so in love! But now I realise it was the voice I loved, not him. What a voice he has! He only has to start singing and I melt, he can wrap me round his little finger. And he knows it, the scoundrel! Did you see the way he started singing just now, the cheap manipulator? Thank goodness the bell interrupted him, my head was already starting to spin!'

'A handsome gentleman,' the staff captain acknowledged, trying to suppress a yawn. 'Probably gets his fair share of crumpet. Is that what the drama's all about?'

'They told me about him!' Glyceria Romanovna exclaimed with her eyes flashing. 'There are always plenty of "well-wishers" in the world of theatre. But I didn't believe them. And then I saw it with my own eyes! And where? In my own drawing room! And who with? That old floozy Koturnova! I'll never set foot in that desecrated apartment again! Or in Petersburg either!'

'So you're moving to Moscow, then?' the staff captain summed up. It was clear from his tone of voice that he was impatient to put an end to this trivial conversation and settle into his newspaper.

'Yes, we have another apartment in Moscow, on Ostozhenka Street. *Georges* sometimes takes an engagement for the winter at the Bolshoi.'

At this, Rybnikov finally concealed himself behind *Evening Russia* and the lady was obliged to fall silent. She nervously picked up the *Russian Assembly*, ran her eyes over the article on the front page and tossed it aside, muttering:

'My God, how vulgar! Completely undressed, in the road! Could she really have been stripped totally and completely naked? Who is this Countess N.? Vika Olsufieva? Nelly Vorontsova? Ah, it doesn't matter anyway.'

Outside the windowpane, dachas, copses of trees and dreary vegetable patches drifted by. The staff captain rustled his newspaper, enthralled.

Lidina sighed, then sighed again. She found the silence oppressive.

'What's that you find so fascinating to read?' she eventually asked, unable to restrain herself.

'Well, you see, it's the list of officers who gave their lives for the tsar and the fatherland in the sea battle beside the island of Tsushima. It came through the European telegraph agencies, from Japanese sources. The scrolls of mourning, so to speak. They say they're going to continue it in forthcoming issues. I'm looking to see if any of my comrades-in-arms are there.' And Vasilii Alexandrovich started reading out loud, with expression, savouring the words. 'On the battleship *Prince Kutuzov-Smolensky*: junior flagman, Rear Admiral Leontiev; commander of the vessel, Commodore Endlung; paymaster of the squadron, State Counsellor Ziukin; chief officer, Captain Second Rank von Schwalbe . . .'

'Oh, stop!' said Glyceria Romanovna, fluttering her little hand. 'I don't want to hear it! When is this terrible war ever going to end!'

'Soon. The insidious enemy will be crushed by the Christian host,' Rybnikov promised, setting the newspaper aside to take out a little book, in which he immersed himself with even greater concentration.

The lady screwed her eyes up short-sightedly, trying to make out the title, but the book was bound in brown paper.

The train's brakes screeched and it came to a halt.

'Kolpino?' Lidina asked in surprise. 'Strange, the express never stops here.'

Rybnikov stuck his head out of the window and called to the duty supervisor.

'Why are we waiting?'

'We have to let a special get past, Officer, it's got urgent military freight.'

While her companion was distracted, Glyceria Romanovna seized the chance to satisfy her curiosity. She quickly opened the book's cover, held her pretty lorgnette on a gold chain up to her eyes and puckered up her face. The book that the staff captain had been reading so intently was called *TUNNELS AND BRIDGES: A concise guide for railway employees.*

A telegraph clerk clutching a paper ribbon in his hand ran up to the station supervisor, who read the message, shrugged and waved his little flag.

'What is it?' asked Rybnikov.

'Don't know if they're coming or going. Orders to dispatch you and not wait for the special.'

The train set off.

'I suppose you must be a military engineer?' Glyceria Romanovna enquired.

'What makes you think that?'

Lidina felt embarrassed to admit that she had peeped at the title of the book, but she found a way out – she pointed to the leather tube.

'That thing. It's for drawings, isn't it?'

'Ah, yes.' Vasilii Alexandrovich lowered his voice. 'Secret documents. I'm delivering them to Moscow.'

'And I thought you were on leave. Visiting your family, or your parents, perhaps.'

'I'm not married. Where would I get the earnings to set up a family? I'm dog poor. And I haven't got any parents, I'm an orphan. And in the regiment they used to taunt me for a Tatar because of my squinty eyes.'

After the stop at Kolpino the staff captain brightened up somewhat and became more talkative, and his broad cheekbones even turned slightly pink.

Suddenly he glanced at his watch and stood up.

'*Pardon*, I'll just go out for a smoke.'

'Smoke here, I'm used to it,' Glyceria Romanovna told him graciously. 'Georges smokes cigars. That is, he used to.'

Vasilii Alexandrovich smiled in embarrassment.

'I'm sorry. When I said a smoke, I was being tactful. I don't smoke, an unnecessary expense. I'm actually going to the WC, on a call of nature.'

The lady turned away with a dignified air.

The staff captain took the tube with him. Catching his female companion's indignant glance, he explained in an apologetic voice:

'I'm not allowed to let it out of my hands.'

Glyceria Romanovna watched him go and murmured:

'He really is quite unpleasant.' And she started looking out of the window.

But the staff captain walked quickly through second class and third class to the carriage at the tail of the train and glanced out on to the brake platform.

There was an insistent, lingering blast on a whistle from behind.

The conductor-in-chief and a gendarme sentry were standing on the platform.

'What the hell!' said the conductor. 'That can't be the special. They telegraphed to say it was cancelled!'

The long train was following them no more than half a verst away, drawn by two locomotives, puffing out black smoke. A long tail of flat wagons cased in tarpaulin stretched out behind it.

The hour was already late, after ten, but the twilight had barely begun to thicken – the season of white nights was approaching.

The gendarme looked round at the staff captain and saluted.

'Begging your pardon, Your Honour, but please be so good as to close the door. Instructions strictly forbid it.'

'Quite right, old fellow,' Rybnikov said approvingly. 'Vigilance, and all the rest of it. I just wanted to have a smoke, actually. Well, I'll just do it in the corridor here. Or in the WC.'

And he went into the toilet, which in third class was cramped and not very clean.

After locking himself in, Vasilii Alexandrovich stuck his head out of the window.

The train was just moving on to an antediluvian bridge, built in the old Count Kleinmichel style, which spanned a narrow little river.

Rybnikov stood on the flush lever and a hole opened up in the bottom of the toilet. Through it he could clearly see the sleepers flickering past.

The staff captain pressed some invisible little button on the tube and stuffed the narrow leather case into the hole – the diameter matched precisely, so he had to employ a certain amount of force.

When the tube had disappeared through the hole, Vasilii Alexandrovich quickly moistened his hands under the tap and walked out into the vestibule of the carriage, shaking the water from his fingers.

A minute later, he was already walking back into his own compartment.

Lidina looked at him severely – she still had not forgiven him for that 'call of nature' – and was about to turn away, when she suddenly exclaimed:

'Your secret case! You must have forgotten it in the toilet!'

An expression of annoyance appeared on Rybnikov's face, but before he could answer Glyceria Romanovna there was a terrifying crash and the carriage lurched and swayed.

The staff captain dashed to the window. There were heads protruding from the other windows too, all of them looking back along the line.

At that point the line curved round in a small arc and they had a clear view of the tracks, the river they had just crossed and the bridge.

Or rather, what was left of it.

The bridge had collapsed at its precise centre, and at the precise moment when the line of heavy military flat wagons was crossing it.

The catastrophe was an appalling sight: a column of water and steam, splashed up into the air as the locomotives crashed down into the water, upended flat wagons with massive steel structures tumbling off them and – most terrible of all – a hail of tiny human figures showering downwards.

Glyceria Romanovna huddled against Rybnikov's shoulder and started squealing piercingly. Other passengers were screaming too.

The tail-end carriage of the special, probably reserved for officers, teetered on the very edge of the break. Someone seemed to jump out of the window just in time, but then the bridge support buckled and the carriage went plunging downwards too, into the heap of twisted and tangled metal protruding from the water.

'My God, my God!' Lidina started screaming hysterically. 'Why are you just looking? We have to do something!'

She dashed out into the corridor. Vasilii Alexandrovich hesitated for only a second before following her.

'Stop the train!' the small lady gabbled hysterically, throwing herself on the conductor-in-chief, who was running towards the leading carriage. 'There are wounded men there! They're drowning! We have to save them!'

She grabbed him by the sleeve so tenaciously that the railwayman had no choice but to stop.

'What do you mean, save them? Save who? In that shambles!' Pale as death, the captain of the train crew tied to pull himself free. 'What can we do? We have to get to a station, to report this.'

Glyceria Romanovna refused to listen and pounded him on the chest with her little fist.

'They're dying, and we just leave them? Stop! I demand it!' she squealed. 'Press that emergency brake of yours, or whatever you call it!'

Hearing her howling, a dark-complexioned man with a little waxed moustache put his head out of the next compartment. Seeing the captain of the train hesitate, he shouted menacingly:

'Don't you dare stop! I've got urgent business in Moscow!'

Rybnikov took Lidina gently by the elbow and started speaking soothingly:

'Really and truly, madam. Of course, it's a terrible disaster, but the only thing we can do to help is telegraph as soon as possible from the next . . .'

'Ah, to hell with all of you!' shouted Glyceria Romanovna.

She darted to the emergency handle and pulled it.

Everyone in the train went tumbling head over heels to the floor. The train gave a hop and started screeching sickeningly along the rails. There were howls and screams on every side – the passengers thought their train had crashed.

The first to recover his senses was the man with the dark complexion, who had not fallen, but only banged his head against the lintel of the door.

With a cry of 'You rrrotten bitch, I'll kill you!' he threw himself on the hysterical woman, who had been stunned by her fall, and grabbed her by the throat.

The small flames that glinted briefly in Vasilii Alexandrovich's eyes suggested that he might possibly have shared the swarthy gentleman's bloody intentions to some extent. However, there was more than just fury in the glance that the staff captain cast at Glyceria Romanovna as she was being strangled – there was also something like stupefaction.

Rybnikov sighed, grabbed the intemperate dark-haired man by the collar and tossed him aside.

The fourth syllable,
in which a hired gun
sets out on the hunt

The phone rang at half past one in the morning. Before he even lifted the receiver to answer, Erast Petrovich Fandorin gestured to his valet to hand him his clothes. A telephone call at this hour of the night could only be from the Department, and it had to be about some emergency or other.

As he listened to the voice rumbling agitatedly in the earpiece, Fandorin knitted his black eyebrows tighter and tighter together. He switched hands, so that Masa could slip his arm into the sleeve of a starched shirt. He shook his head at the shoes – the valet understood and brought his boots.

Erast Petrovich did not ask the person on the phone a single question, he simply said:

'Very well, Leontii Karlovich, I'll be there straight away.'

Once he was dressed, he stopped for a moment in front of the mirror. He combed his black hair threaded with grey (the kind they call 'salt-and-pepper'), ran a special little brush over his entirely white temples and his neat moustache, in which there was still not a single silver hair. He frowned after running his hand across his cheek, but there was no time to shave.

He walked out of the apartment.

The Japanese was already sitting in the automobile, holding a travelling bag in his hand.

The most valuable quality of Fandorin's valet was not that he did everything quickly and precisely, but that he knew how to manage without unnecessary talk. From the choice of footwear, Masa had guessed there was a long journey in prospect, so he had equipped himself accordingly.

With its mighty twenty-horsepower engine roaring, the twin-cylinder Oldsmobile surged down Sadovaya Street, where Fandorin was lodging, and a minute later it was already gliding across the Chernyshevsky Bridge. A feeble drizzle was trickling down from the grey, unconvincing night sky, and glinting on the road. The remarkable 'Hercules' brand non-splash tyres glided over the black asphalt.

Two minutes later the automobile braked to a halt at house number 7 on Kolomenskaya Street, where the offices of the St Petersburg Railway Gendarmerie and Police were located.

Fandorin set off up the steps at a run, with a nod to the sentry, who saluted him. But his valet remained sitting in the Oldsmobile, and even demonstratively turned his back.

From the very beginning of the armed conflict between the two empires, Masa – who was Japanese by birth, but a Russian citizen according to his passport – had declared that he would remain neutral, and he had stuck scrupulously to this rule. He had not delighted in the heroic feats of the defenders of Port Arthur, nor had he rejoiced at the victories of Japanese armies. But most importantly of all, as a matter of principle, he had not stepped across the threshold of any military institutions, which at times had caused both him and his master considerable inconvenience.

The valet's moral sufferings were exacerbated still further by the fact that, following several arrests on suspicion of espionage, he had been obliged to disguise his nationality. Fandorin had procured a temporary passport for his servant in the name of a Chinese gentleman, so that now, whenever Masa left the house, he was obliged to put on a wig with a long pigtail. According to the document, he bore the impossible name of 'Lianchan Shankhoevich Chaiunevin'. As a consequence of all these ordeals, the valet had lost his appetite and grown lean, and had even given up breaking the hearts of housemaids and seamstresses, with whom he had enjoyed vertiginous success during the pre-war period.

These were hard times, not only for the false Lianchan Shankhoevich, but also for his master.

When Japanese destroyers attacked the Port Arthur squadron without warning, Fandorin was on the other side of the world, in the Dutch West Indies, where he was conducting absolutely fascinating research in the area of underwater navigation.

At first Erast Fandorin had wanted nothing to do with a war between two countries that were both close to his heart, but as the advantage swung more and more towards Japan, Fandorin gradually lost interest in the durability of aluminium, and even in the search for the galleon *San Felipe*, which had gone down with its load of gold in the year AD 1708 seven miles south-south-east of the island of Aruba. On the very day when Fandorin's submarine finally scraped its aluminium belly across the stump of the Spanish mainmast protruding from the sea bottom, news came of the loss of the battleship *Petropavlosk*, together with Commander-in-Chief Admiral Makarov and the entire crew.

The next morning Fandorin set out for his homeland, leaving his associates to deal with raising the gold bars to the surface.

On arriving in St Petersburg, he contacted an old colleague from his time in the Third Section, who now occupied a highly responsible post, and offered his services: Erast Petrovich knew that Russia had catastrophically few specialists on Japan, and he had spent several years living in the Land of the Rising Sun.

The old acquaintance was quite delighted by Fandorin's visit. He said, however, that he would like to make use of Erast Petrovich in a different capacity.

'Of course, there aren't enough experts on Japan, or on many other subjects,' said the general, blinking rapidly with eyes red from lack of sleep, 'but there is a far worse rent in our garments, which leaves us exposed, pardon me for saying so, at the most intimate spot. If you only knew, my dear fellow, what a calamitous state our counter-espionage system is in! Things have more or less come together in the army in the field, but in the rear, the confusion is appalling, monstrous. Japanese agents are everywhere, they act with brazen impudence and resourcefulness, and we don't know how to catch them. We have no experience. We're used to civilised spies, the European kind, who do their work under cover of an embassy or foreign companies. But the Orientals break all the rules. I'll tell you what worries me most,' said the important man, lowering his voice. 'Our railways. When the war's happening tens of thousands of versts away from the factories and the conscription centres, victory and defeat depend on the railways, the primary circulatory system of the organism of the state. The entire empire has just one artery from Peter to Arthur. Atrophied, with a feeble pulse, prone to thrombosis and – worst of all – almost completely unprotected. Erast Petrovich, dear fellow, there are two things that I dread in this situation: Japanese sabotage and Russian slovenliness. You have more than enough experience of intelligence work, thank God. And then, they told me that in America you qualified as an engineer. Why not get back in harness, eh? On any terms you like. If you want, we'll reinstate you in government service; if you want, you can be a freelance, a hired gun. Help us out, will you, put your shoulder to the wheel.'

And so Fandorin found himself engaged at the capital's Department of Railway Gendarmerie and Police in the capacity of a 'hired gun' – that is, a consultant receiving no salary, but endowed with extremely far-reaching powers. The goal set for the consultant was as follows: to develop a security system for the railways, test it in the zone under his jurisdiction and then pass it on to be used by all the Railway Gendarmerie departments of the empire.

It was hectic work, not very much like Erast Fandorin's preceding activities, but fascinating in its own way. The Department's jurisdiction extended to two thousand versts of railway lines, hundreds of stations and terminuses, bridges, railway line reservations, depots and workshops – and all this had to be protected against possible attack by the enemy. While the provincial department of gendarmes had several dozen employees, the railway department had more than a thousand. The scale and the responsibility were beyond all comparison. In addition, the duty regulations for the railways' gendarmes exempted them from performing the functions of a political police, and for Fandorin that was very important: he was not fond of revolutionaries, but he regarded with even greater revulsion the methods by which the Okhrana and the Special Section of the Department of Police endeavoured to eradicate the nihilist contagion. In this sense, Erast Petrovich regarded working for the Railway Gendarmerie Department as 'clean work'.

Fandorin did not know much about railways, but he could not be classed as a total dilettante. He was, after all, a qualified engineer in the area of self-propelled machines, and twenty years earlier, while investigating a rather complicated case, he had worked on a railway line for a while in the guise of a trainee.

During the year just past, the 'hired gun' had achieved a great deal. Gendarme sentries had been established on all trains, including passenger trains; a special regime had been introduced for guarding bridges, tunnels, crossings and points, flying brigades on handcars had been created, and so on and so forth. The innovations introduced in the St Petersburg department were quickly adapted in the other provinces and so far (fingers firmly crossed) there had not been a single major accident, not a single act of sabotage.

Although Fandorin's official position was a strange one, they had grown accustomed to Erast Petrovich in the Department and regarded him with great respect, referring to him as 'Mr Engineer'. His superior, Lieutenant General von Kassel, had grown used to relying on his consultant in all matters and never took any decisions without his advice.

And now Leontii Karlovich Kassel was waiting for his assistant in the doorway of his office.

Catching sight of the engineer's tall, dashing figure at the end of the corridor, he went rushing towards it.

'Of all things, the Tezoimenitsky Bridge!' the general shouted before he was even close. 'We wrote to the minister and warned him the bridge was dilapidated and unsafe! And now he rebukes me and threatens me: says that if this turns out to be Japanese sabotage – I'll stand trial for it. How in hell can it be sabotage? The Tezoimenitsky Bridge hasn't been repaired since 1850! And here's the result for you: it couldn't bear the weight of a military transport carrying heavy artillery. The ordnance is ruined. There are large numbers of dead. And worst of all, the line to Moscow has been disrupted!'

'A good thing it happened here, and not beyond Samara,' said Erast Petrovich, following von Kassel into the office and closing the door. 'Here we can send trains by an alternative route along the Novgorod line. But is it certain the bridge collapsed and this is not sabotage?'

Leontii Karlovich frowned.

'Oh, come, now, how can it be sabotage? You ought to know, you developed the regulations yourself. Sentries on the bridge, the rails checked every half-hour, gendarmes on duty on the brake platforms of all trains – my territory is in perfect order. Tell me instead, if you can, what our unfortunate homeland has done to deserve such disasters. We're straining ourselves to the very limit as it is. What about Tsushima, eh? Have you read the newspaper reports? A total debacle, and not a single enemy vessel sunk. Where did it come from, this Japan? When I entered the service, no one had even heard of such a country. And now it's sprung up out of nowhere, in just a few years, like a mushroom overnight. Why, it's totally unheard of.'

'Why d-do you say it's unheard of?' Fandorin replied with his habitual light stammer. 'Japan began modernising in 1868, thirty-seven years ago. Less time than that passed from the moment Peter the Great ascended the throne until the battle of Poltava. Before that, there was no such power as Russia, then it suddenly sprang up out of nowhere, also like a m-mushroom, overnight.'

'Oh, come on, that's history,' the general said dismissively, crossing himself with broad sweeps of his hand. 'I'll tell you what it is. It's God punishing us for our sins. Punishing us harshly, as he did the Egyptian pharaoh, with miraculous disasters. So help me . . .' – Leontii Karlovich glanced round at the door and dropped his voice to a whisper – ' . . . we've lost the war.'

'I d-don't agree,' Erast Petrovich snapped. 'Not on a single point. Nothing miraculous has occurred. That is one. What has happened is only what should have been expected. It's hardly surprising that Russia has not won a single battle. It would have been an absolute miracle if she had. Our enlisted man is no match for the Japanese soldier – he has less stamina, less learning and less martial spirit. Let us assume that the Russian officer is not bad, but the Japanese officer is simply superb. And then, what can we say about the generals (please don't take this personally, Your Excellency); ours are fat and lack initiative, the Japanese generals are lean and forceful. If we are still holding out somehow, the only reason is that it is easier to defend than attack. But don't be alarmed, Leontii Karpovich. We may lose the battles, but we shall win the war. And that is t-two. We are immeasurably stronger than the Japanese in the most important thing of all: we have economic might, human and natural resources. Time is on our side. Commander-in-Chief Linevich is acting entirely correctly, unlike Kuropatkin; he is drawing out the campaign, building up his strength. The longer it goes on, the weaker the Japanese become. Their treasury is on the brink of bankruptcy, their lines of communication are being extended further and further, their reserves are being drained. All we have to do is avoid large-scale battles, and victory is in the b-bag. Nothing could have been more stupid than to drag the Baltic fleet halfway round the world to be devoured by Admiral Togo.'

As the general listened to his assistant, his face grew brighter but, having begun on a bright note, Fandorin concluded his optimistic discourse on a gloomy one.

'The crash on the Tezoimenitsky Bridge frightens me more than the loss of our navy squadron. Without a fleet, at least we will just about win the war, but if tricks like this start happening on the main railway line supplying the front, Russia is done for. Have them couple the inspector's carriage to a locomotive. Let's go and take a look.'

The fifth syllable,
which features
an interesting passenger

By the time the inspector's carriage reached the scene of the disaster on the rocky banks of the Lomzha river, night had grown weary of pretending to be dark at all, and the clear morning light was streaming down from the sky in all its glory.

A quite incredible amount of top brass had gathered at the stub end of the Tezoimenitsky Bridge – the Minister of War, and the most august Inspector General of Artillery, and the Minister of Railways, and the Chief of the Gendarmes Corps, and the Director of the Department of Police, and the Head of the Provincial Gendarmes Department. There were as many as half a dozen saloon carriages, each with its own locomotive, drawn up one after another in a queue.

There, above the precipice, gold braid glittered, spurs and adjutant's aiguillettes jingled, imperious bass voices rumbled peremptorily, and down below, at the water's edge, chaos and death prevailed. Rising up in the middle of the Lomzha was a shapeless heap of wood and iron, with the broken bones of the bridge drooping down over it; one of the mangled and twisted locomotives had buried its nose in the far bank and was still smoking, while the rectangular black tender of the other protruded from the water like a cliff. The wounded had already been taken away, but there was a long line of dead lying on the sand, covered with tarpaulins.

The latest heavy guns, intended for the Manchurian army, had tumbled off the flat wagons: some had sunk and some had been scattered across the shallows. On the opposite bank a mobile crane was jerking its jib absurdly as it tugged at the mounting of a monster with a twisted barrel, but it was obvious that it could not cope and would never pull it out.

Leontii Karlovich set off towards the topmost brass, but Fandorin skirted round the islet of gold epaulettes and walked up to the very edge of the cliff. He stood there for a while, looking, then suddenly started climbing down the inclined surface. Down by the water, he leapt agilely on to the roof of a submerged carriage, and from there clambered on to the next support of the bridge, from which the crooked rails were dangling. The engineer scrambled up the sleepers as if they were the rungs of a ladder, and was soon on the far side of the river.

There were fewer people here. Standing some distance away, about fifty paces, was an express train – the one that had managed to slip across the bridge just before the collapse. The passengers were gathered in little knots beside the carriages.

On the surviving section of the bridge and beside the water, men in civilian clothes, all dressed differently but all, nonetheless, as alike as brothers, were swarming about with a businesslike air. Among them Fandorin recognised Evstratii Pavlovich Mylnikov, with whom he had once worked in Moscow.

A gendarme corporal in a wet, torn uniform was standing rigidly to attention in front of Mylnikov – it looked as if his report was already in full spate. But the court counsellor was not looking at the corporal, he was looking at Fandorin.

'Bah,' he said, throwing his arms wide, as if he was about to embrace the engineer. 'Fandorin! What are you doing here? Ah, yes, you're in the RGD now, they told me. Sorry for invading your territory, but it's an order from the very top: investigate as a matter of emergency, involve all the contiguous departments. Got us up out of our feather bed. Go get 'em, they said, pick up that trail, you old bloodhound. Well, the part about the feather bed's not true.' Mylnikov bared his yellow teeth in what should have been a smile, but his eyes remained cold and narrowed. 'When would humble sleuths like us ever see our feather beds these days? I envy you railway sybarites. I spent the night on the chairs in the office, as I usually do. But then again, as you can see, I got here first. Look, I'm interrogating your lads, to see if it was a Japanese mine.'

'Mr Engineer,' the corporal said excitedly, turning to Fandorin, 'tell His Honour, will you? Do you remember me? I'm Loskutov, I use to work in Farforovaya, on the crossing. You inspected us in winter and you were well pleased. You gave orders for me to be promoted. I did everything all right and proper, just like we're supposed to! I climbed over the whole lot myself, ten minutes before the express. It was all clear! And how could the enemy have crept through on to the bridge? I've got sentries at both ends!'

'So it was completely clear?' Fandorin asked to make certain. 'Did you look carefully?'

'Why, I . . . Just look at that . . .' The corporal choked and tugged his peaked cap off his head. 'By Christ the Lord! Seven years . . . You ask anyone you like how Loskutov does his duty.'

The engineer turned to Mylnikov:

'What have you managed to find out?'

'The picture's clear,' Mylnikov said with a shrug. 'The usual old Rooshian nonsense. The express train was travelling in front. It stopped at Kolpino and was supposed to let the special with the field guns go past. Then this telegraph clerk passes on a telegram: Carry on, the special's delayed. Someone messed things up somewhere. As soon as the express has cleared the bridge, the army train catches up with it from behind. A heavy brute, as you can see for yourself. Should have shot across at full speed, as required, then nothing would have happened. But it must have started to brake, and the supports caved in. The railway top brass will be in for it now.'

'Who sent the telegram about the special b-being delayed?' asked Fandorin, leaning forward eagerly.

'Well, that's just it. No one sent any such telegram.'

'And where's the telegraph clerk who supposedly received it?'

'We're searching. Haven't found him yet – his shift was already over.'

The corner of the engineer's mouth twitched.

'You're not searching hard enough. Get a verbal portrait, a photo if you can, and put him on the all-Russian wanted list, urgently.'

'The telegraph clerk? On the all-Russian list?'

Fandorin beckoned the court counsellor with his finger, took him aside and said in a quiet voice:

'This is sabotage. The bridge was blown up.'

'How do you make that out?'

Fandorin led the sleuths' boss across to the break and started climbing down the dangling rails. Mylnikov clambered after him, gasping and crossing himself.

'L-look.'

The hand in the grey glove pointed to a charred and splintered sleeper and a rail twisted like a paper streamer.

'Our experts will arrive any minute now. They are certain to discover particles of explosive . . .'

Mylnikov whistled and pushed his bowler hat on to the back of his head.

The detectives hung there above the black water, swaying slightly on the improvised ladder.

'So the gendarme's lying when he says he inspected everything? Or even worse, he's in on it? Shall we arrest him?'

'Loskutov – a Japanese agent? Rubbish. Then he would have run for it, like the Kolpino t-telegraph clerk. No, no, there wasn't any mine on the line.'

'Then how'd it happen? There wasn't any mine, but there was an explosion?'

'That's the way it is, though.'

The court counsellor frowned thoughtfully and set off up the sleepers.

'Go and report this to the top brass . . . Now won't there be a real song and dance.'

He waved to the agents and shouted:

'Hey, get me a boat!'

However, he didn't get into the boat, he changed his mind.

He watched Fandorin walking away towards the express train, scratched the back of his head and went dashing after him.

The engineer glanced round at the sound of tramping feet and nodded towards the motionless train.

'Was there really such a small distance between the trains?'

'No, the express halted farther along, on the emergency brake. Then the driver reversed. The conductors and some of the passengers helped to get the wounded out of the water. It's not so far to a station this side as on the other. They drove a farm cart over and took them off to hospital . . .'

Fandorin summoned the conductor-in-chief with an imperious gesture and asked:

'How many passengers on the train?'

'All the seats were sold, Mr Engineer. That makes three hundred and twelve. I'm sorry, but when can we get moving again?'

Two of the passengers were standing quite close by: an army staff captain and an attractive-looking lady. Both covered from head to foot in mud and green slime. The officer was pouring water on to his companion's handkerchief from a kettle, and she was energetically scrubbing her mud-smeared face. Both of them were listening to the conversation curiously.

A platoon of railway gendarmes approached at a trot from the bridge. The commanding officer ran up first and saluted.

'Mr Engineer, we're here at your disposal. There are two platoons on the other bank. The experts have started work. What will our orders be?'

'Cordon off both sides of the bridge and the banks. Let no one near the break, not even if they hold the rank of general. Otherwise we renounce all responsibility for the investigation – tell them that. Tell Sigismund Lvovich to look for traces of explosive . . . But no, don't bother, he'll see that for himself. Give me a clerk and four of your brightest soldiers. Yes, and one more thing: put a cordon round the express train as well. Let none of the passengers or train staff through without my permission.'

'Mr Engineer,' the captain of the train's crew exclaimed plaintively, 'we've been standing here for over four hours.'

'And you'll b-be standing here for a long time yet. I have to draw up a complete list of the passengers. We'll question all of them and check their credentials. We'll start from the final carriage. And you, Mylnikov, would do better to turn your attention to that telegraph clerk who disappeared. I can manage things here without you.'

'Of course, right enough, it's your move,' said Mylnikov, and he even waved his arms, as if to say: I'm leaving, I'm not claiming any rights here. However, he didn't leave.

'Sir, madam,' the conductor-in-chief said to the officer and lady in a dejected voice. 'Please be so good as to return to your seats. Did you hear? They're going to check your documents.'

'Disaster, Glyceria Romanovna,' Rybnikov whispered. 'I'm done for.'

Lidina gasped as she examined a lace cuff stained with blood, but then jerked her head up sharply.

'Why? What's happened?'

In those slightly red and yet still beautiful eyes, Vasilii Alexandrovich read an immediate readiness for action and once again, after all the numerous occasions during the night, he marvelled at the unpredictability of this capital-city cutie.

The way Glyceria Romanovna had behaved during the efforts to save the drowning and wounded had been absolutely astounding: she didn't sob and wail, or throw a fit of hysterics; in fact she didn't cry at all, simply bit on her bottom lip at the most painful moments, so that by dawn it had swollen up quite badly. Rybnikov shook his head as he watched the frail little lady dragging a wounded soldier out of the water and binding up his bleeding wound with a narrow rag torn off her silk dress.

Once, overcome by the sight, the staff captain had murmured to himself: 'It's like Nekrasov, that poem "Russian Women"'. And he glanced around quickly, to see whether anyone had heard this comment that fitted so badly with the image of a grey little runt of an officer.

After Vasilii Alexandrovich had saved her from the dark-complexioned neurasthenic, and especially after several hours of working together, Lidina had started acting quite naturally with the staff captain, as if he were an old friend – she, too, had evidently changed her opinion of her travelling companion.

'Why, what's happened? Tell me!' she exclaimed, gazing at Rybnikov with fright in her eyes.

'I'm done for all round,' Vasilii Alexandrovich whispered, taking her by the arm and leading her slowly towards the train. 'I went to Peter without authorisation, my superiors didn't know about it. My sister's unwell. Now they'll find out – it's a catastrophe . . .'

'The guardhouse, is it?' Lidina asked, distressed.

'Never mind the guardhouse, that's no great disaster. The terrible part is something else altogether . . . Remember you asked about my tube? Just before the explosion? Well, I really did leave it in the toilet. I'm always so absentminded.'

Glyceria Romanovna put her hand over her lips and asked in a terrible whisper:

'Secret drawings?'

'Yes. Very important. Even when I went absent without leave, I didn't let them out of my sight for a moment.'

'And where are they? Haven't you taken a look there, in the toilet?'

'They've disappeared,' Vasilii Alexandrovich said in a sepulchral voice, and hung his head. 'Someone took them. That's not just the guardhouse, it means a trial, under martial law.'

'How appalling!' said the lady, round-eyed with horror. 'What can be done?'

'I want to ask you something,' said Rybnikov, stopping as they reached the final carriage. 'Before anyone's looking, I'll duck in under the wheels and afterwards I'll choose my moment to slip down the embankment and into the bushes. I can't afford to be checked. Don't give me away, will you? Tell them you've got no idea where I went to. We didn't talk during the journey. What would you want with a rough type like me? And take my little suitcase that's on the rack with you, I'll call round to collect it in Moscow. Ostozhenka Street, wasn't it?'

'Yes, the Bomze building.'

Lidina glanced round at the big boss from St Petersburg and the gendarmes, who were also moving towards the train.

'Will you help me out, save me?' asked Rybnikov, stepping into the shadow of the carriage.

'Of course!' A determined, even reckless expression appeared on Glyceria Romanovna's little face – just like earlier, when she had made a dash for the emergency brake. 'I know who stole your drawings! That repulsive specimen who attacked me! That's why he was in such a great hurry! And I wouldn't be surprised if he blew up the bridge too!'

'Blew it up?' Rybnikov gasped in amazement, struggling to keep up with what she was saying. 'How do you make that out? How could he blow it up?'

'How should I know, I'm not a soldier! Perhaps he threw some kind of bomb out of the window! I'll save you all right! And there's no need to go crawling under the carriage!' she shouted, darting off towards the gendarmes so impulsively that the staff captain was too late to hold her back, even though he tried.

'Who's in charge here? You?' Lidina asked, running up to the elegant gentleman with the grey temples. 'I have important news!'

Screwing his eyes up in alarm, Rybnikov glanced under the carriage, but it was too late to duck in under there now – many eyes were already gazing in his direction. The staff captain gritted his teeth and set off after Lidina.

She was holding the man with grey hair by the sleeve of his summer coat and jabbering away at incredible speed:

'I know who you want! There was a man here, an obnoxious type with dark hair, vulgarly dressed, with a diamond ring – a huge stone, but not pure water. Terribly suspicious! In a terrible hurry to get to Moscow. Absolutely everybody stayed, and lots of them helped get the men out of the river, but he grabbed his travelling bag and left. When the first wagon arrived from the station for the wounded, he bribed the driver. He gave him money, a lot of money, and drove away. And he didn't take a wounded man with him!'

'Why, that's true,' the captain of the train put in. 'A passenger from the second carriage, compartment number six. I saw him give the peasant a hundred-rouble note – for a wagon! And he rode off to the station.'

'Oh, be quiet, will you, I haven't finished yet!' Lidina said, gesturing at him angrily. 'I heard him ask that peasant: "Is there a shunting engine at the station?" He wanted to hire the engine, to get away as quickly as possible! I tell you, he was terribly suspicious!'

Rybnikov listened anxiously, expecting that now she would tell them about the stolen tube, but clever Glyceria Romanovna kept quiet about that highly suspicious circumstance, astounding the staff captain yet again.

'A m-most interesting passenger,' the gentleman with the grey temples said thoughtfully, and gestured briskly to a gendarmes officer. 'Lieutenant!

Send to the other side. My Chinese servant is across there in the inspector's carriage, you know him. Tell him to come at the d-double. I'll be at the station.'

And he strode off rapidly along the train.

'But what about the express, Mr Fandorin?' the lieutenant shouted after him.

'Send it on its way!' the man with the stammer shouted back without stopping.

A dull fellow with a simple sort of face and a dangling moustache who was hanging about nearby snapped his fingers – two nondescript little men came running up to him, and the three of them started whispering to each other.

Glyceria Romanovna returned to Rybnikov victorious.

'There now, you see, it's all settled. No need for you to go chasing through the bushes like a hare. And your drawings will turn up.'

But the staff captain wasn't looking at her, he was looking at the back of the man whom the lieutenant had called 'Fandorin'. Vasilii Alexandrovich's yellowish face was like a frozen mask, and there were strange glimmers of light flickering in his eyes.

NAKA-NO-KU

The first syllable,
in which Vasilii Alexandrovich
takes leave

They said goodbye as friends and, of course, not for ever – Rybnikov promised that as soon as he was settled in, he would definitely come to visit.

'Yes, do, please,' Lidina said severely, shaking his hand. 'I'll be worried about that tube of yours.'

The staff captain assured her that he would wriggle out of it somehow now and parted from the delightful lady with mixed feelings of regret and relief, of which the latter was by far the stronger.

After shaking his head to drive away inappropriate thoughts, the first thing he did was pay a visit to the telegraph office at the station. A telegram was waiting there for him to collect: 'Management congratulates brilliant success objections withdrawn may commence project receive goods information follows'.

Apparently this acknowledgement of his achievements, plus the withdrawal of certain objections, was very important to Rybnikov. His face brightened up and he even started singing a song about a toreador.

Something in the staff captain's manner changed. His uniform still sat on him baggily (after the adventures of the night, it had become even shabbier), but Vasilii Alexandrovich's shoulders had straightened up, the expression in his eyes was more lively, and he wasn't dragging his leg any more.

Running up the stairs to the second floor, where the offices were located, he seated himself on a broad windowsill offering a clear view of the entire wide, empty corridor and took out a notebook with pages full of aphorisms for every occasion in life. These included the old byword: 'A bullet's a fool, a bayonet's a fine fellow' and 'The Russian harnesses up slowly, but he rides fast' and 'Anyone who's drunk and clever has two landholdings in him', and the last of the maxims that had caught Vasilii Alexandrovich's interest was: 'You may be Ivanov the Seventh, but you're a fool. A. P. Chekhov'.

Chekhov was followed by blank pages, but the staff captain took out a flat little bottle of colourless liquid, shook a drop on to the paper and rubbed it with his finger, and strange symbols that looked like intertwined snakes appeared on the page. He did the same thing with the next few pages – and the outlandish squiggles came wriggling out of nowhere on to them as well. Rybnikov studied them closely for some time. Then he thought for a while, moving his lips and memorising something. And after another minute or two the serpentine scribbles disappeared all by themselves.

He went back to the telegraph office and sent off two urgent telegrams – to Samara and Krasnoyarsk. The content of both was identical: a request to come to Moscow 'on agreed business' on 25 May and a statement that a room had been booked in 'the same hotel'. The staff captain signed himself with the name 'Ivan Goncharov'.

And with that, urgent business was apparently concluded. Vasilii Alexandrovich went downstairs to the restaurant and dined with a good appetite, without counting the kopecks – he even allowed himself cognac. He also gave the waiter a tip that was not extravagant, but quite respectable.

And that was only the start of this army scarecrow's miraculous transformation.

From the station, the staff captain went to a clothing shop on Kuznetsky Most. He told the salesman that he had been discharged 'for good' when he was wounded, and wished to acquire a decent wardrobe.

He bought two good summer suits, several pairs of trousers, shoes with spats and American ankle boots, an English cap, a straw boater and half a dozen shirts. He changed there, put the tattered uniform away in his suitcase and told them to wrap his sword in paper.

And then there was this: Rybnikov arrived at the shop in a plain, ordinary cab, but he drove off in a lacquered four-wheeler, the kind that charge you fifty kopecks just for getting in.

The dapper passenger got out at Vuchtel's typographical emporium and told the driver not to wait for him. He had to pick up an order – a hundred *cartes de visite* in the name of a correspondent from the Reuters telegraph agency, and, moreover, the first name and patronymic on the cards were his, Rybnikov's – Vasilii Alexandrovich – but the surname was quite different: Sten.

And the freshly minted Mr Sten (but no, in order to avoid confusion, let him remain Rybnikov) made his departure from there on a regular five-rouble rocket, telling the driver to deliver him to the Saint-Saëns boarding house, but first to call in somewhere for a bunch of white lilies. The driver, a real sport, nodded respectfully: 'Understood, sir.'

The railings of the absolutely charming empire-style villa ran along the actual boulevard. If the garland of small coloured lanterns decorating the gates was anything to go by, the boarding house must have looked especially festive during the evening hours. But just at the moment the courtyard and the stand for carriages were empty and the tall windows were filled with the blank white of lowered curtains.

Rybnikov asked whether this was Countess Bovada's house and handed the doorman his card. Less than a minute later a rather portly lady emerged from the depths of the house, which proved to be far more spacious on the inside than it appeared to be from the outside. No longer young, but not yet old, she was very well groomed and made up so skilfully that it would have taken an experienced eye to spot any traces of cosmetic subterfuge.

At the sight of Rybnikov, the countess's slightly predatory features seemed to tighten and shrink for a brief moment, but then they immediately beamed in a gracious smile.

'My dear friend! My highly esteemed . . .' – she squinted sideways at the calling card. 'My highly esteemed Vasilii Alexandrovich! I am absolutely delighted to see you! And you haven't forgotten that I love white lilies! How sweet!'

'I never forget anything, Madam Beatrice,' said the former staff captain, pressing his lips to the hand that glittered with rings.

At these words his hostess involuntarily touched her magnificent ash-blonde hair, arranged in a tall style, and glanced in concern at the back of the gallant visitor's lowered head. But when Rybnikov straightened up, the charming smile was beaming once again on the countess's plump lips.

In the decor of the salon and the corridors, pastel tones were prevalent, with the gilt frames of copies of Watteau and Fragonard gleaming on the walls. This rendered even more impressive the contrast with the study to which Her Excellency led her visitor: no frivolity or affectation here – a writing desk with account books, a bureau, a rack for papers. It was obvious that the countess was a thoroughly businesslike individual, and not in the habit of wasting time idly.

'Don't be alarmed,' said Vasilii Alexandrovich, taking a seat in an armchair and crossing his legs. 'Everything is in order. They are pleased with you, you are as useful here as you were previously in Port Arthur and Vladivostok. I have not come to you on business. You know, I'm tired. I decided to take a period of leave, live quietly for a while.' He smiled cheerfully. 'I know from experience that the wilder things are around me, the calmer I feel.'

Countess Beauvade took offence.

'This is not some wild place, this is the best-run establishment in the city! After only a year of work my guest house has acquired an excellent reputation! Very respectable people come to us, people who value decorum and calm.'

'I know, I know,' Rybnikov interrupted her, still with the same smile. 'That is precisely why I came straight here from the train, dear Beatrice. Decorum and calm are exactly what I need. I won't be in the way, will I?'

His hostess replied very seriously.

'You shouldn't talk like that. I'm entirely at your disposal.' She hesitated for a moment and asked delicately, 'Perhaps you would like to relax with one of the young ladies? We have some capital ones. I promise you'll forget your tiredness.'

'I'd better not,' said the telegraph correspondent, declining politely. 'I may have to stay with you for two or three weeks. If I enter into a special

33

relationship with one of your ... boarders, it could lead to jealousy and squabbling. We don't want that.'

Beatrice nodded to acknowledge the reasonableness of his argument.

'I'll put you in a three-room apartment with a separate entrance. It's a section for clients who are prepared to pay for total privacy. That will be the most convenient place for you.'

'Excellent. Naturally, your losses will be reimbursed.'

'Thank you. In addition to being secluded from the main part of the house, where it is sometimes quite noisy at night, the apartment has other conveniences. The rooms are connected by secret doors, which might prove apposite.'

Rybnikov chuckled.

'I bet it also has false mirrors, conveniently positioned for taking photographs in secret. Like in Arthur, remember?'

The countess smiled and said nothing.

Rybnikov was pleased with his apartment. He spent a few hours arranging it, but not at all in the usual meaning of that word. His domestic bustle had nothing to do with the cosy comforts of home.

Vasilii Alexandrovich went to bed after midnight and took a right royal rest, the kind he had not had in a long time – he slept for an entire four hours, twice as long as usual.

The second syllable,
in which Masa
violates his neutrality

The passenger from compartment number six did not disappoint Erast Petrovich. On the contrary, the theory appeared ever more promising as time went on.

At the station Fandorin found the driver of the wagon that had transported the passenger who was in such a great hurry away from the banks of the Lomzha. The pretty lady's testimony was confirmed when the peasant said that the German had indeed forked out a hundred roubles.

'Why do you say he is German?' the engineer asked.

The driver was surprised.

'Well, why would any Russian shell out a hundred note when the price is fifteen kopecks at the outside?' Then he thought and added, 'And he had a queer way of speaking too.'

'Exactly how was it "queer"?' Erast Petrovich enquired eagerly, but the local couldn't explain that.

It was much harder to establish where the dark-haired man had gone on to from there. The stationmaster claimed ignorance, the duty supervisor bleated and avoided Fandorin's eyes, the local gendarme stood to attention and pretended to be a total imbecile. Then, recalling what his invaluable witness had said, the engineer asked point blank where the shunting engine was.

The gendarme instantly came out in large beads of sweat, the duty supervisor turned pale and the stationmaster turned red.

It turned out that the engine, in contravention of all the rules and regulations, had borne the dark-haired man off, full steam ahead, in pursuit of the passenger train that had passed through an hour ahead of the express. The berserk passenger (concerning his nationality, the opinions of the witnesses differed: the stationmaster thought he was a Frenchman, the duty supervisor thought he was a Pole, and the gendarme thought he was a 'Yid boy') had thrown so much money about in all directions that it was impossible to resist.

No doubts remained: this was the man Fandorin wanted.

The train that the interesting passenger had set out to chase arrived in Moscow at a quarter to ten, so there was just barely enough time left.

The engineer sent a telegram to the Moscow representative of the Department and an identical one to the head of the Volokolamsk section, Lieutenant Colonel Danilov, telling them to meet the suspect (there follow a detailed description) at the station but not to detain him under any circumstances, simply assign the smartest plainclothes agents they had to shadow him; and to do nothing more until Erast Petrovich arrived.

Because of the wreck, all traffic on the Nicholas line had come to a halt. A long queue of passenger and goods trains had formed in the St Petersburg direction, but in the Moscow direction the line was clear. Fandorin requisitioned the very latest five-axle 'compound engine' locomotive and, accompanied by his faithful valet, set off to the east at a speed of eighty versts an hour.

Erast Petrovich had last been in his native city five years earlier – in secret, under an assumed name. The higher authorities of Moscow were not fond of the retired state counsellor; indeed, they disliked him so greatly that even the briefest of stays in Russia's second capital city could end very unpleasantly for him.

After Fandorin returned to government service without any of the normal formalities being observed, an extremely strange situation had arisen: although he enjoyed the confidence of the government and was invested with extremely wide-ranging powers, the engineer continued to be regarded as *persona non grata* in the province of Moscow and endeavoured not to extend his journeys beyond the station of Bologoe.

But shortly after the New Year an incident had occurred that put an end to these years of exile, and if Erast Petrovich had not yet got around to visiting his native parts, it was only because of his extraordinarily excessive workload.

Standing beside the driver and gazing absentmindedly into the hot blaze of the firebox, Fandorin thought about the imminent encounter with the city of his youth and the event that had made this encounter possible.

It was an event that shook Moscow, in the literal sense as well as the figurative one. The governor-general of Moscow, Fandorin's bitter enemy, had been blown to pieces by a Social Revolutionary bomb right in the middle of the Kremlin.

For all his dislike of the deceased, a man of little worth, who had caused only harm to the city, Erast Petrovich was shocked by what had happened.

Russia was seriously ill, running a high fever, shivering hot and cold by turns, with bloody sweat oozing from her pores, and it was not just a matter of the war with Japan. The war had merely brought to light what was already clear in any case to any thinking individual: the empire had become an anachronism, a dinosaur with a body that was huge and a head that was too small, a creature that had outlived its time on earth. Or rather, the actual dimensions of the head were huge, it was swollen up with a multitude of ministries and committees, but hidden at the centre of this head was a tiny little brain, uncomplicated by any convolutions. Any decision that was even slightly complex, any movement of the unwieldy carcass, was impossible without a decision of will by a single individual whose wisdom, unfortunately, fell far short of Solomon's. But even if he had been an intellectual titan, how was it possible, in the age of electricity, radio and X-rays, to govern a country single-handed, during the breaks between lawn tennis and hunting?

So the poor Russian dinosaur was reeling, tripping over its own mighty feet, dragging its thousand-verst tail aimlessly across the earth. An agile predator of the new generation sprang at it repeatedly, tearing out lumps of flesh, and deep in the entrails of the behemoth, a deadly tumour was burgeoning. Fandorin did not know how to heal the ailing giant, but in any case bombs were not the answer – the jarring concussion would totally confuse the immense saurian's tiny little brain, the gigantic body would start twitching convulsively in panic, and Russia would die.

As usual, it was the wisdom of the East that helped purge his gloomy and barren thoughts. The engineer fished out of his memory an aphorism that suited the case: 'The superior man knows that the world is imperfect, but does not lose heart'.

The factor that had disrupted the harmony of Erast Petrovich's soul should be arriving at the Nicholas station in Moscow any minute now.

He could only hope that Lieutenant Colonel Danilov would not blunder . . .

Danilov did not blunder. He met his visitor from St Petersburg in person, right beside the reserve line at which the 'compound' arrived. The lieutenant colonel's round face was glowing with excitement. As soon as they had shaken hands he started his report.

He didn't have a single good agent – they had all been lured into the Okhrana's Flying Squad, where the pay and the gratuities were better, and there was more freedom. And therefore, knowing that the engineer would not have alarmed him over something trivial, Danilov had decided to reprise the good old days, taken his deputy, Staff Captain Lisitsky, a very capable officer, to help him and followed the mark himself.

Now the engineer understood the reason for bold Nikolai Vasilievich's agitation. The lieutenant colonel had had enough of sitting in his office, he was weary of having no real work to do, that was why he had gone dashing off so eagerly to play cops and robbers. 'I'll have to tell them to transfer him to work in the field,' Fandorin noted to himself as he listened to the adventurous tale of how Danilov and his deputy had dressed up as petty merchants and how deftly they had arranged the surveillance in two cabs.

'In Petrovsko-Razumovskoe?' he asked in surprise. 'In that d-dump?'

'Ah, Erast Petrovich, it's easy to see you haven't been around for quite a while. Petrovsko-Razumovskoe's a fashionable dacha district now. For instance, the dacha to which we trailed the dark-haired man is rented by a certain Alfred Radzikovski for a thousand roubles a month.'

'A thousand?' Fandorin echoed in astonishment. 'What kind of Fontaine-bleau is that?'

'A Fontainebleau is exactly what it is. A huge great garden with its own stables, even a garage. I left the staff captain to continue the surveillance, he has two corporals with him, in civvies, naturally. Reliable men but, of course, not professional sleuths.'

'Let's go,' the engineer said briskly.

Lisitsky – a handsome fellow with a rakishly curled moustache – proved to be a very capable fellow. He hadn't wasted his time sitting in the bushes, he had found out a great deal.

'They live on a grand scale,' he reported, occasionally slipping into a Polish accent. 'Electricity, telephone, even their own telegraph apparatus. A bathroom with a shower! Two carriages with thoroughbred trotters! An automobile in the garage! A gym with exercise bicycles! Servants in lace pinafores! Parrots this size in the winter garden!'

'How do you know about the parrots?' Fandorin asked incredulously.

'Why, I was there,' Staff Captain Lisitsky replied with a cunning air. 'I tried to get a job as a gardener. They didn't take me – said they already had one. But they let me take a peep into the conservatory – one of them is a great lover of plants.'

'One?' the engineer asked quickly. 'How many are there?'

'I don't know, but it's a fair-sized group. I heard about half a dozen voices. And, by the way, between themselves they talk Polish.'

'But what about?' the lieutenant colonel exclaimed. 'You know the language!'

The young officer shrugged.

'They didn't say anything significant with me there. They praised the dark-haired bloke for something, called him a "real daredevil". By the way, his name's Yuzek.'

'They're Polish nationalists from the Socialist Party, I'm sure of it!' Danilov exclaimed. 'I read about them in a secret circular. They've got mixed up with the Japanese, who promised to make independence for Poland a condition if they win. Their leader went to Tokyo recently. What's his name again . . .'

'Pilsudski,' said Erast Petrovich, examining the dacha through a pair of binoculars.

'That's it, Pilsudski. He must have got money in Japan, and instructions.'

'It l-looks like it . . .'

Something was stirring at the dacha. A blond man standing by the window in a collarless shirt with wide braces shouted something into a telephone. A door slammed loudly once, twice. Horses started neighing.

'It looks like they're getting ready for something,' Lisitsky whispered in the engineer's ear. 'They started moving about half an hour ago now.'

'The Japs' spies don't seem any too bothered about us,' the lieutenant colonel boomed in his other ear. 'Of course, our counter-espionage is pretty lousy, right enough, but this is just plain cheeky: setting themselves up in comfort like this, five minutes away from the Nicholas railway station. Wouldn't I just love to nab the little darlings right now. A pity it's out of our jurisdiction. The Okhrana boys and the provincial gendarmes will eat us alive. If they were on the railway right of way, now that would be a different matter.'

'I tell you what we can do,' Lisitsky suggested. 'We'll call our platoon and put the dacha under siege, but we won't take it, we'll inform the police. Then they won't make any fuss about it.'

Fandorin didn't join in the discussion – he was turning his head this way and that, trying to spot something. He fixed his gaze on a freshly trimmed wooden pole sticking up out of the ground beside the road.

'A telephone pole . . . We could listen to what they're saying . . .'

'How?' the lieutenant colonel asked in surprise.

'Tap the line, from the pole.'

'Sorry, Erast Petrovich, I don't have a clue about technical matters. What does "tap the line" mean?

Fandorin, however, didn't bother to explain anything – he had already made his decision.

'One of the platforms on our Nicholas line is c-close by here . . .'

'That's right, the Petrovsko-Razumovskoe way station.'

'There must be a telephone apparatus there. Send a gendarme. But be quick, don't waste a second. He runs in, cuts the wire right at the wall, takes the telephone and comes straight back. No wasting time on explanations, he just shows his identification document, that's all. At the double, now!'

A few moments later they heard the tramping of rapidly receding boots as the corporal rushed off to carry out his mission. About ten minutes after that he came dashing back with the severed telephone and wire.

'Lucky it's so long,' the engineer said happily, and astounded the gendarmes by taking off his elegant coat, clutching a folding penknife in his teeth and shinning up the pole.

After fiddling with the wires for a bit, he came back down, holding the earpiece in his hands, with its wire leading up into the air.

'Take it,' he said to the staff captain. 'Since you know Polish, you can do the listening.'

Lisitsky was filled with admiration.

'What a brilliant idea, Mr Engineer! How incredible that no one ever thought of it before! Why, you could set up a special office at the telephone exchange! Listen to what suspicious individuals are saying! What tremendous benefit for the fatherland! And so very civilised, in the spirit of technological progr . . .' The officer broke off in mid-word, raised a warning finger and informed them in a terrible whisper, 'They're calling! The central exchange!'

The lieutenant colonel and the engineer leaned forward eagerly.

'A man . . . asking for number 398 . . .' Lisitsky whispered jerkily. 'Another man . . . Speaking Polish . . . The first one's arranging to meet . . . No, it's a gathering . . . On Novo-Basmannaya Street . . . In the Varvarin Company building . . . An operation! He said "operation"! That's it, he cut the connection.'

'What kind of operation?' asked Danilov, grabbing his deputy by the shoulder.

'He didn't say. Just "the operation", that's all. At midnight, and it's almost half past nine already. No wonder they're bustling about like that.'

'On Basmannaya? The Varvarin Company Building?' Erast Petrovich repeated, also whispering without even realising it. 'What's there, do you know?'

The officers exchanged glances and shrugged.

'We need an address b-book.'

They sent the same corporal running back to the way station – to dart into the office, grab the *All Moscow* guidebook off the desk and leg it back as quickly as possible.

'The men at the way station will think the railway gendarme service is full of head cases,' the lieutenant colonel lamented, but mostly for form's sake. 'Never mind, we'll return it all afterwards – the telephone and the book.'

The next ten minutes passed in tense anticipation, with them almost tearing the binoculars out of each other's hands. They couldn't see all that well because it was starting to get dark, but all the lights were on in the dacha and hasty shadows flitted across the curtains.

The three of them went dashing to meet the panting corporal. Erast Petrovich, as the senior in rank, grabbed the tattered volume. First he checked what telephone number 398 was. It proved to be the Great Moscow Hotel. He moved on to the *Listing of Buildings* section, opened it at Novo-Basmannaya Street, and the blood started pounding in his temples.

The building that belonged to the Varvarin Company contained the administrative offices of the District Artillery Depot.

The lieutenant colonel glanced over the engineer's shoulder and gasped.

'Why, of course! Why didn't I realise straight away . . . Novo-Basmannaya Street. That's where they have the warehouses for the shells and dynamite that they send to the army in the field! They always have at least a week's supply of ammunition! But, gentlemen, that's ... Why, it's unheard of! Monstrous! If they're planning to blow it up – almost half of Moscow will be blown to pieces! Why, those lousy Poles! Begging your pardon, Boleslav Stefanovich, I didn't mean ...'

'What can you expect from socialists,' said Staff Captain Lisitsky, interceding for his nation. 'Pawns in the hands of the Japanese, that's all. But what about those Orientals! Genuine new Huns! Absolutely no concept of civilised warfare!'

'Gentlemen, gentlemen,' Danilov interrupted, with his eyes blazing. 'There's a silver lining to this cloud! The artillery stores adjoin the workshops of the Kazan railway, and that's ...'

'... that's our territory!' Lisitsky concluded for him. 'Bravo, Nikolai Vasilievich! We'll get by without the provincials!'

'And without the Okhrana!' his boss said with a predatory smile.

The lieutenant colonel and the staff captain worked a genuine miracle of efficiency: in two hours they set up a sound, thoroughly planned ambush. They didn't trail the saboteurs from Petrovsko-Razumovskoe – that was too risky. At night the lanes in the dacha village were empty and, as luck would have it, the moon was shining with all its might. It was more rational to concentrate all their efforts at a single spot, where the plotters had arranged their gathering.

Danilov brought out all the current members of the section for the operation, apart from those who were standing duty – sixty-seven men altogether.

Most of the gendarmes were set around the inside of the depot's perimeter wall, with orders to 'lie there quietly and not stick their heads up'. Lisitsky was the man in command on the spot. The lieutenant colonel himself took ten of his best men and hid in the management building.

To obtain permission for the railway gendarmes to run their own show on the territory of the artillery administration, they had to get the Director of Depositories, an old general who had fought against Shamil some fifty years previously, out of his bed. He got so agitated that it never even entered his head to nitpick about the finer points of jurisdiction – he just agreed to everything immediately and kept swallowing heart drops all the time.

Seeing that Danilov was managing perfectly well without him, the engineer distanced himself from the supervision of the ambush. He and Masa stationed themselves in an entrance opposite the gates of the depot. Fandorin chose the spot quite deliberately. If the gendarmes, who were not used to this kind of operation, let any of the saboteurs get away, then Erast Petrovich would block their path, and they would not get away from him! However, Danilov, elated by the preparations, understood the engineer's decision in his own way, and a note of slight condescension appeared in the lieutenant colonel's tone of voice, as if to say: Well, of course, I'm not criticising, you're a civilian, you're not obliged to put yourself in the way of a bullet.

Just as soon as everyone had taken up their positions and the nervous general had followed instructions by putting out the light in his office before pressing his face up against the windowpane, they heard the chiming of the clock in the tower on Kalanchovskaya Square, and a minute later three open carriages came rolling into the street from two directions – two from the Ryazan Passage and one from the Yelokhovsky Passage. The carriages met in front of the administration building and men got out of them (Fandorin counted five, and another three who stayed on the coach boxes). They started whispering to each other about something.

The engineer took out of his pocket a beautiful small, flat pistol, manufactured to order at the Browning factory in Belgium, and tugged on the breech. His valet demonstratively turned away.

Well then, come on, Erast Petrovich thought to himself, trying to hurry the Poles along, and sighed – there was not much hope that Danilov's fine eagles would take anyone alive. But never mind, at least one of the villains had to stay with the horses. The lucky man would escape a gendarme's bullet and fall into Fandorin's hands.

The discussions ended. But instead of moving towards the doors of the administration building or straight to the gates, the saboteurs got back into their carriages, cracked their whips and all three carriages dashed away from the depot, picking up speed, in the direction of Dobraya Sloboda.

Had they noticed something? Had they changed their plan?

Erast Petrovich ran out of the gateway.

The carriages had already disappeared round the corner.

The engineer pulled his splendid coat off his shoulders and set off at a run in the same direction.

His servant picked up the abandoned coat and jogged after him, puffing and panting.

When Lieutenant Colonel Danilov and his gendarmes darted out on to the porch, Novo-Basmannaya Street was already empty. The sound of hoofbeats had faded into the distance, and the moon was shining placidly in the sky.

It turned out that Erast Petrovich Fandorin, a responsible member of a highly serious government agency, a man no longer in the prime of youth, could not only shin up telephone poles, but could also run at a quite fantastic speed, while making no sound and remaining virtually invisible – he ran close to the walls, where the shadows of night were thickest of all, skirting round the patches of moonlight or vaulting over them with a prodigious leap. More than anything else, the engineer resembled a phantom, careering along the dark street on some otherworldly business of his own. It was a good thing he didn't run into anybody out walking late – the poor devil would have been in for a serious shock.

Fandorin caught up with the carriages quite soon. After that he started running more gently, in order to keep his distance.

The pursuit, however, did not continue for long.

The carriages halted behind the Von-Dervizov Grammar School for Girls. They were parked wheel to wheel, and one of the drivers gathered all the reins into a bundle, while the other seven men set off towards a two-storey building with a glass display window.

One of them fiddled with the door for a moment, then waved his hand, and the whole group disappeared inside.

Erast Petrovich stuck his head out from round the corner, trying to work out how to creep up on the driver, who was standing on his box, gazing around vigilantly in all directions. All the approaches were brightly lit by the moon.

At this point Masa came panting up. Realising from Fandorin's expression that his master was about to take decisive action, he threw his false pigtail over his shoulder and whispered angrily in Japanese:

'I shall only intervene if the supporters of His Majesty are going to kill you. But if you start killing the supporters of His Majesty the Mikado, then do not count on my help.'

'Oh, drop it,' Erast Petrovich replied in Russian. 'Don't get in my way.'

There was a muffled scream from the house. No further delay was possible.

The engineer ran soundlessly to the nearest lamp-post and hid behind it. He was now only ten paces away from the driver.

Taking a monogrammed cigar case out of his pocket, Fandorin tossed it away from him.

The driver started at the jingling sound and turned his back to the lamp-post.

That was exactly what was required. Fandorin covered the distance between them in three bounds, jumped up on to the footboard and pressed the driver's neck. The driver went limp, and the engineer carefully laid him out on the cobblestones, beside the inflated tyres.

From here he could make out the sign hanging above the door.

'IOSIF BARANOV. DIAMOND, GOLD AND SILVER ITEMS,' the engineer read, and muttered:

'I don't understand a thing.'

He ran up to the window and glanced in – he could make out the glow of several electric torches in the shop, but it was still dark inside, with only agile shadows darting about. Suddenly the interior was illuminated by an unbearably bright glow, a rain of fiery sparks scattered in all directions, and Fandorin could make out glass counters with men scurrying along them and the door of a safe, with a man leaning over it, holding a blowtorch – the very latest model. Erast Petrovich had seen one like it in a picture in a French magazine.

A man who looked like the nightwatchman had been tied up and was sitting on the floor with his back against the wall: his mouth was covered with sticking plaster, blood was flowing from a wound where he had been hit over the head, and his frantic eyes were glaring wildly at the satanic flame.

'What has the Japanese secret service c-come to?' exclaimed Fandorin, turning to his valet, who had just walked up. 'Can Japan really be so short of money?'

'The servants of His Majesty the Mikado do not stear,' replied Masa, surveying the picturesque scene. 'These are bandits. "Moscow Daredevirs" – I read about them in the newspaper; they make raids in automobiles or fast carriages – they very fond of progress.' The Japanese servant's face lit up in a smile. 'That's good! Master, I can herp you!'

Erast Petrovich himself had already realised that he was the victim of a misunderstanding – he had mistaken ordinary Warsaw bandits on tour in Moscow for saboteurs. All that time had been wasted for nothing!

But what about the dark-haired man, the passenger from compartment number six, who had fled the scene of the catastrophe in such a suspicious manner?

That's very simple, the engineer replied to his own question. A daring robbery was committed two days ago in St Petersburg, all the newspapers wrote about it in purple prose. An unidentified individual in a mask stopped the carriage of Countess Vorontsova, robbed Her Excellency, quite literally, of her last thread of clothing and left her there in the road, naked apart from her hat. The spicy part was that the countess had quarrelled with her husband that very evening, and she was moving to her parents' house, secretly taking all her jewels with her. No wonder Lisitsky said that the inhabitants of the dacha called the dark-haired man 'a real daredevil' – he had pulled off the job in St Petersburg and got back here in time for the Moscow operation.

If not for his bitter disappointment and annoyance with himself, Erast Petrovich would probably not have interfered in a mere criminal case, but his fury demanded an outlet – and he felt sorry for the nightwatchman – what if they slit his throat?

'Take them when they start coming out,' he whispered to his servant. 'One for you, one for me.'

Masa nodded and licked his lips.

But fate decreed otherwise.

'Nix it, gents!' someone shouted desperately – he must have seen the two shadows outside the window.

In an instant the acetylene glow went out and instead of it a crimson-red gunshot came crashing out of the pitch darkness.

Fandorin and his Japanese valet jumped in opposite directions with perfect synchronisation. The shop window shattered with a deafening jangle.

They carried on firing from the shop, but it was already completely pointless.

'Whoever jumps out is yours,' the engineer jabbered rapidly.

He crouched down, rolled agilely over the windowsill covered with shards of glass and dissolved into the dark entrails of the shop.

From inside came the sounds of men yelling and cursing in Russian and

Polish, and short, sharp blows. Every so often the room was lit up by the flashes of shots.

A man in a check cap came flying out of the door with his head pulled down into his shoulders. Masa caught the fugitive with an uppercut and laid him out with a blow to the nape of the neck. He rapidly tied him up and dragged him over to the carriages, where the driver Fandorin hàd half throttled was lying.

Soon another one jumped out through the window and took to his heels without looking back. The Japanese easily overtook him, grabbed him by the wrist and twisted it gently. The bandit squealed and hunched over in pain.

'Easy, easy,' Masa coaxed his prisoner as he quickly tied his wrists to his ankles with his belt.

He carried him over to the other two and went back to his original position.

There was no more noise from inside the shop. Masa heard Fandorin's voice.

'One, two, three, four ... where's number five? Ah, there he is – five. Masa, how many have you got?'

'Three.'

'That tallies.'

Erast Petrovich thrust his head out through the rectangle rimmed with barbs of glass.

'Run to the depot and bring the gendarmes. And quick about it, or this lot will come round and we'll be off again.'

The servant ran off in the direction of Novo-Basmannaya Street.

Fandorin untied the watchman and gave him a few slaps on the cheeks to bring him to his senses. But the watchman didn't want to come to his senses – he muttered and screwed up his eyes, quivered and hiccupped. In medical terms it was called 'shock'.

While Erast Petrovich was rubbing his temples and feeling for a nerve point just below his collarbone, the stunned bandits began to stir.

One muscly hulk, who had taken an impeccable blow to the chin from a shoe only five minutes earlier, sat up on the floor and started shaking his head. Fandorin had to leave the hiccupping watchman in order to give the reanimated bandit a second helping.

No sooner had that one dived nose first into the floor than another one came round, got up on all fours and started crawling nimbly towards the door. Erast Petrovich dashed after him and stunned him.

A third one was already stirring in the corner, and things were also getting confused out on the street, where Masa had arranged his bandit ikebana: by the light of the street lamp Fandorin could see the driver trying to unfasten the knot on one of his partner's elbows with his teeth. It occurred to Fandorin that now he was like a clown in a circus who has thrown several balls up in the air and doesn't know how he's going to deal with them all. While he's picking one up off the floor, the others come showering down.

He dashed to the corner. A dark-haired bandit (could it be Yuzek himself?) had not only come round, he had already managed to take out a knife. A quick blow, and another one to make sure. The bandit lay down.

Then a rapid dash to the carriages – before those three could crawl away.

Damn it, where had Masa got to?

But Fandorin's valet had not managed to reach Lieutenant Colonel Danilov, who was hanging about cluelessly with his men at the Varvarin Company building.

At the very first corner an agile fellow flung himself under Masa's feet and another two fell on him from above, twisting his arms behind his back.

Masa growled and even tried to bite, but they had his arms twisted tightly, in true professional style.

'Evstratii Pavlovich! We've got one! A Chink! Tell us, Chinky, where's the shooting?'

They pulled Masa's pigtail and the wig flew off his head.

'He's in disguise!' the same voice shouted triumphantly. 'But he's a slanty-eyed git all right, a Jap! A spy, Evstratii Pavlovich!'

Another man, wearing a bowler hat, walked up and praised his men.

'Good lads.'

He leaned down to Masa.

'Good evening to you, Your Japanese Honour. I'm Court Counsellor Mylnikov, Special Section, Department of Police. What's your name and rank?'

The prisoner tried to give the court counsellor a vicious kick on the shin, but he missed. Then he started hissing and cursing in some foreign tongue.

'No point in swearing,' Evstratii Pavlovich rebuked him. 'You're caught now, so you can stop chirping. You must be an officer of the Japanese general staff, a nobleman? I'm a nobleman too. So let's deal honestly with each other. What were you up to here? What's all this shooting and running about? Give me a light here, Kasatkin.'

The yellow circle of electric light picked out a narrow-eyed face contorted in fury and a head of short-cropped, shiny black hair.

Mylnikov started babbling in confusion:

'Why, it's . . . How do you do, Mr Masa . . .'

'Rong time, no see,' hissed Fandorin's valet.

The third syllable,
in which Rybnikov
gets into a jam

In recent months Vasilii Alexandrovich Rybnikov (now Sten) had lived a feverish, nervous life, dealing with hundreds of different matters every day and getting no more than two hours' sleep a night (which, however, was quite enough for him – he always woke as fresh as a daisy). But the telegram of congratulations he had received the morning after the crash at the Tezoi-menitsky Bridge had relieved the former staff captain of routine work, allowing him to concentrate completely on his two main missions or, as he thought of them, 'projects'.

The brand-new Reuters correspondent did everything that needed to be done at the preliminary stage in the first two days.

In preparation for the main 'project' (this involved the onward delivery of a large consignment of certain goods), it was sufficient to send the consignee with the frivolous name of Thrush a letter by the municipal post, telling him to expect delivery in one or two weeks, everything else as formerly agreed.

The second 'project', which was of secondary importance, but even so very significant indeed, also required very little fuss or bother. In addition to the aforementioned telegrams to Samara and Krasnoyarsk, Vasilii Alex-androvich ordered from a glass-blowing workshop two slim spirals to match a drawing that he supplied, whispering confidentially to the receiving clerk that they were parts of an alcohol purification device for home use.

By inertia or as a pendant, so to speak, to his hectic life in Peter, Rybnikov spent another day or two running round the military institutions of Moscow, where a correspondent's calling card ensured him access to all sorts of well-informed individuals – everyone knows how we love the foreign press. The self-styled reporter discovered a great deal of curious and even semi-confidential information, which, when properly assembled and analysed, became completely confidential. After that, however, Rybnikov thought better of it and put an end to all his interviewing. In comparison with the projects that he had been charged to carry out, this was petty business, and there was no point in taking any risks for it.

With an effort of will, Vasilii Alexandrovich suppressed the itch for action that had been developed by long habit and forced himself to spend more time at home. Patience and the need to remain in a state of quiescence are a severe trial for a man who is not used to sitting still for a single minute, but even here Rybnikov proved up to the challenge.

He transformed himself in an instant from an energetic, active individual into a sybarite who sat in his armchair at the window for hours at a stretch and strolled around his apartment in a dressing gown. The new rhythm of his life coincided perfectly with the regimen of the carefree inhabitants of 'Saint-Saëns', who woke up at about midday and strolled round the house in curlers and carpet slippers until seven in the evening.

Vasilii Alexandrovich established a wonderful relationship with the girls in no time at all. On the first day the young ladies were still uncertain of the new boarder, and so they made eyes at him, but very soon the rumour spread that he was Beatrice's *sweetheart*, and the tentative romantic approaches ceased immediately. On the second day 'Vasenka' had already become a general favourite. He treated the girls to sweets and listened to their tittle-tattle with interest and, in addition to that, he tinkled on the piano, crooning sentimental romances in a pleasant, slightly mawkish tenor.

Rybnikov really was interested in spending time with the girls at the boarding house. He had discovered that their tittle-tattle, if correctly directed, could be every bit as useful as dashing from one fake interview to another. Countess Bovada's boarding house was a substantial establishment, men of position visited it. Sometimes they discussed work matters with each other in the salon and later on, in a separate room, when they were in a tender and affectionate mood, they might let slip something absolutely intriguing. They must have assumed that the empty-headed young ladies would not understand anything anyway. And indeed, the girls were certainly no match for Sophia Kovalevskaya when it came to intellect, but they had retentive memories and they were terribly fond of gossiping.

And so, tea parties at the piano not only helped Vasilii Alexandrovich to kill the time, they also provided a mass of useful information.

Unfortunately, during the initial period of the staff captain's voluntary life as a hermit, the young ladies' imagination was totally engrossed by the sensation that had set the entire old capital buzzing. The police had finally caught the famous gang of 'daredevils'. Everyone in Moscow was writing and talking more about this than about Tsushima. They knew that a special squad of the very finest sleuths had been sent from St Petersburg to capture the audacious bandits – and Muscovites found that flattering.

A redheaded Manon Lescaut who went by the nickname of 'Wafer' was known to have been frequented by one of the 'daredevils', a handsome Pole and genuine fancy morsel, so now Wafer was wearing black and acting mysteriously. The other girls envied her.

During these days Vasilii Alexandrovich several times caught himself thinking about his companion in the compartment in the train – possibly because Lidina was the total opposite of the sentimental but coarse-spirited inhabitants of the 'Saint-Saëns'. Rybnikov recalled Glyceria as she made a dash for the emergency brake handle, or with her pale face and bitten lip, binding up a torn artery in a wounded man's leg with a scrap of her dress.

Surprised at himself, the hermit drove these pictures away; they had nothing to do with his life and his present interests.

For his constitutional he went for a walk along the boulevards, as far as the Cathedral of the Saviour and back again. Vasilii Alexandrovich did not know Moscow very well, and therefore he was terribly surprised when he looked at a sign with the name of a street that led up and away at an angle from the Orthodox cathedral.

The street was called 'Ostozhenka'.

'The Bomze building on Ostozhenka Street,' Vasilii Alexandrovich heard a soft voice say, clipping its consonants in the Petersburg style as clearly as if she were there.

He strolled for a while along the street with its asphalt roadway and lines of beautiful buildings, but soon came to his senses and turned back.

Nonetheless, after that time he got into the habit of making a loop to take in Ostozhenka Street when he reached the end of his horseshoe route on the boulevards. Rybnikov also walked past the Bomze apartment building –

a smart four-storey structure. Vasilii Alexandrovich's indolence had put him in a strange mood, and as he glanced at the narrow Viennese windows, he even allowed himself to daydream a little about what could never possibly happen in a million years.

And then his dreams caught him out.

On the fifth day of his walks, as the false reporter, tapping his cane, was walking down along Ostozhenka Street to Lesnoi Passage, someone called him from a carriage.

'Vasilii Alexandrovich! Is that you?'

The resounding voice sounded happy.

Rybnikov froze on the spot, mentally cursing his own thoughtlessness. He turned round slowly, putting on a surprised expression.

'Where did you get to?' Lidina chirped excitedly. 'Shame on you, you promised! Why are you in civilian clothes? An excellent jacket, you look much better in it than in that terrible uniform! What about the drawings?'

She asked the last question in a whisper, after she had already jumped down on to the pavement.

Vasilii Alexandrovich warily shook the slim hand in the silk glove. He was nonplussed, which only happened to him very rarely – you might even say that it never happened at all

'A bad business,' he mumbled eventually. 'I am obliged to lie low. That's why I'm in civvies. And that's why I didn't come, too . . . You know, it's best to keep well away from me just now.' To make this more convincing, Rybnikov glanced round over his shoulder and lowered his voice. 'You go on your way, and I'll walk on. We shouldn't attract attention.'

Glyceria Romanovna's face looked frightened, but she didn't move from the spot.

She glanced round too, and then spoke right into his ear.

'A court martial, right? What is it – hard labour? Or . . . or worse?'

'Worse,' he said, moving away slightly. 'There's nothing to be done. It's my own fault. I'm to blame for everything. Really, Glyceria Romanovna, my dear lady, I'll be going.'

'Not for anything in the world! How can I abandon you in misfortune? You probably need money, don't you? I have some. Accommodation? I'll think of something. Good Lord, what terrible bad luck!' Tears glinted in the lady's eyes.

'No, thank you. I'm living with . . . with my aunt, my late mother's sister. I don't want for anything. See what a dandy I am . . . really, people are looking at us.'

Lidina took hold of his elbow. 'You're right. Get into the carriage, we'll put the top up.'

And she didn't wait for him to answer, she put him in – he already knew he could never match the stubbornness of this woman. Remarkably enough, although Vasilii Alexandrovich's iron will did not exactly weaken at that moment, it was, so to speak, *distracted*, and his foot stepped up on to the running board of its own accord.

They took a drive round Moscow, talking about all sorts of things. The raised hood of the carriage lent even the most innocent subject an intimacy that Rybnikov found alarming. He decided several times to get out at the next corner, but somehow he didn't get around to it. Lidina was concerned about one thing above all – how to help this poor fugitive who had the merciless sword of martial law dangling over his head.

When Vasilii Alexandrovich finally took his leave, he had to promise that he would come to Prechistensky Boulevard the next day. Lidina would be riding in her carriage, catch sight of him as though by chance, call him and he would get in again. Nothing suspicious, a perfectly normal street scene.

As he gave his promise, Rybnikov was certain that he would not keep it, but the next day the will of this man of iron was affected once again by the inexplicable phenomenon already mentioned above. At precisely five o'clock the correspondent's feet brought him to the appointed place and the ride was repeated.

The same thing happened the next day, and the day after that.

There was not even a hint of flirting in their relationship – Rybnikov kept a very strict watch on that. No hints, glances or – God forbid! – sighs. For the most part their conversations were serious, and the tone was not at all the one in which men usually talk to beautiful ladies.

'I like being with you,' Lidina confessed one day. 'You're not like all the others. You don't show off, you don't pay compliments. I can tell that for you I'm not a creature of the female sex, but a person, an individual. I never thought that I could be friends with a man and it could be so enjoyable!'

Something must have changed in the expression on his face, because Glyceria Romanovna blushed and exclaimed guiltily:

'Ah, what an egotist I am! I'm only thinking about myself! But you're on the edge of a precipice!'

'Yes, I am on the edge of a precipice . . .' Vasilii Alexandrovich murmured desolately, and the way he said it was so convincing that tears sprang to Lidina's eyes.

Glyceria Romanovna thought about poor Vasya (that was what she always called him to herself) all the time now – before their meetings and afterwards too. How could she help him? How could she save him? He was disoriented, defenceless, not suited to military service. How stupid to put an officer's uniform on someone like that! It was enough just to remember what he looked like in that get-up! The war would end soon, and no one would ever remember about those papers, but a good man's life would be ruined for ever.

Every time she appeared at their meeting elated, with a new plan to save him. She suggested hiring a skilled draughtsman who would make another drawing exactly the same. She thought of appealing for help to a high-ranking general of gendarmes, a good friend of hers, who wouldn't dare refuse.

Every time, however, Rybnikov turned the conversation on to abstract subjects. He was reluctant and niggardly in speaking about himself. Lidina wanted very much to know where and how he had spent his childhood, but all that Vasilii Alexandrovich told her was that as a little boy he loved to catch dragonflies and let them go later from the top of a high cliff, to watch them darting about in zigzags above the void. He also loved imitating the voices of the birds – and he actually mimicked a cuckoo, a magpie and a blue tit so well that Glyceria Romanovna clapped her hands in delight.

On the fifth day of their drives Rybnikov returned to his apartment in a particularly thoughtful mood. First, because there were fewer than twenty-four hours remaining until both 'projects' moved into a crucial stage. And secondly, because he knew he had seen Lidina for the last time that day.

Glyceria Romanovna had been especially endearing today. She had come up with two plans to save Rybnikov: one we have already mentioned, about the general of gendarmes, and a second, which she particularly liked, to arrange for him to escape abroad. She described the advantages of this idea enthusiastically, coming back to it again and again, although he said straight away that it wouldn't work – they would arrest him at the border post.

The fugitive staff captain strode along the boulevard with his jaw thrust out determinedly, so deep in thought that he didn't glance at his mirror-bright watch at all.

Once he had reached the boarding house, though, and was inside his separate apartment, his habitual caution prompted him to peep out from behind the curtains.

He gritted his teeth: standing at the opposite pavement was a horse cab with its hood up, despite the bright weather. The driver was staring hard at the windows of the 'Saint-Saëns'; the passenger could not be seen.

Scraps of thoughts started flitting rapidly through Rybnikov's head.

How?

Why?

Countess Bovada?

Impossible.

But no one else knows.

The old contacts had been broken off, new ones had not yet been struck up.

There could only be one explanation: that damned Reuters Agency. One of the generals he had interviewed had decided to correct something or add something, phoned the Reuters Moscow office and discovered there was no Sten assigned there. He had taken fright, informed the Okhrana . . . But even if that was it – how had they found him?

And here again there was only one probable answer: by chance.

Some particularly lucky agent had recognised him in the street from a verbal description (ah, he should at least have changed his wardrobe!), and now was trailing him.

But if it was a chance occurrence, things could be set right, Vasilii told himself, and immediately felt calmer.

He estimated the distance to the carriage: sixteen – no, seventeen – steps.

His thoughts grew even shorter, even more rapid.

Start with the passenger, he's a professional . . . A heart attack . . . I live here, help me carry him in, old mate . . . Beatrice would be annoyed. Never mind, she was in this up to her neck. What about the cab? In the evening, that could be done in the evening.

He finished thinking it all out on the move. He walked unhurriedly out on to the steps, yawned and stretched. His hand casually flourished a long cigarette holder – empty, with no *papirosa* in it. Rybnikov also extracted a small, flat pillbox from his pocket and took out of it something that he put in his mouth.

As he walked past the cabby, he noticed the man squinting sideways at him.

Vasilii Alexandrovich paid no attention to the driver. He gripped the cigarette holder in his teeth, quickly jerked back the flap of the cab – and froze.

Lidina was sitting in the carriage.

Suddenly deathly pale, Rybnikov jerked the cigarette holder out of his mouth, coughed and spat into his handkerchief.

Not looking even slightly embarrassed, she said with a cunning smile:

'So this is where you live, Mr Conspirator! Your auntie has a lovely house.'

'You followed me?' said Vasilii Alexandrovich, forcing out the words with a struggle, thinking: One more second, a split second, and . . .

'Cunning, isn't it?' Glyceria Romanovna laughed. 'I switched cabs, ordered the driver to drive at walking pace, at a distance. I said you were my husband and I suspected you of being unfaithful.'

'But . . . what for?'

She turned serious.

'You gave me such a look when I said "until tomorrow" . . . I suddenly felt that you wouldn't come tomorrow. And you wouldn't come again at all. And I don't even know where to look for you . . . I can see that our meetings are a burden on your conscience. You think you're putting me in danger. Do you know what I've thought of?' Lidina exclaimed brightly. 'Introduce me to your aunt. She's your relative, I'm your friend. You have no idea of the power of two women who join forces!'

'No!' said Rybnikov, staggering back. 'Absolutely not!'

'Then I shall go in myself,' Lidina declared, and her face took on the same expression it had worn in the corridor of the train.

'All right, if you want to so badly . . . But I have to warn my aunt. She has a bad heart, and she's not very fond of surprises in general,' said Vasilii Alexandrovich, spouting nonsense in his panic. 'My aunt runs a boarding house for girls from noble families. It has certain rules. Let's do it tomorrow . . . Yes, yes, tomorrow. In the early eve—'

'Ten minutes,' she snapped. 'I'll wait ten minutes, then I'll go in myself.'

And she emphatically raised the small diamond watch hanging round her neck.

Countess Bovada was an exceptionally resourceful individual, Rybnikov already knew that. She understood his meaning from a mere hint, didn't waste a single second on questions and went into action immediately.

Probably no other woman would have been capable of transforming a bordello into a boarding house for daughters of the nobility in ten minutes.

After exactly ten minutes (Rybnikov was watching from behind the curtains) Glyceria Romanovna paid her cabby and got out of the carriage with a determined air.

The door was opened for her by the respectable-looking porter, who bowed and led her along the corridor towards the sound of a pianoforte.

Lidina was pleasantly surprised by the rich decor of the boarding house. She thought it rather strange that there were nails protruding from the walls in places – as if pictures had been hanging there, but they had been taken down. They must have been taken away to be dusted, she thought absent-mindedly, feeling rather flustered before her important conversation.

In the cosy salon two pretty girls in grammar school uniform were playing the 'Dog's Waltz' for four hands.

They got up, performed a clumsy curtsy and chorused: '*Bonjour, madame.*'

Glyceria Romanovna smiled affectionately at their embarrassment. She had once been a shy young thing just like them, she had grown up in the artificial world of the Smolny Institute: childish young dreams, reading Flaubert in secret, virginal confessions in the quiet of the dormitory . . .

Vasya was standing there, by the piano – with a bashful look on his plain but sweet face.

'My auntie's waiting for you. I'll show you the way,' he muttered, letting Lidina go on ahead.

Fira Ryabchik (specialisation 'grammar school girl') held Rybnikov back for a moment by the hem of his jacket.

'Vas, is that your ever-loving? An interesting little lady. Don't get in a funk. It'll go all right. We've locked the others in their rooms.'

Thank God that she and Lionelka didn't have any make-up on yet because it was still daytime.

And there was Beatrice, already floating out of the doors to meet them like the Dowager Empress Maria Fyodorovna.

'Countess Bovada,' she said, introducing herself with a polite smile. 'Vasya has told me so much about you!'

'Countess?' Lidina gasped.

'Yes, my late husband was a Spanish grandee,' Beatrice explained modestly. 'Please do come into the study.'

Before she followed her hostess, Glyceria Romanovna whispered:

'So you have Spanish grandees among your kin? Anyone else would certainly have boasted about that. You are definitely unusual.'

In the study things were easier. The countess maintained a confident bearing and held the initiative firmly in her own grip.

She warmly approved of the idea of an escape abroad. She said she would obtain documents for her nephew, entirely reliable ones. Then the two ladies' conversation took a geographical turn as they considered where to evacuate their adored 'Vasya'. In the process it emerged that the Spanish grandee's widow had travelled almost all over the world. She spoke with special affection of Port Said and San Francisco.

Rybnikov took no part in the conversation, merely cracked his knuckles nervously.

Never mind, he thought to himself. It's the twenty-fifth tomorrow, and after that it won't matter.

The fourth syllable,
in which Fandorin
feels afraid

Sombre fury would be the best name to give the mood in which Erast Petrovich found himself. In his long life he had known both the sweetness of victory and the bitterness of defeat, but he could not remember ever feeling so stupid before. This must be the way a whaler felt when, instead of impaling a sperm whale, his harpoon merely scattered a shoal of little fish.

But how could he possibly have doubted that the thrice-cursed dark-haired man was the Japanese agent responsible for the sabotage? The absurd concatenation of circumstances was to blame, but that was poor comfort to the engineer.

Precious time had been wasted, the trail was irredeemably lost.

The mayor of Moscow and the detective police wished to express their heartfelt gratitude to Fandorin for catching the brazen band of crooks, but Erast Petrovich withdrew into the shadows, and all the glory went to Mylnikov and his agents, who had merely delivered the bound bandits to the nearest police station.

There was a clearing of the air between the engineer and the court counsellor, and Mylnikov did not even attempt to be cunning. Gazing at Fandorin with eyes bleached colourless by his disappointment in human-kind, Mylnikov admitted without the slightest trace of embarrassment that he had set his agents on the case and come to Moscow himself because he knew from the old days that Fandorin had a uniquely keen nose, and it was a surer way of picking up the trail than wearing out his own shoe leather. He might not have picked up any saboteurs, but he hadn't come off too badly – the hold-up artists from Warsaw would earn him the gratitude of his superiors and a gratuity.

'And instead of name-calling, you'd be better off deciding what's the best way for you and me to rub along,' Mylnikov concluded amicably. 'What can you do without me? That railway outfit of yours doesn't even have the right to conduct an investigation. But I do, and then again, I've brought along the finest sleuths in Peter, grand lads, every last one of them. Come on, Fandorin, let's come to friendly terms, comradely like. The head will be yours, the arms and legs will be ours.'

The proposal made by this rather less than honourable gentleman was certainly not devoid of merit.

'On a friendly basis, so be it. Only bear in mind, Mylnikov,' Fandorin warned him, 'if you take it into your head to be cunning and act behind my b-back, I shan't beat about the bush. I shan't write a complaint to your superiors, I'll simply press the secret *bakayaro* point on your stomach, and that will be the end of you. And no one will ever guess.'

There was no such thing as a *bakayaro* point, but Mylnikov, knowing how skilled Fandorin was in all sorts of Japanese tricks, turned pale.

'Don't frighten me, my health's already ruined as it is. Why should I get cunning with you? We're on the same side. I'm of the opinion that without your Japanese devilry, we'll never catch the fiend who blew up that bridge. We have to fight fire with fire, sorcery with sorcery.'

Fandorin raised one eyebrow slightly, wondering whether the other man could be playing the fool, but the court counsellor had a very serious air, and little sparks had lit up in his eyes.

'Do you really think old Mylnikov has no brains and no heart? That I don't see anything or ponder what's going on?' Mylnikov glanced round and lowered his voice. 'Who is our sovereign, eh? The Lord's anointed, right? So the Lord should protect him from the godless Japanese, right? But what's happening? The Christ-loving army's taking a right battering, left, right and centre. And who's battering it? A tiny little nation with no strength at all. That's because Satan stands behind the Japanese, he's the one who's giving the yellow bastards their strength. And the Supreme Arbiter of fate has forsaken our sovereign, He doesn't want to help. Just recently I read a secret report in the Police Department, from the Arkhangelsk province. There's a holy man prophesying up there, an Old Believer: he says the Romanovs were given three hundred years to rule and no longer, that's the limit they were set. And those three hundred years are running out. And the whole of Russia is bearing the punishment for that. Doesn't that sound like the truth?'

The engineer had had enough of listening to this drivel. He frowned and said:

'Stop all this street sleuth's drivel. If I want to discuss the fate of the tsarist dynasty, I won't choose to do it with a member of the Special Section. Are you going to work or just arrange stupid provocations?'

'Work, work,' said Mylnikov, dissolving in spasms of wooden laughter, but the sparks were still dancing in his eyes.

Meanwhile the experts had concluded their examination of the site of the disaster and presented a report that completely confirmed Fandorin's version of events.

The explosion of moderate force that had caused the collapse was produced by a charge of melinite weighing twelve to fourteen pounds – that is, its power was approximately equal to a six-inch artillery shell. Any other bridge on the Nicholas line would probably have survived a shock of that power, but not the decrepit Tezoimenitsky, especially while a heavy train was crossing it. The saboteurs had chosen the spot and the moment with professional competence.

An answer had also been found to the riddle of how the perpetrators had managed to place a mine on a tightly guarded target and explode it right under the wheels of the military train. At the point of the fracture, the experts had discovered scraps of leather from some unknown source and microscopic particles of dense laboratory glass. After racking their brains for a while, they offered their conclusion: a long, cylindrical leather case and a narrow spiral glass tube.

That was enough for Erast Petrovich to reconstruct a picture of what had happened.

The melinite charge had been placed in a leather package, something like a case for a clarinet or other narrow-bodied wind instrument. There had not been any hard casing at all – it would only have made the mine heavier and weakened the blast. The explosive used was chemical, with a retardant – the engineer had read about those. A glass tube holding fulminate of mercury is pierced by a needle, but the fulminate does not flow out immediately, it takes thirty seconds or a minute, depending on the length and shape of the tube.

No doubt remained: the bomb had been dropped from the express travelling directly in front of the special.

The situation by which the two trains were in dangerously close proximity to each other had been arranged by artifice, using the false telegram that was passed on by the telegraph clerk at Kolpino (who, naturally, had disappeared without a trace).

Fandorin racked his brains for a while over the question of exactly how the mine had been dropped. Through the window of a compartment? Hardly. The risk was too great that when the case hit the covering of the bridge, it would go flying off into the river. Then he guessed – through the flush aperture in the toilet. That was what the narrow case was for. Ah, if only that witness hadn't interfered, with her comments about the suspicious dark-haired man! He should have acted as he had planned to do from the start: make a list of the passengers, and question them too. Even if he'd had to let them all go, he could have interrogated them again now – they would definitely have remembered a travelling musician, and it was quite probable that he wasn't alone, but in a group . . .

Once the mystery of the disaster had been solved, Erast Petrovich had no time for wounded pride, for more compelling concerns came to light.

The engineer's work in the Railway Gendarmerie (or, as Mylnikov called it, the 'Randarmerie') had already been going on for an entire year already, directed to a single goal: to protect the most vulnerable section in the anatomy of the ailing Russian dinosaur – its one major artery. The enterprising Japanese predator that had been attacking the wounded giant from all sides must realise sooner or later that he did not need to knock his opponent off its feet, it was enough simply to gnaw through the single major vessel of its blood supply – the Trans-Siberian main line. Left without ammunition, provisions and reinforcements, the Manchurian army would be doomed.

The Tezoimenitsky Bridge was no more than a test run. Traffic over it would be completely restored in two weeks, and meanwhile trains were making a detour via the Pskov-Starorusskoe branch, losing only a few hours. But if a similar blow were to be struck at any point beyond Samara, from where the main line extended as a single thread for eight thousand versts, it would bring traffic to a halt for at least a month. Linevich's army would be left in a catastrophic position. And apart from that, what was to stop the Japanese from arranging one act of sabotage after another?

Of course, the Trans-Siberian was a new line, built using modern technology. And the last year had not been wasted – a decent system of security was up and running, and the Siberian bridges could in no way be compared with the Tezoimenitsky – you wouldn't blow them up with ten pounds of melinite dumped through the outlet of a water closet. But the Japanese were shrewd, they would come up with something else. The worst thing had already happened – they had already launched their war on the railways. Just wait and see what would come next.

This thought (which was, unfortunately, quite incontrovertible) made Erast Petrovich feel afraid. But the engineer belonged to that breed of people in whom the response to fear is not paralysis or panic-stricken commotion, but the mobilisation of all their mental resources.

'Melinite, melinite,' Fandorin repeated thoughtfully as he strode around the office that he had taken on temporary loan from Danilov. He snapped the fingers of the hand he was holding behind his back, puffed on his cigar and stood at the window for a long time, screwing his eyes up against the bright May sky.

There could be no doubt that the Japanese would also use melinite for subsequent acts of sabotage. They had tested the explosive on the Tezoimenitsky Bridge and the results had been satisfactory.

Melinite was not produced in Russia, the explosive was deployed only in the arsenals of France and Japan, and the Japanese called it *simose* or, as distorted by the Russian newspapers, '*shimoza*'. It was *simose* that was given most of the credit for the victory of the Japanese fleet at Tsushima: shells packed with melinite had demonstrated far greater penetrative and explosive power than the Russian powder shells.

Melinite, or picric acid, was ideally suited for sabotage work: powerful, easy to combine with detonators of various kinds and also compact. But even so, to sabotage a large modern bridge would require a charge weighing several *poods*. Where would the saboteurs get such a large amount of explosive and how would they convey it?

This was the key point – Erast Petrovich realised that straight away – but before he advanced along his primary line of search, he put certain precautions in place on his secondary one.

In case the melinite theory was mistaken and the enemy was intending to use ordinary dynamite or gun cotton, Fandorin gave instructions for a secret circular to be sent to all the military depots and arsenals, warning them of the danger. Of course, this piece of paper would not make the guards any more vigilant, but thieving quartermasters would be more afraid of selling explosive on the side, and that was precisely the way that such lethal materials usually found their way into the hands of Russia's terrorist bombers.

Having taken this safety measure, Erast Petrovich concentrated on the routes for transporting melinite.

They would deliver it from abroad, and most likely from France (they couldn't bring it all the way from Japan!).

You can't ship a load of at least several *poods* in a suitcase, thought Fandorin, twirling in his fingers a test tube of light yellow powder that he had acquired from an artillery laboratory. He raised it to his face and absentmindedly drew the sharp smell in through his nose – the same 'fatal aroma of *shimoza*' that the Russian war correspondents were so fond of mentioning.

'Well now, p-perhaps,' Erast Petrovich murmured.

He quickly got up, ordered his carriage to be brought round, and a quarter of an hour later he was already on Maly Gnezdnikovsky Lane, at the Police Telegraph Office. There he dictated a telegram that set the operator, who had seen all sorts of things in his time, blinking rapidly.

The fifth syllable, consisting almost completely of face-to-face conversations

On the morning of 25 May, Countess Bovada's boarder received news of the arrival of the Delivery and the Shipment on the same day, as had been planned. The organisation was working with the precision of a chronometer.

The Delivery consisted of four one-and-a-half-*pood* sacks of maize flour, sent from Lyons for the Moscow bakery 'Werner and Pfleiderer'. The consignment was awaiting the consignee at the Moscow Freight Station depot on the Brest line. It was all very simple: turn up, show the receipt and sign. The sacks were extremely durable – jute, waterproof. If an overly meticulous gendarme or railway thief poked a hole in one to try it, the yellow, coarse-grained powder that poured out would pass very well for maize flour in wheat-and-rye-eating Russia.

Things were a little more complicated with the Shipment. The sealed wagon was due to arrive by way of a roundabout route from Naples to Batumi, and from there by railway via Rostov to the Rogozhsk shunting yard. According to the documents, it belonged to the Office of Security Escorts and was accompanied by a guard consisting of a corporal and two privates. The guard was genuine, the documents were fake. That is, the crates really did contain, as the transport documents stated, 8,500 Italian 'Vetterli' rifles, 1,500 Belgian 'Francotte' revolvers, a million cartridges and blasting cartridges. However, this entire arsenal was not intended for the needs of the Escorts Office, but for a man who went by the alias of Thrush. According to the plan developed by Vasilii Alexandrovich's father, large-scale disturbances were supposed to break out in Moscow, putting a rapid end to the Russian tsar's enthusiasm for the Manchurian steppes and Korean concessions.

The wise author of the plan had taken everything into account: the fact that the Guards were in St Petersburg, while the old capital had only a scrappy ragbag garrison made up of second-class reservists, and that Moscow was the transport heart of the country, and that the city had 200,000 hungry workers embittered by privation. Ten thousand reckless madcaps could surely be found among them, if only there were weapons. A single spark, and the workers' quarters would be bristling with barricades.

Rybnikov began as he had been taught in his childhood – that is, with the hardest thing.

The staff captain arrived at the shunting yard. He introduced himself and was given an escort of a minor bureaucrat from the goods arrival section, and they set off to line number three to meet the Rostov special. The clerk felt timid in the company of the gloomy officer, who tapped impatiently on the planking with the scabbard of his sabre. Fortunately, they did not have to wait long – the train arrived exactly on the dot.

The commander of the guard, a corporal who was well past the prime of youth, moved his lips as he read the document presented to him by the staff captain, while the draymen whom Rybnikov had hired drove up to the platform one by one.

But then there was a hitch – there was absolutely no sign of the half-platoon that was supposed to guard the convoy.

Cursing the Russian muddle, the staff captain ran to the telephone. He came back white-faced with fury and let loose a string of such intricately obscene curses that the clerk shrank in embarrassment and the sentries wagged their heads respectfully. There obviously wasn't going to be any half-platoon for the staff captain.

Having raged for the appropriate length of time, Rybnikov took hold of the corporal by the sleeve.

'Look, mate, what's your name ... Yekimov, as you can see, this is one almighty cock-up. Help me out here, will you? I know you've done your duty and you're not obliged, but I can't send it off without a guard, and I can't leave it here either. I'll see you all right: three roubles for you and one each for your fine lads here.'

The corporal went to have a word with the privates, who were as long in the tooth and battered by life as he was.

The deal they struck was this: in addition to the money, His Honour would give them a paper saying the squad could spend two days on the town in Moscow. Rybnikov promised.

They loaded up and drove off. The staff captain at the front in a cab, then the drays with the crates, the sentries on foot, one on the left, one on the right, the corporal bringing up the rear of the procession. Pleased with the remuneration and leave pass they had been promised, the privates strode along cheerfully, holding their Mosin rifles at the ready. Rybnikov had warned them to keep their eyes skinned – the slanty-eyed enemy never slept.

Rybnikov had booked a warehouse on the River Moscow in advance. The draymen carried the Shipment in, took their money and left.

The staff captain carefully put the receipt from a member of the workmen's co-operative away in his pocket as he walked over to the sentries from Rostov.

'Thanks for the help, lads. I'll settle up now, a bargain's a bargain.'

The riverside wharf in front of the warehouse was deserted, and the river water, iridescent from patches of oil, splashed under the planking.

'But Your Honour, where are the guards?' Yekimov asked, gazing around. 'It's kind of odd. An arms depot with no guards.'

Instead of answering, Rybnikov jabbed him in the throat with a finger of steel, then turned towards the privates. One of them was just about to lend the other some tobacco – and he froze like that, with his mouth hanging open, so the crude shag missed the paper and went showering past. Vasilii Alexandrovich hit the first one with his right hand and the second with his left. It all happened very quickly: the corporal's body was still falling, and his two subordinates were already dead.

Rybnikov dropped the bodies under the wharf, after first tying a heavy rock to each one of them.

He took off his cap and wiped the sweat off his forehead.

Right, then, it was only half past ten and the most troublesome part of the job was already over.

It only took ten minutes to collect the Delivery. Vasilii Alexandrovich arrived at the Moscow Freight Station in tarred boots, a long coat and a cloth cap – a regular shop counterman. He carried the sacks out himself, wouldn't even let the cabby help, in case he might ask for an extra ten kopecks. Then he transported the 'maize flour' from the Brest line to the Ryazan–Uralsk line, because the Delivery's onward route led towards the east. On the way across to the other side of the city, he repacked the goods and at the station he checked it in as two lots, with different receipts.

And that put an end to his scurrying about from one railway station to another. Rybnikov wasn't in the least bit tired; on the contrary, he was filled with a fierce, vigorous energy – he had grown weary of idleness and, of course, he was inspired by the importance of his actions.

Expertly dispatched, received on time, competently delivered, he thought. That was the way invincibility was shaped. When everyone acted in his own place as if the outcome of the entire war depended on him alone.

He was slightly concerned about the 'dummies' summoned from Samara and Krasnoyarsk. What if they were late? But it was no accident that Rybnikov had chosen those precise two out of the notebook filled with snaky squiggles. The Krasnoyarsk man (Vasilii Alexandrovich thought of him as

'Tunnel') was greedy, and his greed made him dependable, and the Samara man (his code name was 'Bridge') might not be outstandingly dependable, but he had compelling reasons not to be late – he was a man with not much time left.

And his calculations had proved correct; neither of the 'dummies' had let him down. Rybnikov was already aware of this when he left the station for the agreed hotels – the 'Kazan' and the 'Railway'. The hotels were located close to each other, but not actually adjacent. The last thing he needed was for the two dummies to get to know each other through some grotesque coincidence.

At the Railway Hotel, Vasilii Alexandrovich left a note: 'At three. Goncharov'. The note at the Kazan Hotel read: 'At four: Goncharov'.

Now it was time to deal with the man with the alias of Thrush, the consignee of the Shipment.

In this matter Rybnikov employed particular caution, for he knew that the Social Revolutionaries were kept under close surveillance by the Okhrana, and the revolutionary riff-raff had plenty of traitors among their own ranks. He could only hope that Thrush realised this as well as he, Rybnikov, did.

Vasilii Alexandrovich made a call from a public telephone (a most convenient innovation that had only recently appeared in the old capital). He asked the lady to give him number 34-81.

He spoke the prearranged words:

'A hundred thousand pardons. May I ask for the honourable Ivan Konstantinovich to come to the phone?'

After a second's pause, a woman's voice replied:

'He's not here at present, but he will be soon.'

That meant Thrush was in Moscow and prepared to meet.

'Please be so good as to let Ivan Konstantinovich know that Professor Stepanov wishes to invite him to his seventy-third birthday.'

'Professor Stepanov?' the woman asked, bemused. 'To his seventy-third?'

'Yes, that is correct.'

The go-between didn't need to understand the meaning, her job was to pass on precisely what he said. In the figure 73, the first numeral indicated the time, and the second was a position in a list of previously agreed meeting places. Thrush would understand: at seven o'clock, at place number 3.

If anybody had eavesdropped on Rybnikov's conversation with the man from Krasnoyarsk, he probably would not have understood a thing.

'More account books?' asked Tunnel, a sturdy man with a moustache and eyes that were constantly half closed. 'We should raise the price. Everything's so expensive nowadays.'

'No, not books,' said Vasilii Alexandrovich, standing in the middle of the cheap hotel room and listening carefully to the footsteps in the corridor. 'A special delivery. Payment too. Fifteen hundred.'

'How much?' the other man gasped.

Rybnikov pulled out a bundle of banknotes.

'There. You'll receive the same again in Khabarovsk. If you do everything right.'

'Three thousand?'

The Krasnoyarsk man's eyebrows twitched and twitched again, but they didn't rise up on to his forehead. It's not easy to gape in astonishment with eyes used to watching the world through a peephole.

The man whom Vasilii Alexandrovich had christened Tunnel had no idea about this nickname, or about the real activities of the people who paid for his services so generously. He was convinced that he was assisting illegal gold miners. The 'Statute on Private Gold-Mining' required prospecting co-operatives to hand over their entire output to the state in exchange for so-called 'assignations' at a price lower than the market level and with all sorts of other deductions into the bargain. And everybody knew that when the law was unjust or irrational, people found ways to get round it.

Tunnel occupied a post that was extremely useful to the Organisation – he escorted the postal wagons along the Trans-Siberian main line. When he carried notebooks filled with columns of figures from the European part of the empire to the Far East and back, he assumed that this was financial correspondence between the miners and the dealers in black-market gold.

But Rybnikov had fished the postman out of his own cunning little note-book for a different purpose.

'Yes, three thousand,' he said firmly. 'And no one pays money like that for nothing, you know that.'

'What do I have to carry?' asked Tunnel, licking his lips, which had turned dry with excitement.

Rybnikov snapped:

'Explosive. Three *poods*.'

The postman started blinking, thinking it over. Then he nodded.

'For the diggings? To smash the rocks?'

'Yes. Wrap the crates in sackcloth, like packages. Do you know tunnel No. Twelve on the Baikal Bypass Line?'

'The "Half-Tunnel"? Everyone knows that.'

'Throw the crates off exactly halfway through, at marker 197. Our man will pick them up afterwards.'

'But . . . er, won't it go off bang?'

Rybnikov laughed.

'It's obvious you know nothing about using explosives. Haven't you ever heard of detonators? Go off bang – don't talk nonsense.'

Satisfied with this reply, Tunnel spat on his fingers, preparing to count the money, and Vasilii Alexandrovich smiled to himself: It won't go off bang, it will make a boom that sets the Winter Palace shaking. Then just let them try to rake out the smashed rock and drag out the flattened wagons and locomotive.

The Baikal Bypass Tunnel, which had been built at huge expense and opened only recently, ahead of schedule, was the final link in the Trans-Siberian. The military trains used to line up in immense queues at the Lake Baikal ferry crossing, but now the line pulsated three times faster than before. The Half-Tunnel was the longest one on the line; if it was put out of action, the Manchurian army would be back on short rations again.

And that was only half of Rybnikov's dual 'project'.

The second half was to be implemented by the man staying at the Kazan Hotel, with whom Vasilii Alexandrovich spoke quite differently – not curtly and abruptly, but soulfully, with compassionate restraint.

He was a man still quite young, with a sallow complexion and protruding Adam's apple. He made a strange impression: the subtle facial features, nervous gesticulations and spectacles fitted uncomfortably with the worn pea jacket, calico shirt and rough boots.

The man from Samara coughed up blood and was in love, but his feelings were not requited. This made him hate the whole world, especially the world close to him: the people around him, his native city, his own country. There was no need for secrecy with him – Bridge knew who he was working for and he carried out his assignments with lascivious vengefulness.

Six months earlier, on the instructions of the Organisation, he had left university and taken a job as a driver's mate on the railway. The heat of the firebox was consuming the final remnants of his lungs, but Bridge was not clinging to life, he wanted to die as soon as possible.

'You told our man that you wish to go out with a bang. I'll give you the opportunity to do that,' Rybnikov declared in ringing tones. 'This bang will be heard right across Russia, right round the world, in fact.'

'Tell me, tell me,' the consumptive said eagerly.

'The Alexander Bridge in Syzran . . .' said Rybnikov, and paused for effect. 'The longest in Europe, seven hundred *sazhens*. If it is sent crashing into the Volga, the main line will come to a halt. Do you understand what that means?'

The man he called Bridge smiled slowly.

'Yes, yes. Collapse, defeat, disgrace. Surrender. You Japanese know where to strike! You deserve the victory!' The former student's eyes blazed brightly and he spoke faster and faster with every word. 'It can be done! I can do it! Do you have powerful explosive? I'll hide it in the tender, under the coal. I take one slab into the cabin. I throw it in the firebox, it explodes, fireworks!'

He burst into laughter.

'On the seventh span,' Rybnikov put in gently. 'That's very important. Otherwise it might not work. On the seventh, don't get that wrong.'

'I won't! I go on duty the day after tomorrow. A goods train to Chelya-binsk. The driver will get what's coming to him, the bastard, he's always sneering at my cough, calls me "Tapeworm". I feel sorry for the stoker, though, he's only a young boy. But I'll get him off. At the last station I'll catch his hand with the shovel. Tell him never mind, I'll shovel the coal myself. But what about our deal?' Bridge exclaimed with a sudden shudder. 'You haven't forgotten about our deal?'

'How could we?' asked Rybnikov, setting his hand to his heart. 'We remember. Ten thousand. We'll hand it over exactly as you instructed.'

'Not hand it over, drop it off,' the sick man cried out nervously. 'And the note: "In memory of what might have been". I'll write it myself, you'll get it wrong.'

And he wrote it there and then, splattering ink about.

'She'll understand . . . And if she doesn't, so much the better,' he muttered with a sniff. 'Here, take it.'

'But bear in mind that the individual who is so precious to you will only receive the money and the note on one condition – if the bridge collapses. Don't get the count wrong, the seventh span.'

'Don't worry,' said the man from Samara, shaking a tear from his eyelashes. 'If there's one thing consumption has taught me, it's precision – I have to take my pills at the right time. But don't you trick me. Give me your word of honour as a samurai.'

Vasilii Alexandrovich drew himself up to attention, wrinkled up his forehead and narrowed his eyes. Then he performed a fanciful gesture that he had just invented and solemnly declared:

'My word of honour as a samurai.'

The most important face-to-face conversation was set for seven o'clock in the evening, in a cab drivers' inn close to the Kaluga Gates (place number three).

The place had been well chosen: dark, dirty, noisy, but not uproarious. In this place they didn't drink beverages that heated the brain, but tea, in large amounts, entire samovars of it. The clientele was well mannered and incurious – they'd seen quite enough of the hustle and bustle of the streets, and of their own passengers, during the day. Now all they wanted was to sit in peace and quiet and make staid conversation.

Vasilii Alexandrovich arrived ten minutes late and immediately made for the table in the corner, which was occupied by a sturdy man with a beard, an expressionless face and a piercing gaze that was never still for a moment.

Rybnikov had been watching the entrance to the inn for the last hour from the next gateway and had spotted Thrush as he walked up. When he was certain Thrush wasn't being trailed, he went in.

'My greetings to Kuzmich,' he shouted from a distance, holding up one hand with the fingers spread wide. Thrush didn't know what he looked like, and they had to act out a meeting between old friends.

The revolutionary was not in the least surprised, and he replied in the same tone:

'Aha, Mustapha. Sit down, you old Tartar dog, we'll have a spot of tea.'

He squeezed Rybnikov's hand tightly and slapped him on the shoulder for good measure.

They sat down.

At the next table a large party was sedately consuming tea with hard bread rings. They glanced incuriously at the two friends and turned away again.

'Are they following you?' Vasilii Alexandrovich said quietly, asking the most important question first. 'Are you sure there's no police agent in your group?'

'Certainly they're following me, quite definitely. And we have a stooge. We're leaving him alone for the time being. Better to know who – they'll only plant another one, and then try to figure out who it is.'

'They are following you?' Rybnikov tautened like a spring and cast a rapid glance in the direction of the counter – there was an exit into a walk-through courtyard behind it.

'They're following me, so what?' the Socialist Revolutionary said with a shrug. 'Let them follow, when it doesn't matter. And when it does, I can give them the slip, I'm well used to it. So don't you get nervous, my bold samurai. I'm clean today.'

It was the second time in one day that Vasilii Alexandrovich had been a called a samurai, but this time the mockery was obvious.

'You are Japanese, aren't you?' the consignee of the Shipment asked, crunching on a lump of sugar and slurping tea noisily from his saucer. 'I read that some of the samurais are almost indistinguishable from Europeans.'

'What the hell difference does it make whether I'm a samurai or not?' Rybnikov asked, out of habit slipping into the tone of the person he was talking to.

'True enough. Let's get down to business. Where are the goods?'

'I took them to a warehouse on the river, as you asked. Why do you need them on the river?'

'I just do. Where exactly?'

'I'll show you later.'

'Who else knows, apart from you? Unloading, transporting, guarding – that's quite an operation. Are they reliable people? Know how to keep a still tongue in their heads?'

'They'll be as silent as the grave,' Rybnikov said seriously. 'I'll wager my head on that. When will you be ready to collect?'

Thrush scratched his beard.

'We're thinking of floating some of the goods, a small part, down the Oka, to Sormovo. A barge will come up from there tomorrow at nightfall. We'll collect it then.'

'Sormovo?' said Vasilii Alexandrovich, narrowing his eyes. 'That's good. A good choice. What's your plan of action?'

'We'll start with a strike on the railways. Then a general strike. And when the authorities start getting the jitters, let the Cossacks loose or do a bit of shooting – the combat squads will be out in a flash. Only this time we'll manage without cobblestones, the weapon of the proletariat.'

'When are you going to start?' Rybnikov asked casually. 'I need it to be within a month.'

The revolutionary's stony face twisted into an ironic grin.

'Running out of steam, are you, sons of the Mikado? On your last legs?'

A snigger ran round the room and Vasilii Alexandrovich started in surprise – surely they couldn't have heard?

He jerked round, and then immediately relaxed.

Two grey-bearded cab drivers had just staggered into the inn, both well oiled. One had missed his footing and fallen, and the other was trying to help him up, muttering:

'Never mind, Mityukha, a horse has got four legs, and it still stumbles . . .'

Someone shouted from one of the tables:

'A horse like that's ready for the knacker's yard!'

People cackled with laughter.

Mityukha was about to curse his mockers roundly, but the waiters swooped on him and in half a jiffy they had shoved the two drunken cabbies out: There, don't you go bringing shame on our establishment.

'Ah, old Mother Russia,' Thrush chuckled with another crooked grin. 'Never mind, soon we'll give her such a jolt, she'll jump right out of her pants.'

'And set off at a run with a bare backside, into the bright future?'

The revolutionary looked intently into the cold eyes of the other man.

I shouldn't have mocked him, Rybnikov realised immediately. That was going too far.

He held that glance for a few seconds, then pretended that he couldn't hold out and lowered his eyes.

'You and we have only one thing in common,' the SR said contemptuously. 'A lack of bourgeois sentiment. Only we revolutionaries *no longer* have any, while you young predators *don't yet* have any – you haven't reached that age yet. You use us, we use you, but you, Mr Samurai, are not my equal. You're no more than a cog in a machine, and I'm the architect of tomorrow, savvy?'

He is like a cat, Vasilii Alexandrovich decided. Lets you feed him, but he won't lick your hand – the most he'll do is purr, and even that's not very likely.

He had to reply in the same style, but without aggravating the confrontation.

'All right, Mr Architect, to hell with the fancy words. Let's discuss the details.'

Thrush even left like a cat, without saying goodbye.

When he had clarified everything he needed to know, he simply got up and darted out through the door behind the counter, leaving Vasilii Alexandrovich to exit via the street.

In front of the inn cabbies were dozing on their coach boxes, waiting for passengers. The first two were the drunks who had been ejected from the inn. The first one was completely out of it, snoring away with his nose down against his knees. The second was more or less holding up, though – he even shook his reins when he caught sight of Rybnikov.

But Vasilii Alexandrovich didn't take a cab at the inn – that would contravene the rules of conspiracy. He walked quite a long way before he stopped one that happened to be driving past.

At the corner of Krivokolenny Street, at a poorly lit and deserted spot, Rybnikov put a rouble note on the seat, jumped down on to the road – gently, without even making the carriage sway – and ducked into a gateway.

As they say, God takes care of those who take care of themselves.

The sixth syllable,
in which a tail and ears
play an important part

Special No. 369-B was expected at precisely midnight, and there was no reason to doubt that the train would arrive on the dot – Fandorin was being kept informed of its progress by telegraph from every station. The train was travelling 'on a green light', with priority over all others. Freight trains, passenger trains and even expresses had to give way to it. When the locomotive with only a single compartment carriage went hurtling past an ordinary train that had inexplicably come to a halt at the station in Bologoe or Tver, the worldly-wise passengers said to each other: 'Higher-ups in a hurry. Must be some kind of hitch in Moscow'.

The windows of the mysterious train were not only closed, but completely curtained over. During the entire journey from the present capital to the old one, 369-B stopped only once, to take on coal, and then for no more than fifteen minutes.

They were waiting to meet the mysterious train outside Moscow, at a small way station surrounded by a double cordon of railway gendarmes. A fine, repulsive drizzle was falling, and the lamps were swaying in a gusting wind, sending sinister shadows scuttling furtively across the platform.

Erast Petrovich arrived ten minutes before the appointed time, listened to Lieutenant Colonel Danilov's report on the precautions that had been taken and nodded.

Court Counsellor Mylnikov, who had been informed of the imminent event only an hour earlier (the engineer had called for him without any forewarning), couldn't keep still: he ran round the platform several times, always coming back to Fandorin and asking: 'Who is it we're waiting for?'

'You'll see,' Fandorin replied briefly, glancing every now and then at his gold Breguet.

At one minute to twelve they heard a long hoot, then the bright lights of the locomotive emerged from the darkness.

The rain started coming down harder, and the valet opened an umbrella over the engineer's head, deliberately standing so that the drops ran off on to Mylnikov's hat. However, Mylnikov was so worked up that he didn't notice – he merely shuddered when a cold rivulet ran in under his collar.

'The head of your division, is it?' he asked when he made out the compartment carriage. 'The chief of the Corps?' And finally, lowering his voice to a whisper: 'Not the minister himself, surely?'

'Exclude all unauthorised individuals!' Fandorin shouted when he spotted a linesman at the end of the platform.

Gendarmes went dashing off with a loud tramping of boots, to carry out the order.

The 369-B came to a halt. Evstratii Pavlovich Mylnikov thrust out his chest and whipped off his bowler, but when the clanging of iron and screeching of brakes stopped, his ears were assaulted by a strange sound very similar to the diabolical ululations that tormented his ailing nerves at night. Mylnikov gave his head a shake to drive away the dark spell, but the howling only grew louder, and then he quite clearly heard barking.

An officer in a leather pea jacket skipped smartly down the steps, saluted Fandorin and handed him a package bearing a mysterious inscription in black: RSEUDPWUHPHHDAPO.

'What's that?' Mylnikov asked in a faltering voice, suspecting that he was dreaming all this – the engineer's appearance in the middle of the night, the drive through the rain, the dogs' barking and the unpronounceable word on the envelope,

Fandorin decoded the abbreviation:

'The Russian Society for the Encouragement of the Use of Dogs in Police Work under the Honorary Presidency of His Highness Duke Alexander Petrovich of Oldenburg. Very well, L-Lieutenant, you can bring them out. The horseboxes are waiting.'

Police officers started emerging from the carriage one after another, each leading a dog on a leash. There were German shepherds and giant schnauzers and spaniels, and even mongrels.

'What is all this?' Mylnikov repeated perplexedly. 'What's it for?'

'This is Operation Fifth Sense.'

'Fifth? Which one's the fifth?'

'Smell.'

Operation Fifth Sense had been planned and prepared with the utmost dispatch in a little over two days.

In the urgent telegram of 18 May that had so greatly astonished the experienced police telegraph clerk, Fandorin had written to his chief: 'REQUEST URGENTLY GATHER DUKE'S DOGS DETAILS FOLLOW'.

Erast Petrovich was an enthusiastic supporter and even, to some extent, inspirer of the initiative undertaken by the Duke of Oldenburg, whose idea was to establish in Russia a genuine, scientifically organised police dog service on the European model. This was a new area, little studied as yet, but it had immediately been given massive backing.

Coaching a good dog to track down a specific smell required only a few hours. The amount of *simose* needed was allocated from the Artillery Department and work began: fifty-four police instructors thrust the noses of their shaggy helpers into the yellow powder, the air was filled with reproachful and approving exclamations, peals of barking and the cheerful sound of sugar crunching between dog's teeth.

Melinite had an acrid smell and the tracker dogs recognised it easily, even among sacks of common chemical products. Following a brief training course, His Highness's protégés set off on their work assignments: twenty-eight dogs went to the western border – two to each of the fourteen crossing points – and the rest went on the special train to Moscow, to receive further instructions from the engineer Fandorin.

Working by day and night in two shifts, the handlers led the dogs through the carriages and depots of all the railway lines of the old capital. Mylnikov did not believe in Fandorin's plan, but he didn't try to interfere, just looked on. In any case, the court counsellor had no ideas of his own on how to catch the Japanese agents.

On the fifth day, Erast Petrovich finally received the long-awaited telephone call in the office where he was studying the most vulnerable points of the Trans-Siberian Railway, all marked on a map with little red flags.

'We've got it!' an excited voice shouted into the receiver over the sound of deafening barking. 'Mr Engineer, I think we've got it! This is trainer Churikov calling from the Moscow Freight Station on the Brest line! We haven't touched a thing, just as you ordered!'

Erast Petrovich telephoned Mylnikov immediately.

They dashed to the station from different directions, arriving almost simultaneously.

Trainer Churikov introduced his bosses to the heroine of the hour, a Belgian sheepdog of the Grunendal breed:

'Mignonette.'

Mignonette sniffed at Fandorin's shoes and wagged her tail. She bared her fangs at Mylnikov.

'Don't take offence, she's in pup,' the handler said hastily. 'But it makes the nose keener.'

'Well, what is it you've found?' the court counsellor demanded impatiently.

Churikov tugged on the dog's lead and she plodded reluctantly towards the depot, glancing back at the engineer. At the entrance she braced her paws against the ground and even lay down, making it very clear that she was in no hurry to go anywhere. She squinted up at the men to see whether they would scold her.

'She's acting up,' the trainer said, sighing. He squatted down, scratched the bitch's belly and whispered something in her ear.

Mignonette graciously got up and set off towards the stacks of crates and sacks.

'There now, there, watch,' said Churikov, throwing up one hand.

'Watch what?'

'The ears and the tail!'

Mignonette's ears and tail were lowered. She walked slowly along one row, and then another. Halfway along the third, her ears suddenly jerked erect and her tail shot up and then sank back down and stayed there, pressed between her legs. The tracker dog sat down and barked at four neat, medium-sized jute sacks.

The consignment had arrived from France and was intended for the Werner and Pfleiderer Bakery. It had been delivered on the morning train from Novgorod. The contents were a yellow powder that left a distinctive oily sheen on the fingers – no doubt about it, it was melinite.

'It crossed the border before the dogs got there,' Fandorin said after checking the accompanying documentation. 'Right then, Mylnikov, we have work to do.'

They decided to do the work themselves and not trust it to the detectives. Erast Petrovich dressed up as a railwayman and Mylnikov as a loader. They installed themselves in the next goods shed, which gave them an excellent view of the depot and the approaches to it.

The consignee arrived for his delivery at 11.55.

The rather short man, who looked like a shop hand, presented a piece of paper, signed the office book and carried the sacks to a closed wagon himself.

The observers were glued to their binoculars.

'Japanese, I think,' Erast Petrovich murmured.

'Oh, come on!' Mylnikov exclaimed doubtfully, fiddling with the little focusing wheel. 'As Russian as they come, with just a touch of the Tatar, the way it ought to be.'

'Japanese,' the engineer repeated confidently. 'Perhaps with an admixture of European blood, but the form of the eyes and the nose . . . I've seen him before somewhere. But where, and when? Perhaps he simply looks like one of my Japanese acquaintances . . . Japanese faces are not noted for their variety – anthropology distinguishes only twelve basic types. That's because of their insular isolation. There was no influx of b-blood from other races.'

'He's leaving!' Evstratii Pavlovich exclaimed, interrupting the lecture on anthropology. 'Quick!'

But there was no need to hurry. A whole fleet of cabs and carriages of various kinds had been assembled to carry out surveillance around the city, and an agent was sitting in every one, so the mark couldn't get away.

The engineer and the court counsellor lowered themselves on to the springy seat of the carriage bringing up the rear of this cavalcade, which was giving a convincing imitation of a busy stream of traffic, and set off slowly through the streets.

The buildings and lamp-posts were decorated with flags and garlands. Moscow was celebrating the birthday of the Empress Alexandra Fyodorovna far more sumptuously than in previous years. There was a special reason for that: the sovereign's wife had recently presented Russia with an heir to the throne, after four little girls – or 'blank shots', as Mylnikov expressed it disrespectfully.

'But they say the little lad's sickly, there's a hex on him,' Evstratii Pavlovich said, and sighed. 'The Lord's punishing the Romanovs.'

This time the engineer didn't bother to reply and merely frowned at this provocative gibberish.

Meanwhile the mark demonstrated that he was a conjuror. At the freight station he had loaded four sacks into his closed wagon, but at the left luggage office of the Ryazan-Uralsk line he took out three wooden crates and eight small bundles wrapped in shiny black paper. He let the wagon go. Of course, the agents stopped the wagon round the very first bend, but all they found in it were four empty jute sacks. For some reason the melinite had been extracted from them and repacked.

The clerk at the left luggage office stated that the crates and the bundles had been left as two separate items, with different receipts.

But Fandorin received all this information only later. Since the putative Japanese proceeded on his way from the station as a pedestrian, the engineer and the court counsellor took the surveillance into their own hands once again.

They followed the mark at the greatest possible distance and dispatched the sleuths into the reserve. The most important thing now was not to frighten off the live bait that might attract some other fish.

The shop hand called into two hotels close to the station – the 'Kazan' and the 'Railway'. They prudently decided not to go barging in, and they wouldn't have had time in any case – the mark spent no more than a minute inside each building.

Erast Fandorin was scowling darkly – his worst fears had been confirmed: the Ryazan-Uralsk line was part of the great transcontinental line on which the engineer's red pencil had marked at least a hundred vulnerable sectors. For which one of them were the items handed in at the left luggage office intended?

From the station square the mark set off into the centre and circled around in the city for quite a long time. On several occasions he suddenly stopped his cabby right there in the middle of a street and let him go, but he failed to shake off the superbly organised surveillance.

Shortly after seven o'clock in the evening, he entered a cab drivers' inn close to Kaluga Square. Since he had spent the previous hour hiding in the gateway of the next building, he had to have an appointment here, and this was an opportunity that must not be missed.

As soon as the mark entered the inn (that happened at nine minutes past seven), Mylnikov summoned the Flying Brigade's special carriage with his whistle. This carriage was a highly convenient innovation in modern detective work: it contained a selection of costumes and items of disguise to suit every possible occasion.

The engineer and the court counsellor dressed up as cabbies and staggered unsteadily into the tavern.

After casting an eye round the dark room, Evstratii Pavlovich pretended that he couldn't stay on his feet and collapsed on the floor. When Fandorin leaned down over him he whispered:

'That's Lagin with him. Codename Thrush. An SR. Extremely dangerous. How about that . . .'

The important point had been established, so rather than loiter in the tavern in open view, they allowed themselves to be thrown out in the street.

After stationing four agents at the back entrance, they hurriedly discussed their alarming discovery.

'Our agents abroad inform us that Colonel Akashi, the senior Japanese foreign agent, is meeting with political émigrés and buying large deliveries of weapons,' Mylnikov whispered, leaning down from the coach box of his government carriage. 'But that's a long way off, in places liked Paris and London, and this is old mother Moscow. We couldn't have slipped up there, surely? Give the local loudmouths Japanese rifles, and we'll have real trouble . . .'

Erast Petrovich listened with his teeth gritted. Provoking a revolution in the enemy's rear – a démarche unheard of in the practice of war in Europe – was a hundred times more dangerous than any bombs on railway lines. It threatened not just the outcome of the military campaign, but the fate of the Russian state as a whole. The warriors of the Land of Yamato knew what real war was: there were no means that were impermissible, there was only defeat or victory. How the Japanese had changed in a quarter of a century!

'The **** Asian ***s!' Mylnikov cursed obscenely, as if he had overheard Fandorin's thoughts. 'There's nothing holy! How do you fight bastards like that?'

But was this not what Andrei Bolkonsky was talking about before the Battle of Borodino, the engineer objected – not out loud to Mylnikov, naturally, but to himself. Chivalry and war practised by the rules are stupid nonsense, according to the most attractive character in the whole of Russian literature. Kill prisoners, do not negotiate. No indulging noble sentiments. War is not amusement.

But even so, the side that indulges noble sentiments is the one that will win, Fandorin suddenly thought, but before he could follow this paradoxical idea through to its conclusion, the agent stationed by the door gave the signal, and he had to clamber up on to his coach box at the double.

The shop hand came out alone. He looked at the line of cabs (every last one belonging to the Okhrana), but didn't take one. He walked away some distance and stopped a passing cabby – another false one, naturally.

But in the end all of Mylnikov's cunning was wasted. In some incomprehensible manner, the mark disappeared from the carriage. The detective impersonating the driver did not notice when and how this happened: first there was a passenger, and then there wasn't – just a crumpled rouble note lying on the seat in mockery.

This was annoying, but not fatal.

First, there was still the SR Lagin, alias Thrush – they had a man in his inner circle. And secondly, near the left luggage office, an ambush was set up, for which Fandorin had especially high hopes, since the arrangements were made through the Railway Gendarmerie, without Mylnikov involved.

The clerk was given a thoroughly detailed briefing by the engineer. As soon as the 'shop hand' appeared, or anyone else came to present the familiar receipts, he was to press a button that had been installed specially. A lamp would go on in the next room, where a squad was waiting, and the officer in charge would immediately telephone Fandorin, and then, depending on his orders, either make an arrest or continue secret surveillance (through an eyehole) until plainclothes agents arrived. And. of course, the clerk would make sure the luggage was not given out too quickly.

'Now we've got the slanty-eyed macaque like this,' Mylnikov gloated, grabbing a tight fistful of air in his strong fingers.

The seventh syllable,
in which it emerges
that not all Russians love Pushkin

A few days before the long-awaited 25 May, the Moscow life of Vasilii Alexandrovich Rybnikov was punctuated by an episode that may appear insignificant in comparison with subsequent events, but not to mention it at all would amount to dishonesty.

It happened during the period when the fugitive staff captain was languishing in the tormenting embrace of idleness, which, as already mentioned above, even led him to commit certain acts rather uncharacteristic of him.

In one of his idle moments, he visited the Address Bureau located on Gnezdnikovsky Lane and started making enquiries about a certain person in whom he was interested.

Rybnikov did not even think of buying a two-kopeck request form; instead he demonstrated his knowledge of psychology by engaging the clerk in soulful conversation, explaining that he was trying to find an old army comrade of his deceased father. He had lost sight of this man a long time ago and understood perfectly well what a difficult task it was, so he was willing to pay for the all the work involved at a special rate.

'Without a receipt?' the clerk enquired, raising himself slightly above the counter to make sure that there were no other customers in the premises.

'Why, naturally. What use would it be to me?' The expression in the staff captain's yellowish-brown eyes was imploring and his fingers casually twirled a rather thick-looking wallet. 'Only it's not likely that this man is living in Moscow at present.'

'That's all right, sir. Since it will be a *special rate*, it's quite all right. If your acquaintance is still in government service, I have lists of all the departments. If he is retired, then, of course, it will be difficult . . .'

'He's still in service, he is!' Rybnikov assured the clerk. 'And with a high rank. Perhaps even the equivalent of a general. He and my late father were in the Diplomatic Corps, but I heard that before that he was with the Police

Department or, perhaps, the Gendarmes Corps. Perhaps he could have gone back to his old job?' He delicately placed two paper roubles on the counter.

The clerk took the money and declared cheerfully:

'It often happens that diplomats are transferred to the gendarmes and then back again. That's government service for you. In what name does he rejoice? What is his age?'

'Erast Fandorin. Fan-dor-in. He must be about forty-eight or forty-nine now. I was informed that he resides in St Petersburg, but that is not definite.'

The address wizard rummaged through his plump, tattered books for a long time. Every now and then he declared:

'No one by that name listed with the ministry of foreign affairs ... Not with Gendarmes Corps HQ ... Not with the Railway Gendarmerie ... At the ministry of internal affairs they have a Ferendiukin, Fedul Kharitonovich, director of the Detective Police Material Evidence Depot. Not him?'

Rybnikov shook his head.

'Maybe you could look in Moscow? I recall that Mr Fandorin was a native Muscovite and resided here for a long period.'

He proffered another rouble, but the clerk shook his head with dignity.

'A Moscow enquiry is two kopecks. My direct responsibility. I won't take anything. Anyway, it only takes a moment.' And indeed, he very soon declared: 'No one by that name, either living or working here. Of course, I could look through previous years, but that would be by way of an exception ...'

'Fifty kopecks a year,' replied the perspicacious client: it was a pleasure doing business with a man like him. At this point the enquiries started dragging on a bit. The clerk took out the annual directories volume by volume and moved from the twentieth century back into the nineteenth, burrowing deeper and deeper into the strata of the past.

Vasilii Alexandrovich had already reconciled himself to failure when the clerk suddenly exclaimed:

'I have it! Here, in the book for 1891! That will be ... er ... seven roubles!' And he read it out: '"E. P. Fandorin, state counsellor, deputy for special assignments to governor-general of Moscow. Malaya Nikitskaya Street, annexe to the house of Baron Evert-Kolokoltsev". Well, if your acquaintance held a position like that fourteen years ago, he definitely must be an Excellency by now. Strange that I couldn't find him in the ministry listings.'

'It is strange,' admitted Rybnikov, absentmindedly counting through the reddish notes protruding from his wallet.

'You say the Department of Police or the gendarmes?' the clerk asked, narrowing his eyes cunningly. 'You know the way things are there: a man may seem to exist, and even hold an immensely high rank, but for the general public, it's as if he didn't exist at all.'

The customer batted his eyelids for a moment and then livened up a little.

'Why, yes. My father said that Erast Petrovich worked on secret matters at the embassy!'

'There, you see. And you know what ... My godfather works just close by here, on Maly Gnezdnikovsky Lane. At the police telegraph office. Twenty years he's been there, he knows everyone who's anyone ...'

There followed an eloquent pause.

'A rouble for you, and one for your godfather.'

'Where do you think you're going?' the clerk shouted at a peasant who had stuck his nose in at the door. 'Can't you see it's half past one? It's my lunch hour. Come back in an hour! And you, sir' – this was to Vasilii Alexandrovich, in a whisper – 'wait here. I'll be back in a flash.'

Of course, Rybnikov did not wait in the office. He waited outside, taking up a position in a gateway. You could never tell. This petty bureaucrat might not be as simple as he seemed.

However, the precaution proved unnecessary.

The bureaucrat came back a quarter of an hour later, alone and looking very pleased.

'A quite eminent individual! As they say, widely known in very narrow circles,' he announced when Rybnikov popped up beside him. 'Pantelei Ilich told me so much about your Fandorin! It turns out that he was a very important man. In the old days, under Dolgorukov.'

As he listened to the story of the former greatness of the governor's special deputy, Vasilii Alexandrovich gasped and threw his hands up in the air, but the greatest surprise was waiting for him at the very end.

'And you're lucky,' said the bureaucrat, flinging his arms wide dramatically, like a circus conjuror. 'This Mr Fandorin of yours is in Moscow, he arrived from Peter. Pantelei Ilich sees him every day.'

'In Moscow?' Rybnikov exclaimed. 'Really! Well, that is a stroke of luck. Do you know if he'll be here long?'

'No way of telling. It's something highly important, government business. But Pantelei didn't say what it was, and I didn't ask. That's not for the likes of us to know.'

'Certainly, that's right ...' There was a peculiar expression in Rybnikov's slightly narrowed eyes as their glance slid over the other man's face. 'Did you tell your godfather that one of Erast Petrovich's acquaintances was looking for him?'

'No, I asked as if I was the one who was interested.'

He's not lying, Vasilii Alexandrovich decided. He decided to keep both roubles for himself. His eyes widened again to assume their normal expression. And the clerk never knew that his little life had just been hanging on the very slimmest of threads.

'It's very good that you didn't. I'll arrange a surprise for him – in memory of my late dad. Won't Erast Petrovich be delighted!' Rybnikov said with a radiant smile.

But when he walked out, his face started twitching nervously.

That was the same day that Glyceria Romanovna came to their meeting with a new idea for saving Rybnikov: to appeal for help to her good friend, the head of the Moscow Gendarmes Office, General Charme. Lidina assured him that Konstantin Fyodorovich Charme was a dear old man whose name suited him perfectly, and he would not refuse her anything.

'But what good will that do?' asked Rybnikov, trying to fight her off. 'My dear, I am a state criminal: I lost secret documents and I went on the run. How can your general of gendarmes help with that?'

But Glyceria Romanovna exclaimed heatedly:

'You're wrong! Konstantin Fyodorovich himself explained to me how much depends on the official who is assigned to handle a case. He can make things go badly or make them go well. Ah, if we could find out who is dealing with you!'

And then, giving way to the impulse of the moment, Vasilii Alexandrovich suddenly blurted out:

'I do know. You've seen him. Do you remember, beside the bridge – that tall gentleman with the grey temples?'

'The elegant one, in the light-coloured English coat? I remember, a very impressive man.'

'His name is Fandorin, Erast Petrovich Fandorin. He has come to Moscow from St Petersburg especially to catch me. For God's sake, don't ask anyone to intercede – you'll only make them suspect that you are harbouring a deserter. But if you could find out cautiously, in passing, what kind of man he is, what kind of life he leads, what his character is like, that might help me. Every little detail is important here. But you must act delicately!'

'You men have nothing to teach us about delicacy,' Lidina remarked condescendingly, already figuring out how she would go about this business. 'We'll set this misfortune right, just let me sleep on it.'

Rybnikov didn't thank her, but the way he looked at her gave her a warm feeling in her chest. His yellow eyes no longer seemed like a cat's, as they had during the first minutes of their acquaintance – she thought of them now as 'bright coffee-coloured' and found them very expressive.

'You're like the Swan Queen,' he said with a smile. '"Dearest Prince, do not pine so, for this wonder I do know. In friendship's name, do not be sad, I shall help you and be glad."'

Glyceria Romanovna frowned.

'Pushkin! I can't stand him!'

'What? But surely all Russians adore Pushkin, don't they?'

Rybnikov suddenly realised that in his astonishment he had expressed himself rather awkwardly, but Lidina attached no importance to his strange words.

'How could he write: '"Your end, your children's death, with cruel joy I do behold"? What kind of poet is it that rejoices at the death of children? So much for "a star of captivating happiness"!'

And the conversation turned from a serious subject to Russian poetry, which Rybnikov knew quite well. He said that his father, a passionate admirer of Pushkin's lyre, had cultivated the taste in him as a child.

And then 25 May had come, and Vasilii Alexandrovich had entirely forgotten the inconsequential conversation – there was more important business afoot.

The 'dummies' had been instructed to collect the packages from the left luggage office at dawn, just before they set off. The postman would cover the three crates with sackcloth, daub them with sealing wax and conceal them among his parcels – the best possible hiding place. Bridge's job was even easier, because Vasilii Alexandrovich had done half the work for him: while riding in the closed wagon, he had tipped the melinite into eight cardboard boxes and wrapped each one in anthracite-black paper.

They were both going on the same eastbound express, only Bridge was travelling on his railway worker's pass, in third class, and Tunnel was in the mail coach. Then their paths would part. The former would change to the locomotive of a freight train at Syzran, and in the middle of the Volga he would throw the boxes into the firebox. The latter would ride on as far as Lake Baikal.

For the sake of good order, Rybnikov decided to make certain that the agents collected the baggage by observing in person – naturally, without letting them see him.

As night was drawing to an end, he left the boarding house dressed in the style of a 'little man', with a crooked peaked cap and a collarless shirt under a jacket.

Casting a brief glance at the edge of the sky, which was just turning pink, he slipped into his role and jogged off along Chistoprudny Lane like a stray mongrel.

SHIMO-NO-KU

The first syllable,
in which iron stars
rain down from the sky

The putative Japanese had now been lost, and the Moscow Okhrana was tailing Thrush, so the efforts of the Petersburgians were concentrated entirely on the left luggage office. The items had been deposited there for twenty-four hours, which indicated that they would be called for no later than midday.

Fandorin and Mylnikov took up position in a secret observation post the evening before. As has already been mentioned, railway gendarmes were concealed in close proximity to the left luggage office, and Mylnikov's agents were also taking turns to stroll around the square in front of the station, so the two bosses installed themselves comfortably in the premises of Lyapunov's Funeral Services, which were located opposite the station, offering a superlative panoramic view. The American glass of the shop window was also very handy for their purpose, being funereal black and only allowing light through in one direction.

The two partners did not switch on the light – they had no real need for it anyway, since there was a street lamp burning nearby. The night hours dragged by slowly.

Every now and then the telephone rang – it was their subordinates reporting that the net had been cast, all the men were in position and vigilance was not slackening.

Fandorin and Mylnikov had already discussed everything to do with the job, but the conversation simply would not gel when it came to more abstract subjects – the ranges of the two partners' interests were simply too different.

The engineer was not concerned, the silence did not bother him, but it drove the court counsellor wild.

'Did you ever happen to meet Count Loris-Melikov?' he asked.

'Certainly,' replied Fandorin, 'but no more than that.'

'They say the man had a great mind, even though he was Armenian.'

Silence.

'Well, what I'm getting at is this. I've been told that before he retired His Excellency had a long tête-à-tête with Alexander III, and he made all sorts of predictions and gave him lots of advice: about a constitution, about concessions to foreigners, about foreign politics. Everyone knows the late tsar wasn't exactly bright. Afterwards he used to laugh and say: "Loris tried to frighten me with Japan – just imagine it! He wanted me to be afraid of Japan". That was in 1881, when no one even thought Japan was a proper country! Have you heard that story?'

'I have had occasion to.'

'See what kind of ministers Alexander II, the old Liberator, had. But Sandy number three had no time for them. And as for *his* son, our Nicky, well, what can you say ... The old saying's true: If He wants to punish someone, He'll take away their reason. Will you at least say something! I'm talking sincerely here, straight from the heart. My soul's aching for Russia.'

'S-so I see,' Fandorin remarked drily.

Not even taking a meal together brought them any closer, especially since each of them ate his own food. An agent delivered a little carafe of rowanberry vodka, fatty bacon and salted cucumbers for Mylnikov. The engineer's Japanese servant treated him to pieces of raw herring and mar- inaded radish. Polite invitations from both parties to sample their fare were both declined with equal politeness. At the end of the meal, Fandorin lit up a Dutch cigar and Mylnikov sucked on a eucalyptus pastille for his nerves.

Eventually, at the time determined by nature, morning arrived.

The street lamps went out in the square, rays of sunlight slanted through the steam swirling above the damp surface of the road and sparrows started hopping about on the pavement under the window of the undertaker's office.

'There he is!' Fandorin said in a low voice: for the last half-hour he had been glued to his binoculars.

'Who?'

'Our man. I'll c-call the gendarmes.'

Mylnikov followed the direction of the engineer's binoculars and put his own up to his eyes.

A man with a battered cap pulled right down to his ears was ambling across the broad, almost deserted square.

'That's him all right!' the court counsellor said in a bloodthirsty whisper, and immediately pulled a stunt that was not envisaged in the plan: he stuck his head out through a small open windowpane and gave a deafening blast on his whistle.

Fandorin froze with the telephone receiver in his hand.

'Have you taken leave of your senses?'

Mylnikov grinned triumphantly and tossed his reply back over his shoulder:

'Well, what did you expect? Didn't think Mylnikov would let the railway gendarmes have all the glory, did you? You can sod that! The Jap's mine, he's mine!'

From different sides of the square, agents dashed towards the little man, four of them in all. They trilled on their whistles and yelled menacingly.

'Stop!'

The spy listened and stopped. He turned his head in all directions. He saw there was nowhere to run, but he ran anyway – chasing after an empty early tram that was clattering towards Zatsepa Street.

The agent running to cut him off thought he had guessed his enemy's intentions – he darted forward to meet the tramcar and leapt nimbly up on to the front platform.

Just at that moment the Japanese overtook the tram, but he didn't jump inside; running at full speed, he leapt up and grabbed hold of a rung of the dangling ladder with both hands, and in the twinkling of an eye, he was up on the roof.

The agent who had ended up inside the tram started dashing about between the benches – he couldn't work out where the fugitive had disappeared to. The other three shouted and waved their arms, but he didn't understand their gesticulations, and the distance between them and the tram was gradually increasing.

Spectators at the station – departing passengers, people seeing them off, cab drivers – gaped at this outlandish performance.

Then Mylnikov clambered out of the open window almost as far as his waist and howled in a voice that could have brought down the walls of Jericho:

'Put the brake on, you idiot!'

Either the agent heard his boss's howling, or he twigged for himself, but he went dashing to the driver, and immediately the brakes squealed, the tram slowed down and the other agents started closing in on it rapidly.

'No chance, he won't get away!' Mylnikov boasted confidently. 'Not from my aces he won't. Every one of them's worth ten of your railway boneheads.'

The tram had not yet stopped, it was still screeching along the rails, but the little figure in the jacket ran along its roof, pushed off with one foot, performed an unbelievable somersault and landed neatly on a newspaper kiosk standing at the corner of the square.

'An acrobat!' Mylnikov gasped.

But Fandorin muttered some short word that obviously wasn't Russian and raised his binoculars to his eyes.

Panting for breath, the agents surrounded the wooden kiosk. They raised their heads, waved their arms, shouted something – the only sounds that reached the undertaker's premises were 'f***! – f***! – f***!'

Mylnikov chortled feverishly.

'Like a cat on a fence! Got him!'

Suddenly the engineer exclaimed:

'*Shuriken!*'

He flung aside his binoculars, darted out into the street and shouted loudly:

'Look out!'

But too late.

The circus performer on the roof of the kiosk spun round his own axis, waving his hand through the air rapidly – as if he were thanking the agents on all four sides. One by one, Mylnikov's 'aces' tumbled on to the paved surface.

A second later the spy leapt down, as softly as a cat, and dashed along the street towards the gaping mouth of a nearby gateway.

The engineer ran after him. The court counsellor, shocked and stunned for a moment, darted after him.

'What happened? What happened?' he shouted.

'He'll get away!' Fandorin groaned.

'Not if I have anything to do with it!'

Mylnikov pulled a revolver out from under his armpit and opened fire on the fugitive like a real master, on the run. He had good reason to pride himself on his accuracy, he usually felled a moving figure at fifty paces with the first bullet, but this time he emptied the entire cylinder and failed to hit the target. The damned Japanese was running oddly, with sidelong jumps and zigzags – how can you pop a target like that?

'The bastard!' gasped Mylnikov, clicking the hammer of his revolver against an empty cartridge case. 'Why aren't you firing?'

'There's no p-point.'

The shooting brought the gendarmes tearing out of the station after breaking their cover for the ambush. The public started to panic, there was shouting and jostling, and waving of umbrellas. Local police constables' whistles could be heard trilling from various directions. But meanwhile the fugitive had already disappeared into the gateway.

'Along the side street, the side street!' Fandorin told the gendarmes, pointing. 'To the left!'

The light-blue uniforms rushed off round the building. Mylnikov swore furiously as he clambered up the fire escape ladder, but Erast Petrovich stopped and shook his head hopelessly.

He took no further part in the search after that. He looked at the gendarmes and police agents bustling about, listened to Mylnikov's howls from up above his head and set off back towards the square.

A crowd of curious gawkers was jostling around the kiosk, and he caught glimpses of a policeman's white peaked cap.

As he walked up, the engineer heard a trembling, senile voice declaiming:

'So is it said in prophecy: and iron stars shall rain down from the heavens and strike down the sinners . . .'

Fandorin spoke sombrely to the policeman:

'Clear the public away.'

Even though Fandorin was in civilian garb, the policeman realised from his tone of voice that this man had the right to command, and he immediately blew on his whistle.

To menacing shouts of 'Move aside! Where do you think you're shoving?' Fandorin walked round the site of the slaughter.

All four agents were dead. They were lying in identical poses, on their backs. Each had an iron star with sharp, glittering points protruding from his forehead, where it had pierced deep into the bone.

'Lord Almighty!' exclaimed Mylnikov, crossing himself as he walked up.

Squatting down with a sob, he was about to pull a metal star out of a dead head.

'Don't touch it! The edges are smeared with p-poison!'

Mylnikov jerked his hand away.

'What devil's work is this?'

'That is a *shuriken*, also known as a *syarinken*. A throwing weapon of the "Furtive Ones", a sect of hereditary sp-spies that exists in Japan.'

'Hereditary?' The court counsellor started blinking very rapidly. 'Is that like our Rykalov from the detective section? His great-grandfather served in the Secret Chancellery, back in Catherine the Great's time.'

'Something of the kind. So that's why he jumped on to the kiosk . . .'

Fandorin's last remark was addressed to himself, but Mylnikov jerked his head up and asked:

'Why?'

'To throw at standing targets. You and your "cat on a fence". Well, you've made a fine mess of things, Mylnikov.'

'Never mind the mess,' said Mylnikov, with tears coursing down his cheeks. 'If I made it, I'll answer for it, it won't be the first time. Zyablikov, Raspashnoi, Kasatkin, Möbius . . .'

A carriage came flying furiously into the square from the direction of Bolshaya Tartarskaya Street and a pale man with no hat tumbled out of it and shouted from a distance:

'Evstratpalich! Disaster! Thrush has got away! He's disappeared!'

'But what about our plant?'

'They found him with a knife in his side!'

The court counsellor launched into a torrent of obscenity so wild that someone in the crowd remarked respectfully:

'He's certainly making himself clear.'

But the engineer set off at a brisk stride towards the station.

'Where are you going?' shouted Mylnikov.

'To the left luggage office. They won't come for the melinite now.'

But Fandorin was mistaken.

The clerk was standing there, shifting from one foot to the other in front of the open door.

'Well, did you catch the two boyos?' he asked when he caught sight of Fandorin.

'Which b-boyos?'

'You know! The two who collected the baggage. I pressed on the button, like you told me to. Then I glanced into the gendarme gentlemen's room. But when I looked, it was empty.'

The engineer groaned as if afflicted with a sudden, sharp pain.

'How l-long ago?'

'The first one came exactly at five. The second was seven or eight minutes later.'

Fandorin's Breguet showed 5.29.

The court counsellor started swearing again, only not menacingly this time, but plaintively, in a minor key.

'That was while we were creeping round the courtyards and basements,' he wailed.

Fandorin summed up the situation in a funereal voice:

'A worse debacle than Tsushima.'

The second syllable,
entirely about railways

The interdepartmental conflict took place there and then, in the corridor. In his fury, Fandorin abandoned his usual restraint and told Mylnikov exactly what he thought about the Special Section, which was fine for spawning informers and agents provocateurs, but proved to be absolutely useless when it came to real work and caused nothing but problems.

'You gendarmes are a fine lot too,' snarled Mylnikov. 'Why did your smart alecs abandon the ambush without any order? They let the bombers get away with the melinite. Now where do we look for them?'

Fandorin fell silent, stung either by the justice of the rebuke or that form of address – 'you gendarmes'.

'Our collaboration hasn't worked out,' said the man from the Department of Police, sighing. 'Now you'll make a complaint to your bosses about me, and I'll make one to mine about you. Only none of that bumph is going to put things right. A bad peace is better than a good quarrel. Let's do it this way: you look after your railway and I'll catch Comrade Thrush. The way we're supposed to do things according to our official responsibilities. That'll be safer.'

Hunting for the revolutionaries who had established contact with Japanese intelligence obviously seemed far more promising to Mylnikov than pursuing unknown saboteurs who could be anywhere along an eight-thousand-verst railway line.

But Fandorin was so sick of the court counsellor that he replied contemptuously:

'Excellent. Only keep well out of my sight.'

'A good specialist always keeps out of sight,' Evstratii Pavlovich purred, and he left.

And only then, bitterly repenting that he had wasted several precious minutes on pointless wrangling, did Fandorin set to work.

The first thing he did was question the receiving clerk in detail about the men who had presented the receipts for the baggage.

It turned out that the man who took the eight paper packages was dressed like a workman (grey collarless shirt, long coat, boots), but his face didn't match his clothes – the clerk said he 'wasn't that simple'.

'What do you mean by that?'

'He was educated. Glasses, hair down to his shoulders, a big, bushy beard like a church sexton. Since when does a worker or a craftsman look like that? And he's ill. His face is all white and he kept clearing his throat and wiping his lips with a handkerchief.'

The second recipient, who had shown up a few minutes after the one in glasses, sounded even more interesting to the engineer – he spotted an obvious lead here.

The man who took away the three wooden crates had been dressed in the uniform of a railway postal worker! The clerk could not possibly be mistaken about this – he had been working in the Department of Railways for a good few years.

Moustache, broad cheekbones, middle-aged. The recipient had a holster hanging at his side, which meant that he accompanied the mail carriage, in which, as everybody knew, sums of money and precious packages were transported.

Fandorin could already feel a presentiment of success, but he suppressed that dangerous mood and turned to Lieutenant Colonel Danilov, who had just arrived.

'In the last twenty minutes, since half past five, have any trains set off?'

'Yes indeed, the Harbin train. It left ten minutes ago.'

'Then that's where they are, our boyos. Both of them,' the engineer declared confidently.

The lieutenant colonel was doubtful.

'But maybe they went back into the city? Or they're waiting for the next train, to Paveletsk? It's at six twenty-five.'

'No. It is no accident that they showed up at the same time, with just a few minutes between them. That is one. And note what time that was – dawn. What else of any importance happens at this station between five and six, apart from the departure of the Harbin train? And then, of course, the third point.' The engineer's voice hardened. 'What would saboteurs want with the P-Paveletsk train? What would they blow up on the Paveletsk line? Hay and straw, radishes and carrots? No, our subjects have gone off on the Harbin train.'

'Shall I send a telegram to stop the train?'

'Under no circumstances. There is melinite on board. Who knows what these people are like? If they suspect something is wrong, they might blow it up. No delays, no unscheduled stops. The bombers are already on their guard, they're nervous. No, tell me instead where the first stop is according to the timetable.'

'It's an express. So it will only stop in Vladimir – let me just take a look ... At nine thirty.'

*

The powerful locomotive commandeered by Danilov overhauled the Harbin express at the border of the province of Moscow and thereafter maintained a distance of one verst, which it only reduced just before Vladimir.

It came flying on to the next line only a minute after the express. Fandorin jumped down on to the platform without waiting for the locomotive to stop. The scheduled train halted at the station for only ten minutes, so every minute was precious.

The engineer was met by Captain Lenz, the head of the Vladimir Railway Gendarmes Division, who had been briefed about everything in detail by telephone. He goggled wildly at Fandorin's fancy dress (greasy coat, grey moustache and eyebrows, with temples that were also grey, only there had been no need to dye them) and wiped his sweaty bald patch with a handkerchief, but did not ask any questions.

'Everything's ready. This way, please.'

He reported about everything else on the run, as he tried to keep up with Erast Petrovich.

'The trolley's waiting. The team has been assembled. They're keeping their heads down, as ordered . . .'

The station postal worker, who had been informed of the basic situation, was loitering beside a trolley piled high with correspondence. To judge from the chalky hue of his features, he was in a dead funk. The room was packed with light-blue uniforms – all the gendarmes were squatting down, and their heads were bent down low too. That was so that no one would see them from the platform, through the window, Fandorin realised.

He smiled at the postal worker.

'Calm down, calm down, nothing unusual is going to happen.'

He took hold of the handles and pushed the trolley out on to the platform.

'Seven minutes,' the gendarmes captain whispered after him.

A man in a blue jacket stuck his head out of the mail carriage, which was coupled immediately behind the locomotive.

'Asleep, are you, Vladimir?' he shouted angrily. 'What's taking you so long?'

Long moustache, middle-aged. Broad cheekbones? I suppose so, Erast Petrovich thought to himself, and whispered to his partner again:

'Stop shaking, will you? And yawn, you almost overslept.'

'There you go . . . Couldn't keep my eyes open. My second straight day on duty,' the Vladimir man babbled, yawning and stretching.

Meanwhile the disguised engineer was quickly tossing the mail in through the open door and weighing things up, wondering whether he should grab the man with the long moustache round the waist and fling him on to the platform. Nothing could be easier.

He decided to wait first and check whether there were three wooden crates measuring 15 × 10 × 15 inches in there.

He was right to wait.

He climbed up into the carriage and began dividing the Vladimir post into three piles: letters, parcels and packages.

The inside of the carriage was a veritable labyrinth of heaps of sacks, boxes and crates.

Erast walked along one row, then along another, but he didn't see the familiar items.

'What are you doing wandering about?' someone barked at him out of a dark passage. 'Get a move on, look lively! Sacks over this way, square items over there. Are you new, or something?'

This was a surprise: another postman, also about forty years old, with broad cheekbones and a moustache. Which one was it? A pity he didn't have the clerk from the left luggage office with him.

'Yes, I'm new,' Fandorin droned in a deep voice, as if he had a cold.

'And old too, from the look of you.'

The second postal worker came over to the first one and stood beside him. They both had holsters with Nagant revolvers hanging on their belts.

'Why are your hands shaking – on a spree yesterday, were you?' the second one asked the Vladimir man.

'Just a bit . . .'

'But didn't you say this was your second day on duty?' the first one, with the long moustache, asked in surprise.

The second one stuck his head out of the door and looked at the station building.

Which one of them? Fandorin tried to guess, slipping rapidly along the stacks. Or is it neither? Where are the crates of melinite?

Suddenly there was a deafening clang as the second postman slammed the door shut and pushed home the bolt.

'What's up with you, Matvei?' the one with the long moustache asked, surprised again.

Matvei bared his yellow teeth and cocked the hammer of his revolver with a click.

'I know what I'm doing! Three blue caps in the window, and all of them staring this way! I've got a nose for these things!'

Incredible relief was what Erast Petrovich felt at that moment – so he hadn't wasted his time smearing lead white on his eyebrows and moustache and it had been worthwhile breathing locomotive soot for three hours.

'Matvei, have you gone crazy?' the one with the long moustache asked in bewilderment, gazing into the glittering gun barrel.

The Vladimir postal worker got the idea straight away and pressed himself back against the wall.

'Easy, Lukich. Don't stick your nose in. And you, you louse, tell me, is this loader of yours a nark? I'll kill you!' The subject grabbed the local man by the collar.

'They made me do it . . . Have pity . . . I've only one year to go to my pension . . .' said the local man, capitulating immediately.

'Hey, my good man, don't be stupid!' shouted Fandorin, sticking his head out from behind the crates. 'There's nowhere you can go anyway. Drop the wea . . .'

He hadn't expected that – the subject fired without even bothering to hear him out.

The engineer barely managed to squat down in time, and the bullet whistled by just above his head.

'Ah, you stinking rat!' Fandorin heard the man that the saboteur had called Lukich cry indignantly.

There was another crash, then two voices mingling together – one groaning, the other whining.

Erast Petrovich crept to the edge of the stack and glanced out.

Things had taken a really nasty turn.

Matvei was ensconced in the corner, holding the revolver out in front of him. Lukich was lying on the floor, fumbling at his chest with bloody fingers. The Vladimir postal worker was squealing with his hands up over his face.

Bluish-grey powder smoke swayed gently in the ghastly light of the electric lamp.

From the position that Fandorin had occupied, nothing could have been easier than to shoot the villain, but he was needed alive and preferably not too badly damaged. So Erast Petrovich stuck out the hand holding his Browning and planted two bullets in the wall to the subject's right.

Exactly as required, the subject retreated from the corner behind a stack of cardboard boxes.

Shooting continuously (three, four, five, six, seven), the engineer jumped out, ran and threw himself bodily at the boxes – they collapsed, burying the man hiding behind them.

After that it took only a couple of seconds.

Erast Petrovich grabbed a protruding leg in a cowhide boot, tugged the saboteur out into the light of day (of the electric lamp, that is) and struck him with the edge of his hand slightly above the collarbone.

He had one.

Now he had to catch the other one, in glasses, who had collected the paper parcels.

Only how was he to find him? And was he even on the train at all?

But he didn't have to search for the man in glasses – he announced his own presence.

When Erast Petrovich drew back the bolt and pushed open the heavy door of the mail carriage, the first thing he saw was people running along the platform. And he heard frightened screams and women squealing.

Captain Lenz was standing beside the carriage, looking pale and behaving strangely: instead of looking at the engineer, who had just escaped deadly danger, the gendarme was squinting off to one side.

'Take him,' said Fandorin, dragging the saboteur, who had still not come round, to the carraige door. 'And get a stretcher here, a man's been wounded.' He nodded at the stampeding public. 'Were they alarmed by the shots?'

'No, not that. It's a real disaster, Mr Engineer. As soon as we heard the shots, my men and I rushed out on to the platform, thinking we could help

you . . . Then suddenly there was a wild, crazy howl from that carriage there
. . .' Lenz pointed off to one side. '"I won't surrender alive!" That's when it
started . . .'

Two gendarmes lugged away Matvei, under arrest, and Erast Petrovich
jumped down on to the platform and looked in the direction indicated.

He saw a green third-class carriage with not a single soul anywhere near
it – but he glimpsed white faces with wide-open mouths behind the windows.

'He has a revolver. And a bomb,' Lenz reported hastily. 'He must have
thought we came dashing out to arrest him. He took the conductor's keys
and locked the carriage at both ends. There are about forty people in there.
He keeps shouting: "Just try getting in, I'll blow them all up!"'

And at that moment there was a blood-curdling shriek from the carriage.

'Get back! If anybody moves, I'll blow them all to kingdom come!'

However, he hasn't blown them up yet, the engineer mused. Although
he has had the opportunity. 'I tell you what, Captain. Carry all the crates
out of the mail carriage quickly. We'll work out later which ones are ours.
And observe every possible precaution as you carry them. If the melinite
detonates, you'll be building a new station afterwards. That is, not you, of
course, b-but somebody else. Don't come after me. I'll do this alone.'

Erast Petrovich hunched over and ran along the line of carriages. He
stopped at the window from which the threats to 'blow everyone to kingdom
come' had been made. It was the only one that was half open.

The engineer tapped delicately on the side of the carriage: tap-tap-tap.

'Who's there?' asked a surprised voice.

'Engineer Fandorin. Will you allow me to come in?'

'What for?'

'I'd like to t-talk to you.'

'But I'm going to blow everything in here to pieces,' said the voice,
puzzled. 'Didn't you hear that? And then, how will you get in? I won't open
the door for anything.'

'That's all right, don't worry. I'll climb in through the window, just don't
shoot.'

Erast Petrovich nimbly hauled himself up and in through the window as
far as his shoulders, then waited for a moment, so that the bomber could
get a good look at his venerable grey hair, before creeping into the carriage
slowly, very slowly.

Things looked bad: the young man in spectacles had thrust his revolver
into his belt, and he was holding one of the black packages. In fact, he had
already thrust his fingers inside it – Fandorin assumed he was clutching the
glass detonator. One slight squeeze and the bomb would detonate, setting
off the other seven. There they were, on the upper bunk, covered with
sackcloth.

'You don't look like an engineer,' said the youth, as pale as death, examining the dusty clothing of the false loader.

'And you don't look like a p-proletarian,' Erast Petrovich parried.

The carriage had no compartments; it consisted of a long corridor with wooden benches on both sides. Unlike the people clamouring on the platform, the hostages were sitting quietly – they could sense the nearness of death. There was just a woman's voice tearfully murmuring a prayer somewhere.

'Quiet, you idiot, I'll blow the whole place up!' the youth shouted in a terrible deep voice, and the praying broke off.

He's dangerous, extremely dangerous, Fandorin realised as he looked into the terrorist's wide, staring eyes. He's not playing for effect, not throwing a fit of hysterics – he really will blow us up.

'Why the delay?' asked Erast Petrovich.

'Eh?'

'I can see that you are not afraid of death. So why are you putting it off? Why don't you crush the detonator? There is something stopping you. What?'

'You're strange,' said the young man in glasses. 'But you're right . . . This is all wrong. It isn't how it should all happen . . . I'm selling myself cheap. It's frustrating. And she won't get her ten thousand . . .'

'Who, your mother? Who will she not get the money from, the Japanese?'

'What mother!' the youth cried, gesturing angrily. 'Ah, what a wonderful plan it was! She would have racked her brains, wondered who did it, where it was from. Then she would have guessed and blessed my memory. Russia would have cursed me, but she would have blessed me!'

'The one you love?' Fandorin said with a nod, starting to understand. 'She is unhappy, trapped, this money would save her, allow her to start a new life?'

'Yes! You can't imagine what a hideous abomination Samara is! And her parents and brothers! Brutes, absolute brutes! Never mind that she doesn't love me, that's all right! Who could love a living corpse, coughing up his own lungs? But I'll reach out to her even from the next world, I'll pull her out of the quagmire . . . That is, I would have done . . .'

The young man groaned and started shaking so violently that the black paper rustled in his hands.

'She won't get the money because you failed to blow up the bridge? Or the tunnel?' Erast Petrovich asked quickly, keeping his eyes fixed on that deadly package.

'A bridge, the Alexander Bridge. How do you know that? But what difference does it make? Yes, the samurai won't pay. I shall die in vain.'

'So you are doing all this because of *her*, for the ten thousand?'

The youth in glasses shook his head.

'Not only that. I want to take revenge on Russia. It's a vile, abominable country!'

Fandorin sat down on the bench, crossed his legs and shrugged.

'You can't do Russia any great harm now. Well, you'll blow up the carriage. Kill and maim forty poor third-class passengers, and the lady of your heart will be left to languish in Samara.' He paused to give the young man a chance to reflect on that, then said forcefully: 'I have a better idea. You give me the explosive, and then the girl you love will get her ten thousand. And you can leave Russia to her fate.'

'You'll deceive me,' the consumptive whispered.

'No. I give you my word of honour,' said Erast Petrovich, and he said it in a voice that made it impossible not to believe.

Patches of ruddy colour bloomed on the bomber's cheeks.

'I don't want to die in a prison hospital. Better here, now.'

'Just as you wish,' Fandorin said quietly.

'Very well. I'll write her a note . . .'

The youth pulled a notebook out of his pocket and scribbled in it feverishly with a pencil. The parcel with the bomb was lying on the bench and now Fandorin could easily have grabbed it. But the engineer didn't budge.

'Only, please, be brief,' he said. 'I feel sorry for the passengers. After all, every second is torment for them. God forbid, someone might have a stroke.'

'Yes, yes, just a moment . . .'

He finished writing, folded the page neatly and handed it over.

'It has the name and address on it . . .'

Only then did Fandorin take the bomb and hand it out through the window, after first calling the gendarmes. The other seven followed it: the youth in glasses took hold of them carefully and handed them to Erast Petrovich, who lowered them out through the window.

'And now go out, please,' said the doomed man, cocking the hammer of his revolver. 'And remember: you gave your word of honour.'

Looking into the youth's bright-blue eyes, Erast Petrovich realised that it was pointless to try to change his mind, and walked towards the door.

The shot rang out behind his back almost immediately.

The engineer arrived back at home, feeling weary and sad, as the day was ending. At the station in Moscow he was handed a telegram from Petersburg: 'All's well that ends well but we need the Japanese I hope the ten thousand is a joke'.

That meant he would have to pay the *Belle Dame sans merci* of Samara out of his own pocket, but that was not why he was feeling sad – he simply could not stop thinking about the young suicide, with all his love and hate. And Erast Petrovich's thoughts also kept coming back again and again to the man who had thought of a way to make practical use of someone else's misery.

They hadn't learned much about this resourceful individual from the arrested postman. Nothing new at all, really. They still had no idea where to look for the man. And it was even more difficult to predict at which point he would strike his next blow.

Fandorin was met in the doorway of his government apartment by his valet. Observing neutrality had been particularly difficult for Masa today. All the time his master was away, the Japanese had muttered sutras and he had even tried to pray in front of an icon, but now he was the very image of dispassion. He ran a quick glance over Erast Petrovich to see whether he was unhurt. Seeing that he was, Masa screwed his eyes up in relief and immediately said indifferently in Japanese:

'Another letter from the head of the municipal gendarmes.'

The engineer frowned as he unfolded the note, in which Lieutenant General Charme insistently invited him to come to dinner today at half past seven. The note ended with the words: 'Otherwise, I really shall take offence'.

Yesterday there had been an identical invitation, left without a reply for lack of time.

It was awkward. An old, distinguished general. And in an adjacent government department – he couldn't offend him.

'Wash, shave, dinner jacket, white tie, top hat,' the engineer told his servant in a sour voice.

The third syllable,
in which Rybnikov
gives free rein to his passion

On 25 May, Glyceria Romanovna drove along the boulevard in vain – Vasya did not come. This upset her, but not too badly. First, she knew where to find him now, and secondly, she had something to do.

Lidina drove straight from the boulevard to see Konstantin Fyodorovich Charme at his place of work. The old man was absolutely delighted. He threw some officers or other with documents out of his office, ordered hot chocolate to be served and was generally very sweet with his old-fashioned gallantry.

It was not at all difficult to turn the conversation to Fandorin. After idle chat about their common acquaintances in St Petersburg, Glyceria Romanovna told him how she had nearly been caught up in the appalling crash on the bridge, with graphic descriptions of what she had seen and what she had been through. She dwelt in detail on the *mysterious* gentleman with grey temples who was in charge of the investigation.

Just as Lidina had calculated, this emphatic epithet had its effect.

'He may be mysterious to you, but not to me,' the general said with a condescending smile. 'That's Fandorin from the Petersburg Railway Gendarmerie. Highly intelligent man, cosmopolitan, a great original. He's handling a very important case in Moscow at present. I have been warned that my collaboration might be required at any moment.'

Glyceria Romanovna's heart sank: 'an important case'. Poor Vasya!

But she gave no sign of her dismay. Instead, she pretended to be curious:

'Cosmopolitan? A great original? Ah, dear Konstantin Fyodorovich, introduce me to him! I know nothing is impossible for you!'

'No, no, don't even ask. Erast Petrovich has a reputation as a heartbreaker. Could it be that even you have not remained indifferent to his marble features? Take care, I shall become jealous and have you put under secret surveillance,' the general threatened her jokingly.

But, of course, his stubbornness did not last long – he promised to invite the Petersburgian to dinner that very evening.

Glyceria Romanovna put on her silvery dress, the one which, in her own mind, she called '*fatale*', scented herself with sensuous perfume and even made up her eyes a little, something that she usually did not do. She looked so fine that for five minutes she simply couldn't go out on to the stairs – she carried on admiring herself in the mirror.

But the odious Fandorin did not come. Lidina sat there all evening, listening to the flowery compliments of her host and the conversations of his boring guests.

As they were saying goodnight, Konstantin Fyodorovich spread his hands and shrugged.

'Your mystery man didn't come. He didn't even condescend to answer my note.'

She tried to persuade the general not to be angry – perhaps Fandorin was on an important investigation. And she said:

'You have such a lovely home! And your guests are all so wonderful. I tell you what, arrange another dinner tomorrow, with the same set. And write a bit more determinedly to Fandorin, so that he will definitely come. Do you promise?'

'For the pleasure of seeing you in my home again, I would do anything. But why are you so interested in Fandorin?'

'It's not a matter of him,' said Lidina, lowering her voice confidentially. 'It's just idle curiosity. A caprice, if you like. It's simply that I'm very solitary now, I need to be out in society more. I didn't tell you. I'm leaving Georges.'

The general appreciated being taken into her confidence. Glancing round at his tedious wife, he immediately suggested lunch out of town the next day, but Glyceria Romanovna quickly scotched that. And in point of fact, the general was quite content with a little moderate flirtation with the attractive young woman; he had brought up the subject of lunch at the Yar restaurant only out of habit, like an old, retired hussar steed champing at the bit when he hears the distant sound of the bugle.

The next day Fandorin did come, although he was late. And in effect, nothing more was required of him – Lidina had no doubts about how charming she was. Today she looked every bit as fine as yesterday. Even finer, because she'd had the idea of putting on an embroidered Mauritanian cap and lowering a transparent, absolutely ethereal veil from it across her face.

The strategy she chose was the simplest, but it was certain.

At first she did not look at him at all, but she was amiable with the most handsome of the guests – a horse guardsman who was the governor-general's adjutant.

Later she reluctantly acceded to her host's repeated requests to perform Mr Poigin's audacious romance 'Do not go, stay a while with me', accompanying herself on the piano. Glyceria Romanovna's voice was not very strong, but it had a very pleasant timbre and its effect on men was infallible. As she sang the passionate promise to 'quench languorous love with caresses of fire', she looked by turn at all the men, apart from Fandorin.

When she calculated that the subject should be in the required state of readiness – that is, he should by now be sufficiently intrigued and piqued – Lidina gathered herself to strike the final blow and even set off towards the *causeuse* on which Fandorin was sitting, but their host spoiled her plan.

He walked over to the guest and struck up an idiotic conversation about work, praising some railway gendarmes captain called Lisitsky, who had come to him recently with a very interesting proposal – to set up a permanent station at the municipal telephone exchange.

'An excellent idea your subordinate had,' the general rumbled. 'That's the gendarme spirit for you. It wasn't the civilians in the Department who came up with it, but one of our own! I've already given instructions to allocate the apparatus required and a special room. Lisitsky said that the idea of eavesdropping on conversations was yours.'

'Not "eavesdropping", but "listening in". And the staff captain is also being too modest. I had nothing to do with it.'

'Perhaps you could lend him to me to get things started? A competent officer.'

Lidina sighed, realising that the assault would have to be postponed to a more convenient moment.

That moment arrived when the gentlemen followed the new-fangled custom of withdrawing to the smoking room before the meal. By that time Glyceria Romanovna had conclusively established herself as the queen of the evening, and the subject, of course, was not in the slightest doubt that he was the least attractive of all the squires in the present company. The fact that Fandorin kept glancing stealthily at his watch suggested that he was no longer anticipating any pleasure from the soirée, but was calculating when it would be acceptable for him to beat a retreat.

It was time!

She walked briskly (there was no point in delaying any further) up to the man with the greying dark hair, who was puffing on a small, aromatic cigar, and declared:

'I remember! I remember where I've seen you before! At the bridge that was blown up. It's not easy to forget such an unusual face.'

The investigator (or whatever it was he was called in his own department) started and fixed Lidina with the gaze of his slightly narrowed blue eyes – she had to confess that they went very well with his silver-shot hair. Anybody would have started at a compliment like that, especially when it was entirely unexpected.

'Yes indeed,' he said slowly, getting to his feet. 'I recall that t-too. I think you were not alone, but with some army man . . .'

Glyceria Romanovna gestured carelessly.

'He's a friend of mine.'

It was too soon to start talking about Vasya. Not that she had any plan of action worked out in advance – she followed only her inspiration – but you should never, under any circumstances, let a man see that you wanted something from him. He should remain convinced that he was the one who wanted something and it lay in your will to give that precious *something* or not give it. You first had to arouse the hope, then take it away, then titillate his nostrils once again with that magical fragrance.

A clever woman who wished to bind a man to her could always sense to which type he belonged: those who sooner or later will have to be fed, or those who should remain eternally hungry – so that they will be more tractable.

On examining Fandorin more closely, Lidina immediately realised that he was not the Platonic admirer type. If he was led a dance for too long, he would simply shrug his shoulders and walk away.

Which meant that the problem shifted automatically from the tactical phase to the moral or, in unequivocal terms (and Lidina always tried to be supremely honest with herself), it could be formulated thus: could she carry her flirtation with this man all the way through – in order to save Vasya?

Yes, she was prepared for this sacrifice. Having realised that, Glyceria Romanovna experienced a strangely tender feeling and immediately set about justifying such a step.

First, it would not be debauchery, but the very purest self-sacrifice – and not even out of passionate infatuation, but out of selfless, sublimely exalted friendship.

Secondly, it would serve Astralov right – he deserved it.

Of course, if Fandorin had been fat, with warts and bad breath, there could have been no question of any such sacrifice, but although the anglicised investigator was no longer young, he was perfectly good-looking. In fact, more than merely good-looking . . .

This entire maelstrom of thoughts swept through Lidina's mind in a single second, so there was no perceptible pause in the conversation.

'I noticed that you haven't taken your eyes off me all evening,' she said in a low, vibrant voice, and touched his arm.

Of course he hadn't! She had done everything to make sure that the guests could not forget her for a single moment.

The dark-haired man did not protest, but inclined his head honestly.

'But I didn't look at you. Not at all.'

'So I n-noticed.'

'Because I was afraid . . . I had the feeling that you didn't turn up here purely by chance. That fate had brought us together. And that made me feel afraid.'

'F-fate?' he asked, with that barely perceptible stammer of his.

He had the right expression in his eyes – attentive and also, she thought, bewildered.

Lidina decided not to waste any time on pointless talk. There was no avoiding what had to be. And she plunged recklessly, head first, into the whirlpool.

'You know what? Let's leave. Damn the dinner. Let them talk, I don't care.'

If Fandorin hesitated, then it was only for an instant. His eyes flashed with a metallic glint and his voice sounded stifled.

'Why not, let's go.'

On the way to Ostozhenka Street he behaved very oddly. He didn't squeeze her arm or try to kiss her or even make conversation.

Glyceria Romanovna remained silent too, trying to work out the best way to behave with this strange man.

And why was he so tense? With his lips clenched firmly together and his eyes fixed on the driver.

Oh, these still waters must definitely run deep! She felt a sweet swooning sensation somewhere inside and rebuked herself angrily: Don't be such a woman, this is not a romantic adventure, you have to save Vasya!

At the entrance Fandorin behaved even more surprisingly.

He let the lady go ahead, but didn't walk in straight away himself; he paused, and then entered very rapidly, almost leaping in.

He ran up the stairway first, keeping his hand in his coat pocket all the time.

'Maybe he's gaga,' Lidina suddenly thought in fright. '*Cock-a-doodle in the head*, as they say nowadays.'

But it was too late to back out now.

Fandorin moved her aside and bounded forward. He swung round and pressed his back against the wall of the hallway. He rapidly turned his gaze left, right, upwards.

A little black pistol had appeared in his hand out of nowhere.

'What's wrong with you?' Glyceria Romanovna exclaimed, seriously frightened.

The insane investigator asked:

'Well, where is he?'

'Who?'

'Your lover. Or superior. I really don't know yet what your relationship with him is.'

'Who are you talking about?' Lidina babbled in a panic. 'I don't under—'

'The one who set you this assignment,' Fandorin interrupted impatiently, listening very carefully. 'The staff captain, your travelling companion. It was him who ordered you to entice me here, wasn't it? But he's not in the apartment, I would sense it. Where is he?'

She threw her hands up to her chest. He knew, he knew everything! But how?

'Vasya's not my lover,' she gabbled, realising through intuition rather than reason that now was the time to tell the truth. 'He's my friend, and I really want to help him. Don't ask me where he is, I won't tell you. Erast Petrovich, dear man, I want to ask you for clemency.'

'For what?'

'For clemency! A man committed a foolish error. From your military point of view it might be considered a crime, but it's nothing more than absentmindedness! Surely absentmindedness ought not to be punished so severely!'

The man with dark hair wrinkled up his forehead and put the pistol away in his pocket.

'I don't q-quite understand . . . Who are you talking about?'

'Why about him, about him! Vasya Rybnikov! Yes, I know, he lost that drawing of yours, but now do you have to destroy a good man? Why, it's monstrous! The war will be over in a month, or maybe six, and he has to serve hard labour? Or even worse? It's not human, it's not Christian, you must agree!' And this all flooded out so sincerely and soulfully that the tears sprang to her own eyes.

Even this cold fish Fandorin was touched – he gazed at her in surprise bordering on utter amazement.

'How could you think I was trying to save my lover!' Glyceria Romanovna declared bitterly, following up quickly on her advantage. 'If I loved one man, how could I entice another? Yes, at first I intended to enchant you, in order to help Vasya, but . . . but you really have turned my head. I confess, I even forgot why I wanted to lead you on . . . You know, I felt a kind of twinge here . . .' She set her hand slightly below her bodice in order to emphasise the line of her bust, which was quite lovely enough already.

Glyceria Romanovna uttered several more phrases in the same vain in a voice muffled with passion, without worrying too much about their plausibility – everyone knew how gullible and susceptible men were to that kind of talk, especially when the prey was so close and so accessible.

'I'm not asking you for anything. And I won't ask. Let's forget about everything . . .'

She threw her head back and turned it slightly to one side. First, this was her best angle. And secondly, the position made it very convenient to kiss her.

A second passed, then another, and another.

But no kiss came.

Opening her eyes and squinting sideways, Lidina saw that Fandorin was not looking at her, but off to one side. But there was nothing of any interest there, just the telephone apparatus hanging on the wall.

'He lost a drawing? Is that what Rybnikov told you?' the investigator said thoughtfully. 'He lied to you, madam. That man is a Japanese spy. If you don't want to tell me where he is, you do not have to. I shall find out today in any case. G-goodbye.'

He swung round and walked out of the apartment.

Glyceria Romanovna's legs almost buckled under her. A spy? What monstrous suspicion! She had to warn him immediately. It turned out that the danger was even more serious than he thought! And then, Fandorin had said that he would find out today where Vasya was hiding!

She grabbed the telephone earpiece, but suddenly felt afraid that the investigator might be listening from the stairway. She opened the door – no one there, nothing but rapid footsteps on the stairs.

She went back in and telephoned.

'Saint-Saëns Boarding House,' a woman's voice cooed in the earpiece. She could hear the sounds of a piano playing a jolly polka.

'I need to talk to Vasilii Alexandrovich urgently!'

'He's not here.'

'Will he be back soon?'

'He doesn't report to us.'

What an ill-mannered maid! Lidina stamped her foot in frustration.

There was only one answer: she must go there and wait for him.

The doorman gaped at the visitor as if it was some devil with horns on his head who had arrived, not an elegantly dressed, highly respectable lady, and he blocked the entrance with his chest.

'Who do you want?' he asked suspiciously.

The same sounds of rollicking music she had heard on the telephone came out through the doorway. In a respectable boarding house, after ten o'clock in the evening?

Ah yes, today was 26 May, wasn't it, the end of the school year, Glyceria Romanovna recalled. There must be a graduation party in the boarding house, that was why there were so many carriages in the courtyard – the parents had come. It was hardly surprising that the doorman did not wish to admit an outsider.

'I'm not here for the party,' Lidina explained to him. 'I need to wait for Vasilii Alexandrovich. He will probably arrive soon.'

'He's already come back. Only this isn't the way to his rooms, you need to go in over there,' said the doorman, pointing to the small wing.

'Ah, how stupid of me! Naturally, Vasya can't live with the girl boarders!'

She ran up the steps with a rustle of silk. She rang the bell hastily and then started knocking as well.

The windows of the apartment were dark. Not a shadow stirring, not a sound.

Tired of waiting, Lidina shouted:

'Vasilii Alexandrovich! It's me! I have something urgent and terribly important to tell you!'

And the door opened immediately, that very second.

Rybnikov stood in the doorway, staring silently at his unexpected visitor.

'Why is it dark in your rooms?' she asked – in a whisper for some reason.

'I think the electrical transformer has burnt out. What's happened?'

'But you have candles, don't you?' she asked, walking in, and immediately, still on the threshold, stumbling over the words in her agitation, she started telling him the bad news: how she had met the official dealing with his case by chance, at someone's home, and this man thought Vasilii Alexandrovich was a spy.

'We have to explain to him that the drawing was stolen from you! I'll be a witness, I'll tell them about that nasty specimen on the train. You can't imagine the kind of man Fandorin is. A very serious gentleman, eyes like ice! He should be looking for that swarthy character, not you! Let me explain everything to him myself!'

Rybnikov listened to her incoherent story without speaking as he lit the candles in the candelabra one after another. In the trembling light Glyceria Romanovna thought his face seemed so tired, unhappy and haunted that she choked on her pity.

'I'll do anything for you! I won't leave you!' Lidina exclaimed, clutching impetuously at his hands.

He gave a sudden jerk and strange sparks lit up in his eyes, completely transforming his ordinary appearance. His face no longer seemed pitiful to Glyceria Romanovna – oh no! Black and red shadows ran across his face; he looked like Vrubel's *Demon* now.

'Oh God, my darling, my darling, I love you . . .' Lidina babbled, stunned by the realisation. 'How could I . . . You are the dearest thing that I have!'

She reached out to him with her arms, her face, her entire body, trembling in anticipation of his movement in response.

But the former staff captain made a sound like a snarl and shrank back.

'Leave,' he said in a hoarse voice. 'Leave immediately.'

Lidina could never remember running out into the street.

Rybnikov stood there for a while in the entrance hall, absolutely motionless, gazing at the little flames of the candles with his face set in a stiff, lifeless mask.

Then there was a quiet knock at the door.

He leapt across in a single bound and wrenched the door open.

The countess was standing on the porch.

'I'm sorry for bothering you,' she said, peering into the semi-darkness. 'It's noisy in the house tonight, so I came to ask whether our guests are bothering you. I could tell them that a string has broken in the piano and set up the gramophone in the small drawing room. That would be quieter . . .'

Sensing something strange in her lodger's behaviour, Countess Bovada stopped in mid-phrase.

'Why are you looking at me like that?'

Without speaking, Vasilii Alexandrovich took hold of her hand and pulled her towards him.

The countess was a hard-headed woman and extremely experienced, but she was bewildered by the suddenness of this.

'Come on,' said the transformed Rybnikov, jerking her in after him.

She followed him, smiling mistrustfully.

But when Vasilii Alexandrovich forced his lips against hers with a dull moan and clasped her in his strong arms, the smile on the plump, beautiful face of the Spanish grandee's widow changed first to an expression of amazement and, later, to a grimace of passion.

Half an hour later Beatrice was unrecognisable, weeping on her lover's shoulder and whispering words that she had not spoken for many years, since her early girlhood.

'If you only knew, if you only knew,' she kept repeating as she wiped away the tears, but what exactly he ought to know, she was unable to explain.

Rybnikov barely managed to bundle her out.

When he was finally left alone, he sat down on the floor in an awkward, complicated pose. He stayed like that for exactly eight minutes. Then he got up, shook himself like a dog and made a telephone call – exactly half an hour before midnight, as arranged.

And at the same time, at the far side of the boulevard ring, Lidina, who had not yet removed her evening wrap and her hat, was standing in front of the mirror in her hallway, weeping bitterly.

'It's finished . . . My life is finished,' she whispered. 'Nobody, nobody needs me . . .'

She swayed, caught her foot on something that rustled and cried out. The entire floor of the hallway was covered with a living carpet of scarlet roses. If poor Glyceria Romanovna's nose had not been blocked by her sobbing, she would have caught the intoxicating scent on the stairway.

From out of the dark depths of the apartment came entrancing sounds, creeping stealthily at first, then flowing in a burgeoning flood. The magical voice sang Count Almaviva's serenade.

'*Ecco, ridente in cielo spunta la bella aurora . . .*'

The tears gushed out of Glyceria Romanovna's lovely eyes faster than ever.

The fourth syllable,
in which the name of the Japanese God
is taken in vain

The very moment that Evstratii Pavlovich finished reading the urgent message from the senior member of the squad that had arrived from St Petersburg to replace the agents slain by the metal stars, he jumped up from his desk and dashed to the door – he even forgot about his bowler hat.

The duty carriages were standing ready at the entrance to the Okhrana building, and the drive from Gnezdnikovsky Lane to Chistoprudnaya Street was about ten minutes, if you drove like the wind.

'Heigh-ho, heigh-ho,' the court counsellor kept repeating to himself, trying to read the note once again – it was not easy: the carriage was bouncing over the cobbled street, there was not enough light from the street lamps, and Smurov had scrawled the note like a chicken scribbling with its foot. It was quite obvious that the highly experienced agent who had been charged with following Fandorin's movements was seriously agitated – the letters jumped and skipped, the lines were lopsided.

I took over the watch at 8 from sen. agent Zhuchenko, at the house of General Charme. Silver Fox emerged from the entranceway at three minutes to 9, accompanied by a little lady who has been given the code name Bimbo. They took a cab to Ostozhenka Street, the Bomze House. Silver Fox emerged at 9.37 and five minutes later Bimbo came running out. I sent two men to follow Silver Fox, Kroshkin and I followed Bimbo – I was quite impressed by how agitated she seemed. She drove to Chistoprudny Boulevard and let her carriage go at the Saint-Saëns Boarding House. She walked up on to the porch of the wing. She knocked and rang the bell, but the door was not opened for a long time. From the position I had taken up, I observed a man peep out of the window, look at her and hide. There is a bright lantern outside the building just there and I got a good look at his face. It seemed familiar to me. After a while I remembered where I had seen it: in Peter, on Nadezhdinskaya Street (code name Kalmyk). And then I realised that his description fitted the Acrobat, as described in the briefing circular. It's him, Evstratii Pavlovich, I swear it's him!

Sen. agent Smurov

The way the report was written violated the regulations, and the manner of its conclusion was entirely impermissible, but the court counsellor was not annoyed with Smurov about that.

'Well, what's he up to? Still there?' Mylnikov snapped at the senior agent as soon as he jumped down from the carriage.

Smurov was sitting in the bushes, behind the fence of the small park in the square, from where there was an excellent view of the yard of the Saint-Saëns, flooded with the bright light of coloured lanterns.

'Yes, sir. Have no doubt, Evstratii Pavlovich, I've got Kroshkin watching round the other side. If the Kalmyk had climbed out of the window, Kroshkin would have whistled.'

'All right, tell me what's happened.'

'Right, then,' said Smurov, raising his notebook to his eyes. 'Bimbo didn't stay long with Kalmyk, only five minutes. She ran out at 10.38, wiping away her tears with a handkerchief. At 10.42 a woman emerged from the main entrance, we called her Peahen. She walked up on to the porch and went inside. Peahen stayed until 11.20. She emerged sobbing and slightly unsteady on her feet. That's all there is.'

'What does this slit-eyed fiend get up to, to upset all the women like that?' asked Mylnikov, astonished. 'Well, never mind, now we'll upset him a little bit too. So, Smurov, I've brought six men along with me. I'll leave one with you. You three are on the windows. And I'll take the others and get the Jap. He's tricky all right, but we weren't exactly born yesterday either. And then, it's dark in there. He must have gone to bed. Worn out from all those women.'

They doubled over and ran across the yard. Before walking up on to the porch, they took off their boots – they didn't want any clattering now.

The court counsellor's men were hand picked. Pure gold, not men. He didn't have to explain anything to them, gestures were enough.

He snapped his fingers at Sapliukin, and Sapliukin immediately leaned down over the lock. He fiddled about a bit with his picklock, putting in a drop of oil where it was needed. In less than a minute, the door was opened soundlessly.

Mylnikov entered the dark hallway first, holding at the ready a most convenient little doodad – a rubber club with a lead core. The Jappo had to be taken alive, so Fandorin wouldn't cut up nasty afterwards.

After he clicked a little button on his secret torch, Evstratii Pavlovich picked out three white doors with the beam: one straight ahead, one on the left, one on the right.

He pointed with his finger: you go straight on, you go this way, you go that way, only shshhhh.

He stayed in the hallway with Lepinsh and Sapliukin, ready to dash through the door from behind which they heard the agreed signal: the squeaking of a mouse.

They stood there, huddled up in their tension, waiting.

A minute went by, then two, and three, and five.

Vague nocturnal rustlings came from the apartment; somewhere behind the wall a gramophone was wailing. A clock started striking midnight – so loudly and suddenly that Mylnikov's heart almost jumped out of his chest.

What were they mucking about at in there? It only took a moment, just glance in and turn your head this way and that. Had they just disappeared into thin air, or what?

The court counsellor suddenly realised that he wasn't feeling the thrill of the hunt any longer. And his passionate eagerness had evaporated without a trace – in fact, he felt repulsive, chilly shudders running down his spine. 'Those damn nerves. I'll just nab this Jappo, and then I'll go on the mineral water treatment,' Evstratii Pavlovich promised himself.

He gestured to his agents to stay put and cautiously stuck his nose inside the door on the left.

It was absolutely quiet in there. And empty, as Mylnikov soon convinced himself by shining his torch about. So there had to be a way through into the next room.

Stepping soundlessly across the parquet, he walked out into the middle of the floor.

What the devil! A table, chairs. A window. A mirror on the wall facing the window. There wasn't any other door. And agent Mandrykin wasn't there.

He tried to cross himself, but the club grasped in his hand got in the way.

Feeling the cold sweat breaking out on his forehead, Evstratii Pavlovich went back to the hallway.

'Well?' Sapliukin asked with just his lips

The court counsellor just gestured irritably at him. He glanced into the room on the right.

It was exactly like the one on the left – the furniture, the mirror and the window.

Not a soul, empty!

Mylnikov went down on his hands and knees and shone his torch under the table, although it was impossible to imagine that an agent could have decided to play hide-and-seek.

Evstratii Pavlovich tumbled back into the hallway, muttering: 'Oh, our Lord, and the Blessed Virgin.'

He pushed the agents aside and rushed through the door leading straight ahead – clutching his revolver this time, not his club.

It was the bedroom. A washbasin in the corner, with a bath, a toilet bowl and some other white porcelain contraption screwed to the floor behind a curtain.

No one! The chipped moon squinted in derisively at Mylnikov through the window.

He menaced it with his revolver and started flinging open the cupboard doors with a crash. He glanced under the bed, even under the bath.

The Japanese had disappeared. And he had taken with him three of Mylnikov's best agents.

Evstratii Pavlovich felt afraid that he might have lost his reason. He shouted hysterically:

'Sapliukin! Lepinsh!'

When the agents failed to reply, he dashed back to the hallway.

Only there was no one there any longer.

'Oh, Lord Jesus!' the court counsellor wailed beseechingly, dropping his revolver and crossing himself with broad gestures. 'Dispel the sorcery of the Japanese devil!'

When the thrice-repeated sign of the cross failed to help, Evstratii Pavlovich finally realised that the Japanese God was stronger than the Russian one and fell to his knees before His Squintyness.

He rested his forehead on the floor and crawled towards the door, howling loudly: 'Banzai, banzai, banzai.'

The final syllable,
the longest one of all

How could he have failed to recognise her straight away? Well, yes, certainly, he was tired, he was tormented by boredom, waiting impatiently for when he could leave. And, of course, she looked quite different: that first time, at dawn near the sabotaged bridge, she was pale and exhausted, in a dress that was muddy and soaking wet, and this time she glowed with a delicate, well-groomed beauty, and the veil had blurred the features of her face. But even so, some sleuth he was!

Then, when she approached him herself and mentioned the bridge, it was like being struck by lightning. Erast Petrovich had recognised her and remembered her testimony, which had led to his fatal, shameful error, and – most importantly – he had remembered her companion.

At the Moscow Freight Station, when he looked through his binoculars and saw the man who had received the melinite, Fandorin realised immediately that he had seen him somewhere before but, confused by those Japanese facial features, he had taken a wrong turning, imagining that the spy resembled one of his old acquaintances from his time in Japan. But it was all much simpler than that! He had seen this man, dressed in a staff captain's uniform, at the site of the catastrophe.

Now everything had fallen into place.

The special had been blown up by the Acrobat, as Mylnikov had so aptly christened him. The Japanese saboteur was travelling in the express train, accompanied by his female accomplice – this Lidina woman. How cunningly she had sent the gendarmes off on a false trail!

And now the enemy had decided to strike a blow at the person who was hunting him. One of the favourite tricks of the sect of stealthy ones, it was called 'The rabbit eats the tiger'. Well, not to worry, there was also a Russian saying: 'The mouse hunts the cat'.

Glyceria Romanovna's invitation to go to her apartment had not taken the engineer by surprise – he was prepared for something of the sort. But even so, he tensed up inside when he asked himself whether he could cope with such a dangerous opponent on his own.

'If I don't cope, that's my karma, let them fight on without me,' Erast Petrovich thought philosophically – and he went.

But at the house on Ostozhenka Street he behaved with extreme caution. Karma was all very well, but he had no intention of playing giveaway chess.

That only made the disappointment all the greater when he realised that the Acrobat was not in the apartment. Fandorin didn't beat about the bush after that. The dubious lady's part in everything had to be clarified there and then, without delay.

She was not an agent, he realised that straight away. If she was an accomplice, she was an unwitting one and had not been initiated into any secrets. True, she knew where to find the Acrobat, but she would never tell Fandorin, because she was head over heels in love. He couldn't subject her to torture, could he?

At this point Erast Petrovich's eye fell on the telephone apparatus, and the whole idea came to him in an instant. A spy of this calibre had to have a telephone number for emergency contacts.

After frightening Lidina as badly as he could, Fandorin ran down the stairs, out into the street, took a cab and ordered the driver to race as fast as he could to the Central Telephone Exchange.

Lisitsky had set himself up very comfortably in his new place of work. The young ladies on the switchboards had already given him lots of embroidered doilies and he had a bowl of home-made biscuits, jam and a small teapot standing on the desk. The dashing staff captain seemed to be popular here.

On seeing Fandorin, he jumped up, pulled off his earphones and exclaimed enthusiastically:

'Erast Petrovich, you are a true genius! This is the second day I've been sitting here and I never weary of repeating it! Your name should be incised in gold letters on the tablets of police history. You cannot imagine how many curious and savoury facts I have learned in these two days!'

'I c-cannot,' Fandorin interrupted him. 'Apartment three, the Bomze House, Ostozhenka Street – what's the number there?'

'Just a moment,' said Lisitsky, glancing into the directory. '37-82.'

'Check what calls have been made from 37-82 in the last quarter of an hour. Q-quickly!'

The staff captain shot out of the room like a bullet and came back three minutes later.

'A call to number 114-22. That's the Saint-Saëns Boarding House, on Chistoprudny Boulevard, I've already checked it. It was a brief conversation, only thirty seconds.'

'That means she didn't find him in . . .' Fandorin murmured. 'What boarding house is that? There wasn't one by that name in my time. Is it educational?'

'After a fashion.' Lisitsky chuckled. 'They teach the science of the tender passion. It's a well-known establishment, belongs to a certain Countess Bovada. A highly colourful individual, she figured in one of our cases. And they know her well in the Okhrana too. Her real name is Anfisa Minkina. Her life story is a genuine Boussenard novel. She has travelled right round the world. A shady character, but she is tolerated because from time to time she provides services to the relevant government departments. Of an intimate, but not necessarily sexual, nature,' the jolly staff captain said, and laughed again. 'I told them to connect me to the boarding house. There are two numbers registered there, so I've connected to both. Was I right?'

'Yes, well done. Sit here and listen. And meanwhile I'll make a call.'

Fandorin telephoned his apartment and told his valet to make his way to Chistoprudny Boulevard and observe a certain house.

Masa paused and asked:

'Master, will this be interfering in the course of the war?'

'No,' Erast Petrovich reassured him, prevaricating somewhat, but he had no other choice at the moment. Mylnikov was not there, and the railway gendarmes would not be able to provide competent surveillance. 'You will simply watch the Saint-Saëns Boarding House and tell me if you see anything interesting. The Orlando electric theatre is close by, it has a public telephone. I shall be at number . . .'

'20-93,' Lisitsky prompted him, with an earphone pressed to each ear.

'A call, on the left line!' he exclaimed a minute later.

Erast Petrovich grabbed an extension earpiece and heard a blasé man's voice:

'. . . Beatrice, my little sweetheart, I'm aflame, I just can't wait any longer. I'll come straight to your place. Get my room ready, do. And Zuleika, it must be her.'

'Zuleika is with an admirer,' a woman's voice, very gentle and pleasant, replied at the other end of the line.

The man became flustered.

'What's that you say, with an admirer? With whom? If it's Von Weilem, I'll never forgive you!'

'I'll prepare Madam Frieda for you,' the woman cooed. 'Remember her, the large lady with the wonderful figure. She's a true whiplash virtuoso, every bit as good as Zuleika. Your Excellency will like her.'

The staff captain started shaking with soundless, suppressed laughter. Fandorin dropped his earpiece in annoyance.

During the next hour there were many calls, some of an even more spicy nature, but all of them in Lisitsky's left ear – that is, on number 114-22. Nothing on the other line.

It came to life at half past eleven, with a call from the boarding house. A man requested number 42-13.

'42-13 – who's that?' the engineer asked in a whisper, while the young lady was putting through the connection.

The gendarme was already rustling the pages. He found the number and ran his thumbnail under the line of print.

Fandorin read it: 'Windrose Restaurant'.

'Windrose Restaurant,' said a voice in the earpiece. 'Can I help you?'

'My dear fellow, could you please call Mr Miroshnichenko to the telephone? He's sitting at the table by the window, on his own,' the Saint-Saëns said in a man's voice.

'Right away, sir.'

A long silence, lasting several minutes.

And then a calm baritone voice at the restaurant end asked:

'Is that you?'

'As we agreed. Are you ready?'

'Yes. We'll be there at one in the morning.'

'There's a lot of it. Almost a thousand crates,' the boarding house warned the restaurant.

Fandorin gripped his earpiece so tightly that his fingers turned white. Weapons! A shipment of Japanese weapons, it had to be!

'We have enough men,' the restaurant replied confidently.

'How will you move it? By water?'

'Naturally. Otherwise, why would I need a warehouse on the river?'

Just at that moment little lamps started blinking on the telephone apparatus on the desk in front of Lisitsky.

'That's the special line,' the officer whispered, grabbing the receiver and twirling a handle. 'For you, Erast Petrovich. I think it's your servant.'

'You listen!' Fandorin said with a nod at the earpiece, and took the receiver. 'Yes?'

'Master, you told me to tell you if anything interesting happened,' Masa said in Japanese. 'It's very interesting here, come.'

He didn't try to explain anything – evidently there were a lot of people in the electric theatre.

In the meantime the conversation between Windrose and Saint-Saëns had ended.

'Well, d-did he tell him the place?' the engineer asked, turning to Lisitsky impatiently.

The gendarme spread his hands helplessly.

'It must have been during the two seconds when you put the receiver down and I hadn't picked it up yet . . . All I heard was the one at the restaurant saying: "Yes, yes, I know". What are your instructions? Shall I send squads to the Windrose and Saint-Saëns?'

'No need. You won't find anyone at the restaurant now. And I'll deal with the guest house myself.'

As he flew along the dark boulevards in the carriage, Fandorin thought about the terrible danger hanging over the ancient city – no, over the thousand-year-old state. Black crowds, armed with rifles from Japan (or wherever), would choke the throats of the streets with the nooses of barricades. A formless, bloody stain would creep in from the outskirts to the centre and a ferocious, protracted bloodbath would begin, in which there would be no victors, only dead and defeated.

The great enemy of Erast Petrovich's life – senseless and savage Chaos – stared out at the engineer through the blank wall eyes of dark windows, grinned at him with the rotten mouths of ravenous gateways. Rational, civilised life shrank to a frail strand of lamps, glimmering defencelessly along the pavement.

Masa was waiting for him by the railings.

'I don't know what's going on,' he said quickly, leading Fandorin along the edge of the pond. 'That bad man *Myrnikov* and five of his men crept into the house, through that porch over there. That was . . . twerve minutes ago,' he said, glancing with delight at the gold watch that Erast Petrovich had given him for the Mikado's fiftieth birthday. 'I terephoned you straight away.'

'Ah, how appalling!' the engineer exclaimed miserably. 'That jackal picked up the scent and he's ruined everything again!'

His valet replied philosophically:

'There's nothing you can do about it now, anyway. Ret's watch what happens next.'

So they started watching.

There were single windows on the left and right of the door. They had no light in them.

'Strange,' whispered Erast Petrovich. 'What are they doing there in the dark? No shots, no shouts . . .'

And that very second there was a shout – not very loud, but filled with such utter animal terror that Fandorin and his servant both leapt up without a word, breaking their cover, and went running towards the house.

A man crawled out on to the porch, working his elbows and knees rapidly.

'Banzai! Banzai!' he howled over and over again.

'Let's go!' said the engineer, looking round at Masa, who had stopped. 'What's wrong with you?'

His servant stood there with his arms crossed, the mute embodiment of affronted feelings.

'You deceived me, Master. That man is Japanese.'

There was no point in trying to persuade him. And anyway, Fandorin felt ashamed.

'He is not Japanese,' said Fandorin. 'But you're right: you'd better go. If neutrality is not to be compromised.'

The engineer sighed and moved on. The valet sighed and plodded away.

Three shadows came flying out, one after another, from round the corner of the boarding house – three men in identical coats and bowler hats.

'Evstratii Pavlovich!' they clamoured, taking hold of the crawling man and setting him on his feet. 'What's wrong?'

Mylnikov howled and tried to break free of their grip.

'I am Fandorin,' said Erast Petrovich, moving closer.

The agents exchanged glances, but they didn't say anything – obviously no further introductions were required.

'He's cracked up,' one of them, a little older than the others, said with a sigh. 'Evstratii Pavlovich hasn't been himself for quite a while now, our lads have noticed. But this time he's really flipped his lid.'

'The Japanese God . . . . Banzai . . . Get thee behind me . . .' the afflicted man repeated, twitching and jerking.

So that he would not get in the way, Fandorin pressed on his artery, and the court counsellor quietened down. He hung his head, gave a snore and slumped in the grip of his deputies.

'Let him lie down for a while, nothing will happen to him. Right now, follow me!' the engineer ordered.

He walked quickly round the rooms, switching on the electric light everywhere.

The apartment was empty, lifeless. The only movement was a curtain fluttering at an open window.

Fandorin dashed over to the windowsill. Outside was the courtyard, and after that a vacant lot and the gloomy silhouettes of buildings.

'He got away! Why was no one posted under the window? That's not like Mylnikov!'

'Well, I was standing there,' one of the agents started explaining. 'Only when I heard Evstratpalich shout, I ran. I thought he needed a hand . . .'

'Where are our lads?' the older one asked, looking around in amazement.

'Mandrykin, Lepinsh, Sapliukin, Kutko and that other one, what's his name, with the big ears. Did they go after him, through the window? They should have whistled . . .'

Erast Petrovich set about examining the apartment more closely. In the room to the left of the entrance hall, he discovered a few drops of blood on the carpet. He touched it – it was fresh.

He glanced around, set off confidently towards the sideboard and pulled open the door, which was slightly ajar. There, protruding slightly from the inner space, was a small crossbow, gripped in a carpenter's vice. It had been fired.

'Well, well, familiar tricks,' the engineer murmured, and started feeling the floor at the spot where he found the blood. 'Aha, and here's the spring. He hid it under the parquet . . . But where's the body?'

He turned his head to the right and the left. Then walked towards the mirror hanging on the wall facing the window. He fingered the frame, but couldn't find a switch, and simply smashed his fist into the brilliant surface.

The agents, who were blankly following 'Silver Fox's' actions, gasped – the mirror jangled and collapsed into a black niche.

'So that's where it is,' the engineer purred in satisfaction, clicking a switch. A small door opened up in the wallpaper.

There was a tiny boxroom behind the false mirror. At the far end of it was a window that gave an excellent view of the next space, the bedroom. Half of the secret hiding place was taken up by a camera on a tripod, but that was not what interested Fandorin.

'With big ears, you say?' the engineer asked, bending down and examining something on the floor. 'Is this him?'

He dragged out a dead body, holding it under the armpits. There was a short, thick arrow protruding from its chest.

The agents clustered round their dead comrade, but the engineer was already hurrying into the opposite room.

'The same trick,' he announced to the senior agent, who had followed him in. 'A secret spring under the parquet. A crossbow concealed in the cupboard. Instantaneous death – the point is smeared with poison. And the body is over there' – he pointed to the mirror. 'You can check for yourself.'

But in this secret space, which was exactly like the previous one, there were three bodies.

'Lepinsh,' the agent said with a sigh, dragging out the top one. 'Sapliukin. And Kutko's underneath . . .'

The fifth body was found in the bedroom, in the gap behind the wardrobe.

'I don't know how he managed to deal with them on his own . . . It probably happened like this,' said Fandorin, recreating the scene. 'The ones who went into the side rooms were killed first, by the arrows, and they were spirited away – "through the l-looking glass". This one, in the bedroom, was killed with a bare hand – at least, there are no visible signs of injury. Sapliukin and this one, what's his name, Lepinsh, have had their cervical vertebrae smashed. Lepinsh's open mouth suggests that he caught a glimpse of his killer, but no more than that. The Acrobat killed these two in the hallway, dragged them into the room on the right and threw them on top of Kutko. The one thing I don't understand is how Mylnikov survived. He must have amused the Japanese with his cries of "Banzai". But that's enough idle speculation. Our most important job is still ahead of us. You,' he said, prodding one of the agents with his finger, 'collect your deranged superior and take him to the Kanatchikovo mental clinic. And you two come with me.'

'Where to, Mr Fandorin?' asked the one who was a little older.

'To the River Moscow. Damnation, half past twelve already, and we still have to look for a needle in a haystack!'

Not an easy trick, finding a warehouse on the River Moscow when you don't know which one it is. The old capital didn't have a cargo port, and the goods wharves began at the Krasnokholmsky Bridge and stretched downstream for several versts, with breaks, all the way to Kozhukhovo.

They started looking from Taganka, at the wharf of the Volga Basin Steamship Line and Trading Company. Then came the landing stage of the Kamensky Brothers Trading House, the warehouses of Madam Kashina's Nizhny Novgorod Steamship Company, the freight sheds of the Moscow River Partnership, and so on, and so forth.

They searched like this: they rode along the waterfront in a cab, gazing into the darkness and listening for any noise there might be. Who else would work at this desolate hour of the night, apart from men who had something to hide?

Occasionally they went down to the river and listened to the water – most of the moorings were on the left bank, but once in a while there were some on the right bank too.

They went back to the carriage and drove on.

Erast Petrovich became gloomier and gloomier with every minute that passed.

The search was dragging on – the Breguet in his pocket jangled twice. As though in reply, the clock on the tower of the Novospassky Monastery struck two, and the engineer's thoughts turned to matters divine.

The survival of the autocratic monarchy depends on the people's belief in its mystical, supernatural origin, Fandorin thought sombrely. If that faith is undermined, Russia will suffer the same fate as Mylnikov. The people are observing the course of this wretched war and every day they are convinced that the Japanese God is stronger than the Russian one, or that he loves his anointed one more than ours loves the Tsar Nicholas. A constitution is the only possible salvation, mused the engineer – despite his mature age, he had not yet outgrown his tendency to idealism. The monarchy must shift the fulcrum of its authority from religiosity to rationality. The people must comply with the will of the authorities because they are in agreement with that will, not out of the fear of God. But if armed revolt breaks out now, it is the end of everything. And it no longer matters whether the monarchy is able to drown the rebellion in blood or not. The genie will escape from the bottle, and the throne will come crashing down anyway – if not now, then in a few years' time, during the next convulsion . . .

Large, paunchy iron tanks glinted in the darkness – the oil storage facilities of the Nobel Company. At this point the river made a bend.

Erast Petrovich touched the driver on the shoulder to make him stop. He listened, and from somewhere on the water in the distance he could hear the clear sound of regular mechanical grunting.

'Follow me,' said the engineer, beckoning to the agents.

They jogged through a clump of trees. The breeze carried the smell of crude oil to their nostrils – the Postyloe Lake was somewhere close by, behind the trees.

'That's it!' gasped the senior agent (his name was Smurov). 'Looks like them, all right!'

Down below, at the bottom of a low slope, was the dark form of a long wharf, with several barges moored at it, and one of them, the smallest, was coupled to a steep-sided little tugboat under steam. It was its panting that Fandorin's sharp hearing had detected.

Two loaders carrying a crate ran out of a warehouse abutting the wharf and disappeared into the hold of the little barge. After them another one appeared, with something square on his shoulders, and ran down the same gangplank.

'Yes, that's them,' Fandorin said with a smile, instantly forgetting his apocalyptic visions. 'The s-sansculottes are in a hurry.'

'The who?' asked agent Kroshkin, intrigued by the unfamiliar word.

Smurov, who was better read, explained.

'They were armed militants, same as the SRs are. Haven't you ever heard of the French Revolution? No? What about Napoleon? Well, that's something at least.'

Another loader ran out of the warehouse, then three at once, lugging along something very heavy. The flame of a match flared up in the corner of the berth and a second or two later shrank to a red dot. There were two more men standing there.

The smile on the engineer's face was replaced by a thoughtful expression.

'There are quite a lot of them . . .' Erast Petrovich looked around. 'What's that dark form over there? A bridge?'

'Yes, sir. A railway bridge. For the ring road under construction.'

'Excellent! Kroshkin, over in that direction, beyond Postyloe Lake, is the Kozhukhovo Station. Take the cab and get there as quick as you can. There must be a telephone at the station. Call Lieutenant Colonel Danilov at number 77-235. If the lieutenant colonel is not there, speak to the duty officer. Describe the s-situation. Tell him to put the watch and the duty detail, everyone they can find, on hand trolleys. And send them here. That's all, run now. Only give me your revolver. And a supply of shells, if you have them. They're no good to you, but we might find a g-good use for them.'

The agent dashed off back to the carriage at full tilt.

'Right then, Smurov, let's creep a bit closer. There's an excellent stack of rails over there.'

While Thrush was lighting his pipe, Rybnikov glanced at his watch.

'A quarter to three. It will be dawn soon.'

'It's all right, we'll get it done. The bulk of it's already been loaded.' The SR nodded at a big barge. 'There's just the stuff for Sormovo left. That's nothing, only a fifth of the load. Look lively now, comrades, look lively!'

They may be your comrades, but you're not lugging any crates, Vasilii Alexandrovich thought in passing as he tried to calculate when would be best to bring up the most important subject – the timing of the uprising.

Thrush set off unhurriedly towards the warehouse. Rybnikov followed him.

'When's the Moscow load going?' he asked, meaning the big barge.

'The rivermen will move it to Fili tomorrow. Then on to somewhere else from there. We'll keep moving it from place to place, so it won't attract unwanted attention. And the small one here will go straight to Sormovo now, down the Moscow river, then the Oka.'

Almost no crates were left in the warehouse now, there were just flat boxes of wires and remote control devices.

'How do you say "*merci*" in your language?' Thrush asked with a grin.

'*Arigato.*'

'So, it's a big proletarian *arigato* to you, Mr Samurai. You've done your job, we'll manage without you now.'

Rybnikov broached the most important subject, speaking in a grave voice.

'Well, then. The strike has to start within the next three weeks. And the uprising within six weeks . . .'

'Don't give me orders, Marshal Oyama. We'll figure all that out for ourselves,' the SR interrupted. 'We're not going to dance to your tune. I think we'll hit them in the autumn.' He grinned. 'Until then you can keep plucking away at Tsar Nick's feathers and fluff. Let the people see him stripped naked. That's when we'll lamp him hard.'

Vasilii Alexandrovich smiled back at him. Thrush never even guessed that at that second his life and the lives of his eight comrades hung by a thread.

'But that's really not right. We agreed,' said Rybnikov, raising his hands reproachfully.

Sparks of mischief glinted in the revolutionary leader's eyes.

'To keep a promise made to a representative of an imperialist power is a bourgeois prejudice,' he declared, and puffed on his pipe. 'And what would "see you around" be in your language?'

A workman nearby hoisted the final box on to his back and said in surprise:

'This is far too light. Not empty, is it?'

He put it back down on the ground.

'No,' explained Vasilii Alexandrovich, opening the lid. 'It's a selection of leads and wires for various purposes. This one is a fuse, this is a camouflage lead and this one, with the rubber covering, is for underwater mines.'

Thrush was interested in that. He took out the bright-red coil and examined it. He caught the metal core between his finger and thumb – it slipped out of the waterproof covering easily.

'A smart idea. Laying mines underwater? Maybe we could knock off the royal yacht? I have this man in my team, a real desperate character . . . I'll have to think about it.'

The loader picked up the box and ran out on to the wharf.

Meanwhile Rybnikov had taken a decision.

'All right, then, autumn it is. Better late than never,' he said. 'But the strike in three weeks. We're counting on you.'

'What else can you do?' Thrush answered casually over his shoulder. 'That's all, samurai, this is the parting of the ways. Hop it back to your everloving Japanese mother.'

'I'm an orphan,' said Vasilii Alexandrovich, smiling with just his lips, and he thought once again how good it would be to break this man's neck – in order to watch his eyes bulge and turn glassy just before he died.

At that moment the silence ended.

'Mr Engineer, it looks like that's all. They've finished,' Smurov whispered.

Fandorin could see for himself that the loading had been completed. The barge had settled almost right down to the waterline. It might look small, but apparently it was capacious – it took a lot of space to accommodate a thousand crates of weapons.

There was the last man clambering up the gangway – from the way he was walking, his load was not heavy at all, and then seven, no eight, handrolled cigarettes were lit on the barge, one after another.

'They've done a bit of moonlighting. Now they'll have a smoke and sail away,' the agent breathed in his ear.

Kroshkin ran off to get help at a quarter to three, the engineer calculated. Let's assume he got to a phone at three. It would take him five minutes, maybe ten, to get Danilov or the duty officer to understand what was going on. Agh, I should have sent Smurov, he's better with words. So we'll assume they get the watch out at ten minutes, no, a quarter, past three. They won't set out before half past three. And it takes at least half an hour to get from Kalanchovka Street to the Kozhukhovo Bridge on a handcar. No point in expecting the gendarmes any earlier than four. And it's three twenty-five . . .

'Get your gun out,' Fandorin ordered, taking his Browning in his left hand and Kroshkin's Nagant in his right. 'On the count of four, fire in the direction of the barge.'

'What for?' asked Smurov, startled. 'Look how many of them there are! And how can they get off the river anyway? When help arrives, we'll overtake them on the bank!'

'How do you know they won't sail the barge out of the city, where there are no people, or transfer the weapons to carts before it gets light? No, they have to b-be arrested. How many cartridges do you have?'

'Seven in the cylinder and seven spares, that's all. We're secret policemen, not some kind of Bashibazouks . . .'

'Kroshkin had fourteen as well. I have only seven, I don't carry a spare clip. Unfortunately, I'm no janissary either. Thirty-five shots – that's not many for half an hour. But there's nothing to be done about it. This is what we do. You loose off the first cylinder without a pause, to produce an impression. But after that use the bullets sparingly, make every one count.'

'It's a bit far,' said Smurov, judging the distance. 'They're half hidden by the side of the barge. It's hard enough to hit a half-length figure from this far away, even during the day.'

'Don't aim at the men – they are your own compatriots, after all. Fire to prevent anyone getting across from the barge on to the tug. Ready, three, four!'

Erast Petrovich pointed his pistol up into the air (with its short barrel, it was almost useless at that distance, anyway) and pressed the trigger seven times.

'Well, how about that,' drawled Thrush when he heard the rapid firing.

He stuck his head out of the door cautiously. So did Rybnikov.

The flashes of shots glinted above a heap of rails dumped about fifty paces from the wharf.

The response from the barge was erratic shooting from eight barrels.

'Narks. They've tracked us down,' Thrush said coolly, summing up the situation. 'But there are only a few of them. Three or four at the most. It's a snag, but we'll soon fix it. I'll shout and tell the lads to outflank them from both sides . . .'

'Wait!' said Vasilii Alexandrovich, grabbing him by the shoulder and speaking very rapidly. 'You mustn't get drawn into a battle. That's what they want you to do. There aren't many of them, but they must have sent for support. It's not hard to intercept a barge on the river. Tell me, is there anyone on the tug?'

'No, they were all on loading.'

'The police only got here recently,' Rybnikov said confidently. 'Otherwise there'd be an entire company of gendarmes here already. That means they didn't see the loading of the main barge; we've spent almost an hour loading the one for Sormovo. Listen here, Thrush. The Sormovo load can be sacrificed. Save the big barge. Leave, and you can come back again tomorrow. Go, go. I'll lead the police away.'

He took the coil of red cable from the SR, stuffed it into his pocket and ran out into the open, zigzagging from side to side.

The black silhouettes on the barge disappeared as if by magic, along with the scarlet sparks of light. But a second later the white flashes of shots glinted above the side of the vessel.

Another figure dashed from the warehouse to the barge, weaving and dodging – the engineer watched its movement with especial interest.

At first the bullets whistled high over their heads, but then the revolutionaries found their range and the little lumps of lead ricocheted off the rails, with a nauseating whine and a scattering of sparks.

'Oh Lord, death's come for me!' gasped Smurov, ducking right down behind the stack every now and then.

Fandorin kept his eyes fixed on the barge, ready to fire as soon as anyone tried to slip across to the tug.

'Then don't be shy,' said the engineer. 'Why be afraid? All those people waiting for you and me in the next world. They'll greet you like a long-lost friend. And such people, too. Not the kind we have nowadays.'

Amazingly enough, the argument advanced by Fandorin worked.

The police agent raised his head a little.

'And Napoleon's waiting too?'

'Napoleon too. Do you like Napoleon?' the engineer murmured absent-mindedly, screwing up his left eye. One of the revolutionaries, more quick-witted than the others, had decided to clamber from the barge on to the tug.

Erast Petrovich planted a bullet in the cladding, right in front of the bright spark's nose. The man ducked back down into shelter behind the barge's side.

'Keep your eyes open and your wits about you,' Fandorin told his partner. 'Now they've realised it's time for them to leave, they'll creep across one at a time. Don't let them, fire across their path.'

Smurov didn't answer.

The engineer glanced at him quickly and swore.

The police agent was slumped with his cheek against the rails, the hair on the back of his head was soaked in blood, and one open eye was staring, mesmerised, off to the side. He was dead . . .

I wonder if he'll meet Napoleon? Fandorin thought fleetingly. Just at that moment he could not afford to indulge in sentimentality.

'Comrade helmsman, into the wheelhouse!' a voice yelled out loud and clear on the barge. 'Quickly now!'

The figure that had hidden at the bow of the barge started climbing into the tug again. Fandorin heaved a sigh and fired to kill. The body fell into the water with a splash.

Almost immediately another man tried, but he was clearly visible against the white deck housing and Erast Petrovich was able to hit him in the leg. In any case, the shot man started roaring, so he must still be alive.

The cartridges Erast Petrovich got from Kroshkin had run out. Fandorin took the dead man's revolver, but there were only three bullets in the cylinder. And there were still an entire eighteen minutes left until four o'clock.

'Boldly now, comrades!' the same voice shouted. 'They're almost out of bullets. Cut the mooring lines.'

The stern of the barge started creeping away from the wharf; the gang-planks creaked and plunged into the water.

'Forward, on to the tug! All together, comrades!'

There was no way of stopping that.

When the whole gang of men went rushing to the bow of the barge, Fandorin did not even bother to fire – what was the point?

The tug spewed a shower of sparks out of its funnel, and started flapping at the water with its paddle wheels. The cables stretched taut with a twang.

They set off at 3.46 – the engineer checked his watch.

He had managed to delay them for twenty-one minutes. At the cost of two human lives.

He set off along the bank, moving parallel to the barge.

At first keeping up was not hard, but then he had to break into a run – the tug was gradually picking up speed.

As Erast Petrovich was passing the railway bridge he heard the rumble of steel wheels from up above, on top of the embankment. A large handcar crowded with men came hurtling out of the darkness at top speed.

'This way! This way!' shouted Fandorin, waving his hand, and fired into the air.

The gendarmes came running down the incline towards him.

'Who's in c-command?'

'Lieutenant Bryantsev!'

'There they are,' said Erast Petrovich, pointing to the receding barge. 'Get half the men across the bridge to the other side. Follow on both sides. When we overtake the barge, fire at the wheelhouse of the tug. Until they surrender. At the double!'

The strange pursuit of a barge sailing down a river by gendarmes on foot did not last for long.

The return fire from the tug rapidly fell off as the revolutionaries became more and more reluctant to show themselves above the iron sides. The glass in the wheelhouse windows had been smashed by bullets and the helmsman was steering the vessel without sticking his head up, by guesswork. The result was that half a verst from the bridge the tug ran on to a shoal and stopped. The current started slowly swinging the barge round sideways.

'Cease fire,' ordered Fandorin. 'Call on them to surrender.'

'Lay down your arms, you blockheads!' the lieutenant shouted from the riverbank. 'Where can you go? Surrender!'

There really was nowhere for the SRs to go. The sparse, pre-dawn mist swirled above the water, the darkness was dissolving before their very eyes, and gendarmes were lying in ambush on both sides of the river, so they couldn't even get away one at a time, by swimming.

The survivors huddled together beside the wheelhouse – it looked as if they were conferring.

Then one of them straightened up to his full height.

It was him!

Even at that distance it was impossible not to recognise Staff Captain Rybnikov, alias the Acrobat.

The men on the tug started singing tunelessly, and the Japanese spy took a run-up and vaulted across on to the barge.

'What's he up to? What's he doing?' the lieutenant asked nervously.

'Our proud "Varangian" surrenders to no foe, for mercy no one is pleading!' they sang on the tug.

'Shoot, shoot!' Fandorin exclaimed when he saw a small flame flare up like Bengal fire in the Acrobat's hands. 'That's a stick of dynamite!'

But it was too late. The stick went flying into the hold of the barge and the false staff captain grabbed a lifebelt from the side of the tug and leapt into the river.

A second later the barge reared up, snapped in two by several powerful explosions. The front half surged up and covered the tug. Chunks of wood and metal flew into the air and blazing fuel spread across the water.

'Get down!' the lieutenant roared desperately, but even without his command the gendarmes were already dropping to the ground, covering their heads with their arms.

The bent barrel of a rifle embedded itself in the ground beside Fandorin. Bryantsev gazed in horror at a hand grenade that had thudded down beside him. It was spinning furiously, with its factory grease glittering.

'Don't worry, it won't go off,' the engineer told him. 'It's got no detonator.'

The officer got up, looking abashed.

'Is everyone all right?' he bellowed briskly. 'Line up for a roll-call. Hey, Sergeant Major!' he shouted, folding his hands to form a megaphone. 'How are your men?'

'One got caught, Yeronner!' a voice replied from the other bank.

On this side two men had been hurt by pieces of debris, but not seriously.

While the wounded were being bandaged up, the engineer went back to the bridge, where he had spotted a buoy-keeper's hut earlier.

He rode back to the site of the explosion in a boat. The buoy-keeper was rowing, with Fandorin standing in the bow, watching the chips of wood and blotches of oil that covered the entire surface of the river.

'May I join you?' Bryantsev had asked. A minute later, already in the boat, he asked, 'What are you watching for? The revolutionary gentlemen are on the bottom, that's clear enough. The divers will come and raise the bodies later. And the cargo – what they can find of it.'

'Is it deep here?' the engineer asked, turning to the oarsman.

'Round here it would be about two *sazhens*. Maybe three in some spots. In summer, when the sun gets hot, it'll be shallower, but it's deep as yet.'

The boat floated slowly downstream. Erast Petrovich gazed fixedly at the water.

'That one who threw the dynamite was a really desperate fellow. The lifebelt didn't save him. Look, it's floating over there.'

Yes, there was the red-and-white ring of cork, swaying on the waves.

'Right th-then, row over there!'

'What do you want that for?' asked the lieutenant, watching as Fandorin reached for the lifebelt.

Once again Erast Petrovich did not condescend to answer the garrulous officer. Instead he murmured:

'Aha, that's where you are, my boyo.'

He pulled the ring out of the water, exposing to view a red rubber tube attached to its inside surface.

'A familiar trick,' the engineer said with a condescending smile. 'Only in ancient times they used bamboo, not a rubber cable with the core pulled out.'

'What's that enema tube for? And what trick do you mean?'

'Bottom walking. But now I'll show you an even more interesting trick. Let's note the time.' And Fandorin pinched the tube shut.

One minute went by, then another.

The lieutenant looked at the engineer in increasing bewilderment, but the engineer kept glancing from the water to the second hand of his watch and back.

'Phenomenal,' he said with a shake of his head. 'Even for them . . .'

Halfway through the third minute a head suddenly appeared out of the water about fifteen *sazhens* from the boat.

'Row!' Fandorin shouted at the boatman. 'Now we'll take him! He didn't stay on the bottom, so we'll take him!'

And, of course, they did take him – there was nowhere for the cunning Acrobat to escape to. But then, he didn't try to resist. While the gendarmes bound his arms, he sat there with a detached expression on his face and his eyes closed, dirty water streaming out of his hair and green slime clinging to his shirt.

'You are a strong player, but you have lost,' Erast Fandorin told him in Japanese.

The prisoner opened his eyes and studied the engineer for a long time. But it still was not clear if he had understood or not.

Then Fandorin leaned down and uttered a strange word:

'*Tamba.*'

'When your number's up, it's up,' the Acrobat remarked indifferently, and that was the only thing he said.

He maintained his silence in the Krutitsk garrison jail, where he was taken from the place of arrest.

All the top brass came to conduct the interrogation – from the gendarmes, and the military courts, and the Okhrana – but neither by threats nor promises were they able to get a single word out of Rybnikov. After being thoroughly searched and dressed in a coarse prisoner's jacket and trousers, he sat there motionless. He didn't look at the generals, only occasionally glanced at Erast Petrovich Fandorin, who took no part in the interrogation and generally stood a little distance away.

After labouring in vain over the stubborn prisoner all day long until the evening, the top brass ordered him to be taken away to a cell.

The cell was a special one, for especially dangerous miscreants. For

Rybnikov they had taken additional security measures: the bed and stool had been replaced with a palliasse, the table had been taken out and the kerosene lamp removed.

'We know these Japanese, we've read about them,' the commandant told Fandorin. 'He smashes his head open against a sharp corner, and we have to answer for it. Or he'll pour burning kerosene over himself. He can just sit there with a candle instead.'

'If a man like that wishes to die, it is not possible to prevent him.'

'Ah, but it's very possible. A month ago I had an anarchist, a terrible hard case, he spent two weeks lying swaddled, like a newborn infant. He growled, and rolled around on the floor, and tried to smash his head open against the wall – he didn't want to die on the gallows. But I still delivered the fellow to the executioner in good order.'

The engineer grimaced in revulsion and remarked:

'This is no anarchist.' And he left, with a strangely heavy feeling in his heart.

The engineer was haunted and unsettled by the strange behaviour of a prisoner who had ostensibly surrendered, but at the same time clearly had no intention of providing any evidence.

Once he found himself in a cell, Vasilii Alexandrovich spent some time in an activity typical of prisoners – he stood under the small barred window, gazing at a patch of evening sky.

Rybnikov was in a good mood.

The two goals for which he had surfaced from the waters of the River Moscow, instead of remaining on its silty bottom, had both been achieved.

First, he had confirmed that the main barge, loaded with eight hundred crates, had remained undiscovered.

Secondly, he had looked into the eyes of the man he had heard so much about and had thought about for so long.

That seemed to be all.

Except . . .

He sat down on the floor, picked up the short pencil left for the prisoner in case he might wish to provide written testimony, and wrote a letter in Japanese cursive script that began with the invocation 'Father!'

Then he yawned, stretched and lay down at full length on the palliasse.

He fell asleep.

Vasilii Alexandrovich had a glorious dream. He was dashing along in an open carriage that shimmered with all the colours of the rainbow. There was pitch darkness all around him, but far away, right on the very horizon, a bright, even light was glowing. He was not riding alone in the miraculous chariot, but he could not see the faces of his companions, because his gaze was constantly directed forward, towards the source of that rapidly approaching radiance.

The prisoner slept for no more than a quarter of an hour.

He opened his eyes. He smiled, still under the influence of his magical dream.

Vasilii Alexandrovich's fatigue had evaporated completely. His entire being was filled with lucid strength and diamond-hard resolution.

He reread the letter to his father and burned it in the candle flame without a moment's hesitation.

Then he undressed to the waist.

The prisoner had a flesh-coloured plaster attached to the skin just below his left armpit. It was camouflaged so artfully that the prison warders had failed to notice it when they searched him.

Rybnikov tore the plaster off, revealing a narrow razor blade. He seated himself comfortably and, with a rapid circular movement, made a single cut all the way round the edge of his face. He caught the edge of the skin with his fingernails and pulled it all off, from the forehead to the chin, and then, without making a single sound, he slashed the blade across his own throat.

BOOK 2

BETWEEN THE LINES

Japan, 1878

A BUTTERFLY'S FLIGHT

The omurasaki butterfly gathered itself for the flight from one flower to another. It cautiously spread its small, white-flecked, azure wings and rose a mere hair's breadth into the air, but just at that moment, from out of nowhere, a violent gust of wind swooped down on the weightless creature, tossed it way up high into the sky and held it there, carrying it in a mere few minutes all the way from the hills to the plain, with its sprawling city; the wind swirled its captive round above the tiled roofs of the native quarters, drove it in zigzags over the regular geometry of the Settlement, flung it in the direction of the sea and then faded away, its impetus exhausted.

With its freedom restored, the omurasaki flew almost right down on to the green surface that looked like a meadow, but spotted the deception just in time and soared back up before the transparent spray could reach it. It fluttered around for a while above the bay, where the beautiful sailing ships and ugly steamships were standing at anchor, but failed to find anything interesting in this sight and turned back towards the pier.

There the butterfly's attention was attracted by a crowd of people waiting to meet passengers – seen from above, the brightly coloured spots of women's caps, hats and bouquets of flowers made it look like a flowery meadow. The omurasaki circled for a minute or so, choosing the most attractive-looking target, made its choice and settled on a carnation in the buttonhole of a gaunt gentleman who gazed out at the world through a pair of blue spectacles.

The carnation was a lush scarlet colour, cut only very recently, and the bespectacled gentleman's thoughts were a smooth stream of aquamarine, so the omurasaki started settling in thoroughly, folding its wings together, opening them and folding them back together again.

... I just hope he'll be a competent worker, and not some featherbrain, the owner of the carnation thought, not noticing that his buttonhole had become even more imposing than before. This dandy had a long, shimmering name: Vsevolod Vitalievich Doronin. He held the post of Consul of the Russian Empire in the port city of Yokohama, and he wore dark glasses, not out of any love of mystery (he already had more than enough of that in his job), but because of chronic conjunctivitis.

Vsevolod Vitalievich had come to the pier on business – to meet a new diplomatic colleague (name: Erast Petrovich Fandorin; title: Titular Counsellor). Doronin, however, did not entertain any real hope that the man would prove to be an efficient functionary. Reading a copy of Fandorin's service record had left him distinctly dissatisfied on all counts: this boy of twenty-two was already a ninth-grade civil servant (so he was someone's protégé), he had begun his government service in the police (phooh!), and afterwards he had been commandeered to the Third Section (what could he have done to deserve that?), and he had tumbled directly from the pinnacle of the San Stefano negotiations all the way down to a posting in a third-rate embassy (he must have come badly unstuck somewhere).

Doronin had been left without an assistant for more than seven months now, because his brilliant bosses in Petersburg had sent Vice-Consul Weber off to Hankow – supposedly temporarily, but it looked as if it would be for a very long time indeed. Vsevolod Vitalievich now handled all current business himself: he met Russian ships and saw them off, oversaw the interests of sailors discharged to shore, buried the ones who died and investigated the seamen's brawls. And all this even though he – a man of strategic intellect and a long-term resident of Japan – had certainly not been appointed to Yokohama for that kind of petty tomfoolery. The question currently being decided was where Japan and, with it, the entire Far East would come to rest – under the wing of the double-headed eagle or the sharp claws of the British lion.

In the pocket of his frock coat the consul had a rolled-up copy of the *Japan Gazette*, containing a telegram from the Reuters agency, printed in bold type: 'The tsar's ambassador Count Shuvalov has left London. War between Great Britain and Russia is now more likely than ever'. An obnoxious business. We just barely managed to get the better of the wretched Turks, how can we possibly fight the British? A matter of 'God grant our little calf will gore the wolf'. We'll raise a racket, of course, rattle the sabres a bit, but then our ardour will cool ... The sly sons of Albion wish to subjugate the entire world. Oh, we'll hand them the Far East on a plate, the way we've already handed them the Middle East, along with Persia and Afghanistan.

The omurasaki twitched its little wings in alarm, sensing the ominous purple hue flooding Vsevolod Vitalievich's thoughts, but just at that moment the consul raised himself up on tiptoe and fixed his gaze on a passenger in a brilliant-white tropical suit and blinding pith helmet. Fandorin or not Fandorin? Come on, white swan, fly lower, let's take a look at you.

From considerations of state the consul's thoughts turned back to everyday concerns, and the butterfly immediately settled down.

How much time and ink had been wasted on something so absolutely obvious, thought Vsevolod Vitalievich. Surely it was quite clear that without an assistant he could not possibly engage in any strategic work – he had no time for it. The nerve centre of Far Eastern politics was not located in Tokyo, where His Excellency, Mr Ambassador, was stationed, but here. Yokohama was the most important port in the Far East. This was the place where all the cunning British manoeuvres were concocted, the control centre for all that underhand plotting. Why, it was as clear as day, but how long they had dragged things out!

Well, all right, better late than never. This Fandorin here, initially appointed as second secretary at the embassy, had now been transferred to the Yokohama consulate, in order to release Vsevolod Vitalievich from routine work. Mr Ambassador had probably taken this veritably Solomonic decision himself, after checking the titular counsellor's service record. He had not wished to keep such a recondite individual about his own person. So there you are, dearest Vsevolod Vitalievich, take what is of no use to us.

The snow-white colonialist stepped on to the quayside and no more doubt remained. Definitely Fandorin, every point of the description fitted. Dark hair, blue eyes and the most significant distinguishing feature – prematurely grey temples. But oh, he was dolled up as if he were going on an elephant hunt!

The initial impression was not reassuring. The consul sighed and moved forward to meet him. The omurasaki butterfly flitted its wings in response to this upheaval, but remained on the flower, still unnoticed by Doronin.

Oh, deary me, look at his finger – a diamond ring, Vsevolod Vitalievich noted as he bowed in greeting to the new arrival. And a moustache curled into little loops, if you please! Not a single hair out of place on those temples! And that languorous, blasé expression in the eyes! Griboedov's Chatsky, to an absolute T. Pushkin's Onegin: 'And, like everything in the world, travelling palled on him'.

Immediately after they had introduced themselves, he asked, with an ingenuous air:

'Do tell me at once, Erast Petrovich, did you see Fuji? Did she hide from your eyes or reveal herself to you?' And then he explained confidentially: 'It's a kind of omen I have. If a person has seen Mount Fuji as he approaches the shore, it means that Japan will open her soul to him. But if capricious Fuji has shut herself off behind the clouds – then, alas. Though you may live here for ten years, you will neither see, nor understand, the most important things of all.'

Actually, Doronin knew perfectly well that Fuji could not possibly have been visible from the sea today, owing to the low clouds, but he needed to take this Childe Harold from the Third Section down a peg.

However, the titular counsellor was neither flustered, nor upset.

He merely remarked, with a slight stammer:

'I don't b-believe in omens.'

Well naturally. A materialist. All right, let's give him a nip from the other side.

'I am acquainted with your service record,' said Vsevolod Vitalievich, raising his eyebrows admiringly. 'What a career you have made, you have even been decorated! Abandon a brilliant stage like that for our modest backwater? There can only be one reason for it: you must have a great love for Japan! Am I right?'

'No,' the latter-day Onegin said with a shrug, squinting at the flower in the consul's buttonhole. 'How can one love what one does not know?'

'Why, most certainly one can!' Doronin assured him. 'And with far greater ease than objects that are only too familiar to us ... Hmm, is that your luggage?'

This von-baron had so many things that almost a dozen porters were required to carry them: suitcases, boxes, bundles of books, a huge three-wheeled velocipede and even a *sazhen*-long clock made in the image of London's Big Ben.

'A beautiful item. And useful. I confess, I prefer a pocket watch myself,' said the consul, unable to resist a sardonic comment, but he promptly took himself in hand, put on a radiantly polite smile and extended one arm in the direction of the shoreline. 'Welcome to Yokohama. A splendid city, you will like it!'

This final phrase was uttered entirely without irony. In three years Doronin had developed a genuine affection for this city that grew larger and lovelier by the day.

Just twenty years ago there had been a tiny fishing village here, but now, thanks to the meeting of two civilisations, a truly magnificent modern port had sprung up, with a population of fifty thousand, of whom almost one fifth were foreigners. A little piece of Europe at the very end of the world. Vsevolod Vitalievich was especially fond of the Bund – a seaside esplanade with beautiful stone buildings, gas street lamps and an elegant public.

But Onegin, having cast an eye over this magnificent sight, pulled a sour face, which only served to confirm Doronin's decision not to like his new work fellow. He passed his verdict: a pompous, preening peacock and supercilious snob. 'And I'm a fine fellow too, putting on a carnation for his sake,' thought the consul, gesturing irritably for Fandorin to follow him. He pulled the flower out of his buttonhole and flung it away.

The butterfly soared into the air, fluttered its wings above the heads of the Russian diplomats and, mesmerised by the whiteness of it, settled on Fandorin's helmet.

Why did I have to dress up in this clown's outfit? the owner of the miraculous headgear thought in purple anguish. The moment he stepped on the gangway and surveyed the public on the quayside, Erast Petrovich had made a highly unpleasant discovery for anyone who attaches importance to correct dress. When one is dressed correctly, people around you look you straight in the face; they do not gape open-mouthed at your attire. It is the portrait that should attract attention, not the frame. But exactly the opposite was happening here. The outfit purchased in Calcutta, which had appeared perfectly appropriate in India, looked absurd in Yokohama. From the appearance of the crowd, it was clear that in this city people did not dress in the colonial fashion, but in a perfectly normal manner, European-style. Fandorin pretended not to notice the inquisitive glances (which he thought seemed derisive) and strove with all his might to maintain an air of equanimity. There was only one thought in his mind – that he must change as soon as possible.

Even Doronin seemed staggered by Erast Petrovich's gaffe – Fandorin could sense it from the consul's barbed glance, which not even the dark glasses could conceal.

Observing Doronin more closely, Erast Petrovich followed his customary habit and employed deductive analysis to construct a cognitive image. Age – forty-seven or forty-eight. Married, with no children. Disposition – intelligent, choleric, inclined to caustic irony. An excellent professional. What else? He had bad habits. The circles under his eyes and a sallow complexion indicated an unhealthy liver.

But the young functionary's first impression of Yokohama was not at all favourable. He had been hoping to see a picture from a lacquered casket: multi-tiered pagodas, little teahouses, junks with webbed-membrane sails skimming across the water – but this was an ordinary European seafront. Not Japan, more like Yalta. Was it really worth travelling halfway round the globe for this?

The first thing Fandorin did was to get rid of the idiotic helmet – in the simplest way possible. First he took it off as if he was suddenly feeling hot. And then, as they walked up the stairway to the esplanade, he surreptitiously set the colonialist contrivance down on a step and left it there – if anybody wanted it, they were welcome.

The omurasaki did not wish to be parted from the titular counsellor. Forsaking the helmet, it fluttered its wings just above the young man's broad shoulder, but did not actually alight – it had spotted a more interesting landing place: a colourful tattoo, glistening with little drops of sweat, on a rickshaw man's shoulder: a dragon in blue, red and green.

The butterfly's legs brushed against the taut bicep and the fleet-winged traveller caught the local man's guileless, brownish-bronze thought ('*Kayui!*'),* after which its brief life came to an end. Without even looking, the rickshaw man slapped his open hand against his shoulder, and all that was left of the exquisite creature was a little blob of greyish blue.

> Careless of beauty
> And ever fearless of death:
> A butterfly's flight.

---

* 'That tickles!' (Japanese).

THE OLD *KURUMA*

'Mr Titular Counsellor, I was expecting you on the SS *Volga* a week ago, on the first of May,' said the consul, halting beside a red-lacquered gig that had clearly seen better days. 'For what reason were you pleased to be delayed?'

The question, despite being posed in a strict tone of voice, was essentially simple and natural, but for some reason it embarrassed Erast Petrovich.

The young man coughed and his face fell.

'I'm sorry. When I was changing ships, I c-caught a cold . . .'

'In Calcutta? In a temperature of more than a hundred degrees?'

'That is, I mean, I overslept . . . In general, I missed the boat and was obliged to wait for the next steamer.'

Fandorin suddenly blushed, turning almost the same colour as the gig.

Tut-tut-tut! thought Doronin, gazing at Fandorin in delighted amazement and shifting his spectacles to the end of his nose. So much for Onegin! We don't know how to lie. How splendid.

Vsevolod Vitalievich's bilious features softened and sparks glinted in those lacklustre eyes with the reddish veins.

'So it's not a clerical error in the service record, we really are only twenty-two, it's just that we make ourselves out to be a romantic hero,' the consul purred, by which he only embarrassed the other man even more. Cutting loose entirely, he winked and said:

'I bet it was some young Indian beauty. Am I right?'

Fandorin frowned and snapped: 'No,' but he did not add another word, and so it remained unclear whether there was no young beauty at all, or there was, but she was not Indian.

The consul did not pursue the immodest interrogation. Not a trace was left of his earlier hostility. He took the young man by the elbow and pulled him towards the gig.

'Get in, get in. This is the most common form of transport in Japan. It is called a *kuruma*.'

Erast Petrovich was surprised to see that there was no horse harnessed to the carriage. For a moment a quite fantastic image was conjured up in his mind: a magic carriage, dashing along the street on its own, its shafts held out ahead of it like crimson antennae.

The *kuruma* accepted the young man with obvious pleasure, rocking him on its threadbare but soft seat. But it greeted Doronin inhospitably, jabbing a broken spring into his scraggy buttock. The consul squirmed, arranging himself more comfortably, and muttered:

'This chariot has a vile soul.'

'What?'

'In Japan every creature, and even every object, has its own soul. At least, so the Japanese believe. The scholarly term for it is "animism" . . . Aha, and here are our little horses.'

Three locals, whose entire wardrobe consisted of tight-fitting drawers and twisted towels coiled tightly round their heads, grasped the bridle in unison, shouted 'hey-hey-tya!' and set off with their wooden sandals clattering along the road.

'See the troika dashing along snowy Mother Volga,' Vsevolod Vitalievich sang in a pleasant light tenor, and laughed.

But Fandorin half-rose off the seat, holding on to the side of the gig, and exclaimed:

'Mr Consul! How can one use human beings like animals! It's . . . it's barbaric!'

He lost his balance and fell back on to the cushion.

'Accustom yourself to it,' Doronin said, laughing, 'otherwise you'll have to move around on foot. There are hardly any cab drivers at all here. And these fine fellows are called *dzinrikisya*, or "rikshas", as the Europeans pronounce it.'

'But why not use horses to pull carriages?'

'There are not many horses in Japan, and they are expensive, but there are a lot of people, and they are cheap. A riksha is a new profession – ten years or so ago, no one had ever heard of it. Wheeled transport is regarded as a European novelty here. One of these poor fellows here runs about sixty versts a day. But then, by local standards, the pay is very good. If he is lucky, he can earn half a yen, which is a rouble in our money. Although rikshas don't live long – they overstrain themselves. Three or four years, and they go to pay their respects to the Buddha.'

'But that is monstrous!' Fandorin exploded, swearing to himself that he would never use this shameful form of transport again. 'To set such a low price on one's own life!'

'You will have to get used to that too. In Japan life is worth no more than a kopeck – whether it's someone else's or your own. And why should the heathens settle for half-measures? After all, there is no Last Judgement in store for them, merely a long cycle of reincarnations. Today – that is, in this life – you drag the carriage along, but if you drag it honestly, then tomorrow someone else will be pulling *you* along in the *kuruma*.'

The consul laughed, but somehow ambiguously; the young functionary thought he heard a note of something like envy in that laugh, rather than ridicule of the local beliefs.

'Please observe that the city of Yokohama consists of three parts,' Doronin explained, pointing with his stick. 'Over that way, where the roofs are clumped close together, is the Native Town. Here, in the middle, is the actual Settlement: banks, shops, institutions. And on the left, beyond the river, is the Bluff. That's something like a little piece of Good Old England. Everyone who is even slightly better off makes his home there, well away from the port. Generally speaking, it's possible to live a quite civilised life here, in the European fashion. There are a few clubs: rowing, cricket, tennis, horse riding, even gastronomic. I think they will be glad to welcome you there.'

As he said that, he glanced back. Their red 'troika' was being followed by an entire caravan of vehicles carrying Fandorin's luggage, all drawn by the same kind of yellow-skinned horsemen, some by a pair, some by just one. Bringing up the rear of the cavalcade was a cart loaded with athletic equipment: there were cast-iron weights, and a boxer's punchball, and gleaming on top of it all was the polished steel of the aforementioned velocipede – the patented American 'Royal Crescent Tricycle'.

'All foreigners except the embassy employees try to live here, not in the capital,' the long-time Yokohama resident boasted. 'Especially since it's only an hour's journey to the centre of Tokyo by railway.'

'There is a railway here too?' Erast Petrovich asked dismally, feeling his final hopes for oriental exoticism evaporating.

'And a most excellent one!' Doronin exclaimed with enthusiasm. 'This is how the modern Yokohamian lives nowadays: he orders tickets for the theatre by telegraph, gets into the train, and a hour and a quarter later he is already watching a kabuki performance!'

'I'm glad that it is at least kabuki, and not operetta . . .' the newly minted vice-consul remarked, surveying the seafront glumly. 'But listen, where are all the Japanese women in kimonos, with fans and umbrellas? I can't see a single one.'

'With fans?' Vsevolod Vitalievich chuckled. 'They're all in the teahouses.'

'Are those like the local cafés? Where they drink Japanese tea?'

'One can take a drink of tea, of course. Additionally. But people visit those places to satisfy a different need.' Doronin manipulated his fingers in a cynical gesture that might have been expected from a spotty grammar-school boy, but certainly not from the Consul of the Russian Empire – Erast Petrovich even blinked in surprise. 'Would you like to pay a visit? Personally, I abstain from tea parties of that kind, but I can recommend the best of the establishments – it is called "Number Nine". The sailor gentlemen are highly satisfied with it.'

'N-no,' Fandorin declared. 'I am opposed on principle to venal love, and I consider brothels an affront to both the female and the male sexes.'

Vsevolod Vitalievich smiled as he squinted sideways at his companion, who had blushed for the second time, but he refrained from any comment.

Erast Petrovich rapidly changed the subject.

'And the samurai with two swords? Where are they? I have read so much about them!'

'We are riding through the territory of the Settlement. The only Japanese who are allowed to live here are shop workers and servants. But you will not see samurai with two swords anywhere now. Since the year before last the carrying of cold steel has been forbidden by imperial decree.'

'What a shame!'

'Oh yes,' said Doronin with a grin. 'You've really lost a lot there. It was a quite unforgettable sensation – squinting timidly at every son of a bitch with two swords stuck in his belt. Wondering if he'd just walk past, or swing round and take a wild slash at you. I'm still in the habit, when I walk through the Japanese quarters, of glancing behind me all the time. You know, I came to Japan at a time when it was considered patriotic to kill *gaijins*.'

'Who is that?'

'You and I. *Gaijin* means "foreigner". They also call us *akahige* – "red-haired", *ketojin*, meaning "hairy", and *saru*, namely "monkeys". And if you go for a stroll in the Native Town, the little children will tease you by doing this . . .' The consul removed his spectacles and pulled his eyelids apart with his fingers. 'That means "round-eyed", and it is considered very offensive. But never mind, at least they don't just carve you open for no reason at all. Thanks to the Mikado for disarming his cut-throats.'

'But I read that a samurai's sword is an object of reverent obeisance, l-like a European nobleman's sword,' said Erast Petrovich, sighing – disappointments were raining down one after another. 'Did the Japanese knights really abandon their ancient tradition as easily as that?'

'There was nothing at all easy about it. They were in revolt all last year, it went as far as a civil war, but Mr Okubo is not a man to be trifled with. He wiped out the most turbulent and the rest changed their tune.'

'Okubo is the minister of internal affairs,' Fandorin said with a nod, demonstrating a certain knowledge of local politics. 'The French newspapers call him the First Consul, the Japanese Bonaparte.'

'There is a similarity. Ten years ago there was a *coup d'état* in Japan . . .'

'I know. The restoration of the Meiji, the re-establishment of the power of the emperor,' the titular counsellor put in hastily, not wishing his superior to think him a total ignoramus. 'The samurai of the southern principalities overthrew the power of the shoguns and declared the Mikado the ruler. I read about it.'

'The southern principalities – Satsuma and Choshu – are like Corsica in France. And Corsican corporals were even found – three of them: Okubo, Saigo and Kido. They presented His Imperial Majesty with the respect and adoration of his subjects, and quite properly reserved the power for themselves. But triumvirates are an unstable sort of arrangement, especially when they contain three Bonapartes. Kido died a year ago, Saido quarrelled with the government and raised a rebellion, but he was routed and, in accordance with Japanese tradition, committed hara-kiri. Which left Minister Okubo as the only cock in the local henhouse . . . You're quite right to note this down,' the consul remarked approvingly, seeing Fandorin scribbling away with a pencil in a leather-covered notebook. 'The sooner you fathom all the subtle points of our local politics, the better. By the way, you'll have a chance to take a look at the great Okubo this very day. At four o'clock there will be a ceremonial opening of a House for the Re-education of Fallen Women. It is an entirely new idea for Japan. It had never occurred to anyone here before to re-educate the courtesans. And the funds for this sacred undertaking have not been provided by some missionary club, but a Japanese philanthropist, a certain Don Tsurumaki. The crème de la crème of the Yokohama beau monde will be there. And the Corsican himself is expected. He is hardly likely to show up for the formal ceremony, but he will almost certainly come to the Bachelors' Ball in the evening. It is an entirely unofficial function and has nothing to do with the re-education of loose women – quite the opposite in fact. You will not find it boring. "He returned and went, like Chatsky, from the ship straight to the ball".'

Doronin winked again as he had done recently, but the titular counsellor did not feel attracted to these bachelor delights.

'I will take a look at Mr Okubo some other time ... I'm rather exhausted after the journey and would prefer to rest. So if you will permit ...'

'I will not permit,' the consul interrupted with affected severity. 'The ball is de rigueur. Regard it as your first official assignment. You will see many influential people there. And our maritime agent Bukhartsev will be there, the second man in the embassy. Or, perhaps, even the first,' Vsevolod Vitalievich added with a suggestive air. 'You will meet him, and tomorrow I shall take you to introduce yourself to His Excellency ... Ah, but here is the consulate. *Tomare!** he shouted to the rickshas. 'Remember the address, my good fellow, Number Six, the Bund Esplanade.'

Erast Petrovich saw a stone building with a yard flanked by two wings running towards the street.

'My apartment is in the left wing, yours is in the right wing, and the office is there, in the middle,' said Doronin, pointing beyond the railings – the formal wing at the back of the courtyard was topped off by a Russian flag. 'Where we serve is where we live.'

As the diplomats got down on to the pavement, the *kuruma* gently rocked Erast Petrovich lovingly in farewell, but peevishly snagged the consul's trousers with the end of a spring.

Whinging and cursing
Vicious potholes in the road:
My old *kuruma*.

---

* 'Stop!' (Japanese)

A HERO'S EYES

In the reception area a very serious young Japanese man, wearing a tie and steel-rimmed spectacles, rose to his feet to greet the new arrivals. Standing on the desk among the files and heaps of papers were two little flags – Russian and Japanese.

'Allow me to introduce you,' said Doronin. 'Shirota. He has been working with me for more than seven years now. Translator, secretary and invaluable assistant. My guardian angel and clerk, so to speak. I trust you will get on well together.'

Taking the name 'Shirota' for the Russian word meaning 'orphan', Fandorin was rather surprised that the consul thought it necessary to inform him of his colleague's unfortunate family situation at the moment of introduction. No doubt the sad event must have taken place only recently, although there was no sign of mourning in the clerk's manner of dress, with the possible exception of his black satin oversleeves. Erast Petrovich bowed in sympathy, expecting a continuation, but Doronin did not say anything.

'Vsevolod Vitalievich, you have forgotten to tell me his name,' the titular counsellor reminded his superior in a low voice.

'Shirota is his name. When I had just arrived here, I felt terribly homesick for Russia. All the Japanese looked the same to me and their names sounded like gibberish. I was stuck here all on my lonesome, there wasn't even a consulate then. Not a single Russian sound or Russian face. So I tried to surround myself with locals whose names sounded at least a little bit more familiar. My valet was Mikita, just like the Russian name. That's written with three hieroglyphs, and means "Field with three trees". Shirota was my translator, the name means "White field" in Japanese. And I also have the extremely charming – as in the Russian word *obayanie* – Obayasi-san, to whom I shall introduce you later.'

'So the Japanese language is not so very alien to the Russian ear?' Erast Petrovich asked hopefully. 'I should very much like to learn it as soon as possible.'

'It is both alien and difficult,' said Vsevolod Vitalievich, dashing his hopes. 'The discoverer of Japan, St Franciscus Xaverius, said: "This speech was invented by a concourse of devils in order to torment the devotees of the faith". And such coincidences can sometimes play mean tricks. For instance, my surname, which in Russian is perfectly euphonious, causes me no end of bother in Japan.'

'Why?'

'Because "*doro*" means "dirt" and "*nin*" means "man". "Dirty man" – what sort of name is that for the consul of a great power?'

'And what is the meaning of "Russia" in Japanese?' asked the titular counsellor, alarmed for the reputation of his homeland.

'Nothing good. It is written with two hieroglyphs: *Ro-koku*, "Stupid country". Our embassy has been waging a complicated diplomatic struggle for years now, to have a different hieroglyph for "*ro*" used in the documents, one that signifies "dew". So far, unfortunately, with no success.'

The clerk Shirota took no part in the linguistic discussion, but simply stood there with a polite smile on his face.

'Is everything ready for the vice-consul to be accommodated?' Doronin asked him.

'Yes, sir. The official apartment has been prepared. Tomorrow morning the candidates for the position of valet will come. They all have very good references, I have checked them. Where would you like to take your meals, Mr Fandorin? If you prefer to dine in your rooms, I will find a cook for you.'

The Japanese spoke Russian correctly, with almost no accent, except that he occasionally confused 'r' and 'l' in some words.

'That is really all the same to me. I follow a very simple d-diet, so there is no need for a cook,' the titular counsellor explained. 'Putting on the samovar and going to the shop for provisions are tasks that a servant can deal with.'

'Very well, sir,' Shirota said with a bow. 'And are we anticipating the arrival of a Mrs Vice-Consul?'

The question was formulated rather affectedly, and Erast Petrovich did not instantly grasp its meaning.

'No, no. I am not married.'

The clerk nodded, as if he had been prepared for this answer.

'In that case, I can offer you two candidates to choose from in order to fill the position of a wife. One for three hundred yen a month, fifteen years old, never previously married, knows one hundred English words. The second is older, twenty-one, and has been married twice. She has excellent references from the previous husbands, knows a thousand English words and is less expensive – two hundred and fifty yen. Here are the photographs.'

Erast Petrovich blinked his long eyelashes and looked at the consul in consternation.

'Vsevolod Vitalievich, there's something I don't quite . . .'

'Shirota is offering you a choice of concubines,' Doronin explained, examining the photos with the air of a connoisseur. They showed doll-like young ladies with tall, complicated hairstyles. 'A wife by contract.'

The titular counsellor wrinkled up his brow, but still did not understand.

'Everyone does it. It is most convenient for officials, seamen and traders who are far from home. Not many bring their family here. Almost all the officers of our Pacific fleet have Japanese concubines, here or in Nagasaki.

The contract is concluded for a year or two years, with the option to extend it. For a small sum of money you obtain domestic comfort, care and attention and the pleasures of the flesh into the bargain. If I understand correctly, you are no lover of brothels? Hmm, these are fine girls. Shirota is a good judge in this matter,' said Doronin, and tapped his finger on one of the photos. 'My advice to you is: take this one, who is slightly older. She has already been married to foreigners twice, you won't have to re-educate her. Before me, my Obayasi lived with a French sea captain and an American speculator in silver. And on the subject of silver . . .' Vsevolod Vitalievich turned to Shirota. 'I asked for the vice-consul's salary for the first month and relocation allowance for settling in to be made ready – six hundred Mexican dollars in all.'

The clerk inclined his head respectfully and started opening the safe.

'Why Mexican?' Fandorin asked as he signed the account book.

'The most tradable currency in the Far East. Not too convenient, certainly,' the consul remarked, watching Shirota drag a jangling sack out of the safe. 'Don't rupture yourself. There must be about a *pood* of silver here.'

But Erast Petrovich lifted the load with no effort, using just his finger and thumb – evidently he made good use of those cast-iron weights that he carried about in his luggage. He was about to put the bag on a chair, but he became distracted and started studying the portraits hanging above Shirota's desk.

There were two of them. Gazing out at Fandorin on the left was Alexander Sergeevich Pushkin, and on the right was a plump-cheeked Oriental with his thick eyebrows knitted in a menacing lour. The titular counsellor was already very familiar with the engraving from the portrait by Kiprensky, and it held no great interest for him, but he was intrigued by the second portrait. It was a garishly coloured wood-block print that could not have been expensive, but it had been done so expertly that the irascible fat man seemed to be glaring straight into the vice-consul's eyes. A fat neck with naturalistic folds of flesh could be seen under the open, gold-embroidered collar, and the forehead of the Japanese was tightly bound in a white bandana with a scarlet circle at its centre.

'Is he some kind of poet?' Fandorin enquired.

'Not at all. That is the great hero Field Marshal Saigo Takamori,' Shirota replied reverently.

'The one who rebelled against the government and committed suicide?' Erast Petrovich asked in surprise. 'Surely he is regarded as a traitor to the state?'

'He is. But he is still a great hero. Field Marshal Saigo was a sincere man. And he died a beautiful death.' A wistful note appeared in the clerk's voice. 'He ensconced himself on a mountain with samurai from his native Satsuma. The government soldiers surrounded him on all sides and started shouting: "Surrender, Your Excellency! We will deliver you to the capital with honour!" But the field marshal did not capitulate. He fought until he was hit in the stomach by a bullet, and then told his adjutant: "Chop my head from my shoulders".'

Fandorin gazed at the heroic field marshal without speaking. How expressive those eyes were! The rendition of the portrait was truly masterful.

'But why do you have Pushkin here?'

'A great Russian poet,' Shirota explained, then thought for a moment and added, 'Also a sincere man. He died a beautiful death.'

'There is nothing the Japanese like better than someone who died a beautiful death,' Vsevolod Vitalievich said with a smile. 'But it's too soon for us to die, gentlemen, there is a slew of work to be done. What's our most urgent business?'

'The corvette *Horseman* has ordered a hundred *poods* of salt beef and a hundred and fifty *poods* of rice,' said Shirota, taking several sheets of paper out of a file as he started his report. 'The first mate of the *Cossack* has requested a repair dock to be arranged in Yokosuka as soon as possible.'

'These are matters that fall within the competence of the brokers,' the consul explained to Fandorin. 'The brokers are local traders who act as intermediaries and answer to me for the quality of deliveries and work performed. Carry on, Shirota.'

'A note from the municipal police, asking if they should release the assistant engineer from the *Boyan*.'

'Reply telling them to keep him until tomorrow. And first let him pay for the broken shop window. What else?'

'A letter from the spinster Blagolepova,' said the clerk, holding out an opened envelope to the consul. 'She informs us that her father has died and asks us to issue a death certificate. She also petitions for the payment of a gratuity.'

Doronin frowned and took the letter.

'"Passed away suddenly" ... "completely alone now" ... "do not leave me without support" ... "at least something for the funeral" ... Hmm, yes. There you are, Erast Petrovich. The routine but nonetheless sad side of a consul's work. We care not only for the living, but also the dead subjects of the Russian Empire.'

He glanced at Fandorin with an expression that combined enquiry with guilt.

'I realise perfectly well that this is infamous on my part ... You have barely even arrived yet. But you know, it would be a great help to me if you could visit this Blagolepova. I still have to write a speech for the ceremony today, and it is dangerous to put off the inconsolable spinster until tomorrow. She could turn up here at any moment and give us a performance of the lamentations of Andromache ... Would you go, eh? Shirota will show you the way. He can draw up everything that's required and take any necessary action, you'll only have to sign the death certificate.'

Fandorin, who was still contemplating the portrait of the hero who had been beheaded, was about to say: 'Why, certainly', but just at that moment the young man thought he saw the field marshal's black-ink eyes glint as if they were alive – and not aimlessly, but to convey some kind of warning. Astonished, Erast Petrovich took a step forward and even leaned towards the picture. The miraculous effect instantly disappeared, leaving nothing but mere painted paper.

'Why, certainly,' said the titular counsellor, turning towards his superior. 'This very moment. Only, with your permission, I shall change my outfit. It is entirely unsuitable for such a doleful mission. But who is this young lady?'

'The daughter of Captain Blagolepov, who would appear to have departed this life.' Vsevolod Vitalievich crossed himself, but rather perfunctorily, without any particular air of devoutness. 'May heaven open its gates to him, as they say, although the recently deceased's chances of gaining entry there are none too great. He was a pitiful individual, totally degenerate.'

'He took to drinking?'

'Worse. He took to smoking.' Seeing his assistant's bewilderment, the consul explained. 'An opium addict. A rather common infirmity in the East. In actual fact, there is nothing so very terrible about smoking opium, any more than there is about drinking wine – it's a matter of knowing where to draw the line. I myself like to smoke a pipe or two sometimes. I'll teach you – if I see that you are a level-headed individual, unlike Blagolepov. But you know, I can remember him as a quite different man. He came here five years ago, on a contract with the Postal Steamship Company. Served as captain on a large packet boat, going backwards and forwards between here and Osaka. He bought a good house and sent for his wife and daughter from Vladivostok. Only his wife died soon afterwards, and in his grief, the captain took to the noxious weed. Little by little the habit consumed everything: his savings, his job, his house. He moved to the Native Town, and for foreigners that is regarded as the ultimate downfall. The captain's daughter was really worn out, she was almost starving.'

'If he lost his position, why do you still call him "captain"?'

'By force of habit. Recently Blagolepov had been sailing a little steam launch, taking people on cruises round the bay. He didn't sail any farther than Tokyo. He was his own captain, and able seaman, and stoker. One in three persons. At first the launch was his property, then he sold it. He worked for a salary, and for the tips. The Japanese were happy to hire him, it was a double curiosity for them: to go sailing in a miraculous boat with a chimney, and to have a *gaijin* dancing attendance on them. Blagolepov squandered everything he earned in the opium den. He was a hopeless case, and now he's given up the ghost . . .'

Vsevolod Vitalievich took a few coins out of the safe.

'Five dollars for her for the funeral, as prescribed by the regulations.' He sighed a little and took another two silver discs out of his pocket. 'And give her these, without a receipt. A ship's chaplain will read the burial service, I'll arrange for that. And tell Blagolepova that she should go back to Russia as soon as she's buried him, this is no place for her. God forbid she could end up in a brothel. We'll give her a third-class ticket to Vladivostok. Well, go on, then. My congratulations on starting your new job at the consulate.'

Before he left the room, Erast Petrovich could not resist glancing round at the portrait of Field Marshal Saigo once again. And once again he thought he glimpsed some kind of message in the hero's gaze – either a warning or a threat.

> Three ancient secrets:
> Rising sun and dying moon,
> And a hero's eyes.

THE BLUE DIE DOES NOT
LIKE BADGER

Semushi scratched his hump with a rustling sound and raise his hand to indicate that bets were no longer being taken. The players – there were seven of them – swayed back on their heels, all of them trying to appear impassive.

Three for 'evens' and four for 'odds', Tanuki noticed, and although he had not staked anything himself, he clenched his fists in agitation.

Semushi's fleshy hand covered the little black cup, the dice clacked against its bamboo walls (that magical sound!) and the two little cubes, red and blue, came flying out on to the table.

The red one halted almost immediately with the 4 upwards, but the blue one clattered on to the very edge of the rice-straw mats.

'Evens!' thought Tanuki, and the next moment the dice stopped with the 2 upwards. Just as he thought! But if he'd placed a bet, the detestable little cube would have landed on 1 or 3. It had taken a dislike to Tanuki – that had been proved time and time again.

Three players received their winnings and four reached into their pockets to get out new coins. Not a single word, not a single exclamation. The rules of the ancient noble game prescribed absolute silence.

The hunchbacked host gestured to the waitress to pour sake for the players. The girl squatted down beside each one of them and filled their beakers. She squinted quickly at Semushi, saw that he was not looking, and quickly crawled across on her knees to Tanuki and poured some for him, although she was not supposed to.

Naturally, he did not thank her, and even deliberately turned his back. You had to be strict with women, unapproachable, that roused their spirit. If only the rolling dice could be managed that easily!

At the age of eighteen, Tanuki already knew that not many women could refuse him. That is, of course, you had to be able to sense whether a woman could be yours or not. Tanuki could sense this very clearly, it was a gift he had. If there was no chance, he didn't even look at a woman. Why waste the time? But if – from a glance or the very slightest movement, or a smell – he could tell that there was a chance, Tanuki acted confidently and without any unnecessary fuss. The main thing was that he knew he was a good-looking man, he was handsome and knew how to inspire love.

Then what could he want, one might wonder, with this skinny servant girl? After all, he wasn't hanging about here for his own amusement, he was on an important job. A matter of life and death, you might say, but still he hadn't been able to refrain. The moment he saw the girl, he realised straight away that she was *his kind*, and without even pausing to think, he had applied all his skill in the way he acted with her: he put on a haughty face with a sultry expression in his eyes. When she came closer, he turned away; when she was at a distance, he kept his eyes fixed on her. Women notice that straight away. She had already tried to talk to him several times, but Tanuki maintained his mysterious silence. On no account must he open his own mouth too early.

It wasn't so much that he was amused by the game with the servant girl – it was more that it helped to relieve the boredom of waiting. And then again, free sake was no bad thing either.

He had been hanging about in Semushi's dive since yesterday morning. He had already blown almost all the money he had been given by Gonza, even though he only placed a bet every one and a half hours at the most. The accursed blue die had gobbled up all his coins, and now he only had two left: a small gold one and a large silver one, with a dragon.

Since yesterday morning he had neither eaten nor slept, only drunk sake. His belly ached. But his *hara* could endure it. Far worse was the fact that his head had started to spin – either from the cold or the sweetish smoke that came drifting from the corner where the opium smokers were lying and sitting: three Chinese, a red-haired sailor with his eyes closed and his mouth blissfully open, two rikshas.

Foreigners – *akuma* take them, let them all croak, but he felt sorry for the rikshas. They were both former samurai, that was obvious straight away. Their kind found it hardest of all to adapt to a new life. These were changed times, the samurai weren't paid pensions any more – let them work, like everyone else. Only what if you didn't know how to do anything except wave a sword about? But they'd even taken away the poor devils' swords . . .

Tanuki guessed again – this time it would be 'odds', and it was! Two and 5!

But the moment he put up the silver yen, the dice betrayed him again. As usual, the red one settled first, on a 5. How he implored the blue one: give me odds, give me odds! And of course, it rolled over into a 3. His last coin but one had gone for nothing.

Snuffling in his fury, Tanuki put down his beaker, so that the servant could splash some sake into it, but this time the mischievous girl poured some for everyone except him – she was probably offended because he wasn't looking at her.

It was stuffy in the room, the players were sitting there naked to the waist, wafting themselves with fans. If only he had a snake tattoo on his shoulder. Maybe not with three rings, like Obake's, and not five, like Gonza's – just one would do. Then the rotten girl would look at him differently. But never mind, if he carried out his assignment diligently, Gonza had promised him not only a fiery-red snake on his right shoulder, but even a chrysanthemum on each knee!

The very reason that Tanuki had been entrusted with this important mission was that he did not have a single decoration on his skin. He had not had any chance to earn them. But the hunchback would not have let in anyone with tattoos. That was why Fudo and Gundari had been put on the door, to prevent any Yakuza from other clans getting in. Fudo and Gundari told customers to roll up their sleeves and inspected their backs and chests. If they saw decorated skin, they threw the man out straight away.

Semushi was cautious, it was not easy to reach him. His 'Rakuen' gambling den had a double door: they let you in one at a time, then the first door was locked with some cunning kind of mechanism; on guard behind the inner door were Fudo and Gundari, two guards named in honour of the redoubtable buddhas who guarded the Gates of Heaven. The heavenly buddhas were truly terrible – with goggling eyes and tongues of flame instead of hair, but this pair were even worse. They were Okinawans, skilled in the art of killing with their bare hands.

There were another four guards in the hall as well, but there was no point in even thinking about them. Tanuki's assignment was clear, he just had to let his own people in, and after that they would manage without him.

Bold Gonza had been given his nickname in honour of Gonza the Spear-Bearer from the famous puppet play – he was a really great fighter with a bamboo stick. Dankichi certainly deserved his nickname of Kusari, or 'Chain', too. He could knock the neck off a glass bottle with his chain, and the bottle wouldn't even wobble. Then there was Obake the Phantom, a master of the *nunchaku*, and Ryu the Dragon, a former *sumotori* who weighed fifty *kamme** – he didn't need any weapon at all.

Tanuki didn't have anything with him either. First, they wouldn't have let him in with a weapon. And secondly, he could do a lot with his hands and feet. He only looked inoffensive – short and round like a little badger (hence his nickname).[†] And anyway, since the age of eight, he had practised the glorious art of jujitsu, to which, in time, he had added the Okinawan skill of fighting with the feet and legs. He could beat anyone – except, of course, for Ryu; not even a *gaijin*'s steam *kuruma* could shift him from the spot.

The plan thought up by the cunning Gonza had seemed quite simple at first.

Walk into the gambling den as if he wanted to play a bit. Wait until Fudo or Gundari, it didn't matter which, left his post to answer a call of nature or for some other reason. Then go flying at the one who was still at the door, catch him with a good blow, open the bolt, give the prearranged shout and avoid getting killed in the few seconds before Gonza and the others came bursting in.

It was a rare thing for a novice to be given a first assignment that was so complicated and so responsible. In the normal way of things, Badger should have remained a novice for at least another three or four years, he was much

---

* A measure of weight equal to 3.75 kilograms
† In Japanese, '*tanuki*' means badger

too young for a fully fledged warrior. But the way things were nowadays, sticking to the old customs had become impossible. Fortune had turned her face away from the Chobei-gumi, the oldest and most glorious of all the Japanese gangs.

Who had not heard of the founder of the gang, the great Chobei, leader of the bandits of Edo, who defended the citizens against the depredations of the samurai? The life and death of the noble Yakuza were described in kabuki plays and depicted in Ukio-e engravings. The perfidious samurai Mizuno lured the hero, unarmed and alone, into his house by deception. But the Yakuza made short work of the entire band of his enemies with his bare hands, leaving only the base Mizuno alive. And he told him: 'If I escaped alive from your trap, people would think that Chobei was too afraid for his own life. Kill me, here is my chest'. And with a hand trembling in fear Mizuno impaled Chobei on his spear. How could you possibly imagine a more exalted death?

Tanuki's grandfather and his father had belonged to the Chobei-gumi. Since his early childhood, he had dreamed of growing up, joining the gang and making a great and respected career in it. First he would be a novice, then a warrior, then he would be promoted to the *wakashu*, the junior commanders, then to the *wakagashira*, the senior commanders, and at the age of about forty, if he survived, he would become the *oyabun* himself, a lord with the power of life and death over fifty valiant men, and they would start writing plays about his great feats for the kabuki theatre and the Bunraku puppet theatre.

But over the last year the clan had almost been wiped out. The enmity between two branches of the Yakuza lasts for centuries. The *Tekiya*, to which the Chobei-gumi belonged, were patrons of petty trade: they protected the street vendors and peddlers against the authorities, for which they received the gratitude prescribed by tradition. But the *Bakuto* made their living from games of chance. Those treacherous bloodsuckers never stayed anywhere for long, they flitted from place to place, leaving ruined families, tears and blood in their wake.

How well the Chobei-gumi had established themselves in the new city of Yokohama, which was positively seething with trade. But the predatory *Bakuto* had turned up, bent on seizing another clan's territory. And how crafty they turned out to be! The hunchbacked owner of the 'Rakuen' didn't act openly, with the two clans meeting in an honest fight and slashing away with their swords until victory is won. Semushi had proved to be a master at setting underhand traps. He informed against the *oyabun* to the authorities, then challenged the warriors to a battle, and there was a police ambush waiting there. The survivors had been picked off one by one, with ingenious patience. In a few short months the gang had lost nine-tenths of it membership. It was said that the hunchback had patrons in high places, that the top command of the police was actually in his pay – an entirely unprecedented disgrace!

And that was how it happened that at the age of eighteen, long before the normal time, Tanuki had moved up from the novices to become a fully fledged member of the Chobei-gumi. True, at the present time there were only five warriors left in the clan: the new *oyabun* Gonza, Dankichi with his chain, Obake with his *nunchaku*, the man-mountain Ryu and himself, Tanuki.

That wasn't enough to keep watch over all the street trade in the city. But it was enough to get even with the hunchback.

So here was Badger, exhausted by the fatigue and the strain of it all, waiting for the second day for the moment to arrive when there would be only one guard left on the door. He couldn't deal with two, he knew that very well. And he could only deal with one if he ran at him from behind.

Fudo and Gundari had gone away – to sleep, to eat, to rest – but the one who left was always immediately replaced by one of the men on duty in the gambling hall. Tanuki had sat there for an hour, ten hours, twenty, thirty – but all in vain.

Yesterday evening he had gone out for a short while and walked round the corner to where the others were hiding in an old shed. He had explained the reason for the delay.

Gonza told him: Go and wait. Sooner or later one man will be left on the door. And he gave Tanuki ten yen – to lose.

In the morning Tanuki had gone out again. His comrades were already tired, of course, but their determination to avenge themselves had not weakened. Gonza gave him another five coins and said: That's all there is.

Now it was getting on for evening again, the entrance to the 'Rakuen' was still guarded as vigilantly as ever, and on top of everything else, Badger had only one final yen left.

Surely he wouldn't have to leave without completing his assignment? Such disgrace! It would be better to die! To throw himself at both terrifying monsters and take his chances!

Semushi scratched his sweaty chest that was like a round-bellied barrel and jabbed a finger in Tanuki's direction.

'Hey, kid, have you moved in here to stay? You just keep on sitting there, but you don't play much. Either play or get lost. Have you got any money?'

Badger nodded and took out his gold coin.

'Then stake it!'

Tanuki gulped and put his yen down on the left of the line, where money was staked on 'odds'. He changed his mind and moved it to 'evens'. Then he changed his mind again and wanted to move it back, but it was too late. Semushi had raised his hand.

The dice rattled in the little cup. The red one landed on 2. The blue one rolled round in a semicircle on the straw mats and landed on 3.

Tanuki bit his lip to stop himself howling in despair. His life was ending, destroyed by a vicious little six-sided cube. Ending in vain, pointlessly.

Of course, he would try to overpower the guards. Drift quietly towards the door, hanging his head low. He would strike the long-armed Fudo first. If he could hit the *minch* point on the chin and put his jaw out of joint, Fudo would lose all interest in fighting. But then he wouldn't take Gundari by surprise, and that meant that Tanuki's life would simply be thrown away. He wouldn't be able to able to open the door, or let Gonza in . . .

Badger looked enviously at the smokers. They just carried on sleeping, and nothing mattered a damn to them. If he could just lie there like that, gazing up at the ceiling with a senseless smile, with a thread of saliva dangling out of his mouth and his fingers lazily kneading the fragrant little white ball . . .

He sighed and got to his feet decisively.

Suddenly Gundari opened the little window cut into the door. He glanced out and asked: 'Who is it?'

Three people came into the room one after another. The first was a Japanese with a foreign haircut and clothes. He grimaced fastidiously while the guards searched him and didn't look around. Then a white woman came in, or maybe a girl – you could never tell how old they were, twenty or forty. Terribly ugly: huge big arms and legs, hair a repulsive yellow colour and a nose like a raven's beak. Tanuki had already seen her here yesterday.

Gundari searched the yellow-haired woman, while Fudo searched the third of the newcomers, an astoundingly tall, elderly *gaijin*. He looked round the den curiously: he looked at the players, the smokers, the low counter with the beakers and jugs. If not for his height, the *gaijin* would have looked like a human being: normal hair – black with venerable grey at the temples.

But when the longshanks came closer, Tanuki saw that he was a monster too. The *gaijin*'s eyes were an unnatural colour, the same colour as the abominable die that had ruined unfortunate Badger.

You do not toss it,
You are the one who is tossed
By the die of chance.

THE BLUE DIE LOVES THE *GAIJIN*

Things were not good at the house of Captain Blagolepov. And it was not even a matter of the departed lying on the table in his old patched tunic with the copper five-kopeck pieces over his eye-sockets (had he brought them with him from Russia, especially for this occasion?). Everything in this decrepit dwelling was permeated with the smell of poverty and chronic, mildewed misery.

Erast Petrovich looked round the dark room with a pained air: tattered straw mats on the floor, the only furniture the aforementioned unvarnished table, two rickety chairs, a crooked cupboard and a set of shelves with just one book or, perhaps, an album of some kind. Under the icon in the corner a slim little candle was burning, the kind that were sold in Russia at five for half a kopeck. The most distressing elements were the pitiful attempts to lend this kennel at least some semblance of home comfort: the embroidered doily on the bookcase, the wretched curtains, the lampshade of thick yellow card.

The spinster Sophia Diogenovna Blagolepova was well matched to her dwelling. She spoke in a quiet little voice, almost a whisper, sniffing with her red nose; she was swathed in a faded, colourless shawl and seemed to be on the point of breaking into protracted floods of tears.

In order to avoid provoking this outpouring of grief, Fandorin comported himself sadly but sternly, as became a vice-consul in the performance of his official responsibilities. The titular counsellor felt terribly sorry for the spinster, but he was afraid of women's tears and disliked them. Owing to inexperience, his condolences did not turn out very well.

'P-please allow me for my part, that is, on behalf of the state of Russia, which I represent here ... That is, of course, not I, but the c-consul ...' Erast Petrovich babbled unintelligibly, stammering more than usual in his agitation.

When Sophia Diogenovna heard the state mentioned, she gaped at him in fright with her faded blue eyes and bit the edge of her handkerchief. Fandorin lost the thread of his thought and fell silent.

Fortunately Shirota helped him out. It seemed that this kind of mission was nothing new to the clerk.

'Vsevolod Vitalievich Doronin has asked us to convey to you his profound condolences,' the clerk said with a ceremonial bow. 'Mr Vice-Consul will sign the necessary documents and also present you with a financial subsidy.'

Recollecting himself, Fandorin handed the spinster the five coins from the state and the two from Doronin, to which, blushing slightly, he added another handful of his own.

This was the correct manoeuvre. Sophia Diogenovna ceased her sobbing, gathered the Mexican silver together in her palm, counted it quickly and also gave a low bow, displaying the plait arranged in a loop on the back of her head.

'Thank you for not leaving a poor orphan without support.'

Her thick hair was a beautiful golden-wheat colour. Blagolepova could probably have been rather good-looking, if not for her chalky complexion and the expression of stupid fright in her eyes.

Shirota was making signs to the functionary: he had pinched his finger and thumb together and was running them through the air. Ah, he meant the receipt.

Erast Petrovich shrugged, as if to say: It's too awkward, later. But the Japanese himself presented the lady with the paper, and she signed with a pencil in a curly flourish.

Shirota sat down at the table, took out a sheet of paper and a travelling inkwell and prepared to write out the death certificate.

'What were the cause and the circumstances of the demise?' he asked briskly.

Sophia Diogenovna's face instantly melted into a tearful grimace.

'Papa came home in the morning at about seven o'clock. He said, I feel bad, Sophia. I've got this aching in my chest . . .'

'In the morning?' Fandorin asked. 'Was he working at night, then?'

He was sorry he had asked. The tears poured down in torrents from Blagolepova's eyes.

'No-o,' she howled. 'He'd been in the "Rakuen" all night long. It's a place like a tavern. Only in our taverns they drink vodka, and in theirs they smoke a noxious weed. I went there at midnight and implored him: "Father, let's go home. You'll spend everything on smoking again, and our apartment isn't paid for, and the oil for the lamp has run out . . . " He wouldn't come, he drove me away. He almost beat me . . . And when he dragged himself home in the morning, there was nothing in his pockets, they were empty . . . I gave him tea. He drank a glass. Then he suddenly looked at me and said: "That's that. Sophia, I'm dying. Forgive me, my daughter". And he put his head on the table. I started shaking him, but he was dead. He was staring sideways, with his mouth open . . .'

At that point the sad narrative broke off, drowned in sobbing.

'The circumstances are clear,' Shirota declared solemnly. 'Shall we write: "Sudden death from natural causes"?'

Fandorin nodded and shifted his gaze from the sobbing spinster to the deceased. What a strange fate! To die at the end of the world from the heady Chinese poison . . .

The clerk scraped his pen over the paper, Sophia Diogenovna cried, the vice-consul gazed morosely at the ceiling. The ceiling was unusual, faced with planks. So were the walls. As if they were inside a crate. Or a barrel.

For lack of anything else to do, Erast Petrovich walked over and touched the rough surface with his hand.

'Papa put that up with his own hands,' Blagolepova said in an adenoidal voice. 'So it would be like in a mess room. When he was a cabin boy, the ships were still all wood. One day he looked at the wall and suddenly waved his hand and shouted out: "A name is a mortal's fate, and there's no getting away from it! The name you're given decides the way you live your whole life. Haven't I flapped about all over the place? I ran away to sea from the seminary, I've sailed the seven seas, but even so I'm ending my life as Diogenes – in a barrel".'

And, moved by her reminiscences, she started gushing even more profusely. The titular counsellor, wincing in sympathy, handed Sophia Diogenovna his handkerchief – her own needed to be wrung out.

'Thank you, kind man,' she sobbed, blowing her nose into the fine cambric. 'And I should be even more grateful, grateful for ever, if you could only liberate my property.'

'What property?'

'The Japanese man Papa sold the launch to didn't pay him all the money. He didn't give him it all at once, he said: "You'll smoke yourself to death". He paid it out in parts, and he still owed seventy-five yen. That's a lot of money! There was no paper contract between them, that's not the Japanese custom, so I'm afraid that the hunchback won't give me it, he'll deceive a poor orphan.'

'Why hunchb-back?'

'Why, he has a hump. He's got one at the front and another one at the back. A genuine monster and a bandit. I'm afraid of him. Couldn't you go with me, Mr Vice-Consul, since you're a diplomat from our great homeland, eh? I'd pray to God for you with all my strength!'

'The consulate does not engage in the collection of debts,' Shirota said quickly. 'It is not appropriate.'

'I could go in a private capacity,' the soft-hearted vice-consul suggested. 'Where can I find this man?'

'It's not far, just across the river,' said the spinster, immediately stopping her crying and gazing hopefully at Fandorin. '"Rakuen", it's called, that means "Heavenly Garden" in their language. Papa worked for the boss there. He's called Semushi, it means Hunchback. Papa gave everything he earned at sea to that bloodsucker, for the drug.'

Shirota frowned.

'The "Rakuen"? I know it. An absolutely infamous establishment. The *Bakuto* (they are very bad men) play dice there, and they sell Chinese opium. It is shameful, of course,' he added in an apologetic tone of voice, 'but Japan is not to blame. Yokohama is an open port, it has its own customs. However, a diplomat cannot appear in the "Rakuen" under any circumstances. There could be an Incident.'

The final word was pronounced with special emphasis and the clerk even raised one finger. Erast Petrovich did not wish to be involved in an Incident, especially not on his first day of work as a diplomat, but how could he abandon a defenceless young woman in distress? And then again, it would be interesting to take a look at an opium den.

'The regulations of the consular service enjoin us to render assistance to our compatriots who find themselves in extremity,' Fandorin said sternly.

The clerk did not dare to argue with the regulations. He sighed and resigned himself to the inevitable.

They set out for the den on foot. Erast Petrovich had refused in principle to take a riksha from the consulate, and he did not yield now.

The young man found everything in the native quarter curious: the hovels nailed together haphazardly out of planks, and the paper lanterns on poles, and the unfamiliar smells. The Japanese people seemed exceptionally ugly to the young functionary. Short and puny, with coarse faces, they walked in a fussy manner with their heads pulled down into their shoulders. The women were especially disappointing. Instead of the wonderful, bright-coloured kimonos that Fandorin had seen in pictures, the Japanese women were dressed in washed-out, formless rags. They walked in tiny little steps on their monstrously bandy legs, and their teeth were absolutely black! Erast Petrovich made this appalling discovery when he saw two busybodies gossiping on a corner. They bowed to each other every second and smiled broadly, looking like two black-toothed witches.

But even so, the titular counsellor liked it much better here than on the decorous Bund. This was it, the real Japan! It might be plain and dowdy, but even this place had its merits, thought Erast Petrovich, drawing his first conclusions. Despite the poverty, it was clean everywhere. That was one. The simple people were extremely polite and he could not sense any air of abjection about them. That was two. Fandorin could not think of a third argument in favour of Japan quite yet, and he postponed any further conclusions until later.

'The shameful quarter starts at the other side of the Ivy Bridge,' said Shirota, pointing to a arched wooden bridge. 'Teahouses, beer parlours for the sailors. And the "Rakuen" is there too. There, you see it? Over there by the pole with a head on it.'

As he stepped on to the bridge, Erast Petrovich looked in the direction indicated and froze. A woman's head with an intricate hairstyle was hanging on a tall pole. The young man wanted to turn away immediately, but he held his glance still for a moment, and after that he could not turn away. The dead face was frighteningly, magically lovely.

'That is a woman by the name of O-Kiku,' the clerk explained. 'She was the finest courtesan in the "Chrysanthemum" establishment – the one over there, with the red lantern at the entrance. O-Kiku fell in love with one of her clients, a kabuki actor. But he grew cold towards her, and then she poisoned him with rat poison. She poisoned herself too, but she vomited, and the poison did not take effect. They washed out her stomach and then cut off her head. Before the execution, she composed a beautiful haiku, a verse of three lines . . .'

Shirota closed his eyes, concentrated and declaimed in a singsong voice:

'A tempest at night,
But dawn brings complete silence –
A flower's dream ends.'

And he explained:

'The flower is herself because "kiku" means "chrysanthemum". The hurricane is her passion, the silence is her forthcoming execution, and the dream is human life . . . The judge ordered her head to be kept outside the door of the tearoom for a week – as a lesson to the other courtesans and to punish the proprietress. Not many clients will favour a shop sign like that.'

Fandorin was impressed by the story he had been told, and by Japanese justice, and most of all by the wonderful poem. But Sophia Diogenovna remained unmoved. She crossed herself at the sight of the severed head without any excessive fright – in all the years she had lived in Japan, she must have become accustomed to the peculiarities of the Japanese system of justice. Blagolepova was far more interested in the 'Rakuen' – the young lady gazed at the stout oak door with eyes wide in terror.

'There is nothing for you to be afraid of, madam,' Erast Petrovich reassured her, and was about to enter, but Shirota slipped ahead of him.

'No, no,' he declared with a most decisive air. 'This is my responsibility.'

He knocked and stepped into a small dark passage that reminded Fandorin of the antechamber of a bathhouse. The door immediately slammed shut, evidently impelled by a concealed spring.

'That's a procedure they have here. They let people in one at a time,' Blagolepova explained.

The door opened again, as if of its own accord, and Fandorin let the lady go ahead.

Sophia Diogenovna babbled 'Merci' and disappeared into the antechamber.

Finally, it was the titular counsellor's turn.

For five seconds he stood in total darkness, then another door opened in front of him, admitting a smell of sweat and tobacco and another unfamiliar, sweetish aroma. 'Opium', Erast Petrovich guessed, sniffing the air.

A short, thickset, strong-looking fellow (predatory facial features, wearing a bandana with squiggles on it round his forehead) started slapping the functionary on the sides and feeling under his armpits. A second fellow, who looked exactly the same, brusquely searched Sophia Diogenovna at the same time.

Fandorin flushed, prepared to put an end to this intolerable impudence there and then, but Blagolepova said rapidly:

'It's all right, I'm used to it. They have to do this, they get far too many wild characters coming here.' And she added something in Japanese, in a tone that sounded soothing.

Shirota had already been let through – he was standing a little to one side, with a perfectly clear air of disapproval.

But the vice-consul found it all very interesting.

At first glance the Japanese den of iniquity reminded him very strongly of a Khitrovka tavern of the very worst kind. Only in Khitrovka it was very much dirtier and the floor was covered with gobs of spittle, but here, before stepping on to the straw mats covering the floor, he had to take off his shoes.

Sophia Diogenovna became terribly embarrassed, and Fandorin could not immediately understand why. Then he noticed that the poor spinster had no stockings, and he delicately averted his eyes.

'Now, which man here is the one who owes you money?' he asked brightly, gazing around.

His eyes quickly accustomed themselves to the dim lighting. There were motionless figures lying and sitting on straw mattresses in the far corner. No, one of them moved: a gaunt Chinese with a long plait blew on the wick of an outlandish-looking lamp that was standing beside him; he used a needle to turn a little white ball that was heating over the flame, then stuffed the ball into the opening of a long pipe and took a long draw. He shook his head for a few moments, then flopped back on to a bolster and took another draw.

In the middle of the room about half a dozen or so gamblers were sitting at a table with tiny little legs. Several other men were not playing, but watching – all exactly the same as in some Daredevil Inn or Half-Bottle Tavern.

Fandorin identified the owner without any prompting. The half-naked man with an unnaturally bloated upper body shook some kind of small cup, then tossed two little cubes on to the table. That was clear enough – they were playing dice. But it was astonishing that the result of the game didn't arouse any emotions at all in the men sitting round the table. In Russia the winners would have burst into a string of joyful obscenities and the loser would have sworn obscenely too, but viciously. However, these men silently sorted out the money, most of which went to the hunchback, and then started sipping some kind of murky liquid from little cups.

Taking advantage of the break, Sophia Diogenovna walked up to the owner, bowed obsequiously and started asking him about something. The hunchback listened sullenly and drawled: 'Heh-eh-eh' once, as if he was surprised at something. (Erast Petrovich guessed that this was his reaction to the news of the captain's death.) He heard the woman out, shook his head sharply and muttered: '*Nani-o itterunda!*' – and then several brief, rumbling phrases.

Blagolepova started crying quietly.

'What? Does he refuse?' Fandorin asked, touching the lady's sleeve.

She nodded.

'This man says he has paid the captain in full. The captain has spent the entire launch from the funnel to the anchor on opium,' Shirota translated.

'He's lying!' Sophia Diogenovna exclaimed. 'Papa couldn't have smoked enough for all the money! He told me himself that there were still seventy-five yen left!'

The owner gestured with one hand and spoke to Fandorin in appalling English:

'Want play? Want puh-puh? No want play, no want puh-puh – go-go.'

Shirota whispered, looking round anxiously at the well-muscled young fellows with the white bandanas on their foreheads, who were slowly approaching the table from different sides of the room:

'There's nothing we can do. There's no receipt – we can't prove anything. We must leave, or else there could be an Incident.'

Sophia Diogenovna was weeping quietly, inconsolably. Fandorin's cambric handkerchief was already soaked through, and she took out her own, which had dried off slightly.

'What kind of game is this?' Erast Petrovich asked curiously. 'Is it d-difficult?'

'No, it is absolutely simple. It is called "Choka-hanka" – that is, "Odds and evens". If you place money to the left of that line there, it means you are betting on evens. If you place it on the right, you are betting on odds.' The clerk spoke in nervous haste, all the while tugging the vice-consul towards the door with his finger and thumb. 'Do let us go. This is absolutely not a good place.'

'Well then, I'll try it too. I believe at the current rate the yen is worth two roubles?'

Erast Petrovich squatted down awkwardly, took out his wallet and counted out fifteen red ten-rouble notes. That made exactly seventy-five yen. The embassy functionary put his stake to the left of the line.

The owner of the den was not at all surprised by the sight of banknotes with a portrait of the bearded Mikhail Fyodorovich Romanov; Russians had evidently been rather frequent visitors to the 'Rakuen'. But the hunchback was surprised by the size of the stake, for none of the other players had put more than five yen on the table.

Everything went very quiet. The idle onlookers moved closer, with the guards in white bandanas who had given poor Shirota such a bad fright towering over them. A stocky, round-faced Japanese with a little waxed ponytail on the shaven back of his head had been about to move towards the door, but his attention was caught too. He changed his mind about leaving and froze on the spot.

The little cup swayed in the hunchback's strong hand and the dice rattled against its thin walls – a sweep of the arm, and the two little dice went tumbling across the low table. The red one rolled over a few times and stopped, showing five dots on its upper surface. The blue one skipped as far as the very edge and stopped right in front of Erast Petrovich, displaying three dots.

A sigh ran round the table.

'Did I win?' Erast Petrovich asked Shirota.

'Yes!' the clerk said in a whisper. His eyes were blazing in elation.

'Well then, tell him that he owes me seventy-five yen. He can give the money to Miss Blagolepova.'

Erast Petrovich started getting up, but the owner grabbed his arm.

'No! Must play three! Rule!'

'He says that under the rules of the establishment, you have to play at least three times,' said Shirota, pale-faced, although Fandorin had already understood the meaning of what was said.

The clerk apparently tried to argue, but the owner, who had just tipped a heap of yen on to the table, started shifting them back towards him. It was clear that he would not let the money go without repeating the game.

'Leave it,' Erast Petrovich said with a shrug. 'If he wants to play, we'll play. It will be worse for him.'

Once again the dice rattled in the little cup. Now everyone on the room had gathered round the table, apart from the apathetic smokers and the two guards at the door, but even they stood up on tiptoe, trying to get at least a glimpse of something over the bowed backs.

The only person who was bored was the titular counsellor. He knew that by a mysterious whim of fate he always won in any game of chance, even in games of which he did not know the rules. So why should he be concerned about a stupid game of 'Odds and evens'? In his place another man would have become a millionaire ages ago, or else gone insane, like Pushkin's Herman in *The Queen of Spades*, who was unable to endure the mystical whimsicality of Fortune. But Fandorin had made it a rule always to trust in miracles and not attempt to squeeze them into the pigeonholes of human logic. If miracles happened, then Thank You, Lord – looking a gift horse in the mouth was bad form.

Erast Petrovich barely even glanced at the table when the dice were cast for the second time. Once again the blue die was slower to settle than the red one.

The spectators shed their reserve and the air rang with exclamations.

'They are saying: "The blue die has fallen in love with the *gaijin*!"' Shirota, red-faced now, shouted in the titular counsellor's ear and started raking the heap of white and yellow coins towards him.

'Madam, there is your father's money,' said Fandorin, setting aside the heap of money lost by the owner in the previous game.

'*Damare!*' the hunchback roared at the spectators.

He looked terrifying. His eyes were bloodshot, his Adam's apple was trembling, his humped chest was heaving.

The servant girl dragged a jangling sack across the floor. The owner untied the laces with trembling hands and began quickly setting out little columns on the table, each column containing ten coins.

He's going to try to win it all back, Erast Petrovich realised, and suppressed a yawn.

One of the bruisers guarding the door finally succumbed and set off towards the table, which was almost completely covered with little silver columns that gleamed dully.

This time the hunchback shook the little cup for at least a minute before he could bring himself to throw. Everyone watched his hands, mesmerised. Only Fandorin, firmly convinced of the immutability of his gambler's luck, was gazing around curiously.

And that was why he saw the chubby-faced Japanese edging slyly towards the door. Why was he being so furtive? Had he not settled his bill? Or had he filched something?

The dice struck against the wood and everyone leaned down over the table, shouldering each other aside, but Fandorin was observing the young moon-faced youth.

His behaviour was quite astonishing. Once he had backed away as far as the guard, who was totally absorbed in the game, even though he had remained at the door, Moon-face struck the guard on the neck with his open hand in a fantastically rapid movement. The big brute collapsed on to the floor without a sound and the sneak thief (if he was a thief) was away and gone: he slid the bolt open soundlessly and slipped outside.

Erast Petrovich merely shook his head, impressed by such adroitness, and turned back to the table. What had he staked his money on? Evens, wasn't it?

The little red cube had stopped on 2, the blue one was still rolling. A second later a dozen throats let out a roar so loud that the titular counsellor was deafened.

Shirota hammered his superior on the back, shouting something inarticulate. Sophia Diogenovna gazed at Fandorin through eyes radiant with happiness.

The blue die was lying there, displaying six large black dots.

> Oh why does it love
> Only the indifferent,
> The fleet tumbling die?

THE FLAG OF A GREAT POWER

Pushing his way through the others, Shirota started scooping the silver back into the sack. The room was filled with a melancholy jingling sound, but the music did not continue for long.

A loud, furious bellow issued simultaneously from several throats and a rabble of most daunting-looking natives came bursting into the room.

The first to run in was a moustachioed, hook-nosed fellow with his teeth bared in a ferocious grin and a long bamboo pole in his hands. Another two flew in behind him, bumping their shoulders together in the doorway – one slicing an iron chain through the air with a whistle, the other holding an odd-looking contrivance: a short wooden rod attached to a cord with an identical wooden rod at the other end. Tumbling in after them came a hulk of such immense height and stature that in Moscow he would have been shown at a fairground – Erast Petrovich had not even suspected that there were specimens like this to be found among the puny Japanese nation. Rolling in last of all came the titch who had recently gone out, so his strange behaviour was finally explained.

Two gangs arguing with each other over something, Erast Petrovich realised. Exactly the same as at home. Only our cut-throats don't take off their shoes.

This final observation was occasioned by the fact that, before the attackers stepped on to the rice-straw mats, they kicked off their wooden sandals. And then there was a kind of brawl that Fandorin had never seen before, although, despite his young age, the titular counsellor had already been involved in several bloody altercations.

In this unpleasant situation, Erast Petrovich acted rationally and coolly: he caught Sophia Diogenovna as she swooned in horror, dragged her into the farthest corner and shielded her with his body. Shirota was there beside him in an instant, repeating an unfamiliar word in a panicky voice: 'Yakuza, Yakuza!'

'What's that you're saying?' Fandorin asked him as he watched the battle develop.

'Bandits! I warned you! There's going to be an Incident! Ah, this is an Incident!'

And the clerk was quite right about that – a most serious incident was shaping up.

The gamblers and idle onlookers scattered in all directions. First they pressed themselves back against the wall and then, taking advantage of the absence of any guards on the door, they ran for it. Fandorin could not follow their sensible example – he could not abandon the young lady, and the disciplined Shirota clearly had no intention of abandoning his superior. The clerk even attempted, in turn, to shield the diplomat with his own body, but Erast Petrovich moved the Japanese aside – he was blocking his view.

The young man was rapidly seized by the excitement that seizes any individual of the male sex at the sight of an affray, even if it has nothing to do with him and he is an altogether peaceable individual. The breathing quickens, the blood flows twice as fast, the hands fold themselves into fists and, in defiance of reason, in defiance of the instinct of self-preservation, the desire arises to dash headlong into the free-for-all, doling out blind, fervent blows to left and right.

In this fight, however, almost no blind blows were struck. Perhaps even none at all. The fighters did not bawl out profanities, they only grunted and screeched furiously.

The attackers' leader seemed to be the man with the moustache. He was the first to throw himself into the fray and smack the surviving doorman very deftly across the ear with the end of his pole – apparently only lightly, but the man fell flat on his back and did not get up again. The pair who had followed the man with the moustache started lashing out, one with his chain and the other with his piece of wood, and they laid out the three guards in white bandanas.

But that was not the end of the battle – far from it.

Unlike the frenetic fellow with the moustache, the hunchback did not go looking for trouble. He stayed behind his men, shouting out instructions. New warriors came dashing out from back rooms somewhere, and the attackers also started taking punishment.

The hunchback's fighters were armed with long daggers (or perhaps short swords; Erast Petrovich would have found it hard to give a precise definition of those blades fifteen to twenty inches long) and they handled their weapons rather deftly. One might have expected a bamboo pole and a short wooden rod, or the bare hands with which the giant and the titch fought, to be useless against steel, but nonetheless, the scales were clearly not tipping in the 'Rakuen's' favour.

Chubby Face struck out with his feet as well as his hands, managing to hit one man on the forehead and another on the chin. His elephantine comrade acted more majestically and simply: with a nimbleness that was quite incredible for such vast dimensions, he grabbed an opponent by the wrist of the hand clutching a dagger and jerked, flinging him first to the floor and then against the wall. His massive ham-like hands, completely covered with red tattoos, possessed a truly superhuman strength.

The only persons present to remain indifferent to the battle were the spinster Blagolepova, still in a swoon, and the opium addicts in their state of bliss, even though every now and then the blood from some severed artery splashed as far as the mattresses. Once the latest victim of the mountainous man-thrower crashed down on to a dozing Chinaman, but the temporary resident of paradisiacal pastures merely smiled dreamily.

The white bandanas backed towards the counter, losing warriors on the way: some lay with their heads split open, some groaned as they clutched a broken arm. But the raiders suffered losses too: the virtuoso master of the wooden rod impaled his chest on a sharp blade; the chain-bearer fell, skewered from both sides. The chubby-faced prancer was still alive, but he had taken a heavy blow to the temple from a sword-hilt and was sitting on the floor, doltishly wagging his half-shaved head.

But now the hunchback was squeezed into a corner and his two most dangerous enemies – the tattooed giant and the man with the moustache under a hook-nose – were advancing on him.

The owner pressed his hump against the counter, flipped over with amazing agility and ended up on the other side. But that was hardly likely to save him.

The raiders' leader stepped forward and started twirling his weapon through the air in a whistling figure of eight, just barely touching it with his fingertips.

The hunchback raised his hand. And a six-chamber revolver glinted in it.

'And about time too,' Erast Petrovich remarked to his assistant. 'He c-could have thought of that a bit sooner.'

The face of the bandit with the moustache was suddenly a mask of amazement, as if he had never even seen a firearm before. The hand holding the pole whirled upwards, but the shot rang out too quickly. The bullet struck the bandit on the bridge of the nose and knocked him off his feet. Blood oozed out of the black hole slowly and reluctantly. The dead man's face was still frozen in an expression of bewilderment.

The last remaining raider was also dumbfounded. His plump lower lip drooped and his narrow eyes started blinking rapidly in their cushions of fat.

The hunchback shouted out some kind of order. One of the guards got up off the floor, swaying on his feet. Then a second, and a third, and a fourth.

They took a firm grip of the giant's arms, but he gave a light, almost casual shrug, and the white bandanas went flying off and away. Then the owner of the dive calmly discharged the other five cartridges into the hulk's chest. The huge man only jerked as the bullets ripped into his massive body. He swayed for a moment or two, wreathed in powder smoke, and sat down on the straw mats.

'At least half a dozen c-corpses,' said Erast Petrovich, summing up the outcome of the fight. 'We have to call the police.'

'We have to get away as quickly as possible!' protested Shirota. 'What a terrible Incident! The Russian vice-consul at the scene of a bandit massacre. Ah, what a blackguard that man Semushi is.'

'Why?' Fandorin asked in amazement. 'After all, he was defending his own life and his establishment. They would have killed him otherwise.'

'You do not understand. Genuine Yakuza will have nothing to do with gunpowder! They kill only with cold steel or their bare hands! What a disgrace! What is Japan coming to! Let's go!'

Roused by the shots, Sophia Diogenovna sat up and pulled in her feet. The clerk helped her to get up and pulled her towards the exit.

The consular functionary followed but he kept looking around. He saw the guards dragging the dead behind the counter, carrying and leading away the wounded. They pinned the stunned titch's arms behind his back and emptied a jar of water over him.

'What are you doing?' Shirota called from the doorway. 'Hurry!'

'Wait for me outside. I'll just c-collect my winnings.'

But the titular counsellor did not move towards the table where the silver was lying in a blood-spattered heap, he moved towards the counter – the owner was standing there and the Yakuza who had been seized had been dragged across to him.

The hunchback asked him something. Instead of replying, the titch tried to kick him in the crotch, but the blow was feeble and poorly directed – the prisoner had obviously not yet recovered his wits fully. The owner hissed viciously and started kicking the short, sturdy youth – in the stomach, on the knees, on the ankles.

The titch didn't make a sound.

Wiping the sweat off his forehead, the hunchback asked another question.

'He wants to know if there is anyone else left in the Chobei-gumi,' a voice whispered in Erast Petrovich's ear.

It was Shirota. He had led Sophia Diogenovna outside and come back – he took his responsibilities very seriously.

'Left where?'

'In the gang. But the Yakuza won't tell him, of course. They'll kill him now. Let us leave this place. The police will be here soon, they must have been informed already.'

Three men in white bandanas grunted as they dragged the dead man-mountain across the floor. The mighty arms flopped about helplessly. The tips of both little fingers were missing.

The servant girl busily sprinkled white powder on the straw mats and immediately wiped them with a rag, and the red blotches disappeared as if by magic. Meanwhile the owner put a thin cord round the prisoner's neck and pulled the noose tight. He tugged and tugged, and when the Yakuza's face was suffused with blood, he asked the same question again.

The titch lashed out despairingly at his tormentor with his foot once again, but once again to no avail.

Then the hunchback evidently decided that there was no point in wasting any more time. His flat face spread into a grim smile and his right hand started slowly winding the cord on to his left wrist. The captive started wheezing, his lips started clutching vainly at the air, his eyes bulged out of their sockets.

'Right then, translate!' Fandorin ordered the clerk. 'I am a representative of the consular authority of the city of Yokohama, which is under the jurisdiction of the great powers. I demand that you put an end to this summary execution immediately.'

Shirota translated, but what came out was much longer than what Fandorin had said, and at the end he performed a weird trick: he took out of his pocket two little flags, Russian and Japanese (the same ones that Erast Petrovich had recently seen on his desk), and performed a strange manipulation with them – he raised the red, white and blue tricolour high in the air and leaned the red and white flag over sideways.

'What was that you showed them?' the puzzled vice-consul asked.

'I translated what you said and added on my own behalf that if he kills the bandit, he will have to kill you as well, and then our emperor will have to apologise to the Russian emperor, and that will bring terrible shame on Japan.'

Erast Petrovich was astounded that such an argument could have any effect on the owner of a bandit den. Japanese cut-throats were clearly different from Russian ones after all.

'But the flags? Do you always carry them with you?'

Shirota nodded solemnly.

'I always have to remember that I serve Russia, but at the same time remain a Japanese subject. And then, they are so beautiful!'

He bowed respectfully, first to the Russian flag, then to the Japanese one.

After a moment's thought, Erast Petrovich did the same, only he began with the flag of the Land of the Rising Sun.

Meanwhile there was strange, bustling activity taking place in the room. They took the noose off the captive Yakuza's neck, but for some reason laid him out on the floor, and four guards sat on his arms and legs. From the evil grin on the hunchback's face, it was clear that he had thought up some new infamy.

Two male servants came running into the room – one was holding a bizarre-looking piece of metal, and the other a small chalice of black ink.

The half-pint started squirming with every part of his body, he shuddered and howled in misery. Erast Petrovich was astounded – after all, this man had just demonstrated absolute fearlessness in the face of imminent death!

'What's happening? What are they about to do to him? Tell them I won't allow them to torture him!'

'They are not going to torture him,' the clerk said sombrely. 'The owner of the establishment intends to tattoo the hieroglyph *ura* on his forehead. It means "traitor". It is the mark used by Yakuza to brand renegades who have committed the worst of all crimes – betraying their own. For this they deserve death. A man cannot possibly live with this brand, and he cannot commit suicide either, because his body will be buried in the slaughterhouse quarter. What appalling villainy! No, Japan is not what she used to be. The honest bandits of former times would never have done anything so vile.'

'Then we must stop this!' Fandorin exclaimed.

'Semushi will not back down, or he will lose face in front of his men. And we cannot force him. This is an internal Japanese matter, it lies beyond consular jurisdiction.'

The owner seated himself on the prostrate man's chest, set his head in a wooden vice and dipped the piece of metal into the inkwell – and it became clear that the face of the elaborate contrivance was covered with little needles.

'Villainy always falls within jurisdiction,' Erast Petrovich said with a shrug, stepping forward and seizing the owner by the shoulder.

He nodded at the heap of silver, pointed at the prisoner and said in English: 'All this against him. Stake?'

The hunchback visibly wavered. Shirota also took a step forward, stood shoulder to shoulder with Fandorin and lifted up the Russian flag, making it clear that the entire might of a great empire stood behind the vice-consul's suggestion.

'OK. Stake,' the owner agreed in a hoarse voice, getting up.

He snapped his fingers, and the bamboo cup and dice were handed to him with a bow.

> Would that you always
> inspired only true respect,
> my own country's flag!

A COBBLED STREET RUNNING
DOWN A HILL

They did not linger in the vicinity of the 'Rakuen'. Without a word being spoken, they immediately turned the corner and strode off at a smart pace. Certainly, Shirota tried to assure Fandorin that the hunchback would not dare to pursue them, because taking back someone's winnings was not the *Bakuto* custom, but he himself did not appear entirely convinced of the inviolability of bandit traditions and kept looking round. The clerk was lugging the sack of silver. Erast Petrovich was leading the young lady along by the elbow and the Yakuza who had been beaten at dice was plodding along behind, still seeming not quite to have recovered from all his ordeals and so many twists of fate.

They stopped to catch their breath only when they were already out of the 'quarter of shame'. Rikshas ran along the street, the decorous public strolled along the lines of shop windows and the cobbled road leading down to the river was brightly illuminated by gas lamps – twilight had descended on the city.

And here the titular counsellor was beset by a triple ordeal.

The example was set by the spinster Blagolepova. She embraced him passionately round the neck (in so doing, striking him a painful blow on the back with the bundle containing the captain's legacy) and watered his cheek with tears of gratitude. The young man was called 'a saviour', 'a hero', 'an angel' and even 'a darling'.

And that was only the beginning.

While Fandorin, dumbstruck by that 'darling', comforted the lady by cautiously stroking her heaving shoulders, Shirota waited patiently. But the moment Erast Petrovich freed himself from the maiden's embraces, the clerk bowed to him, almost right down to the ground, and froze in that position.

'Good Lord, Shirota, now what are you doing?'

'I am ashamed that there are people like Semushi in Japan,' the clerk said in a flat voice. 'And this on the day of your arrival! What must you think of us!'

Fandorin was about to explain to this patriot that there were very many bad people in Russia too, and he knew very well that a people should be judged by its best representatives, not its worst, but then the vice-consul was struck by another blow.

The plump-faced bandit stopped glancing round repeatedly at the bridge, panted, dropped at Erast Petrovich's feet and suddenly started banging his firm forehead against the road!

'He is thanking you for saving his honour and his life,' Shirota translated.

'Please tell him that his gratitude is accepted and to get up quickly,' the titular counsellor said nervously, glancing round at the people in the street.

The bandit got up and bowed from the waist.

'He says that he is a soldier of the honourable Chobei-gumi gang, which no longer exists.'

Fandorin found the term 'honourable gang' so intriguing that he said:

'Ask him to tell me about himself.'

'*Hai, kashikomarimashita,*'* said the 'soldier', bowing once again, and then, with his arms pressed to his sides, he began reporting in true military style, his eyes staring fixedly at the superior officer whose role Erast Petrovich was playing.

'He comes from a family of hereditary *machi-yakko* and is very proud of it. (These are also noble Yakuza, who defend little people against the tyranny of the authorities. Well, and they also collect tribute from them, of course),' said Shirota, mingling translation with comment. 'His father had only two fingers on his hand. (That is a Yakuza custom: if a bandit has committed some offence and wishes to apologise to the gang, he cuts off a section of a finger.) He himself, of course, does not remember his father – he has heard about him from other people. His mother also came from a respected family, her entire body was covered in tattoos, right down to the knees. When he was three years old, his father escaped from jail, hid in a lighthouse and sent word to his wife – she worked in a teahouse. His mother tied the child to her back and hurried to join her husband at the lighthouse, but she was followed and the warders of the jail were informed. They surrounded the lighthouse. His father did not wish to return to jail. He stabbed his wife in the heart and himself in the throat. He wanted to kill his little son too, but could not do it, and simply threw him into the sea. However, karma did not allow the child to drown – he was fished out and taken to an orphanage.'

'Why, what a b-brute his dear papa was!' Erast Petrovich exclaimed, dumbfounded.

Shirota was surprised.

'Why a brute?'

'Well, he killed his own wife and threw his own s-son off a cliff!'

'I assure you that he would not have killed his own wife for anything, unless she had asked him to do it. They did not wish to be parted, their love was stronger than death. This is very beautiful.'

'But what has this to do with the infant?'

'Here in Japan we take a different view of this matter, I beg your pardon,' the clerk replied severely. 'The Japanese are conscientious people. Parents are responsible for their child, especially if he is very young. The world is so cruel! How is it possible to cast a defenceless creature to the whim of fate?

---

* I obey (Japanese)

It is simply inhuman! A family should hold together and not be separated. The most touching thing about this story is that the father could not bring himself to stab his little son with a knife . . .'

While this dialogue was taking place between the vice-consul and his assistant, the titch engaged Sophia Diogenovna in conversation and asked some question that made the spinster sob and burst into bitter tears.

'What's wrong?' Fandorin exclaimed without hearing Shirota out. 'Has this bandit offended you? What did he say to you?'

'No-o,' Blagolepova sniffed. 'He asked . . . he asked how my esteemed father was ge-ge-getting on.'

Once again moisture gushed from the young lady's eyes – apparently her tear glands produced it in genuinely unlimited amounts.

'Did he really know your father?' Erast Petrovich asked in surprise.

Sophia Diogenovna blew her nose into the wet handkerchief and was unable to reply, so Shirota readdressed the question to the Yakuza.

'No, he did not have the honour of being acquainted with the yellow-haired lady's father, but last night he saw her come to the "Rakuen" for her parent. He was a very sociable man. Opium makes some people fall asleep but others, on the contrary, become merry and talkative. The old captain was never quiet for a moment, he was always talking, talking.'

'What did he talk about?' Fandorin asked absentmindedly, taking out his watch.

A quarter to eight. If he had to go to this notorious Bachelors' Ball with the consul, it would be a good idea to take a bath and tidy himself up first.

'About how he took three passengers to Tokyo, to the Susaki mooring. How he waited for them there and then brought them back. They spoke the Satsuma dialect. They thought the *gaijin* would not understand, but the captain had been sailing Japanese waters for a long time and had learned to understand all the dialects. The Satsuma men had long bundles with them, and there were swords in the bundles, he made out one of the hilts. Very odd, covered with *kamiyasuri* . . .' – at this point Shirota hesitated, unsure of how to translate this difficult word. '*Kamiyasuri* is a kind of paper, covered all over in particles of glass. It is used to make the surface of wood smooth . . .'

'Glasspaper?'

'Yes, yes indeed! Glasspaper,' said Shirota, repeating the word so that he would not forget it again.

'But how can a sword hilt be covered with glasspaper? It would lacerate your palm.'

'Of course, it is not possible,' the Japanese agreed, 'but I am merely translating.'

He told the Yakuza to continue.

'Those men said very bad things about Minister Okubo, they called him Inu-Okubo, that is "the Dog Okubo". One of them, a man with a withered arm who was their leader, said: "Never mind, he will not get away from us tomorrow". And when the captain brought them back to Yokohama, they told him to be at the same place tomorrow an hour before dawn and paid him a good advance. The captain told everyone who was nearby about this. And he said he would sit there for a little longer and then go to the police and they would give him a big reward for saving the minister from the plotters.'

As he translated the bandit's story Shirota frowned more and more darkly.

'This is very alarming information,' he explained. 'Former samurai from the principality of Satsuma hate their fellow Satsuman. They regard him as a traitor.'

They started asking the titch about this, but he laughed and waved his hand disdainfully.

'He says this is all nonsense. The captain was totally sizzled with opium, he was tripping over his own tongue. He must have imagined it. Where would Satsuma samurai get the money to pay for a steam launch? They are all ragged tramps. If they wanted to kill the minister, they would walk to Tokyo. And then, who has ever heard of covering the hilt of a sword with glasspaper? The old *gaijin* simply wanted people to listen to him, so he spun a tall story.'

Erast Petrovich and Shirota exchanged glances.

'Right, get him to tell us all the d-details. What else did the captain say? Did anything happen to him?'

The Yakuza was surprised that his story had aroused such great interest, but he was diligent in his reply.

'He didn't say anything else. Only about the reward. He kept going to sleep, then waking up and talking about the same thing. He probably really did carry some passengers, but as for the swords, they were an opium dream, everybody said so. And nothing unusual happened to the captain. He sat there until dawn, then suddenly got up and left.'

'Suddenly? Exactly how d-did it happen?' enquired Fandorin, who did not like this story about the mysterious samurai at all – especially in the light of Blagolepov's sudden demise.

'He simply got up and left.'

'For no reason at all?'

The Yakuza started thinking hard.

'The captain was sitting there, dozing. With his back to the room. I think someone walked past behind him and woke him. Yes, yes! Some old man, totally doped. He staggered and swung his arm and caught the captain on the neck. The captain woke up and swore at the old man. Then he said: "Boss, I'm not feeling too well, I'll be going". And he left.'

When he finished translating, Shirota added on his own behalf:

'No, Mr Titular Counsellor, there's nothing suspicious in that. The captain must have felt a pain in his heart. He got as far as his home and then died there.'

Erast Petrovich did not respond to this piece of deduction, but a slight narrowing of his eyes suggested that he was not entirely satisfied with it.

'His hand caught his neck?' he murmured thoughtfully.

'What?' asked Shirota, who had not heard.

'What is this bandit going to do now? His gang has been massacred, after all,' Fandorin asked, but without any great interest: he simply did not wish to let the clerk know what he was thinking for the time being.

The bandit replied briefly and vigorously.

'He says he is going to thank you.'

The determined tone in which these words were spoken put the titular counsellor on his guard.

'What does he mean by that?'

Shirota explained with obvious approval:

'Now you are his *onjin* for the rest of his life. Unfortunately, there is no such word in the Russian language.' He thought for moment. 'Benefactor to the grave. Can one say that?'

'To the g-grave?' Fandorin said with a shudder.

'Yes, to the very grave. And he is your debtor to the grave. For not only did you save him from death, you also spared him indelible disgrace. For that, it is our custom to pay with supreme gratitude, even with our very life itself.'

'What would I want with his life? Tell him "don't mention it", or whatever it is you say, and let him go on his way.'

'When people say those words with such sincerity, they do not go on their own way,' Shirota said reproachfully. 'He says that from now on, you are his master. Wherever you go, he goes.'

The titch gave a low bow and stuck his little finger up in the air, which seemed rather impolite to Erast Petrovich.

'Well, what does he say? Why does he not leave?' asked the young Russian.

'He will not leave. His *oyabun* has been killed, and so he has decided to devote his life to serving you. In proof of his sincerity, he offers to cut off his little finger.'

'Oh, let him go to the d-devil!' Fandorin exclaimed indignantly. 'Tell him to hop it.'

The clerk did not dare argue with the annoyed vice-consul and started translating, but then stopped short.

'In Japanese it is not possible to say simply "hop", you have to explain where to.'

If not for the presence of a lady, Fandorin would gladly have provided the precise address, since his patience was running out – his first day in Japan had proved exhausting in the extreme.

'Hop down the hill, like a grasshopper,' said Fandorin, gesturing towards the waterfront with one hand.

A look of puzzlement flashed across the titch's face, but immediately disappeared.

'*Kashikomarimashita*,' he said, and nodded.

He gathered himself, raised one foot off the ground and hopped off down the slope.

Erast Petrovich frowned. The blockhead could slip and break his leg on those cobbles. But damn him anyway, the vice-consul had more important business.

'Tell me, Shirota, can you recommend a reliable doctor, capable of performing an autopsy?'

'Reliable? Yes, I know a very reliable doctor. His name is Mr Lancelot Twigs. He is a sincere man.'

A rather strange recommendation for a medical man, thought the vice-consul.

From down below came a regular thudding, gradually growing more rapid – it was Fandorin's debtor to the grave hopping down the cobbled street like a grasshopper.

Bruises will they bring,
the roadway's rough cobblestones.
Honour's path is hard.

A PERFECTLY HEALTHY CORPSE

'I don't understand a thing,' said Dr Lancelot Twigs, peeling off the gloves covered in brownish-red spots and pulling the sheet up over the lacerated body. 'The heart, liver and lungs are in perfect order. There's no sign of any haemorrhaging in the brain – there was no need for me to saw open the brainpan. God grant every man such excellent health after the age of fifty.'

Fandorin glanced round at the door behind which Sophia Diogenovna had remained in Shirota's care. The doctor had a loud voice, and the anatomical details he had mentioned might induce another outburst of hysterical sobbing. But then, how would this simple young woman know English?

The autopsy had taken place in the bedroom. They had simply removed the skinny mattress from the wooden bed, spread out oiled paper on the planks, and the doctor had set about his joyless task. Erast Petrovich had played the role of his assistant, holding a lantern and turning it this way and that, following the doctor's instructions. At the same time, he himself tried to look away, so that he would not – God forbid! – collapse in a faint at the appalling sight. That is, when the doctor said: 'Just take a look at that magnificent stomach!' or 'What a bladder! I wish I had one like that! Just look at it, will you!', Fandorin turned round, he even nodded and grunted in agreement, but sensibly kept his eyes tightly shut. The smell alone was quite sufficient for the titular counsellor. It seemed as if this torture would never end.

The doctor was elderly and staid, but at the same time exceptionally talkative. His faded blue eyes had a genial glow to them. He had carried out his job conscientiously, from time to time running one hand over a bald spot surrounded by a faint halo of gingerish hair. But when it emerged that the cause of Captain Blagolepov's death simply refused to be clarified, Twigs became excited, and the sweat started flowing freely across his bald cranium.

After one hour, two minutes and forty-five seconds (the exhausted Erast Petrovich had been timing things with his watch) Twigs finally capitulated.

'I am obliged to state that this is a perfectly healthy corpse. This was a heroically robust organism, especially when one considers the protracted use by the deceased of the dried lacteal juice of the seed cases of *Papaver somniferum*. Nothing, apart perhaps from traces of tobacco resins ingrained in the throat and a slight darkening of the lungs – here, see?' (Without even looking, Erast Petrovich said: 'Oh, yes'.) 'He has the heart of an ox. And it suddenly goes and stops, for no reason at all. I've never seen anything like it. You should have seen my poor Jenny's heart.' Twigs sighed. 'The muscles were like threadbare rags. When I opened up the thoracic cavity, I simple wept for pity. The poor soul had a really bad heart, the second birth wore it out completely.'

Erast Petrovich already knew that Jenny was the doctor's deceased wife and that he had decided to perform her autopsy in person, because both of his daughters also had weak hearts, like their mother, and he needed to take a look to see what the problem was – ailments of that kind were often inherited. It turned out to be a moderately severe prolapse of the bicuspid valve and, possessing that important piece of information, the doctor had been able to arrange the proper treatment for his adored little ones. Fandorin listened to this amazing story, not knowing whether he should feel admiration or horror.

'Did you check the cervical vertebrae carefully?' Erast Petrovich asked, not for the first time. 'As I said, he might have been struck on the neck, from behind.'

'There's no trauma. Not even a bruise. Only a little red spot just below the base of the skull, as if from a slight burn. But it's quite out of the question for a trifle like that to have any serious consequences. Perhaps there was no blow?'

'I don't know,' said the young man, already regretting that he had started this rigmarole of the autopsy. Who knew what might stop the heart of an inveterate opium addict?

The dead man's clothing was hanging on a chair. Erast Petrovich looked thoughtfully at the badly worn back of the tunic, the patched shirt with the buttoned collar – the very cheapest kind, celluloid. And suddenly he leaned down.

'There was no blow as such, but there was a touch!' he exclaimed. 'Look, right here, the imprint left by a f-finger. Although it could have been Blagolepov's own hand,' the vice-consul added disappointedly. 'He was fastening his collar, and he took a grip ...'

'Well, that's not hard to clear up.' The doctor took out a large magnifying glass and squatted down beside the chair. 'Aha. The thumb of the right hand.'

'You can tell that from a glance?' asked Fandorin, astounded.

'Yes, I've taken a bit of an interest. You see, my friend Henry Folds, who works in a hospital in Tokyo, made a curious discovery. While studying the prints left by fingers on old Japanese ceramics, he discovered that the pattern on the pads of the fingers is never repeated ...' Twigs walked over to the bed, took the dead man's right hand and examined the thumb through the magnifying glass. 'No, this is a quite different thumb. No doubt at all about it ... And so Mr Folds proposed a curious hypothesis, according to which ...'

'I have read about fingerprints,' Erast Petrovich interrupted impatiently, 'but the European authorities do not see any practical application for the idea. Why don't you check if it matches the spot with the mark that you spoke about?'

The doctor unceremoniously raised the dead head with its top sawn off and doubled right over.

'Yes, it probably does. But what of that? There was a touch, but there was no blow. Where the burn came from is not clear, but I assure you that no one has ever died from a cause like this.'

Fandorin sighed and gave in. 'Very well, stitch him up. I ought not to have bothered you.'

While the doctor worked away with his needle, the titular counsellor went out into the next room. Sophia Diogenovna leaned eagerly towards him with an expression on her face as if she were expecting the miraculous news that her father was not dead at all, and the English doctor had just established the fact scientifically.

Fandorin blushed and said:

'We n-needed to establish the cause of death medically. It is routine.'

The young lady nodded, and the hope faded from her face.

'And what was the cause?' enquired Shirota.

Embarrassed, Erast Petrovich coughed into his hand and repeated the medical abracadabra that had stuck in his mind.

'Prolapse of the biscuspid valve.'

The clerk nodded respectfully, but Sophia Diogenovna started crying quietly and inconsolably, as if this news had finally laid her low.

'And what am I to do now, Mr Vice-Consul?' she asked, her voice breaking. 'I feel afraid here. What if Semushi suddenly shows up, for the money? Is there any way I can spend the night at your office? I could manage somehow on the chairs, no?'

'Very well, let's go. We'll think of something.'

'I'll just collect my things.'

The young lady ran out of the room.

Silence fell. The only sound was the doctor whistling as he worked. Then something clattered on the floor and Twigs swore: 'Damned crown!', from which Fandorin speculated that the Anglo-Saxon had dropped the top of the braincase.

Erast Petrovich suddenly felt unwell and, in order not to hear anything else nasty, he started a conversation – he asked why Shirota had called the doctor 'a sincere man'.

The clerk was pleased at the question – he too seemed to find the silence oppressive, and he started telling the story with relish.

'It is a very beautiful story, they even wanted to write a kabuki theatre play about it. It happened five years ago, when Twigs-sensei was still in mourning for his esteemed wife and his esteemed daughters were little girls. While playing the card game of bridge at the United Club, the sensei quarrelled with a certain bad man, a doerist. The doerist had arrived in Yokohama recently and started beating everyone at cards, and if anyone took offence, he challenged them to fight. He had already shot one man dead and seriously wounded another two. Nothing happened to the doerist for this, because it was a duel.'

'Aha, a duellist!' Fandorin exclaimed, after puzzling over the occasional alternating l's and r's in Shirota's speech, which was absolutely correct in every other way.

'Yes, yes, a doerist,' Shirota repeated. 'And so this bad man challenged the sensei to fight with guns. The doctor was in a dreadful situation. He did not know how to shoot at all, and the doerist would certainly have killed him, and his daughters would have been left orphans. But if the sensei refused to fight a duel, everyone would have turned their backs on him, and his daughters would have been ashamed of their father. But he did not want his daughters to feel ashamed. And then Mr Twigs said that he accepted the challenge, but he needed a delay of five days in order to prepare himself for death as befits a gentleman and a Christian. And he also demanded that the seconds must name the very longest distance that was permitted by the doering code – a full thirty paces. The doerist agreed contemptuously, but demanded in return that there must be no limit to the number of shots and the duel must continue until there was "a result". He said he would not allow a duel of honour to be turned into a comedy. For five days the sensei saw no one. But at the appointed hour on the appointed day he came to the site of the duel. People who were there say he was a little pale, but very intense. The opponents were set thirty paces away from each other. The doctor removed his frock coat, and put cotton wool in his ears. And when the second waved the handkerchief, he raised his pistol, took careful aim and shot the doerist right in the centre of the forehead!'

'That's incredible!' Erast Petrovich exclaimed. 'What a stroke of luck! The Almighty certainly took mercy on Twigs!'

'That was what everyone in the Settlement thought. But what had happened soon came to light. The manager of the shooting club revealed that Mr Twigs had spent all five days in the firing range. Instead of praying and writing a will, he learned how to fire a duelling pistol, at the precise distance of thirty paces. The sensei became a little deaf, but he learned to hit the centre of the target and never miss. And why not, he had fired thousands of rounds! Anyone in his place would have achieved the same result.'

'Oh, well done!'

'Some said what you say, but others were outraged and abused the doctor, saying it was not "fair play". One young pup, a lieutenant in the French marines, got drunk and started mocking the doctor in public for cowardice. The sensei heaved a sigh and said: "You are very young and do not yet understand what responsibility is. But if you consider me a coward, I am willing to fight a duel with you on the same terms" – and as he spoke, he looked straight at the centre of the young pup's forehead, so intently that the Frenchman sobered up completely and apologised. That is the kind of man that Dr Twigs is,' Shirota concluded admiringly. 'A sincere man!'

'Like Pushkin and Field Marshal Saigo?' Erast Petrovich asked, and couldn't help smiling.

The clerk nodded solemnly.

It must be admitted that when the doctor emerged from the bedroom, even Fandorin saw him with different eyes. He noticed certain features of Twigs' appearance that were not apparent at a casual glance: the firm line of the chin, the resolute, massive forehead. A very interesting specimen.

'All patched and sewn up, looking fine,' the doctor announced. 'That will be a guinea and two shillings, Mr Fandorin. And another six pence for a place in the morgue. Ice is expensive in Yokohama.'

When Shirota left to fetch a cart to transport the body, Twigs took hold of one of Erast Petrovich's buttons with his finger and thumb and said with a mysterious air:

'I was just thinking about that thumbprint and the little red spot . . . Tell me, Mr Vice-Consul, have you ever heard of the art of *dim-mak*?'

'I b-beg your pardon?'

'You have not,' the doctor concluded. 'And that is not surprising. Not much is known about *dim-mak*. Possibly it is all a load of cock and bull . . .'

'But what is *"dim-mak"*?'

'The Chinese art of deferred killing.'

Erast Petrovich shuddered and looked hard at Twigs to see whether he was joking.

'What does that mean?'

'I don't know the details, but I have read that there are people who can kill and heal with a single touch. Supposedly they are able to concentrate a certain energy into some kind of ray and affect certain points of the body with it. You have heard of acupuncture?'

'Yes, I have.'

'*Dim-mak* would seem to operate with the same anatomical principles, but instead of a needle, it uses a simple touch. I have read that those who have mastered this mysterious art can cause a fit of sharp pain or, on the contrary, render a man completely insensitive to pain, or temporarily paralyse him, or put him to sleep, or kill him . . . And moreover, not necessarily at the moment of contact, but after a delay.'

'I don't understand what you're talking about!' exclaimed Fandorin, who was listening to the doctor with increasing bewilderment.

'I don't understand it myself. It sounds like a fairy tale . . . But I recalled a story I once read, about a master of *dim-mak* who struck himself on a certain point and fell down dead. He wasn't breathing and his heart wasn't beating. His enemies threw him to the dogs to be eaten, but after a while he woke up alive and well. And there's another story I've read, about a certain Chinese ruler who was kissed on the foot by a beggar. Some time later a pink spot appeared at the sight of the kiss, and a few hours after that, the king suddenly fell down dead . . . Damn it!' the doctor exclaimed in embarrassment. 'I'm getting like those blockheaded journalists who make up all sorts of wild tales about the East. It's just that while I was sewing our friend up, I kept thinking about the mark on his neck, so I remembered . . .'

It was hard to imagine that a staid, sedate individual like Dr Twigs could have decided to play a hoax on anyone, but it was also hard for a convinced rationalist, such as Erast Petrovich considered himself to be, to believe in deferred killing.

'Mm, yes,' the titular counsellor said eventually. 'In the East, of course, there are many phenomena still unstudied by European science ...'

And on that polite comment the mystical conversation came to an end.

They said goodbye to Twigs in the street. The doctor got into a riksha, raised his hat and rode away. Two locals laid the poor captain's body, wrapped in a sheet, on a cart.

Erast Petrovich, Shirota and the sobbing Sophia Diogenovna set out on foot to the consulate, because Fandorin refused once again to 'use human beings as horses', and the clerk and the young lady also did not wish to ride in style, since the titular counsellor was travelling on his own two feet.

At the very first street lamp, there was a surprise waiting for the vice-consul.

The chubby-faced Yakuza, whom Erast Petrovich had already completely forgotten, loomed up out of the darkness.

He froze in a low bow, with his arms pressed to his sides,. Then he straightened up and fixed his benefactor with a severe, unblinking gaze.

'I hopped as far as the river,' Shirota translated, gazing at the bandit with obvious approval. 'What other orders will there be, Master?'

'How sick I am of him!' Fandorin complained. 'Now I wish that they had put that brand on his forehead! Listen, Shirota, am I never going to get rid of him now?'

The clerk looked carefully into the stubborn fellow's eyes.

'He is a man of his word. The only way is to tell him to put an end to his own life.'

'Lord above! All right. At least get him to tell me what his n-name is.'

Shirota translated the reply from the former soldier of the Chobei-gumi gang:

'His name is Masahiro Sibata, but you can call him simply Masa.'

Erast Petrovich glanced round at a squeak of wheels and doffed his top hat – it was the carters pushing along the cart on which the 'perfectly healthy corpse' had set off to the morgue after the doctor. Lying at its head were a pair of low boots and neatly folded clothing.

Vain fuss all around,
only he is at repose,
who has joined Buddha

SPARKS OF LIGHT ON A
KATANA BLADE

'Three samurai? Swords wrapped in rags. They called Okubo "a dog"? This could be very, very serious!' Doronin said anxiously. 'Everything about it is suspicious, and especially the fact that they used the launch. It's the best way of getting right into the heart of the city, bypassing the road posts and the toll gates.'

Erast Petrovich had caught Vsevolod Vitalievich at home, in the left wing of the consulate. Doronin had already returned from the opening of the charitable establishment and the supper that had followed it, and he was getting changed for the Bachelors' Ball. The consul's gold-embroidered uniform was hanging over a chair and a plump Japanese maid was helping him into his dinner jacket.

Fandorin was very much taken by his superior's apartment: with its furnishings of light rattan, it was very successful in combining Russianness with Japanese exoticism. For instance, on a small table in the corner there was a gleaming, fat-sided samovar, and through the glass doors of a cupboard, carafes of various colours could be seen, containing liqueurs and flavoured vodkas, but the pictures and scrolls on the walls were exclusively local in origin, and the place of honour was occupied by a stand with two samurai swords, while through an open door there was a view of an entirely Japanese room – that is, with no furniture at all and straw flooring.

The hazy circumstances of Blagolepov's death interested Vsevolod Vitalievich far less than his three nocturnal passengers. This reaction actually seemed rather extreme to Fandorin at first, but Doronin explained the reason for his alarm.

'It is no secret that the minister has many enemies, especially among the southern samurai. In Japan attempts at political assassinations are almost as frequent as in Russia. At home, of course, the dignitaries are killed by revolutionaries, and here by reactionaries, but that makes little difference to the case – society and the state suffer equally serious damage from leftist zealots as from rightist ones. Okubo is a key figure in Japanese politics. If the fanatics can get to him, the entire direction, the entire orientation, of the empire will change, in a way that is highly dangerous for Russia. You see, Fandorin, Minister Okubo is a protagonist of evolution, the gradual development of the internal forces of the country under strict governmental control. He is an animal trainer who cracks his whip and does not allow the tiger to break out of its cage. The tiger is the ancestral, deep-rooted militancy of the aristocracy here, and the cage is the Japanese archipelago. What was it that tore the notorious triumvirate of the three Japanese Corsicans apart? The question of war. The mighty party that was led by our Shirota's favourite hero, Marshal Saigo, wanted to conquer Korea immediately. The reason why Okubo gained the upper hand over all his opponents at that time was that he is cleverer and more cunning. But if he is killed, power will inevitably go to those who support rapid development based on expansion, the poets of the great Japanese Empire of Yamato. Although, God knows, there are already too many empires in the world – any minute now they will all start wrangling with each other and sinking their steel talons into each other's fur . . .'

'Wait,' Fandorin said with a frown, holding open the leather-bound notebook intended for collecting information about Japan, but not yet writing anything in it. 'What does that matter to Russia? If Japan does attack Korea, then what do we care?'

'Tut-tut-tut, such puerile talk, and from a diplomat,' the consul said reproachfully, and clicked his tongue. 'Learn to think in terms of state policy, strategically. You and I have been an empire for a long time now, and everything that happens on the globe matters to empires, my dear. Especially in Korea. For the Japanese, the Korean Peninsula will be no more than a bridge to China and Manchuria, and we have had our own sights on those for a very long time. Have you never heard of the project to create Yellow Russia?'

'I have, but I don't like the idea. For goodness' sake, Vsevolod Vitalievich, God grant us the grace to solve our own internal problems.'

'He doesn't like it!' the consul chuckled. 'Are you in the tsar's service? Are you paid a salary? Then be so good as to do your job, and let those who have been entrusted with responsibility do the thinking and give the orders.'

'But how is it possible not t-to think? You yourself do not greatly resemble a person who follows orders without thinking!'

Doronin's face hardened.

'You are right about that. Naturally, I think, I have my own judgement, and as far as I can I try to bring it to the attention my superiors. Although, of course, sometimes, I'd like . . . But then, that does not concern you,' said the consul, suddenly growing angry and jerking his hand so that his cufflink fell to the floor.

The servant girl kneeled down, picked up the little circle of gold, took the consul's arm and set his cuff to rights.

'*Domo, domo,*' Vsevolod Vitalievich thanked her, and the girl smiled, revealing crooked teeth that spoiled her pretty little face rather badly.

'You should have a word with her, to get her to smile without parting her lips,' Fandorin remarked in a low voice, unable to restrain his response.

'The Japanese have different ideas about female beauty. We value large eyes, they value small ones. We value the shape of the teeth, they value only the colour. Irregularity of the teeth is a sign of sensuality, regarded as highly erotic. Like protruding ears. And the legs of Japanese beauties are best not mentioned at all. The habit of squatting on their haunches has made most women here bandy-legged and pigeon-toed. But there are gratifying exceptions,' Doronin suddenly added in a completely different, affectionate tone of voice, looking over Erast Petrovich's shoulder.

Fandorin glanced round.

A woman in an elegant white-and-grey kimono was standing in the doorway of the Japanese room. She was holding a tray with two cups on it. Fandorin thought her white-skinned, smiling face seemed exceptionally lovely.

The woman walked into the drawing room, stepping soundlessly on small feet in white socks, and offered the guest tea.

'And this is my Obayasi, who loves me according to a signed contract.'

Erast Petrovich had the impression that the deliberate crudeness of these words was the result of embarrassment – Vsevolod Vitalievich was gazing at his concubine with an expression that was gentle, even sentimental.

The young man bowed respectfully, even clicking his heels, as if in compensation for Doronin's harshness. The consul spoke several phrases in Japanese and added:

'Don't be concerned, she doesn't know any Russian at all. I don't teach her.'

'But why not?'

'What for?' Doronin asked with a slight frown. 'So that after me she can sign a marriage contract with some sailor? Our bold seafarers think very highly of a "little madam" if she can chat even a little in Russian.'

'Isn't that all the same to you?' the titular counsellor remarked rather drily. 'She will have to live somehow, even after your love by contract expires.'

Vsevolod Vitalievich flared up:

'I shall make provisions for her. You shouldn't imagine that I'm some kind of absolute monster! I understand your gibe, I deserved it, I shouldn't have been so flippant. If you wish to know, I respect and love this lady. And she returns my feelings, independent of any contracts, yes indeed, sir!'

'Then you should get married properly. What is there to stop you?'

The flames that had blazed up in Doronin's eyes went out.

'You are pleased to joke. Conclude a legal marriage with a Japanese concubine? They would throw me out of the service, for damaging the reputation of Russian diplomats. And then what? Would you have me take her to Russia? She would pine away there, with our weather and our customs. People there would stare at her as if she were some kind of monkey. Stay here? I should be expelled from civilised European society. No, the fiery steed and trembling doe cannot be yoked ... But everything is excellent as it is. Obayasi does not demand or expect anything more from me.'

Vsevolod Vitalievich turned slightly red, because the conversation was encroaching farther and farther into territory that was strictly private. But in his resentment at the consul's treatment of Obayasi, Fandorin was not satisfied with that.

'But what if there's a child?' he exclaimed. 'Will you "make provisions" for him too? In other words, pay them off?'

'I can't have a child,' Doronin said with a grin. 'I mention it without the slightest embarrassment, because it has nothing to do with sexual impotence. On the contrary.' His bilious smile widened even further. 'In my young days, I was very keen on the ladies, and I ended up with a nasty disease. I was pretty much cured, but the likelihood of having any progeny is almost zero – such is the verdict of medicine. That, basically, is why I have never concluded a legal marriage with any modest maiden of the home-made variety. I did not wish to disappoint the maternal instinct.'

Obayasi obviously sensed that the conversation was taking an unpleasant turn. She bowed once again and walked out as soundlessly as she had come in. She left the tray with the tea on the table.

'Well, enough of that,' the consul interrupted himself. 'You and I are behaving far too much like Russians ... Intimate talk like that requires either long friendship or a substantial amount of drink, and we are barely acquainted and completely sober. And therefore, we had better get back to business.'

Assuming an emphatically businesslike air, Vsevolod Vitalievich started bending his fingers down one by one.

'First, we have to tell Lieutenant Captain Bukhartsev about everything – I have already mentioned him to you. Secondly, write a report to His Excellency. Thirdly, if Okubo arrives at the ball, warn him about the danger ...'

'I still d-don't understand, though ... Even if Blagolepov did not imagine the suspicious things that his passengers said in his opium dream, what need is there to get so worked up? They have only cold steel. If they had revolvers or carbines, they would hardly be likely to lug their medieval swords around with them. Can such individuals really represent a danger to the most powerful politician in Japan?'

'Ah, Erast Petrovich, do you really think the Satsumans are unacquainted with firearms or were unable to obtain the money for a couple of revolvers? Why, one night journey on the launch must cost more than a used Smith and Wesson. This is a different issue. In Japan it is considered unseemly to kill an enemy with a bullet – for them, that is cowardice. A sworn enemy, and especially one as eminent as Okubo, has to be cut down with a sword or, at the very least, stabbed with a dagger. And furthermore, you cannot even imagine how effective the *takana*, the Japanese sword, is in the hands of a genuine master. Europeans have never even dreamed of the like.'

The consul picked up one of the swords from the stand – the one that was somewhat longer – and flourished it carefully in his left hand, without drawing it from the scabbard.

'Naturally, I do not know how to fence with a *katana* – that has to be studied from childhood. And it is preferable to study *the Japanese way* – that is, to devote your entire life to the subject that you are studying. But I take lessons in *battojiutsu* from a certain old man.'

'Lessons in what?'

'*Battojiutsu* is the art of drawing the sword from the scabbard.'

Erast Petrovich could not help laughing.

'Merely drawing it? Is that like the true duellists of Charles the Ninth's time? Shake the sword smartly, so that the scabbard flies off by itself?'

'It's not a matter of a smart shake. Do you handle a revolver well?'

'Not too badly.'

'And, of course, you are convinced that, with a revolver, you will have no trouble in disposing of an adversary who is armed with nothing but a sword?'

'Naturally.'

'Good,' Vsevolod Vitalievich purred, and took a revolver out of a drawer. 'Are you familiar with this device? It's a Colt.'

'Of course I am. But I have something better.'

Fandorin thrust his hand in under the tail of his frock coat and took a small, flat revolver out of a secret holster. It was hidden so cleverly that the guards at the 'Rakuen' had failed to discover it.

'This is a Herstal Agent, seven chambers. They are p-produced to order.'

'A lovely trinket. Now put it back. Good. And now can you take it out very, very quickly?'

Erast Petrovich threw out the hand holding the revolver with lightning speed, aiming directly at his superior's forehead.

'Superb! I suggest a little game. On the command of "three!" you will take out your Herstal, and I shall take out my *katana*, and we'll see who wins.'

The titular counsellor smiled condescendingly, put the revolver back in the holster and folded his arms in order to give his rival a head start, but Doronin out-swanked him by raising his right hand above his head.

He gave the command:

'One . . . two . . . three!'

It was impossible to follow the movement that the consul made. All Erast Petrovich saw was a glittering arc that was transformed into a blade, which froze into immobility before the young man could even raise the hand holding the revolver.

'Astounding!' he exclaimed. 'But it's not enough just to draw the sword, you have to cover the distance of one and a half *sazhens* between us. In that time I would have already taken aim and fired.'

'You're right. But I did warn you that I have only learned to draw the sword. I assure you that my teacher of swordsmanship would have sliced you in half before you pulled the trigger.'

Erast Petrovich did not try to argue – the trick had impressed him.

'And have you heard anything about the art of deferred killing?' he asked cautiously. 'I think it is called *dim-mak*.'

He told the consul what he had heard from Dr Twigs.

'I've never heard of anything of the sort,' Doronin said with a shrug, admiring the flashes of light on the sword blade. 'I think it's a tall tale of the same genre as the fantastic stories about the ninja.'

'About whom?'

'During the Middle Ages there were clans of spies and hired assassins, they were called ninja. The Japanese simply love blathering all sorts of nonsense with a mystical air to it.'

'But if we accept that this Chinese *dim-mak* actually does exist,' Fandorin continued, pursuing his line of thought, 'could the Satsuma samurai know the art?'

'The devil only knows. From a theoretical point of view, it's possible. Satsuma is a land of seagoers, ships from there go all over South-East Asia. And in addition, it's a mere stone's throw away from the Ryukyu islands, where the art of killing with bare hands has flourished since ancient times ... All the more important, then, that we take measures. If Blagolepov's three passengers are not ordinary crazies, but masters of secret skills, the danger is even more serious. Somehow this threesome don't seem like loony fanatics. They sailed across the bay to Tokyo for some reason, and they took precautions – we must assume that they deliberately hired a foreigner in the belief that he would not understand their dialect and would not be conversant with Japanese affairs. They paid him generously and gave him an advance against the next journey. Serious gentlemen. You believe that they killed Blagolepov because he was talking too much and planned to go to the police?'

'No. It was some old man who killed him. More likely than not, he has nothing to do with all this. But even so, I can't get the captain's strange death out of my mind ...'

Vsevolod Vitalievich narrowed his eyes, blew a speck of dust off his sword and said thoughtfully:

'Strange or not, perhaps the old opium addict simply croaked on his own – but it gives us an excellent pretext to set up our own investigation. Why, of course! A Russian subject has expired in suspicious circumstances. In such cases, under the status of the Settlement, the representative of the injured party – that is, the Consul of the Russian Empire – has the right to conduct an independent investigation. You, Fandorin, have served in the police and had dealings with the Third Section, so you hold all the aces. Try to pick up the trail of the passengers from that night. Not yourself, of course.' Doronin smiled. 'Why put your own life in danger? As the vice-consul, you will merely head up the investigation, but the practical work will be carried out by the municipal police – they are not accountable to the Japanese authorities. I'll send an appropriate letter to Sergeant Lockston. But we'll warn the minister today. That's all, Fandorin. It's after ten, time to go and see Don Tsurumaki. Do you have a dinner jacket?'

The titular counsellor nodded absentmindedly – his thoughts were occupied with the forthcoming investigation.

'No doubt in mothballs and unironed?'

'Unironed, but with no m-mothballs – I wore it on the ship.'

'Excellent, I'll tell Natsuko to iron it immediately.'

The consul said something to the maid in Japanese, but Fandorin said:

'Thank you. I already have my own servant.'

'Good gracious! When did you manage to arrange that?' Doronin asked, staggered. 'Shirota wasn't planning to send you any candidates until tomorrow.'

'It just happened,' Erast Petrovich replied evasively.

'Well, well. Honest and keen, I trust?'

'Oh yes, very keen,' the younger man replied with a nod, avoiding the first epithet. 'And one other thing. I brought some new equipment with me in my luggage – a Remington typewriter with interchangeable Russian and Latin typefaces.'

'Yes, yes, I saw the advertisement in the *Japan Daily Herald*. It really is a very fine device. How is it they describe it?'

'A most convenient item for printing official documents,' Fandorin replied enthusiastically. 'It occupies only one corner of a room and weighs a little over four *p-pood*s. I tried it on the ship. The result is magnificent! But . . .' He lowered his eyes with a guilty expression. ' . . . we need an operator.'

'Where can we get one? And there is no provision for that position on the consulate staff.'

'I could teach Miss Blagolepova. And I would pay her salary out of my own pocket. After all, she would make my work considerably easier.'

The consul gave his assistant a searching look and whistled.

'You are an impetuous man, Fandorin. Barely even ashore yet, and you have already got mixed up in some nasty business, found a servant for yourself and taken care of your comforts of the heart. Apparently you will not be requiring an indigenous concubine.'

'That's not it at all!' the titular counsellor protested indignantly. 'It is simply that Sophia Diogenovna has nowhere to go. She has been left without any means of subsistence, after all . . . and an operator really would b-be of use to me.'

'So much so that you are prepared to support that operator yourself? Are you so very rich, then?'

Erast Petrovich replied with dignity:

'I won a considerable sum at dice today.'

'What an interesting colleague I do have,' the consul murmured, slipping the glittering sword blade back into the scabbard with a rakish whistle.

Like life's white hoarfrost
on death's winter windowpane,
the glints on the blade.

THE ERMINE'S GLASSY STARE

The dinner jacket had been ironed painstakingly but clumsily and it was somewhat puckered. However, the new servant had polished up the patent leather shoes until they glittered like crystal and the black top hat also gleamed brightly. And Doronin presented his assistant with a white carnation for a buttonhole. In short, when Erast Petrovich took a look at himself in the mirror, he was satisfied.

They set out in the following order: Vsevolod Doronin and Miss Obayasi at the front in a *kuruma*, followed by Fandorin on his tricycle.

Despite the late hour, the Bund promenade was still lively, and the eyes of people out for a stroll were drawn to the impressive sight of the cyclist riding by – the men gazed hostilely, the ladies with interest.

'You are creating a furore!' Doronin shouted jovially.

But Fandorin was thinking that Obayasi in her elegant grey and white kimono looked far more exquisite than the fashionable European ladies in their impossible hats and frilly dresses with bustles at the waist.

They rode across a bridge and up a low hill, and then Fandorin's eyes were greeted by a truly amazing sight, a picture illuminated by the moon: prim-looking villas, cast-iron railings with monograms, hedges – in short, an absolutely British town, that had been miraculously transported ten thousand miles from the Greenwich meridian.

'That is Bluff,' said the consul, pointing proudly. 'All the best society lives here. A genuine piece of Europe! Can you believe that ten years ago this was a wasteland? Just look at those lawns! And they say they have to be mown for three hundred years.'

Taking advantage of the fact that the road had widened, Erast Petrovich drew level with the *kuruma* and said in a low voice:

'You said this was a bachelor ball . . .'

'You mean Obasi? "Bachelor" has never meant "without women", merely "without wives". The European wives are too haughty and boring, they'll spoil any celebration. Concubines are a different matter. That's where Don Tsurumaki is so clever, he knows how to take the best from the East and the West. From the former, an aversion to hypocrisy; from the latter, the achievements of progress. You'll see for yourself soon. Don is a Japanese of the new generation: that is what they call them, "the new Japanese". They are today's masters of life. Some come from the samurai, some from the merchants, but there are some like our own Russian self-made men of common origin, who have suddenly become millionaires. The man we are going to visit was once known by the plebeian name of Jiro, which means simply "second son", and he had no surname at all, because in the old Japan commoners were not expected to have one. He took his surname recently, from the name of his native village. And to make it sound more impressive, he added the hieroglyph "*don*", meaning "cloud",' and became Donjiro, but after a while somehow the ending was forgotten and only Don-san was left, that is "Mr Cloud". And he really is like a cloud. Tumultuous, expansive, thunderous. The most un-Japanese of all Japanese. A kind of jolly bandit. You know, the kind who make good friends and dangerous enemies. Fortunately, he and I are friends.'

The two rikshas pulling the carriage stopped at a pair of tall open-work gates, beyond which the new arrivals could see a lawn illuminated by torches and, a little farther away, a large two-storey house with its windows glowing cheerfully, hung with coloured lanterns. A slowly moving procession of carriages and local *kurumas* stretched along the avenue leading to the house – the guests were getting out at the steps of the front porch.

'Tsurumaki is a village to the west of Yokohama,' Doronin continued, keeping one hand on the handlebars of Fandorin's tricycle, because Erast Petrovich was scribbling in a notepad and occasionally pressing his foot down on the pedal. 'Our former Jiro grew rich from construction contracts under the previous regime of the Shogun. Construction contracts have always been a shady and risky business, at all times and in all countries. The workers are a wild bunch. Keeping them under control requires strength and cunning. Don set up his own brigade of overseers, excellently trained and well armed, all the work was done on schedule and the clients were not concerned about the means used to achieve this result. When civil war broke out between the supporters of the Shogun and the supporters of the Mikado, he immediately realised which way the wind was blowing and joined the revolutionaries. He organised his supervisors and workers into fighting units – they were called "Black Jackets", from the colour of their work clothes. He fought a war for a couple of weeks, and he has been reaping the rewards ever since. Now he is a politician, and an entrepreneur, and a philanthropist. Mr Cloud has opened the country's first English school and a technical college, and even built a model prison – clearly in memory of his own past, which is itself enveloped in thick clouds. Without Don, our settlement would simply wither away. Half of the clubs and drinking establishments belong to him, the useful contacts with government officials, the profitable supply contracts – everything passes through him. The governors of the four surrounding prefectures come to him for advice, and even some ministers do the same ...' At this point Doronin stop in mid-phrase and jerked his chin cautiously to one side. 'Incidentally, there is an individual far more influential than Don. The senior foreign adviser of an imperial government, and the main enemy of Russian interests. The Right Honourable Algernon Bullcox in person.'

As Bullcox and his companion came closer, he cast a casual glance at the waiting guests and led his companion up to the steps. He was a most colourful gentleman: exuberant, fiery-red hair, sideburns covering half his face, a keen (indeed, predatory) glance and a white sabre scar on his cheek.

'What is so honourable about him, this Bullcox?' Fandorin asked in surprise.

Doronin chuckled.

'Nothing. I was referring to his title. Bullcox is a "Right Honourable", the youngest son of the Duke of Bradfordshire. One of those young, ambitious climbers that they call "the hope of the empire". He had a brilliant career in India. Now he is trying to conquer the Far East. And I am afraid that he will conquer it.' Doronin sighed. 'There is simply no comparison between our strength and the strength of the British – in both naval and diplomatic terms ...'

Catching the eye of the Right Honourable, the consul bowed coolly. The Briton inclined his head slightly and turned away.

'We still greet each other, as yet,' Doronin remarked. 'But if, God forbid, war should break out, we can expect anything at all from him. He is one of that breed who do not play by the rules and never accept that any goal is unachievable ...'

The consul went on to say something else about pernicious Albion, but at that precise moment something strange happened to Erast Petrovich – he could hear his superior's voice, he even nodded in reply, but he completely stopped understanding the meaning of the words. And the reason for this inexplicable phenomenon was trivial, even paltry. Algernon Bullcox's female companion, to whom Fandorin had so far paid no attention, suddenly turned round.

Absolutely nothing else at all happened. She simply looked round, and that was all. But in that second the titular counsellor's ears were filled with the chiming of silvery bells, his mind lost the ability to distinguish words and something altogether incredible happened to his vision: the surrounding world shrank to a small circle, leaving the periphery shrouded in darkness – but that circle was so distinct and so bright that every detail included in it seemed positively radiant. And the unknown lady's face was caught in this magical circle – or perhaps everything happened the other way round: the light radiating from that face was too bright, and that was why everything around went dark.

With an effort of will, Erast Petrovich tore himself away from the astounding sight for a moment to look at the consul – could he really not see it? But Vsevolod Vitalievich was moving his lips as if nothing had happened, producing inarticulate sounds, and apparently had not noticed anything out of the ordinary. So it's an optical illusion, whispered Fandorin's reason, which was accustomed to interpreting all phenomena from a rational viewpoint.

Never before had the sight of a woman, even the most beautiful, had such an effect on Erast Petrovich. He fluttered his eyelashes, squeezed his eyes shut and opened them again – and, thank the Lord, the enchantment disappeared. The titular counsellor saw before him a young Japanese woman –

a rare beauty, but no mirage, a living woman of flesh and blood. She was tall for a native woman, with a supple neck and exposed white shoulders. A nose with a slight crook in it, an unusual form to the elongated eyes stretching out towards the temples, a small mouth with plump lips. The beauty smiled in response to some remark from her beau, revealing her teeth – fortunately they were perfectly even. The only thing that might have been regarded as a defect from the viewpoint of the European canon were the charming, but distinctly protruding ears, nonchalantly exposed to view by the tall hairstyle. However, this regrettable prank of nature did nothing at all to spoil the overall impression. Fandorin recalled that Doronin had said protruding ears were considered a sign of sensuality in Japan.

But even so, the most striking thing about the woman was not the features of her face, but the vivacity that filled them and the grace of her movements. This became clear after the single second for which the Japanese woman had paused to allow the vice-consul to examine her so thoroughly, when she flung the end of her necklet back over her shoulder. This impetuous, fleeting gesture caused the glowing circle to reappear – although not quite as dramatically as the first time. The head of an ermine came to rest against the beauty's back.

Erast Petrovich started recovering his wits and even thought abstractedly that she was not so much beautiful as exotic. Indeed, she herself was rather like a predatory beast with precious fur – an ermine or a sable.

The lady carried on looking in Fandorin's direction – not, unfortunately, at his fine manly figure, but at his tricycle, which was a strange sight among the carriages and *kurumas*. Then she turned away, and Erast Petrovich felt a twinge in his heart, as if he had suffered some painful loss.

He looked at that white neck, the black curls on the back of that head, those ears protruding like two petals, and suddenly remembered something he had read somewhere: 'A true beauty is a beauty from all sides and all angles, no matter what point you observe her from'. A clasp in the form of an archer's bow glinted in the stranger's hair.

'E-er, why, you're not listening to me,' said the consul, touching the young man's sleeve. 'Lost in admiration of Miss O-Yumi, are you? No point in that.'

'Who is sh-she?'

Erast Petrovich tried very hard to make the question sound casual, but clearly did not succeed very well.

'A courtesan. A "Dame aux Camelias", but of the very highest class. O-Yumi began in the local brothel "Number Nine",' where she was wildly successful. She has excellent English, but can also make herself understood in German and Italian. She herself chooses who to be with. Do you see that clasp in her hair, shaped like a bow? "*Yumi*" means a bow. No doubt it is a hint at Cupid. At present she is kept by Bullcox, and has been for quite a long time. Don't gape at her, my dear boy. This bird of paradise flies too high for the likes of you and me. Bullcox is not only a handsome devil, he is rich too. Respectable ladies consider him a most interesting man, an attitude encouraged in no small measure by his reputation as a terrible hellraiser.'

Fandorin shrugged one shoulder.

'I was only looking at her out of curiosity. And I am not attracted to venal women. In general, I cannot even imagine how it is possible to b-be' – [here the titular counsellor's cheeks turned pink –] 'with a tainted woman who has belonged to God knows who.'

'Oh, how young and – pardon me – foolish you are,' Doronin said with a thoughtful smile. 'Firstly, a woman like that cannot belong to anyone. Everyone belongs to her. And secondly, my young friend, women are not tainted by love, they merely acquire radiance. But in any case, your sniffing should be categorised as "sour grapes".'

Their turn came to walk up on to the porch where the host was receiving his guests. Erast Petrovich gave his tricycle into the care of a valet and walked up the steps. Doronin led his concubine by the arm. For a brief moment she was beside the 'tainted woman', and Fandorin was astounded at how different these two Japanese women were: one endearing, meek and serene, while the other had an aura of glorious danger.

O-Yumi was just offering the host her hand for a kiss. He leaned down, so that his face was completely hidden, leaving in view just a fleshy nape and a red Turkish fez with a dangling tassel.

The ermine necklet slid down a long elbow glove and the Japanese beauty tossed it back over her shoulder again. Fandorin caught a momentary glimpse of a delicate profile and the moist gleam of eyes under trembling lashes.

Then the courtesan turned away, but the beady glass eyes of the furry ermine continued to observe the vice-consul.

Either it will bite,
Or tickle you with its fur,
The nimble ermine.

THE SILVER SLIPPER

The courtesan laughed as she said something to him, and the 'new Japanese' straightened up.

Fandorin saw a ruddy face, overgrown almost right up to the eyebrows with a thick black beard, a pair of exceptionally lively eyes and a lush mouth. Don Tsuramaki grinned, exposing remarkably firm teeth, and gave Bullcox a friendly slap on the shoulder.

Doronin was right: there was almost nothing Japanese in their host's manner and appearance – except for the slant of his eyes and his low stature.

A huge, thick cigar was smoking in his short-fingered hand, his large stomach was tightly bound in with a scarlet silk waistcoat, and an immense black pearl glinted on his tie.

'O-oh, my Russian friend!!' Don exclaimed in a booming voice. 'Welcome to an old bachelor's den! The incomparable Obayasi-san, *yoku ira-syshaimashita!*'* And this must be the assistant you have been waiting for so impatiently. What a fine young man! I'm afraid he will change my girls' minds about being re-educated!'

A hot palm squeezed the titular counsellor's hand tightly, and that was the end of the introduction: Tsurumaki gave a howl of joy and dashed over to embrace some American captain.

An interesting specimen, thought Erast Petrovich, looking around. A genuine dynamo electric machine.

An orchestra was playing in the hall, compensating for the dubious quality of its performance with bravura crashing and rumbling.

'Our volunteer fire brigade,' Vsevolod Vitalievich remarked. 'They're rather poor musicians, but there aren't any others in the city.'

The guests chattered cheerfully, standing in little groups, strolling about on the open terrace, helping themselves to refreshments from the long tables. Fandorin was surprised by the number of meat dishes – all sorts of ham, gammon, sausage, roast beef and quails.

Doronin explained.

'Until recent times the Japanese were vegetarians. They regard eating meat as a sign of enlightenment and progress, in the same way as our aristocrats regard drinking koumiss and chewing on sprouted grain.'

Most of the male guests were Europeans and Americans, but the majority

---

* 'Welcome' (Japanese)

of the women were Japanese. Some, like Obayasi, were wearing kimonos and others, like O-Yumi, had dressed up in the Western style.

An entire flower garden of beauties had gathered round a thin, fidgety gentleman who was showing them some pictures. He was Japanese, but dressed more meticulously than any dandy on London's Bond Street: a sparkling waistcoat, a gleaming brilliantined parting, a violet in his buttonhole.

'Prince Onokoji,' the consul whispered to Fandorin. 'The local arbiter of fashion. Also a product of progress, in a sense. There were no princes like that in Japan before.'

'And this, ladies, is a Madras cap from Bonnard,' Fandorin heard the prince say in an effeminate voice, burring his r's in the Parisian fashion, even though he was speaking English. 'The very latest collection. Note the frills and especially the bow. Seemingly so simple, but what elegance!'

Vsevolod Vitalievich shook his head.

'And he is descended from the *daimyo*, the ruling princes! The next province belonged entirely to his father. But now the appanage principalities have been abolished and the former *daimyo* have become state pensioners. Some, like this fop, have taken to their new status eagerly. No cares, no need to support a pack of samurai, live to please yourself, pluck the blossoms of pleasure and delight. Onokoji, of course, ruined himself instantly, but he is fed and kept by our generous Mr Cloud – in gratitude for the patronage that the prince's daddy extended to the bandit.'

Erast Petrovich moved off to one side to jot down in his notepad this useful information about progressive meat-eating and the *daimyo* receiving pensions. At the same time he tried to dash off a quick sketch of O-Yumi's profile: the curve of the neck, the nose with the smooth crook, the quick glance from under lowered eyelids. But it didn't look like her – there was something missing.

'Ah, there's the man we need,' said the consul, beckoning Fandorin.

Two men were talking in the corner, beside a column: the Right Honourable Bullcox, whom Fandorin already knew, and another gentleman, whose monocle and gaunt physique suggested that he might also be English. The conversation did not appear to be a friendly one; Bullcox was laughing hostilely and the other man was curling his thin lips angrily. The 'Dame aux Camelias' was not with them.

'That is Captain Bukhartsev,' said Lieutenant Vsevolod Vitalievich, leading his assistant across the hall. 'He's sparring with our British foe.'

Erast Petrovich looked more closely at the maritime agent, but still could not discover any indications of Russianness in this gentleman. The representatives of two rival empires were as alike as brothers. If one had to choose, then Bullcox could more easily be taken for a Slav, with his exuberant locks and open, energetic features.

No four-way conversation ensued, however. With a curt nod to Fandorin, who had been introduced to him by the consul, the Englishman announced that a lady was waiting for him and walked away, leaving the Russians to each other. Fandorin did not like the lieutenant captain's handshake – what strange sort of manner was that, to offer just the tips of the fingers? Mstislav Nikolaevich (the maritime agent's first name and patronymic) clearly wished to distance himself immediately and demonstrate that he was the most important one there.

'Abominable little Englishman,' Bukhartsev hissed through his teeth, watching Bullcox walk away through narrowed eyes. 'How dare he! "You should not forget that Russia ceased to be a great power twenty years ago!" How do you like that? I told him: "We have just defeated the Ottoman Empire, and you can't even deal with the pitiful Afghans!"'

'A fine riposte,' Vsevolod Vitalievich said approvingly. 'What did he say to that?'

'He tried to preach at me. "You are a civilised man. Surely it is clear that the world will only gain if it learns to live the British way?".'

This assertion set Fandorin thinking. What if the Englishman was right? If one had to choose how the world should live – the British way or the Russian way ... But at that point Erast Petrovich pulled himself up short. Firstly, for being unpatriotic, and, secondly, for posing the question incorrectly. First one had to decide whether it would be a good thing for the whole world to live according to a single model, no matter how absolutely wonderful it might be.

He pondered this complex question, at the same time listening to Doronin telling the agent in a low voice abut Captain Blagolepov's sinister passengers.

'Nonsense,' said Bukhartsev with a frown, but after a moment's thought, he said brightly, 'Although, go ahead. At least we'll demonstrate to the minister how greatly Russia is concerned for his safety. Let him remember we are his real friends, not the English.'

Just then their host, visible from a distance owing to his remarkable fez, went dashing towards the doors, where some kind of commotion was developing: some guests moved forward and others respectfully backed away, and a Japanese in a modest grey frock coat walked slowly into the hall. He halted in the doorway and greeted the assembled company with an elegant bow. His intelligent, narrow face, adorned with a drooping moustache, lit up in a pleasant smile.

'Ah, and here is our Bonaparte, speak of the devil,' the consul said to Fandorin. 'Let's move a bit closer.'

The minister's retinue jostled behind him. In contrast with the great man himself, they were decked out in sumptuous uniforms. It occurred to Erast Petrovich that perhaps Okubo really was imitating the Corsican: he had also liked to surround himself with gold-feathered peacocks, while he went about in a grey frock coat and frayed three-cornered hat. This was the grand chic of genuine, self-assured power.

'Well hello, you old bandit. Hello, you slanty-eyed Danton,' said the minister, shaking his host's hand with a jolly laugh.

'And hello to you, Your Equally Slanty-Eyed Excellency,' Tsurumaki responded in the same tone.

Erast Petrovich was rather shaken, both by the epithet and the familiarity. He glanced involuntarily at the consul, who whispered out of the corner of his mouth:

'They're old comrades-in-arms, from before the revolution. And that "slanty-eyed" business is just play-acting for the Europeans – it's no accident that they're speaking English.'

'Why "Danton", though?' Fandorin asked.

But Doronin did not need to answer – Tsurumaki did that for him.

'Take care, Your Excellency, if you cling to power so tightly, Dantons and Robespierres will be lining up against you. All the civilised countries have a constitution and a parliament, but what do we have in Japan? An absolute monarchy is a brake on progress, and you can't understand that!'

Although Don smiled, it was clear that the only jocular thing about his words was the tone in which they were spoken.

'It's too soon for you Asiatics to have a parliament,' the minister disagreed in a serious voice. 'First educate yourselves, and then we'll see.'

'Now do you understand why Russia likes Okubo so much?' asked Vsevolod Vitalievich, unable to resist the urge to seditious irony, although he spoke cautiously, directly into Fandorin's ear.

Bukhartsev, who had not heard this freethinking remark, said briskly:

'We won't be able to get to the minister now. But never mind, I can see the person we need.' He pointed to a military officer who was standing apart from the other members of the retinue. 'That is the vice-intendant of police, Kinsuke Suga. Although he is only the vice-intendant, everyone knows Suga is the true head of the imperial police. His superior is a purely decorative figure, a member of the Kyoto aristocracy.'

Bukhartsev squeezed through the crush, gestured to the policeman, and a moment later all four of them were in a quiet corner together, away from the crowd.

Having quickly disposed of the social formalities, the lieutenant captain got down to business. He was a sensible man after all – he stated the essence of the matter clearly, succinctly and yet comprehensively.

Suga listened, knitting his thick eyebrows together. He touched his curled moustache a couple of times and ran his hand nervously over his short-cropped brush of hair. Erast Petrovich had not yet learned to tell the age of locals, but to look at, the vice-intendant seemed about forty-five. The titular counsellor did not push himself forward, he stood behind the maritime agent and the consul, but the policeman addressed his response to him.

'Mr Vice-Consul, have you not confused anything here? The launch definitely went to Susaki that night, not to any other mooring?'

'I could not have confused that even if I wished to. I don't know Tokyo at all, I'm haven't even been there yet.'

'Thank you, you have gathered very important information,' said Suga, still addressing Fandorin directly, which caused a grimace of dissatisfaction to flit across the lieutenant captain's face. 'You know, gentlemen, that the steamship 'Kasuga-maru', the first modern ship that we have built without foreign help, is moored at Susaki. Last night His Excellency was there – at a banquet to mark the launching of the steamship. The Satsumans found out about that somehow and probably intended to lie in wait for the minister on his way back. Everyone knows that His Excellency moves about without any guards at any time of the day or night. If the officers of the ship, having taken a drink or two, had not got the idea of unharnessing the horses and pulling the carriage by hand, the assassins would certainly have carried out their criminal plan. You say that they ordered the launch again for the end of this night?'

'Yes, that is c-correct.'

'That means they know that today His Excellency will go back from here in the small hours. They could easily land at some mooring in Simbasi or Tsukiji, steal through the dark streets and set up an ambush at the minister's residence in Kasumigaseki. Gentlemen, you are doing our country a truly invaluable service! Come with me, I will take you to His Excellency.'

Suga whispered in the minister's ear and led him out of the respectful circle of guests towards the Russian diplomats

'Tomorrow all the local newspapers will write about this,' Bukhartsev said with a self-satisfied smile. 'It could even get into the *Times*, but not on the front page, of course: "The Strong Man of Japan Conspires with the Russian".'

The report on the situation was run through for a third time, this time in Japanese. Erast Petrovich caught a few familiar words: 'Fandorin', 'Rosia', '*katana*', 'Susaki', 'Kasuga-maru' – and the endlessly repeated '*satsumajin*' probably meant 'Satsumans'. The vice-intendant of police spoke forcefully and bowed frequently, but not subserviently, more as if he were nudging his phrases forward with his shoulders.

An expression of annoyance appeared on the minister's tired face and he replied sharply. Suga bowed again, even more insistently.

'What's happening?' Bukhartsev asked in a low voice – he obviously did not know Japanese.

'He refuses to accept a guard, but Suga is insisting,' Doronin translated quietly, then cleared his throat and said in English: 'Your Excellency, permit me to remark that you are behaving childishly. After all, in the final analysis, it is not a matter of your life, but of the future of the country that His Majesty the Emperor has entrusted to your management. And in any case, the guard is a temporary measure. I am sure that your police will make every effort to find the conspirators quickly. And for my part, as a consul, I will set up an investigative group in Yokohama – no, no, naturally not in connection with the anticipated attempt on Your Excellency's life (that would be interference in internal affairs), but in connection with the suspicious circumstances surrounding the demise of a Russian subject.'

'And I shall assign my most capable men to assist the investigative group, which will give you the support of the Japanese authorities,' put in Suga, also speaking English. 'I swear, Your Excellency, that the police guard will not bother you for long. The miscreants will be seized within a few days.'

'All right,' Okubo agreed reluctantly. 'I will tolerate it for three days.'

'Three days might not be enough,' Fandorin suddenly declared from behind the backs of the state officials. 'A week.'

Bukhartsev glanced round in horror at the violator of etiquette. Suga and Doronin also froze, evidently afraid that the minister would explode and tell them to go to hell and take their guard with them.

But Okubo looked intently at Erast Petrovich and said:

'Are you the man who has been assigned to lead the investigation? Very well, I give you one week. But not a single day longer. I cannot allow some cranks to limit my freedom of movement. And now, gentlemen, please excuse me, I have to talk to the British consul.'

He nodded and moved away.

'He did that deliberately,' Bukhartsev said in Russian with a sour face. 'To restore the balance. There won't be any article in the *Times*.'

But his voice was drowned out by Suga.

'Well done, Mr Fandorin! I would never have dared talk to His Excellency in that tone of voice. A whole week – that is wonderful! It means the minister has fully understood the seriousness of the threat. He would never have accepted bodyguards before. He believes in fate. He often repeats: "If I am still needed by my country, nothing will happen to me. And if I am no longer needed, then it is my destiny".'

'How shall we organise the investigation, General?' Bukhartsev enquired briskly. 'Which of your deputies will you attach to the consular group?'

The vice-intendant, however, addressed Fandorin, not the maritime agent.

'Your superior told me that you have worked in the police. That is very good. I will not give you a bureaucrat from the administration, but one of my inspectors – naturally, one who speaks English and knows Yokohama well. But I must warn you: the Japanese police are not much like the other police forces of the world. Our people are efficient, but they lack initiative – after all, not so long ago, they were all samurai, and a samurai was taught from the cradle not to think, but to obey. Many cling too tightly to the old traditions and simply cannot get used to firearms. They shoot incredibly badly. But never mind, my material may be in a rough state, but it is gold, pure 24 carat gold.' Suga spoke quickly and energetically, emphasising his words by waving his fist. 'Yes, my samurai have a long way to go to match the British constables and the French agents as far as police training is concerned, but they do not take bribes, they are diligent and willing to learn. Give us time, and we will create the finest police force in the world!'

Fandorin liked these passionate words, and the vice-intendant himself, very much. If only, he thought, our police force was run by enthusiasts like this, instead of stuffy gentlemen from the Department of Police. He was particularly struck by the fact that the police did not take bribes. Was that possible, or did the Japanese general have his head in the clouds?

Discussion of the details of future collaboration was interrupted by an unexpected event.

'Ee-ee-ee-ee!' a bevy of female voices squealed with such reckless enthusiasm that the men abandoned their conversation and looked round in amazement.

Don Tsurumaki was dashing across the hall.

'Surprise!' he shouted, pointing with a laugh to the curtain that covered one of the walls. That was where the squeal had come from.

The conductor waved his baton dashingly, the firemen rendered a thunderous, rollicking little motif, and the curtain parted to reveal a line of girls in gauzy skirts. They were Japanese, but they were under the command of a redheaded, long-limbed Frenchwoman.

'*Mes poules, allez-op!*' she shouted, and the girls in the line all hoisted their skirts and kicked one leg up into the air.

'A cancan!' the guests murmured. 'A genuine cancan!'

The dancers did not kick their legs up so very high, and the limbs themselves were perhaps rather short, but nonetheless the audience was absolutely delighted. The famous Parisian attraction must have been quite a curiosity in Japan – the surprise was an obvious success.

Erast Petrovich saw Obayasi gazing spellbound at the cancan – she turned pink and put her hand over her mouth. The other ladies were also staring wide-eyed at the stage.

The titular counsellor looked round for O-Yumi.

She was standing with her Briton, beating out the furious rhythm with her fan and moving her finely modelled head slightly as she followed the dancers' movements. Suddenly O-Yumi did something odd that probably no one but Fandorin could have seen – they were all so engrossed in the cancan. She lifted up the hem of her dress and kicked up her leg in its silk stocking – very high, above her head, far higher than the dancers. It was a long, shapely leg, and the movement was so sudden that the silver slipper slipped off her foot. After performing a glittering somersault in the air, this ephemeral object started falling and was caught deftly by Bullcox. The Englishman and his lady friend laughed, then the Right Honourable went down on one knee, took hold of the foot without a slipper, held the slim ankle slightly longer than was necessary and put the slipper back in its place.

Erast Petrovich felt a sharp, painful sensation and turned his eyes away.

With a true beauty,
Her simple silver slippers
Can also fly high

THE FIRST RAY OF SUNLIGHT

Late in the night, closer to the end of that interminable day, Erast Petrovich was sitting in the office of the head of the municipal police. They were waiting for the third member of the investigative group, the Japanese inspector.

In the not so distant past, Sergeant Walter Lockston had served as a guardian of the law in some cattle town in the Wild West of America, and he had retained all the manners of that uncivilised place. The sergeant sat there with his feet up on the table, swaying on his chair; his uniform cap was pushed forward almost as far as his nose, like a cowboy hat, he had a dead cigar protruding from the corner of his mouth and two massive revolvers hanging on his belt.

The policeman never stopped talking for a moment, cracking jokes and doing everything possible to demonstrate that he was a regular down-to-earth fellow, but Fandorin became more and more convinced that Lockston was not as simple as he was pretending to be.

'The career I've had, you wouldn't believe it,' he said, stretching out his vowels mercilessly. 'Normal people get promoted from sergeants to marshals, but with me it's all backwards. In that dump that had five thousand cows to five hundred people, where the crime of the century was the theft of sixty-five dollars from the local post office, I was called a marshal. And here in Yokohama, where there are almost ten thousand people, not counting the danged hordes of slanty-eyed locals, I'm only a sergeant. And at the same time, my assistant's a lieutenant. Ain't that a hoot! That's the way it's set up. A sergeant, eh? When I write letters home, I have to lie, I sign them "Captain Lockston". That's what I should rightfully be, a captain. This sergeant business is some European contrivance of yours. So tell me, Rusty, do you have sergeants in Russia?'

'No,' replied Erast Petrovich, who had already resigned himself to that appalling 'Rusty', which was the result, on the one hand, of Lockston's inability to pronounce the name 'Erast' and, on the other, of the grey hair on the titular counsellor's temples. The only thing that irritated him was the stubbornness with which the office's incumbent avoided talking about the matter at hand. 'We don't have sergeants in the police. Walter, I asked you what you know about that establishment, the "Rakuen"?'

Lockston took the cigar out of his mouth and spat brown saliva into the wastepaper basket. He looked at the Russian with his watery, slightly bulging eyes and seemed to realise that this man would not give up that easily. He screwed up his copper-red face into a wince and said reluctantly:

'You see, Rusty, the Rakuen is on the other side of the river, and that's not the Settlement. That's to say, legally speaking it's our territory, but white folks don't live there, only yellowbellies. So we don't usually stick our noses in there. Sometimes the Jappos stab each other to death, it happens all the time. But until they touch the white folk, I do nothing. That's something like an unspoken agreement that we have.'

'But in this case there is a suspicion that a Russian subject has been killed.'

'So you told me,' Lockston said with a nod. 'And you know what I have to say to that? Bullshit, drivel. If your Mr B. kicked the bucket because some drunk happened to catch him on the neck with a finger, the old man must have been on his last legs already. What damned kind of murder is that? Let me tell you what a real murder looks like. This one time at Buffalo Creek . . .'

'But what if Blagolepov *was* murdered?' the embassy official interrupted after he had listened to several harrowing stories from the criminal history of the cowboy town.

'Well then . . .' The sergeant screwed his eyes up fiercely. 'Then the slanty-eyes will answer to me for it. If it really is one of their lousy oriental tricks, they'll regret they ever did the dirt on my territory. The year before last at the Ogon-basi bridge (and that, note, is already outside the bounds of the Settlement) they stabbed a French officer-boy. From behind, sneaky-like. This psychopath, an ex-samurai, turned nasty because his kind had been forbidden to carry swords. Whatever happens here, for them the whites are always to blame. So I called out all my lads and caught the son of a bitch, he hadn't even washed the blood off his sword yet. How he begged me to let him slice his belly open! Well, screw him. I dragged him round the native quarter on a rope, to let the yellowbellies get a good look, and afterwards I strung him up with the same rope, no messing. Of course, the Jappos made a big scandal of it. Said they ought to have tried the psycho themselves and chopped his head off, the way they do things round here. I don't think so. I prefer to pay my own debts. And if I come to believe that your compatriot didn't kick the bucket on his own, but some Jap gave him a hand . . .' Lockston didn't finish what he was saying: he simply slammed his fist down eloquently on the desk.

'Do you know the inspector who has been assigned to us from the Japanese police? The g-gentleman is called Goemon Asagawa.'

Erast Petrovich deliberately spoke about the Japanese with emphatic correctness, making it clear that he did not like the sergeant's choice of words. The American seemed to take the hint.

'I know him. He's in charge of the station on Wagon Street, that's in the Native Town. Of all the yellow . . . Of all the Japanese, Go is the smartest. We've worked together a couple of times already, on mixed cases when the mischief-makers were whites and yell . . . I mean natives. He's a really young guy, only thirty, but experienced. He's been in the police about fifteen years.'

'How is that possible?' Fandorin asked in surprise.

'Well, he's a hereditary *yoriki*.'

'Who?'

'A *yoriki*, it's like a precinct cop. Under the old regime, the shoguns, the usual thing was for every trade, even every job, to pass from father to son. For instance, if your father was a water-carrier, then you're going to spend your entire life carting around barrels of water. If your old man was the deputy head of the fire brigade, then you'll be the deputy head too. That was why everything here fell apart on them – there was no point in straining yourself, you couldn't jump any higher than your dear old dad anyway. And Go's from a family of *yoriki*. When his father was killed by a robber, the lad was only thirteen. But order is order: he hung two swords on his belt, picked up a truncheon and went to work. He told me that the first year he carried the long sword under his arm so that it wouldn't drag along the ground.'

'But can a b-boy really maintain order in an entire neighbourhood?'

'He can here, because the Jappos . . . the Japanese don't look at the man so much, they look at the position and the rank. And then, they respect the police here – they're all samurai to a man. And then, Rusty, bear in mind that guys who were born into *yoriki* families have been taught the whole body of police science since they were little kids: how to catch a thief, how to disarm robbers and tie them up, and they can handle a truncheon in a fight like our cops have never even dreamed of. I think Go could do plenty when he was thirteen.'

Erast Petrovich listened with great interest.

'And how is their police organised now?'

'On the English model. There are out-of-work samurai everywhere you look now, so there's no shortage of volunteers. If you're interested in the details, ask Go – here he comes.'

Fandorin looked out of the window at the well-lit square and saw a tall Japanese in a black uniform jacket and white trousers, with a sword hanging at his side. He was walking towards the station, swinging his right arm in military style.

'You see he has a revolver on his belt,' said Lockston, pointing. 'That's unusual for a native. They prefer to use a stick or, at a pinch, a sword.'

Inspector Asagawa was taciturn and calm, with a still face and quick eyes that were surely highly observant. The titular counsellor liked him. The Japanese began by ceremoniously but quite decisively putting the noisy sergeant in his place.

'I am glad to see you too, Mr Lockston. Only please, if it is not too difficult for you, call me Goemon and not Go, although we Japanese feel more comfortable when we are addressed by our surnames. No thank you, I won't have any coffee. Concerning my health and so forth, with your permission, we can talk later about that. My superiors have informed me that I come under the command of the vice-consul. What are your orders, Mr Fandorin?'

In this way the conversation was immediately set on business lines.

Erast Petrovich briefly described their goal.

'Gentlemen, we have to find three samurai from Satsuma whom the

Russian subject Captain Blagolepov carried on his launch last night. We have to ascertain if these men were involved in his sudden death.'

Fandorin didn't say anything about the political background to the investigation. Asagawa understood and apparently approved – at least, he nodded.

'Well, and how are we going to find them and ascertain that?' asked Lockston.

'These men hired the captain to take them to Tokyo again before dawn today, they even p-paid him an advance. So our first action will be as follows: we will go to the spot where the launch is moored and see if the Satsumans show up at the agreed time or not. If they do not, it means they know that the captain is dead. That will serve to strengthen the suspicion that they are involved in his death. That is one.'

'What's the point?' the sergeant asked with a shrug. 'So it will strengthen the suspicion. But where do we look for those three, that's the catch.'.

'The daughter of the deceased told me that most of her father's clients were supplied by the owner of the Rakuen. I assume that these three also made their arrangements with the owner of the launch and not with the captain. I can't be completely certain of that, but let us not forget that the suspicious blow to his neck was inflicted inside the Rakuen. Which brings me to the second stage of this investigation: if the Satsumans do not show up, we shall turn our attention to Mr Semushi.'

Lockston chewed on his cigar, thinking over what Fandorin had said, but the Japanese was already on his feet.

'In my humble judgement, your plan is very good,' he said briefly. 'I shall take ten experienced police officers. We shall surround the mooring and wait.'

'And I'll take six of the lads, the entire night shift,' said the sergeant, also getting up.

Erast Petrovich summed up the situation.

'So, if the Satsumans come, they are no longer under suspicion of the captain's death. We hand them over to the Japanese police, who can deal with finding out who they are and what their intentions were. If the Satsumans do not come, the investigation remains within the competence of the consulate and the m-municipal police . . .'

'And make no mistake, we'll find those sons of bitches, wherever they are,' the American put in. 'We'll go straight from the mooring to the hunch-backed Jappo's place and shake the very soul out of him.'

Fandorin couldn't help it, he shuddered at that 'Jappo' and was about to rebuke the sergeant for his intemperate speech, but it turned out that Inspector Asagawa had no intention of letting his nation be insulted.

'The Japanese soul, Mr Lockston, is hidden deeper than it is in white people. It is not so easy to shake out, especially with a man like Semushi. He is an *akunin*, of course, but by no means a weakling.'

'Who is he?' Fandorin asked, knitting his brows together at the sound of an unfamiliar word.

'An *akunin* is like an evil man or a villain,' Asagawa tried to explain. 'But not entirely . . . I don't think the English language has a precise translation for it. An *akunin* is an evil man, but he is not petty, he is a strong man. He has his own rules, which he defines for himself. They do not conform to the prescriptions of the law, but an *akunin* will sacrifice his life for the sake of his rules, and so he inspires respect as well as hate.'

'There is no word for that in Russian either,' Fandorin admitted after a moment's thought. 'But g-go on.'

'Semushi undoubtedly breaks the law. He is a cruel and cunning bandit. But he is not a coward, otherwise he could not hold on to his position. I have been working my way towards him for a long time. I have arrested him twice: for smuggling and on suspicion of murder. But Semushi is one of a new breed. He does not act like the bandits of former times. And most importantly of all, he has protectors in high places . . .'

Asagawa hesitated and stopped, as if realising that he had said too much.

He doesn't want to hang out his dirty laundry in front of foreigners, Fandorin guessed, and decided to leave any questions for later, when he got to know the inspector better

'Know what I have to say to you guys?' said Lockston, narrowing his eyes sceptically. 'We're not going to get anywhere. We won't prove the old dope-smoker was bumped off. With just a finger. It's not possible.'

'And is it possible for the touch of a finger to leave a burn mark on the neck, through a celluloid collar?' Fandorin countered. 'All right, it's too early to argue about that. Let's go to the mooring and wait for the samurai. If they don't come, we'll work on the owner of the Rakuen. But Mr Asagawa is right – we can't go at this like a bull at a gate. Tell me, Inspector, do you have agents in civilian dress . . . that is, I mean, not in uniforms, but in kimonos?'

The Japanese smiled gently.

'The kimono is formal wear. But I understand your question, Mr Vice-Consul. I have very good agents – in Japanese clothing and in European frock coats. We will put Semushi under secret surveillance.'

'And from what my servant can tell me, I shall compose a verbal p-portrait of the man who touched Blagolepov's neck. But let us not get ahead of ourselves. Perhaps the Satsumans will show up after all?'

The deceased Captain Blagolepov's launch was tied up among fishing boats at a berth a long way from the Settlement.

The ambush was already in place two hours before the dawn. The Japanese police were ensconced under the decking of the jetty, on the launch itself and on the boats beside it. Lockston and his constables were posted on the shore, in a warehouse.

It was very dark and very quiet;, the only sound was the breathing of the bay, and every now and then the moon peeped out for a short while from behind the clouds. Erast Petrovich had found the prospect of sitting in the warehouse with the white policeman uninteresting. He wanted to be with Asagawa and his men in the immediate vicinity of the launch. The titular counsellor and four of the Japanese policemen had taken up a post under the pier, up to their knees in water. After a quarter of an hour Fandorin started feeling cold, and half an hour after that his teeth were chattering wildly, but he had to put up with it in order not to disgrace himself in front of the locals.

When there was moonlight filtering through between the boards of the pier, the young man examined his silent companions. Not one of them had a firearm, or even cold steel – only long staffs. But during the fight at the Rakuen, Erast Petrovich had seen how effective this weapon was in the hands of a master, so he contemplated the Japanese men's unimpressive equipment with respect.

What surprised the titular counsellor most of all was that four of the ten men brought by Asagawa were wearing spectacles. It was absolutely impossible to imagine a Russian constable in glasses – the very idea was enough to make a cat laugh. But for the Japanese officers it seemed to be in the accepted order of things. Unable to quell his curiosity, Fandorin quietly asked the inspector what was the reason for this phenomenon – was it perhaps a national disposition to short-sightedness?

The inspector replied seriously and comprehensively. He explained that from the day they were born men of the samurai class had a predilection for reading and self-education. And the pursuit of book-learning was particularly well developed in the police – which was good for the job, but bad for the eyesight. Nonetheless, this activity was enthusiastically encouraged by the high command, for now, in these times of progress, the representatives of authority should be educated individuals – otherwise the public would lose all respect for them, and contempt for the representatives of authority was detrimental to society.

So there was Erast Petrovich with his teeth chattering, up to his knees in water, pondering the terrible mistake that the government of his homeland had made by not involving the landed gentry in socially useful activity following the liberation of the peasantry. If only at that point they had disbanded the appalling Russian police – illiterate, corrupt through and through – and started taking young men from the nobility as police constables in the cities and rural districts. What a wonderful idea – a police force that is more educated and more high-minded that its fellow citizens, a police force that is a model for emulation! Russia had so many starry-eyed idlers with a grammar-school education! And now they were living totally useless lives, or else youthful idealism and the energy of unspent passion drove them to join the revolutionaries. What a loss for the state and society!

When he hit his forehead against a rough beam of timber, Erast Petrovich realised that his mind had slipped imperceptibly into the drowsy realm of daydreams. Noble police constables – what an absurd fantasy!

He shook his head to drive sleep away and took his watch out of his pocket. Three minutes after four. The gloom was starting to brighten.

And when the first, hesitant ray of sunlight stretched out across the dark-blue waters of the bay, it finally became clear that the Satsumans would not come.

It seemed like the end,
No hope left. But suddenly –
The first ray of sun.

A *MAMUSI'S* HEART

While his master was sleeping, Masa managed to do many important jobs. A thoughtful, responsible approach was what was required here – after all, it's not every day that a man starts a new life.

Masa did not know much about *gaijins*, and he knew almost nothing at all about his master, and, naturally, that made him feel a bit timid – he didn't want to make a mess of things, but his spirit was filled with the zeal of devotion, and that was the most important thing.

Shirota-san had explained Masa's duties to him the day before: do the housekeeping, buy provisions, prepare food, clean clothes – in short, do everything to meet his master's every need. Masa had been given twenty yen to cover outgoings and also his salary for a month in advance.

The salary was generous, and he spent it as befitted a devoted retainer, that is, on acquiring an appearance worthy of his position.

The Yakuza known as Badger had died with the Chobei-gumi gang. Now the same body was inhabited by a man called Sibata-san – no, better 'Mister Masa' – who had to live up to his calling.

The first thing Masa did was pay a visit to the barber and have his lacquered pigtail shaved off. Of course, the result was not very beautiful to see: white on top and black at the sides, like an old *gaijin's* bald patch. But Masa's hair grew with remarkable speed: in two days the back of his head would be covered with stubble and in a month he would have a wonderful stiff brush. It would be clear straight away that the owner of a head like that was a modern individual, a man of European culture. Like in that song everyone was singing in Tokyo:

> Tap a lacquer-pigtailed head
> For full elucidation.
> Hear the dull and obtuse thud
> Of musty, crass stagnation.
>
> Tap a trim and tidy head
> For full elucidation.
> Hear the clear, progressive note
> Of bright illumination.

Masa knocked on the freshly trimmed crown of his own head and was pleased with the sound. And while his hair was growing, he could wear a hat – he bought a fine felt bowler, only very slightly frayed, for just thirty sen in a second-hand clothes shop.

He bought his outfit in the same place: jacket, shirt-front and cuffs, check trousers. He tried on a heap of shoes, boots and half-boots, but decided to wait for a while with the *gaijin* footwear – it was very stupid and uncomfortable, and took such a long time to put on and take off. He kept his wooden *geta*.

Having transformed himself into a genuine foreigner, he visited one of his former girlfriends, who had taken a job with the family of an American missionary: first, to show off his newly acquired chic and, secondly, to ask about the habits and customs of *gaijins*. He obtained a great deal of surprising and very useful information, although not without some difficulty, because the brainless girl pestered him with her amorous advances and slobbered all over him. But he had come on serious business, after all, not just to fool about.

Now Masa felt sufficiently prepared to set to work.

It was a real stroke of luck that his master didn't come back until dawn and slept almost until midday – there was enough time to prepare everything properly.

Masa put together an elegant breakfast: he brewed some wonderful barley tea, then took a wooden plate and set out on it pieces of sea centipede, yellow sea-urchin caviar and transparent slices of squid; he arranged the marinated plums and salted radish beautifully; he boiled the most expensive rice and sprinkled it with crushed seaweed; and he could feel especially proud of the absolutely fresh, snow-white tofu and fragrant tender-brown *natto* paste of fermented soybeans. The tray was decorated according to the season with small yellow chrysanthemums.

He carried this beautiful display into the bedroom, where he sat down on the floor without making a sound and started waiting for his master to wake up at last. But his master didn't open his eyes; he was breathing calmly and quietly, and the only movement was the trembling of his long eyelashes.

Ai, this was not good! The rice would get cold! The tea would stand for too long!

Masa thought and thought about what to do, and a brilliant idea occurred to him.

He filled his lungs right up with air and gave a great sneeze.

A-tishoo!

His master jerked upright on the bed, opened his strange-coloured eyes and gazed in amazement at his seated retainer.

Masa bowed low, begged forgiveness for the noise he had made and held out one hand spattered with saliva, as if to say: It couldn't be helped, an impulse of nature.

And then straight away, with a broad smile, immediately held out to his master the magnificent earthenware chamber pot that he had bought for ninety sen. Masa had learned from his former girlfriend that foreigners put this object under the bed for the night and did their *gaijin* business in it.

But his master did not seem pleased to see the chamber pot and waved his hand, as if to say: Take it away, take it away. Evidently Masa should have bought the white one, not the pink one with beautiful flowers.

Then Masa helped his master get washed, examining his white skin and firm muscles as he did so. He wanted very much to take a look at how a *gaijin*'s male parts were arranged, but for some reason the master sent his faithful servant out of the room before he washed the lower part of his body.

The breakfast was a magnificent success.

Of course, he had to spend some time teaching his master to use the chopsticks, but *gaijins* had nimble fingers. That was because they were descended from monkeys – they admitted that themselves, and they weren't ashamed of it at all.

Masa's master delighted him with his excellent appetite, and he had an interesting way of swallowing his food. First he bit off a small piece of centipede, then he wrinkled his face right up (no doubt in delight) and finished it off very quickly, washing it down greedily with barley tea. He gagged on the tea and started coughing, his mouth opened wide and his eyes gaped. That was like the Koreans – they belched when they wanted to show how delicious something was. Masa made a mental note that he must prepare twice as much next time.

After breakfast there was a language lesson. Shirota-san had said that the master wanted to learn Japanese – not like the other foreigners, who forced their servants to learn their language.

The lesson went like this.

The master pointed at various parts of his face and Masa told him their Japanese names: eye – *meh*, forehead – *hitai*, mouth – *kuti*, eyebrow – *mayu*. His pupil wrote these down in a notebook and repeated them diligently. His pronunciation was funny, but of course Masa didn't permit himself even a tiny little smile.

The master drew a human face on a separate page and indicated its various parts with little arrows. That was clear enough. But then he started asking about something that Masa didn't understand.

He could make out some words: 'Rakuen' and *satsumajin* – but what they referred to remained a mystery. His master pretended to be sitting there with his eyes closed, then he jumped up, staggered, waved one arm about and prodded Masa in the neck, then pointed to the face he had drawn and said, as if he was asking a question:

'*Meh? Kuti?*'

Eventually, having reduced Masa to a state of complete bewilderment, he sighed, ruffled up his hair and sat down.

And then the most unusual part began.

The master ordered Masa to stand facing him, held out his clenched fists and started gesturing, as if he was inviting Masa to kick him.

Masa was horrified and for a long time he refused: how could he possibly kick his *onjin*? But then he remembered an interesting detail about the *gaijins'* intimate life, something that his former girlfriend had told him. She had spied on what the missionary and his wife did when they were in the bedroom and seen her mistress, wearing nothing but a black bodice (apart from her riding boots), beating the sensei with a whip on his bare *o-siri*, and him asking her to hit him again and again.

That must be how the *gaijins* did things, Masa guessed. He bowed respectfully and struck his master in the chest with his foot, not very hard – right between absurdly extended fists.

The master fell over on to his back, but jumped up straight away. He clearly liked it and asked Masa to do it again.

This time he started springing about and following Masa's every movement closely, so Masa couldn't hit him straight away. The secret of ju-jitsu, or 'the art of soft combat', is to follow your opponent's breathing. Everyone knows that strength enters into you with the air, and it leaves you with the air too; breathing in and out is the alternation of strength and weakness, fullness and emptiness. So Masa waited until his in-breath coincided with his master's out-breath and repeated the attack.

His master fell down again, and this time he was really pleased. *Gaijins* truly were different from normal people, after all.

Having received what he wanted, the master put on a beautiful uniform and went to the central part of the building, to serve the Russian emperor. Masa did a bit of tidying and took up a position at the window, with a view of the garden and the opposite wing, where the consul lived (how could servants work for a man with such a shameful name?).

In the morning Masa's eye had been caught by the consul's maid, a girl by the name of Natsuko. His instinct told him it would be worthwhile spending a bit of time on her – it could lead to something.

He could see the girl doing the cleaning, moving from room to room, but she didn't look out of the window.

Masa opened the curtains a bit wider, put a mirror on the windowsill and started pretending to shave – exactly the way his master did. Masa's cheeks were round and remarkably smooth, no beard grew on them, the Buddha be praised, but why shouldn't he lather them up with fragrant foam?

Working away gravely with the brush, Masa moved the mirror about a bit, trying to direct a spot of sunlight into Natsuko's eyes.

He had to break off for a while, because Shirota-san and the dead captain's yellow-haired daughter came out into the garden. They sat down on a bench under a young gingko tree and the interpreter began reading something out loud from a book, waving his hand about at the same time. Every now and then he cast a sideways glance at the young lady, but she sat with her eyes lowered and didn't look at him at all. Such a learned man, but he had no idea how to court women, Masa thought, feeling sorry for Shirota-san. He ought to turn away from her completely and be casual, uttering only an occasional word. Then she wouldn't turn her nose up, she'd start worrying that perhaps she wasn't attractive enough.

They sat there for about a quarter of an hour, and when they left they forgot the book, leaving it on the bench. It was lying there with the front cover facing upwards. Standing up on tiptoe, Masa was able to make out the cover – it showed a *gaijin* with frizzy hair and curly hair on his cheeks at both sides, exactly like the orang-utan Masa had seen in the Asakusa park last week. There were lots of curiosities on show there: a performance by a master of passing wind, and a woman who smoked with her navel, and a spider-man with an old man's head and the body of a five-year-old child.

He started fiddling with the mirror again, turned it this way and that, and eventually, after about half an hour, he was successful. Natsuko started showing interest in the ray of light that kept getting in her eyes. She turned her head right and left, glanced out of the window and saw the vice-consul's servant. By that time, of course, Masa had already set the mirror on the windowsill and was making wild eyes as he waved a sharp razor about in front of his face.

The girl froze with her mouth open – he saw that very clearly out of the corner of his eye. He knitted his eyebrows together, because women appreciate sternness in a man; he pushed his cheek out with his tongue, as his master had done earlier, and turned sideways on to Natsuko, so she wouldn't feel shy about examining her new neighbour more closely.

In about an hour's time he should go out into the garden. As if he needed to clean his master's sword (the narrow one in a beautiful scabbard with a gilded hilt). He could be sure Natsuko would also find herself something to do out there.

The maid stared at him for about a minute and then disappeared.

Masa stuck his head out of the window: it was important to understand why she had gone away – whether her mistress had called her or he had failed to make a strong enough impression.

There was a faint rustling sound behind him.

Erast Petrovich's valet tried to turn round, but he was suddenly overcome by an irresistible urge to sleep. Masa yawned, stretched and slid down on to the floor. He started snoring.

Roused from sleep by a deafening sound of uncertain origin, Erast Petrovich jerked upright on the bed and for a brief moment felt frightened: there was an outlandish Oriental sitting on the floor, dressed in check trousers, a white shirt-front and a black bowler hat. The Oriental was watching the titular counsellor intently, and when he saw that Erast Petrovich had woken up, he swayed forward, like a bobbling Chinese doll.

And then Fandorin recognised his new servant. What was his name? Ah, yes, Masa.

The breakfast prepared by this native Sancho Panza was a nightmare. How could they eat that slimy, smelly, cold stuff? And raw fish! And gooey rice that stuck to the roof of your mouth! And it was better not even to think about what that sticky diarrhoea-coloured glue was made of. Not wishing to offend the Japanese, Fandorin quickly swallowed all this poison and washed it down with tea, but the tea seemed to have been brewed out of fish scales.

The attempt to compose a verbal portrait of the suspicious old man from the Rakuen ended in failure – it couldn't be done without an interpreter, and the titular counsellor had not yet decided whether it was appropriate to let Shirota know all the details of the investigation.

But on the other hand, the introductory lesson on Japanese pugilism was a tremendous success. English boxing proved to be quite powerless against it. Masa moved with incredible speed and he struck with strength and precision. How right it was to fight with the legs instead of the arms! The lower limbs were so much stronger and longer! This was a skill well worth learning.

Then Erast Petrovich put on his uniform with the red cuffs and went to the consular premises to present himself to his superior with all due cere-mony – for after all, this was his first day in his new position.

Doronin was sitting in his office, dressed in a frivolous shantung two-piece suit, and he gestured at the uniform as if it were a piece of silly nonsense.

'Tell me, quickly!' he exclaimed. 'I know you got back early in the morning, and I've been waiting impatiently for you to wake up. Naturally, I understand that you came back empty-handed, otherwise you would have come to report straight away, but I want to know all the details.'

Fandorin briefly expounded the meagre results of the investigation's first operation and announced that he was ready to perform his routine duties, since he had nothing else to deal with for the time being – until information was received from the Japanese agents who were following the hunchback.

The consul pondered that for a moment.

'So, what do we have? The instigators didn't show up, thereby only deepening our suspicions. The Japanese police are searching for three men who speak the Satsuma dialect and have swords. And the hilt of one man's sword, the one who has a withered arm, is covered with glasspaper (if the captain didn't imagine it). At the same time your group has focused its attention on the owner of the Rakuen and the mysterious old man whom your servant saw near Blagolepov. We'll get a verbal portrait – I'll have a word with Masa myself. I tell you what, Fandorin. Forget your vice-consular duties for the present, Shirota will manage on his own. You need to study the Settlement and its surroundings as soon as possible. It will make your detective work easier. Let's take a pedestrian excursion around Yokohama. Only get changed first.'

'With great pleasure,' Erast Petrovich said, and bowed. 'But first, if you will p-permit me, I shall take a quarter of an hour to show Miss Blagolepova the principles of the typewriter.'

'Very well. I shall call for you at your quarters in half an hour.'

*

In the corridor he met Sophia Diogenovna – she seemed to have been waiting for the young man. When she saw him, she blushed and pressed the book she was holding tight against her chest.

'There, I left it behind in the garden,' she whispered, as if she were making excuses for something. 'Kanji Mitsuovich, Mr Shirota, gave me it to read . . .'

'Do you like Pushkin?' asked Fandorin, glancing at the cover and wondering whether he ought to offer the young spinster his condolences on the occasion of her father's demise once again, or whether enough had been said already. He decided it would be better not to – she might burst into floods of tears again.

'He writes quite well, but it's very long-winded,' Sophia Diogenovna replied. 'We were reading Tatyana's letter to the object of her passion. Some girls are really so daring. I would never have dared . . . but I really love poetry. Before Papa took to smoking, sailor gentlemen often used to visit us, they wrote things in my album. One conductor from the St Pafnutii composed very soulful poems.'

'And what did you like best?' Erast Petrovich asked absentmindedly.

The young lady lowered her eyes and whispered.

'I can't recite it . . . I'm too embarrassed. I'll write it out for you and send it later, all right?'

At this point 'Kanjii Mitsuovich' glanced out of the door leading to the office. He gave the vice-consul a strange look, bowed politely and announced that the writing machine had been unpacked and installed.

The titular counsellor led the new operator off to introduce her to this great achievement of progress.

Half an hour later, exhausted by his pupil's inept diligence, Erast Petrovich went to get changed for the proposed excursion. He took his boots off in the entrance hall and unbuttoned his short undercoat and shirt, in order not to delay Vsevolod Vitalievich, who was due to appear at any minute.

'Masa!' the titular counsellor called as he walked into the bedroom. He spotted his servant immediately. He was sleeping peacefully on the floor under the open window, and hovering over him was a little old Japanese man in worker's clothes: grey jacket, narrow cotton trousers, straw sandals over black stockings.

'What's g-going on here? And who are you, anyway?' Fandorin began, but broke off, first because he realised that the native man was hardly likely to understand English and, secondly, because he was astounded by the little old man's behaviour.

The old man smiled imperturbably, transforming his face into a radiant mass of wrinkles, slipped his hands into his broad sleeves and bowed – he was wearing a close-fitting cap on his head.

'What's wrong with Masa?' Fandorin asked, unable to resist uttering further pointless words. He dashed across to his sweetly snuffling valet and leaned down over him – Masa really was asleep.

What kind of nonsense was this!

'Hey, wait!' the titular counsellor shouted to the old man, who was ambling towards the door.

When the little old man didn't stop, the vice-consul overtook him in two bounds and grabbed him by the shoulder. Or rather, he tried to. Without even turning round, the Japanese swayed imperceptibly to one side, and the vice-consul's figures clutched at empty air.

'Dear man, I d-demand an explanation,' said Erast Petrovich, growing angry. 'Who are you? And what are you doing here?'

His tone of voice, and the situation in general, should have rendered these questions comprehensible without any translation.

Realising that he would not be allowed to leave, the old man turned to face the vice-consul. He wasn't smiling any more. The black eyes, glittering like two blazing coals, observed Fandorin calmly and attentively, as if they were deciding some complicated but not particularly important problem. This cool gaze finally drove Fandorin into a fury.

This Oriental was damned suspicious! He had clearly sneaked into the building with some criminal intent!

The titular counsellor reached out his hand to grab the thief (or, perhaps, spy) by the collar. This time the old man didn't dodge; without taking his hands out of his sleeves, he simply struck Fandorin on the wrist with his elbow.

The blow was extremely light, almost insubstantial, but the titular counsellor's arm went completely numb and dangled uselessly at his side – the elbow must have hit some kind of nerve centre.

'Why, damn you!' Erast Petrovich exclaimed.

He delivered a superb left hook, which should have flattened the obnoxious old man against the wall, but his fist merely described a powerful arc through the empty air. The inertia spun Fandorin round his own axis and left him standing with his back to the Japanese.

The villainous intruder immediately took advantage of this and struck him on the neck with his other elbow, again very lightly, but the young man's knees buckled. He collapsed flat on his back and was horrified to feel that he couldn't move any part of his body.

It was like a nightmare!

The most terrifying thing of all was the searing, blazing gaze of the old man's eyes; it seemed to penetrate into the prostrate vice-consul's very brain.

The old man leaned down, and that was when the most incredible thing of all happened.

He finally took his hands out of his sleeves.

In his right hand he was clutching a greyish-brown snake with small, beady, glittering eyes. Gripped tight by the neck, it was straining its jaws open.

The prone man groaned – that was all he had the strength for.

The snake slithered smoothly out of the sleeve and fell on to Fandorin's chest in a springy coil. He felt its touch on his skin, at the spot where his collar was unbuttoned – a cold, rough sensation.

The diamond-shaped head swayed very close, only a few inches away from his face. Erast Petrovich heard the quiet, fitful hissing, he saw the sharp little fangs, the forked tongue, but he couldn't even stir a finger. Ice-cold sweat trickled down off his forehead.

He heard a strange clicking sound – it was made by the old man, who seemed to be urging the reptile to hurry.

The jaws swayed towards Fandorin's throat and he squeezed his eyes shut, with the thought that nothing could possibly be more terrible than this horror. Even death would be a blessed release.

Erast Petrovich opened his eyes again – and didn't see the snake.

But it had been here, he had felt its movements.

The reptile had apparently decided to settle down more comfortably on his chest – it curled up into a ball and its tail crept in under his shirt and slithered ticklishly across his ribs.

With a struggle, Fandorin focused his eyes on the old man – he was still gazing directly at his paralysed victim, but something in his eyes had changed. Now, if anything, they were filled with surprise. Or was it curiosity?

'Erast Petrovich!' a voice called from somewhere far away. 'Fandorin! Is it all right if I come in?'

What happened after that took less than a second.

In two absolutely silent leaps the old Japanese was by the window; he jumped up, somersaulted in the air, propping one hand against the windowsill as he flew over it, and disappeared.

And then Vsevolod Vitalievich appeared in the doorway – in a panama hat and carrying a cane, ready for their pedestrian excursion.

A prickling sensation ran across Fandorin's neck, and he discovered that he could turn his head.

He turned it, but he couldn't see the old man any more – just the curtain swaying at the window.

'Now, what's this I see? An adder!' Doronin shouted. 'Don't move!'

The startled snake darted off Erast Petrovich's chest and made for the corner of the room.

The consul dashed after it and started beating it with his cane – so furiously that the stick broke in half at the third blow.

The titular counsellor raised the back of his head off the carpet – the paralysis seemed to be gradually passing off.

'Am I asleep?' he babbled, barely able to control his tongue. 'I dreamed I saw a snake . . .'

'It was no dream,' said Doronin, wrapping his handkerchief round his fingers and squeamishly lifting the reptile up by its tail.

He examined it, shifting his spectacles down to the end of his nose, then carried it to the window and threw it out. He cast a disapproving glance at Masa and heaved a sigh.

Then he took a chair, sat down facing his feebly stirring assistant and fixed him with a severe stare.

'Now then, my dear,' the consul began sternly. 'Let's have no nonsense, everything out in the open. What an angel he made himself out to be yesterday! Doesn't go to brothels, has never even heard of opium addicts . . .' Doronin drew a deep breath in through his nose. 'Not a whiff of opium here, though. So you prefer injections? Do you know what they call what has happened to you? Narcotic swoon. Don't shake your head, I wasn't born yesterday! Shirota told me about your heroics yesterday in the gambling den. A fine servant you've picked up for yourself! Did he procure the drug for you! Of course, who else! He took some himself, and obliged his master at the same time. Tell me one thing, Fandorin. Only honestly now! How long have you been addicted to drugs?'

Erast Fandorin groaned and shook his head.

'I believe you. You're still so young, don't destroy yourself! I warned you: the drug is deadly dangerous if you're not capable of keeping yourself in hand. You were very nearly killed just now – by an absurd coincidence! A *mamusi* crept into the room while both of you were in a narcotic trance – that is, in a completely helpless state!'

'Who?' the titular counsellor asked in a weak voice. 'Who c-crept in?'

'A *mamusi*. A Japanese adder. It's a gentle-sounding name, but in May, after the winter hibernation, *mamusis* are extremely dangerous. If one bites you on the arm or leg, that's not too bad, but a bite on the neck is certain death. Sometimes *mamusis* swim into the Settlement along the canals from the paddy fields and they get into courtyards, or even houses. Last year one of those reptiles bit the son of a Belgian businessman and they couldn't save him. Well, why don't you say something?'

Erast Petrovich didn't say anything, because he didn't have the strength for any explanations. And what could he have said? That there was an old man in the room, with eyes like blazing coals, and then he just flew out of the window? That would only have reinforced the consul's certainty that his assistant was an inveterate drug addict who suffered from hallucinations. Better postpone the fantastic story until later, when his head stopped spinning and his speech was articulate again.

And in all honesty, the young man himself was no longer absolutely sure that it had all been real. Did things like that actually happen?

'But I didn't imagine the little old man with the snake in his sleeve who can jump so high. And I have reliable p-proof of that. I'll present it to you a little later,' Fandorin concluded, and glanced round at his listeners: Sergeant Lockston, Inspector Asagawa and Dr Twigs.

The titular counsellor had spent the entire previous day flat on his back, slowly recovering, and his strength had been completely restored only after ten hours of deep sleep.

And now here, in the police station, he was telling the members of the investigative group the incredible story of what had happened to him.

Asagawa asked:

'Mr Vice-Consul, are you quite certain that it was the same old man who struck the captain in the Rakuen?'

'Yes. Masa didn't see him in the bedroom, but when, with the help of an interpreter, I asked him to describe the man from the Rakuen, the descriptions matched: height, age and even that special, piercing gaze. It's him, no doubt about it. After having made this interesting g-gentleman's acquaintance, I am quite prepared to believe that he inflicted a fatal injury on Blagolepov with a single touch. *"Dim-mak"*, I think it's called – isn't that right, Doctor?'

'But why did he want to kill you?' asked Twigs.

'Not me. Masa. The old conjuror had somehow found out that the investigation had a witness who could identify the killer. The plan, obviously, was to put my valet to sleep and set the *mamusi* on him, so that it would look like an unfortunate accident – especially since the same thing had already happened in the Settlement before. My sudden appearance prevented the plan from being carried through. The visitor was obliged to deal with me, and he did it so deftly that I was unable to offer the slightest resistance. I can't understand why I'm still alive . . . there's a whole host of questions – enough to set my head spinning. But the most important one is: how did the old man know that there was a witness?'

The sergeant, who had not uttered a single word so far, but merely sucked on his cigar, declared:

'We're talking too much. In front of outsiders, too. For instance, what's this Englishman doing here?'

'Mr Twigs, did you bring it?' Fandorin asked the doctor instead of answering the sergeant's question.

The doctor nodded and took some long, flat object, wrapped in a piece of cloth, out of his briefcase.

'Here, I kept it. And I sacrificed my own starched collar, so the dead man wouldn't have to lie in the grave with a bare neck,' said Twigs as he unwrapped a celluloid collar.

'Can you c-compare the prints?' asked the titular counsellor, unwrapping a little bundle of his own and taking out a mirror. 'It was lying on the windowsill. My m-mysterious guest touched the surface with his hand as he turned his somersault.'

'What kind of nonsense is this?' muttered Lockston, watching as Twigs examined the impressions through a magnifying glass.

'The thumb is the same!' the doctor announced triumphantly. 'This print is exactly like the one on the celluloid collar. The delta pattern, the whorl, the forks – it all matches!'

'What's this? What's this?' Asagawa asked quickly, moving closer. 'Some innovation in police science?'

Twigs was delighted to explain.

'It's only a hypothesis as yet, but a well-tested one. My colleague Dr Folds from the Tsukiji Hospital describes it in a learned article. You see, gentlemen, the patterns on the cushions of our fingers and thumbs are absolutely unique. You can meet two people who are as alike as two peas, but it's impossible to find two perfectly identical fingerprints. They already knew this in medieval China. Instead of signing a contract, workers applied their thumbprint – the impression cannot be forged . . .'

The sergeant and the inspector listened open-mouthed as the doctor went into greater historical and anatomical detail.

'What a great thing progress is!' exclaimed Asagawa, who was normally so restrained. 'There are no mysteries that it cannot solve!'

Fandorin sighed.

'Yes there are. How do we explain, from the viewpoint of science, what our sp-sprightly old man can do? Delayed killing, induced lethargy, temporary paralysis, an adder in his sleeve . . . Mystery upon mystery!'

'*Shinobi,*' said the inspector.

The doctor nodded:

'I thought of them too, when I heard about the *mamusi* in his sleeve.'

> So much wisdom there,
> And so many mysteries –
> A *mamusi*'s heart

SNOW AT THE NEW YEAR

'That's a classic trick of theirs. If I remember correctly, it's called *mamusi-gama*, "the snake sickle", isn't it?' Twigs asked the Japanese inspector. 'Tell the vice-consul about it.'

Asagawa replied respectfully.

'You'd better tell it, Sensei. I'm sure you are far better read on this matter and also, to my shame, know the history of my country better.'

'Just what are these *shinobi*?' Lockston exclaimed impatiently.

'The "Stealthy Ones",' the doctor explained, finally grasping the helm of the conversation firmly. 'A caste of spies and hired killers – the most skilful in the entire history of the world. The Japanese love to pursue any skill to perfection, so they attain the very highest levels both in what is good and what is bad. These semi-mythical knights of the cloak and dagger are also known as *rappa*, *suppa* or ninja.'

'Ninja?' the titular counsellor repeated, remembering that he had already heard that word from Doronin. 'Go on, Doctor, go on!'

'The things they write about the ninja are miraculous. Supposedly, they could transform themselves into frogs, birds and snakes, fly through the sky, jump from high walls, run across water and so on, and so forth. Of course, most of this is fairy tales, some of them invented by the *shinobi* themselves, but some things are true. I have taken an interest in their history and read dissertations written by famous masters of *ninjutsu*, "the secret art", and I can confirm that they could jump from a sheer wall twenty yards high; with the help of special devices, they could walk through bogs; they crossed moats and rivers by walking across the bottom and did all sorts of other genuinely fantastic things. This caste had its own morality, a quite monstrous one from the viewpoint of the rest of humanity. They elevated cruelty, treachery and deceit to the rank of supreme virtues. There was even a saying: "as cunning as ninja". They earned their living by taking commissions for murder. It cost an immense amount of money, but the ninja could be relied on. Once they took a commission, they never deviated from it, even if it cost them their lives. And they always achieved their goal. The *shinobi* code encouraged treachery, but never in relation to the client, and everyone knew that.

'They lived in isolated communities and they prepared for their future trade from the cradle. I'll tell you a story that will help you to understand how the young *shinobi* were raised.

'A certain famous ninja had powerful enemies, who managed to kill him and cut off his head, but they weren't absolutely certain that he was the right man. They showed their trophy to the man's eight-year-old son and asked: "Do you recognise him?" The boy didn't shed a single tear, because that would have shamed the memory of his father, but the answer was clear from his face in any case. The little ninja buried the head with full honours and then, overcome by his loss, slit his stomach open and died, without a single groan, like a true hero. The enemies went back home, reassured, but the head they had shown the boy actually belonged to a man he did not know, whom they had killed in error.'

'What self-control! What heroism!' exclaimed Erast Petrovich, astounded. 'So much for the Spartan boy and his fox cub!'

The doctor smiled contentedly.

'You liked the story? Then I'll tell you another one. It's also about self-sacrifice, but from a quite different angle. This particular plot could not very well have been used by European novelists like Sir Walter Scott or Monsieur Dumas. Do you know how the great sixteenth-century general Uesugi was killed? Then listen.

'Uesugi knew they were trying to kill him, and he had taken precautions that prevented any killer from getting anywhere near him, but even so, the ninja accepted the commission. The task was entrusted to a dwarf – dwarf ninja were prized especially highly, they were deliberately raised using special clay jugs. This man was called Jinnai, and he was less than three feet tall. He had been trained since his childhood to act in very narrow and restricted spaces.

'The killer entered the castle by way of a crevice that only a cat could have got through, but not even a mouse could have squeezed through into the prince's chambers, so Jinnai was obliged to wait for a very long time. Do you know what place he chose to wait in? One that the general was bound to visit sooner or later. When the prince was away from the castle and the guards relaxed their vigilance somewhat, Jinnai slipped through to His Excellency's latrine, jumped down into the cesspit and hid himself up to the throat in the appetising slurry. He stayed there for several days, until his victim returned. Eventually Uesugi went to relieve himself. As always, he was accompanied by his bodyguards, who walked in front of him, behind him and on both sides. They examined the privy and even glanced into the hole, but Jinnai ducked his head down under the surface. And then he screwed some canes of bamboo together to make a spear and thrust it straight into the great man's anus. Uesugi gave a bloodcurdling howl and died. The samurai who came running in never realised what had happened to him. The most amazing thing is that the dwarf remained alive. While all the commotion was going on above him, he sat there hunched up, breathing through a tube, and the next day made his way out of the castle and informed his *jonin* that he had completed his task . . .'

'Who d-did he inform?'

'His *jonin*, that's the general of the clan, the strategist. He accepted commissions, decided which of his *chyunins*, or officers, should be charged with planning an operation, while the actual killing and spying were done by the *genins*, or soldiers. Every *genin* strove to achieve perfection in some narrow sphere in which he had no equals. For instance, in soundless walking, *shinobi-aruki*; or in *intonjutsu* – moving without making a sound or casting a shadow; or in *fukumi-bari* – poison-spitting.'

'Eh?' said Lockston, pricking up his ears. 'In what?'

'The ninja put a hollow bamboo pipe in his mouth, with several needles smeared with poison lying in it. A master of *fukumi-bari* could spit them out in a volley to quite a significant distance, ten or fifteen paces. The art of changing one's appearance rapidly was particularly prized by the *shinobi*. They write that when the famous Yaemon Yamada ran through a crowd, eyewitnesses later described six different men, each with his own distinguishing features. A *shinobi* tried not to show other people his real face in any case – it was reserved for fellow clan-members. They could change their appearance by acquiring wrinkles or losing them, changing their manner of walking, the form of their nose and mouth, even their height. If a ninja was caught in a hopeless situation and was in danger of being captured, he killed himself, but first he always mutilated his face – his enemies must not see it, even after his death. There was a renowned *shinobi* who was known as Sarutobi, or Monkey Jump, a name he was given because he could leap like a monkey: he slept on the branches of trees, simply leapt over spears that were aimed at him and so forth. One day, when he jumped down off the wall of the Shogun's castle, where he had been sent to spy, Sarutobi landed in a trap and the guards came rushing towards him, brandishing their swords. Then the ninja cut off his foot, tied a tourniquet round his leg in an instant and started jumping on his other leg. But when he realised he wouldn't get away, he turned towards his pursuers, reviled them in the foulest possible language and pierced his own throat with his sword: but first, as it says in the chronicle, "he cut off his face".'

'What does that mean, "cut off his face"?' asked Fandorin.

'It's not clear exactly. It must be a figurative expression that means "slashed", "mutilated", "rendered unrecognisable".'

'And what was it you s-said about a snake? *Mamusi-gama*, wasn't it?'

'Yes, the "Stealthy Ones" were famous for making very skilful use of animals to achieve their goals: messenger pigeons, hunting hawks, even spiders, frogs and snakes. That is the origin of the legend about them being able to transform themselves into any kind of animal. *Shinobi* very often used to carry adders about with them, and the snakes never bit them. A snake could come in useful for preparing a potion – the ninja would squeeze a few drops of venom out of it; or for releasing into an enemy's bed; or even just as a deterrent. A "sickle-snake" was when a *mamusi* was tied to the handle of a sickle. By waving this exotic weapon about, a ninja could reduce a whole crowd of people to panic and then exploit the stampede to make his escape.'

'It fits! It all fits!' Erast Petrovich said excitedly, jumping to his feet. 'The captain was killed by a ninja using his secret art. And I saw that man yesterday! Now we know who to look for! An old *shinobi* with links to the Satsuman samurai.'

The doctor and the inspector exchanged glances. Twigs had a slightly confused air, and the Japanese shook his head, as if in gentle reproof.

'Mr Twigs has given us a very interesting lecture,' Asagawa said slowly, 'but he forgot to mention one important detail ... There have not been any devious *shinobi* for three hundred years.'

'It's true,' the doctor confirmed in a guilty voice. 'I probably should have warned you about that at the very beginning, in order not to lead you astray.'

'Where did they g-go to?'

There was a note of genuine disappointment in the titular counsellor's voice.

'Apparently I shall have to carry my "lecture", as the inspector called it, right through to the end,' said the doctor, setting his hands on his chest as if asking for Asagawa's forgiveness. 'Three hundred years ago the "Stealthy Ones" lived in two valleys divided off from each other by a mountain range. The major clan occupied the Iga valley, hence their name: *iga-ninja*. Fifty-three families of hereditary spies ruled this small province, surrounded on all sides by sheer cliffs. The "Stealthy Ones" had something like a republic, governed by an elected *jonin*. The final ruler was called Momochi Tamba, and legends circulated about him even during his lifetime. The emperor granted him an honorary crest with seven moons and an arrow. The chronicle tells of how a wicked sorceress put a curse on Kyoto in a fit of fury: seven moons lit up in the sky above the emperor's capital, and all the people in the city trembled in terror at this unprecedented disaster. The emperor called on Tamba to help. He took one look at the sky, raised his bow and unerringly dispatched an arrow into the moon that was the sorceress's disguise. The villainous woman was killed, and the evil apparition was dispelled. God only knows what actually happened, but the very fact that stories like that circulated about Tamba indicates that his reputation must have been truly legendary. But, to his own cost, the mighty *jonin* quarrelled with an even more powerful man, the great dictator Nobunaga. And this is no fairy tale, it's history.

'Three times Nobunaga sent armies to wage war on the province of Iga. The first two times the small number of ninja defeated the samurai. They attacked the punitive expedition's camp at night, starting fires and sowing panic; they wiped out the finest commanders; they changed into the enemy's uniform and provoked bloody clashes between different units of the invading army. Thousands of warriors lay down their lives in the mountain gorges and passes ...

'Eventually Nobunaga's patience gave out. In the Ninth Year of Celestial Justice, that is, in the year 1581 of the Christian calendar, the dictator came to Iga with an immense army, several times larger than the population of the valley. The samurai exterminated all living creatures along their way: not just women and children, but domestic cattle, wild mountain animals, even lizards, mice and snakes – they were afraid that they were transformed *shinobi*. Worst of all was the fact that the invaders were assisted by the ninja from the neighbouring province of Koga, the *koga-ninja*. They it was who ensured Nobunaga's victory, since they knew all the cunning tricks and stratagems of the "Stealthy Ones".

'Momochi Tamba and the remnants of his army made their stand in an old shrine on the mountain of Hijiama. They fought until they were all killed by arrows and fire. The last of the "Stealthy Ones" slit their own throats, after first "cutting off" their faces.

'The death of Tamba and his men basically put an end the history of the *shinobi*. The *koga-ninja* were rewarded with the rank of samurai and henceforth served as guards at the Shogun's palace. Wars came to an end, there was peace in the country for two hundred and fifty years and there was no demand for the skills of the *shinobi*. In their rich, idle new service, the former magicians of secret skills lost all their abilities in just a few generations. During the final period of the shogunate, before the revolution, the descendants of the "Stealthy Ones" guarded the women's quarters. They grew fat and lazy. And the most important event in their lives now was a snowfall.'

'What?' asked Erast Petrovich, thinking that he must have misheard.

'That's right.' The doctor laughed. 'A perfectly ordinary snowfall which, by the way, doesn't happen every year in Tokyo. If snow fell on New Year's Day, they held a traditional amusement at the palace: the female servants divided up into two armies and pelted each other with snowballs. Two teams squealing in excitement – one in white kimonos, the other in red – went to battle to amuse the Shogun and his courtiers. In the middle, keeping the two armies apart, stood a line of ninja, dressed in black uniforms. Naturally, most of the snowballs hit their faces, now rendered quite obtuse by centuries of idleness, and everyone watching rolled about in laughter. Such was the inglorious end of the sect of appalling assassins.'

One more page turning,
A new chapter in the book.
Snow at the New Year

A WHITE HORSE IN A LATHER

Fandorin, however, was not convinced by this story.

'I'm used to putting my trust in the facts. And they testify that the *shinobi* have not disappeared. One of your idle, bloated guards managed to carry the secrets of this terrible trade down through the centuries.'

'Impossible,' said Asagawa, shaking his head. 'When they became palace guards, the *shinobi* were granted the title of samurai, which means they undertook to live according to the laws of bushido, the knight's code of honour. They didn't become stupid, they simply rejected the villainous arsenal of their ancestors – treachery, deceit, underhand murder. None of the Shogun's vassals would have secretly preserved such shameful skills and passed them on to his children. I respectfully advise you to abandon this theory, Mr Vice-Consul.'

'Well, and what if it isn't a descendant of the medieval ninja?' the doctor exclaimed. 'What if it's someone who taught himself? After all, there are treatises with detailed descriptions of the ninja's methods, their instruments, their secret potions! I myself have read the *Tale of the Mysteries of the Stealthy Ones*, written in the seventeenth century by a certain Kionobu from a renowned *shinobi* family. And after that there was the twenty-two-volume work *Ten Thousand Rivers Flow into the Sea*, compiled by Fujibayashi Samuji-Yasutake, a scion of yet another family respected among the ninja. We can assume that there are other, even more detailed manuscripts not known to the general public. It would have been quite possible to resurrect the lost art using these instructions!'

The inspector did not answer, but the expression on his face made it quite clear that he did not believe in the probability of anything of the kind. Moreover, it seemed to Fandorin that Asagawa was not much interested in discussing the *shinobi* in any case. Or was that just Japanese reserve?

'So,' said Erast Petrovich, casting a keen glance at the inspector as he started his provisional summing-up. 'So far we have very little to go on. We know what Captain Blagolepov's presumed killer looks like. That is one. But if this man does possess the skills of the *shinobi*, then he can certainly alter his appearance. We have two identical thumbprints. That is two. But we do not know if we can rely on this method of identification. That leaves the third lead: the owner of the Rakuen. Tell me, Agasawa-san, has your investigation turned anything up yet?'

'Yes,' the Japanese replied imperturbably. 'If you have finished analysing your theory, with your permission I shall report on the results of *our* efforts.'

'B-by all means.'

'Last night, at sixteen minutes past two, Semushi left the Rakuen via a secret door that my agents had discovered earlier. As he walked along the street he behaved very cautiously, but our men are experienced and the hunchback did not realise he was being followed. He went to the *godaun* of the Sakuraya Company in the Fukushima quarter.'

'What is a g-*godaun*?'

'A warehouse, a goods depot,' Lockston explained quickly. 'Go on, go on! What did he do there, in the *godaun*? How long did he stay there?'

Without hurrying, Asagawa took out a small scroll completely covered with hieroglyphs and ran his finger down the vertical lines.

'Semushi spent fourteen minutes in the *godaun*. Our agents do not know what he did there. When he came out, one of my men followed him, the other stayed behind.'

'That's right,' Fandorin said with a nod and immediately felt embarrassed – the inspector clearly knew his business and had no need of the vice-consul's approval.

'Seven minutes after that,' Asagawa continued in the same even voice, 'three men came out of the *godaun*. It is not known if they were Satsumans, since they did not speak to each other, but one was holding his left arm against his side. The agent is not entirely certain, but he got the impression that the arm was twisted.'

'The man with the withered arm!' the sergeant gasped. 'Why didn't you say anything earlier, Go?'

'My name is Goemon,' the Japanese corrected the American – apparently he was more protective of his name than Fandorin. But he left the question unanswered. 'The agent entered the *godaun* and carried out a search, trying not to disturb anything. He found three finely made *katanas*. One *katana* had an unusual hilt, covered with glasspaper . . .'

At this point all three listeners started talking at once.

'It's them! It's them!' said Twigs, throwing his hands up in the air.

'Damnation!' said Lockston, flinging his cigar away. 'Damn you to hell, you tight-lipped whore.'

Fandorin expressed the same idea, only more articulately:

'And you only tell us this now? After we've spent the best part of an hour discussing events that happened in the sixteenth century?'

'You are in charge, I am your subordinate,' Asagawa said coolly. 'We Japanese are accustomed to discipline and subordination. The senior speaks first, then the junior.'

'Did you hear the tone that was spoken in, Rusty?' the sergeant asked, with a sideways glance at Fandorin. 'That's the reason I don't like them. The words are polite, but the only thing on their minds is how to make you look like a dumb cluck.'

Still looking only at the titular counsellor, the Japanese remarked:

'To work together, it is not necessary to like each other.'

Erast Petrovich did not like it any more than Lockston when he was 'made to look like a dumb cluck', and so he asked very coolly:

'I assume, Inspector, that these are all the facts of which you wish to inform us?'

'There are no more facts. But there are hypotheses. If these are of any value to you, with your permission . . .'

'Out with it, d-damn you. Speak, don't d-drag things out!' Fandorin finally exploded, but immediately regretted his outburst – the lips of the intolerable Japanese trembled in a faint sneer, as if to say: I knew you were the same kind, only pretending to be well bred.

'I am speaking. I am not dragging things out.' A polite inclination of the head. 'The three unknown men left the *godaun* unarmed. In my humble opinion, this means two things. Firstly, they intend to come back. Secondly, somehow they know that Minister Okubo is now well guarded, and they have abandoned their plan. Or have decided to wait. The minister's impatience and his dislike of bodyguards are well known.'

'The *godaun*, of c-course, is under observation?'

'Very strict and precise observation. Top specialists have been sent from Tokyo to assist me. As soon as the Satsumans show up, I shall be informed immediately, and we will be able to arrest them. Naturally, with the vice-consul's sanction.'

The final phrase was pronounced in such an emphatically polite tone that Fandorin gritted his teeth – the odour of derision was so strong.

'Thank you. But you seem to have d-decided everything without me.'

'Decided – yes. However, it would be impolite to make an arrest without you. And also without you, of course, Mr Sergeant.' Another derisively polite little bow.

'Sure thing,' said Lockston, with a fierce grin. 'That's all we need, for the local police to start treating the Settlement like its own territory. But what I have to tell you guys is this. Your plan is shit. We need to get down to that *godaun* as quickly as possible, set up an ambush and nab these perpetrators on their way in. While they're still unarmed and haven't got to their swords yet.'

'With all due respect for your point of view, Mr Lockston, these men cannot be "nabbed while they're still unarmed and haven't got to their swords yet".'

'And why so?'

'Because Japan isn't America. We need to have proof of a crime. There is no evidence against the Satsumans. We have to arrest them with their weapons in their hands.'

'Agasawa-san is right,' Fandorin was obliged to admit.

'You're a new man here, Rusty, you don't understand! If these three are experienced *hitokiri*, that is, cut-throats, they'll slice up a whole heap of folks like cabbage!'

'Or else, which is even more likely, they'll kill themselves and the investigation will run into a dead end,' the doctor put in. 'They're samurai! No, Inspector, your plan is definitely no good!'

Agasawa let them fume on for a little longer, then said:

'Neither of these two things will happen. If you gentlemen would care to relocate to my station, I could show you how we intend to carry out the operation. And what's more, it's only a five-minute walk from the station to the Fukushima quarter.'

The Japanese police station, or *keisatsu-syho*, was not much like Sergeant Lockston's office. The municipal bulwark of law enforcement made a formidable impression: a massive door with a bronze sign-plate, brick walls, iron roof, steel bars on the windows of the prison cell – all in all, a true *bulwark*, and that said it all. But Asagawa's offices were located in a low house with walls of wooden planks and a tiled roof – it looked very much like a large shed or drying barn. True, there was a sentry on duty at the entrance, wearing a neat little uniform and polished boots, but this Japanese constable was quite tiny and he also had spectacles. Lockston snickered as he walked past him.

Inside the shed was very strange altogether.

The municipal policemen paraded solemnly, even sleepily, along the corridor, but here everyone dashed about like mice; they bowed rapidly on the move and greeted their superior abruptly. Doors were constantly opening and closing. Erast Petrovich glanced into one of them and saw a row of tables with a little clerk sitting at each one, all of them rapidly running brushes over pieces of paper.

'The records department,' Asagawa explained. 'We regard it as the most important part of police work. When the authorities know who lives where and what he does, there are fewer crimes.'

A loud clattering sound could be heard from the other side of the corridor, as if an entire swarm of mischievous little urchins were wildly hammering sticks against the boards. Erast Petrovich walked across and took advantage of his height to look in through the little window above the door.

About twenty men in black padded uniforms and wire masks were bludgeoning each other as hard as they could with bamboo sticks.

'Swordsmanship classes. Obligatory for all. But we're not going there. We're going to the shooting gallery.'

The inspector turned a corner and led his guests out into a courtyard that Fandorin found quite astonishing, it was so clean and well tended. The tiny little pond with its covering of duckweed and bright red carp tracing out majestic circles in the water was especially fine.

'My deputy's favourite pastime,' Asagawa murmured, apparently slightly embarrassed. 'He has a particular fondness for stone gardens . . . That's all right, I don't forbid it.'

Fandorin looked round, expecting to see sculptures of some kind, but he didn't see any plants carved out of stone – nothing but fine gravel with several crude boulders lying on it, arranged without any sense of symmetry.

'As I understand it, this is an allegory of the struggle between order and chaos,' said the doctor, nodding with the air of a connoisseur. 'Quite good, though perhaps a little unsubtle.'

The titular counsellor and the sergeant exchanged glances. The former with a baffled frown, the latter with a smirk.

They walked underground, into a long cellar illuminated by oil lamps. Targets and boxes of empty shell cases indicated that this was the firing range. Fandorin's attention was drawn to three straw figures the height of a man. They were dressed in kimonos, with bamboo swords in their hands.

'I most humbly request the respected vice-consul to listen to my plan,' said Asagawa. He turned up the wicks in the lamps and the basement became lighter. 'At my request, Vice-Intendant Suga has sent me two men who are good shots with a revolver. I tested them on these models, neither of them ever miss. We will allow the Satsumans to enter the *godaun*. Then we will arrive to arrest them. Only four men. One will pretend to be an officer, the other three ordinary patrolmen. If there were more, the Satsumans really might commit suicide, but in this case they will decide that they can easily deal with such a small group. They will take out their swords, and then the "officer" will drop to the floor – he has already played his part. The three "patrolmen" (they are the two men from Tokyo and myself) take their revolvers out from under their cloaks and open fire. We will fire at their arms. In that way, firstly, we will take the miscreants armed and, secondly, ensure that they cannot escape justice.'

The American nudged Erast Petrovich in the side with his elbow.

'Hear that, Rusty? They're going to fire at the arms. It's not all that easy, Mr Go. Everyone knows what kind of marksmen the Japanese make! Maybe the plan's OK, but you're not the ones who should go.'

'Who, then, if you will permit me to ask? And permit me to remind you that my name is Goemon.'

'OK, OK, so it's Gouemon. Who's going to go and aerate those yellow- . . . those Satsumans? In the first place, of course, me. Tell me, Rusty, are you a good shot?'

'Fairly good,' Erast Petrovich replied modestly – he could plant all bullets in the cylinder on top of each other. 'Naturally, from a long-barrelled weapon and with a firm support.'

'Excellent. And we know all about you, Doc – you shoot the way you handle a scalpel. Of course, you're an outsider and you're not obliged to perform in our show, but if you're not afraid.'

'No, no,' said Twigs, brightening up. 'You know, I'm not at all afraid of shooting now. Hitting the target is much easier than sewing up a muscle neatly or putting in stitches.'

'Attaboy, Lance! There you have your three "patrolmen", Go. I'll dress Rusty and Lens up in uniforms and we'll be like three thick-headed municipal policemen. OK, so we'll take you as the fourth – supposedly as our interpreter. You can make idle chat with us and then drop to the ground, and we'll do the rest. Right, guys?'

'Of course!' the doctor exclaimed enthusiastically, very pleased at the prospect of being included.

Erast Petrovich thought how once a man had held a gun in his hand, even a man of the most peaceable of professions, he could never forget that sensation. And he would be eager to feel it again.

'Pardon me for being so meticulous, but may I see how well you shoot, gentlemen?' Asagawa asked. 'I would not dare, of course, to doubt your word, but this is such an important operation and I am responsible for it, both to the vice-intendant and the minister himself.'

Twigs rubbed his hands together.

'Well, as for me, I'll be glad to show you. Will you be so good as to loan me one of your remarkable Colts, sir?'

The sergeant handed him a revolver. The doctor took off his frock coat, exposing his waistcoat. He wiggled the fingers of his right handle slightly, grasped the handle of the gun, took careful aim and his first shot broke one of the straw figure's wrists – the bamboo sword fell to the floor.

'Bravo, Lance!'

Twigs gagged at the powerful slap on his back. But the inspector shook his head.

'Sensei, with all due respect . . . The bandits will not stand and wait while you take aim. This is not a European duel with pistols. You have to fire very, very quickly, and also take into account that your opponent will be moving at that moment.'

The Japanese pressed some kind of lever with his foot and the figures started rotating on their wooden base, like a carousel.

Lancelot Twigs batted his eyelids and lowered the revolver.

'No . . . I never learned to do that . . . I can't.'

'Let me try!'

The sergeant moved the doctor aside. He stood with his feet wide apart, squatted down slightly, grabbed his Colt out of the holster and fired off four shots one after the other. One of the straw figures flopped off the stand and clumps of straw went flying in all directions.

Asagawa walked over and bent down.

'Four holes, two in the chest, two in the stomach.'

'What did you expect! Walter Lockston never misses.'

'It won't do,' said the Japanese, straightening up. 'We need them alive. We have to fire at their arms.'

'Aha, you try it! It's not as easy as it sounds!'

'I'll try it now. Would you mind spinning the turntable? Only, as fast as possible, please. And you, Mr Vice-Consul, give the command.'

The sergeant set the figures whirling so fast that they were just a blur.

Asagawa stood there, holding his hand in his pocket.

'Fire!' shouted Fandorin, and before he had even finished pronouncing this short word, the first shot rang out.

The inspector fired without taking aim, from the hip. Both figures stayed where they were.

'Aha!' Lockston howled triumphantly. 'Missed!'

He stopped swaying the lever with his foot, the figures slowed down, and it became clear that the hand in which one of them was holding its sword had twisted slightly.

The doctor walked over and bent down.

'Right in the tendon. With a wound like that, a man couldn't even hold a pencil.'

The sergeant's jaw dropped.

'Damnation, Go! Where in hell did you learn to do that?'

'Yes, indeed,' Fandorin put in. 'I've never seen anything like it, not even in the Italian circus, when the bullet maestro shot a nut off his own daughter's head.'

Asagawa lowered his eyes modestly.

'You could call it the "Japanese circus",' he said. 'All I have done is combine two of our ancient arts: *battojutsu* and *inu-omono*. The first is . . .'

'I know, I know!' Erast Petrovich interrupted excitedly. 'It's the art of drawing a sword from its scabbard at lightning speed. It can be learned! But what is *inu-omono*?'

'The art of shooting at running dogs from a bow,' the miracle marksman replied, and the titular counsellor's enthusiasm wilted – this was too high a price to pay for miraculous marksmanship.

'Tell me, Asagawa-san,' said Fandorin, 'are you sure that your other two men fire as well as that?'

'Far better. That is why my target is the man with the withered arm, one well-placed bullet will be enough for him. But no doubt Mr Vice-Consul also wishes to demonstrate his skill. I'll just order the targets' arms to be reattached.'

Erast Petrovich merely sighed.

'Th-thank you. But I can see the Japanese police will conduct this operation in excellent fashion without involving us.'

However, there was no operation; once again the net that had been cast remained without a catch. The Satsumans did not return to the *godaun*, either in the daytime, the evening twilight or the darkness of night.

When the surrounding hills turned pink in the rays of the rising sun, Fandorin told the downcast inspector:

'They won't come now.'

'But it can't be! A samurai would never abandon his *katana*!'

By the end of the night there was almost nothing left of the inspector's derisive confidence. He turned paler and paler and the corners of his mouth twitched nervously – it was clear that he was struggling to maintain the remnants of his self-control.

After the mockery of the previous day, Fandorin did not feel the slightest sympathy for the Japanese.

'You shouldn't have relied so much on your own efforts,' he remarked vengefully. 'The Satsumans spotted your men following them. No doubt samurai do value their swords highly, but they value their own skins even more. I'm going to bed.'

Asagawa flinched in pain.

'But I'll stay and wait,' he forced out through clenched teeth, without any more phrases such as 'with your permission' or 'if Mr Vice-Consul will be so kind as to allow me'.

'As you wish.'

Erast Petrovich said goodbye to Lockston and the doctor and set off home.

The deserted promenade was shrouded in gentle, transparent mist, but the titular counsellor was not looking at the smart façades of the buildings, or the damply gleaming road – his gaze was riveted to that miracle not of human making that is called 'sunrise over the sea'. As the young man walked along he thought that if everybody started their day by observing God's world filling up with life, light and beauty, then squalor and villainy would disappear from the world – there would be no place for them in a soul bathed in the light of dawn.

It should be said that, owing to the course that Erast Petrovich's life had taken, he was capable of abandoning himself to such beautiful reveries only when he was alone, and even then only for a very short time – his relentless reason immediately arranged everything in due order. 'It's quite possible that contemplating the sunrise over the sea would indeed reduce the incidence of crime during the first half of the day, only to increase it during the second half,' the titular counsellor told himself. 'Man is inclined to feel ashamed of his moments of sentimentality and starry-eyed idealism. Of course, for the sake of equilibrium, one could oblige the entire population of the earth to admire the sunset as well – another very fine sight. Only then it's frightening to think how the overcast days would turn out . . .'

Fandorin heaved a sigh and turned away from the picture created by God to the landscape created by people. In this pure, dew-drenched hour the latter also looked rather fine, although by no means as perfect: there was an exhausted sailor sleeping under a street lamp with his cheek resting on his open palm, and on the corner an overly diligent yard keeper was scraping away with his broom.

Suddenly he dropped his implement and looked round, and at that very second Fandorin heard a rapidly approaching clatter and a woman screaming. A light two-wheeled gig came tearing wildly round the corner of the promenade. It almost overturned as one wheel lifted off the road, but somehow it righted itself again – the horse swerved just before the parapet, but it slowed its wild career only for a split second. Shaking its head with a despairing whinny and shedding thick flakes of lather, it set off at a crazy gallop along the seafront, rapidly approaching Fandorin.

There was a woman in the gig, holding on to the seat with both hands and screaming piercingly, her tangled hair fluttering in the wind – her hat must have flown off much earlier. Everything was clear – the horse had taken fright at something and bolted, and the lady had not been able to keep hold of the reins.

Erast Petrovich did not analyse the situation, he did not try to guess all the possible consequences in advance, he simply leapt off the pavement and started running in the same direction as the careering gig – as fast as it is possible to run when running backwards all the time.

The horse had a beautiful white coat, but it was craggy and low in the withers. The titular counsellor had already seen horses like this here in Yokohama. Vsevolod Vitalievich had said that it was a native Japanese breed, known for its petulant character, poorly suited to working in harness.

Fandorin had never stopped a bolting horse before but once, during the recent war, he had seen a Cossack manage it very deftly indeed and, with his usual intellectual curiosity, he had asked how it was done. 'The important thing, squire, is that you keep your hands off the bridle,' the young soldier had confided. 'They don't like that when they've got their dander up. You jump on her neck and bend her head down to the ground. And don't yell and swear at her, shout something sweet and soothing: "There, my little darling, my little sweetheart". She'll see sense then. And if it's a stallion, you can call him "little brother" and "fine fellah".'

When the crazed animal drew level with him as he ran, Erast Petrovich put theory into practice. He jumped and clung to the sweaty, slippery neck, and immediately realised he did not know whether this was a stallion or a mare – there hadn't been time to look. So to be on the safe side, he shouted out 'sweetheart' and 'fine fellah' and 'little brother' and 'darling'.

At first it did no good. Perhaps he needed to do his coaxing in Japanese, or the horse didn't like the weight on its neck, but the representative of the petulant breed snorted, shook its head and snapped at the titular counsellor's shoulder with its teeth. When it missed, it started slowing its wild pace a little.

After another two hundred strides or so, the wild gallop finally came to an end. The horse stood there, trembling all over, with clumps of soapy lather slithering down its back and rump. Fandorin released his grip and got to his feet, staggering a little. The first thing he did was clarify the point that had occupied his mind throughout the brief period when he was playing the part of a carriage shaft.

'Aha, so it's a d-darling,' Erast Petrovich muttered, and then he glanced at the lady he had rescued.

It was the Right Honourable Algernon Bullcox's kept woman, she of the magical radiance, O-Yumi. Her hairstyle was destroyed and there was a long strand hanging down over her forehead, her dress was torn and he could see her white shoulder with a scarlet scratch on it. But even in this condition the owner of the unforgettable silver slipper was so lovely that the titular counsellor froze on the spot and fluttered his long eyelashes in bewilderment. It isn't any kind of radiance, he thought. It's *blinding beauty*. That's why they call it that, because it's as if it blinds you . . .

The thought also occurred to him that dishevelment was almost certainly not as becoming to him as it was to her. One sleeve of the titular counsellor's frock coat had been completely torn off and was dangling at his elbow, the other sleeve had been chewed on by the mare, his trousers and shoes were black with grime and, most horrible of all, of course, was the acrid smell of horse sweat with which Erast Petrovich was impregnated from head to foot.

'Are you unhurt, madam?' he asked in English, backing away a little in order not to insult her sense of smell. 'There is b-blood on your shoulder...'

She glanced at the scrape and lowered the edge of the dress even further, revealing the hollow under her collarbone, and Fandorin swallowed the end of his phrase.

'Ah, I did that myself. I caught myself with the handle of the whip,' the Japanese woman replied, and brushed away the bright coral-coloured drop carelessly with her finger.

The courtesan's voice was surprisingly low and husky – unattractive by European standards – but there was something in its timbre that made Fandorin lower his eyes for a moment.

Taking a grip on himself, he looked into her face again and saw that she was smiling – she seemed to find his embarrassment amusing.

'I see you were not very badly frightened,' Erast Petrovich said slowly.

'I was, very. But I have had time to calm down. You embraced my Naomi so ardently.' Sparks of cunning glinted in her eyes. 'Ah, you are a real hero! And if I, for my part, were a real Japanese woman, I should spend the rest of my days repaying my debt of gratitude. But I have learned many useful things from you foreigners. For instance, that it is possible simply to say "thank you, sir" and the debt is paid. Thank you, sir. I am most grateful to you.'

She half-rose off her seat and performed a graceful curtsy.

'Don't mention it,' said Fandorin. As he inclined his head, he saw that damned dangling sleeve and pulled it right off quickly. He wanted very much to hear the sound of her voice again and asked: 'Did you go out for a drive this early in the day? It is not five o'clock yet.'

'I drive to the headland every morning to watch the sun rising over the sea. It is the finest sight in all the world,' O-Yumi replied, pushing a lock of hair behind her little protruding ear, which was bright pink from the light shining through it.

Erast Petrovich looked at her in amazement – it was as if she had read his recent thoughts.

'And do you always rise so early?'

'No, I go to bed so late,' the amazing woman said, laughing. Unlike her voice, her laughter was not husky at all, but clear and vibrant.

And now Fandorin wanted her to laugh some more. But he didn't know how to make it happen. Perhaps say something humorous about the horse?

The titular counsellor absentmindedly patted the mare on the rump. It gave him a sideways glance from an inflamed eye and whinnied pitifully.

'I'm terribly upset about my hat.' O-Yumi sighed as she carried on tidying up her hair. 'It was so beautiful! It blew off, and now I'll never find it. That's the price of patriotism for you. My friend warned me that a Japanese horse would never walk well in harness, but I decided to prove he was wrong.'

She meant Bullcox, Erast Petrovich guessed.

'She won't bolt now. She just needs to be led by the reins for a while . . . If you will p-permit me . . .'

He took the mare by the bridle and led her slowly along the promenade. Fandorin wanted very badly to glance back, but he kept himself in hand. After all, he was no young boy, to go gaping at beautiful women.

The silence dragged on. Erast Petrovich, we know, was being firm with himself, but why did she not say anything? Did women who have just been rescued from mortal danger really remain silent, especially in the presence of their rescuer?

A minute went by, then a second, and a third. The silence ceased to be a pause in the conversation and began acquiring some special meaning of its own. It is a well-known fact, at least in belles-lettres, that when a woman and a man who barely know each other do not speak for a long time, it brings them closer than any conversation.

Eventually the titular counsellor gave way and pulled the bridle very slightly towards himself, and when the mare shook its head in his direction, he half-turned, squinting at the Japanese woman out of the corner of his eye.

Apparently the thought of staring at his back had never even entered her head! She had turned away and opened a little mirror, and was busy with her face – she had even brushed her hair and pinned it up already, and powdered her little nose. So much for a significant silence!

Furious at his own stupidity, Fandorin handed the reins to O-Yumi and said firmly:

'There, my lady. The horse is completely calm now. You can drive on, only take it gently and don't let go of the reins.'

He raised the hat that had somehow miraculously remained on his head and was about to bow, but hesitated, wondering whether it was polite to leave without introducing himself. On the other hand, would that not be too much – to pay this dissolute woman the same courtesy as a society lady?

Courtesy won the day

'P-pardon me, I forgot to introduce myself. I . . .'

She stopped him with a wave of her hand.

'Don't bother. The name will tell me very little. And I shall see what is important without any name.'

She gave him a long, intent stare and her tender lips started moving soundlessly.

'And what do you see?' Fandorin asked, unable to repress a smile.

'Not very much as yet. You are loved by luck and by things, but not by destiny. You have lived twenty-two years in the world, but in fact you are older than that. And that is not surprising. You have often been within an inch of death and you have lost half of your heart, and that ages people rapidly . . . Well, then. Once again, thank you, sir. And goodbye.'

When he heard her mention half of his heart, Erast Petrovich shuddered. But the lady shook the reins with a piercing yell of '*Yoshi, ikoo!*' and set the mare off at a spanking trot, despite his warning.

The horse called Naomi ran obediently, twitching its white pointed ears in a regular rhythm. Its hoofs beat out a jolly, silvery tattoo on the road.

And at journey's end
You remember a white horse
Dashing through the mist

THE FINAL SMILE

That day he saw her again. Nothing surprising in that – Yokohama was a small town.

Erast Petrovich was making his way back to the consulate along Main Street in the evening, after a meeting with the sergeant and the inspector, and he saw the flame-haired Bullcox and his concubine drive by in a brougham. The Englishman was dressed in something crimson (Fandorin hardly even glanced at him); his companion was wearing a black, figure-hugging dress and a hat with an ostrich feather and a gauzy veil that did not conceal her face, but seemed merely to envelop her features in a light haze.

The titular counsellor bowed slightly, trying to make the movement express nothing but quite ordinary courtesy. O-Yumi did not respond to the bow, but she gave him a long, strange look, and Erast Fandorin tried to penetrate its meaning for a long time afterwards. Seeking something, slightly uneasy? Yes, that was probably it: she seemed to be trying to make out something concealed in his face, simultaneously hoping and fearing to find it.

With some effort, he forced himself to put this nonsense out of his mind and redirect his thoughts to important matters.

They next time they met was the next day, in the afternoon. Lieutenant Captain Bukhartsev had come from Tokyo to find out how the investigation was progressing. Unlike in the first meeting, the maritime agent behaved like a perfect angel. His attitude to the titular counsellor had changed completely – his manner was polite, he spoke little and listened attentively.

They learned nothing new from him, only that Minister Okubo was being guarded night and day, he hardly ever left his residence, and was in a terrible rage as a result. He might not hold out for the promised week.

Erast Petrovich briefly outlined the state of affairs to his compatriot. The Satsumans had disappeared without trace. The watch being kept on the hunchback had been intensified, since it had now been established for certain that he was in league with the conspirators, but so far the secret surveillance had not yielded anything useful. The owner of the Rakuen spent all his time at his gambling den; in the early morning he went home to sleep, then came back to the den. And there were no leads.

Fandorin also showed Bukhartsev the items of evidence they had collected – they were displayed on the sergeant's desk especially for the occasion: the three swords, the celluloid collar and the mirror.

The lieutenant captain examined the last two items though a magnifying glass, then examined the fleshy pad of his own thumb for a long time through the same magnifying glass, shrugged and said: 'Twaddle.'

As the vice-consul was showing the maritime agent to his carriage, he held forth on the importance of the job Fandorin had been given.

'. . . We can either increase the effectiveness of our influence to unprecedented heights – that is, if you manage to catch the killers – or undermine our reputation and provoke the displeasure of the all-powerful minister, who will not forgive us for putting him in a cage,' Mstislav Nikolaevich pontificated confidentially in a hushed voice.

The titular counsellor listened with a slight frown – first, because he knew all this already in any case, and, secondly, because he was irritated by the familiar way in which the embassy popinjay had set one hand on his shoulder.

Bukhartsev suddenly broke off in mid-word and whistled.

'What a pretty little monkey!'

Fandorin looked round.

For a moment he didn't recognise her, because this time she had a tall, complicated hairstyle and was dressed in the Japanese manner, in a white kimono with blue irises, and holding a little light-blue parasol. Erast Petrovich had seen beauties like that in *ukiyo-e* prints, but after spending several days in Japan, he had decided that the elegant, charming female figures of the *ukiyo-e* were a mere fabrication, like all the other fantasies of European '*japonisme*', but O-Yumi was every bit as lovely as the beauties immortalised by the Japanese artist Utamaro, whose works were now sold in the saloons of Paris for substantial amounts of money. She floated by, with a sideways glance at Erast Petrovich and his companion. Fandorin bowed, Bukhartsev gallantly raised one hand to the peak of his cap.

'Oh, the neck, the neck!' the maritime agent moaned. 'I adore those collars of theirs. More provocative in their own way than our low necklines.'

The high collar of the kimono was lowered at the back. Erast Petrovich was unable to tear his eyes away from the delicate curls on the back of the head and the vulnerable hollow in the neck, and especially from the ears that protruded in such a touchingly childish fashion. She must still be a real child in terms of years, he suddenly thought. Her mocking wit is no more than a mask, a defence against the coarse and cruel world in which she has spent her life. Like the thorns on a rose bush.

He took his leave of Bukhartsev absentmindedly, barely even turning his head towards him – he was still watching that slim figure walking away, floating across the square.

Suddenly O-Yumi stopped, as if she had sensed his gaze.

She turned round and walked back.

Realising that she was not simply walking back, but coming towards him, Fandorin took a few steps towards her.

'Be wary of that man,' O-Yumi said rapidly, swaying her chin to indicate the direction in which the lieutenant captain had driven off. 'I don't know who he is, but I can see he is pretending to be your friend, while he really wishes you harm. He has written a report denouncing you today, or he will write one.'

When she finished speaking, she tried to walk away, but Erast Petrovich blocked her path. Two bearded, emaciated faces observed this scene curiously through the barred windows of the police station. The constable on duty at the door also looked on with a grin.

'You're very fond of making a dramatic exit, but this time I demand an answer. What is this nonsense about a report? Who told you about it?'

'His face. Or rather, a wrinkle in the corner of his left eye, in combination with the line and colour of his lips.' O-Yumi smiled gently. 'Don't look at me like that. I am not joking or playing games with you. In Japan we have the ancient art of *ninso*, which allows us to read a person's face like an open book. Very few people possess this skill, but there have been masters of *ninso* in our family for the last two hundred years.'

Before he came to Japan, of course, the titular counsellor would have laughed at hearing a tall tale like this, but now he knew that in this country there really were countless numbers of the most incredible 'arts', and so he didn't laugh, but merely asked:

'Reading a face like a book? Something like physiognomics?'

'Yes, only much broader and more detailed. A *ninso* master can interpret the shape of the head, and the form of the body, and the manner of walking and the voice – in short, everything that a person tells the outside world about himself. We can distinguish a hundred and forty-four different gradations of colour on the skin, two hundred and twelve types of wrinkles, thirty-two smells and much, much more. I am far from complete mastery of the skills that my father possesses, but I can precisely determine a man's age, thoughts, his recent past and immediate future . . .'

When he heard about the future, Fandorin realised that he was being toyed with after all. What a credulous fool he was!

'Well, and what have I been doing today? No, better still, tell me what I have been thinking about,' he said with an ironic smile.

'In the morning you had a headache, here.' Her light fingers touched Fandorin's temple, and he started – either in surprise (she was right about the headache), or simply at her touch. 'You were prey to sad thoughts. That often happens to you in the morning. You were thinking about a woman who no longer exists. And you were also thinking about another woman, who is alive. You were imagining all sorts of scenes that made you feel heated.'

Erast Petrovich blushed bright red and the sorceress smiled cunningly, but did not elaborate on the subject.

'This is not magic,' she said in a more serious voice. 'Merely the fruit of centuries of research pursued by highly observant individuals, intent on their craft. The right half of the face is you, the left half is people connected with you. For instance, if I see a little *inshoku*-coloured pimple on the right temple, I know that this person is in love. But if I see the same pimple on the left temple, then someone is in love with them.'

'No, you are mocking me after all!'

O-Yumi shook her head.

'The recent past can be determined from the lower eyelids. The immediate future from the upper eyelids. May I?'

The white fingers touched his face again. They ran over his eyebrows and tickled his eyelashes. Fandorin felt himself starting to feel drowsy.

Suddenly O-Yumi recoiled, her eyes gazing at him in horror.

'What ... what's wrong?' he asked hoarsely – his throat had suddenly gone dry.

'Today you will kill a man!' she whispered in fright, then turned and ran off across the square.

He almost went dashing after her, but took a grip on himself just in time. Not only did he not run, he turned away and took a slim manila out of his cigar case. He succeeded in lighting it only with his fourth match.

The titular counsellor was trembling – no doubt in fury.

'Jug-eared m-minx!' he hissed through his teeth. 'And I'm a fine one, listening wide-eyed like that!'

But what point was there in trying to deceive himself? She was an astounding woman! Or perhaps it wasn't just her? The thought was electrifying. *There is some strange connection between us*. He was astonished by the idea, but he didn't carry it through to the end, he didn't have time, for at that moment something happened that shook all thoughts about mysterious beauties out of the young man's head.

First there was a sound of breaking glass, then someone bellowed despairingly:

'Stop! Stop the bloody ape!'

Recognising Lockston's voice, Fandorin went dashing back to the station. He ran along the corridor, burst into the sergeant's office and saw the sergeant swearing furiously as he tried to climb out of the window, but rather awkwardly – the sharp splinters of glass were getting in his way. There was an acrid smell of burning in the room, and smoke swirling just below the ceiling.

'What happened?'

'That there ... son of a bitch ... the lousy snake!' Lockston yelled, pointing with his finger.

Fandorin saw a man in a short kimono and a straw hat, running fast in the direction of the promenade.

'The evidence!' the sergeant gasped, and smashed his great fist into the window frame. The frame went flying out into the street.

The American jumped out after it.

At the word 'evidence', Erast Petrovich turned to look at the desk, where the swords, the collar and the mirror had been lying only ten minutes earlier. The cloth covering of the desk was smouldering and some papers on it were still blazing. The swords were still there, but the celluloid collar had curled up into a charred tube, and the molten surface of the mirror was slowly spreading out, its surface trembling slightly.

But there was no time to contemplate this scene of destruction. The titular counsellor vaulted over the windowsill and overtook the bison-like sergeant in a few rapid bounds. He shouted:

'What caused the fire?'

'He'll get away!' Lockston growled instead of answering. 'Let's cut through the Star.'

The fugitive had already disappeared round a corner.

'He came in! Into my office! He bowed!' Lockston yelled, bursting in through the back door of the Star saloon. 'Then suddenly there was this egg! He smashed it on the table! Smoke and flames!'

'What do you mean, an egg?' Fandorin yelled back.

'I don't know! There was a pillar of flame! And he threw himself backwards out the window! Damned ape!'

That explained the part about the ape, but Fandorin still didn't understand about the fiery egg. The pursuers dashed though the dark little saloon and out on to the sun-drenched Bund. They glimpsed the straw hat about twenty strides ahead, manoeuvring between the passers-by with incredible agility. The 'ape' was rapidly pulling away from the pursuit.

'It's him!' Erast Petrovich gasped, peering at the low, skinny figure. 'I'm sure it's him!'

A constable on duty outside a money-changing shop was cradling a short rifle in the crook of his arm.

'What are you gawping at?' Lockston barked. 'Catch him!'

The constable shot off so eagerly that he overtook his boss and the vice-consul, but even he couldn't overhaul the criminal.

The running man swerved off the promenade into an empty alley and leapt across the little bridge over the canal in a single bound. A respectable clientele was sitting under the striped awning of Le Café Parisien there. A long lanky figure jumped up from one of the tables – Lancelot Twigs.

'Gentlemen, what's the matter?'

Lockston just waved a hand at him. The doctor dashed after the members of the investigative group, shouting:

'But what's happened? Who are you chasing?'

The fugitive had built up a lead of a good fifty paces, and the distance was increasing. He raced along the opposite side of the canal without looking back even once.

'He'll get away!' the constable groaned. 'That's the native town, a genuine maze!'

He snatched a revolver out of its holster, but didn't fire – it was a bit too far for a Colt.

'Give me that!'

The police chief tore the carbine out of the constable's hands, set his cheek against the butt, swung the barrel into line with the nimble fugitive and fired.

The straw hat went flying in one direction and its owner in the other. He fell, rolled over several times and stayed lying there with his arms flung out.

The people in the café started clamouring and jumping up off their chairs.

'Right then. Phew!' said Lockston, wiping the sweat off his face with his sleeve. 'You're witnesses, gentlemen. If I hadn't fired, the criminal would have got away.'

'An excellent shot!' Twigs exclaimed with the air of a connoisseur.

They walked across the bridge without hurrying: the victorious sergeant with his smoking carbine at the front, followed by Fandorin and the doctor, and then the constable, with the idle public at a respectful distance.

'If you've k-killed him outright, we'll have no leads,' Erast Petrovich said anxiously. 'And we don't have the fingerprints any more.'

The American shrugged.

'What do we need them for, if we have the one who made them? I was aiming for his back. Maybe he's alive?'

This suggestion was immediately confirmed, and in a most unexpected manner.

The man on the ground jumped to his feet as if nothing had happened and darted off along the canal at the same fast pace as before.

The public gasped. Lockston started blinking.

'Damn me! Ain't he a lively one!'

He raised the carbine again, but it wasn't a new-fangled Winchester, only a single-shot Italian Vetterli. The sergeant threw the useless weapon to the constable with a curse and pulled out a Colt.

'Here, let me!' the doctor said eagerly. 'You won't hit him!' He almost grabbed the revolver out of Lockston's hands, then stood in the picturesque pose of a man fighting a duel and closed one eye. A shot rang out.

The fugitive fell again, this time face down.

Some people in the crowd applauded. Lockston stood there scratching his chin while his subordinate reloaded the carbine. Fandorin was the only one who ran forward.

'Don't be in such a hurry!' Twigs called to stop him, and explained coolly: 'He's not going anywhere now. I broke his spine at the waist. Cruel, of course, but if he's a student of those *shinobi*, the only way to take him alive is to paralyse him. Take your Colt, Walter. And thank the gods that at this time of the day I always take tea at the Parisien. Otherwise there's no way . . .'

'Look!' Fandorin exclaimed.

The fallen man got up on all fours, then stood up, shook himself like a wet dog and dashed on, leaping along with huge steps.

This time no one gasped or yelled – everyone gaped in silent bewilderment.

Lockston opened fire with his revolver, but kept missing, and the doctor grabbed at his arm, trying to get him to hand over the weapon again – they had both forgotten about the second revolver on the sergeant's belt.

Erast Petrovich quickly estimated the distance (about seventy paces, and the grey hovels of the native town were no more than a hundred away) and turned to the constable.

'Have you loaded it? Give it to me.'

He took aim according to all the rules of marksmanship. He held his breath and aligned the sight. He made only a slight adjustment for movement – the shot was almost straight in line with the running man. One bullet, he mustn't miss.

The enchanted fugitive's legs were twinkling rapidly. No higher than the knees, or you might kill him, the titular counsellor told the bullet, and pressed the trigger.

Got him! The figure in the kimono fell for the third time. Only this time the pursuers didn't stand still, they dashed forward as fast as they could.

They could see the wounded man moving, trying to get up. Then he did get up and hopped on one leg, but lost his balance and collapsed. He crept towards the water, leaving a trail of blood.

The most incredible thing of all was that he still didn't look round even once.

When they were only about twenty paces away from the wounded man, he stopped crawling – clearly he had realised that he wouldn't get away. He made a rapid movement – and a narrow blade glinted in the sun.

'Quick! He's going to cut his throat!' the doctor shouted.

But that wasn't what the *shinobi* did. He ran the blade rapidly round his face, as if he wanted to set it in an oval frame. Then he grabbed at his chin with his left hand, tugged with a dull growl – and a limp rag went flying through the air, landing at Erast Petrovich's feet. Fandorin almost stumbled when he realised what it was – the skin of a face, trimmed and torn off; red on one side, with the other side looking like mandarin peel.

And then the man finally turned round.

In his short life, Erast Petrovich had seen many terrible things; some visions from his past still woke him at night in a cold sweat. But nothing on earth could have been more nightmarish than that crimson mask with its white circles of eyes and the grinning teeth.

'*Kongojyo!*' the lipless mouth said quietly but distinctly, opening wider and wider.

The hand with the bloody knife crept slowly up to the throat.

Only then did Fandorin think to squeeze his eyes shut. And he stood like that until the fit of nausea and dizziness passed off.

'So that's what "cutting off your face" means!' he heard Dr Twigs say in an excited voice. 'He really did cut it off, it's not a figure of speech at all!'

Lockston reacted the most calmly of all. He leaned down over the body, which – God be praised – was lying on its stomach. Two holes in the kimono, one slightly higher, one slightly lower, exposed a glint of metal. The sergeant ripped the material apart with his finger and whistled.

'So that's what his magic is made of!'

Under his kimono, the dead man was wearing thin tempered-steel armour.

While Lockston explained to the doctor what had happened at the station, Fandorin stood to one side and tried in vain to still the frantic beating of his heart.

His heart was not racing because of the running, or the shooting, or even the ghastly sight of that severed face. The vice-consul had simply recalled the words that a husky woman's voice had spoken a few minutes earlier: 'Today you will kill a man'.

'So Mr Fandorin was right after all,' the doctor said with a shrug. 'It really was an absolutely genuine ninja. I don't know where and how he learned the secrets of their trade, but there's no doubt about it. The steel plate that saved him from the first two bullets is called a *ninja-muneate*. The fire egg is a *torinoko*, an empty shell into which the *shinobi* introduce a combustible mixture through a small hole. And did you see the way he grinned before he died? I've come across a strange term in books about the ninja – the Final Smile – but the books didn't explain what it was. Well now, not a very appetising sight!'

How fiercely I yearn
To smile with a carefree heart
At least at the last

EARLY PLUM RAIN

Doronin stood at the window, watching the rivulets run down the glass. '*Baiu*, plum rain,' he said absentmindedly. 'Somewhat early, it usually starts at the end of May.'

The vice-consul did not pursue the conversation about natural phenomena and silence set in again.

Vsevolod Vitalievich was trying to make sense of his assistant's report. The assistant was waiting, not interrupting the thought process.

'I tell you what,' the consul said eventually, turning round. 'Before I sit down to write a report for His Excellency, let's run thought the sequence of facts once more. I state the facts and you tell me if each point is correct or not. All right?'

'All right.'

'Excellent. Let's get started. Once upon a time there was a certain party who possessed almost magical abilities. Let us call him No-Face.' (Erast Fandorin shuddered as he recalled the 'final smile' of the man who had killed himself earlier in the day.) 'Employing his inscrutable art, No-Face killed Captain Blagolepov – and so adroitly that it would have remained a dark secret, if not for a certain excessively pernickety vice-consul. A fact?'

'An assumption.'

'Which I would nonetheless include among the facts, in view of subsequent events. Namely: the attempt to kill your Masa, the witness to the killing. An attempt committed in a manner no less, if not even more, exotic than the murder. As you policemen say, the criminal's signatures match. A fact?'

'Arguably.'

'The criminal did not succeed in eliminating Masa – that damned vice-consul interfered once again. So now, instead of one witness, there were two.'

'Why didn't he kill me? I was completely helpless. Even if the snake didn't bite me, he could probably have finished me off in a thousand other ways.'

Doronin pressed his hand against his chest modestly.

'My friend, you are forgetting that just at that moment your humble servant appeared on the scene. The murder of the consul of a great power would be a serious international scandal. There has been nothing of the kind since Griboedov's time. On that occasion, as a sign of his contrition, the Shah of Persia presented the Tsar of Russia with the finest diamond in his crown, which weighed nine hundred carats. What do you think,' Vsevolod Vitalievich asked brightly, 'how many carats would they value me at? Of course, I'm not an ambassador, only a consul, but I have more diplomatic experience that Griboedov did. And precious stones are cheaper nowadays ... All right, joking aside, the fact is that No-Face did not dare to kill me or did not want to. As you have already had occasion to realise, in Japan even the bandits are patriots of their homeland.'

Erast Petrovich was not entirely convinced by this line of reasoning, but he did not object.

'And by the way, I do not hear any words of gratitude for saving your life,' said the consul, pretending his feelings were hurt.

'Thank you.'

'Don't mention it. Let's move on. After the unsuccessful bit of theatre with the "creeping thing", No-Face somehow finds out that the investigation has another strange, incredible piece of evidence – the prints of his thumb. Unlike Bukhartsev and – yes, I admit it – your humble servant, No-Face took this circumstance very seriously. And I can guess why. You drew up a verbal portrait of the man whom Masa saw at the Rakuen, did you not?'

'Yes.'

'Does it match the description of your uninvited guest?'

'Marginally. Only as far as the height is concerned – little over four foot six inches – and the slender build. However, in Japan that kind of physique is not unusual. As for all the rest ... At the gambling den, Masa saw a doddery old man with a stoop, a trembling head and pigmentation spots on his face. But my old m-man was quite fresh and sprightly. I wouldn't put his age at more than sixty.'

'There now,' said the consul, raising one finger. 'The ninja were known to be masters at changing their appearance. But if Mr Folds's theory is correct, it is impossible to change the prints of your fingers. The similarity of the prints on the collar and the mirror confirms that. But in any case, No-Face decided on a desperately audacious move – to destroy the evidence right there in the office of the chief of police. He tried to get away, but failed. It is curious that before he died he said: "*Kongojyo*".'

'Did I remember it correctly?'

'Yes, "*Kongojyo*" means "Diamond Chariot".'

'What?' the titular counsellor asked in amazement. 'In what sense?'

'This is not the time to launch into a detailed lecture on Buddhism, so I'll give you a brief, simplified explanation. Buddhism has two main branches, the so-called Vehicles, or Chariots. Everyone who desires liberation and light can choose which of them to board. The Lesser Chariot speeds along the road leading to the salvation of only your own soul. The Greater Chariot is for those who wish to save all of mankind. The devotee of the Lesser Road strives to attain the status of an arhat, an absolutely free being. The devotee of the Greater Road can become a bodhisattva – an ideal being, who is filled with compassion for the whole of creation, but does not wish to achieve Liberation while all others are in bondage.'

'I like the b-bodhisattvas best,' Erast Petrovich remarked.

'That is because they are closer to the Christian idea of self-sacrifice. I am a misanthropist and should prefer to become an arhat. I'm only afraid that I'm rather lacking in righteousness.'

'And what is the Diamond Chariot?'

'It is an entirely distinct branch of Buddhism, extremely complex and abounding in mysteries. The uninitiated know very little about it. According to this teaching, a man can attain Enlightenment and become a Buddha while still alive, but this requires a special firmness of faith. That is why the chariot is called diamond – there is nothing in nature harder than diamond.'

'I don't understand anything at all,' Fandorin said after a moment's thought. 'How is it possible to become a Buddha and attain enlightenment, if you commit murders and other abominations?'

'Well, let's assume that's no great problem. How many vile tricks do our holy sermonisers play on us, all in the name of Christ and the salvation of our souls? It's not a matter of the teaching. I know monks of the Singon sect who profess the path of the Diamond Chariot. They work away, enlightening themselves without interfering with anyone. They don't let anyone else into their business, but they don't take any interest in anyone else's. And they are not fanatical in the least. It is hard to imagine any of them cutting off his face with a howl of *"Kongojyo!"*. And, above all, I have never heard of this formula having any magical significance . . . You see, in Japanese Buddhism, it is believed that certain sutras or verbal formulas possess magical power. There is the sacred invocation *"Namu Amida Butsu"*, there is the Lotus Sutra, *"Namu-myoho-rengekyo"*. The monks repeat them thousands of times, believing that this advances them along the Path of the Buddha. Probably there is some fanatical sect that uses *"Kongojyo"* as an exclamation . . .' Vsevolod Vitalievich spread his hands and shrugged. 'Unfortunately, there is no way for a European to get to the bottom of these matters. We'd better get back to No-Face before we lose our way in the thickets of Buddhism. Let us check the sequence of events. Question: Why was Blagolepov killed? Answer: Because he was blabbing to all and sundry about his passengers from the night before. There doesn't seem to have been any other reason to set a master of such subtle killing techniques on such a worthless little man. Correct?'

'Correct.'

'No-Face is a ninja, and history tells us that they are hired for money. It's an entirely different question where a ninja could appear from in 1878 – perhaps now we shall never find out. But since a man has appeared who has decided to live and die according to the laws of this sect, then his mode of life must also have been the same. In other words, he was a mercenary. Question: Who hired him? Answer: We don't know. Question: Why was he hired?'

'To shield and guard three samurai from Satsuma?' Fandorin suggested.

'Most probably. Hiring a master like that must cost a great deal of money. Where would former samurai get that from? So there are serious players in the wings of this game, able to place stakes large enough to break the bank. We know who the bank is – it's Minister Okubo. I shall write all this down in my report to the ambassador. I shall add that the owner of a gambling den is the leader, messenger or intermediary of the Satsuman killers. The Japanese police have him under observation and at the present time that is our only lead. What do you say, Fandorin. Have I missed anything in my analysis of the situation?'

'Your analysis is perfectly good,' the titular counsellor declared.

'*Merci*.' The consul raised his dark glasses and rubbed his eyes wearily. 'However, my superiors appreciate me less for my analytical competence than for my ability to propose solutions. What shall I write in the summary of my report?'

'Conclusions,' said Fandorin, also walking over to the window to look at the leaves of the acacias swaying in the rain. 'Four in number. The conspirators have an agent in police circles. That is one.'

Doronin shuddered.

'How do you deduce that?'

'From the facts. First the killer discovered that I had a witness to Blagolepov's murder. Then someone warned the samurai about the ambush at the *g-godaun*. And finally the <u>ninja</u> knew about the thumbprints and where they were being kept. There can only be one conclusion: someone from my group, or someone who receives information about the course of the investigation, is connected with the conspirators.'

'Such as me, for instance?'

'Such as you, for instance.'

The consul knitted his brows together and paused for a moment.

'Very well, the first conclusion is clear. Go on.'

'The hunchback undoubtedly knows that he is being followed and under no circumstances will he contact the Satsumans. That is two. Therefore, we shall have to force the hunchback to act. That is three. However, in order to make sure there are no more leaks, the operation will have to be conducted without the knowledge of the municipal and Japanese police. That is four. And that is all.'

Having thought over what had been said, Doronin shook his head sceptically.

'Well, so that's the way of it. But what does "force him to act" mean? How do you envisage that?'

'Semushi has to escape from surveillance. Then he will definitely go dashing to find his accomplices. And he will lead me to them. But to carry out this operation, I need approval to take independent action.'

'What action, precisely?'

'I don't know yet,' the titular counsellor replied dispassionately. 'Whatever action is n-necessary.'

'You don't want to tell me,' Doronin guessed. 'Well, that's right. Otherwise, if your operation fails, you'll note me down as a spy.' He drummed his fingers on the windowpane. 'You know what, Erast Petrovich? In order not to compromise the experiment, I shall not write to the ambassador about your conclusions. And as for the authority to act, consider that you have been granted it by your immediate superior. Act as you think necessary. But just one thing . . .' The consul hesitated momentarily. 'Perhaps you would agree to take me, not as your confidant, but as your agent? It will be hard for you, on your own, with no help. Of course, I am no ninja, but I could carry out some simple assignment.'

Fandorin looked Vsevolod Vitalievich up and down and politely refused.

'Thank you. The embassy secretary, Shirota, will be enough for me. Although . . . no. I think perhaps I need to speak with him first . . .'

The titular counsellor hesitated – he remembered that the Japanese had been behaving strangely recently, blenching and blushing for no reason, giving Fandorin sideways glances; the secretary's attitude to the vice-consul, initially exceedingly friendly, had clearly undergone a change.

Erast Petrovich decided to find out what the matter was without delay.

He went to the administrative office, where the spinster Blagolepova was hammering away deafeningly on the keys of the Remington. When she saw Fandorin, she blushed, adjusted her collar with a swift gesture and started hammering even more briskly.

'I need to have a word with you,' the titular counsellor said in a quiet voice, leaning across Shirota's desk.

Shirota jerked in his seat and turned pale.

'Yes, and I with you. It is high time.'

Erast Petrovich was surprised. He enquired cautiously:

'You wished to speak to me? About what?'

'No, you first.' The secretary got to his feet and buttoned up his frock coat determinedly. 'Where would you like it to be?'

To the accompaniment of the Remington's hysterical clattering, they walked out into the garden. The rain had stopped, glassy drops were falling from the branches and birds were singing overhead.

'Tell me, Shirota, you have linked your life with Russia. May I ask why?'

The secretary listened to the question and narrowed his eyes tensely. He answered crisply, in military style, as if he had prepared his answer in advance.

'Mr Vice-Consul, I chose to link my life with your country, because Japan needs Russia very much. The East and the West are too different, they cannot join with each other without an intermediary. Once, in ancient times, Korea served as a bridge between Japan and great China. Now, in order to join harmoniously with great Europe, we need Russia. With the assistance of your country, which combines within itself both the East and the West, my homeland will flourish and join the ranks of the great powers of the world. Not now, of course, but in twenty or thirty years' time. That is why I work in the Russian consulate . . .'

Erast Petrovich cleared his throat with an embarrassed air – he had not been expecting such a clear-cut response, and the idea that a backward oriental country could transform itself into a great power in thirty years was simply laughable. However, there was no point in offending the Japanese.

'I see,' Fandorin said slowly, feeling that he had not really achieved his goal.

'You also have a very beautiful literature,' the secretary added, and bowed, as if to indicate that he had nothing more to add.

There was a pause. The titular counsellor wondered whether he ought to ask straight out: 'Why do you keep looking daggers at me?' But from the viewpoint of Japanese etiquette, that would probably be appallingly impolite.

Shirota broke the silence first.

'Is that what the vice-consul wished to speak to me about?'

There was a note of surprise in his voice.

'Well, actually, y-yes . . . But what did you wish to speak to me about?'

The secretary's face turned from white to crimson. He gulped and then cleared his throat.

'About the captain's daughter.' Seeing the amazement in the other man's eyes, he explained: 'About Sophia Diogenovna.'

'What has happened?'

'Mr Vice-Consul, do you . . . do you ruv her?'

Because the Japanese had mispronounced the 'l' in the crucial word, and even more because the very supposition was so unthinkable, Erast Petrovich did not immediately understand the meaning of the question.

The evening before, on returning home from the police station, the young man had discovered a powerfully scented envelope with nothing written on it on the small table in his bedroom. When he opened it, he found a pink sheet of paper. Traced out on it, in a painstaking hand with flourishes and squiggles, were four lines of verse:

> My poor heart can bear this no more
> Oh, come quickly to help me now!
> And if you do not come, you know
> I shall lose my life for you.

Bemused, Fandorin had gone to consult Masa. He showed him the envelope, and his servant ran through a brief pantomime: a long plait, large round eyes, two spheres in front of his chest. 'The spinster Blag- olepova,' Erast Petrovich guessed. And then he immediately remembered that she had promised to write out her favourite stanza of love poetry from her album, a piece composed by the conductor from the St Pafnutii. He stuck the sheet of paper into the first book that came to hand and forgot all about it.

But now it seemed there was a serious emotional drama being played out.

'If you love Miss Blagolepova, if your in-ten-tions are hon-our-ab-le, I will stand aside . . . I understand, you are her com-pat-ri-ot, you are handsome and rich, and what can I offer her?' Shirota was terribly nervous, he pronounced the more difficult words with especial care and avoided looking in Fandorin's eyes, lowering his head right down on to his chest. 'But if . . .' His voice started to tremble. 'But if you intend to exploit the de-fence-less-ness of a solitary young woman . . . Do you wish to?'

'Do I wish to what?' asked the titular counsellor, unable to follow the thread of the conversation – he found deductive reasoning far easier than talk on intimate matters.

'Exploit the de-fence-less-ness of a solitary young woman.'

'No, I do not.'

'Not at all, at all? Only honestly!'

Erast Petrovich pondered, to make sure the reply would be quite honest. He recalled the spinster Blagolepova's thick plait, her cow's eyes, the verse from her album.

'Not at all.'

'So, your in-ten-tions are hon-our-ab-le,' said the poor secretary, and he became even gloomier. 'You will make Sophia Diogenovna a pro-po-sal?'

'Why on earth should I?' said Fandorin, starting to get angry. 'I have no interest in her at all!'

Shirota raised a brighter face for a moment, but immediately narrowed his eyes suspiciously.

'And you did not go to the Rakuen and risk your life there, and you do not now pay her salary out of your own pocket because you love her?'

Erast Petrovich suddenly felt sorry for him.

'The idea never even entered my head,' the vice-consul said in a gentle voice. 'I assure you. I do not find anything at all about Miss Blagolepova attractive . . .' He stopped short, not wishing to hurt the lovelorn secretary's feelings. 'No, that is . . . she is, of course, very p-pretty and, so to speak . . .'

'She is the finest girl in the world!' Shirota exclaimed sternly, interrupting the vice-consul. 'She . . . she is a captain's daughter! Like Masha Mironova from Pushkin's *Captain's Daughter*! But if you do not love Sophia Diogenovna, why have you done so much for her?'

'Well, how could I not do it? You said it yourself: solitary, defenceless, in a foreign country . . .'

Shirota sighed and declared solemnly:

'I love Miss Blagolepova.'

'I had g-guessed as much.'

The Japanese suddenly bowed solemnly – not in the European manner, with just the chin, but from the waist. And he didn't straighten up immediately, only after five seconds had passed.

Now he looked straight into Fandorin's face, and there were tears glistening in his eyes. In his agitation, all his 'l's' became 'r's' again.

'You are a nobur man, Mr Vice-Consur. I am your eternar debtor.'

Soon half of Japan will be my eternal debtors, Erast Petrovich thought ironically, not wishing to admit to himself that he was touched.

'There is onry one bitter thing.' Shirota sighed. 'I sharr never be abur to repay your nobirity.'

'Oh, yes you will,' said the titular counsellor, taking him by the elbow. 'Let's go to my rooms. That damned p-plum rain has started falling again.'

Raise no umbrella
When the sky is scattering
Its springtime plum rain

SIRIUS

The night smelled of tar and green slime – that was from the dirty River Yosidagawa splashing near by, squeezed in between the *godauns* and the cargo wharves. Erast Petrovich's valet was sitting at the agreed spot, under the wooden bridge, pondering the vicissitudes of fate and waiting. When Semushi appeared, the master would howl like a dog – Masa had taught him how. In fact they had spent a whole hour on a *renshu* duet, until the neighbours came to the consulate and said they would complain about the Russians to the police if they didn't stop torturing that poor dog. They had been forced to abandon the *renshu* rehearsal, but the master could already do it quite well. .

There were lots of dogs in Yokohama, and they often howled at night, so neither Semushi nor the police agents would be suspicious. The main concern was something else – not to confuse the sound with a genuine dog. But Masa hoped he wouldn't get confused. It would be shameful for a vassal not to be able to tell his master's noble voice from the howl of some mongrel.

Masa had to sit under the bridge very quietly, without moving at all, but he could do that. In his former life, when he was still an apprentice in the honourable Chobei-gumi gang, he had sat and waited on watch duty or in an ambush many, many times. It wasn't boring at all, because an intelligent man could always find something to think about.

It was absolutely out of the question to make any noise or move about, because there was a police agent, disguised as a beggar, hanging about on the wooden bridge right over his head. When someone out late walked by, the agent started intoning sutras through his nose, and very naturally too – a couple of times a copper coin even jangled against the planking. Masa wondered whether the agent handed in the alms to his boss afterwards or not. And if he did, whether the coppers went into the imperial treasury.

There were detectives stationed all the way along the road leading from the Rakuen to Semushi's home: one agent at every crossroads. Some were hiding in gateways, some in the ditch. The senior agent, the most experienced, prowled along after Semushi. He was shrouded in a grey cloak, he had soundless felt sandals on his feet, and he could hide so quickly that no matter how many times you looked round, you would never spot anyone behind you.

Hanging back about fifty paces behind the senior agent were another three – just in case something unforeseen happened. Then the senior agent would give them a quick flash from the lamp under his cloak, and they would run up to him.

That was how strictly they were following Semushi, there was no way he could get away from the police agents. But the master and Masa had thought and thought and come up with a plan. As soon as the Vice-Consul of the Russian Empire started howling in the distance, Masa had to . . .

But just at that moment Masa heard a wail that he recognised immediately. Erast Petrovich howled quite authentically, but even so, not like one of Yokohama's stray mutts – there was something thoroughbred about that melancholy sound, as if it were being made by a bloodhound or, at the very least, a basset.

It was time to move from thought to action.

Masa strolled silently under the planks until he was behind the 'beggar's' back. He took three small steps on tiptoe, and when the agent turned round at the rustling sound, he leapt forward and smacked him gently below the ear with the edge of his hand. The 'beggar' gave a quiet sob and tumbled over on to his side. A whole heap of coppers spilled out of his cup.

Masa took the coins for himself so that everything would look right and, in general, they would come in handy. His Imperial Highness could manage without them somehow.

He squatted down beside the unconscious man in the shadow of the parapet and started watching.

There was a fine drizzle falling, but the corner from which Semushi ought to appear was lit up by two street lamps. The hunchback would walk across the little bridge over the canal, then cut across a plot of wasteland to the bridge over the Yosidagawa. So he would have the junction of the river and the canal on his right, one bridge ahead of him, another behind him, and nothing on his left but the dark wasteland – and that was the whole point of the plan.

There was the squat, lumpish figure. The hunchback moved with a heavy, plodding walk, waddling slightly from side to side.

It probably wasn't easy lugging a hump around all the time, thought Masa. And how easy could it be to live with a deformity like that? When he was little, the other boys must have teased him. When he grew a bit, the girls all turned their noses up. That was why Semushi had turned out so villainous and spiteful. Or maybe it wasn't because of that at all. On the street where Masa grew up, there had been a hunchback, a street sweeper. Even more hunched and crooked than this one, he could barely hobble along. But he was kind, everyone liked him. And they used to say: He's so good because the Buddha gave him a hump. It wasn't the hump that mattered, but what kind of *kokoro* a man had. If the *kokoro* was right, a hump would only make you better, but if it was rotten, you would hate the whole wide world.

Meanwhile, the owner of a vicious *kokoro* had crossed the little bridge.

Erast Petrovich's servant told himself: 'Now the master will pull the string' – and at that very moment there was a loud crash. Suddenly, out of the blue, a cart that was standing on the little bridge had lurched over sideways – its axle must have snapped. The large barrel standing on the cart smashed down on to the ground and burst open, releasing a stream of black tar that flooded the planking surface – no one could walk or drive across now . . .

Semushi swung round when he heard the crash and put his hand inside his jacket, but he saw that nothing dangerous had happened. There wasn't a single soul to be seen. The cart driver must have left his goods close to the market yesterday and settled down in some nearby eating-house where he could get a meal and a bed for the night. But his *kuruma* was old and decrepit, ready to break down at any moment.

The hunchback stood still for a minute or so, turning his head in all directions. Finally he was satisfied and walked on.

A grey shadow appeared on the far side of the bridge – Masa could see it. It stepped into the black puddle and stuck there.

Of course it did! Masa had bought the tar himself. He had chosen the very lousiest kind, as runny as possible and so sticky you could never get out of it.

There was a gleam of light – that had to be the agent signalling to the others. Three more shadows appeared. They started rushing about on the bank, not knowing what to do. One decided to risk it after all and got stuck fast too.

Then Semushi looked round, enjoyed the sight for a moment, shrugged and went on his way. What was it to him? He knew there were probably agents up ahead as well.

When the hunchback reached the river, Masa growled and dashed out to meet him. He was holding a *wakizashi*, a short sword, and brandishing it wildly – it was a treat to see the way the blade glinted in the light of the street lamp.

'For the Chobei-gumi!!' Masa shouted out, but not too loudly: so that Semushi could hear, but the stuck policemen couldn't. 'Do you recognise me, Hunchback? You're done for now!'

He deliberately leapt out sooner than he should have done if he really wanted to kill the rotten snake.

Semushi had time to recoil and pull out his revolver, that vile weapon of cowards. But Masa wasn't afraid of the revolver – he knew that the senior police agent, a man with very deft hands, had filed down the hammer the day before yesterday.

The hunchback clicked once, and twice, but didn't bother to click a third time, he spun round and took to his heels. At first he ran back towards the little bridge. Then he realised he'd get stuck in the tar and the police agents wouldn't save him. He turned sharply to the right, which was the way he was supposed to go.

Masa caught up with him and, to give him a real scare, slashed him on the arm, just above the elbow, with the very tip of the blade. The hunchback yelped and made up his mind – he set off across the wasteland, into the darkness. The wasteland was large, it stretched all the way to Tobemura, where they executed criminals and afterwards displayed their severed heads on poles. Previously, when he was still Badger, Masa had been certain that sooner or later he would end up in Tobemura too, goggling down at people with his dead eyes, frightening them. That wasn't very likely now, though. The top of a pole was no place for the head of Sibata Masahiro, liege vassal of Mr Fandorin.

He sliced the sword through the air just behind the back of Semushi's head a couple of times, then stumbled and sprawled full length on the ground. He deliberately cursed, as if he had hurt his leg badly. And now he ran more slowly, limping along.

He shouted:

'Stop! Stop, you coward! You won't get away anyway!'

But by now the hunchback should have realised that he would get away – not only from the unlucky avenger, but also from the agents of the Yokohama police. That was why this place had been chosen: on the wasteland you could see anyone running after you from a long way away.

Masa gave a final, helpless shout:

'It doesn't matter, I'll finish you the next time.'

And then he stopped.

The wasteland was long, but Semushi couldn't get off it, because the river was on his right and the canal was on his left. Right at the far end, by the bridge to Tobemura, Shirota-san was waiting in the bushes. He was an educated man, of course, but he had no experience in matters like this. He had to be helped.

Brushing away his sweat with one hand, Masa ran towards the bank of the Yosidagawa, where there was a boat waiting. A few thrusts of the pole, and he'd be on the other side. If he ran as fast his legs could carry him, he would be just in time – this way was shorter than going across the wasteland. And if he was a bit late – that was why Shirota-san was there. He could show Masa which way Semushi had turned.

The bow of the boat sliced through the black, oily water. Masa pushed the pole against the spongy bottom, repeating to himself:

'Ii-ja-nai-ka! Ii-ja-nai-ka!'

Fandorin's valet was in a very cheerful mood. His master's head was pure gold. He should join the Yakuza – he could make a great career.

Ah, how funny the policemen had looked, floundering in the tar!

The rain came to an end and the stars emerged, scattered across the sky like diamonds, growing brighter and brighter with every minute.

Erast Petrovich walked home slowly, because he was not looking down at his feet, but up, admiring the heavenly illuminations. One particular star right over by the horizon, at the very edge of the sky, was shining especially beautifully. It had a bluish, sad kind of light. The titular counsellor's knowledge concerning the heavenly bodies and constellations was scant: he could recognise only the two bears, Great and Small, and so the name of the spark of blue light was a mystery to him. Fandorin decided it could be called Sirius.

The vice-consul was in an equable and tranquil mood. What was done was done, he could not change anything now. The head of the inquiry had quite unceremoniously, with deliberate intent, affronted the Law: he had impeded the police in the performance of their duty and conspired in the escape of a man suspected of a serious crime against the state. If Semushi got away from Masa and Shirota, the only thing left for him to do would be to confess, and that would be followed by resignation in disgrace and, probably, a trial.

Once inside his deserted apartment, Erast Petrovich took off his frock coat and trousers and sat down in the drawing room in just his shirt. He didn't turn the light on. After a little while he suddenly snapped his fingers, as if a good idea had just occurred to him, but the result of this enlightenment was strange: Fandorin simply put on his hairnet and hid his upper lip under a moustache cover, after first curling up the sides of his moustache with little tongs. God only knows why the young man did all this – he was clearly not preparing to go to bed, he didn't even go into the bedroom.

For about half an hour the titular counsellor sat in the armchair without a single thought in his head, twirling an unlit cigar in his fingers. Then someone rang the doorbell.

Erast Petrovich nodded, as if that was exactly what he had been expecting. But he didn't pull on his trousers; on the contrary, he took off his shirt.

The bell trilled again, louder this time. Without hurrying, the vice-consul slipped his arms into the sleeves of a silk dressing gown and tied the tasselled belt. He stood in front of the mirror and imitated a yawn. And only after that did he light the kerosene lamp and walk towards the hallway.

'Asagawa, is that you?' he asked in a sleepy voice when he saw the inspector outside the door. 'What's happened? I gave my servant leave, so I . . . Why are you j-just standing there?'

But the Japanese did not come in. He bowed abruptly and said in an unsteady voice:

'There can be no forgiveness for me . . . My men have let Semushi get away. I . . . I have nothing to say to excuse myself.'

The light of the lamp fell on Asagawa's miserable face. A *lost* face, thought Erast Petrovich, and he felt sorry for the inspector, for whom losing face before a foreigner must have been double torment. However, the situation required severity, otherwise Fandorin would have to launch into explanations and be forced to lie.

The vice-consul counted to twenty in his head and then, without saying a word, he slammed the door in the Japanese policeman's face.

Now he could go into the bedroom. There wouldn't be any news from Masa and Shirota before morning. It would be good to get a little sleep at least – tomorrow would probably be a hard day.

But his agitation had not completely subsided. Sensing that he wouldn't be able to get to sleep straight away, Fandorin took the second volume of

Goncharov's *The Frigate Pallada* from the drawing room: it was the best possible bedtime reading.

The gas burner in the bedroom hissed, but did not ignite. Erast Petrovich was not surprised – gas lighting had reached Yokohama only recently, and the way it functioned was far from ideal. For occasions like this there was a candlestick beside the bed.

The young man found his way through the pitch darkness to the little table and felt for the matches.

The room was illuminated by a gentle, flickering light.

Fandorin dropped his dressing gown on the floor, turned round and cried out.

Lying there in the bed, with her elbow propped on the pillow, watching him with a still, shimmering gaze, was O-Yumi. Her dress, bodice and silk stockings were hanging over the footboard of the bed. The blanket had slipped down to expose her blindingly white shoulder.

The vision sat up, so that the blanket slipped down to her waist, a supple hand reached out for the candelabra and carried it to her lips – and once again it was dark.

Erast Petrovich almost groaned – he felt such piercing pain at the disappearance of the lovely apparition.

He cautiously reached out with one hand, afraid of discovering nothing but emptiness in the darkness. But what his fingers touched was hot, smooth, alive.

A husky voice said:

'I thought you were never going to come in . . .'

The sheet rustled and gentle but surprisingly strong hands embraced Fandorin round the neck and pulled him forward . . .

The scent of skin and hair set the pulse pounding in Fandorin's temples.

'Where did you . . .' he whispered breathlessly, but didn't finish – hot lips covered his mouth.

Not another word was spoken in the bedroom. In the world into which the titular counsellor had been drawn by those gentle hands and fragrant lips, there were no words, there could not be any, they would only have confused and disrupted the enchantment.

After his recent adventure in Calcutta, which had led to his missing the steamship, Erast Petrovich regarded himself as an experienced man of the world, but in O-Yumi's embrace he did not feel like a man, but some incredible musical instrument – sometimes a seductive flute, sometimes a divine violin or a sweet reed pipe, and the virtuoso magical musician played on all of them, mingling heavenly harmony with earthly algebra.

In the brief intermissions the intoxicated vice-consul attempted to babble something, but the only reply was kisses, the touch of tender fingertips and quiet laughter.

When grey streaks of dawn started filtering in through the window, Fandorin made an incredible effort of will and surfaced from the hypnotic haze. He had enough strength for only a single question – the most important one of all, nothing else had any meaning. He put his hands on her temples and held her so that those huge eyes filled with mysterious light were very close.

'Will you stay with me?'

She shook her head.

'But . . . but you will come again?'

O-Yumi also put her hands on his temples, made a light circular movement and pressed gently, and Fandorin instantly fell asleep without realising it. He simply fell into a deep sleep and didn't even feel her hands gently supporting his head as they laid it on the pillow.

At that moment Erast Petrovich was already dreaming. In his dream he was rushing straight up to the sky in a blue chariot that glittered with an icy sheen, rushing higher and higher. His road led to a star that was drawing the diamond chariot towards it with its transparent rays. Little gold stars went rushing past, wafting fresh, icy breezes into his face. Erast Petrovich felt very good, and the only thing he remembered was that he mustn't look back, no matter what – or he would fall and be dashed to pieces.

But he didn't look back. He rushed onwards and upwards, towards the star. The star called Sirius.

It shines, unaware
Even of its own true name.
The star Sirius

HORSE DUNG

Fandorin was woken by someone patting him gently but insistently on the cheek.

'O-Yumi,' he whispered, and saw before him a face with slanting eyes, but, alas, it was not the sorceress of the night, but the secretary Shirota.

'I beg your pardon,' said the secretary, 'but you simply would not wake up, and I was starting to feel alarmed . . .'

The titular counsellor sat up in bed and looked around. The bedroom was illumined by the slanting rays of the early sun. There no O-Yumi, nor any sign at all of her recent presence.

'Mr Vice-Consul, I am ready to make my report,' Shirota began, holding a sheet of paper at the ready.

'Yes, yes, of course,' Fandorin muttered, glancing under the blanket.

The bedsheet was crumpled, but that didn't mean anything. Maybe there was something left – a long hair, a crumb of powder, a scarlet trace of lipstick?

Not a thing.

Had it all been a dream?

'Following your instructions, I concealed myself in the bushes beside the fork at which the two roads separate. At forty-three minutes past two a running man appeared from the direction of the wasteland . . .'

'Sniff that!' Fandorin interrupted, burying his nose in the pillow. 'What is that scent?'

The secretary took the pillow and conscientiously drew air in through his nose.

'That is the aroma of *ayameh*. What is that in Russian, now. . . . iris.'

The titular counsellor's face lit up in a happy smile.

It wasn't a dream!

She had been here! It was the aroma of her perfume!

'Iris is the main aroma of the present season,' Shirota explained. 'Women scent themselves with it and they steep the laundry in it at the washhouses. In April the aroma of the season was wistaria, in June it will be azalea.'

The smile slid off Erast Petrovich's face.

'May I continue?' the Japanese asked, handing back the pillow.

And he continued his report. A minute later Fandorin had completely stopped thinking about the scent of irises and his nocturnal apparition.

*

The paddy fields shone unbearably brightly in the sunlight, as if the entire valley had been transformed into one immense cracked mirror. The dark cracks in the effulgent surface were the boundaries that divided the plots into little rectangles, and in each rectangle there was a figure in a broad straw hat, pottering through the water, bent double. The peasants were weeding the rice fields.

At the centre of the fields there was a small, wooded hill, crowned by a red roof with its edges curled upwards. Erast Petrovich already knew that it was an abandoned Shinto shrine.

'The peasants don't go there any more,' said Shirota. 'It's haunted. Last year they found a dead tramp by the door. Semushi was right to choose a place like this to hide. It's a very fine refuge for a bad man. And it has a clear view of all the approaches.'

'And what will happen to the shrine now?'

'Either they will burn it down and build a new one, or they will perform a ceremony of purification. The village elder and the *kannusi*, the priest, have not decided yet.'

A narrow embankment no more than five paces wide ran through the fields to the shrine. Erast Petrovich examined the path to the hill carefully, then the moss-covered steps leading up to the strange red wooden gateway: just two verticals and a crosspiece, an empty gateway with no gates and no fence. A gateway that did not separate anything from anything.

'That is the *torii*,' the secretary explained. 'The gate to the Other World.'

Well, that made sense, if it led to the Other World.

The titular counsellor had an excellent pair of binoculars with twelve-fold magnification, a souvenir of the siege of Plevna.

'I can't see Masa,' said Fandorin. 'Where is he?'

'You are looking in the wrong direction. Your servant is over there, in the communal plot. Farther left, farther left.'

The vice-consul and his assistant were lying in the thick grass at the edge of a rice field. Erast Petrovich caught Masa in the twin circles. He was no different from the peasants: entirely naked, apart from a loincloth, with a fan hanging behind his back. Except perhaps that his sides were rounder than those of the other workers.

The round-sided peasant straightened up, fanned himself and looked round towards the village. It was definitely him: fat cheeks and half-closed eyes. He looked close enough for Fandorin to flick him on the nose.

'He has been here since the morning. He took a job as a field-hand for ten sen. We agreed that if he noticed anything special, he would hang the fan behind his back. See, the fan is behind his back. He has spotted something!'

Fandorin focused his binoculars on the hill again and started slowly examining the hunchback's hiding place, square by square.

'Did he come straight here from Yokohama? He d-didn't stop off anywhere along the way?'

'He came straight here.'

What was that white patch there, among the branches?

Erast Petrovich turned the little wheel and gave a quiet whistle. There was a man sitting in a tree. The hunchback? What was he doing up there?

But last night Semushi had been wearing a dark brown kimono, not a white one.

The man sitting in the tree turned his head. Fandorin still couldn't make out the face, but the shaved nape glinted.

No, it wasn't Semushi! His hair was cut in a short, stiff brush.

Fandorin moved the binoculars on. Suddenly something glinted in the undergrowth. Then again, and again.

Just adjust the focus slightly.

Oho!

A man wearing a kimono with its hem turned up was standing on an open patch of ground. He was absolutely motionless. Beside him was bamboo pole stuck into the earth.

Suddenly the man moved. His legs and trunk didn't stir, but his sword scattered sparks of sunlight and severed bamboo rings flew off the pole: one, two, three, four. What incredible skill!

Then the miraculous swordsman swung round to face the opposite direction – apparently there was another pole there. But Erast Petrovich was not watching the sword blade any longer, he was looking at the left sleeve of the kimono. It was either twisted or tucked up.

'Why did you strike the ground with your fist? What did you see?' Shirota whispered eagerly in his ear.

Fandorin handed him the binoculars and pointed him in the right direction.

'Kataudeh!' the secretary exclaimed. 'The man with the withered arm!' So the others must be there!'

The vice-consul wasn't listening, he was scribbling something rapidly in his notebook. He tore the page out and started writing on another one.

'Right now, Shirota. Go to the Settlement as fast you can. Give this to Sergeant Lockston. Tell him the d-details yourself. The second note is for Inspector Asagawa.'

'Also as fast as I can, right?'

'No, on the contrary. You must walk slowly from Lockston to the Japanese police station. You can even drink tea along the way.'

Shirota gaped at the titular counsellor in amazement. Then he seemed to get the idea and he nodded.

The sergeant arrived with his entire army of six constables armed with carbines.

Erast Petrovich was waiting for the reinforcements on the approach to the village. He praised them for getting there so quickly and briefly explained the disposition of forces.

'What, aren't we going to rush them?' Lockston asked, disappointed. 'My guys are just spoiling for a scrap.'

'N-no scrap. We're two miles from the Settlement, beyond the consular jurisdiction.'

'Damn the jurisdiction, Rusty! Don't forget: these three degenerates killed a white man! Maybe not in person, but they're all in the same gang.'

'Walter, we have to respect the laws of the country in which we find ourselves.'

The sergeant turned sulky.

'Then why the hell did you write: "as quickly as possible and bring long-range weapons"?'

'Your men are needed to put a cordon round the area. Set them out round the edge of the fields, in secret. Get your constables to lie on the ground and cover themselves with straw, with a distance of two to three hundred paces between them. If the criminals try to leave through the water, fire warning shots, drive them back on to the hill.'

'And who's going to nab the bandits?'

'The Japanese police.'

Lockston narrowed his eyes.

'Why didn't you just call the Japs? What do you need the municipals for?'

The titular counsellor didn't answer and the sergeant nodded knowingly.

'To make sure, right? You don't trust the yellow-bellies. You're afraid they'll let them get away. Maybe even *deliberately*, right?'

This question went unanswered too.

'I'm going to wait for Asagawa in the village. You're responsible for the other three sides of the square,' said Fandorin.

He had to wait for a long time – obviously, before Shirota visited the Japanese police station, he had not only drunk tea, but dined as well.

When the sun reached its zenith, the workers started moving back to their houses to rest before their afternoon labours. Masa came back with them.

He explained with gestures that all three samurai were there, and the hunchback was with them. They were keeping a sharp lookout in all directions. They couldn't be taken by surprise.

Erast Petrovich left his valet to keep an eye on the only path that led to the shrine, while he set out to the other side of the village, to meet the Japanese police.

Three hours later a dark spot appeared on the road. Fandorin raised the binoculars to his eyes and gasped. An entire military column was approaching in marching formation from the direction of Yokohama. Bayonets glittered and officers swayed in their saddles in the cloud of dust.

The titular counsellor dashed forward to meet the troops, waving his arms at them from a distance to get them to stop. God forbid that the men on the hill should notice this bristling centipede!

Riding at the front was the vice-intendant of police himself, Kinsuke Suga. Catching sight of Fandorin's gesticulations, he raised his hand and the column halted.

Erast Petrovich did not like the look of the Japanese soldiers: short and skinny, with no moustaches, uniforms that hung on them like sacks, and they had no bearing at all. He remembered Vsevolod Vitalievich telling him that military conscription had been introduced here only very recently and peasants didn't want to serve in the army. Of course not! For three hundred years commoners had been forbidden to carry arms, the samurai chopped their heads off for that. And the result was a nation that consisted of an immense herd of peasant sheep and packs of samurai sheepdogs.

'Your Excellency, why didn't you bring the artillery too?' Fandorin exclaimed angrily as he raced up to the top man.

Suga chuckled contentedly and twirled his moustache.

'If it's needed, we will. Bravo, Mr Fandorin! How on earth did you manage to track down these wolves? You're a genuine hero!'

'I asked the inspector for ten capable agents. Why have you brought an entire regiment of soldiers?'

'It's a battalion,' said Suga, flinging one leg across the saddle and jumping down. His orderly took the reins immediately. 'As soon as I got Asagawa's telegram, I telegraphed the barracks of the Twelfth Infantry Battalion, it's stationed only a mile from here. And I dashed here by train. The railway is a fine invention too!'

The vice-intendant positively radiated energy and enthusiasm. He gave a command in Japanese and the word passed along the line 'Chutaicyo, Chu-taicyo, Chutaicyo!'* Three officers came running towards the head of the column, holding their swords down at their sides.

'We shall need the army for setting an external cordon,' Suga explained. 'Not one of the villains must slip away. You needn't have been so worried, Fandorin, I wasn't going to bring the soldiers any closer. The company commanders will now form the men up into a chain and locate them round the large square. They won't see that from the hill.'

The shoddy-looking soldiers moved with remarkable nimbleness and coordination. Not soaring eagles, of course, but they are rather well drilled, thought Fandorin, correcting his first impression.

In about a minute the battalion had reformed into three very long ranks. One of them stayed where it was, the other two performed a half-about-face and marched off to the left and the right.

Only now could Fandorin see that there was a group of police standing at the end of the column – about fifteen of them, including Asagawa, but the Yokohama inspector was behaving modestly, not like a commander at all. Most of the policemen were middle-aged, severe-looking individuals, the kind that we in Russia call old campaigners. Shirota was there with them – judging from the green colour of his face, he could barely stay on his feet. That was only natural: a sleepless night, nervous stress and the long dash all the way to Yokohama and back again.

---

* Company commanders, company commanders, company commanders! (Japanese)

'The finest fighters in our police,' Suga said proudly, indicating the men. 'Soon you'll see them in action.'

He turned to one of his deputies and started speaking Japanese.

The embassy secretary started, recalling his official duties, and walked up to the titular counsellor.

'The adjutant is reporting that they have already spoken to the village elder. The peasants will work as usual, without giving away our presence in any way. They're going to hold a meeting now. There is a very convenient place.'

The 'very convenient place' proved to be the communal stables, permeated with the stench of dung and horse sweat. But the broad chinks in the wall provided an excellent view of the field and the hill.

The vice-intendant sat on a folding stool, the other police officers stood in a half-circle and the operational staff set about planning the operation. Suga did most of the talking. Confident, brisk, smiling – he was clearly in his element.

'. . . His Excellency objects to the commissar, Mr Iwaoka, that there is no point in waiting for night to come,' Fandorin's interpreter babbled in his ear. 'The weather is expected to be clear, there will be a full moon and the fields will be like a mirror, with every shadow visible from afar. Better during the day. We can creep up to the hill disguised as peasants weeding the fields.'

The police officers droned approvingly in agreement. Suga spoke again.

'His Excellency says that there will be two assault groups, each of two men. Any more will look suspicious. The other members of the operation must remain at a distance from the hill and wait for the signal. After the signal they will run straight through the water without worrying about disguise. The important thing here is speed.'

This time everyone started droning at once, and very ardently, and Inspector Asagawa, who had not opened his mouth until this moment, stepped forward and started bowing like a clockwork doll, repeating over and over: 'Kakka, tanomimas nodeh! Kakka, tanomimas nodeh!'

'Everybody wants to be in an assault group,' Shirota explained. 'Mr Asagawa is requesting permission to atone for his guilt. He says that otherwise it be very difficult for him to live in this world.'

The vice-intendant raised his hand and silence fell immediately.

'I wish to ask the Russian vice-consul's opinion,' Suga said to Fandorin in English. 'What do you think of my plan? This is our joint operation. An operation of two "vices".'

He smiled. Now everyone was looking at Fandorin.

'To be quite honest, I'm surprised,' the titular counsellor said slowly. 'Assault g-groups, an infantry cordon – this is all very fine. But where are the measures to take the conspirators alive? After all, their contacts are really more important to us than they are.'

Shirota translated what had been said – evidently not all the policemen knew English.

The Japanese glanced at each other strangely, one even snickered, as if the *gaijin* had said something stupid.

The vice-intendant sighed. 'We shall, of course, try to capture the criminals, but we are not likely to succeed. Men of this kind are almost never taken alive.'

Fandorin did not like this response, and his suspicions stirred again more strongly than ever.

'Then I tell you what,' he declared. 'I must be in one of the assault groups. In that case I give you my guarantee that you will receive at least one of the c-conspirators alive and not dead.'

'May I enquire how you intend to do this?'

The vice-consul replied evasively:

'When I was a prisoner of the Turks, they taught me a certain trick, but I had better not tell you about it in advance, you will see for yourselves.'

His words produced a strange impression on the Japanese. The policemen started whispering and Suga asked doubtfully:

'You were a prisoner?'

'Yes, I was. During the recent Balkan campaign.'

The commissar with the grey moustache gazed at Erast Petrovich with clear contempt, and the way the others were looking could certainly not have been called flattering.

The vice-intendant walked over and magnanimously slapped Fandorin on the shoulder.

'Never mind, all sorts of things happen in war. During the expedition to Formosa, Guards Lieutenant Tatibana, a most courageous officer, was also taken prisoner. He was badly wounded and unconscious, and the Chinese took him away in a hospital cart. Of course, when he came round, he strangled himself with a bandage. But there isn't always a bandage.'

Then he repeated the same thing in Japanese for the others (Erast Petrovich made out the name 'Tatibana') and Shirota explained quietly:

'In Japan it is believed that a samurai should never be taken prisoner. An absurd idea, of course. A prejudice,' the secretary added hastily.

The titular counsellor became furious. Raising his voice, he repeated stubbornly:

'I must be in the assault group. I insist on it. P-permit me to remind you that without me and my deputies, there would not even be any operation.'

A discussion started among the Japanese, and Fandorin was clearly the subject of it, but his interpreter expounded the essence of the argument briefly and rather apologetically.

'It . . . Generally speaking . . . The gentlemen of the police are discussing the colour of your skin, your height, the size of your nose . . .'

'May I ask you to undress to the waist?' Suga suddenly asked, turning towards the titular counsellor.

And, to set an example, he removed his tunic and shirt first. The vice-intendant's body was firm and compact, and although his stomach was large, it was not at all flabby. But it was not the details of the general's anatomy which caught Erast Petrovich's attention, but the old gold cross dangling on the convex, hairless chest. Catching Fandorin's glance, Suga explained.

'Three hundred years ago our family were Christians. Then, when European missionaries were expelled from the country and their faith was forbidden, my forebears renounced the alien religion, but kept the cross as a relic. It was worn by my great-great-great-grandmother, Donna Maria Suga, who preferred death to renunciation. In her memory, I have also accepted Christianity – it is not forbidden to anyone any longer. Are you undressed? Right, now look at me and at yourself.'

He stood beside Fandorin, shoulder to shoulder, and the reason why they had had to get undressed became clear.

Not only was the vice-consul an entire head taller than the other man, his skin also gleamed with a whiteness that was quite clearly not Japanese.

'The peasants are almost naked,' said Suga. 'You will tower over the field and sparkle like snowy Mount Fuji.'

'But even so,' the titular counsellor declared firmly, 'I must be in the assault g-group.'

They gave up trying to persuade him after that. The policemen grouped around their commander, talking in low voices. Then the one with the grey moustache shouted loudly: 'Kuso! Umano kuso!'

The vice-intendant laughed and slapped him on the shoulder.

'What did he s-say?'

Shirota shrugged.

'Commissar Iwaoka said: "Dung. Horse dung".'

'Did he mean me?' Erast Perovich asked furiously. 'Tell him that in that c-case he . . .'

'No, no, how could you think that!' the secretary interrupted him, while still listening to the conversation. 'This is something else . . . Inspector Asagawa is asking what to do about your height. Peasants are never such ranky beanpours. Did I get that right?'

'Yes, yes.'

Fandorin watched Commissar Iwaoka's actions suspiciously. The commissar moved out of the group, removed his white glove and scooped up a handful of dung.

'Mr Sasaki from the serious crimes group says you are a genuine kirin, but that is all right, because the peasants never straighten up.'

'Who am I?'

'A kirin – it's a mythical animal. Like a giraffe.'

'Aah . . .'

The man with the grey moustache walked up, bowed briefly and slapped the lump of dung straight on to the Russian diplomat's chest. The vice-consul was stupefied.

'There,' Shirota translated. 'Now you no longer look like the snowy peak of Mount Fuji.'

Commissar Iwaoka smeared the foul-smelling, yellow-brown muck across Erast Petrovich's stomach.

Fandorin grimaced, but he endured it.

The true noble man
Is so pure that even dung
Cannot besmirch him

TIGER ON THE LOOSE

It turned out to be possible to get used to a foul smell. The stench of the dung stopped tormenting the titular counsellor's nose quite soon. The flies were far worse. Attracted by the appetising aroma, they flew to congregate on poor Fandorin from all over the Japanese archipelago or, at the very least, from all over the prefecture of Kanagawa. At first he tried to drive them away, then he gave up, because a peasant flapping his hands about might attract attention. He gritted his teeth and endured the nauseating tickling of the multitude of little green brutes busily crawling over his back and chest and face.

The doubled-over diplomat moved along slowly, up to his knees in water, pulling up some kind of vegetation. No one had bothered to explain to him what the weeds looked like, so he was very probably disposing of shoots of rice, but that was the last thing the sweat-drenched vice-consul was worried about. He hated rice, and flooded-field farming, and his own stubbornness, which had secured him a place in an assault group.

The other member of his group was the instigator of the anointment with dung, Iwaoka of the grey moustache. Although, in fact, the commissar no longer had his dashingly curled moustache – he had shaved it off before the operation began, in order to look more like a peasant. Erast Petrovich had managed to save his own moustache, but he had moistened it and let it dangle at the corners of his mouth like two small icicles. This was the only consolation now left to the titular counsellor – in every other respect Iwaoka had come off far more comfortably.

First, the flies took absolutely no interest in him at all – smelly Erast Petrovich was quite enough for them. Secondly, the commissar moved through the champing mud without any visible effort, and the weeding seemed to be no problem to him – every now and then he stopped and rested, waiting for his lagging partner. But Fandorin's envy was provoked most powerfully of all by the large white fan with which the prudent Japanese had armed himself. The titular counsellor would have paid any price now, simply to be able to waft the air on to his face and blow off the accursed flies.

His straw hat, lowered almost all the way down to his chin, had two holes in it so that he could observe the shrine without raising his head. The two 'peasants' had covered the two hundred paces separating the hill from the edge of the field in about an hour and a half. Now they were trampling mud about thirty feet from dry land, but they mustn't go any closer, in order not to alarm the lookout. He already had his eyes fixed on them as it was. They turned this way and that to let him see that they were men of peace, harmless, there was nowhere they could be hiding any weapons.

The support group, consisting of six policemen minus uniforms, was keeping its distance. There was another support group at work on the other side; it couldn't be seen from here.

The vice-intendant was still nowhere to be seen, and Fandorin started feeling concerned about whether he would be able to straighten up when the time for action finally arrived. He cautiously kneaded his waist with one hand, and it responded with an intense ache.

Suddenly, without raising his head, Iwaoka hissed quietly.

It had started!

Two people were walking along the path to the shrine: striding along solemnly in front was the Shinto priest or *kannusi*, in black robes and a hood, and trotting behind him came the female servant of the shrine, or *miko*, in a white kimono and loose scarlet trousers, with long straight hair hanging down at both sides of her face. She stumbled, dropping some kind of bowl, and squatted down gracefully. Then she ran to catch up with the priest, wiggling her hips awkwardly like a young girl. Fandorin couldn't help smiling. Well done, Asagawa, what fine acting!

In front of the steps, the *kannusi* halted, lowered a small twig broom into the bowl and started waving it in all directions, singing something at the same time – Suga had begun the ritual of purification. The vice-intendant's moustache was now dangling downwards, like Fandorin's, and a long, thin grey beard had been glued to His Excellency's chin.

The commissar whispered:

'Go!'

The sentry was surely watching the unexpected visitors, he wouldn't be interested in the peasants now.

Erast Petrovich started moving towards the hill, trying not to splash through the water. Fifteen seconds later they were both in the bamboo thickets. There was liquid mud flowing down over the titular counsellor's ankles.

Iwaoka went up the slope first. He took a few silent steps, stopped to listen, then waved to his partner to say: Come on, it's all right.

And so Fandorin climbed to the top of the hill, staring at the commissar's broad, muscular back.

They lay down under a bush and started looking around.

Iwaoka had picked the ideal spot. From here they could see the shrine, and the stone steps with the two figures – one black, one red and white – slowly climbing up them. On every step Suga stopped and waved his twig broom about. His nasal chant was slowly getting closer.

Up at the top, Semushi was waiting in the sacred gateway. He was wearing just a loincloth – in order to demonstrate his deformity, one must assume – and bowing abjectly right down to the ground.

He's pretending to be a cripple who has found refuge in the abandoned shrine, Fandorin guessed. He wants to make the priest feel sorry for him.

But what about the others?

There they were, the cunning devils.

The Satsumans had hidden behind the shrine – Suga and Asagawa couldn't see that, but from here in the bushes they had a very good view.

Three men in light kimonos were standing, pressing themselves up against the wall, about a dozen paces away from the commissar and the titular counsellor. One, with his withered left arm strapped to his side, was peeping cautiously round the corner, the two others kept their eyes fixed on him.

All three of them had swords, Fandorin noted. They had obtained new ones from somewhere, but he couldn't see any firearms.

The man with the withered arm looked as if he was well past forty – there were traces of grey in the plait glued to the crown of his head. The other two were young, mere youths.

Then the 'priest' noticed the tramp. He stopped chanting his incantations, shouted something angrily and started walking quickly up the steps. The *miko* hurried after him.

The hunchback flopped down on to his knees and pressed his forehead against the ground. Excellent – it would be easier to grab him.

The commissar seemed to think the same. He touched Fandorin on the shoulder: Time to go!

Erast Petrovich stuck his hand into his loincloth and pulled out a thin rope from round his waist. He rapidly wound it round his hand and his elbow, leaving a large loop dangling.

Iwaoka nodded sagely and demonstrated with his fingers: the one with the withered arm is yours, the other two are mine. That was rational. If they were going to take someone alive, of course it ought to be the leader.

'But where's your weapon?' Fandorin asked, also in gestures.

The commissar didn't understand at first. Then he smiled briefly and held out the fan, which turned out not to be made of paper or cardboard, but steel, with sharply honed edges.

'Wait, I go first,' Iwaoka ordered.

He moved soundlessly along the bushes, circling round behind the Satsumans.

Now he was right behind them: an intent expression on his face, his knees slightly bent, his feet stepping silently across the ground.

The samurai didn't see him or hear him – the two young ones were looking at the back of their leader's head, and he was following what was happening on the steps.

Suga was acting for all he was worth: yelling, waving his arms about, even striking the 'tramp' on the back of the neck with his twig broom a couple of times. The *miko* stood slightly to one side of the hunchback, with her eyes lowered modestly.

Erast Petrovich got up and started swaying his lasso back and forth.

One more second and it would start.

Iwaoka would drop one and get to grips with another. When they heard a noise, Suga and Asagawa would grab the hunchback. The titular counsellor's job was to throw the lasso accurately and pull it good and tight. Not such a difficult trick if you had the knack, and Erast Petrovich certainly did. He had done a lot of practising in his Turkish prison, to combat the boredom and inactivity. It would all work out very neatly.

He didn't understand how it happened: either Iwaoka wasn't careful enough, or the Satsuman turned round by chance, but it didn't work out neatly at all.

The last samurai, the youngest, looked round when the commissar was only five steps away. The young man's reactions were simply astounding.

Before he had even finished turning his head, he squealed and jerked his blade out of the scabbard. The other two leapt away from the wall as if they had been flung out by a spring and also drew their weapons.

A sword glinted above Iwaoka's head and clanged against the fan held up to block it, sending sparks flying. The commissar turned his wrist slightly, opened his strange weapon wider and sliced at the air, almost playfully, but the steel edge caught the Satsuman across the throat. Blood spurted out and the first opponent had been disposed of. He slumped to the ground, grabbing at his throat with his hands, and soon fell silent.

The second one flew at Iwaoka like a whirlwind, but the old wolf easily dodged the blow. With a deceptively casual movement, he flicked the fan across the samurai's wrist and the sword fell out of the severed hand. The samurai leaned down and picked the *katana* up with his other hand, but the commissar struck again, and the samurai tumbled to the ground with his head split open.

All this took about three seconds. Fandorin still hadn't had a chance to throw his lasso. He stood there, whirling it above his head in whistling circles, but the man with the withered arm moved so fast that he couldn't choose the moment for the throw.

The steel blade clashed with the steel fan, and the fearsome opponents leapt back and circled round each other, ready to pounce again.

When the man with the withered arm slowed down, Erast Petrovich seized the moment and threw his lasso. It went whistling through the air – but the Satsuman leapt forward, knocked the fan aside, swung round his axis and slashed at Iwaoka's legs.

Something appalling happened: the commissar's feet stayed where they were, but his severed ankles slipped off them and stuck in the ground. The old campaigner swayed, but before he fell, the sword blade sliced him in half – from his right shoulder to his left hip. The body settled into a formless heap.

Celebrating his victory, the man with the withered arm froze on the spot for a mere second, but that was enough for Fandorin to make another throw. This one was faultlessly precise and the broad noose encircled the samurai's shoulders. Erast Petrovich allowed it to slip down to his elbows and tugged it towards him, forcing the Satsuman to spin round his own axis again. In just a few moments, the prisoner had been bound securely and laid out on the ground. Snarling furiously and baring his teeth, he writhed and twisted, even trying to reach the rope with his teeth, but there was nothing he could do.

Suga and Asagawa dragged over the hunchback with his wrists tied to his ankles, so that he could neither walk nor stand – when they let go of him, he tumbled over on to his side. There was a wooden gag protruding from his mouth, with laces that were tied at the back of his head.

The vice-intendant walked over to the commissar's mutilated body and heaved a deep sigh, but that was as far as the expression of grief went.

When the general turned towards Fandorin, he was smiling.

'We forgot about the signal,' he said cheerfully, holding up his whistle. 'Never mind, we managed without any back-up. We've taken the main two villains alive. That's incredibly good luck.'

He stood in front of the man with the withered arm, who had stopped thrashing about on the ground and was lying there quite still, pale-faced, with his eyes squeezed tight shut.

Suga said something harsh and kicked the prone man contemptuously, then grabbed him by the scruff of the neck and stood him on his feet.

The samurai opened his eyes. Never before had Fandorin seen such sheer animal fury in a human stare.

'An excellent technique,' said Suga, fingering the noose of the lasso. 'We'll have to add it to our repertoire. Now I understand how the Turks managed to take you prisoner.'

The titular counsellor made no comment – his didn't want to disappoint the Japanese police chief. In actual fact he had been captured with a brigade of Serbian volunteers who had been cut off from their own lines and used up all their cartridges. According to the samurai code, apparently they should have choked themselves with their own shoulder belts . . .

'What is that for?' Erast Petrovich asked, pointing to the gag in the hunchback's mouth.

'So that he won't take it into his head . . .'

Suga never finished what he was saying. With a hoarse growl, the man with the withered arm pushed the general aside with his knee, lunged forward into a run and smashed his forehead into the corner of the shrine at full speed.

There was a sickening crunch and the bound man collapsed face down. A red puddle started spreading rapidly beneath him.

Suga bent down over the samurai, felt the pulse in the man's neck and waved his hand hopelessly.

'The *hami* is needed to prevent the prisoner from biting off his own tongue,' Asagawa concluded for his superior. 'It is not enough simply to take enemies like this alive. You have to prevent them dying afterwards as well.'

Fandorin said nothing, he was stunned. He felt guilty – and not just because he had not bound an important prisoner securely enough. He was feeling even more ashamed of something else.

'There's something I have to tell you, Inspector,' he said, blushing as he led Asagawa aside.

The vice-intendant was left beside the remaining prisoner: he checked to make sure the ropes were pulled tight. Once he was convinced that everything was in order, he went to inspect the shrine.

In the meantime Fandorin, stammering more than usual, confessed his perfidious deceit to the inspector. He told him about the tar, and about his suspicions concerning the Japanese police.

'I know I have c-caused you a great deal of unpleasantness and damaged your reputation with your s-superiors. I ask you to forgive me and bear no grudge . . .'

Asagawa heard him out with a stony face; only the slight trembling of his lips betrayed his agitation. Erast Petrovich was prepared for a sharp, well-deserved rebuff, but the inspector surprised him.

'You could have never admitted anything,' he said in a quiet voice. 'I would never have known the truth, and you would have remained an impeccable hero. But your confession required even greater courage. Your apology is accepted.'

He bowed ceremoniously. Fandorin replied with a precisely similar bow.

Suga came out of the shrine, holding three bundles in his hands.

'This is all there is,' he said. 'The search specialists will take a more thorough look later. Maybe they'll find some kind of hiding place. I'd like to know who helped these villains, who supplied them with new swords. Oh, I have plenty to talk about with Mr Semushi! I'll question him myself,' said the vice-intendant, with a smile so ferocious it made Erast Petrovich wonder whether the interrogation would be conducted in accordance with civilised norms. 'Everyone is in line for decorations. A high order for you, Fandorin-san. Perhaps even . . . *Miro!*' the general exclaimed suddenly, pointing to Semushi. '*Hami!*'

The titular counsellor saw that the wooden gag was no longer protruding from between the hunchback's teeth, but dangling on its laces. Inspector Agasawa dashed towards the prisoner, but too late – Semushi opened his mouth wide and clenched his jaws shut with a snarl. A dense red torrent gushed out of his mouth on to his bare chest.

There was a blood-curdling roar that faded into spasmodic gurgling. Suga and Asagawa prised open the suicide's teeth and stuffed a rag into his mouth, but it was clear that the bleeding could not be stopped. Five minutes later Semushi stopped groaning and went quiet.

Asagawa was a pitiful sight. He bowed to his superior and to Fandorin, insisting that he had no idea how the prisoner could have chewed through the lace – it had evidently not been strong enough and he, Asagawa, was to blame for not checking it properly.

The general listened to all this and waved his hand dismissively. His voice sounded reassuring. Fandorin made out the familiar word '*akunin*'.

'I was saying that it's not possible to take a genuine villain alive, no matter how hard you try,' said Suga, translating his own words. 'When a man has a strong *hara*, there's nothing you can do with him. But the mission is a success in any case. The minister will be delighted, he's sick to death of sitting under lock and key. The great man has been saved, for which Japan will be grateful to Russia and to you personally, Mr Vice-Consul.'

That evening Erast Petrovich betrayed his principles and rode home in a *kuruma* pulled by three rikshas. After all his emotional and physical tribulations, the titular counsellor was absolutely worn out. He couldn't tell what had undermined his strength more – the bloody spectacle of the two suicides or the hour and a half spent weeding, but the moment he got into the *kuruma*, he fell asleep, muttering:

'I'm going to sleep all night, all day and all night again . . .'

The conveyance in which the triumphant victors rode back to the consulate presented a truly unusual sight: snoring away in the middle was the secretary Shirota, wearing a morning coat and a string tie; this respectable-looking gentleman was flanked by two semi-naked peasants, sleeping soundly with their heads resting on his shoulders, and one of them was caked all over in dried dung.

Alas, however, Erast Petrovich was not given a chance to sleep all night, all day and all night again.

At eleven in the morning, when he was sleeping like a log, the vice-consul was shaken awake by his immediate superior.

Pale and trembling, Vsevolod Vitalievich splashed cold water over Fandorin, drank the liquid remaining in the mug and read out the express message that had just arrived from the embassy:

'*Early this morning Okubo was killed on the way to the imperial palace. Six unidentified men drew concealed swords, killed the postillion, hacked at the horse's legs and stabbed the minister to death when he jumped out of the carriage. The minister had no guards. As yet nothing is known about the killers, but eyewitnesses claim that they addressed each other in the Satsuma dialect. Please report to the embassy immediately with Vice-Consul Fandorin.*'

'How is that possible?' the titular counsellor exclaimed. 'The conspirators were wiped out!'

'It is now clear that the group you have been hunting only existed in order to divert the authorities' energy and attention. Or else the man with the withered arm and his group were given a secondary role once they had attracted the attention of the police. The main group was waiting patiently for its chance. The moment Okubo broke his cover and was left without any protection, the killers struck. Ah, Fandorin, I fear this is an irredeemable blow. And the worst disaster is still to come. The consequences for Russia will be lamentable. There is no one to tame the beast, the cage is empty, the Japanese tiger will break free.'

The zoo is empty,
All the visitors have fled.
Tiger on the loose

THE SCENT OF IRISES

Six morose-looking gentlemen were sitting in the office of the Russian ambassador: five in black frock coats and one in naval uniform, also black. The frivolous May sun was shining outside the windows of the building, but its rays were blocked out by thick curtains, and the room was as gloomy as the general mood.

The nominal chairman of the meeting was the ambassador himself, Full State Counsellor Kirill Vasilievich Korf, but His Excellency hardly even opened his mouth, maintaining a significant silence and merely nodding gravely when Bukhartsev, sitting on his right, had the floor. The seats on the left of the plenipotentiary representative of the Russian Empire were occupied by another two diplomatic colleagues, the first secretary and a youthful attaché, but they did not participate in the conversation, and in introducing themselves, they had murmured their names so quietly that Erast Petrovich could not make them out.

The consul and vice-consul were seated on the other side of the long table, which gave the impression, if not of direct confrontation, then at least of a certain opposition between Tokyoites and Yokohamans.

First they discussed the details of the assassination: the attackers had revolvers, but they fired only into the air, to cause fright and confusion; the unfortunate Okubo had tried to protect himself from the sword blades with his bare hands, so his forearms were covered in slashes; the fatal blow had split the brilliant minister's head in half; from the scene of the killing, the conspirators had gone straight to the police to surrender and had submitted a written statement, in which the dictator was declared a usurper and enemy of the nation; all six were former samurai from Satsuma, their victim's home region.

Fandorin was astounded.

'They surrendered? They didn't try to kill themselves?'

'There's no point now,' the consul explained. 'They've done their job. There will be a trial, they will make beautiful speeches, the public will regard them as heroes. Plays will be written about them, and prints will be made. And then, of course, they'll chop their heads off, but they have secured themselves an honourable place in Japanese history.'

After that they moved on to the main item on the agenda – discussing the political situation and forecasting imminent changes. Two of the men – the consul and the maritime agent – argued, the others listened.

'Japan will now inevitably be transformed from our ally into our rival and, with time, our sworn enemy,' Vsevolod Vitalievich prophesied morosely. 'Such, I fear, is the law of political physics. Under Okubo, an advocate of strict control over all aspects of social life, Japan was developing along the Russian path; a firm vertical structure of power, state management of the basic industrial sectors, no democratic games. But now the hour of the English party has been ushered in. The country will turn on to the British path – with a parliament and political parties, with the development of private capital on a large scale. And what is the British model of development, gentlemen? It is outward extension and expansion, a gaseous state, that is, the urge to fill all available space: a weak Korea, a decrepit China. That is the ground on which we will meet the Japanese tiger.'

Lieutenant Captain Bukhartsev was not alarmed in the least by the prospect that the Yokohama consul had outlined.

'What tiger are you talking about, sir? This is quite absurd. It's no tiger, it's a pussy cat, and a scabby, mangy one at that. Japan's annual budget is only a tenth of Russia's. And what can I say about their military forces? The Mikado's peacetime army is thirty-five thousand men. The Tsar's is almost a million. And what kind of soldiers do the Japanese have? They barely come up to the chests of our brave lads. And their navy! In the line of duty, I visited a battleship they bought recently in England. I could have laughed till I cried! Tiny little Lilliputs, crawling all over Gulliver. How do they intend to manage the turret mechanism for twelve-inch guns? Are five of them going to jump up and hang on the wheel? And as for Korea and China, oh, come now, Vsevolod Vitalievich! With God's help, the Japanese might just liberate the island of Hokkaido!'

The ambassador liked what Bukhartsev had said – he smiled and started nodding. But out of the blue Doronin asked:

'Tell me, Mstislav Nikolaievich, whose homes are cleaner – the Russian peasants', or the Japanese peasants'?'

'What has that go to do with the point?'

'The Japanese say: "If the homes are clean, the government is respected and stable". Our homes, my dear compatriots, are not clean – in fact, they are very unclean. Filth, drunkenness and, at the slightest provocation, the red cock crows under the landowner's roof. We, my dear sirs, have bombers. Opposition is considered *bon ton* among our educated young people, but for the Japanese it is patriotism and respect for the authorities. And as for the difference in physique, that can be compensated for in time. We say: Healthy in body, healthy in mind. The Japanese are convinced of the opposite. And you know, I agree with them on that. Four-fifths of our population are illiterate, but they have passed a law on universal education. Soon every child here will go to school. Patriotism, a healthy mind and education – that is the recipe for the feed that will allow this "mangy pussy cat" to grow into a tiger very quickly indeed. And, in addition, do not forget the most important treasure that the Japanese possess, one that is, unfortunately, very rare in our parts. It is called "dignity".'

The ambassador was surprised.

'I beg your pardon, how do you mean that?'

'In the most direct sense possible, Your Excellency. Japan is a country of politeness. Every individual, even the very poorest, conducts himself with dignity. A Japanese fears nothing so much as to forfeit the respect of those around him. Yes, today this is a poor, backward country, but it stands on a firm foundation, and therefore it will realise its aspirations. And that will happen far more quickly than we think.'

Bukhartsev did not continue the sparring – he merely glanced at the ambassador with a smile and spread his hands eloquently.

And then His Excellency finally pronounced his own weighty word.

'Vsevolod Vitalievich, I value you as a fine connoisseur of Japan, but I also know that you are an enthusiast. Staying too long in one place has its negative aspects: one starts viewing the situation through the eyes of the locals. This is sometimes useful, but don't get carried away, don't get carried away. The late Okubo used to say that he would not be killed *as long as* his country needed him. I understand fatalism of that sort, I take the same view of things and consider that, since Okubu is no longer with us, he had exhausted his usefulness. Naturally, you are right when you say that Japan's political course will change now. But Mstislav Nikolaevich is also right: this Asiatic country does not have and cannot have the potential of a great power. It will possibly become a more influential and active force in the Far Eastern zone, but never a potential player. That is what I intend to state in my report to His Excellency the Chancellor. And henceforth the main question will be formulated in this way: Which tune will Japan dance to? – the Russian or the English?' The baron sighed heavily. 'I fear we shall find this rivalry hard going. The Britons have a stronger hand to play. And apart from that, we are still committing unforgivable blunders.' His Excellency's voice, which had so far been neutral and measured, took on a strict, even severe tone. 'Take this business of hunting the false assassins. The entire diplomatic corps is abuzz with whispers that Okubo was killed because of a Russian plot. Supposedly we deliberately handed the police a few ragamuffins, leaving the real killers free to plot and strike unhindered. Today at lawn tennis the German ambassador remarked with a subtle smile: "Had Okubo ceased to be useful?" I was dumbfounded. I said: "Your Excellency, where could you have got such information?" It turned out that Bullcox had already found time to visit him. Oh, that Bullcox! It's not enough for him that Britain has been relieved of its main political opponent, Bullcox wants to cast suspicion on Russia as well. And you gentlemen from Yokohama unwittingly assist his machinations!'

By the end of his speech, the ambassador was thoroughly annoyed and, although he had been addressing the 'gentlemen from Yokohama', he had not looked at the consul, but at Erast Petrovich, and his gaze was anything but benign.

'It is as I reported to Your Excellency. On the one hand – connivance, and on the other – irresponsible adventurism.'

The two parties – the conniving (that is, Vsevolod Vitalievich) and the irresponsibly adventurist (that is, Fandorin) – exchanged surreptitious glances. Things were taking a very nasty turn.

The baron chewed on his dry Ostsee lips, raised his watery eyes to the ceiling and frowned. However, no lightning bolt ensued, things went no farther than a roll of thunder.

'Well then, you gentlemen from Yokohama, from now on, please stick to your immediate consular duties. There will be plenty of work for you, Fandorin: arranging supplies for ships, repairing ships, assisting sailors and traders, summarising commercial data. But do not stick your nose into political and strategic matters, they are beyond you. We have a military man, a specialist, for that.'

Well, it could have been worse.

They drove from the diplomatic quarter with the beautiful name of the Tiger Gates to the Shimbashi Station in the ambassador's carriage – His Excellency was a tactful individual and he possessed the major administrative talent of being able to give a subordinate a dressing-down without causing personal offence. The carriage with the gilded coat of arms on the door was intended to sweeten the bitter pill that the baron forced the Yokohamans to swallow.

To Erast Petrovich, the city of Tokyo seemed remarkably like his own native Moscow. That is to say, naturally, the architecture was quite different, but the alternating hovels and palaces, narrow streets and waste lots were entirely Muscovite, and the fashionable Ginja Street, with its neat brick houses, was precisely like prim Tverskaya Street, pretending as hard as it could to be Nevsky Prospect.

The titular counsellor kept looking out of the window, contemplating the melange of Japanese and Western clothes, hairstyles and carriages. But Doronin gazed wearily at the velvet wall, and the consul's conversation was dismal.

'Russia's own leaders are its ruin. What can be done so that the people who rule are those who have the talent and vocation for it, not those with ambition and connections? And our other misfortune, Fandorin, is that Mother Russia has her face turned to the West, and her back to the East. And furthermore, we have our nose stuck up the West's backside, because the West couldn't give a damn for us. But we expose our defenceless derrière to the East, and sooner or later the Japanese will sink their sharp teeth into our flabby buttocks.'

'But what is to be done?' asked Erast Petrovich, watching a double-decker omnibus drive past, harnessed to four stunted little horses. 'Turn away from the West to the East? That is hardly possible.'

'Our eagle is double-headed, so that one head can look to the West, and the other to the East. We need to have two capitals. And the second one should not be Moscow, but Vladivostok.'

'But I've read that Vladivostok is an appalling dump, a mere village!'

'What of it? St Petersburg wasn't even a village when Peter stretched out his hand and said: "It is nature's command that we break a window through to Europe here". And in this case even the name suits: Vladivostok – Rule the East!'

Since conversation had touched on such a serious topic, Fandorin stopped gazing idly out of the window and turned towards the consul.

'Vsevolod Vitalievich, why should I rule other people's lands if I can't even set my own to rights?'

Doronin smiled ironically.

'You're right, a thousand times right. No conquest can be secure if our own home is tottering. But that doesn't apply only to Russia. Her Imperial Majesty Queen Victoria's house also stands on shaky foundations. The Earth will not belong to either us or the Britons. Because we set about conquering it in the wrong way – by force. And force, Fandorin, is the weakest and least permanent of instruments. Those defeated by it will submit, of course, but they will simply wait for the moment to come when they can free themselves. None of the European conquests in Africa and Asia will last long. In fifty or a hundred years, at most, there will be no colonies left. And the Japanese tiger won't come to anything either – they're learning from the wrong teachers.'

'And from whom should they learn?'

'The Chinese. No, not the empress Tzu Hsi, of course, but the Chinese people's thorough and deliberate approach. The inhabitants of the Celestial Empire will not budge until they have put their own house in order, and that's a long job, about two hundred years. But then afterwards, when the Chinese started feeling cramped, they'll show the world what genuine conquest is. They won't rattle their weapons and send expeditionary forces abroad. Oh no! They'll show the other countries that living the Chinese way is better and more rational. And gradually everyone will become Chinese, although it may take several generations.'

'But I think the Americans will conquer the whole world,' said Erast Petrovich. 'And it will happen within the next hundred years. What makes the Americans strong? The fact that they accept everyone into their country. Anyone who wants to b-be American can be, even if he used to be an Irishman, a Jew or a Russian. There'll be a United States of the Earth, you'll see.'

'Unlikely. The Americans, of course, behave more intelligently than the European monarchies, but they lack patience. Their roots are Western too, and in the West they place too much importance on time. But in fact, time does not even exist, there is no "tomorrow", only an eternal "now". The unification of the world is a slow business, but then, what's all the hurry? There won't be any United States of the Earth, there'll be one Celestial Empire, and then the hour of universal harmony will arrive. Thank God that you and I shall never see that heaven on earth.'

And on that melancholy note the conversation about the future of mankind broke off – the carriage had stopped at the station.

The following morning Vice-Consul Fandorin took up his routine work: compiling a register of Russian ships due to arrive in the port of Yokohama in June and July 1878.

Erast Petrovich scribbled the heading of this boring document in slapdash style (the spinster Blagolepova would type it out again later anyway), but that was as far as the work got. The window of the small office located on the first floor presented a glorious view of the consulate garden, the lively Bund and the harbour roadstead. The titular counsellor was in a sour mood, and his thoughts drifted aimlessly. Propping one cheek on his fist, he started watching the people walking by and the carriages driving along the promenade.

And he saw a sight worth seeing.

Algernon Bullcox's lacquered carriage drove past, moving in the direction of the Bluff. Russia's perfidious enemy and his concubine were perched beside each other on the leather seat like two turtle doves. And, moreover, O-Yumi was holding the Englishman's arm and whispering something in his ear and the Right Honourable was smiling unctuously.

The immoral kept woman did not even glance in the direction of the Russian consulate.

Despite the distance, with his sharp eyes Erast Petrovich could make out a small lock of hair fluttering behind her ear, and then the wind brought the scent of irises from the garden . . .

The pencil crunched in his strong hand, snapped in half.

What was she whispering to him, why were they laughing? And at whom? Could it be at him?

Life is cruel, essentially meaningless and infinitely humiliating, Erast Petrovich thought morosely, glancing at the sheet of paper waiting for the register of shipping. All of life's charms, delights and enticements existed only in order to melt a man's heart, to get him to roll over on to his back, waving all four paws trustingly in the air and exposing his defenceless underbelly. And life wouldn't miss her chance – she'd strike a blow that would send you scuttling away howling, with your tail tucked between your legs.

So what was the conclusion?

It was this: never give way to tender feelings, always remain on your guard, with all weapons at the ready. If you see the finger of fate beckoning, then bite the damn thing off, and the entire hand too, if you can manage it.

With a serious effort of will, the vice-consul forced himself to concentrate on tonnages, itineraries and captains' names.

The empty columns gradually filled up. The Big Ben grandfather clock ticked quietly in the corner.

And at six o'clock in the evening, at the end of the office day, Erast Fandorin, feeling weary and gloomy, went downstairs to his apartment to eat the dinner that Masa had prepared.

None of it ever happened, Erast Petrovich told himself, chewing in disgust on the gooey rice that stuck to his teeth. There never was any lasso clutched in his hand, or any hot pulsing of blood, or any scent of irises. Especially the scent of irises. It was all a monstrous delusion that had nothing at all to do with real life. What did exist was clear, simple, necessary work. And there was also breakfast, lunch and dinner. There was sunrise and sunset. Rule, routine and procedure – and no chaos. Chaos had disappeared, it would not come back again. And thank God for that.

At that point the door creaked behind the titular counsellor's back and he heard someone clear their throat delicately. Without turning round, without even knowing who it was, simply from what he could feel inside, Fandorin guessed that it was chaos – it had come back again.

Chaos took the form of Inspector Asagawa. He was standing in the doorway of the dining room, holding his hat in his hand, and his face was firmly set in an expression of determination.

'Hello, Inspector. Is there something . . .'

The Japanese suddenly toppled to the floor. He pressed the palms of his hands against the carpet and started beating his head against it.

Erast Petrovich snatched off his napkin and jumped to his feet.

'What is all this?'

'You were right not to trust me,' Asagawa blurted out without raising his head. 'I am to blame for everything. It is my fault that the minister was killed.'

Despite the contrite pose, the words were spoken clearly and precisely, without the ponderous formulae of politeness typical of the inspector's usual conversation.

'What's that? Drop all this Japanese c-ceremonial, will you! Get up!'

Asagawa did not get to his feet, but he did at least straighten his back and put his hands on his knees. His eyes – Fandorin could see them very clearly now – were glowing with a steady, furious light.

'At first I was insulted. I thought: How dare he suspect the Japanese police! The leak must have happened on their side, on the side of the foreigners, because we have order, and they do not. But today, when the catastrophe occurred, my eyes were suddenly opened. I told myself: Sergeant Lockston and the Russian vice-consul could have let something slip to the wrong person, about the witness to the murder, about the ambush at the *godaun*, about the fingerprints, but how could they have known when exactly the guards were dismissed and where the minister would go in the morning?'

'Go on, go on!' Fandorin pressed him.

'You and I were looking for three samurai. But the conspirators had planned their attack thoroughly. There was another group of six assassins. And perhaps there were others, in reserve. Why not? The minister had plenty of enemies. The important thing here is this: all these fanatics, no matter how many of them there were, were controlled from one centre and their actions were coordinated. Someone provided them with extremely precise information. The moment the minister acquired guards, the killers went into hiding. And as soon as His Excellency left his residence without any protection, they struck immediately. What does this mean?'

'That the conspirators received information from Okubo's inner circle.'

'Precisely! From someone who was closer to him than you or I! And as soon as I realised this, everything fell into place. Do you remember the tongue?'

'Which tongue?'

'The one that was bitten off! I could not get it out of my mind. I remember that I checked the *hami* and the lace was perfectly all right. Semushi could not have bitten through it, and it could not have come loose – my knots do not come untied ... This morning I went to the stockroom, where they keep the clues and material evidence relating to the case of the man with the withered arm and his gang: weapons, clothes, equipment used – everything we are trying to use in order to establish their identities and get a lead on their contacts. I examined the *hami* very closely. Here it is, look'

The inspector took a wooden gag-bit with dangling tapes out of his pocket.

'The cord has been cut!' Fandorin exclaimed. 'But how could that have happened?'

'Remember the way it was,' said Asagawa, finally getting to his feet and standing beside the vice-consul. 'I walked over to you and we stood there, talking. You asked me to forgive you. But he stayed beside the hunchback, pretending to check how well his binds were tied. Remember?'

'Suga!' the titular counsellor whispered. 'Impossible! But he was with us, he risked his life! He planned the operation and implemented it brilliantly!'

The Japanese laughed bitterly.

'Naturally. He wanted to be on the spot, to make sure that none of the conspirators fell into our hands alive. Remember how Suga came out of the shrine and pointed at the hunchback and shouted: *"Hami!"*? That was because Semushi was taking too long, he couldn't bring himself to do it ...'

'An assumption, n-nothing more,' the titular counsellor said with a shake of his head.

'And is this also an assumption?' asked Asagawa, holding up the severed cord. 'Only Suga could have done that. Wait, Fandorin-san, I still haven't finished what I want to say. Even when I found this terrible, incontrovertible proof, I still couldn't believe that the vice-intendant of police was capable of such a crime. It's absolutely beyond belief! And I went to Tokyo, to the Department of Police.'

'What f-for?'

'The head of the secretariat is an old friend of my father's, also an old *yoriki* ... I went to him and said I had forgotten to keep a copy of one of the reports that I had sent to the vice-intendant.'

Fandorin pricked up his ears.

'What reports?'

'After every conversation and meeting that we had, I had to report to Suga immediately, by special courier. Those were my instructions, and I followed them meticulously. I sent eight reports in all. But when the head of the secretariat gave me the file containing my reports, I found only five of them in it. Three were missing: the one about your servant having seen the presumed killer; the one about the ambush at the *godaun*; and the one about the municipal police holding the fingerprints of the mysterious *shinobi* ...'

The inspector seemed to have said everything he wanted to say. For a while the room was silent while Fandorin thought very hard and Asagawa waited to see what the result of this thinking would be.

The result was a question that the titular counsellor asked, gazing straight into Asagawa's eyes.

'Why did you come to me and not the intendant of police?'

Asagawa was evidently expecting this and had prepared his answer in advance.

'The intendant of police is a vacuous individual, they only keep him in that position because of his high-sounding title. And in addition ...' – the Japanese lowered his eyes, it was obviously hard for him to say something like this to a foreigner – '... how can I know who else was in the conspiracy? Even in the police secretariat there are some who say that the Satsumans are guilty of crimes against the state, of course, but even so they are heroes. Some even whisper that Okubo got what he deserved. That is the first reason why I decided to turn to you ...'

'And what is the second?'

'Yesterday you asked me to forgive you, although you did not have to. You are a sincere man.'

For a moment the titular counsellor could not understand what sincerity had to do with this, but then he decided it must be a failure of translation. No doubt the English phrase 'sincere man', as used by Asagawa, or its Russian equivalent, *'iskrennii chelovek'*, as used by the secretary Shirota to express his respect for Pushkin, Martial Saigo and Dr Twigs, did not adequately convey the essential quality that the Japanese valued so highly. Perhaps it should be 'unaffected' or 'genuine'? He would have to ask Vsevolod Vitalievich about this ...

'But I still do not understand why you have come to me with this,' said Erast Petrovich. 'What can you change now? Mr Okubo is dead. His opponents have the upper hand, and now they will determine the policies of your state.'

Asagawa was terribly surprised.

'How can you ask: "What can you change?" I know nothing about politics, that is not my business, I am a policeman. A policeman is a man who is needed to prevent evil-doing from going unpunished. Desertion of duty, conspiracy and murder are serious crimes. Suga must pay for them. If I cannot punish him, then I am not a policeman. That, as you like to say, is one. And now, two: Suga has insulted me very seriously – he has made me look like a stupid kitten, trying to pounce on a ribbon tied to a string. A sincere man does not allow anyone to treat him like that. And so, if Suga's crime goes unpunished, I am, firstly, not a policeman and, secondly, not a sincere man. Then who am I, if I may be allowed to ask?'

No, a 'sincere man' is what we call a 'man of honour', the titular counsellor guessed.

'Do you want to kill him, then?'

Asagawa nodded.

'Yes, very much. But I will not kill him. Because I am a policeman. Policemen do not kill criminals, they expose them and hand them over to the system of justice.'

'Well said indeed. But how can it be done?'

'I do not know. And that is the third reason why I have come to you. We Japanese are predictable, we always act according to the rules. This is both our strength and our weakness. I am a hereditary *yoriki*, which makes me doubly Japanese. From when I was very little, my father used to say to me: "Act in accordance with the law, and everything else is not your concern". And that is how I have lived until now, I do not know how to live otherwise. You are made differently – that much is clear from the story of the hunchback's escape. Your brain is not shackled by rules.'

That should probably not be taken as a compliment, especially coming from a Japanese, Erast Petrovich thought. But the inspector was certainly right about one thing: you should never allow anyone to make you look a fool, and that was exactly how the wily Suga had behaved with the leader of the consular investigation. A kitten, with a ribbon dangling in front of it on a string?

'Well, we'll see about that,' Fandorin murmured in Russian.

'I already know you well enough,' Asagawa went on. 'You will start thinking about the vice-intendant and you will definitely think of something. When you do – let me know. Only do not come to my station yourself. It is quite possible that one of my men ...' He heaved a sigh, without finishing the phrase. 'Let us communicate with notes. If we need to meet, then in some quiet place, with no witnesses. For instance, in a hotel or a park. Is it a deal?'

The American phrase 'Is it a deal', combined with an outstretched hand, was not Asagawa's style at all. He must have picked that up from Lockston, the titular counsellor surmised as he sealed the agreement with a handshake.

The inspector gave a low bow, swung round and disappeared through the door without saying another word.

It turned out that the Japanese had studied his Russian associate rather well. Erast Petrovich did indeed immediately start thinking about the vice-intendant of police, who had deliberately and cunningly brought about the death of a great man whom it was his professional duty to protect against his numerous enemies.

Fandorin did not think about how to expose the faithless traitor yet. First of all he had to understand what this individual who went by the name of Suga Kinsukeh was like. The best way to do this was to reconstruct the sequence of his actions, for surely it was actions that defined a personality most vividly and accurately of all.

And so, in order.

Suga had taken part in a conspiracy against the minister, and perhaps even led that conspiracy. The threads from the groups hunting the dictator all led back to him. On the evening of 8 May at Don Tsurumaki's ball, the vice-intendant learns that the group led by the man with the withered arm has been discovered. He cannot conceal the alarming news from his superior – the deceit would certainly have been discovered. Instead, Suga acts paradoxically: he takes the initiative and tries to get Okubo to accept extremely tight security measures, and the general supervision of the investigation is quite naturally assigned to Suga, and not any other police official. Suga takes advantage of this to order the Yokohama precinct chief Asagawa to report in detail on all the investigative group's plans – this also appears entirely natural. The vice-intendant tries with consistent obstinacy to protect his associates in the conspiracy from arrest, even taking risks for them. On 9 May he informs No-Face, the master of secret skills, about the evidence that the investigative group is holding. On 10 May he warns the man with the withered arm about the ambush. The situation is completely under control. He only has to hold on for a few more days, until the impatient Okubo rebels and sends his guards and the consular investigation and even the solicitous Suga to hell. Then the conspirators will be able to strike, following their carefully prepared plan, baiting the minister from all sides, like a bear.

Then, however, something unforeseen comes along – in the person of Titular Counsellor Fandorin. On 13 May the man with the withered arm and his group, together with their messenger, the hunchback, are caught in a trap. How does Suga act? Once again, in the face of danger, he seeks to ride the very crest of the wave, by taking personal command of the operation to seize this band of killers, so that not one of the dangerous witnesses will be taken prisoner. Suga's greatest tour de force is the way in which he reverses the course of the game when it has already been half lost, by using the death of one group of assassins to lure the dictator within reach of the swords of another! A brilliant chess move, worthy of a grandmaster.

And what follows from all this?

That this is a brave and resolute man, with a quick, keen mind. And as far as his goals are concerned, he has probably acted out of conviction, confident that he was in the right.

What else could be added to this from Fandorin's personal contact with the man? Exceptional administrative talent. And charm.

A positively ideal individual, Fandorin thought with a chuckle. If not for two small points: calculated cruelty and disloyalty. No matter how strongly you might believe that your ideas were right, to stab someone in the back after he had put his trust in you was simply vile.

Having composed a psychological portrait of the *akunin*, Erast Petrovich moved on to the next phase of his deliberations: how to expose such an enterprising and artful gentleman, who also effectively controlled the entire Japanese police force . . .

The severed cord of the wooden gag could only serve as proof for Asagawa and Fandorin. What was their testimony worth against the word of General Suga?

The reports that had disappeared from the case file? Also useless. Perhaps they had never been in the file at all? And even if they had, and some trace had been left in an office register somewhere, then how in hell's name could they prove who had removed them?

Erast Petrovich pondered until midnight, sitting in an armchair and gazing at the red glow of his cigar. But precisely at midnight his servant came into the dark drawing room and handed him a note that had been delivered by the express municipal post.

The message on the sheet of paper was written in large letters in English: 'Grand Hotel, Room 16. Now!'

Apparently Asagawa had not been wasting his time either. What could he have thought of? Had he found out something?

Fandorin was about to set out to the rendezvous immediately, but an unexpected obstacle arose in the person of Masa.

The Japanese valet was not going to let his master go out alone in the middle of the night. He stuck that idiotic bowler on his head and his umbrella under his arm, and the stubborn line of his jutting chin made it quite clear that he was going to stick close.

Explaining things to him without a common language was difficult, and Fandorin begrudged the time – after all, the note said 'Now!' And he couldn't take this scarecrow with him to the hotel, either. Erast Petrovich was intending to slip into the hotel unnoticed, but with his wooden clogs Masa clattered like an entire squadron of soldiers.

Fandorin was obliged to employ cunning.

He pretended that he had changed his mind about going out. He took off his top hat and cloak and went back into his rooms. He even washed for the night.

But when Masa bowed and withdrew, the titular counsellor climbed on to the windowsill and jumped down into the garden. In the darkness he banged his knee and swore. How absurd to be harassed like this by his own servant!

The Grand Hotel was only a stone's throw away.

Erast Petrovich walked along the deserted promenade and glanced into the foyer.

Luckily for him, the receptionist was dozing behind his counter.

A few silent steps and the nocturnal visitor was already on the stairs.

He ran up to the first floor.

Aha, there was room number 16. The key was sticking out of the lock – very thoughtful, he could enter without knocking, which could easily have attracted the unwelcome attention of some sleepless guest.

Fandorin half-opened the door and slipped inside.

There was a figure silhouetted against the window – but not Asagawa's, it was much slimmer than that.

The figure darted towards the dumbstruck vice-consul, moving like a cat. Long slim fingers clasped his face.

'I have to be with you!' sang that unforgettable, slightly husky voice.

The titular counsellor's nostrils caught a tantalising whiff of the magical aroma of irises.

> Sad thoughts fill the mind,
> Pain fills the heart, and then comes
> That sweet iris scent

LOVE'S CALL

Don't give in, don't give in! his mind signalled desperately to his crazily beating heart. But in defiance of reason, his arms embraced the lithe body of the one who had put the poor vice-consul's soul through such torment.

O-Yumi tore at his collar – the buttons scattered on to the carpet. Covering his exposed neck with rapid kisses and gasping impatiently in her passion, she tugged Fandorin's frock coat off his shoulders.

And then something happened that should have been called a genuine triumph of reason over unbridled, elemental passion.

Gathering all his willpower (a quality with which he was well endowed), the titular counsellor took hold of O-Yumi's wrists and moved them away from him – gently, but uncompromisingly.

There were two reasons for this, both of them weighty.

Erast Petrovich hastily formulated the first of them in this way: What does she take me for, a boy? She disappears when she pleases, whistles for me when she pleases, and I come running? For all its vagueness, this reason was extremely important. In the skirmish between two worlds that is called 'love', there is always monarch and subject, victor and vanquished. And that was the crucial question being decided at that very moment.

The second reason lay outside love's domain. There was a whiff of mystery here, and a very disturbing kind of mystery at that.

'How did you find out that Asagawa and I had agreed to communicate by notes?' Erast Petrovich asked sternly, trying to make out the expression on her face in the darkness. 'And so quickly too. Have you been following us? Eavesdropping on us? Exactly what is your part in this whole business?'

She looked up at him without speaking or moving or trying to free herself, but the touch of her skin scorched the young man's fingers. He suddenly recalled a definition from the grammar school physics textbook: 'The electricity contained in a body gives that body a special property, the ability to attract another body . . .'

Fandorin shook his head and said firmly:

'Last time you slipped away without explaining anything to me. But today you will have to answer my qu-questions. Speak, will you!'

And O-Yumi did speak.

'Who is Asagawa?' she asked, tearing her wrists free of his grasp – the electric circuit was broken. 'Did you think someone else sent you the note?

And you came straight away? All this time I have been thinking of nothing but him, and he . . . What a fool I am!'

He wanted to hold her back, but he could not. She ducked, slipped under his arm and dashed out into the corridor. The door slammed in Erast Petrovich's face. He grabbed hold of the handle, but the key had already turned in the lock.

'Wait!' the titular counsellor called out in horror. 'Don't go!'

Catch her, stop her, apologise.

But no – he heard subdued sobbing in the corridor, and then the sound of light footsteps moving rapidly away.

His reason cringed and shrank, cowering back into the farthest corner of his mind. The only feelings in Fandorin's heart now were passion, horror and despair. The most powerful of all was the feeling of irreparable loss. And what a loss! As if he had lost everything in the world and had nobody to blame for it but himself.

'Damn! Damn! Damn!' the miserable vice-consul exclaimed through clenched teeth, and he slammed his fist into the doorpost.

Curses on his police training! A woman of reckless passion, who lived by her heart – the most precious woman in the whole world – had thrown herself into his embraces. She must have taken great risks to do it, perhaps she could even have risked her life. And he had interrogated her: 'Have you been following?' – 'Have you been eavesdropping?' – 'What's your part in all this?'

Oh, God, how horrible, how shameful!

A groan burst from the titular counsellor's chest. He staggered across to the bed (the very same bed on which heavenly bliss could have been his!) and collapsed on it face down.

For a while Erast Petrovich lay there without moving, but trembling all over. If he could have sobbed, then he certainly would have, but Fandorin had been denied that kind of emotional release for ever.

It had been a long time, a very long time, since he had felt such intense agitation – and it seemed so completely out of proportion with what had happened. As if his soul, fettered for so long by a shell of ice, had suddenly started aching as it revived, oozing thawing blood.

'What is this? What is happening to me?' he kept repeating at first – but his thoughts were about her, not himself.

When his numbed brain started recovering slightly, the next question, far more urgent, arose of its own accord.

'What do I do now?'

Erast Petrovich jerked upright on the bed. The trembling had passed off, his heart was beating rapidly, but steadily.

What should he do? Find her. Immediately. Come what may.

Anything else would mean brain fever, heart failure, the death of his very soul.

The titular counsellor dashed to the locked door, ran his hands over it rapidly and forced his shoulder against it.

Although the door was solid, it could probably be broken out. But then there would be a crash and the hotel staff would come running. He pictured the headline in bold type in the next day's *Japan Gazette*: RUSSIAN VICE-CONSUL FOUND DEBAUCHING IN GRAND HOTEL.

Erast Petrovich glanced out of the window. The first floor was high up, and in the darkness he couldn't see where he was jumping. What if there was a heap of stones, or a rake forgotten by some gardener?

These misgivings, however, did not deter the crazed titular counsellor. Deciding that it was obviously his fate for the day to climb over windowsills and jump out into the night, he dangled by his hands from the window and then opened his fingers.

His was lucky with his landing – he came down on a lawn. He brushed off his soiled knees and looked around.

It was an enclosed garden, surrounded on all sides by a high fence. But a little thing like that did not bother Fandorin. He took a run up, grabbed hold of the top of the fence, pulled himself up nimbly and sat there.

He tried to jump down into the side street, but couldn't. His coat-tail had snagged on a nail. He tugged and tugged, but it was no good. It was fine, strong fabric – the coat had been made in Paris.

'RUSSIAN VICE-CONSUL STUCK ON TOP OF FENCE,' Erast Petrovich muttered to himself. He tugged harder, and the frock coat tore with a sharp crack.

Oops-a-daisy!

In ten paces Fandorin was on the Bund, which was brightly lit by street lamps, even though it was deserted.

He had to call back home.

In order to find Bullcox's address – that was one. And to collect his means of transport – that was two. It would take too long to walk there, and even if he compromised his principles, there was no way he could take a *kuruma* – he didn't want any witnesses to this business.

Thank God, he managed to avoid the most serious obstacle, by the name of 'Masa': there was no light in the window of the small room where the meddlesome valet had his lodgings. He was asleep, the bandit.

The vice-consul tiptoed into the hallway and listened.

No, Masa wasn't asleep. There were strange sounds coming from his room – either sobs or muffled groans.

Alarmed, Fandorin crept over to the Japanese-style sliding door. Masa did not care for European comfort and he had arranged his dwelling to suit his own taste: he had covered the floor with straw mats, removed the bed and bedside locker and hung bright-coloured pictures of ferocious bandits and elephantine sumo wrestlers on the walls.

On closer investigation, the sounds coming through the open door proved to be entirely unambiguous, and in addition, the titular counsellor discovered two pairs of sandals on the floor: one larger pair and one smaller pair.

That made the vice-consul feel even more bitter. He heaved a sigh and consoled himself: Well, let him. At least he won't latch on to me.

Lying on the small table in the drawing room was a useful brochure entitled 'Alphabetical List of Yokohama Residents for the Year 1878'. By the light of a match, it took Erast Petrovich only a moment to locate the address of 'His Right Honourable A.-F.-C. Bullcox, Senior Adviser to the Imperial Government' – 129, The Bluff. And there was a plan of the Settlement on the table too. House number 129 was located at the very edge of the fashionable district, at the foot of Hara Hill. Erast Petrovich lit another match and ran a pencil along the route from the consulate to his destination. He whispered, committing it to memory:

'Across Yatobashi Bridge, past the customs post, past Yatozaka Street on the right, through the Hatacho Qu-quarter, then take the second turn to the left . . .'

He put on the broad-brimmed hat he had worn for taking turns around the deck during the evenings of his long voyage. And he swathed himself in a black cloak.

His carried his means of transport – the tricycle – out on to the porch very carefully, but even so, at the very last moment he caught the large wheel on the door handle. The doorbell trilled treacherously, but there was no catching Fandorin now.

He pulled the hat down over his eyes, leapt up on to the saddle at a run and started pressing hard on the pedals.

The moon was shining brightly in the sky – as round and buttery as the lucky lover Masa's face.

On the promenade the titular counsellor encountered only two living souls: a French sailor wrapped in the arms of a Japanese tart. The sailor opened his mouth and pushed his beret with a pom-pom to the back of his head: the Japanese girl squealed.

And with good reason. Someone black, in a flapping cloak, came hurtling at the couple out of the darkness, then went rustling by on rubber tyres and instantly dissolved into the gloom.

At night the Bluff, with its Gothic bell towers, dignified villas and neatly manicured lawns, seemed unreal, like some enchanted little town that had been spirited away from Old Mother Europe at the behest of some capricious wizard and dumped somewhere at the very end of the world.

Here there were no tipsy sailors or women of easy virtue, everything was sleeping, and the only sound was the gentle pealing of the chimes in the clock tower.

The titular counsellor burst into this Victorian paradise in a monstrously indecent fashion. His 'Royal Crescent' tricycle startled a pack of homeless dogs sleeping peacefully on the bridge. In the first second or so they scattered, squealing, but, emboldened by seeing the monster of the night fleeing from them, they set off in pursuit, barking loudly.

And there was nothing that could be done about it.

Erast Petrovich waved his arm at them and even kicked one of them with the toe of his low boot, but the dratted curs simply wouldn't leave him alone – they chased after the vice-consul, sticking to his heels and barking even more loudly.

He pressed harder on the pedals, which was not easy, because the street ran uphill, but Fandorin had muscles of steel and, after another couple of minutes in pursuit, the dogs started falling behind.

The young man arrived at house number 129 soaked in sweat. However, he was not feeling tired at all – he cared nothing for any trials or tribulations now.

The right honourable patron of the most precious woman in all the world resided in a two-storey mansion of red brick, constructed in accordance with the canons of the glorious Georgian style. Despite the late hour, the house was not sleeping – the windows were bright both downstairs and upstairs.

As he studied the local terrain, Erast Petrovich was surprised to realise that he had been here before. Nearby he could see tall railings with fancy lacework gates and, beyond them, a familiar white palazzo with columns – Don Tsurumaki's estate, where Erast Petrovich had seen O-Yumi for the first time.

Bullcox's domain was both smaller and less grandiose than his neighbour's – and that was very opportune: to scale the ten-foot-high railings of the nouveau-riche Japanese magnate's estate would have required a ladder, while hopping over the Englishman's wooden fence was no problem at all.

Without pausing long for thought, Erast Petrovich hopped over. But he had barely even taken a few steps before he saw three swift shadows hurtling towards him across the lawn – they were huge, silent mastiffs, with eyes that glinted an ominous phosphorus-green in the moonlight.

He was obliged to beat a rapid retreat to the fence, and he only just made it in time.

Perched on the narrow top with his feet pulled up, gazing at those gaping jaws, the titular counsellor instantly conceived the appropriate headline for this scene: HAPLESS LOVER CHASED BY MASTIFFS.

What a disgrace, what puerile tomfoolery, the vice-consul told himself, but he didn't come to his senses, he merely bit his lip – he was so furious at his own helplessness.

O-Yumi was so very close, behind one of those windows, but what could he do about these damned dogs?

The titular counsellor was fond of dogs, he respected them, but right now he could have shot these accursed English brutes with his trusty Herstal, without the slightest compunction. Ah, why had progress not yet invented silent gunpowder?

The mastiffs didn't budge from the spot. They gazed upwards, scraping their clawed feet on the wooden boards. They didn't actually bark – these aristocratic canines had been well trained – but they growled.

Erast Petrovich suddenly heard rollicking plebeian barking from the end of the street. Looking round, he saw his recent acquaintances – the homeless dogs from the Yatobashi Bridge. Surely they couldn't have followed my scent, he thought to himself, but then he saw that the mongrels were chasing after a running man.

The man was waving his arm about – there was a pitiful yelp. He swung his arm in the other direction – another yelp, and the pack dropped back.

Masa, it was Fandorin's faithful vassal, Masa! He had a wooden club in his hand, with another, identical, one attached to it by a chain. Fandorin already knew that this unprepossessing but effective weapon was called a *nunchaku*, and Masa could handle it very well.

The valet ran up and bowed to his master sitting on the fence.

'How did you find me?' Erast Petrovich asked, and tried to say the same thing in Japanese: *Do-o . . . vatasi . . . sagasu?*

His Japanese lessons had not been a waste of time – Masa understood! He took a sheet of paper, folded into four, out of his pocket, and opened it out.

Ah yes, the plan of the Settlement, with a pencil line leading from the consulate to house number 129.

'This is not work. *Sigoto iie*. Go, go,' said the titular counsellor, waving his hand at Masa. 'There's no danger, do you understand? *Kiken – iie. Wakaru?*'

'*Wakarimas,*' the servant said with a bow. '*Mochiron wakarimas. O-Yumi-san.*'

Erast Petrovich was so surprised that he swayed and almost went crashing down off the fence – on the wrong side. Somehow he recovered his balance. Oh, servants, servants! It was an old truism that they knew more far more about their masters than the masters suspected. But how? Where from?

'How d-do you know? *Do-o wakaru?*'

The Japanese folded his short-fingered hands together and pressed them to his cheek – as if he were sleeping. He murmured:

'O-Yumi, O-Yumi . . . Darring . . .'

Darring?

Had he really been repeating her name in his sleep?

The titular counsellor lowered his head, sorely oppressed by a feeling of humiliation. But Masa jumped up and glanced over the fence. Having ascertained the reason for the vice-consul's strange position, he started turning his head left and right.

'*Hai,*' he said. '*Shosho o-machi kudasai.*'

He ran over to the pack of dogs that was barking feebly at the fence of the next house. He picked up one canine, turned it over, sniffed it and tossed it away. He did the same with another. But he kept hold of the third one, tucked it under his arm and walked back to his master. The mongrels bore this high-handed treatment in silence – they clearly respected strength: only the captive whined pitifully.

'What do you want the dog for?'

Masa somehow managed to climb up on to the fence – about ten paces away from Fandorin – without releasing his live booty.

He swung his legs over, jumped down and dashed for the gate as fast as his legs would carry him. The mastiffs darted after the little titch, ready to tear him to pieces. But the nimble-footed valet opened the latch and flung the mongrel on the ground. It bolted out into the street with a squeal, and then a genuine miracle took place – instead of mauling the stranger, the guard dogs bolted after the mongrel.

It shot away from them, working its little legs furiously. The mastiffs ran after it in a pack, with their heads in line.

Ah, it's a bitch in heat, Fandorin realised. Well done, Masa, brilliant!

The pack also set off at a rush after the terrifying suitors, but maintained a respectful distance. Five seconds later there wasn't a single quadruped left in the street.

Masa walked out through the gate and bowed ceremoniously, gesturing to invite Erast Petrovich through on to the lawn. The vice-consul tossed his cloak into his servant's arms, handed him the hat and went in – not over the fence, but in the conventional manner – through the gate.

In the distance he could hear the loud barking and lingering lovesick howls of the local canine community.

All things forgotten,
Careering along pell-mell,
Answering love's call

THE GARDEN GATE

Erast Petrovich ran across the broad lawn, brightly illuminated by the moonlight. He walked round the house – if he was going to climb in through a window, it would be best to do it at the back, so that he would not be seen by some chance passer-by.

Behind the house he found a garden wrapped in dense shade – just what he needed.

Going up on tiptoe, the adventurer glanced into the first window after the corner. He saw a spacious room – a dining room or drawing room. A white tablecloth, candles burning out, the remains of a supper served for two.

His heart suddenly ached.

So, she dined with one and set out for a tryst with another? Or, even better, she returned from her dramatic rendezvous and calmly sat down to a meal with her ginger-haired patron? Women truly were mysterious creatures. After two more windows, the next room began – the study.

The windows here were slightly open and Fandorin could hear a man's voice speaking, so he acted with caution and first listened to ascertain where the speaker was.

'. . . will be reprimanded, but his superior will bear the greater part of the guilt – he will be obliged to resign in disgrace . . .' said the voice in the study.

The words were spoken in English, but with a distinct Japanese accent, so it was not Bullcox.

However, the senior adviser was also there.

'And our friend will occupy the vacancy?' he asked.

Two men, Fandorin decided. The Japanese is sitting in the far right corner, and Bullcox is in the centre, with his back to the window.

The titular counsellor lifted himself up slowly, inch by inch, and examined the interior of the room.

Shelves of books, a desk, a fireplace with no fire.

The important thing was that O-Yumi was not here. Two men. He could see his rival's fiery locks sticking up from behind the back of one armchair. The other armchair was occupied by a dandy with a gleaming parting in his hair and a pearl glowing in his silk tie. The minuscule man crossed one leg elegantly over the other and swayed his lacquered shoe.

'Not this very moment,' he said with a restrained smile. 'In a week's time.'

Ah, I know you, my good sir, thought Erast Petrovich, narrowing his eyes.

I saw you at the ball. Prince . . . What was it that Doronin called you?

'Well now, Onokoji, that is very Japanese,' the Right Honourable said with a chuckle. 'To reprimand someone, and reward him a week later with promotion.'

Yes, yes, Fandorin remembered, he's Prince Onokoji, the former *daimyo* – ruler of an appanage principality – now a high society lion and arbiter of fashion.

'This, my dear Algernon, is not a reward, he is merely occupying a position that has fallen vacant. But he will receive a reward, for doing the job so neatly. He will be given the suburban estate of Takarazaka. Ah, what plum trees there are there! What ponds!'

'Yes, it's a glorious spot. A hundred thousand, probably.'

'At least two hundred, I assure you!'

Erast Petrovich did not look in the window – he was not interested. He tried to think where O-Yumi might be.

On the ground floor there were another two windows that were dark, but Bullcox was hardly likely to have accommodated his mistress next to his study. So where were her chambers, then? At the front of the house? Or on the first floor?

'All right, then,' he heard the Briton say. 'But what about Prince Arisugawa's letter? Have you been able to get hold of a copy?'

'My man is greedy, but we simply can't manage without him.'

'Listen, I believe I gave you five hundred pounds!'

'But I need a thousand.'

The vice-consul frowned. Vsevolod Vitalievich had said that the prince lived on Don Tsurumaki's charity, but apparently he felt quite free to earn some subsidiary income. And Bullcox was a fine one, too – paying for court rumours and stolen letters. But then, that was his job as a spy.

No, the Englishman would probably not accommodate his native mistress on the front façade of the house – after all, he was an official dignitary. So her window was probably on the back wall . . .

The wrangling in the study continued.

'Onokoji, I'm not a milch cow.'

'And in addition, for the same sum, you could have a little list from Her Majesty's diary,' the prince said ingratiatingly. 'One of the ladies-in-waiting is my cousin, and she owes me many favours.'

Bullcox snorted.

'Worthless. Some womanish nonsense or other.'

'Very far indeed from nonsense. Her Majesty is in the habit of noting down her conversations with His Majesty . . .'

There's no point in my listening to all these abominations, Fandorin told himself. I'm not a spy, thank God. But if some servant or other sees me, I'll cut an even finer figure than these two: 'RUSSIAN VICE-CONSUL CAUGHT EAVESDROPPING'.

He stole along the wall to a drainpipe and tugged on it cautiously, to see whether it was firm. The titular counsellor already had some experience in climbing drainpipes from his previous, non-diplomatic life.

His foot was already poised on the lower rim of brick, but his reason still attempted to resist. You are behaving like a madman, like a thoroughly contemptible, irresponsible individual, his reason told him. Come to your senses! Get a grip on yourself!

'It's true,' Erast Petrovich replied abjectly, 'I have gone completely gaga.' But his contrition did not make him abandon his insane plan, it did not even slow down his movements.

The diplomat scrambled up nimbly to the first floor, propped one foot on a ledge and reached out for the nearest window. He clutched at the frame with his fingers and crept closer, taking tiny little steps. His frock coat was probably covered in dust, but that did not concern Fandorin just at the moment.

He had a far worse problem – the dark window refused to open. It was latched shut, and it was impossible for him to reach the small upper section.

Break it? He couldn't, it would bring the entire household running . . .

The diamond on the titular counsellor's finger – a farewell gift from the lady responsible for his missing the steamship from Calcutta – glinted cunningly.

If Erast Petrovich had only been in a normal, balanced state of mind, he would undoubtedly have felt ashamed of the very idea – how could he use a present from one woman to help him reach another! But his fevered brain whispered to him that diamond cuts glass. And the young man promised his conscience that he would take the ring off and never put it back on again for as long as he lived.

Fandorin did not know exactly how diamond was used for cutting. He took a firm grip on the ring and scored a decisive line. There was disgusting scraping sound, and a scratch appeared on the glass.

The titular counsellor pursed his lips stubbornly and prepared to apply greater strength.

He pressed as hard as he could – and the window frame suddenly yielded.

For just a moment Erast Petrovich imagined that this was the result of his efforts, but O-Yumi was standing in the dark rectangle that had opened up in front of him. She looked at the vice-consul with laughing eyes that reflected two tiny little moons.

'You have overcome all the obstacles and deserve a little help,' she whispered. 'Only, for God's sake, don't fall off. That would be stupid now.' And in an absolutely unromantic but extremely practical manner, she grabbed hold of his collar.

'I came to tell you that I have also been thinking about you for the last two days,' said Fandorin.

The idiotic English language has no intimate form of the second person pronoun, it's always just 'you', whatever the relationship might be, but he decided that from this moment on they were on intimate terms.

'Is that all you came for?' she asked with a smile, holding him by the shoulders.

'Yes.'

'Good. I believe you. You can go back now.'

Erast Petrovich did not feel like going back.

He thought for a moment and said:

'Let me in.'

O-Yumi glanced behind her.

'For one minute. No longer.'

Fandorin didn't try to argue.

He clambered over the windowsill (how many times had he already done that tonight?) and reached his arms out for her, but O-Yumi backed away.

'Oh no. Or a minute won't be long enough.'

The vice-consul hid his hands behind his back, but he declared:

'I want to take you with me!'

She shook her head and her smile faded away.

'Why? Do you love him?' he asked in a trembling voice.

'Not any more.'

'Th-then why?'

She glanced behind her again – apparently at the door. Erast Petrovich himself had not looked round even once, he hadn't even noticed what room this was – a boudoir or a dressing room. To tear his gaze away from O-Yumi's face for even a second seemed blasphemous to him.

'Go quickly. Please,' she said nervously. 'If he sees you here, he'll kill you.'

Fandorin shrugged one shoulder nonchalantly.

'He won't kill me. Europeans don't do that. He'll challenge me to a d-duel.'

Then she started pushing him towards the window with her fists.

'He won't challenge you. You don't know this man. He will definitely kill you. If not today, then tomorrow or the next day. And not with his own hands.'

'Let him,' Fandorin murmured, not listening, and tried to pull her towards him. 'I'm not afraid of him.'

'. . . But before that he'll kill me. It will be easy for him to do that – like swatting a moth. Go. I'll come to you. As soon as I can . . .'

But he didn't let her out of his arms. He pressed his lips against her little mouth and started trembling, only coming to his senses when she whispered:

'Do you want me to be killed?'

He staggered back, gritted his teeth and jumped up on to the windowsill. He would probably have jumped down just as lightly, but O-Yumi suddenly called out:

'No, wait!' – and she held out her arms.

They dashed to each other as precipitately and inexorably as two trains that a fatal chance has set on the same line, hurtling towards each other. What follows is obvious enough: a shattering impact, billows of smoke and flashes of flame, everything thrown head over heels and topsy-turvy, and God only knows who will be left alive in this bacchanalian orgy of fire.

The lovers clung tightly to each other. Their fingers did not caress, they tore, their mouths did not kiss, they bit.

They fell on the floor, and this time there was no heavenly music, no art – only growling, the sound of clothes tearing, the taste of blood on lips.

Suddenly a small but strong hand pressed against Fandorin's chest and pushed him away.

A whisper right in his ear.

'Run!'

He raised his head and glanced at the door with misty eyes. He heard footsteps and absentminded whistling. Someone was coming, moving up from below – no doubt climbing the stairs.

'No!' groaned Erast Petrovich. 'Let him come! I don't care!'

But she was no longer there beside him – she was standing up, rapidly straightening her dishevelled nightgown.

She said:

'You'll get me killed!'

He tumbled over the windowsill, not in the least concerned about how he would fall, although, incredibly enough, he made a better landing than he had earlier on, at the Grand Hotel, and didn't hurt himself at all.

His frock coat then came flying out of the window after him, followed by his left shoe – the titular counsellor hadn't even noticed when he lost it.

He buttoned himself up somehow or other and tucked in his shirt, listening to hear what was happening now up above him.

But there was a loud slam as someone closed the window; after that there were no more sounds.

Erast Petrovich walked round the side of the house and started off across the lawn in the reverse direction – Masa was waiting there, outside the open gate. The vice-consul took only ten steps and then froze as three long, low shadows came tearing in from the street.

The mastiffs!

They had either concluded their male business or, like the ill-fated titular counsellor, withdrawn disappointed, but either way the dogs were back, and they had cut off his only line of retreat.

Fandorin swung round and dashed back into the garden, hurtling along, unable to make out the path, with branches lashing at his face.

The damned dogs were running a lot faster, and their snuffling was getting closer and closer.

The garden came to an end, and there was a fence of iron ahead. Too high to scramble over. And there was nothing to get a grip on.

Erast Petrovich swung round and thrust one hand into the holster behind his back to take out his Herstal, but he couldn't fire – it would rouse the entire house.

The first mastiff growled, preparing to spring.

'RUSSIAN VICE-CONSUL TORN TO PIECES' – the headline flashed through the doomed man's mind. He put his hands over his face and throat, and instinctively pushed his back against the fence. Suddenly there was a strange metallic clang, the fence gave way, and the titular counsellor fell, sprawling flat on his back.

When evening time comes,
In the mystical silence
The garden gate creaks

THE SCIENCE OF *JOJUTSU*

Still not understanding what had happened, Erast Petrovich rose to a squatting position, ready for the hopeless skirmish with three bloodthirsty monsters, but the amazing fence (no, gate!) slammed shut with a squeak of springs.

On the other side a heavy carcass slammed into the iron bars at full pelt. He heard an angry yelp and snarling. Three pairs of furiously glinting eyes gazed at their inaccessible prey.

'Not your day, folks!' shouted the titular counsellor, whose English speech had clearly been vulgarised somewhat by associating with Sergeant Lockston.

He drew in a deep breath, filling his lungs with air, and breathed out again, trying to calm his heartbeat. He looked around: who had opened the gate that saved him?

There was not a soul to be seen.

He saw Don Tsurumaki's palace in the distance and, much closer, a pond overgrown with water lilies, glinting in the moonlight – it was inexpressibly beautiful, with a tiny island, little toy bridges and spiky rushes growing along its banks. He could hear the melancholy croaking of frogs from that direction. The black surface seemed to be embroidered with silver threads – the reflections of the stars.

The vice-consul thought that the dark pavilion by the water's edge looked particularly fine, with the edges of its roof turned up like wings, as if it were preparing to take flight. A weather vane in the form of a fantastic bird crowned a weightless tower.

Erast Petrovich set off along the bank of the pond, gazing around. He was still stupefied. What kind of miracles were these? Someone must have opened the gate, and then closed it. Someone had rescued the nocturnal adventurer from certain death.

Not until the pavilion and the pond had been left behind did Fandorin think to look at the palace.

An elegant building, constructed in the style of the mansions on the Champs Élysées, with a terrace that faced in the direction of the little lake, and on the first floor someone standing behind the elegant balustrade was waving to the uninvited visitor – someone in a long robe and a fez with a tassel.

Erast Petrovich recognised him from the fez: it was the owner of the estate in person. Seeing that he had finally been spotted, Don Tsurumaki gestured invitingly in welcome.

There was nothing to be done. Fandorin could hardly take to his heels. Cursing under his breath, the titular counsellor bowed politely and set off towards the steps of the porch. His supple mind started functioning again, trying to invent some at least vaguely credible explanation for his scandalous behaviour.

'Welcome, young assistant of my friend Doronin!' a rich male voice said above his head. 'The door is open. Come in and join me up here!'

'Th-thank you,' Fandorin replied drearily.

Erast Petrovich walked through the dark hallway, where the orchestra had thundered and skirts had been lifted above kicking legs in the cancan during the Bachelors' Ball, and then up the stairs, as if he were mounting the scaffold.

What should he do? Repent? Lie? What good would it do if he did lie? The Russian vice-consul, fleeing from the British agent's garden. The situation was quite unambiguous: one spy spying on another . . .

But Fandorin had still not realised just how wretched his situation really was.

Walking out on to the stone terrace, he saw a table laid with a magnificent spread of various kinds of ham, salami, fruits, cakes and sweets, as well as an array of sweet liqueurs; candles protruded from candelabra, but they had not been lit – evidently because of the bright moon. But the table was not the problem – there was a powerful telescope on an iron stand beside the balustrade, and its seeing eye was not pointed up at the heavens, but towards Bullcox's house!

Had Don Tsurumaki seen or hadn't he? Erast Petrovich froze on the spot when the thought hit him. But no, the real point was: What exactly had he seen – just a man running away through the garden or . . .

'Well, don't just stand there!' said the Don, puffing on his black briar pipe as he moved towards Fandorin. 'Would you like something to eat? I love eating alone at night. With no forks and no chopsticks – with just my bare hands.' He held up his palms, gleaming with grease and smeared with chocolate. 'Sheer piggishness, of course, but so help me, it's my favourite time of the day. I regale my soul with the sight of the stars and my body with all sorts of delicacies. Take a quail, they were still soaring over the meadow this morning. And there are oysters, absolutely fresh. Would you like some?'

The fat man spoke with such mouth-watering enthusiasm that Erast immediately realised just how hungry he was, and wanted the quail and the oysters. But he had to find out a few things first.

Since his host was in no hurry to interrogate him, the vice-consul decided to seize the initiative.

'Tell me, why do you need a gate leading into the next garden?' he asked, feverishly trying to think of how to approach the most important question.

'Algernon and I are friends . . .' (the name came out as 'Arudzenon' on his

Japanese lips) ' . . . we pay each other neighbourly calls, with no formalities. It's more convenient to go through the garden than round by the street.'

And it's also more convenient for your lodger to sell his secrets, the vice-consul thought, but, naturally, he didn't tell tales on Prince Onokoji. Fandorin recalled that, unlike the other guests, Bullcox and his consort had arrived at the Bachelors' Ball on foot, and they had appeared from somewhere off to one side, not from the direction of the front gates. So they must have used that gate . . .

'But . . . but how did you open it?' Erast Petrovich asked, still avoiding the most important point.

The Don became excited.

'O-oh, I have everything here running on electric power. I'm a great admirer of that remarkable invention! Here, look.'

He took the vice-consul by the elbow and half-led, half-dragged him to a kind of lectern standing beside the telescope. Erast Petrovich saw a bundle of wires running down to the floor and disappearing into a covered channel. On the lectern itself there were several rows of small, gleaming switches. Tsurumaki clicked one of them and the palace came to life, with yellowish-white light streaming out of all its windows. He clicked the switch again, and the house went dark.

'And this here is our gate. Look through the telescope, the telescope.'

Fandorin pressed his eye to the end of the tube and saw the metal railings very close up, only an arm's length away, with three canine silhouettes beyond them. A green spark glinted once again in a bulging eye. What patient brutes they were.

'One, two!' the Don exclaimed, and the gate swung open with a lively jerk, as if it were alive. One of the dogs bounded forward.

'Three, four!'

The gate slammed shut again just as quickly, and the mastiff was flung back into the garden. And serve the son of a bitch right!

Pretending to adjust the focus, Erast Petrovich raised the aim of the telescope slightly. First the wall of the house appeared in the circle of vision, and then the drainpipe, and then the window – and all very close indeed.

'That's enough, enough!' said the lover of electricity, tugging impatiently on his sleeve. 'Now I'll show you something that will really make you gasp. Nobody has seen it yet, I'm saving it for a big social event . . . The pond, watch the pond!'

Click! An emerald glow appeared above the black, shimmering patch of water as the tiny island was flooded with light from electric lamps, and the tiny stone pagoda standing on it was also lit up – but pink, not green.

'European science!' the millionaire exclaimed, with his eyes glittering. 'The wires are laid along the bottom, in a special telegraph cable. And the bulbs have coloured glass, that's the whole trick. How do you like that?'

'Astounding!' Fandorin exclaimed with genuine delight. 'You're a genuine inventor.'

'Oh no, I'm not an inventor. Making discoveries is what you *gaijins* are good at. The Japanese are not inventors, our element is Order, but pioneers are always children of Chaos. But we are really clever at finding good uses for others' inventions, and you can never keep up with us there. Give us time, Mr Fandorin: we'll learn all your tricks, and then we'll show you how clumsily you have used them.'

The Don laughed, and the titular counsellor thought: It doesn't look to me as if your element is Order.

'Are you interested in astronomy?' Erast Petrovich enquired, clearing his throat and nodding at the telescope.

Tsurumaki understood the hidden meaning of the question quite clearly. His laughter rumbled even more freely and his fat cheeks crept upwards, transforming his jolly, sparkling eyes into two narrow slits.

'Yes, astronomy too. But sometimes there are very curious things to be seen on the ground as well!'

He slapped his visitor on the shoulder in familiar fashion, choked on tobacco smoke and doubled over in laughter.

Erast Petrovich flushed bright red – he had seen it, he had seen everything! But what could Fandorin say now?

'Bravo, Fandorin-san, bravo!' said the joker, brushing away his tears. 'Here's my hand!'

The vice-consul shook the proffered hand very feebly and asked morosely: 'What are you so pleased about?'

'The fact that good old Algernon is a . . . what's the English word, now . . . a *cuckord*!'

Erast Petrovich did not immediately realise that the word intended was 'cuckold'. He asked with emphatic coolness, in order to bring the conversation back within the bounds of propriety:

'But you said he was your f-friend.'

'Of course he is! As far as a native princeling can be a white sahib's friend.' The Don's sanguine features dissolved into a smile that was no longer jolly, but frankly spiteful. 'Do you really not know, my dear Fandorin-san, that one of the greatest of pleasures is the feeling of secret superiority over someone who thinks he is superior to you? You have given me a wonderful present. Now every time I look at Bullcox's snobbish features, I shall remember your magnificent leap from the window and the clothes flying through the air, and inside I shall be roaring with laughter. Thank you very, very much for that!'

He tried to shake hands again, but this time the dumbfounded vice-consul hid his hand behind his back.

'Are you offended? You shouldn't be. I have a proposal for you, a secret Japano-Russian alliance, directed against British imperialism.' The Don winked. 'And I am offering you an excellent base for undermining English influence. You see the little pavilion by the water? A fine, secluded spot. I shall give you a key to the gates, and you will be able to get in at any time of the day or night. And I shall present the lovely O-Yumi with a key to the gate in the garden. Make yourselves at home. Feast on love. Only one condition: don't turn out the lamp and don't close the curtains on this side. Consider that the rental charge for the premises . . . Oh, just look at his eyes flash! Oh! I'm joking, I'm joking!'

He burst into laughter again, but to Erast Petrovich these playful jokes about the exalted and fateful power that had bound him and O-Yumi together seemed like unforgivable blasphemy.

'I will ask you never to speak about this l-lady and my relationship with her in that tone again . . .' he began furiously, in a hissing whisper.

'You're in love!' Tsurumaki interrupted with a laugh. 'Head over heels! Oh, you unfortunate victim of *jojutsu*!'

It is quite impossible to be seriously angry with a man who abandons himself to such good-natured merriment.

'What has jujitsu got to do with it?' Erast Petrovich asked in amazement, thinking that Tsurumaki meant the Japanese fighting art that he was studying with his valet.

'Not JUjitsu, but *jOjutsu*! The art of amorous passion. An art of which top-flight courtesans have complete mastery.' The bon vivant's gaze turned thoughtful. 'I too was once snared in the nets of a mistress of *jojutsu*. Not for long, only a month and a half. Her love cost me thirty thousand yen – all that I had in those days. Afterwards I had to start my business all over again, but I don't regret it – it is one of the best memories of my life!'

'You're mistaken, my dear fellow,' said Fandorin, smiling condescendingly. 'Your *jojutsu* has nothing to do with it. I have not paid for love.'

'It is not always paid for with money,' said the Don, scratching his beard and raising his thick eyebrows in surprise. 'O-Yumi not using *jojutsu*? That would be strange. Let's check. Of course, I don't know all the subtle points of this intricate art, but I remember a few things that I experienced for myself. The initial stage is called "*soyokadzeh*". How can I translate that, now . . . "The breath of wind" – that's pretty close. The goal is to attract the attention of the chosen target. To do this the mistress of the art gives the man a chance to show himself in the best possible light. It's a well-known fact that a man loves those who he believes should admire him more than anyone else. If a man prides himself on his perspicacity, the courtesan will arrange things so that he appears before her in all his intellectual brilliance. If he is brave, she will give him a chance to show that he is a genuine hero. Fake bandits can be hired, so that the target can defend a beautiful stranger against them. Or he might suddenly see a beautiful woman fall into the water from a capsized boat. The most audacious courtesans will even risk being maimed by conspiring with a riksha or a coach driver. Imagine a carriage that has run out of control, and a delightful woman sitting in it, screaming pitifully. How can you possibly not go dashing to assist her? At the first stage of *jojutsu* it is very important, firstly, for the target to feel that he is a protector and, secondly, for him to be inspired with lust for the huntress, not merely compassion. To achieve that she is certain to expose, as if by accident, the most seductive part of her body: a shoulder, a foot, a breast, it varies from one individual to another.'

At first Fandorin listened to this story with a scornful smile. Then, when he heard the words about a carriage running out of control, he shuddered. But he immediately told himself: No, no, it's impossible, it's just coincidence. But what about the torn dress, and the alabaster shoulder with the scarlet scratch? a satanic little voice whispered.

Nonsense, the titular counsellor thought with a shake of his head. It really was absurd.

'And what does the second stage consist of?' he enquired ironically.

Tsurumaki took a bite out of a large, luscious red apple and continued with his mouth full.

'It's called "Two on an Island". A very subtle moment. The point is to maintain distance, while demonstrating that there is some special kind of connection between the courtesan and the target – they are bound together by the invisible threads of fate. For this purpose all means are good: the mistress of the art sets spies on the target, gathers information about him, and then many of the ladies also have a good command of *ninso* – that's like your physiognomics, only far, far more subtle.'

The vice-consul turned cold, but the jolly narrator crunched on his apple and implacably drove needle after needle into his poor suffering heart.

'I think they call the third stage "The Scent of a Peach". The target has to be allowed to inhale the seductive aroma of the fruit, but the fruit is still hanging high up on the branch and no one knows whose hands it will fall into. This is to show that the creature provoking his desire is a living, passionate woman, not some incorporeal angel, and she will have to be fought for. At this stage a rival is certain to appear, and a serious one at that.'

How she rode past the consulate with Bullcox, leaning her head on his shoulder! Erast Petrovich recalled. And she didn't even glance in my direction, although I was sitting right there in the window . . .

Oh no, no, no!

The Don squinted up at the moon.

'How does it continue now? Ah yes, but of course! The "Typhoon" stage. Immediately after the despair ("alas and alack, she will never be mine!"), the courtesan arranges a lover's tryst, completely without any warning. Absolutely breathtaking, employing all the secret arts of the bedroom, but not too long. The target must get the real taste of pleasure, but not be sated. After that comes the *"Ayatsuri"* stage. Separation resulting from insuperable difficulties of some kind. *Ayatsuri* is the way a puppet master controls a puppet in the theatre. Have you ever been to a *bunraku* performance? You must go, you have nothing like it in Europe. Our puppets are just like real people, and . . .'

'Stop!' Fandorin cried out, feeling that he could not take any more. 'For God's sake, stop t-talking!'

Crushed, Erast Petrovich brushed a drop of icy sweat off his forehead and forced himself to speak.

'I see now that you are right . . . And I . . . I am grateful to you. If not for you I really would have lost my reason completely . . . In fact, I have already

'... But no more, I will not be a puppet in her hands any longer!'

'Ah, you are wrong there,' Tsurumaki said disapprovingly. 'You still have the very best stage to come: "The Bow String". In your case the title is doubly piquant,' he said with a smile. '"Bow" in Japanese is *yumi*.'

'I know,' Fandorin said with a nod, looking off to one side. A plan was gradually taking shape in the demoralised vice-consul's head.

'This is the stage of total happiness, when both soul and body attain the very summit of bliss and reverberate with delight, like a taut bowstring. In order to highlight the sweetness even more, the mistress of the art adds just a little bitterness – you will certainly never know ...'

'I tell you what,' Erast Petrovich interrupted, staring sombrely into the eyes of the man who had saved him from insanity, but broken his heart. 'That's enough about *jojutsu*. I'm not interested in that. Give me your key, I'll take it from you for one day. And give ... give her the other key, from the gate in the garden. Tell her that I shall be waiting for her in the pavilion, starting from midnight. But not a word about this conversation of ours. Do you promise?'

'You won't kill her, will you?' the Don asked cautiously. 'I mean, it doesn't really matter to me, but I wouldn't like it to be on my estate ... And then Algernon would resent it. And he's not the kind of man I'd like to quarrel with ...'

'I won't do her any harm. On m-my word of honour.'

It took Fandorin an agonisingly long time to walk to the gates. Every step cost him an effort.

'Ah, *jojutsu*?' he whispered. 'So they call it *jojutsu*, do they?'

A host of students,
But such scanty progress made
In passion's science

A ONE-HANDED CLAP

The day that arrived after this insane night was like nothing on earth. In defiance of the laws of nature, it did not move from morning to evening at a uniform rate, but in jerks and bounds. The hands of the clock either stuck fast or leapt over several divisions all at once. However, when the mechanism began striking either eleven or twelve, Erast Petrovich seemed to start thinking seriously and continuously for the first time; one mood was displaced by another, several times his thoughts completely reversed their direction, and tiresome old Big Ben carried on chiming 'bong-bong-bong' and simply would not shut up.

The vice-consul did not show his face in the consular office – he was afraid he would not be able to maintain a conversation with his colleagues. He didn't eat, he didn't drink, and he didn't lie down or sit down even for a minute, he just strode round and round his room. Sometimes he would start talking to himself in a furious whisper, then he would fall silent again. On several occasions his alarmed valet peeped through the crack of the door and sighed loudly, rattling the tray with his master's cold breakfast, but Fandorin neither saw nor heard anything.

To go or not to go, that was the question that the young man was simply unable to answer.

Or, to be more precise, the decision was taken repeatedly, and in the most definitive terms, but then time was affected by the aforementioned paradox, the hands of Big Ben froze and the torment began all over again.

When he had moved a little beyond his initial numbness and entered a state not entirely dissimilar to normality, Erast Petrovich naturally told himself that he would not go to any pavilion. This was the only dignified way out of the horrifyingly undignified situation into which the vice-consul of the Russian Empire had been drawn by the inopportune awakening of his heart. He had to amputate this whole shameful business with a firm hand, and wait until the blood stopped flowing and the severed nerves stopped smarting. In time the wound would certainly heal over, and the lesson would have been learned for the rest of his life. Why create melodramatic scenes, with accusations and hands upraised to the heavens? He had played the fool's part long enough, it was shameful enough to remember, even without that . . .

He was going to send the key back to the Don immediately.

He didn't send it.

He was prevented by an upsurge of rage, rage of the most corrosive sort – that is, not fiery but icy rage, which does not set the hands trembling, but clenches them into fists, the sort of rage that sets the pulse beating slowly and loudly and paints the face with a deadly pallor.

How had he, an intelligent and dispassionate individual, who had passed honourably through numerous trials, allowed himself to be treated like this? And even more importantly, by whom? A venal woman, a calculating intriguer! He had behaved like a pitiful young pup, like a character out of some vulgar harlequinade! He gritted his teeth, recalling how his coat-tail had snagged on a nail, how he had pressed on the pedals to escape from the pack of homeless mongrels . . .

No, he would go, he had to go! Let her see what he, Fandorin, was really like. Not a pitiful, besotted boy, but a firm, calm man who had seen through her satanic game and stepped disdainfully over the trap that had been set for him.

Dress elegantly, but simply: a black frock coat, a white shirt with a turn-down collar – no starch, no neckties. A cloak? He thought yes. And a cane, that was indispensable.

He dressed up, stood in front of the mirror, deliberately ruffled his hair so that a casual lock dangled down across his forehead – and suddenly flushed, as if he had seen himself from the outside.

My God! The harlequinade wasn't over yet, it was still going on!

His fury suddenly receded, his convulsively clenched fingers unfolded. His heart was suddenly desolate and dreary.

Erast Petrovich dropped the cloak on the floor, flung away the cane and leaned wearily against the wall.

What sort of sickness was love? he wondered. Who was it that tortured a man with it, and for what? That is, it was perfectly possible that for other people it was essential and even beneficial, but this potion was clearly counter-indicated for a certain titular counsellor. Love would bring him nothing but grief and disenchantment, or even, as in the present case, humiliation. Such, apparently, was his fate.

He shouldn't go anywhere. What did he want with this alien woman anyway, why did he need her remorse, or fright or annoyance? Would that really make his heart easier?

Time immediately stopped playing its idiotic tricks, the clock started ticking regularly and calmly. That alone was enough to indicate that the correct decision had been taken.

Erast Petrovich spent the rest of the day reading *The Diary of Sea Captain Golovin Concerning His Adventures as a Prisoner of the Japanese in 1811, 1812 and 1813*, but shortly before midnight he suddenly put the book down and set out for Don Tsurumaki's estate without any preparations at all, apart from putting on a peaked cap.

Masa did not try to stop his master and did not ask any questions. He watched as the figure on the tricycle rode away at a leisurely pace, stuck his *nunchaku* into the waistband of his trousers, hung the little bag containing his wooden *geta* round his neck and trotted off in the direction of the Bluff.

The huge cast-iron gates opened remarkably easily and almost soundlessly. As he walked towards the pond along the moonlit path, Erast Petrovich squinted in the direction of the house. He saw the telescope pointing up at the sky and a thickset figure in a dressing gown standing with his face glued to the eyepiece. Apparently today Don Tsurumaki was not interested in earthly spectacles, he was admiring the sky. And the stars really were larger and brighter than Fandorin had seen them since his grammar-school days, when he loved to sit in the planetarium and dream of flights to the moon or Mars. How strange to think that that was only four years ago!

The titular counsellor was certain that he would be the first to arrive at the pavilion and would be sitting there alone in the darkness for a long time, since, no doubt, the sordid science of *jojutsu* required the enamoured fool to suffer the torments of anticipation. However, the moment he opened the door of the pavilion, Erast Petrovich caught the familiar scent of irises, at which his heart first tried to beat faster, but then submitted to the dictates of reason and reverted to its former rhythm.

So O-Yumi had come first. Well, so much the better.

It was quite light in the tiny hallway – the moonlight filtered in through the cracks of the wooden shutters. Fandorin saw paper partitions and two wooden sandals on the floorboards beside the straw mats on the raised platform. Ah yes, the Japanese custom required footwear to be removed before stepping on to the straw mats.

But Erast Petrovich had no intention of removing his footwear. He crossed his arms and deliberately cleared his throat, although, of course, the 'mistress of the art' had already heard that the 'target' had arrived.

The paper partitions slid apart. Standing behind them, holding the two screens, was O-Yumi – with the wide sleeves of a kimono hanging from her arms, which made the woman look like a butterfly. Dramatic, Fandorin thought to himself with a sneer.

He couldn't see the courtesan's face, only her silhouette against a silvery, shimmering background.

'Come in quickly!' the low, husky voice called to him. 'It's so wonderful in here! Look, I've opened the window, there's the pond and the moon. That bandit Tsurumaki knows a thing or two about beauty.'

But Erast Petrovich didn't move.

'What are you doing?' she said, taking a step towards him. 'Come!'

Her fingers reached out for his face, but they were intercepted by a firm hand in a tight-fitting glove.

Now he could see her face – unbearably beautiful, even now, when he knew everything.

No, not everything.

And Fandorin asked the question for which he had come here.

'Why?' he demanded in a severe voice. 'What do you want from me?'

Of course, a true professional would not have done that. He would have realised that he didn't have a clue about anything, that he was still playing the part of a halfwit and a simpleton, and little by little he would have figured out the secret of this latter-day Circe who transformed men into swine. And at the same time he would have paid her back in the same coin.

Erast Petrovich regarded himself as quite a good professional, but to dissemble with a dissembler was disgusting, and it probably wouldn't have worked anyway – his rebellious heart was beating faster than it should in any case.

'I am not as rich and certainly not as influential as your patron. I do not possess any important secrets. Tell me, what did you want from me?'

O-Yumi listened to him in silence, without trying to free herself. He was standing on the wooden floor, she on the straw mats, so that their faces were almost on the same level, separated by only a few inches, but it seemed to Fandorin that he could never understand the expression of those long eyes that glittered so moistly.

'Who knows the answer to that question?' she asked in a quiet voice. 'Why did I need you, and you me? You simply feel that it cannot be otherwise, and nothing else matters.'

It was not so much the words that were spoken, but the tone in which they were spoken, which set Fandorin's fingers trembling. O-Yumi freed one hand, reached out to his face and stroked his cheek gently.

'Don't ask any questions . . . And don't try to understand – it can't be done anyway. Listen to your heart, it will not deceive you . . .'

It will deceive me! Oh yes it will! – the titular counsellor wanted to cry out the words, but he was incautious enough to catch O-Yumi's eye, and after that he couldn't look away again.

'Is that what your art prescribes?' Fandorin asked in a trembling voice, when her hand slid lower, slipping behind his collar and sliding gently across his neck.

'What art? What are you talking about?'

Her voice had become even lower and huskier. She seemed not to be paying any attention to the meaning of what he said, or to understand very well what she was saying herself.

'Jojutsu!' – Erast Petrovich shouted out the abhorrent word. 'I know everything! You pretend to be in love, but all the time you are using jojutsu!'

There, the accusation had been uttered, now her expression would change and the enchantment would be dispelled!

'Why don't you say anything. It's t-true, isn't it?'

It was incredible, but she didn't look even slightly disconcerted.

'What is true?' O-Yumi murmured in the same sleepy voice, still stroking his skin. 'No, it's not true, I'm not pretending . . . Yes, it is true – I love you according to the laws of jojutsu.'

The vice-consul recoiled.

'Aha! You admit it!'

'What is bad about that? Do I take money or presents from you? Do I want something from you? I love as I know how to love. I love as I have been taught. And you can be sure that I have been taught well. *Jojutsu* is the best of all the arts of love. I know, because I have studied the Indian school, and the Chinese school. I will not even speak of the European school – that barbarous nonsense. But even the Chinese and the Indians understand almost nothing about love, they pay too much attention to the flesh . . .'

As she spoke, her rapid, light fingers did their work – unbuttoning, stroking, sometimes sinking their nails into the body of the enchanted titular counsellor.

'More *jojutsu*, is it?' he murmured, hardly even resisting any more. 'What do you call it when the victim has rebelled and you have to subdue him once again? Something picturesque – "Plum Blossom Rain", "Rampant Tiger"?'

O-Yumi laughed quietly.

'No, it's called "Fight Fire with Fire". The best way to extinguish a powerful flame is with a conflagration. You'll see, you'll like it.'

Erast Petrovich at least had no doubt that she was right about that.

A long time later, after both fires had fused together and consumed each other, they lay on the terrace, watching the shimmering surface of the pool. The conversation sprang up and then broke off again, because it was equally good to speak and to remain silent.

'There's one thing I forgot to ask Don,' said Erast Petrovich, lighting up a cigar. 'How does a course of *jojutsu* end? In Europe the lovers live happily ever after. It's not the same here, I suppose?'

'It isn't.' She rose slightly, propping herself up on one elbow. 'A correctly constructed love does not end with death, but with a subtle finale, so that both parties are left with beautiful memories. We do not allow the feeling to die, we cut it, like a flower. This is slightly painful, but afterwards there is no resentment or bitterness left behind. I like you so much! For you I will think up something especially beautiful, you'll see.'

'Thank you with all my heart, but please don't. What's the hurry?' said Erast Petrovich, pulling her towards him. 'The wise old Don told me something very interesting about the stage that is called "The Bow String".'

'Yes, I suppose it is time . . .' she replied in a voice trembling with passion, and took his hand between the palms of her own hands. 'Lesson one. I am the bowstring, you are the shaft of the bow, our love is an arrow that we must shoot straight into the centre of the moon . . . Look at the moon, not at me. When we fire, it will fall and shatter into a thousand fragments . . .'

And Fandorin started looking up into the sky, where the lamp of night was shining serenely – the poor wretch was quite unaware of the fate in store for it.

★

Throughout the next week Erast Petrovich seemed to exist in two worlds with no connection between them – the world of the sun and the world of the moon. The former was hot, but insipid, almost spectral, since the titular counsellor constantly felt that he wanted to sleep. It was only as evening advanced and the shadows first lengthened and then disappeared altogether that Fandorin started to wake up: first the body, reaching out achingly for the night, and then the mind. The enervated, dreamy state seemed to disappear without trace and somewhere inside him a sweet chiming began, gradually growing stronger, and by the moment when the moon finally rolled out onto the sky, the lovesick titular counsellor was completely ready to immerse himself in the *real* world of the night.

In this world everything was beautiful from the very beginning: the whispering flight of the tricycle along the deserted promenade, the metallic grating of the key in the lock of the gates and the rustling of the gravel on the path leading to the pavilion. And then came the most painful and most poignant part of all – would she come or not? Twice O-Yumi did not appear – she had warned him that this was possible, she might not be able to slip out of the house. He sat on the terrace, smoking a cigar, watching the water and listening to the silence. And then the sun peeped out from behind the tops of the trees, and it was time to go back. The titular counsellor walked back to the gates with his head lowered, but the bitterness of the tryst that never happened held a charm all of its own – it meant that the next meeting would be doubly sweet.

But if Fandorin's sharp hearing caught the squeak of the garden gate, and the sound of light footsteps, the world changed instantly. The stars blazed more brightly, but the moon shrank, already aware that it was to fall to earth again and again, shattering into sparkling dust.

There were no words for what happened in those night hours, there could not be any – at least not in any of the languages known to Erast Petrovich. And it was not simply that European speech either falls silent or lapses into crudity when it has to talk of the merging of two bodies. No, this was something different.

When they made love to each other – either greedily and simply, or subtly and unhurriedly – Fandorin's entire being was possessed by the acute awareness, quite inexpressible in words, that *death exists*. From his early childhood he had always known that the life of the body was impossible without the life of the soul – this was what faith taught, it was written in a multitude of beautiful books. But now, in the twenty-third year of his life, under a moon that was falling from the sky, it was suddenly revealed to him that the opposite is also true – the soul will not live on without the body. There will not be any resurrection, or angels, or long-awaited encounter with God – there will be something quite different, or perhaps there will not be anything at all, because the soul does not exist without the body, just as light does not exist without darkness, just as the clapping of one hand does not exist. If the body dies, the soul will die too, and death is absolute and final. He felt this with every particle of his flesh, and it made him terribly afraid, but at the same time somehow very calm.

That was how they loved each other, and there was nothing to add to this.

Heat that knows no cold,
Happiness that knows no grief –
A one-handed clap

A SPRAY OF ACACIA

On one occasion O-Yumi left earlier than usual, when there was no moon any longer, but there was still a long time left until dawn. She didn't give any explanations – she never explained anything anyway: she just said 'It's time for me to go', dressed quickly, ran her finger down his neck in farewell and slipped out into the night.

Erast Petrovich walked towards the gates along the white path that glowed faintly in the gloom, along the edge of the pond and then across the lawn. As he was walking past the house, he looked up, as he usually did, to see whether his host was on the terrace. Yes, there was the stargazer's corpulent figure rising up above the balustrade. The Don politely doffed his fez, Fandorin bowed equally politely and went on his way. In the last few days this silent exchange of greetings had become something like a ritual. The jovial man with the beard had proved more tactful than could have been expected after that first conversation. The Japanese must have delicacy in their blood, thought the titular counsellor, who was in that state of relaxed bliss when one wants to love the entire world and see only the good in people.

Suddenly, out of the corner of his eye, he noticed something strange, an odd, momentary glimmer that should not have been there in a moonless world. Intrigued, Fandorin glanced round at the dark windows of the house and quite clearly saw a spot of light flash across one of the windowpanes, between the curtains, which were not fully closed, and then disappear.

Erast Petrovich stopped. That stealthy ray was very much like the light of a dark lantern, the kind used by window men, housebreakers and other professionals of a similar ilk. There were housebreakers in Russia and in Europe, why should there not be housebreakers in Japan?

Or was it simply one of the servants who didn't want to switch on the electricity, in order not to disturb his master's nocturnal solitude?

The servants at the estate were trained to such a supreme level of competence that they were not even visible, and everything needful seemed to do itself. When Fandorin arrived at his beloved pavilion, everything had always been tidied, there were hors d'oeuvres and fresh candles on the low table, and a vase with an intricately arranged bouquet – different every time – standing in the shadowy niche. When he walked back to the gates at dawn, the titular counsellor saw that the pathways had been thoroughly swept, and the grass of the English lawn was freshly trimmed, although he had not heard a single sound from a broom or garden shears. Only once did he actually see one of the servants. On his way out, he realised that he had dropped his key somewhere. He stood there at the locked gates, rifling through his pockets, and was about to go back to the pavilion, when suddenly a figure in a black jacket and black trousers emerged silently from the pink-coloured mist, bowed, handed him the lost key and immediately dissolved into the haze – Fandorin didn't even have time to thank him.

Well, if it's a servant, I'll just go on my way, the titular counsellor reasoned. But what if it is a thief after all or, even worse, a killer? To save his host from a fiendish criminal plot would be the best possible way to repay him for his hospitality.

He looked all around – naturally, there was not a soul in sight.

He walked over quickly to the window and reviewed the situation. The wall was faced with slabs of undressed, rough-textured granite. Erast Petrovich braced the toe of his shoe in a small hollow, grasped the protruding windowsill with one hand, pulled himself up nimbly and pressed his face to the glass – at the point where the curtains were not drawn close together.

At first he saw absolutely nothing at all – the room was pitch dark. But after about half a minute a trembling circle of light appeared in the far corner and started creeping slowly along the wall, first picking out a shelf with the golden spines of books, then the frame of a portrait, then a map. This was obviously a study or a library.

Erast Petrovich could not make out the person holding the lantern, but since it was obvious that no servant would behave in such a suspicious manner, the vice-consul readied himself for more decisive action. He pressed cautiously on the left frame of the window – it was locked. But when he pressed the right frame, it yielded slightly. Excellent! Possibly this was the very route the uninvited visitor had used to gain access, or perhaps the window had been left half open to air the room, but that was not important now. The important thing was that this nightbird could be nabbed.

If only the window frame didn't creak.

Fandorin started opening the frame slowly, a quarter of an inch at a time, keeping his eyes fixed on the wandering beam of light.

It suddenly stopped, pointing at one of the shelves, which did not look remarkable in any way. There was a gentle thud and the beam stopped trembling.

He had put the lantern down on the floor, the titular counsellor guessed.

Someone standing on all fours appeared or, rather, crept into the circle of light. Narrow shoulders, gleaming black hair, the white stripe of a starched collar. A European?

The titular counsellor pulled himself up higher, so that he could put one knee on the windowsill. Just a little more, and the crack would be wide enough to get through.

But then the damned window frame did creak after all.

The light instantly went out. Abandoning caution, Fandorin pushed the window open and jumped down on to the floor, but could not move any farther than that, since he couldn't see a thing. He held out his hand with the Herstal in it and strained his ears, listening in case his adversary was creeping up on him.

The man might be invisible now, but he was a mystery no longer. In the brief moment before the lantern went out, the hunched-over individual had looked round, and Erast Petrovich had clearly made out a brilliantined parting, a thin face with a hooked nose, and even a white flower in a buttonhole.

His Excellency Prince Onokoji, the high society spy, in person.

The titular counsellor's precautions were apparently unnecessary. The Japanese dandy had no intention of attacking him. In fact, to judge from the absolute silence that filled the study, the prince's trail was already cold. But that was not important now.

Fandorin put his revolver back in its holster and went to find the stairway to the first floor.

Tsurumaki listened to what the vice-consul told him and scratched the bridge of his nose. The grimace that he made suggested that the news was perplexing rather than surprising. He cursed in Japanese and started complaining:

'Oh, these aristocrats . . . he lives under my roof, occupies an entire wing, I pay him a pension of five thousand a month, and it's still not enough. And I know, I know that he deals in secrets and rumours on the side. I use him myself sometimes, for a separate fee. But this is just too much. Our little prince must be completely mired in debt. Ah!' The fat man sighed mournfully. 'If his late father were not my *onjin*, I'd tell him to go to hell. He's trying to get to my safe.'

Erast Petrovich was astounded by such a phlegmatic response.

'I truly admire the Japanese attitude to a debt of gratitude, but it seems to m-me that everything has its limits.'

'Never mind,' said the Don, with a flourish of his briar pipe. 'He can't open the safe in any case. He needs the key for that, and the key is here, I always keep it with me.'

He pulled a little chain up from behind his shirt collar. There was a little gold rose with a thorny stem hanging on it.

'A beautiful trinket, eh? You hold the bud, put it in, the thorns slip into the slots . . . There you have it, the "Open sesame" to my magical Aladdin's cave.'

Tsurumaki kissed the little key and put it away again.

'Don't they scratch?' asked Fandorin. 'I mean the thorns.'

'Of course they scratch, and quite painfully too. But it's the kind of pain that only makes life seem sweeter,' the millionaire said with a wink. 'It reminds me of the glittering little stones and the gold ingots. I can bear it.'

'You keep gold and precious stones at home? But why? There are b-bank vaults for that.'

'I know. I have a bank of my own. With strong, armour-plated vaults. But we blood-sucking spiders prefer to keep our booty in our own web. All the best to you, Fandorin-san. Thank you for the curious information.'

The titular counsellor took his leave, feeling rather piqued: he had wanted to be a rescuer, and instead he had ended up as an informer. But he went outside, looked in the direction of the pavilion hovering over the smooth black surface of the pond, and felt such a keen, overwhelming rush of happiness that his paltry disappointment was instantly forgotten.

However, the 'taut bowstring' reverberated not only in bliss, and not all the arrows that it fired went darting up into the starry sky. A certain poignantly distressful note, some kind of poisoned needle, blighted Erast Petrovich's happiness. At night he had no time for suffering, because love lives only in the here and now, but when he was far from O-Yumi, in his solitude, Fandorin thought of only one thing.

At their first lover's tryst, as he kissed O-Yumi on her delightfully protruding little ear, he had suddenly caught a very faint whiff of tobacco smoke – English pipe tobacco. He had pulled away, about to ask the question – but he didn't ask it. What for? So that she would lie? So that she would answer: 'No, no, it's all over between him and me'? Or so that she would tell the truth and make it impossible for them to carry on meeting?

Afterwards he had been tormented by his own cowardice. During the day he prepared an entire speech, made ready to tell her that things couldn't go on like this, that it was stupid, cruel, unnatural and, in the final analysis, humiliating! She had to leave Bullcox once and for all. He tried a couple of times to start this conversation, but she simply repeated: 'You don't understand. Don't ask me about anything. I can't tell you the truth, and I don't want to lie.' And then she set her hands and lips to work, and he surrendered, and forgot everything else in the world, only to suffer the same resentment and jealousy the next day.

Consul Doronin could undoubtedly see that something out of the ordinary was happening to his assistant, but he didn't ask any questions. Poor Vsevolod Vitalievich was certain that Fandorin was conducting the investigation at night, and he kept his word, he didn't interfere. Sometimes the titular counsellor's conscience bothered him because of this, but it bothered him far less than the smell of English tobacco.

On the sixth night (which was also the second one spent in the pavilion without his beloved) the vice-consul's suffering reached its highest point. Strictly forbidding himself to think about the reason why O-Yumi had not been able to come this time, Erast Petrovich called on logic to help: if there is a difficult problem, a solution has to be found – what could possibly be easier for a devotee of analytical theory?

And what was the result? A solution was found immediately, and it was so simple, so obvious, that Fandorin was amazed at his own blindness.

He waited for the evening, arrived at the pavilion earlier than usual and, as soon as he heard O-Yumi's footsteps approaching, he ran out to meet her.

'What a b-blockhead I am!' Erast Petrovich declared, taking hold of her hand. 'You don't have to be afraid of Bullcox. We'll get married. You'll be the wife of a Russian subject, and that man won't be able to do anything to you!'

The offer of his heart and his hand was greeted in a most surprising fashion.

O-Yumi burst into laughter, as if she had heard a not very clever but terribly funny joke. She kissed the titular counsellor on the nose.

'Don't be silly. We can't be husband and wife.'

'But why n-not? Because I'm a diplomat? Then I'll resign! Because you're afraid of Bullcox? I'll challenge him to a duel and kill him! Or, if . . . if you feel sorry for him, we'll just go away from here!'

'That's not the problem,' she said patiently, as if she were talking to a child. 'That's not it at all.'

'Then what is?'

'Look at that left eyebrow of yours. It runs in a semicircle, like that . . . And higher up, right here, there's the start of a little wrinkle. You can't see it yet, but it will show through in five years or so.'

'What has a wrinkle got to do with anything?' asked Erast Petrovich, melting at her touch.

'It tells me that you will be loved by very many women, and I probably wouldn't like that . . . And then this slightly lowered corner of the mouth, it testifies that you will not get married again before the age of sixty.'

'Don't make fun of me, I'm really serious! We'll get married and go away. Would you like to go to America? Or New Zealand? Lockston has been there, he says it's the most beautiful place on earth.'

'I'm serious too,' said O-Yumi, taking his hand and running it over her temple. 'Can you feel where the vein is? A *soon* and a quarter from the edge of the eye. That means I shall never marry. And then I have a mole, here . . .'

She parted the edges of her kimono to expose her breasts.

'Yes, I know. And what does that signify, according to the science of *ninso*?' Fandorin asked and, unable to resist, he leaned down and kissed the mole under her collarbone.

'I can't tell you that. But please, don't talk to me again about marriage, or about Algie.'

There was no smile in her eyes any more – a stark, sad shadow flitted though them.

Erast Petrovich could not tell what hurt the most: that name 'Algie', the firmness of the refusal, or the absolutely ludicrous nature of the reasons cited.

'She has turned me into a halfwitted infant . . .' – the thought flashed briefly through Fandorin's mind. He remembered how Doronin had recently said to him: 'What's happening to you, my dear boy? You grow fresher and younger before my very eyes. When you arrived, you looked about thirty, but now you look your real age of twenty-two, even with those grey temples. The Japanese climate and dangerous adventures clearly agree with you.'

Speaking quickly, almost babbling in order not to give himself time to come to his senses, he blurted out:

'If that is how things are, we shan't meet any more. Not until you leave him.'

He said it – and bit his lip, so that he couldn't take back what he had said straight away.

She looked into his eyes without speaking. Realising that he wouldn't hear anything else, she dropped her head. She pulled the lowered kimono back up on to her shoulders and slowly walked out of the pavilion.

Fandorin did not stop her, he did not call out, he did not even watch her go.

He was brought round by a pain in the palms of his hands. He raised his hands to his eyes and stared in bewilderment at the drops of blood, not realising straight away that the marks were made by his fingernails.

'So that's all,' the titular counsellor told himself. 'Better this than become a complete nobody. Farewell, my golden dreams.'

He jinxed himself: there really were no more dreams, because there was no sleep. On arriving home, Erast Petrovich undressed and got into bed, but he couldn't fall asleep. He lay on his side, looking at the wall. He could hardly even see it at first – just a vague greyness in the gloom; and then, as dawn approached, the wall started turning white and faint blotches appeared on it; and then they condensed into rosebuds; and then, after everything else, the sun glanced in at the window, kindling the gilded lines of the painted roses into life.

He had to get up.

Erast Petrovich decided to live as if everything in the world was arranged serenely and meaningfully – it was the only way he could counter the chaos swirling in his soul. He performed his daily weights exercises and respiratory gymnastics, then learned from Masa how to kick a spool of thread off the pillar of the bed, bruising his foot quite painfully in the process.

The physical exercise and the pain were both helpful, they made it easier to focus his will. Fandorin felt that he was on the right path.

He changed into a stripy *tricot* and set off on his usual morning run – to the park, then twenty circuits along the alley around the cricket field.

His neighbours on the Bund, mostly Anglo-Saxons and Americans, were already accustomed to the Russian vice-consul's whims, and on seeing the striped figure swinging its elbows rhythmically, they merely raised their hats in greeting. Erast Petrovich nodded and ran on, focusing on counting his out-breaths. Today he found it harder to run than usual, his breathing simply refused to settle into an even rhythm. Clenching his teeth stubbornly, the titular counsellor speeded up.

... Eight, nine, three hundred and twenty; one, two, three, four, five, six, seven, eight, nine, three hundred and thirty; one, two, three, four ...

Despite the early hour, there was already activity on the cricket pitch: the Athletics Club team was preparing for the Japan Cup competition – the sportsmen were taking turns to throw the ball at the stumps and then dash as quickly as they could to the other end of the wicket.

Fandorin did not get round the pitch. Halfway through his first circuit someone called his name.

There in the thick bushes was Inspector Asagawa, looking pale and drawn, with his eyes blazing feverishly – looking, in fact, very much like Erast Petrovich.

The vice-consul glanced around to see whether anyone was watching.

Apparently not. The players were engrossed in their training, and there was no one else in the park. The titular counsellor ducked into the acacia thickets.

'Well?' the inspector asked, pouncing on Fandorin without so much as a 'hello' or 'how are you'. 'I've been waiting for a week already. I can't bear it any longer. Do you know that yesterday Suga was appointed the intendant of police? The old intendant was dismissed for failing to protect the minister . . . I am burning up inside. I cannot eat, I cannot sleep. Have you thought of anything?'

Erast Petrovich felt ashamed. He could not eat or sleep either, but for a completely different reason. He had not remembered Asagawa even once during the last few days.

'No, n-not yet . . .'

The inspector's shoulders slumped dejectedly, as if he had been deprived of his last hope.

'Yes, of course . . .' he said morosely. 'In your European terms there is nothing to be done here. No clues, no evidence, no witnesses.' He turned even paler and shook his head decisively. 'Well, so be it. If we cannot do it in the European away, I shall act in the Japanese way.'

'What is "the Japanese way"?'

'I shall write a letter to His Majesty the Emperor, expounding all my suspicions concerning Intendant Suga. And I shall kill myself to prove my sincerity.'

'Kill yourself? Not Suga?' exclaimed Fandorin, dumbfounded.

'To kill Suga would not be to punish a criminal, but to commit a new crime. We have an ancient, noble tradition. If you wish to attract the attention of the authorities and the public to some villainy – commit seppuku. A deceitful man will not cut his stomach open.' Asagawa's eyes were inflamed and melancholy. 'But if only you knew, Fandorin-san, how terrible it is to commit seppuku without a second, without someone who will put an end to your suffering with a merciful sword-stroke! Unfortunately, I have no one to turn to with this request, my colleagues will never agree. I am entirely alone . . .' Suddenly he started and seized the vice-consul's arm. 'Perhaps you? Only one stroke! I have a long neck, it will not be hard to hit it!'

Fandorin recoiled and exclaimed:

'G-good Lord Almighty! I have never even held a sword!'

'Only one stroke! I will teach you. If you practise for an hour with a bamboo pole, you will manage it perfectly. I implore you. Do me this invaluable service!'

Seeing the expression on the other man's face, the inspector broke off and took himself in hand with an effort.

'All right,' he said in a dull voice. 'I am sorry for asking you. It was weakness. I am very ashamed.'

But Erast Petrovich was feeling even more ashamed. There were so many things in the world that were more important than wounded vanity, jealousy or an unhappy love! For instance, the aspiration to truth and justice. Moral integrity. Self-sacrifice in the name of justice.

'Listen,' the titular counsellor began agitatedly, squeezing the inspector's slack arm. 'You are an intelligent, modern, educated individual. What sort of barbarity is this – slicing your own stomach open! It's a throwback to the Middle Ages! But the end of the nineteenth century is already in sight! I swear to you that we will think of something!'

But Asagawa would not listen to him.

'I cannot live like this. As a European, you cannot understand this. Let there be no second! I shall not feel the pain. On the contrary, I shall free the pain that is burning me up inside. This villain has betrayed a great man who trusted him! He has kicked me aside with his boot, like a lump of mud! And now he is revelling in his victory. I cannot stand by and see villainy triumph. The criminal Suga is the head of the police! He is admiring himself in the mirror in his new uniform, he is moving into his new estate at Takarazaka! He is certain that the entire world is at his feet! This is intolerable!'

Erast Petrovich wrinkled up his forehead. Takarazaka? He had heard that name before somewhere.

'What estate is th-that?'

'A truly fine estate close to the capital. Suga won it at cards a few days ago. Oh, he is so lucky, his karma is strong!'

And then Fandorin remembered the conversation he had overheard in Bullcox's study. 'Well now, Onokoji, that is very Japanese,' the Englishman had said. 'To reprimand someone, and then reward him with promotion a week later.' And the prince had replied: 'This, my dear Algernon, is not a reward, he is merely occupying a position that has fallen vacant. But he will receive a reward, for doing the job so neatly. He will be given the suburban estate of Takarazaka. Ah, what plum trees there are there! What ponds!'

'What's wrong with you?' the inspector asked, gazing at Fandorin in surprise.

The vice-consul replied slowly:

'I think I know what to do. You and I have no evidence, but perhaps we will have a witness. Or at least an informer. There is someone who knows the true background to the murder.'

And Fandorin told Asagawa about the wily dandy who traded in others' secrets. Asagawa listened avidly, like a condemned man listening to the announcement of his own reprieve.

'Onokoji said that Suga had "done the job neatly"? Then the prince really does know a lot!'

'More than you and I know, in any case. But the most interesting question is who rewarded the new intendant with such a generous gift. Is it possible to find out who the estate belonged to before?'

'One of the deposed Shogun's relatives. But Takarazaka was put up for bidding a long time ago. Anyone at all could have bought it and lost it straight away at cards. We shall find out, it is not difficult.'

'But what can we do with the prince? It's stupid to hope that he will testify voluntarily.'

'Yes, he will,' the inspector declared confidently. 'Voluntarily and frankly.' A bloom had appeared on Asagawa's cheeks, his voice had become brisk and energetic. It was hard to believe that only ten minutes earlier this man had looked like a living corpse. 'Onokoji is pampered and weak. And even more importantly, he is addicted to every possible kind of vice, including the forbidden kind. I have not touched him before, assuming that he was a good-for-nothing idler, basically harmless. And in addition, he has numerous protectors in high places. But now I shall arrest him.'

'For what?'

Asagawa thought for no more than two seconds.

'He goes down to the "Number Nine" almost every day. It's the most famous brothel in Yokohama. Do you know it?'

Fandorin shook his head.

'Ah yes, you haven't been here for long . . . They have merchandise to suit all tastes there. For instance, the owner has a so-called "boarding school", for lovers of little girls. You can find thirteen-year-olds, twelve-year-olds, sometimes even eleven-year-olds. It's illegal, but since only foreign girls work at the "Number Nine", we do not interfere, it is outside our jurisdiction. Onokoji is a great lover of "little ones". I shall order the owner (he is in my debt) to tell me as soon as the prince secludes himself with a young girl. That is when he has to be arrested. I cannot do it myself, unfortunately – the arrest must be carried out by the municipal police.'

'So we'll be working with Sergeant Lockston again,' Erast Petrovich said with a nod. 'And tell me, are there any Russian subjects among the young prostitutes? That would justify my involvement in the matter.'

'I think there is one Polish girl,' Asagawa recalled. 'I do not know what passport she has, though. Probably none at all, since she is a minor.'

'The Kingdom of Poland is part of the Russian Empire, so the unfortunate victim of depravity could be a compatriot of mine. In any case, it is the vice-consul's duty to check. Well now, Inspector, have you changed you mind about slicing open your stomach?'

The titular counsellor smiled, but Asagawa was serious.

'You are right,' he said thoughtfully. 'Seppuku is a throwback to the Middle Ages.'

Something round and hard struck Fandorin in the back. He looked round – it was a cricket ball. One of the sportsmen had thrown very wide of the target.

Erast Petrovich picked up the small, taut leather sphere and flung it to the far end of the pitch. When he turned back again, the inspector was gone – there were only white sprays of acacia swaying on the bushes.

> Intoxicating,
> Astounding the mind, a white
> Spray of acacia

A LITTLE PIECE OF HAPPINESS

'Well now, it's worth a try,' said Vsevolod Vitalievich, narrowing his reddish eyes. 'If you can expose the intendant, that will be a powerful blow struck against the party of war. And your involvement in the investigation will not only free you of all suspicion of Okubo's murder, it will significantly improve the value of Russia's stock in Japan.'

Fandorin had found the consul in his dressing room, taking his morning tea. Doronin's sparse hair was covered with a fine net, and his thin neck with the protruding Adam's apple was visible in the open collar of his shirt.

Obayasi-san bowed and offered the visitor tea, but Erast Petrovich declined, with the lie that he had already had tea. For some reason he had no desire either to eat or drink. But his apathy had disappeared and the beat of his heart was strong and regular. The hunting instinct is every bit as ancient and powerful as the instinct to make love, thought the titular counsellor, glad that he was recovering the habit of rationalising his own feelings.

'We shall not inform the ambassador of your new initiative,' said Doronin, holding out his little finger as he raised his cup to his mouth, but he didn't drink. 'If we do, he will instruct Lieutenant Captain Bukhartsev to deal with it, and *he* will turn the whole business into a grand fiasco.'

Erast Petrovich shrugged.

'Why bother His Excellency with unimportant trifles? This is very small beer: the vice-consul defending the interests of an underage victim of corruption. That's all we're talking about so far.'

And then Vsevolod Vitalievich uttered a most injudicious sentiment.

'Do you know what true patriotism is?' he asked, then raised one finger and declared: 'To act for the good of the Homeland, even if it means going against the will of one's superiors.'

The titular counsellor considered this adventurous maxim. He nodded in agreement.

'Thank you for the aphorism, I f-feel it will prove useful to me in life on more than one occasion. And that being the case, I think I shall not tell you anything more. I shall act like a true patriot, that is, without the sanction of my superiors, at my own discretion. If anything goes wrong, I shall answer for everything. For the time being, let us consider that this conversation of ours never took place.'

Doronin flushed, jumped up off his chair and tore the net off his hair.

'Just what sort of minor role do you think you are assigning to me, my dear sir! Equal shares in the profit, but if the venture makes a loss, please don't be concerned about that? I'm a Russian diplomat, not a stock market speculator!'

Poor Obayasi, frightened by the sudden shouting, froze on the spot and put her hand over her mouth.

Erast Petrovich also got up off his chair.

'Precisely,' he said drily, piqued by that 'my dear sir'. 'You are a diplomat, the consul of the Russian Empire, and you must not think of *your own role*, but the good of the Fatherland.'

The conversation with Lockston was much simpler, with no highbrow introspection.

'So if His Yellow-Bellied Excellency's protectors grab us by the ass, I blame you for everything,' the American summed up. 'My job's a cinch: there was a request from the Russian consulate, and I was obliged to comply. All the notes and protests are your department, Rusty.'

'Precisely so.'

'Then I'm in.' The sergeant chuckled. 'Stick a genuine *daimyo* in the slammer – I like the idea. That'll teach them to go defiling our little girls! And if you can take that skunk Suga down a peg or two, I owe you a crate of genuine bourbon, one dollar ninety-nine a bottle. Why that ape, thinking he could give white men the runaround! There I was with my men, guarding that swamp, while he was pulling his dirty little tricks. Walter Lockston won't let anyone get away with that, especially some lousy, slanty-eyed aboriginal!'

The titular counsellor winced at the American manner of scorning other races and repeated the essential points.

'You wait for the signal. The next time Onokoji shows up at "Number Nine", the owner will plant the young Polish girl on him. Asagawa lets us know immediately. You hurry to the brothel and make an arrest at the scene of the c-crime. Then you summon the Russian vice-consul and the head of the Japanese police.'

They didn't have to wait long for 'the next time'.

That evening a courier arrived at the consulate, bearing an official note from Sergeant Lockston: an underage female, very probably a Russian subject, had been subjected to abuse.

Erast Petrovich responded to the summons immediately, taking the secretary Shirota with him to add greater formality to the proceedings.

The scene that greeted the representatives of Russia in the office of the head of the municipal police was perfectly scandalous. Two people were sitting facing the sergeant, whose visage was set in a predatory smile; Prince Onokoji and a skinny little girl – gaudily made up, but with her hair in plaits, tied with bows. Both arrestees were in a state of complete undress. Lockston had evidently escorted the fornicators to the station in the same condition in which they were caught.

The infuriated *daimyo's* apparel consisted of two sheets (one round his loins, the other thrown across his shoulders) and a pair of silk socks with elastic suspenders.

The presumptive Russian subject was wrapped in a sheet, but by no means tightly, and unlike her accomplice, she gave no sign of being particularly agitated – she kept turning her bright little face this way and that, sniffing all the time, and at the sight of the vice-consul she crossed one leg over the other and toyed coquettishly with her sandal. The knee of this victim of molestation was as skinny as a frog's paw.

'Who is this?' Onokoji squealed in English. 'I demanded the presence of the Japanese authorities! You will answer for this! My cousin is a minister of court!'

'These are representatives of the injured party's state,' Lockston declared solemnly. 'Here you are, Mr Vice-Consul, I relinquish this unfortunate child into your custody.'

Fandorin cast a glance of disgust at the child molester and spoke compassionately to the young girl in Russian.

'What is your name?'

She flirted with her heavily painted eyes, stuck the end of one plait into her mouth and drawled:

'Baska. Baska Zaionchek.'

'How old are you?'

After a moment's thought, the unfortunate child replied:

'Twenty.'

And in an entirely superfluous gesture, she showed him ten outstretched digits twice.

'She says she is twenty years old?' asked the prince, brightening up. 'That is what she told you, right?'

Taking no notice of him, Erast Petrovich said slowly:

'That is a great pity. If you were a juvenile, that is, underage, the Russian Empire, in my person, would have defended you. And then you could count on substantial c-compensation. Do you know what compensation is?'

Baska clearly did know what compensation was. She wrinkled up her forehead and examined the titular counsellor curiously. She jerked her leg, throwing off the sandal, scratched her foot and replied, swallowing her hard Polish 'l':

'I wied to the gentewman. I'm fourteen.' She thought for a little longer. 'I wiw be soon. I'm stiw thirteen.'

This time she put up ten fingers first, then three.

'She is thirteen,' the vice-consul translated for Lockston.

The prince groaned.

'My child, I can only protect your interests if you have Russian citizenship. So tell me, are you a subject of the empire?'

'*Tak*,' Baska said with a nod, crossing herself with three fingers, Orthodox-style, to prove the point – although she did it from left to right, as Catholics did. '*Pan*, the compensation – how much is it?

'She is a Russian subject, we'll take care of her,' Erast Petrovich told the sergeant, and he reassured the girl: 'You'll b-be quite satisfied.'

Her presence was no longer required.

'Why didn't you let the poor creature get dressed?' the vice-consul asked Lockston reproachfully. 'The little child is frozen through. Mr Shirota will take her to her apartment.'

Baska didn't really look chilly at all. On the contrary, keeping her eyes on the interesting man with the dark hair, she opened the sheet as if by accident and Fandorin blinked: the juvenile Zaionchek's breasts were developed well beyond her age. Although the devil only knew how old she really was.

So Shirota led the injured party away and Erast Petrovich stayed to attend to the drawing up of the minutes. And soon after that the representative of the Japanese side turned up – Inspector Asagawa, the head of the indigenous police.

The prince threw himself at the inspector, waving his arms in the air and jabbering something in Japanese.

'Quiet!' Lockston roared. 'I demand that all conversations be conducted in a language comprehensible to the injured party.'

The injured party – in this case Erast Petrovich – nodded sombrely.

'The individual styling himself Prince Onokoji has said he can obtain a promotion for me if I hush this case up,' Asagawa announced imperturbably.

The arrested man gazed round at all three of them with a hunted look and his eyes glinted, as if the realisation was dawning that he had not ended up in the police station by chance. But even so, he drew the wrong conclusion.

'All right, all right.' He chuckled, holding his hands up in a gesture of surrender. 'I can see I've been caught. You arranged it all very neatly. But you are in for a disappointment, gentlemen. Did you think that because I am a prince I have pockets full of money? I am afraid not. I am as poor as a shrine turtle. You won't make much out of me. I'll tell you how all this will end. I'll spend the night in your lock-up and tomorrow someone from the ministry will come and collect me. You'll wind up with nothing.'

'What about the disgrace?' said Asagawa. 'You, a scion of an ancient and glorious line, are involved in a dirty little scandal. Your patrons may perhaps get you released, but then they will break off all relations with you. Society will shun you, as if you had the plague. No more protection, no more charity from relatives.'

Onokoji narrowed his eyes. This man was clearly far from stupid.

'What do you want from me? I can see that you're leading up to something. Tell me straight out. If the price is fair, we'll strike a deal.'

Asagawa and Fandorin exchanged glances.

'Suga,' the inspector said in a quiet voice. 'We want Suga. Tell us everything you know about his part in the assassination of Minister Okubo, and we will let you go.'

The prince's face blenched as rapidly as if he had daubed a paintbrush dunked in lead white across his forehead and cheeks.

'I know nothing about that . . .' he babbled.

'A week ago you told Algernon Bullcox about the reward in store for Suga for doing the job so neatly,' said Fandorin, joining the game. 'Don't deny it, there's no point.'

The prince gaped at the vice-consul in horror – he evidently had not been expecting an attack from this quarter.

'How do you . . .? We were alone in the room, just the two of us!' Onokoji batted his eyelids in confusion.

Erast Petrovich was certain that this puny playboy would flinch and falter now. But instead it was the titular counsellor who flinched.

'Ah!' the prisoner exclaimed. 'It's his concubine, isn't it? She's spying for the Russians? But of course! There weren't any servants in the house, only her!'

'What concubine? Who are you talking about?' Fandorin asked hastily (perhaps rather too hastily). His heart shrank in horror. The very last thing he wanted was to get O-Yumi into trouble! 'You shouldn't chat b-beside open windows where anybody at all might overhear you.'

It was hard to tell whether he had succeeded in diverting Onokoji from his dangerous suspicion with this retort. But the prince refused to speak openly.

'I won't say a thing,' he blurted out sullenly. 'Disgrace may be unpleasant, but my life means more to me . . . Your agent got things confused. I don't know anything of the sort about Intendant Suga.'

And after that he stuck to his guns. Threats of scandal had no effect on him. Onokoji simply kept repeating his demand for the Tokyo police to be informed of the arrest of a member of the higher nobility, a first cousin of four generals and two ministers, a schoolfellow of two Imperial Highnesses, and so on, and so forth.

'Japan will not allow the Prince Onokoji to be held in a foreign lock-up,' he declared in conclusion.

Is he right? was the question in Fandorin's glance at the inspector. Asagawa nodded.

Then what can we do?

'Tell me, Sergeant, I expect you are probably very busy with correspondence, reports and all sorts of documents?' Asagawa asked.

'No, not really,' answered Lockston, surprised.

'Oh, come now,' the inspector insisted. 'You are responsible for the entire Settlement. Citizens of fifteen different states live here, there are so many ships in the port, and you have only one pair of hands.'

'That's true,' the sergeant admitted, trying to understand what the Japanese was driving at.

'I know that under the law you are obliged to inform us of the arrest of a Japanese subject within twenty-four hours, but you might not be able to meet that deadline.'

'Probably not. I'll need two or three days. Maybe even four,' said the American, starting to play along.

'So, I'll receive official notification from you in about four days. I'm very busy as well. Not enough staff, I'm barely keeping up. It could be another three days before I can report to the department.'

Onokoji listened to this conversation with increasing alarm.

'But listen, Inspector!' he exclaimed. 'You're already here! You know that I have been arrested by foreigners.'

'It's not a matter of what I know. I have to be informed about this officially, according to the prescribed procedure,' said Asagawa, raising one finger in admonishment.

The titular counsellor had absolutely no idea what this strange manoeuvre signified, but he did notice the prisoner's face twitch in a strange way.

'Hey, Orderly!' the sergeant shouted. 'Put this one in a cell. And send to the brothel for his clothes.'

'Where will dragging things out like this get us?' Fandorin asked in a low voice when the prince had been led away.

Asagawa didn't answer, he just smiled.

Once again it was night. And once again Erast Petrovich was not sleeping. He wasn't tormented by insomnia, it was as if sleep had ceased to exist, as if the need for it had fallen away. Or perhaps it was all because the titular counsellor was not simply lying in bed – he was listening. He had left the door into the corridor open, and several times he thought he heard the porch creak gently under light footsteps, as if someone was standing there in the darkness, unable to make up their mind to knock. Once, unable to bear it any longer, Fandorin got up, walked through quickly into the hallway and jerked the door open. Naturally, there was nobody on the porch.

When the knock finally did come, it was loud and abrupt. O-Yumi could not possibly knock like that, so Erast Petrovich's heart did not skip a beat. He lowered his feet off the bed and started pulling on his boots. Masa was already leading his nocturnal visitor along the corridor.

The visitor was a constable from the municipal police: the sergeant requested that Mr Vice-Consul come to the station urgently.

Fandorin walked rapidly along the dark Bund, tapping with his cane. Masa plodded along behind, yawning. It was pointless trying to argue with him.

Fandorin's servant did not go into the police station. He sat on the steps, hung his short-cropped head and drifted into a doze.

'The Jap's got convulsions,' Lockston told the vice-consul. 'He's yelling and banging his head against the wall. Has he got epilepsy, then? I told them to tie him up, to stop him harming himself. I sent for you, Asagawa and Dr Twigs. The doc's already here, the inspector hasn't arrived yet.'

Soon Asagawa showed up too. He listened to the sergeant's story without any sign of surprise.

'So soon?' he said, but still didn't explain anything. The inspector's strange composure and the meaning of the 'manoeuvre' were explained when Dr Twigs entered the room.

'Good evening, gentlemen,' he said, greeting the titular counsellor and the inspector. 'It's not epilepsy. It's a perfectly ordinary withdrawal syndrome. Hence the convulsions. This man is an inveterate morphine addict. The veins on his arms are covered in needle marks. And of course, there are the consequences of a hysterical personality and a weak character, but, generally speaking, at that stage a man can't manage without another dose for more than twelve hours.'

'Didn't I tell you, Fandorin-san, that the prince is given to every possible vice that exists,' Asagawa remarked. 'He'll start singing a different tune for us now. Let's go.'

The cell was a recess in the wall of the corridor, fenced off with thick iron bars.

Onokoji was sitting on a wooden bunk with his hands and his feet tied. He was shaking violently and his teeth were chattering.

'Doctor, give me a shot!' he shouted. 'I'm dying! I feel terrible!'

Twigs glanced enquiringly at the others.

Lockston chewed imperturbably on his cigar. Asagawa surveyed the sick man with a satisfied air. Only the vice-consul was clearly ill at ease.

'Never mind,' said the sergeant. 'You'll get out in week or so, you can stick yourself then.'

The prince howled and doubled over.

'This is torture,' Fandorin said in a low voice. 'Say what you will, gentlemen, but I do not wish to obtain information by such methods.'

The inspector shrugged.

'How are we torturing him? He is torturing himself. I don't know how things are in your countries, but in Japanese jails we don't give prisoners narcotics. Perhaps the municipal police have different rules? Do you keep morphine to ease the suffering of morphine addicts?'

'Like hell we do,' said Lockston, shaking his head in admiration. 'Well, Go, you old son of a gun. I could learn a thing or two from you.'

On this occasion Goemon Asagawa did not protest about the American's familiarity, he just smiled at the flattery.

'This is a genuine discovery!' the sergeant continued, waxing more and more enthusiastic. 'Think of the prospects this opens up for police work! What do you do if a criminal clams up and refuses to inform on his accomplices? They used to stretch him on the rack, burn him with red-hot tongs and all the rest of it. But, firstly, that's uncivilised. And secondly, there are some tough nuts you can't crack with any torture. But with this – away you go. All very cultured and scientific! Get a stubborn character like that hooked on morphine and then – bang – stop giving him any. He'll be only too delighted to tell you everything. Listen, Go, I'll write an article about this for the *Police Gazette*. Of course, I'll mention your name. Only the idea is mine, after all. You came across it by chance, but I invented the method. You wouldn't dispute that, would you, my friend?' Lockston asked anxiously.

'I wouldn't, Walter, I wouldn't. You don't even need to mention me at all.' The inspector walked over to the bars and looked at the sobbing prince.

'Tell me, Doctor, could you find an ampoule of morphine and a syringe in that bag of yours?'

'Of course.'

Onokoji straightened up, gazing at Asagawi imploringly.

'Well, Your Excellency, shall we have a talk?' the inspector asked him cordially.

The prisoner nodded, licking his purple lips.

Erast Petrovich frowned, but said nothing – the Japanese inspector was in charge now.

'Thank you, Doctor,' said Asagawi. 'Fill the syringe and leave it with me. You can go home to bed.'

Twigs clearly did not wish to leave. He ran a curious eye over the bound man and rummaged slowly in his bag, opened the ampoule without hurrying and took a long time to examine the syringe.

No one was intending to initiate the doctor into their secret game of backstage politics, but it simply happened anyway.

'Come on, quickly, quickly!' the prince shouted. 'For God's sake! Why are you dawdling like that? One little injection, and I'll tell you all I know about Suga!'

Twigs pricked up his ears at that.

'About whom? Suga? The intendant of police? What has he done?'

There was nothing for it – they had to explain. And so the group that had investigated the case of Captain Blagolepov's strange death was reconstituted. Only now it had a different status. They were not official investigators but, rather, conspirators.

Almost as soon as the prisoner had been untied and injected, he turned pink, started smiling and became jaunty and talkative. He spoke a lot, but told them very little of real substance.

According to Onokoji, the new intendant of police had taken part in the conspiracy against the great reformer because he was nursing a grudge – he felt offended at having been subordinated to a worthless little aristocrat with connections in high places. Being a man of intelligence and cunning, Suga had planned the plot in such a way as to achieve two goals at once: take revenge on the minister, who had failed to appreciate his true worth, and land the responsibility on his immediate superior, in order to take his place. Suga had succeeded wonderfully well. The public, of course, might repeat all sorts of rumours, but once a lion is dead, he ceases to be the king of beasts and becomes plain ordinary carrion, and no one was interested in the late Okubo any more. There were new winds blowing at the highest levels; the dead minister's favourites were making way for appointees from the opposite party.

'Is Suga's involvement in the conspiracy just rumour or authenticated f-fact?' asked Fandorin, disappointed by this frivolous tittle-tattle.

The prince shrugged.

'Naturally, there is no proof, but my information is usually reliable. Otherwise I would have starved to death a long time ago. That skinflint Tsurumaki, who owes everything to our family, pays me such a pitiful allowance that it's barely enough for decent shirts.'

Five thousand yen a month, Fandorin recalled. Twenty vice-consular salaries.

'And who led the c-conspiracy? From whom did Suga receive the estate of Tarazaka as his reward?'

'The samurai of Satsuma set up an entire organisation, and all the members swore to kill the traitor Okubo. Those people prepared for a long hunt, they collected a lot of money. It would have been enough for a dozen estates.'

Further questioning produced nothing. Onokoji repeated the same things over and over again, occasionally veering into high-society gossip, and finally wore his interrogators down.

Eventually, having realised that they wouldn't discover anything else useful, they moved away and tried to work out a plan of further action.

'Apart from the certainty that Suga is guilty and a few other details unconfirmed by any proof, we have nothing,' Erast Petrovich said acidly, no longer doubting that it had been a waste of time to stir up this whole mess. The cunning and morally dubious operation had produced very little.

Asagawa was gloomy too, but he remained determined.

'But even so, we cannot pull back now. Suga must pay for his villainy.'

'How about this?' Lockston suggested. 'The intendant receives an anonymous letter that says: "You think you're a sly dog and you've sold everyone a pup, but you've slipped up, hombre. I've got something on you. I don't give a cuss for Okubo, he got what was coming to him, but I'm in desperate need of money. Come to such-and-such a place at such-and-such a time: I'll give you the evidence, and you give me – let's say, ten thousand". And to make it convincing, slip in a few details about his dirty dealings: the stolen reports, the gag and the estate. At the very least Suga will get alarmed, he'll want to take a look at this blackmailer and see what he's got. If he doesn't send a detachment of police to the rendezvous and comes himself, that alone will give him away, hook, line and sinker. How's that for a plan?' the sergeant asked, giving his comrades a boastful look. 'Not bad, eh?'

The titular counsellor disappointed him.

'Terrible. No good at all. Of course Suga won't come. He's no fool.'

Lockston wouldn't surrender.

'So he'll send some police? I don't think so. He won't want to take the risk. What if the blackmailer really does have some evidence?'

'And there won't be any p-police. More Satsumans will just turn up and slice us to ribbons.'

'Mm, yes, that is very likely,' the doctor admitted.

The inspector didn't say anything, merely frowned even more darkly.

The disputants fell silent.

'Hey! What are you whispering about over there?' Onokoji shouted, walking up to the bars. 'If you don't know how to get Suga's back to the wall, I'll tell you! And in exchange you'll let me out of here. All right?'

The four of them all turned towards the prisoner together and spontaneously moved towards the cell.

The prince held his open hand out through the bars.

'One ampoule in reserve. And the syringe. As an advance.'

'Give them to him,' Asagawa told the doctor. 'If he talks nonsense, we'll take them away again.'

Savouring the moment, the high-society gent kept his audience in suspense for a brief moment while he brushed a speck of dust off his rather crumpled frock coat and adjusted his lapel. He carefully placed the ampoule in his waistcoat pocket, after first kissing it and whispering: 'Oh, my little piece of happiness!' He smiled triumphantly.

'Ah, how little I am appreciated!' he exclaimed. 'And how poorly I am paid. But the moment they need something, they come running to me: "Tell us, find out, pick someone's brains". Onokoji knows everything about everybody. Mark my words, gentlemen. In the century to come, which it is unlikely that I shall live to see, owing to my physical frailty, the most valuable commodity will be information. More valuable than gold, diamonds or even morphine!'

'Stop blabbering!' the sergeant roared. 'Or I'll take it back!'

'See how the red-hairs talk to the scion of an ancient Japanese family,' the prince complained to Asagawa, but when the inspector grabbed him menacingly by the lapels, he stopped playing the fool.

'Mr Suga is a great pedant. A genuine poet of the bureaucratic art. Therein lies the secret of his power. During his years in the police department he has collected a secret archive of hundreds of files.'

'I've never heard about that,' said the inspector, shaking his head.

'Naturally. Neither had I. Until one fine day Suga called me into his office and showed me something. Ah, I am a man of lively fantasy, I flit through life like a butterfly. It is not hard to catch my delicate wings with crude fingers. You, gentlemen, are not the first to have done so ...' The prince sighed woefully. 'On that day, in the course of a conversation that was most unpleasant for me, Suga boasted that he had similar picklocks to open up many highly influential individuals. Oh, Mr Intendant understands perfectly well the great future that lies ahead for information!'

'What did he want from you?' Fandorin asked.

'The same as everyone else. Information about a certain person. And he received it. You see, the contents of my file are such that I did not dare to argue.'

The sergeant chuckled.

'Underage girls?'

'Ah, if only ... But there's no need for you to know about it. What matters to you is that I gave Suga what he wanted, but I didn't want to remain a puppet in his hands for ever afterwards. I turned to certain masters of secret arts for help – not in person, naturally, but through an intermediary.'

'Masters of secret arts?' Twigs exclaimed. 'You wouldn't be talking about *shinobi*, would you?'

The doctor and the vice-consul exchanged glances. Was this really possible?

'Precisely,' Onokoji said, as if that were perfectly normal, and yawned, putting his elegantly manicured hand over his mouth. 'To the dear, kind ninja.'

'S-so . . . So they do exist?'

Lurid images appeared before Erast Petrovich's eyes – first the gaping jaws of the snake, then the red mask of the man with no face. The vice-consul shuddered.

The doctor shook his head mistrustfully.

'If the ninja had survived, people would know about it.'

'Those who need to know, do know,' the prince said with a shrug. 'Those who trade in these arts do not print advertisements in the newspapers. Our family has been employing the services of the Momochi clan for three hundred years.'

'The same clan? The descendants of the great Momochi Tambi, who killed the witch disguised as a moon with his arrow?' the doctor asked in a trembling voice.

'Aha. The very same.'

'So in 1581 on Mount Hijiyama the samurais didn't kill all of them? Who escaped?'

'On which mount?' Onokoji was clearly not well informed about the history of his own country. 'I've no idea. All I know is that the masters of the Momochi clan serve a very narrow circle of clients and charge very dearly for their services. But they know their job well. My intermediary, my late father's senior samurai, contacted them and gave them the commission. The *shinobi* discovered where Suga hides his secrets. If you're interested in the conspiracy against Okubo, you can be certain that all the information you need is kept there. Suga does not destroy documents, they are his investment in the future.'

'I have no doubt that my missing reports are there too!' Asagawa said rapidly, turning to Fandorin.

But the vice-consul was more concerned with the masters of secret arts.

'But how do people contact the ninja?' he asked.

'At our court it was the senior samurai who dealt with that. The prince's most trusted adviser. They always come from the same family and have served *our* family for almost four hundred years. That is, they used to serve . . .' Onokoji sighed. 'There are no more principalities or devoted vassals now. But our senior samurai, a most magnanimous man, carried out my request for old times' sake. He even paid Momochi the advance out of his own funds. An old man with a heart of pure gold – to do that he had to mortgage his family estate. The *shinobi* did a good job and, as I already said, they found the hiding place, But they didn't enter it, they wanted more money for that – those were the terms of the arrangement. And as bad luck would have it, I was going through a dry spell at the time, and I couldn't make the payment. The ninja are very sensitive about that sort of thing. If the client breaks the terms, that's the end of him. They'll kill him, and in some nightmarish fashion too. Oh, they're terrible people, truly terrible.'

'But you seem to be alive, my friend,' Lockston remarked.

The prince was astonished.

'What do I have to do with it? The client was our vassal. And he was the one who had to answer to them. The old man fell ill all of a sudden, out of the blue, with a very strange complaint. His tongue swelled up and fell out of his mouth, then his skin turned black and his eyes melted out of their sockets. The poor fellow screamed in agony for two days and then he died. You know, the *shinobi* are virtuosos at preparing all sorts of unusual potions, both for healing and for killing. They say that the *shinobi* can . . .'

'Oh, damn the *shinobi*!' the sergeant interrupted, to Erast Petrovich's considerable displeasure. 'Where's the hiding place? Did the samurai get a chance to tell you?'

'Yes, the hiding place is always within Suga's reach. Last year they built a new headquarters for the police department, in the Yaesu district. Suga, who was vice-intendant at the time, supervised the building work in person, and unknown to almost anyone, he had a secret room built adjacent to his office. The work was carried out by an American architect, who later drowned. Do you remember that sad story? All the newspapers wrote about it. In gratitude for their good work, the police department organised a steamboat cruise for the architect and the best workers, but then, didn't the boat go and capsize . . . And the best workers included the three who built the secret room.'

'What villainy!' the inspector gasped. 'Now I understand why Suga stayed in his old office when he was put in charge of the department. And everyone in the department admires his modesty!'

'How does one gain access to the secret room?' Fandorin asked.

'I don't know exactly. There's a cunning lever somewhere – that's all the *shinobi* told my old samurai. I don't know any more than that, gentlemen, but you must admit that my information is highly valuable to you. I think you ought to let me go immediately.'

Asagawa and Fandorin glanced at each other.

'We'll see about that when we get back,' said the inspector. 'But you have earned your little bit of happiness.'

Hard though you may try,
You can't pinch off a little
Piece of happiness

Two of them went off on 'the job' (that was what Fandorin called the operation to himself, in criminal style). The doctor, as the father of a family and a law-abiding member of society, did not express any desire to participate in such a risky undertaking. Lockston did express such a desire, but he was refused. Entirely abandoning his Japanese politeness, Asagawa declared that the American smelled of cigar smoke and beer from a mile away and Japanese did not smell like that. And his light blond hair would stand out too clearly in the darkness. At least the Russian vice-consul had hair that was a normal colour. Left alone with Erast Petrovich, the inspector was even less complimentary about the sergeant: 'This matter requires brains, and our American bison knows no other way but to go at something bald-headed.'

The day was spent in preparation. Asagawa went to the police department, supposedly on official business, but really with one very simple goal: he filed down the tongue of the bolt on the window of the toilet. The titular counsellor prepared his outfit for the nocturnal adventure – he bought a costume mask and a close-fitting black fencing costume, and smeared his rubber-soled gymnastic shoes with boot polish.

He tried to catch up on his sleep, but he couldn't.

When it started to get dark, he sent Masa to the Grand Hotel for the evening paper so that he wouldn't follow him, and hurried to catch the last train.

He and the inspector travelled in the same carriage, but they sat at opposite ends and didn't look at each other.

Looking out of the window at the lights drifting by in the darkness, Fandorin was surprised at himself. Why had he got mixed up in this wild adventure? What had made him gamble with his own honour and the honour of his country like this? It was terrible to think what the consequences would be if he, the Russian vice-consul, were caught at night in the office of the intendant of police. What made it worth taking such a risk? The chance to expose a scheming local official who was responsible for the death of another local official? Why, damn the lot of them!

The interests of Russia require it, Fandorin tried to convince himself rather uncertainly. By bringing down Suga, I shall strike a blow at a party hostile to the interests of my Homeland.

He was not convinced. After all, he himself had always said that no interests of the Homeland (at least, its geopolitical interests) could be more important than personal honour and dignity. A most honourable activity, this was – to go rifling through other people's secret hiding places, dressed up like a chimney sweep.

Then he tried to justify things differently, from Asagawa's point of view. There was such a thing as Justice, and also Truth, which it was the duty of every noble man to defend. One could not allow infamous acts to be committed with impunity. By conniving at them or washing one's hands of the matter, one became an accomplice, you insulted your own soul and God.

But for all their grandeur, these highly moral considerations somehow failed to touch the titular counsellor very deeply. It was not a matter of defending Justice. After all, in weaving his plot, Suga could have been guided by his own ideas of Truth, which differed from Fandorin's. In any case, there was no point in Erast Petrovich deceiving himself – he had not embarked on this nocturnal escapade for the sake of words that were written with a capital letter.

He rummaged about inside himself for a bit longer and finally came up with the right reason. Fandorin did not like it, for it was simple, unromantic and even ignominious.

I could not have borne one more sleepless night waiting for a woman who is never going to come again, the titular counsellor told himself honestly. Anything at all, any kind of folly, but not that.

And when the locomotive hooted as it approached the final station of Nihombasi, the vice-consul suddenly thought: I'm poisoned. My brain and my heart have been affected by a slow-acting venom. That is the only possible explanation.

And after thinking that, he calmed down immediately, as if now everything had fallen into place.

While there were still passers-by on the streets, Erast Petrovich maintained his distance from his partner. He walked along with the air of an idle tourist, casually swinging the briefcase that contained his spy's outfit.

But soon they reached the governmental office district, where there were no people, because office hours had finished ages ago. The titular counsellor cut down the distance until he was almost walking in tandem with the inspector. From time to time Asagawa explained something in a low voice.

'You see the white building at the far side of the bridge? That is the Tokyo Municipal Court. It's only a stone's throw from the department.'

Fandorin saw a white three-storey palace in the European Mauritanian style – rather frivolous for an institution of the judiciary. Behind it he could see a high wooden fence.

'Over there?'

'Yes. The estate of the princes Matsudaira used to be there. We won't go as far as the gates, there's a sentry.'

A narrow alley ran off to the left. Asagawa looked round, waved his hand, and the accomplices ducked into the dark, crevice-like passage.

They got changed quickly. The inspector also put on something black and close fitting, tied a kerchief round his head and muffled the lower half of his face in a rag.

'This is exactly how the *shinobi* dress,' he whispered with a nervous giggle. 'Right, forward!'

They gained entrance to the site of the department very easily: Asagawa folded his hands into a stirrup, Fandorin set his foot in it and in an instant he was on top of the fence. Then he helped the inspector to scramble up. The police obviously didn't have enough imagination to believe that miscreants might take it into their heads to break into the holy of holies of law and order voluntarily. In any case, there was no one patrolling the yard – just a figure in a uniform and cap over on the right, striding to and fro at the main entrance.

Asagawa moved quickly and confidently. Hunching over, he ran across to a low building in a pseudo-Japanese style, then along the white wall, past a long series of blank windows. The inspector stopped beside the window at the corner.

'I think this is the one. Help me up.'

He put his arms round Fandorin's neck, then stepped on the vice-consul's half-bent knee with one foot, put the other on his shoulder, and grabbed hold of the window frame. He scraped with something, clicked something, and the small windowpane opened. Asagawa pulled himself up and seemed to be sucked into the black rectangle, so that only the lower half of his body was left outside. Then that disappeared into the window as well, and a few seconds later the large windowpane opened silently.

For form's sake, before entering the building Erast Petrovich noted the time: seventeen minutes past eleven.

The arrangement of the Japanese toilet looked strange to him: a row of low cubicles that could only conceal a seated man up to the shoulders.

Fandorin discovered Asagawa in one of the wooden cells.

'I advise you to relieve yourself,' the black head with the strip of white for the eyes said in a perfectly natural tone of voice. 'It is helpful before hazardous work. To prevent any trembling of the *hara*.'

Erast Petrovich thanked him politely, but declined. His *hara* was not trembling at all, he was simply oppressed by the melancholy presentiment that this business would not end well. Nonsensical thoughts about the next day's newspaper headlines kept drifting into his mind, as they had done on that other memorable night: 'RUSSIAN DIPLOMAT A SPY', 'OFFICIAL NOTE FROM JAPANESE GOVERNMENT TO RUSSIAN EMPIRE' and even 'JAPAN AND RUSSIA BREAK OFF DIPLOMATIC RELATIONS'.

'Will you be much longer?' the vice-consul asked impatiently. 'It's twenty-three minutes past eleven. The nights are short now.'

From the toilet they crept down a long, dark corridor, Asagawa on his twisted-straw sandals and Fandorin on his rubber soles. The department of police was sleeping peacefully. That's what a low level of crime does for you, thought the titular counsellor, not without a twinge of envy. Along the way they encountered only a single office with a light burning, where some kind of night work seemed to be going on, and once a duty officer carrying a candle came out from round a corner. He yawned as he walked past, without even noticing the two black figures pressed back against the wall.

'We're here,' Asagawa whispered, stopping in front of a tall double door.

He put a piece of metal into the keyhole (an ordinary picklock, Erast Petrovich noted), turned it and the accomplices found themselves in a spacious room: a row of chairs along the walls, a secretary's desk, another door in the far corner. It was clearly the reception area. Consul Doronin had told Fandorin that six years earlier there had been a great bureaucratic reform. The functionaries had all been dressed in uniforms instead of kimonos and forced to sit on chairs, not on the floor. The bureaucracy had almost rebelled at first, but had gradually got accustomed to it. What a shame. It must have been very picturesque before. Imagine arriving at a government office, and the heads of department and clerks and secretaries are all dressed in robes and sitting there cross-legged. Fandorin sighed, lamenting the gradual displacement of the variety of life by European order. In a hundred years' time everything would be the same everywhere, you wouldn't be able to tell whether you were in Russia or Siam. How boring.

The room located beyond the reception area was also not in any way remarkable. An ordinary office of some important individual. One broad, short desk, and beyond it a long narrow table. Two armchairs on one side, for official conversations with important visitors. Bookshelves with codes of laws. A photographic portrait of the emperor hanging in the most prominent position. The only unusual thing, from the Japanese point of view, was the crucifixion hanging beside the image of the earthly ruler. Ah, yes, Suga was a Christian, he had a cross hanging round his neck too.

A fine follower of Christ, thought Erast Petrovich, shaking his head, but immediately felt ashamed: As if our own lovers of God don't betray or kill.

Asagawa closed the curtains more tightly, lit an oil lamp and walked up to the titular counsellor. He seemed excited, almost triumphant.

'I don't know if we'll find the hiding place or how all this will end, so I will say now what I must say. I should have come here alone. This is our Japanese business. My business. But I am very grateful to you, Fandorin-san, for volunteering to keep me company. I have more faith in your acumen than I do in my own. Without you, I would almost certainly not find the lever, but you are cunning. Almost as cunning as Intendant Suga.'

Erast Petrovich bowed ceremoniously, but the inspector did not understand the irony. He bowed in reply, only more deeply.

'Do not think I do not understand how much more exalted your sacrifice is than mine. If we are caught, what is that to me, I shall merely take my life and bring disgrace on the clan of Asagawa, which has served the law honestly for two and a half centuries. But you will disgrace your country and your state. You are a very brave man, Fandorin-san.'

They exchanged bows again, this time without even a hint of playfulness on the vice-consul's side, and set about their search.

First they sounded out the two side walls, then divided the office into left and right sections. Unlike the energetic inspector, who nimbly tapped all the skirting boards and floorboards in his half, checked all the items on the desk and then set about the books, Erast Petrovich hardly touched anything at all. He strode around unhurriedly, shining his little American torch on things. An excellent little item, the very latest design. It produced a bright, dense ray of light. When it started to fade – about every one and a half minutes – you had to pump a spring with your fingers, and the torch immediately came back to life.

He stood in front of the portrait for a while. His Majesty the Mikado was shown in military uniform, with epaulettes and a sword. Fandorin thought the young face with the sparse moustache bore the imprint of degeneracy (which was hardly surprising, considering the dynasty's twenty-five centuries of genealogical history), but Emperor Mutsuhito's gaze was searching and intent. Patient, cautious, secretive, unsure of himself, enquiring, thought the vice-consul, practising his physiognomics. A master of *ninso* would undoubtedly have seen far more, but even this was enough to tell that the young royal ruler would go far.

'I've finished my half,' Asagawa declared. 'There's nothing.'

'Would you like to swap? By all means.'

Fandorin walked out into the centre of the room, sat on the conference table and dangled one leg. A quarter past twelve.

An archive was something that you needed often. So the answer was most likely one of two things: either a lever within easy reach that could be operated without getting up from the desk; or, on the contrary, the lever was located right beside the entrance to the secret compartment. Asagawa had examined everything on the desk very thoroughly indeed. So it must be the second option.

There were two walls in which the secret room could be hidden. The wall between the office and reception area could be eliminated, along with the external wall.

Fandorin walked backwards and forwards, scrutinising.

The clock on the wall struck one.

'Have you moved that?' the titular counsellor asked, pointing at the clock.

'Of course,' said Asagawa, wiping the sweat off his forehead. 'I divided the room up into squares, I'm trying not to miss anything.'

Yes, the lever couldn't be in the clock, Fandorin thought. The cleaner might trip it if he started dusting the timepiece. Or the person responsible for winding and adjusting it . . .

'I've run out of squares,' the inspector announced in a dejected voice. 'What can we do? Try again . . .'

One forty-two. Where could the lever be? It wasn't behind the wallpaper or the skirting boards. Or in the bookcase. Asagawa had lifted up the pictures too . . .

Erast Petrovich suddenly froze.

'Tell me, did you touch the emperor's portrait?'

'Of course not. That's impossible!' The inspector actually shuddered at such a blasphemous suggestion.

'But someone dusts it, don't they?'

'That sacred responsibility can only be performed by the owner of the office, with all appropriate respect. In my station no one would dare to touch the portrait of His Majesty that hangs over my desk. People wipe the dust from the emperor's face in the morning, almost as soon as they get to work. With a special silk duster, after first bowing.'

'I see. Well, now I'll show you how the s-secret room opens.'

The titular counsellor took a chair, carried it across to the wall, climbed up on it and took hold of the portrait confidently with both hands. Asagawa gasped.

'Like this,' Erast Petrovich purred, swaying the frame to the left. Nothing happened. 'Well then, like this.'

He swayed the frame to the right – again nothing. Fandorin pulled the portrait towards himself. He tugged it up, he tugged it down. Finally he turned it completely upside down. The poor inspector groaned and whimpered.

'Damn! Could I really be mistaken?'

Erast Petrovich took the emperor down and tapped on the glass. The sound was hollow.

He angrily hung the portrait back up and it swayed to and fro in shock.

The young man felt ashamed. Not for his mistake, but for the lofty condescension with which he had drawled 'I see'. The beam of his torch slid across the wallpaper, lighting up the horizontal beam of the crucifixion from above.

The titular counsellor caught his breath.

'Tell me, who cleans the c-cross? Also the owner of the office?'

Fandorin jumped down on to the floor and moved the chair closer to the crucifixion. He scrambled back up again.

'Of course. The cleaner wouldn't dare. He knows it is a sacred object for your religion.'

'Uh-huh. I can see that.'

The intendant obviously regarded the symbol of the Christian faith with less respect than the portrait of Emperor Mutsuhito – a thin layer of dust had accumulated on the black wood.

Erast Petrovich tried to move the crucifixion, but he couldn't. Shining his torch a bit closer, he saw that the cross was not hung on the wall or nailed to it, but sunk slightly into its surface. Strange! So a special housing had been made for it?

He tried to pull it out. He couldn't. Then he pressed it.

With a barely audible click, the crucifixion sank deeper into the wallpaper, leaving its edges protruding no more than an inch.

A second later there was a melodic clang, and a section of the wall moved aside rapidly, almost springing into the space behind the bookcase. A dark rectangle opened up, slightly lower than the height of a man.

'That's it! The secret hiding place!' Asagawa cried, and glanced round at the door of the reception area, in case he had shouted too loudly.

Fandorin automatically glanced at his watch: two minutes to two.

'Ah, what would I have done without you?' the inspector exclaimed emotionally, almost with tears in his eyes, and dived into the dark hole.

But the vice-consul's attention was caught by the arrangement of the secret room. In cross-section it was clearly visible: a layer of oak boards under the plaster, and then cork. That was why sounding out the walls hadn't helped. The lever released powerful steel springs, which was why the partition jumped aside so fast. Fandorin wondered whether it closed in the same impetuous fashion or whether strength had to be applied.

Having satisfied his technical curiosity, Erast Petrovich followed his accomplice inside.

The repository of secrets proved to be a narrow room, but quite long – about ten paces. Its walls were entirely covered with shelving. Standing on the shelves were perfectly ordinary office files of various thicknesses. Asagawa took them down one by one, exclaimed something in Japanese and put them back again. The vice-consul also took one of the thicker ones. There were hieroglyphs drawn on the cover. The first two were easy, Erast Petrovich recognised them: 'Eastern Capital', that was 'Tokyo', but everything after that was gobbledegook to him.

'What does it say here?'

'Tokyo Provincial Government,' Asagawa said after a swift glance. 'But that's nothing! There are ministers and members of the State Council here, even – you won't believe it – members of the imperial family! Nothing is sacred to this man!'

'And what does he have there about the empress?' Fandorin asked curiously, glancing over the inspector's shoulder.

He couldn't see anything interesting on the page – just some note in the same old hieroglyphic scrawl – but the inspector nudged him away impolitely with his elbow.

'I haven't read it and I won't allow you to! How infamous!'

He tore up the note and a few other pieces of paper in the file with trembling fingers.

'Listen, it's two minutes past two,' the titular counsellor told him, pointing to his watch. 'This isn't what we came here for. Where's the file with the conspirators?'

Owing to his hieroglyphic illiteracy, Erast Petrovich had nothing to occupy himself with. While Asagawa rummaged through the shelves, the young man shone his torch in all directions. He failed to discover anything of interest. There didn't seem to be any lever inside the secret room, it could be opened and closed only from the outside. There were gas burners protruding from the ceiling – evidently the lighting could be switched on from the office, but there was no need for that, the torch and the lamp were quite adequate.

'I have it!' the inspector gasped. 'It says "Okubo" on the spine.' He started leafing feverishly through the pages. 'Here are my missing reports, all three of them! And this is a report from the head of the police in the city of Kagosima. He says that according to reports from his agents, the sword master Ikemura Hyoske and two of his pupils have set out for Tokyo. Description: forty-five years old, a scar on the left side of his neck and his temple, left arm twisted. His nickname is Kamiyasuri – "Glasspaper", because he covers the hilt of his sword with glass paper – his right hand is harder than steel. It's him, the man with the withered arm! Wait, wait, there's more here . . .' Asagawa took out three sheets of paper covered with writing in a strange brown-coloured ink. 'It's an oath. Written in blood. "We, the undersigned, do hereby swear on our honour not to begrudge our lives in the name of an exalted goal – to exterminate the base traitor Okubo . . . " There are three such documents. One of them has six signatures – that is the group that killed the minister. The second document has three signatures, and the first one is Ikemura Hyoske's. Our Satsumans! The third document has four signatures. So there was another group that remained undiscovered. The names are here, it will not be difficult to find the plotters before they can do anything else dangerous . . . We have won, Fandorin-san! We have Suga in our hands! With these oaths and the stolen reports we can pin him down!'

'He was already in our hands anyway,' Erast Petrovich remarked coolly. 'This delightful little archive will cost him his head without any c-conspiracies.'

Asagawa shook his head.

'Surely you do not think that I will allow all these abominations to come pouring out? There is so much filth here, so many family secrets! There would be a wave of suicides, divorces, scandals, resignations in disgrace. No, worse than that! The new minister would take the archive for his own use, he would announce that it has been destroyed, but keep the spiciest items – just in case.'

'Then what is to be done?'

'We are going to destroy all this poison. Without reading it.'

'Very n-noble,' declared Fandorin, who could not have savoured the Japanese secrets even if he had felt any desire to do so. 'But what are these signs? They don't look like hieroglyphs.'

He pointed to a sheet of paper lying at the very bottom of the file. Right at the centre there was a circle with a strange squiggle inside it. Lines ran out from the circle, connecting it with other, smaller circles.

'No, those are not hieroglyphs,' the inspector murmured, peering at the paper. 'At least, not Japanese hieroglyphs. I have never come across any writing like this before.'

'It looks like a diagram of the conspiracy,' Fandorin suggested. 'And in code too. It would be interesting to know who is symbolised by the c-circle at the centre.'

'It must be Suga.'

'Unlikely. He wouldn't have denoted himself with some kind of doodle. He would just have drawn the circle and left it at that.'

They leaned down over the mysterious diagram, with their shoulders pressed against each other. Asagawa must have breathed in a lot of dust, because he sneezed, and the sound echoed loudly under the low vaulted ceiling.

'You're crazy!' Fandorin hissed. 'Quiet!'

The Japanese waved his hand nonchalantly and answered without lowering his voice.

'What does it matter? We no longer have to hide. As soon as we've destroyed the unnecessary documents, I'll call the duty officer and explain that . . .'

But he didn't finish what he was about to say.

Without the slightest warning, the secret door slammed shut with that familiar metallic clang. The wall trembled slightly and the room was suddenly as silent as the grave.

Erast Petrovich's first reaction was purely nervous – he glanced at his watch. It showed eighteen minutes past two

If it is eighteen
Or nineteen minutes past two –
What's the difference?

THE SCALES FALL FROM HIS EYES

For a few minutes the burglars who had fallen into a trap behaved in a perfectly normal and predictable way – they hammered on the impervious partition with their fists, tried to find a joint in the wall with their fingers and searched for some kind of knob or lever. Then Erast Petrovich left all the fussing about to his partner and sat down on the floor with his legs crossed.

'It's p-pointless,' he said in a steady voice. 'There isn't any lever in here.'

'But the door closed somehow! No one came into the office, we would have heard them – I closed the catch!'

Erast Petrovich explained.

'A timing mechanism. Set to twenty minutes. I've read about doors like this. They use them in large bank safes and armoured repositories – where the loot can't be carried out very quickly. Only the owner knows how much time he has before the spring is activated, but anyone who breaks in gets caught. Calm down, Asagawa. We're not going to get out of here.'

The inspector sat down as well, right in the corner.

'Never mind,' he said cheerfully. 'We'll sit here until the morning, then let them arrest us. We have something to show the authorities.'

'No one will arrest us. In the morning Suga will come to work and from the disorder in the office, he'll realise that he's had uninvited visitors. From the chair under the crucifixion, he'll realise that there are mice in the trap. And he'll leave us here to die of thirst. I must admit, I've always been afraid of dying that way . . .'

The words were spoken, however, without any particular feeling. The poisoning of heart and brain had evidently already affected the instinct of self-preservation. So be it, then, thirst it is, Erast Petrovich thought languidly. What difference does it make, in the end?

Fatalism is an infectious thing. Asagawa looked at the waning flame in his lamp and said thoughtfully:

'Don't worry. We won't have time to die of thirst. We'll suffocate before Suga arrives. There's only enough air here for four hours.'

For a while they sat there without speaking, each of them alone with his own thoughts. Erast Petrovich, for instance, thought about something rather strange. It suddenly occurred to him that perhaps none of this really existed at all. The events of the last ten days had been too incredible, and he himself had behaved too absurdly – it was all delirious nonsense. Either a lingering dream or the monstrous visions of the afterlife. After all, no one really knew what happened to a person's soul when it separated from the body. What if there were phantom-like processes that occurred, similar to dreaming? None of it had really happened: not the chase after the faceless assassin, or the pavilion at night beside the pond. In reality, Erast Petrovich's life had been cut short at the moment when the grey and brown *mamusi* fixed its beady stare on his face while he was lying helpless. Or even earlier – when he walked into his bedroom and saw the old Japanese man smiling . . . .

Nonsense, the titular counsellor told himself with a shudder.

Asagawa shuddered too – his thoughts had clearly also taken a wrong turning.

'There's no point in just sitting here,' said the inspector, getting up. 'We still have our duty to perform.'

'But what can we do?'

'Tear out Suga's sting. Destroy the archive.'

Asagawa took several files down off the shelves, carried them into his corner and started tearing the sheets of paper into tiny little scraps.

'It would be better to burn them, of course, but there isn't enough oxygen,' he murmured absentmindedly.

The titular counsellor carried on sitting for a little while, then got up to help. He took a file and handed it to Asagawa, who continued his work of methodical destruction. The paper ripped with a sharp sound and the heap of rubbish in the corner gradually grew higher.

It was getting stuffy. Fine drops of sweat sprang out on the vice-consul's forehead.

'I don't like dying of suffocation,' he said. 'Better a bullet through the temple.'

'Yes?' Asagawa said thoughtfully. 'I think I'd rather suffocate. Shooting yourself is not the Japanese way. It's noisy, and it gives you no chance to feel yourself dying . . .'

'That is obviously a fundamental difference between the European and Japanese cultures . . .' the titular counsellor began profoundly, but this highly interesting discussion was not fated to continue.

Somewhere above them there was a quiet whistle and bluish tongues of trembling flame sprang out of the gas brackets. The secret room was suddenly brightly lit.

Erast Petrovich looked round, raised his head and saw a tiny opening that had appeared in the wall just below the ceiling. A slanting eye was peering out of it at the titular counsellor.

He heard a muffled laugh, and a familiar voice said in English:

'Now there's a surprise. I was expecting anyone at all, but not Mr Russian Diplomat. I knew you were an enterprising and adventurous man, Fandorin-san, but this is really . . .'

Suga! But how had he found out?

The vice-consul did not speak, merely greedily gulping in the air that was seeping into the cramped space through the narrow opening.

'Who told you about my secret place?' the intendant of police asked, and went on without waiting for an answer. 'The only people apart from me who knew of its existence were the architect Schmidt, two stonemasons and one carpenter. But they all drowned . . . Well, I am positively intrigued!'

The most important thing, Erast Petrovich told himself, is not to glance sideways into the corner where Asagawa is hiding. Suga can't see him, he's sure that I'm here alone.

And he also thought what a pity it was that he hadn't taken a few lessons from Doronin in the art of *battojiutsu* – drawing a weapon a high speed. He could have grabbed his Herstal with a lightning-fast gesture and put a bullet in the bridge of this villain's nose. With the little window open they wouldn't suffocate before the morning, and when the morning came, people would arrive and free the prisoners from the trap.

'And you? How did you know I was here?' Fandorin asked to distract the intendant's attention, while he put his hands behind his back and stretched slightly, as if his shoulders were cramped. His fingers found the flat holster.

Out of the corner of his eye he caught a movement in the corner – apparently the inspector was also taking out his weapon. But what was the point? He couldn't hit the little window from there, and Suga would hide at the slightest suspicious rustle.

'The official apartment of the head of police is close by here. The signal went off,' Suga explained willingly, even proudly. 'This may be Asia, but we try to keep up with the latest inventions of progress. I've satisfied your curiosity, now you satisfy mine.'

'Gladly,' the titular counsellor said with a smile and fired.

He fired from the hip, without wasting any time on aiming, but the intendant's reactions were impeccable – he disappeared from the window and the incredibly lucky shot (it didn't hit the wall, but passed straight through the opening) went to waste.

Erast Petrovich was deafened by the roar. He slapped the left side of his head, then the right. The ringing became quieter and he heard Suga's voice:

'. . . something of the kind and I was on my guard. If you behave impolitely and don't answer my questions, I'll close the hatch now and come back in two days to collect the body.'

Asagawa got up without making a sound and pressed his back against the bookshelves. He was holding his revolver at the ready, but Suga wouldn't present himself as a target again now, that was quite clear.

'Yes, come back, do,' said Erast Petrovich, pressing one finger to his lips. 'Collect my mortal remains. And don't forget the glue. It will take you a few years to stick all the thousands of scraps of p-paper from your precious files back together. I've only managed to destroy the contents of seven files so far, but there must be at last two hundred in here.'

Silence. Apparently the intendant was thinking that over.

The inspector gestured to say: Lift me up, so that I can reach the little window. Fandorin shrugged, he didn't really believe in this plan but, when all was said and done, why not try?

He grabbed hold of the shelves and tugged. Files went crashing to the floor and the vice-consul took advantage of the racket to grab Asagawa round the waist, jerk him up to arm's length above his head and press his stomach against the wall, to make it easier to hold him. The Japanese proved not to be so very heavy, about a hundred and fifty pounds, and every morning Fandorin pressed two one-hundred-pound iron weights forty times.

'What are you doing in there?' Suga shouted.

'I knocked the shelves over. Almost by accident!' Erast Petrovich called, and then told the inspector in a low voice: 'Careful! Don't let him spot you!'

A few seconds later Asagawa slapped his comrade on the shoulder to ask to be put down.

'It won't work,' he whispered as his feet touched the floor. 'The window's too small. I can either look or poke the gun out. It's not possible to do both at once.'

'Fandorin! These are my terms,' the intendant announced. He must have been standing right under the window, so he couldn't have seen Asagawa anyway. 'You don't touch any more of the files. You give me the name of the person who told you about the archive. After that I'll let you go. Naturally after searching you to make sure you haven't picked up anything as a souvenir. Then you take the first ship out of Japan. Unless, of course, you prefer to move to the foreign cemetery in Yokohama.'

'He's lying,' the inspector whispered. 'He won't let you go alive.'

'Fair terms!' Fandorin shouted. 'I'll tell you the name. But that's all.'

'All right! Who told you about the archive?'

'A ninja from the Momochi clan.'

The sudden silence suggested that Suga was badly shaken. Which meant he believed it.

'How did you find them?' the intendant asked after a thirty-second silence.

'I won't tell you that. Our agreement was only for the name. Let me out!'

Without looking, he grabbed the first file that came to hand, took out several sheets of paper and started tearing them, holding his hands up close to the opening.

'All right! We have an agreement. Throw your weapon out here!'

Asagawa nodded and flattened himself against the wall – at the spot where the door would open.

Going up on tiptoe, Fandorin tossed his Herstal into the air vent.

The aperture went dark and the eye appeared again. It examined Fandorin carefully.

He stood there tensely, poised to spring into the blind zone if a gun barrel appeared instead of an eye.

'Take your clothes off,' Suga told him. 'Everything. Completely naked.'

'What for?'

'I want to make sure you haven't got another weapon hidden anywhere.'

Seeing Asagawa cautiously cocking the hammer of his revolver with two fingers, Fandorin replied hastily:

'Only don't even think of trying to shoot. I'll jump out of the way before you're even ready. And then that's the end of the agreement.'

'On my word of honour,' the intendant promised.

He was lying, of course, but Fandorin's words had not been meant for him – they were for the inspector, who understood and gestured reassuringly: I won't.

The titular counsellor got undressed slowly, holding up every item of his ensemble for the intendant to see and them dropping it to the floor. Eventually he was left standing there in his birthday suit.

'Well built,' Suga said approvingly. 'Only your belly's too hollow. A man's *hara* should be more substantial than that. Now turn your back to me and raise your hands.'

'So that you can shoot me in the back of my head? Oh, no.'

'All right. Put your clothes under your arm. Take your shoes in the other hand. When I open the door, walk out slowly.'

The cunning door sprang to one side, leaving the way out open.

'We want him alive,' Erast Petrovich mimed with his lips as he walked past Asagawa.

The office was illuminated by a bright light that flickered slightly. Suga was standing on the same chair that the vice-consul had set against the wall so recently. The intendant was holding a large, black revolver (it looked like a Swedish Hagström) and Fandorin's Herstal was lying on the desk.

'NAKED VICE-CONSUL SHOT IN POLICE CHIEF'S OFFICE' – the headline flashed through the junior diplomat's mind.

Nonsense, he won't shoot. This isn't an insulated space, with walls that muffle sound. The duty officers will hear and come running. Why would he want that? But, of course, he's not going to let me out of here alive.

Without stopping, and giving the intendant only a fleeting glance, Fandorin headed straight for the exit.

'Where are you going?' Suga asked in amazement. 'Are you going to walk through the department naked? Put your clothes on. And anyway, they won't let you through. I'll see you out.'

The police chief put his gun away and held up his empty hands: See, I keep my word.

The titular counsellor had never actually had any intention of strolling through the corridors in the altogether. The whole point of the manoeuvre was to distract the intendant's attention from the secret repository and, above all, make him turn his back to it.

It worked!

Suga watched as the vice-consul donned his Mephistophelean outfit, and meanwhile Asagawa darted silently out of the door and trained his gun on the general.

How is this sly dog planning to kill me? Erast Petrovich wondered as he pulled on one of his gymnastic slippers. After all, he can't leave any blood on the parquet.

'You are an interesting man, Mr Fandorin,' Suga rumbled good-naturedly, laughing into his curled moustache. 'I actually like you. I think we have a lot in common. We both like to break the rules. Who knows, perhaps some day fate will throw us together again, and not necessarily as opponents. A period of cooling relations between Russian and Japan will probably set in now, but in about fifteen or twenty years, everything will change. We shall become a great power, your state will realise that we cannot be manipulated, we have to be treated as a friend. And then . . .'

He's talking to distract me, Fandorin realised, seeing the intendant moving closer, almost as if by chance. With his arms casually bent at the elbows and his hands held forward, as if he were gesticulating.

So that was it. He was going to kill without any blood. Using jujitsu, or some other kind of *jitsu*.

Gazing calmly into his adversary's face, the titular counsellor assumed the defensive posture he had been taught by Masa, advancing one half-bent knee and raising his hand in front of himself. Suga's eyes glinted merrily.

'It's a pleasure doing business with you,' he said, chuckling, no longer concealing his preparations for a fight.

Left hand turned palm upward, right arm bent at the elbow, with the hand held behind the back, one foot raised off the floor – a real dancing Shiva. What sort of *jitsu* have I run up against this time? the vice-consul thought with a sigh.

'Now, let's see what you're like in unarmed combat,' the police general purred smugly.

But, thank God, things didn't go as far as unarmed combat.

Choosing his moment, Asagawa bounded across to the intendant and struck him on the neck with the butt of his gun. The hereditary *yoriki's* efficient, virtuoso work was a sheer delight to watch. He didn't let the limp body fall – he dragged it over to a chair and sat it down. In a single movement he uncoiled the rope that was wound round his waist and quickly tied Suga's wrists to the armrests of the chair and his ankles to its legs. Then he stuck a gag-bit in his mouth – the *hami* that was so familiar to Fandorin. In less than twenty seconds the enemy had been bound and gagged in accordance with all the rules of Japanese police craftsmanship.

While the intendant was batting his eyelids as he came round, the victors conferred about what to do next – call the duty officer or wait until the day started and there were plenty of officials in the building. After all, what if the duty officer turned out to be one of Suga's men?

The discussion was interrupted by low grunting from the chair. The general had come round and was shaking his head: he clearly wished to say something.

'Well, I won't take out the *hami*,' said Asagawa. 'Let's do it this way . . .'

He tied down the prisoner's right elbow, but freed the wrist. Then he gave the intendant a sheet of paper and dipped a pen in the inkwell.

'Write.'

Scattering drops of black ink as he scraped the pen over the paper, Suga wrote downwards from the top of the page.

'Let me die,' the inspector translated. 'Damn you, you ignoble traitor!

You'll swallow you full share of disgrace, and your severed head will hang on a pole for all to see.'

Erast Petrovich's attitude was more pacific, but only slightly.

'The diagram,' he reminded Asagawa. 'Let him tell us who is signified by the large circle, and then he can die, if that's what he wants. If he wants to, he'll kill himself in prison, you won't be able to stop him. He'll smash his head open against the wall, like the man with the withered arm, or bite his tongue off at the first interrogation, like the hunchback.'

Asagawa snorted and reluctantly went to get the diagram. When he came back, he stuck the mysterious sheet of paper under the intendant's nose.

'If you tell us who led the conspiracy, I'll let you die. Right here and now. Do you agree?'

After a while – after quite a while – Suga nodded.

'Is this a diagram of the conspiracy?'

A pause. A nod.

'Write the names.'

He wrote in English:

'Just one name.'

And he looked at Fandorin – the agreement was the same, only now they had changed places.

Sensing that if he pressed any harder, the deal could break down, Erast Petrovich said:

'All right. But the most important one.'

The intendant closed his eyes for a few seconds – evidently gathering himself, either for this betrayal or for his own death. Or most likely for both.

He grasped the pen resolutely, dipped it in the inkwell that was held out to him and started slowly scrawling letter after letter – not in hieroglyphs or the Latin alphabet this time, but in *katakana*, the syllabic Japanese alphabet that Fandorin could already read.

'*Bu*', he read. Then '*ru*', '*ko*', '*ku*', '*su*'.

Bu-ru-ko-ku-su?

Bullcox!

Why, of course!

Everything immediately fell into place and the scales fell from the titular counsellor's eyes.

Do you really want
The scales to fall from your eyes
One of these fine days?

A WORD ONCE GIVEN
MUST BE KEPT

They went back to Yokohama on the seven o'clock train, the first. They didn't bother too much about secrecy, sitting next to each other, although they didn't talk. But then, there was no one else in the carriage apart from the vice-consul and the inspector. The second- and third-class carriages were crammed with clerks and shop assistants on their way to work in Yokohama, but it was too early for first-class passengers.

Asagawa dozed lightly for a while and then – oh, those nerves of steel! – fell into a deep, sweet sleep, even smacking his lips occasionally. Fandorin didn't feel like sleeping. It was almost as if his body had completely renounced this trivial pastime. But something told the titular counsellor that there would be no more insomnia.

The medicine that would cure the patient of his painful condition was called 'Bullcox'. Not that Erast Petrovich was thinking about the torment of sleepless nights at this moment, his mind was on something quite different, but at the same time a voice from somewhere in the wings kept whispering to his exhausted body: 'Soon, you will rest soon'.

The titular counsellor's reason, which existed independently of any voices, was concerned with a most important matter – Defining a Sequence of Logical Reasoning.

The sequence that emerged could not possibly have been more elegant.

So, at the head of the conspiracy to which the Napoleon of Japan had fallen victim, stood the Right Honourable Algernon Bullcox, agent of the government of Victoria, Empress of India and Queen of Great Britain.

The motivation for the plot was obvious:

To dispose of a ruler who strove to maintain the balance between the two Great Powers that were vying to seize control of the Pacific Ocean – England and Russia. That was one.

To bring to power the party of expansion, which would require a mighty fleet. Who would help in the forthcoming conquest of Korea? Naturally, the ruler of the waves, Britannia. That was two.

Bullcox could count on a great reward. Why, of course he could! As a result of the operation that he had successfully completed Japan would fall into the zone of British influence, followed by the whole of the Far East. That was three.

From the human point of view, it was also clear that Bullcox was capable of such a sordid, cynical undertaking.

He engaged in spying and did not try very hard to conceal the fact. That was one.

According to O-Yumi (and who could know this villain better than she did, thought Fandorin, stabbing himself in the heart), he was capable of any abominable infamy, he could even send assassins to kill a successful rival or take revenge on a woman who left him. That was two.

Of course, it was highly improbable that he had organised the conspiracy against Okubo with the approval of St James's Palace, but he was an adventurer by nature, an ambitious man who would use any means to secure his own success. That was three.

And now, four. Prince Onokoji had said that the conspirators had a lot of money. But where would poor Satsuman samurai get money? Would they really have been able to reward Suga so generously for the artfulness that he had demonstrated? But the agent of the British crown had access to inexhaustible financial resources. The Right Honourable must have laughed heartily to himself when the high-society gossip-monger told him about the gift of the estate. Bullcox himself must have bought it and then 'lost' it to Suga at cards. Or if not himself, then he had acted through intermediaries – what difference did that make!

The course of his deductive reasoning was unwittingly interrupted by Asagawa, who suddenly snored blissfully in his sleep. Resting on his laurels, almost literally, thought Fandorin. Villainy had been punished, justice had triumphed, harmony had been restored. And the inspector's sleep was not disturbed by any considerations of high politics. Or by the nightmarish events that had taken place two hours earlier in the department of police. The place must be in a fine uproar now. Or it would be very soon.

A cleaner or a zealous secretary, arriving before the start of office hours in order to tidy away a few papers, would glance into the boss's office and see a sight that would make him feel quite unwell . . .

When the intendant named Bullcox, the inspector hissed something to the prisoner in Japanese. Flexing his jaw muscles, he explained his indignation to Fandorin:

'He is an even greater scoundrel than I thought. At least the fanatics from Satsuma believed they were acting in the name of their Homeland, but this one knew they were mere pawns in a game planned by a foreigner!'

Suga bleated.

'We can take out the *hami* now,' said Erast Petrovich, who had still not recovered from his shock – he simply could not understand why this explanation had not occurred to him earlier.

Freed of the gag, the general spat and blurted out hoarsely to Asagawa:

'And aren't you a pawn in the hands of a foreigner?' But then he came to his senses, remembering that he was completely in the inspector's power, and changed his tone of voice. 'I have kept my word. Now it is your turn. Give me a dagger.'

'I don't have a dagger,' Asagawa said with a crooked grimace. 'And if I did,

I wouldn't give it to you. I wouldn't let you stain the noble steel with your filthy blood! Remember how you forced the hunchback to chew his tongue off? Now it is your turn. You've got sharp teeth, go on – if you have the courage. I shall enjoy watching.'

The intendant's eyes narrowed in hatred and glittered with fire.

The vice-consul tried cautiously to bite the tip of his tongue and shuddered. Asagawa was cruel, and no mistake. He was testing Suga's strength of character. If the intendant wavered, he would lose face. Then it would be possible to shake all sorts of things out of him.

None of them spoke. Then there was a strange stifled sound – it was Suga gulping.

No one was watching the door that led into the secret room, so when it slammed shut with a clang, they all started. Could twenty minutes really have gone by since the intendant had pressed the lever?

'You don't want to eat your own tongue,' the inspector remarked smugly. 'Then here is a new proposal. Look here . . .' – he took a revolver out of the general's pocket (Fandorin had not been mistaken, it was a cavalryman's Hagström) and left one bullet in the cylinder. 'Tell us who the other circles represent, and you won't have to gnaw your tongue off.'

The glance that Suga cast at that revolver was beyond description. No Romeo had ever devoured his Juliet with such lust in his eyes, no shipwreck victim had ever gazed so longingly at a speck on the horizon. The titular counsellor was absolutely certain that the general would not be able to resist the temptation. He was certain – and he was mistaken.

On the previous occasion Erast Petrovich had been lucky – he had observed this grisly spectacle from a distance, but this time it all happened just two paces from him.

Suga gave an absolutely feral, inhuman roar, opened his mouth wide, thrust his fleshy, red tongue out as far as it would go and clamped his jaws together. There was a sickening crunch and Fandorin turned away, but even so he had feasted his eyes on the sight long enough for it to remain with him for the rest of his days.

The intendant took longer to die than Semushi. Fandorin realised now that the shock of the pain had been too much for the hunchback. But Suga had a strong heart, and he choked on his own blood. At first he swallowed it convulsively, then it streamed out over his chin and his chest. That probably lasted for a few minutes. And all this time the iron man didn't groan even once.

After the wheezing ended and the suicide slumped limply in his bonds, Asagawa cut him free. The body slid down on to the floor and a red puddle started spreading out across the parquet.

The epitaph pronounced by the inspector was restrained and respectful.

'A strong man. A genuine *akunin*. But the main *akunin* in this story is not Japanese, he is a foreigner. What a disgrace!'

Fandorin was feeling sick. He wanted to get away from this cursed place as quickly as possible, but they spent quite a lot more time there after that.

First they eliminated all signs of their own presence: they collected up the pieces of rope, straightened the portrait of the Mikado, found the bullet fired from Fandorin's Herstal and dug it out.

From the European point of view it looked absolutely absurd: for some reason the head of the imperial police had come to his office in the middle of the night, sat down in a chair, bitten off his own tongue and died. Erast Petrovich could only hope that in Japanese terms it might appear less outlandish.

Then, on Asagawa's insistence, they spent the best part of an hour tearing all the numerous dossiers into tiny scraps of paper. Only then did they finally leave, in the same way as they had entered, that is, via the window of the toilet.

The only part of the archive that they did not destroy was the 'Okubo' file. It contained the page with the coded diagram, the stolen reports and the three sheets of paper with the oath written in blood. In combination with the testimony of the witness, Prince Onokoji, who not only knew about Suga's secret activities, but had connections with Bullcox, this was quite enough. Soon everyone would know why the intendant of police had done away with himself.

But before that the case had to be brought to a conclusion by finding evidence against the Englishman. If that could be managed, Britannia would suffer categorical disgrace, and Russian interests would be completely triumphant. This was a very grave matter – the resident English agent had organised the political assassination of a great man! It would probably lead to the severance of diplomatic relations.

If Bullcox wormed his way out of it and got away scot-free (there was really nothing to snag him with as yet), they would have to be satisfied with having exposed Suga. But that was already quite a lot.

Should he report to Doronin or wait a while? It was probably too soon. First he had to try to catch Bullcox by the tail, and that would probably require him to use methods that were not exactly diplomatic. And then, there was another circumstance, one that was quite insignificant from the viewpoint of high politics, but extremely important to Fandorin. It was precisely this delicate problem, of an entirely personal nature, that he was thinking through as he gazed out of the window at the paddy fields glinting in the sun.

Asagawa suddenly opened his eyes and said thoughtfully, as if he had never been asleep, but had also been immersed in analytical thinking:

'You know, that scoundrel Onokoji deliberately sent us into a trap.'

'Why do you think that?'

'There was no file on Onokoji in the archive.'

Fandorin frowned.

'You mean to say that the *shinobi* carried out their assignment in full? They got into the archive and stole the file of compromising material?'

'If we were able to find the lever, the ninja must certainly have found it. They are far more experienced in such matters, and more cautious. If there were two of them, we must assume that they did not enter the secret room together, as we did, but one stayed on guard outside.

'Then why did they not steal the entire archive? It could have been a powerful instrument of influence for them! Those secrets are worth huge amounts of money!'

The inspector looked at Fandorin in amazement.

'Come now! The Stealthy Ones kill, steal and spy, but they do not engage in blackmail and extortion! That would contradict their traditions and code of honour.'

Yes, Erast Petrovich had forgotten that in Japan everybody, even the villains, always had some kind of code. There was something reassuring about that, somehow.

'So Onokoji did get his f-file? Well, of course. Otherwise, he wouldn't have spoken about Suga's archive so calmly. He got what he wanted, but he didn't wish to pay the Momochi clan for their work. He knew that the senior samurai would be held answerable, not him. The prince used the samurai and condemned him to death.'

'There's no point now in talking about the samurai,' said Asagawa, waving his fist through the air. 'Don't you see? Onokoji knew we would fall into a trap, and he didn't warn us. He was counting on Suga killing us! I swear I'll shake the black soul out of that slimy scoundrel!'

The prince's soul almost took leave of his body without any shaking, just as soon as he heard about the intendant's death.

Lockston was still jangling the key to the cell, Asagawa was still waving his fist menacingly through the bars of the locked door, but the prince needed to be resuscitated. After the inspector's first furious shouts ('Surprised to see us? Did you think Suga would finish us off? It turned out the other way round!') Onokoji had jumped up off the bunk, turned as white as chalk and collapsed in a dead faint.

'Well, would you look at that?' the sergeant said in amazement. 'Bright and chirpy all night, he was, singing Parisian *chansonettes*. Boasting that he'd be free in the morning.'

'Water,' Asagawa said curtly.

They splashed water from the glass into the prisoner's face, slapped him on the cheeks, and the scion of feudal lords came round. He started sobbing and his teeth started chattering.

'Did you . . . Did you kill him? That's it, then, I'm done for.'

The prince was trembling so violently that his head wobbled back and forth on his thin neck. And apparently it was not simply because the effect of the morphine had worn off – Onokoji was in a total panic. At first Fandorin thought he was afraid of Asagawa and vengeance for his treachery. But the titular counsellor soon realised that he was mistaken.

First, the prisoner made no attempt to wriggle out of it. Quite the opposite, in fact!

'I didn't think it was possible, I swear! They told me the trap was a very cunning device! It's his own fault,' the prince babbled, grabbing hold of Erast Petrovich's hand and apparently apologising for the fact that the trap hadn't worked. 'You tell him that, tell him!'

'Tell who?' asked Fandorin, leaning forward bodily in his eagerness. 'We'll certainly tell him, but who?'

Onokoji slapped his palm against his lips. His eyes turned round in terror.

'No one,' he said quickly. Then he groaned pitifully, contradicting himself: 'That's it, he'll kill me now ...'

'Because you were responsible for the intendant's death?'

The aristocrat nodded.

Well, this is one who won't bite his tongue off, the vice-consul thought. And he won't shoot himself either. It looks as if the Englishman won't be able to wriggle his way out of this after all!

'Don't worry, Prince. We'll be able to protect you against him.'

Onokoji just shook his head.

'Do you think we don't know who you are s-so afraid of? We know. Suga told us before he died. It's Bullcox.'

'Bullcox?' said Lockston, wide-eyed in amazement. 'What has Bullcox got to do with all this?'

'Algernon Bullcox was at the head of the conspiracy against Okubo,' Fandorin explained, carefully enunciating every word – more for Onokoji than the sergeant. 'Suga was acting on the Englishman's instructions. Right?'

The question was addressed to the prisoner. He nodded without opening his eyes.

'What kind of nation are these English?' the sergeant exploded. 'India's not enough for them. The seas are not enough! They want to dominate the whole world. And they don't even go about it honestly! Let me tell you this, gentlemen. Old Dame Britannia is getting above herself. It's high time she was put in her place. They've got no business being here in Japan. There are more decent countries that trade honestly and don't go interfering in politics.'

The titular counsellor was entirely in agreement with the American on this point, although he suspected that by 'more decent countries', he did not actually mean the Russian Empire.

'I don't want to be released,' Onokoji said suddenly, looking at Fandorin. 'I'll be killed. Take care of me. I'll be useful to you.'

'You tell us everything you know about Bullcox's secret dealings, and Sergeant Lockston will allow you to live in the municipal prison for as long as necessary.'

'No! He'll find me here in no time at all.'

Seeing that the man was beside himself with fear, Erast Petrovich said gently:

'Very well. I'll give you refuge in the Russian consulate. But only on condition that you are absolutely frank with me.'

'I'll tell you everything. About Bullcox. But not now. I don't feel well. And it will be worse soon. I need another dose. I'll go to sleep and then ... and then we'll talk. Only take me away from here! Quickly! He ... he must know that I've been arrested. He knows about Suga too! And he'll guess straight away. He's very clever!'

Lockston snorted.

'Well, listen to that. That damn lousy Englishman's really got him running scared.'

Suddenly a voice behind him asked:

'Who's that you're talking about, Sergeant? Could it perhaps be me?'

They all looked round. Twigs was standing in the entrance of the cell, wearing a tie and a tight collar, as usual, with his old, scuffed doctor's bag under his arm.

'No, Doc, I wasn't talking about you, I meant . . .' the head of the municipal police began awkwardly, but Asagawa coughed loudly and Lockston finished rather incoherently, 'I was talking about a completely different Englishman . . . a different Englishman.'

Erast Petrovich caught Asagawa's eye and the inspector gave a slight shrug – a gesture that meant: Of course, Twigs-sensei is a most worthy individual, but the state interests and prestige of his homeland are involved here, so we had better keep quiet about Bullcox.

'Well, how did the nocturnal expedition go?' the doctor asked eagerly. 'I must admit, I didn't sleep a wink all night. I was terribly worried about you. Well, come on, tell me, then!'

They told him. Almost everything – the only part they didn't mention was the Right Honourable.

'So, we have evidence against Suga, but we don't have Suga any more?' the doctor summed up, mopping his bald head with a handkerchief. 'But that's marvellous! Why are you all looking so frustrated?'

There was a further exchange of glances, and the inspector shrugged again, but this time with a different meaning: Do what you think best.

'In the intendant's papers we found a diagram with all the inscriptions in strange s-symbols,' said Erast Petrovich, showing the doctor the sheet of paper. 'We know that they are the members of the conspiracy, but we can't read the names . . .'

'Let me take a look . . .'

Twigs moved his spectacles down to the very tip of his nose and peered eagerly at the paper. Then he suddenly turned it upside down.

'Wait, wait . . . I've seen something like this before . . .'

'Remember, Doctor, remember,' all three of them cried together.

'The cryptograms that the ninja used, that's what this is,' Twigs announced triumphantly. 'The *shinobi* had their own system of phonetic writing, for secret correspondence.'

'Intendant Suga was not a *shinobi*,' Asagawa said doubtfully. 'It's not possible. He came from a good samurai family.'

'What does that matter? He could have learned their alphabet, as I tried to do at one time. You know that I'm very interested in the history of the ninja. I can't just read these signs for you off the top of my head, but if

I rummage through my old notes, I might find something and be able to decipher them. I can't promise, but I'll try.'

'We know how to read one of the words,' said Fandorin, pointing to the central circle. 'It's the name of the leader.'

'Oh, that's very important. There are letters here that also occur in the other words. So tell me, what does this say?'

The titular counsellor said the name quietly:

'Bullcox.'

The doctor turned crimson. And when he grasped the full significance of this information, his indignation knew no bounds. He proclaimed a blistering philippic on the subject of rogues and adventurers who besmirch the honour and principles of a great empire, concluding with this:

'If your information is accurate, then the Right Honourable Bullcox is a criminal. He will be exposed and punished as he deserves!'

Asagawa asked incredulously:

'And does it not matter to you that your motherland will suffer?'

Squaring his shoulders proudly and raising one finger, Twigs said:

'The honour of the Motherland, my dear Asagawa, is not maintained by him who conceals her crimes, but by him who is not afraid to purge her of them.'

This rousing maxim was followed by a pause. The others pondered the doctor's words, wondering whether he was right, and, judging from the fact that the inspector winced, the sergeant nodded and the vice-consul sighed, they all reached rather different conclusions.

Asagawa brought the conversation back round to business.

'Since we are all in agreement, I suggest we discuss our plan of action. This is not an easy task. It will require time ... Where are you going?'

The question was addressed to Fandorin, who had suddenly shaken his head, as if coming to some decision, and set off towards the door.

'Consult without me for the time being, g-gentlemen. I have urgent business.'

'Wait! What about me?' shouted Onokoji, dashing over to the bars of his cell. 'You promised to give me refuge!'

Fandorin was so entirely preoccupied with his own idea that words cannot possibly express how reluctant he felt to waste his time dealing with this repulsive specimen.

But he had given his word.

From the beginning,
Enduring until the end –
The Word is the Word

AN AUTUMN LEAF

Masa couldn't sleep all night, he was too anxious.

In the evening, pretending he believed that his master suddenly needed a newspaper, he left the house, but of course he didn't go to any Grand Hotel, he hid behind a tree instead. He followed his master to the station without being seen, and when he saw that the vice-consul was going to Tokyo, he was on the point of buying a ticket himself. Then, however, Inspector Asagawa showed up. From the way that he walked past the master without even saying hello it was quite clear that they had some joint business to deal with.

Masa hesitated. Inspector Asagawa was a real *yoriki*, he couldn't be fooled. He'd spot that he was being followed in an instant. And, moreover, he was a serious man, responsible. The master could be trusted to a man like that.

Anyway, he didn't go. That was why he was in anguish. From all appearances, this business that his master had set out on was no laughing matter. The bag that he had packed in secret contained a night spy's outfit. Oh, how hard was the life of a vassal who could not make himself understood in words to the person he served! If only he knew the language of the northern barbarians, Masa would have told his master: 'You do not have and never will have a more faithful and diligent helper than me. You wound my heart and my honour painfully when you disdain my help. I am obliged to be with you everywhere and always, it is my duty'. Never mind, the master was very clever, every day he knew more and more Japanese words, and the day was not far off when it would be possible to talk to him in proper human language, without making gestures and pulling faces. Then Masa would be able to serve him properly.

But in the meantime he did what he could; first, he didn't sleep; secondly he didn't allow Natsuko into his bed, even though she turned sulky, because she really wanted Masa'a *karada* very badly (never mind, she could wait, the *karada* had to obey the spirit); thirdly he had recited eight hundred and eighty-eight times a dependable incantation against calamities of the night that he had learned from a certain courtesan. The sovereign of that woman's heart was a night bandit. Every time he went off to work, she received no clients, but burned incense and prayed to the big-bellied god Hotei, the patron of all whose fate depended on luck. And every time her beloved returned in the morning with a sack full of booty over his shoulder and, most importantly, alive and unhurt – that was how powerful the incantation was. But one day the stupid woman lost count and, just to be on the safe side, she repeated the prayer more times than necessary. And what happened? That very night the unfortunate robber was seized by the guards, and the next day his head was already grinning at passers-by from the bridge across the Sakuragawa. The courtesan, of course, jabbed a hairpin through her neck, and everyone said that was what she deserved, the irresponsible fool.

To make sure he didn't lose count, Masa gathered rice grains together into little heaps. He recited and added a grain, recited and added a grain. The little heaps of eight grains built up into bigger heaps, consisting of ten little ones. Morning had arrived by the time there were eleven of the big heaps. Masa chanted the prayer unhurriedly another eight times. As he added the final grain to the heap he glanced out of the window and saw a shiny black-lacquered carriage of indescribable beauty drive up to the gates of the consulate, harnessed to a team of four horses. The haughty driver sitting on the box was covered in gold braid and he had feathers in his hat.

The door opened and the master jumped down lightly on to the pavement. He didn't actually have a sack over his shoulders, but he was alive and unhurt. And then, surely a carriage was as good as any sack! Hail to the magical incantation!

Masa dashed over to meet him.

Even more wonderful was the change that had taken place in the master. After that cursed night when he had left the pavilion earlier than usual and stumbled all the way home, like a blind man, the master's face had become like the mask of the Ground Spider in the Noh theatre – dark and stiff – and his nose, which was long enough already, had turned so sharp, it was a ghastly sight.

The reason why O-Yumi-san had chosen the red-haired Englishman was clear: he was much richer, he had a big, beautiful house and eight servants, not just one. The master was suffering terribly from jealousy, and just to look at him plunged Masa into despair too. He even started wondering whether he ought to kill the worthless woman. The master would be sad, of course, but that was still better than destroying your liver by imagining your beloved squirming in someone else's embrace.

But now a miracle had happened, and the evil enchantment had been dispersed. Masa saw that straight away. Thanks to the kind god Hotei, or perhaps for some other reason, the master had been healed. His eyes glowed with confidence and the corners of his mouth were no longer turned down.

'Masa, big job,' he said in Japanese, in a strong voice. 'Very big. Help, all right?'

A man in a crumpled, grimy frock coat climbed out of the carriage, skinny backside foremost, turned round and then swayed so violently that he almost fell.

To judge from his hook-nosed face, pampered skin and elegant little hands, he was an aristocrat.

'He ... live ... home,' the master said, snapping his fingers impatiently because he couldn't immediately remember the words he wanted.

That means he's a guest, Masa realised, and he bowed politely to the stranger, who hiccuped and staggered again. He was either ill or drunk – Masa couldn't tell which.

They went into the building, with the master walking sideways somehow, as if he were shielding his guest from the windows of the Dirty Man.

The master walked along the corridor, thought for a moment and said:

'There. He live there.'

Masa tried to explain that no one could live there, it was a cupboard. There were suitcases, a sack of rice, jars of pickled radish and ginger root in there, but the master wouldn't listen to him.

'Guarudu, guarudu . . .' – he spoke the incomprehensible word twice. Then he muttered 'Dammit' (Masa knew that word, it meant 'chikusho!'), brought the dictionary from his study and translated. 'Guard. You he guard. Understand?'

'Understand,' Masa said with a nod.

He should have said so straight away. Masa grabbed the man with the hooked nose and pushed him into the cupboard. The man started whinging pitifully and sat down limply on the floor.

'Polite,' the master ordered strictly, using the dictionary again. 'Guard. Strict. But polite.'

Very well, politely. Masa brought a mattress, pillow and blanket from his own room and said to the prisoner:

'Please make yourself comfortable.'

The aristocrat tearfully asked the master about something in English. Masa recognised only the familiar word 'puriidz'.

The master sighed deeply and took a little box out of his pocket. There were tiny bottles of some kind of liquid lying in it, and a syringe, like the ones they used for smallpox inoculations. He gave the little box to the sniveller and locked the door of the cupboard.

'Watch. Guard. Strict. Polite,' he repeated, pointing his forefinger up in the air and wagging it about for some reason.

He turned round and almost ran out of the apartment.

He got into the carriage. He drove away.

For the first minute, out of sheer inertia, Erast Petrovich carried on thinking about the witness imprisoned in the cupboard. Masa could be relied on. He wouldn't leave the door and he wouldn't let anyone come close. The devil only knew what the servant thought about all this. Unfortunately, the vice-consul couldn't explain – he didn't have enough words.

The toll of disasters for which the titular counsellor would have to answer was increasing by the hour. Breaking into the lair of the head of police wasn't enough for him, now he had added the concealment of an unauthorised individual on the premises of the consulate without his superior's knowledge. He couldn't tell anyone about the hidden prince, neither Doronin nor Shirota – at least not for the time being.

However, while this high-handed behaviour could at least be kept secret, the next act of folly that the titular counsellor intended to commit would inevitably lead to a high-profile scandal.

Strangely enough, that did not bother Erast Petrovich at all just at the moment.

As he swayed on the cushions of the light carriage that he had hired, the very best that could be found in the fleet of the firm 'Archibald Griffin' ('Excellent horses and also Most Comfortable Carriages for all occasions at an hourly rate'), Fandorin felt very pleased with himself. The idea that made him abandon his colleagues at the height of a supremely important consultation had captivated the titular counsellor with its simplicity and indubitable practicability.

Take O-Yumi from the scoundrel, and have done with it. Not listen to her, give her no time to collect her wits. Simply put her in the carriage and drive her away.

That would be honest and manly, the Russian way.

This was what he should have done at the very beginning, even before Bullcox had been transformed into an arch-villain. What did political conspiracies have to do with love? Nothing. O-Yumi must have been waiting for her beloved to do precisely this. But he had turned flabby, allowed his willpower to flag, got bogged down in despondency and self-pity.

To really do things right, he ought to have dressed up in ceremonial style – tails, top hat. starched shirt, as the importance of the occasion required – but he hadn't wanted to waste a single minute.

The carriage hurtled along the cobbled streets of the Bluff and came to a dashing halt at property number 129. The coach driver removed his hat and opened the door, and the vice-consul descended slowly to the ground. He smoothed down his hair, and twisted up the ends of his moustache with a little brush – they were drooping slightly after his nocturnal adventures – and adjusted his tailcoat.

Well, God speed!

Once inside the wicket gate, he recalled Bullcox's dogs. But the ferocious confrères of Cerberus were nowhere to be seen. They were probably chained up during the day.

Fandorin crossed the lawn with a firm tread. What about O-Yumi? She was probably still sleeping; after all, she didn't go to bed until after dawn . . .

Before he could even touch the bell, the door swung open of its own accord. A haughty footman in livery was standing in the doorway. The titular counsellor handed him a card with a double-headed eagle on it:

Consulat de l'empire de la Russe
Eraste Pétrovich Fandorine
Vice-consul, Conseiller Titulaire
Yokohama, Bund, 6

Only the day before, Shirota had handed him an entire stack of these cards – freshly printed and still smelling of the press.

'I require to see the Right Honourable Algernon Bullcox on urgent business.'

He knew perfectly well that Bullcox could not possibly be home. The Englishman must certainly have been informed already of the mysterious 'suicide' of his accomplice and, of course, he had gone dashing to Tokyo.

Erast Petrovich had even prepared the following respnse:

'Ah, he is not here? Then please inform Miss O-Yumi that I am here. She is sleeping? She will have to be woken. This is a most pressing matter.'

But there was a surprise in store for Fandorin. The doorkeeper bowed as if everything was perfectly in order, asked him to come in and disappeared though a door leading out of the hallway to the left – from his previous, unofficial visit the vice-consul knew that was the location of the study.

Before Erast Petrovich had time to consider the possible implications, the Right Honourable in person came out of the study, wearing a smoking jacket and soft slippers and looking most serene altogether.

'To what do I owe the pleasure, Mr . . . Fendorain?' he asked, with a glance at the card. 'Ah yes, I believe we are acquainted.'

What on earth was happening here? Midday already, and Suga's body had not yet been discovered? Impossible!

Or it had been discovered, but Bullcox, a senior governmental adviser, had not been informed? Out of the question!

Or it had been discovered, but he had not been alarmed by the news? Absurd!

But a fact was a fact: Bullcox had preferred to stay at home. But why?

Erast Petrovich squinted through the half-open door of the study and saw a fire blazing in the hearth. So that was it! He was burning compromising documents! That meant he was really and truly alarmed! He really was an intelligent man. And far-sighted. He had caught the scent of danger!

'Why do you not say anything?' the Briton asked, frowning in annoyance. 'What do you want?'

Fandorin moved the Right Honourable aside and walked into the study.

But there were no papers beside the fireplace, only a pile of dry branches.

'What in damnation is the meaning of this?' asked Bullcox, following him.

Erast Petrovich impolitely answered a question with a question:

'Why have you lit a fire? It's summer now?'

'I heat the fireplace every morning with tamarisk branches. This is a new house, it's damp. And I like the smell of smoke . . . Listen here, sir, you are behaving very strangely. We are hardly even acquainted! Explain to me immediately what is going on! What was your purpose in coming here?'

There was absolutely nothing to lose now, and Fandorin took the plunge, head first into the whirlpool.

'To take away the lady whom you are holding here by force!'

Bullcox's jaw dropped and he started batting his eyelashes, as ginger as his curly locks.

But the titular counsellor, who, in the French expression, *avait déjà jeté son bonnet par-dessus le Moulin*, that is, effectively, he had thrown caution to the wind, proceeded to attack, which, as everyone knows, is the best form of defence in a poor position.

'Intimidating a woman is ignoble and unworthy of a gentleman! But then, what kind of gentleman are you? Out of my way, I'm going to her!'

He tried to walk past, but Bullcox blocked his way and grabbed him by the lapels.

'I'll kill you like a mad dog,' hissed the Englishman, whose own eyes had turned quite rabid.

Erast Petrovich replied in an equally predatory hiss:

'Kill me? Yourself? Oh, hardly. You wouldn't have the courage. You're more likely to send the "Stealthy Ones".'

And he pushed his rival with his uncommonly well-trained arms – so hard that the Right Honourable went flying away and knocked over a chair.

The footman looked in at the crash, and his long English features stretched out even longer.

'What "Stealthy Ones"?' the Briton exclaimed, stunned. 'You're a raving lunatic! I'll file a note of complaint with your government!'

'Go right ahead!' Fandorin growled in Russian.

He tried to run up the stairs, but Bullcox darted after him. He grabbed the Russian by his coat-tail and pulled him back down.

The vice-consul swung round and saw that the senior governmental adviser had assumed a boxer's stance.

Well, boxing was not jujitsu, Erast Petrovich had no cause to be shy here.

He readied himself too: left fist forward, right fist covering the chin.

The first skirmish ended in a draw, with all the blows struck being parried.

In the second clash the vice-consul took a strong poke to the body, but replied with a rather good left hook.

Here the fight was interrupted by a female voice that exclaimed:

'Algie? What's going on?'

O-Yumi was standing on the landing of the staircase in her nightshirt, with a silk shawl on top. Her loose hair was scattered across her shoulders and the sunlight was shining through it.

Erast Petrovich choked.

'It's the Russian!' Bullcoxs exclaimed excitedly. 'He's gone insane! He claims that I'm keeping you here by force. I decided to bring the blockhead to his senses.'

O-Yumi started moving down the steps.

'What's wrong with your ear, Algie? It's all puffy and red. You need to put some ice on it.'

The familial, domestic tone in which these words were spoken, the name 'Algie', spoken twice, and – above all – the fact that she hadn't even looked at him, made Erast Petrovich feel as if he had tumbled impetuously over a precipice.

It was hard to breathe, let alone to speak, but Fandorin turned to O-Yumi and forced out a few hoarse words:

'Just one word. Only one. Me – or – him?'

Bullcox apparently also wanted to say something, but his voice failed him.

Both boxers stood and watched as the black-haired woman walked down the stairs in her light outfit with the sun shining through it.

She reached the bottom and glanced upwards reproachfully at Erast Petrovich. And said with a sigh:

'What a question. You, of course ... Forgive me, Algie. I was hoping everything would end differently for us, but clearly it was not to be.'

The Briton was absolutely crushed. He started blinking, looking from O-Yumi to Fandorin and back again. The Right Honourable's lips trembled, but he still couldn't find any words.

Suddenly Bullcox shouted something inarticulate and went dashing up the steps.

'Let's run!' said O-Yumi, grabbing the titular counsellor by the hand and pulling him after her towards the door.

'What f-for?'

'His armoury room is upstairs!'

'I'm not afraid!' Erast Petrovich declared, but the slim hand jerked him with such surprising strength that he barely managed to stay on his feet.

'Let's run!'

She dragged the titular counsellor along, and he kept looking back, across the lawn. The beautiful woman's hair fluttered in the wind, the hem of her nightdress flapped and ballooned, the backs of her velvet slippers slapped loudly.

'Yumi! For God's sake!' a voice called from somewhere high up.

Bullcox leaned out of a first-floor window, waving a hunting carbine.

Fandorin tried, as far as he could, to cover the woman running in front of him with his own body. A shot rang out, but the bullet missed by a wide margin, he didn't hear it whine.

Looking back again, the titular counsellor saw the Englishman settling his eye to the carbine again, but even at this distance he could see the barrel wobbling – the gunman's hands were shaking wildly.

He didn't need to shout to the driver to set off. He had already set off, in fact, immediately after the first shot – without bothering to wait for his passengers. He just lashed the horses, pulled his head down into his shoulders and didn't look back.

Erast Petrovich opened the door on the run, grabbed his companion round the waist and threw her inside. Then he jumped up on to the seat himself.

'I dropped my shawl and lost one slipper!' O-Yumi exclaimed. 'Ah, how interesting!' Her eyes were wide open and glittering brightly. 'Where are we going, my darling?'

'To my place at the consulate!'

She whispered:
'That means we have an entire ten minutes. Close the blind.'

Fandorin did not notice how they reached the Bund. He was brought round
by a knock at the window. Apparently someone had been knocking for a
while, but he hadn't heard them straight away.

'Sir, sir,' said a voice outside, 'we're here . . . You might add on a bit, for a
fright like that.'

The titular counsellor opened the door slightly and thrust a silver dollar
out through the crack.

'Here you are. And wait.'

He managed more or less to tidy up his suit.

'Poor Algie,' O-Yumi said with a sigh. 'I wanted so much to leave him
according to all the rules. You've gone and spoilt the whole thing. Now his
heart will be filled with bitterness and hate. But never mind. I swear that for
us everything will end beautifully, in proper *jojutsu* fashion. You'll have very,
very good memories of me, we'll separate in the "Autumn Leaf" style.'

The loveliest gift.
A tree gives is its last one –
A gold autumn leaf

INSANE HAPPINESS

'So, that night you rejected me only because you wanted to separate from "poor Algie" according to all the r-rules?' asked Erast Petrovich, looking at her mistrustfully. 'That was the only reason?'

'Not the only one. I really am afraid of him. Did you notice his left earlobe?'

'What?' Fandorin thought he must have misheard.

'From the shape, length and colour of his earlobe, it's clear that he is a very dangerous man.'

'There you go with your *ninso* again! You're just laughing at me!'

'I counted ten dead bodies on his face,' she said quietly. 'And those are only the ones he killed with his own hands.'

Fandorin didn't know whether she was being serious or playing the fool. Or rather, he wasn't absolutely certain that she was playing the fool. And so he asked with a laugh:

'Can you see dead bodies on my face?'

'Of course. Every time one man takes the life of another, it leaves a scar on his soul. And everything that happens in the soul is reflected on the face. You have those traces as well. Do you want me to tell you how many people you have killed?' She held out her hand and touched his cheekbones with her fingers. 'One, two, three . . .'

'St-stop it!' he said, pulling away. 'Better tell me more about Bullcox instead.'

'He doesn't know how to forgive. Apart from the ten that he killed himself, I saw other traces, people for whose deaths he was responsible. There are a lot of them. Far more than there are of the first kind.'

The titular counsellor leaned forward despite himself.

'You mean you can see that too?'

'Yes, it's not hard to read a killer's face, it's moulded so starkly, with sharp contrasts of colour.'

'Positively Lombroso,' murmured Erast Petrovich, touching himself on the cheekbone. 'No, no, it's nothing, go on.'

'The people with the most marks on their faces are front-line generals, artillery officers and, of course, executioners. But the most terrible scars I have ever seen, quite invisible to ordinary people, were on a very peaceable, wonderful man, the doctor in a brothel where I used to work.'

O-Yumi said it as calmly as if she were talking about a perfectly ordinary job – as a seamstress or milliner.

Fandorin felt his insides cringe and he went on hastily, so that she wouldn't notice anything.

'A doctor? How strange.'

'It's not strange at all. Over the years he had helped thousands of girls get rid of their fetuses. Only the doctor had fine, light marks, like ripples on water, but Algie's are deep and bloody. How could I not be afraid of him?'

'He won't do anything to you,' the titular counsellor said sombrely but firmly. 'He won't have time. Bullcox is finished.'

She looked at him in fearful admiration.

'You're going to kill him first, are you?'

'No,' replied Erast Petrovich, opening the blind and peering cautiously at Doronin's windows. 'Any day now Bullcox will be expelled from Japan. In disgrace. Or perhaps even put in prison.'

In was lunchtime. Shirota, as usual, must have taken his 'captain's daughter' to the table d'hôte at the Grand Hotel, but – dammit! – there was a familiar figure hovering in the window of the consul's apartment. Vsevolod Vitalievich was standing there with his arms folded, looking straight at the carriage stuck there at the gates.

The very idea of leading O-Yumi across the yard, in a state of undress, and with only one shoe, was quite unthinkable.

'What are we waiting for?' she asked. 'Let's go! I want to settle into my new home as quickly as possible. Your place is so uncomfortable as it is!'

But they couldn't sneak in like thieves either. O-Yumi was a proud woman, she would feel insulted. And wouldn't he cut a fine figure, embarrassed of the woman he loved!

I'm not embarrassed, Erast Petrovich told himself. It's just that I need to prepare myself. That is one. And she is not dressed. That is two.

'Wait here for now,' he told her. 'I'll be back in a moment.'

He walked across the yard with a brisk, businesslike stride, but he squinted sideways at Doronin's window anyway. He saw Vsevolod Vitalievich turn away with a certain deliberate emphasis. What could that mean?

Clearly he must already know about Suga, and he realised that Fandorin had been involved in some way; waiting at the window was a way of reminding the vice-consul about himself and showing how impatient he was to hear a few explanations; his demonstrative indifference made it clear that he did not intend to demand these explanations – the titular counsellor would decide when the time was right.

Very subtle, very noble and most apposite.

Masa was standing outside the cupboard, as motionless as a Chinese stone idol.

'Well, what has he been like?' Erast Petrovich asked, gesturing to clarify the meaning of the gesture.

His servant reported with the help of mime and gesture: first he cried, then he sang, then he fell asleep, he had to be given the chamber pot once.

'Well done,' the vice-consul said approvingly. '*Kansisuru. Itte kuru.*'

That meant: 'Guard. I go away.'

He looked into his room for a second and went back quickly to the carriage. He opened the door slightly.

'You are not dressed and have no shoes,' he said to the charming passenger, setting down a sack of Mexican silver on the seat beside her. 'Buy yourself some clothes. And, in general, everything that you think you need. And these are my cards with the address. If you need to have something taken in or whatever, I don't know, leave one with the shop assistant, they'll deliver it. When you get back, you can settle in. You are the mistress of the house.'

O-Yumi touched the jingling sack with a smile, but without any great interest, thrust out a little bare foot and stroked Erast Petrovich on the chest with it.

'Ah, what a dunce I am!' he exclaimed. 'You can't even go into a shop in that state!'

He glanced furtively over his shoulder at the consulate and squeezed her slim ankle.

'Why would I go inside?' O-Yumi laughed. 'They'll bring everything I need to the carriage.'

The anti-Bullcox coalition, assembled at full strength, held its meeting in the office of the head of the municipal police. Somehow it turned out that the role of chairman had passed to Asagawa, although he had not been appointed by anyone. The Russian vice-consul, previously acknowledged by all as the leader, ceded his primacy quite willingly. First, having abandoned his brothers-in-arms for the sake of a private matter, Erast Petrovich had, as it were, forfeited his moral right to lead them. And secondly, he knew that his mind and heart were preoccupied with a quite different matter just at the moment. And that matter happened to be a most serious one, which could not be dealt with half-heartedly.

In any case, Asagawa conducted the analytical work surpassingly well without any help from Fandorin.

'So, gentlemen, we have a witness who is prepared to testify. But he is an unreliable individual of dubious character and what he says is of little value without documentary confirmation. We have the Satsuman warriors' oath, signed in blood, but this evidence incriminates only the late Intendant Suga. We also have the police reports confiscated by Suga, but again, they cannot be used against Bullcox. The only unquestionable piece of evidence is a coded diagram of the conspiracy in which the central figure is the senior foreign counsellor of the British imperial government. But in order for this diagram to become proof, we must first decipher it completely. We cannot hand the document over to the authorities before that – we might be making a fatal mistake for, after all, we do not know which other officials are involved in the conspiracy. Since the intendant of police himself was one . . .'

'That's right,' said Lockston, who was puffing on his cigar on the window-sill, beside the open window – in order to spare Dr Twigs' sensitive nose.

'I basically don't trust any of the Jappos ... Apart from you, of course, my good friend Go. Let the doc try to figure out what the squiggles mean. We'll identify all the bad guys and then smash them all at once. Right, Rusty?'

Erast Petrovich nodded in reply to the sergeant, but he looked only at the inspector.

'All this is c-correct, but we don't have much time. Bullcox is a clever man, and he has powerful allies who will stop at nothing. I have no doubt that Bullcox will pay particular attention to my person [the vice-consul cleared his throat in embarrassment at this point] and to you, since it is known that we were working together on investigating the case of the Satsuma trio.'

At this point Erast Petrovich allowed himself to deviate from the truth somewhat, but only in the details. Even if the Englishman had not had personal reasons to hate him, the members of the conspiracy, frightened by the intendant's strange death, would certainly have taken an interest in the vice-consul. He and Suga had been actively involved in the investigation of the conspiracy against Okubo – that was one. The blow struck against the intendant was in the interests of the Russian Empire – that was two. And there was also a three: in his recent confrontation with Bullcox, the titular counsellor had been incautious – his actions had intimated his suspicion that the Briton was intending to burn certain compromising documents. In the emotional heat of the moment, the Right Honourable had probably not paid any attention to this, but later, of course, he would call it to mind. And there could certainly be no doubt that at present he was thinking unceasingly of the Russian diplomat, and with quite exceptional intensity.

It was getting stuffy in the office. Asagawa walked over to the window and stood beside the sergeant in order to take a breath of fresh air, but instead he choked on the ferocious tobacco fumes and started coughing. He waved his hand, scattering the cloud of smoke, and turned his back to the window.

'Perhaps Fandorin-san is right. In any case, extra caution will do no harm. Let's divide up the evidence, so that it is not all kept in the same place. Twigs-sensei will take the diagram – that is obvious. You are our only hope now, Doctor. For God's sake, do not leave your house. No visits, no patients. Say that you are unwell.'

Twigs nodded solemnly and stroked his pocket – obviously that was where the crucial clue was.

'I shall take the police reports, especially since three of them were written by me. That leaves the oaths for you, Sergeant.'

The American took the three sheets of paper covered with brown hiero-glyphs and examined them curiously.

'You can count on me. I'll keep the papers with me, and I won't set foot outside the station. I'll even spend the night here.'

'Excellent, that's the best thing to do.'

'And what will I get?' asked Erast Petrovich.

'You have custody of the only witness. That is quite enough.'

That left Fandorin feeling at a loss.

'Gentlemen ... I was about to ask you to take the prince off my hands. My domestic circumstances have changed somewhat, you see. I can't possibly keep him now ... I'll exchange him for any of the clues. And please, as soon as possible.'

The inspector gave the vice-consul a curious glance, but he didn't ask any questions.

'All right, but it can't be done in daylight – he'll be seen. I tell you what. I know where we can accommodate the prince, there's a good place that he won't escape from. Tonight, just before dawn, bring him to pier number thirty-seven, it's beside the Fujimi bridge.'

'Th-thank you. And what if the doctor doesn't manage to decipher the diagram? What then?'

The Japanese had an answer ready for this eventuality.

'If the sensei does not decipher the diagram, we shall have to act in an unofficial manner. We shall give everything that we know, together with the material evidence and witnesses' testimony, to one of the foreign newspapers. Only not a British one, of course. To the editors of *L'Echo du Japon*, for instance. The French will be absolutely delighted by a sensational story like this. Let Bullcox try to explain everything and demand a retraction. Then all the secrets will come out.'

On the way home Erast Petrovich's eye was caught by the fashion shop 'Madame Bêtise' or, rather, by a huge advertising poster covered with roses and cupids: 'The novelty of the Paris season! Fine and coarse fishnet stockings in all sizes, with moiré ties!' The vice-consul blushed as he recalled a certain ankle. He went into the shop.

The Parisian stockings proved to be wonderfully fine, and on the aforementioned lower limb they ought to look absolutely breathtaking.

Fandorin choose half a dozen pairs: black, lilac, red, white, maroon and a colour called 'Sunrise over the Sea'.

'Which size would you like?' the scented salesman asked.

The titular counsellor was on the brink of confusion – he hadn't thought about the size, but the owner of the shop, Madame Bêtise herself, came to his assistance.

'Henri, the monsieur requires size one. The very smallest,' she cooed, examining the customer curiously (or at least, so it seemed to him).

Yes, indeed, the very smallest, Erast Petrovich realised, picturing O-Yumi's tiny foot. But how did this woman know? Was it some kind of Parisian *ninso*?

The owner turned her face away slightly, still looking at Fandorin, then suddenly lowered her eyes and turned to look at the shelves of merchandise.

She made eyes at me, the titular counsellor deduced, and, even though he was not attracted to Madame Bêtise in the slightest, he squinted at himself in the mirror. And he found that, despite his rather exhausted appearance and creased suit, he was quite positively good-looking.

'So glad to see you, do call more often, Monsieur Diplomat,' a voice called from behind him on his way out.

He was surprised, but only very slightly. Yokahama was a small town. No doubt a tall young man with dark hair and blue eyes and a wonderfully curled moustache, who was always (well, almost always) impeccably dressed, had simply been noticed.

Although there was a fine rain falling (still the same kind, plum rain), Erast Petrovich was in a totally blissful state of mind. People walking towards him seemed to look at him with genuine interest and even, perhaps, gaze after him when he had walked by, the smell of the sea was wonderful and the sight of the ships at the anchorage was worthy of the brush of Mr Aivazovsky. The titular counsellor even tried to sing, something that he would not usually have allowed himself to do. The tune was distinctly bravura, the words entirely frivolous.

> Yokohama, little town,
> See me strolling up and down;
> The town is really very small,
> No need to take a cab at all.

But the little town of Yokohama was even smaller than Fandorin had imagined – as he was soon to discover.

No sooner had Erast Petrovich set foot in the yard of the consulate than someone called his name.

Doronin was loitering in the same window as on the recent previous occasion, but this time he did not turn away or show any signs of tact.

'Mr Vice-Consul!' he shouted in a menacing voice. 'Please be so kind as to call into my office. Immediately, without going round to your apartment!'

And he disappeared, no doubt on his way to the office area.

Fandorin had never seen the highly cultured and restrained Vsevolod Vitalievich in such a fury.

'I didn't ask you about anything! I didn't oblige you to attend the office! I put my trust in you!' the consul seethed rather than shouted, goggling over his blue lenses with his inflamed eyes. 'I assumed that you were occupied with state business, but it appears that you . . . you were engaged in amorous adventures! You burst into the house of the official representative of the British Empire! You abducted his mistress! You provoked an affray! Why are you so surprised? Yokohama is a small town. News, especially the spicy kind, spreads instantaneously here!'

The driver, thought Erast Petrovich. He blabbed to his comrades from 'Archibald Griffin' and they spread it round the town in no time at all. And Bullcox's own servants, too. The kitchen telegraph was the fastest medium of communication.

'Are you at least aware that Intendant Suga has committed suicide? How could you be! And I thought that . . . Ah, you heroic lover!' The consul waved his hand despairingly. 'All sorts of rumours are circulating. Suga didn't shoot himself, he didn't even commit hara-kiri. He chose an ancient, monstrously savage way of leaving this life, one that samurai used if they were captured or suffering severe guilt. Everyone is convinced that the intendant could not forgive himself for Okubo's death, and his undeserved promotion was the final blow. He did not dare to disobey his monarch's will, but felt that he had to expiate his guilt by accepting a martyr's death . . . Well, why don't you say something, Fandorin? Explain yourself, damn you! Say something!'

'I shall speak tomorrow. But for now, please permit me to remind you of the promise that you made me, not to interfere in anything and not to ask any questions. If I fail, I shall answer for everything at once. I have no time to explain now.'

It was well said, with restraint and dignity, but it failed to produce the desired effect.

'That is quite obvious,' the consul hissed, looking not into the other man's eyes, but down and to one side. He waved his hand, this time in disgust, and walked out.

Erast Petrovich also looked down. And there, dangling from the pink paper bag decorated with a ribbon, which he had been handed in the shop, he saw a 'Sunrise over the Sea' fishnet stocking.

The vice-consul returned to his quarters feeling dismal. He opened the door and froze on the spot, barely able to recognise his own hallway.

Hanging on the wall was a large mirror in a lacquered and painted mother-of-pearl frame. There were white and purple irises standing in a vase on a flirtatious little chest and perfuming the air with their scent. The coat stand on which Masa used to keep his master's hats and outer garments was gone – standing in its place was a closed cupboard with doors of woven straw. Above it a large kerosene lamp in a paper shade radiated a soft pink light.

Astounded, Fandorin glanced into the drawing room. There were even more changes there – it was quite impossible to make out all the details, he just got a general impression of something bright, colourful and festive.

In the dining room the titular counsellor saw a table laid in a way that immediately made him feel terribly hungry (something that had not happened to Erast Petrovich at all in the last few days). There were fruits, cheeses, rice balls with red and white fish, pies and cakes, sweets, champagne in an ice bucket.

The vice-consul discovered the fairy who had cast such a miraculous spell on the official government residence in the bedroom. But no, this room could no longer be referred to in such a prosaic, everyday fashion. The broad but simple bed that had been quite adequate for Erast Petrovich was now decorated with a muslin canopy, curtains had appeared at the windows and there was a bright-coloured, fluffy rug on the floor. O-Yumi herself, clad only in her nightshirt (the same one in which she had fled from Bullcox's lair), was standing on a chair, fastening a long scroll with some kind of hieroglyphic inscription to the wall.

'Darling, are you back?' she said, tossing a lock of hair off her forehead. 'I'm so tired! You have a very strange servant. He refused to help me. I had to do everything myself. It's a good thing I learned so much at the tea house.

In that place, until you win respect, you do everything yourself – wash, iron, mend . . . But he really is strange! He stands in the corridor all the time and he wouldn't let me look into the cupboard. What have you got in there? I heard some very odd sounds.'

'That's a secret room. Nothing very interesting, just all sorts of boring diplomatic d-documents,' Fandorin lied. 'I'll order them to be removed tomorrow. But why didn't you buy yourself any clothes?'

She jumped down off the chair without a sound.

'I did. I just took them off so I wouldn't get them dirty. Look, this will be enough for a start.'

She opened the door of the wardrobe, and Erast Petrovich saw that his frock coats and trousers had been squeezed right into the very corner, and four-fifths of the space was occupied by brightly coloured silk, velvet and satin. There were hatboxes on the upper shelf and shoeboxes down below.

'What's that you've got there?' asked O-Yumi, reaching for the pink bag. 'From Madame Bêtise? For me?'

She took out the stockings, turned them over in her hands and wrinkled up her nose.

'Shumiwarui.'

'What?'

'How vulgar! You haven't got a clue about ladies' outfits. I'll probably keep the black ones. But I'll give the others to Sophie. She's certain to like them.'

'T-to whom?' asked poor Erast Petrovich, unable to keep up with the news.

'The yellow-haired fool who taps on that big iron machine.'

'Have you already m-made her acquaintance?'

'Yes, I made friends with her. I gave her a hat, and she gave me a shawl with big red flowers. And I got to know Obayasi-san, your boss's mistress, even better. A sweet woman. I made friends with her too.'

'What else have you managed to do in the three hours since we last saw each other?'

'Nothing else. I bought a few things, started putting the apartment in order and met the neighbours.'

It could not be said that Fandorin was particularly good at counting money, but it seemed to him that there were an awful lot of purchases.

'How did you stretch the money to all this?' he asked admiringly when he spotted a little suede box with a delightful pearl brooch on a small table.

'The money? I spent that in the first two shops.'

'And . . . and how did you pay after that?'

O-Yumi shrugged one bare shoulder.

'The same way as before, when I lived with Algie. I left your cards everywhere.'

'And they gave you c-credit?'

'Of course. By the time I reached the third shop, everybody knew that I was living with you now. Madame Bêtise (I was in her shop too, only

365

I didn't buy these terrible stockings) congratulated me, she said you were very handsome, far more handsome than Bullcox. He's richer, of course, but that's not very important if a man's as handsome as you. I rode back with the blinds open. How everyone stared at me!'

And at me too, thought Erast Petrovich, recalling how people on the street had looked round at him.

Lord, oh Lord . . .

Late in the evening the two of them sat together, drinking tea. Erast Petrovich was teaching her to drink like a Russian cab driver: from the saucer, through a lump of sugar clutched in the teeth, blowing and puffing noisily. O-Yumi, wearing the Russian shawl, with her face glowing red, puffed out her cheeks, gnawed at the sugar with her white teeth and laughed. There was nothing exotic or Japanese about her at that moment, and it seemed to Fandorin that they had lived together in perfect harmony for many years; God grant that they would be together for as many again.

'What is your *jojutsu* good for?' he asked. 'Why did you take it into your head to study that filth that turns something living, passionate and natural into m-mathematics?'

'But isn't that the essence of any art? To break down the natural into its component parts and reassemble them in a new way? I have studied the art of love since I was fourteen.'

'Since you were f-fourteen? Surely that wasn't your own decision?'

'No. My father ordered me to study *jojutsu*. He said: "If you were my son, I would send you to develop your ability to think, your strength and cunning, because these are a man's greatest weapons. But you are a woman, and your greatest weapon is love. If you can completely master this difficult art, the most intelligent, strongest and most cunning men will be like putty in your hands." My father knew what he was talking about. He is the cleverest, strongest and most cunning man I know. I was fourteen years old, I was stupid and I really didn't want to go to study with a mistress of *jojutsu*, but I loved my father, so I obeyed him. And of course, as always, he was right.'

Erast Petrovich frowned, thinking that in any civilised country a loving father who sold his juvenile daughter into a brothel would be packed off to serve hard labour.

'Where is he now, your father? Do you see each other often?'

O-Yumi's face suddenly darkened and her lips clamped firmly together, as if from suppressed pain.

He's dead, the titular counsellor guessed, and, regretting that he had made his beloved suffer, he hastened to make amends for his blunder by gently stroking the hollow at the base of her neck (he had been wanting to do that for a long time anyway).

Much later, lying in bed and staring up at the ceiling, O-Yumi said with a sigh:

'*Jojutsu* is a wonderful science. It is the only thing capable of making a woman stronger than a man. But only until the woman loses her head. I'm afraid that is exactly what is happening to me. How shameful!'

Fandorin closed his eyes tight, feeling himself brimming over with an unbearable, insane happiness.

A stupid question,
This 'to be or not to be',
Once you've been happy

TICKLISH

It was by no means the first time Walter Lockston had spent the night in the office. Under the terms of his contract with the city of Yokohama, the head of the municipal police was provided with an official house, and even furniture, but the sergeant had never got used to those palatial halls. The sofas and chairs stood in their dust covers, the large glass chandelier was never lit up even once, the family bed gathered dust for lack of use – the former inhabitant of the prairies felt more at home on a canvas campbed. It was dreary and depressing to be all alone in a two-storey house, the walls and the ceiling oppressed him. The office was a better place. The familiar cramped space there was all his own, every inch of it: the desk, the safe, the gun shelf. It didn't smell of the emptiness that filled the house. And he slept better here. Walter was always glad to spend the night in the office, and today's excuse couldn't possibly have been more legitimate.

He let the duty constable go home – he was a family man. It was so quiet and peaceful in the station. The lock-up was empty – no sailors on a spree, no drunk clients from 'Number Nine'. Bliss!

He hummed a song about the glorious year of sixty-five as he washed out his shirt. He sniffed his socks and put them back on – he could wear them for one more day. He brewed some strong coffee and smoked a cigar, and then it was time to settle down for the night.

He made himself comfortable on the armchair, took his boots off and put his feet up on a chair. There was a blanket in the office, worn into holes here and there, but it was his favourite blanket, he always had splendid dreams under it.

The sergeant yawned and looked round the room, just to make sure everything was right. Of course, it was hard to imagine English spies or slanty-eyed Jappos trying to creep in and poke around in a police station, but it never hurt to be careful.

The door of the office was locked. So were the window frame and the bars on the window. Only the small windowpane was slightly open, otherwise you could suffocate in here. The distance between the bars was so narrow, a cat could barely get through it.

The rain that had been falling since midday stopped and the moon started shining in the sky, so bright that he had to pull the peak of his cap down over his eyes.

Walter squirmed about, settling down. The sheets of paper with the oaths written in blood crackled inside his shirt. All the weird freaks who live in this world, he thought with a shake of his head.

Lockston always fell asleep quickly, but first (and this was the part he always liked best), coloured pictures of the past flickered through his head, or maybe pictures of things that had never really happened at all. They swirled around, jostling each other for a place in the queue and gradually merged into his first dream, which was the sweetest.

All of this happened now. He saw a horse's head with its pointed ears quivering, dashing hell-for-leather towards a stretch of land overgrown with brownish grass; then a great, high sky with white clouds, the kind you only get over huge open spaces; then a woman who had loved him (or maybe she was pretending) in Lucyville back in sixty-nine; then from somewhere or other a dwarf in a bright-coloured body stocking, whirling around and jumping through a hoop. And this, the final vision to surface out of the depths of his totally forgotten past, maybe even out of his childhood, merged imperceptibly into a dream.

The sergeant murmured wordlessly as he marvelled at the little circus artist, who turned out to be able to fly and blow tongues of flame out of his mouth.

Then a less pleasant dream began, about a house fire – that was because the sleeping man felt hot under the blanket. He started squirming about, the blanket slipped off on to the floor and once again all was well in the realm of dreams.

Walter woke up long after midnight. Not of his own volition, though – he heard a ringing sound somewhere in the distance. Still groggy with sleep, he didn't realise straight away that it was the doorbell, the one that had been hung at the entrance to be used during the night.

The agreement with Asagawa and the Russian vice-consul was this: no matter what happened, the sergeant was not to leave the station. To hell with it if there was a fight, or a knifing, or a murder. It could wait until morning.

And so Lockston turned over on to his side and tried to carry on sleeping, but the jangling continued as loud as ever.

Should he go and take a look? Without going outside, of course – who knew what was out there? It could be a trap. Maybe the bad men had come to get their pieces of paper?

He picked up his revolver and walked silently out into the corridor.

There was a cunning little window made of dark glass in the front door. You could see out of it, but you couldn't see in.

Lockston glanced out and saw a Japanese whore on the porch, wearing a striped kimono, the kind that the staff in the International Hotel had.

The native woman reached up to the bell pull and jerked it with all her might. And then at last she started screeching too.

'Poriceman-san! Me Kumiko, Hoter Intanasyanaru! Troubur! Sairor kirred! Kirred entirery! Birriard room! Fight stick! Howr in head!'

Clear enough. Some sailors had had a fight with the cues in the billiard room and someone had got his skull stove in. The usual stuff.

'Tomorrow morning!' Lockston shouted. 'Tell the boss I'll send a constable in the morning!'

'Impossibur morning! Need now! Sairor die!'

'What am I supposed to do, glue his head back together? Get away, girl, get away. I told you, tomorrow.'

She started ringing again, but the sergeant, reassured, was already walking back along the corridor. No way was the head of police dashing out in the middle of the night for some stupid nonsense like that. Even without the important papers tucked under his shirt, he still wouldn't have gone.

When the bell finally stopped sounding, it was really quiet. Walter couldn't even hear his own footsteps – in the socks his feet moved across the wooden floor without making the slightest sound. If it wasn't for that absolute silence, the sergeant would never have heard the faintest of faint rustling sounds behind the door of the office.

Someone was in there!

Lockston froze and his heart set off at a gallop. He put his ear to the crack of the door – sure thing! Someone was going through the desk, pulling out the drawers.

Why, the sons of bitches, coming up with something like that! Deliberately luring him out of the room, and then . . . But how had they got in? When he went out into the corridor, he locked the door behind him!

Now you'll get yours, you low snakes!

Holding the revolver in his left hand, he slipped the key into the keyhole without making a sound, then turned it, jerked the handle towards him and burst into the room.

'Don't move! I'll kill you!'

And the sergeant would have blasted away, too, but there was a surprise waiting for him, in the form of a tiny figure, about three feet tall, standing by the desk. Just for a moment Walter imagined he was still asleep and dreaming about the dwarf.

But when he clicked the lamp switch and the gas flared up, it wasn't a dwarf at all, but a little Japanese boy, entirely naked.

'Who are you?' Lockston blurted out. 'Where are you from? How did you get in?'

The little imp darted nimbly towards the window, jumped up like a monkey, squeezed sideways through the bars, squirmed into the opening of the small windowpane and would surely have got clean away, but the sergeant was up to the challenge – he dashed across the room just in time to grab him by the foot and drag him back inside.

At least now he had the answer to his third question. The naked urchin had climbed in through the window. Even for him it was a tight fit, as the bruises on his thighs testified. And that was why he was naked – he couldn't have squeezed through in clothes.

Well, how about that! He'd been expecting absolutely anyone – spies, assassins, wily ninja – but instead this little runt had shown up.

'Right, now answer me.' He took hold of the kid's skinny little shoulders and shook him. '*Kataru! Dareh da? Dareh okutta?*'* The little rat gazed unblinkingly at the huge red-faced American. The little upward-turned face – narrow, with a pointed nose – was impassive, inscrutable. A ferret, a genuine ferret, the sergeant thought.

'So, going to keep mum, are you?' he asked menacingly. 'I'll loosen your tongue for you. *Mita ka?*'† He unbuckled his belt and pulled it out of his trousers.

The little lad (he was only about eight, he couldn't possibly have been any older) carried on looking at Lockston with the same indifferent, even weary air, like a little old man.

'Well?' the sergeant roared at him in a terrible voice.

But the strange child wasn't frightened, in fact he seemed to brighten up a bit. In any case, his lips crept out to the sides, as if he was unable to restrain a smile. A little black tube stuck out of his mouth. There was a whistling sound, and the sergeant thought he had been stung on the chest by a wasp.

He looked down in surprise. There was something that glittered sticking out of his shirt, where his heart was. Was that really a needle? But where had it come from?

He wanted to pull it out, but somehow he couldn't raise his hands.

Then suddenly his ears were filled with a low droning and rumbling, and Walter discovered that he was lying on the floor. And now the little boy he had just been looking down on was towering over him – a huge figure, blocking out the entire ceiling.

A massive hand of unbelievable size reached downwards, getting closer and closer. Then everything went dark and all the sounds disappeared. Light fingers ferreted about on his chest, and it felt ticklish.

Vision is the first.
The last sense of all to die
Is the sense of touch.

---

* 'Speak! Who are you? Who sent you?' (distorted Japanese)
† 'See this?' (Japanese)

OFF WITH HIS HEAD

In the twilight at the end of a long day Asagawa paid a visit to Pier 37, a special police mooring for arrested boats. The *Kappa-maru*, a large fishing schooner arrested on suspicion of smuggling, had been standing there for more than two weeks already – in recent times, junks from Hong Kong and Aomin had taken to roaming the bay. They cruised in neutral waters, waiting for a moonless night, when fast boats could put out from the shore to collect crates of wine, sacks of coffee, bundles of tobacco and woven baskets of opium. The Sakai brothers, who owned the schooner, had been caught and were now in jail, but the inspector had thought of a good use for their little ship.

He examined the hold. Dry and roomy. It was immediately obvious that no fish had been carried in it for a long time. A bit cramped as living space, of course, but never mind, it wasn't for royalty. Ah, but in fact it was – it was for a prince, thought Asagawa, and couldn't help smiling.

The idea he had come up with was this. Take the important witness from the vice-consul, put him in the hold of the *Kappa-maru*, move the boat a long way offshore and drop anchor. Take the rubber and the sail away with him and lock the capstan – so that the prince wouldn't take it into his head to weigh anchor in a morphine haze. Let him bob about on the waves for a day or two: he wouldn't escape, and no one could touch him. But the inspector would have to post a sentry at the mooring – to keep an eye on all the confiscated craft, of course.

It was not late yet, and there were still people about near the mooring, but just before dawn there would be no one here. Everything should go quite smoothly. Once he had made sure that the fishing schooner was in good condition, the inspector went home.

The previous night and the day that followed it had been very eventful. In every man's life there is one moment that is the highest point of his existence. Very often we do not realise this and only understand it retrospectively, when we look back: There, that's it, the reason why I was born. But it's already too late, we can't go back to it and we can't put anything right.

Asagawa, however, was aware that he was living through the supreme moment of his life right now, and he was firmly determined not to disappoint his karma. Who could ever have thought that the son and grandson of ordinary *yoriki* would find himself at the centre of high political drama?

Surely it now depended on him which way Japan would turn, which force would rule the country?

It was not in the inspector's character to brag, but today really was a special day, the kind of day that a man could be proud of. And so he allowed himself to feel just a little pride, although he didn't say anything out loud, of course.

The head of the seaboard precinct of the Yokohama police lived on Nogeh Hill, where he rented a room in the Momoya Hotel, a modest establishment, but very neat and clean. The rent was an insignificant sum and the food was beyond all praise (there was an excellent noodle soup shop on the ground floor), and there was also one other circumstance of some importance for a bachelor.

This circumstance (which was female and went by the name of Emiko) was the owner of the Momoya, who immediately brought his supper to his room in person.

Asagawa, having swapped his tight European clothes for a thin *yukata*, sat on a cushion, watching blissfully as Emiko fussed over the meal, sprinkling dried seaweed powder on the hot noodles and pouring the warmed sake from the little jug. The calico-bound file holding the documents had been concealed under the mattress laid out on the floor.

She did not leave even after the inspector had thanked her and started noisily sucking in the scalding hot *soba*, occasionally picking pieces of his favourite pickled radish out of a separate little bowl with his chopsticks. It was clear from the bloom on Emiko's cheeks and her lowered eyes that she was yearning for his amorous attentions. And even though Asagawa was deadly tired and ought to get at least a little sleep before dawn, to offend a woman was impolite. So, having rounded off his meal with a cup of excellent barley tea, he spoke the words that had a special meaning for the two of them:

'How beautiful you are today.'

Emiko blushed and put her broad hands over her face. She murmured:

'Ah, why do you say such things . . .'

But even as she spoke, she was unfastening the cord with which the belt of her kimono was tied.

'Come here,' said the inspector, reaching out his arms.

'I shouldn't. There are customers waiting,' she babbled in a voice hoarse with passion, and pulled the pins out of her hair one after another.

In her impatience, she didn't even unwind her belt completely. She freed one shoulder and pulled the kimono abruptly over her head in a most ungraceful fashion. He liked her best of all like this. It was a shame that today he was in no state to relax and enjoy love.

'I waited all last night . . .' she whispered, crawling on to the bed on hands and knees.

Asagawa glanced to make sure that the file was not sticking out from under the rather thin futon, and lay down first.

When Emiko lowered herself on to him with a moan, the sharp corner dug into his back quite uncomfortably, but there was nothing to be done, he had to bear it.

After his debt of politeness had been paid and Emiko had flitted on her way, Asagawa grunted as he rubbed the bruise on his back and blew out the lamp. Following a habit unchanged since his childhood, he lay on his side, put his hand under his cheek and fell asleep immediately.

All sorts of different sounds came through the paper partitions: the clamour of customers in the noodle shop, the servant girls slipping up and down the stairs, his neighbour – a rice trader – snoring in the next room. All this noise was quite usual and it did not prevent the inspector from falling asleep, even though he was a light sleeper. When a cockroach fell off the ceiling on to the straw mats, Asagawa opened his eyes immediately, and his hand automatically slid in under the wooden pillow, where he kept his revolver. The inspector was woken a second time by the tinkling lid of the china teapot that he always put beside the head of the bed. An earthquake, but only a very small one, Asagawa realised, and went back to sleep.

But after he was woken for the third time, he was not allowed to go to sleep again.

Something extraordinary was happening in the noodle shop. He heard someone yelling in a blood-curdling voice, furniture smashing and then the owner shrieking:

'Asagawa-san!'

That meant he had to go down – Emiko wouldn't disturb him over anything trivial. It must be the foreign sailors getting rowdy again, like the last time. Just recently they had taken to wandering around the native districts – the drink was cheaper there.

The inspector sighed, got up and pulled on his *yukata*. He didn't take his revolver, there was no need. Instead of a firearm, he grabbed his *jitte* – an iron spike with two curved hooks on its sides. In the old days a *jitte* was used to ward off a blow from a sword, but it was also useful for parrying a knife-thrust, or simply hitting someone over the head. Asagawa was a past master in the use of this weapon.

He didn't leave the file in the room, but stuck it in the back of his belt.

To the inspector's relief, it was not foreigners who were getting unruly, but two Japanese. They looked like ordinary *chimpira* – petty thugs of the lowest kind. Not Yakuza, just loudmouths, but very drunk and aggressively boisterous. The table had been turned over and a few bowls had been broken. The old basket weaver Yoichi, who often stayed until late, had a bloody nose. There weren't any other customers, they must all have run off – all except for a fisherman with a face tanned copper-brown by the wind, sitting in the corner. He wasn't bothered at all, just kept picking up noodles with his little sticks without even looking around.

'This is Asagawa-san, a big police boss! Now you'll answer for all this!'

shouted Emiko, who seemed to have suffered too – her hairstyle had slipped over to one side and her sleeve was torn.

It worked.

One *chimpira*, wearing a red headband, backed away towards the door.

'Don't come near us! We're not from round here! We'll go and you'll never see us again.'

And he pulled out a knife, to stop the policeman from interfering.

'What do you mean, you'll go?' Emiko squealed. 'Who's going to pay? Look at all the crockery you've broken! And the table's cracked right across!'

She threw herself at the bullies with her fists up, absolutely fearless.

But the second brawler, with deep pockmarks on his face, swung his fist wildly and struck her on the ear, and the poor woman collapsed on the floor, unconscious. Old Yoichi pulled his head down and went dashing headlong out of the eatery.

Asagawa would not have let the scoundrels get away in any case but, for Emiko's sake, he decided to teach them a serious lesson.

First of all he ran to the door and blocked the way out, so that they couldn't get away.

The two men glanced at each other. The one with the red headband raised his knife to shoulder level and the pockmarked one pulled out a more serious weapon – a short *wakizashi* sword.

'Right, together!' he shouted, and they both threw themselves at Asagawa at once.

But how could they compete with a master of the *jitte*! He easily knocked the knife-thrust aside with his elbow, grabbed the blade of the sword with his hook, tugged, and the *wakizashi* went flying off into the far corner.

Without wasting so much as an instant, Asagawa smacked the man with the red headband across the wrist, so that he dropped the knife. The pock-marked man retreated to the counter and stood with his back to it. The other *chimpira* cowered against him. They weren't kicking up a racket now, or waving their arms about; both their faces were ashen with fear.

Asagawa walked unhurriedly towards them, brandishing his weapon.

'Before you go off to the station, I'll teach you a lesson in how to behave in decent establishments,' he said, furious at the thought that he had been denied his sleep.

Meanwhile the copper-faced fisherman drank the remains of the broth from his bowl and wiped his mouth on his sleeve. He leaned down, picked up the *wakizashi*, weighed it on his palm and suddenly flung it, without any swing at all.

The blade entered the inspector's back slightly above the calico-bound file.

Asagawa looked round with an angry and bewildered look on his face. He swayed, barely able to stay on his feet.

Then, with the speed of lightning, the *chimpira* in the read headband pulled a short, straight sword out from under his clothes and jerked it from right to left, as easily as if he were batting away a fly: the inspector's head leapt off his shoulders and went rolling merrily across the floor.

For a few seconds,
Already off the shoulders,
The head still lives on

THE PHOTOGRAPH OF HIS WIFE

If you wrote the word 'Bullcox' in the syllabic alphabet, you got five letters: *bu-ru-ko-ku-su*. But in the circle at the centre of the mysterious diagram, there were only two. That, however, did not mean a thing: the Japanese loved to shorten foreign words and names that were too long, leaving just the first two letters. So the letters in the circle should be '*bu-ru*'.

The doctor put the notebook that he had taken out the day before on the desk. It contained his five-year-old notes on the history of the Japanese ninja, including the secret alphabet of this clan of professional assassins, carefully copied out from a certain ancient treatise.

The green lamp shone with a peaceful light and the cosy shadows lay thick in the corners of the study. The house was sleeping. Both his daughters, Beth and Kate, had already said their prayers and gone to bed. Following a long-established custom very dear to Twigs' heart, their father had gone to kiss them before they fell asleep – Beth on the right cheek and Kate on the left.

His elder daughter had turned out a genuine beauty, the very image of his dear departed Jenny, thought Twigs (this same thought visited him every evening when he wished his daughters good night). Kate was still an ugly duckling, and if her big, wide mouth and long nose were anything to go by, she was never going to be a good-looker, but he was less worried about her than her elder sister. Beth was the silent type, all she ever wanted to do was read novels, but Kate was bright and lively, the kind of girl that young men liked. The same thing had happened several times already: Beth acquired some new beau and then, before you could blink, he switched his attentions to the younger sister – she was jollier and easier to be with.

In order to keep their correspondence secret, the medieval ninja did not use the standard hieroglyphs, but a special alphabet, the so-called 'shindai letters', a very ancient form of writing reminiscent of the marks left by a snake crawling across wet sand.

Right, then, let's take a look at how the symbol for '*bu*' is written in these squiggles. There it is.

And now '*ru*'. It looks like this.

But what do we have in the circle? Quite different symbols. The first one looks like three snakes.

And the second one is like a whole knot of snakes.

But wait a moment, good sir! Both of these squiggles are also in the alphabet. The first is the syllable 'to', the second is the syllable 'nu', or simply 'n'.

Hmm. Twigs scratched the bridge of his nose, bemused. What on earth is *tonu*? What has *tonu* got to do with anything? It doesn't add up.

Evidently the writing in the diagram was not simply in the secret alphabet of the ninja, it had been additionally enciphered – each letter signified another one. Well now, that was even more interesting.

The doctor drummed his fingers on the table in keen anticipation of a long and fascinating job.

Forward, sir!

Of all the pleasures granted to man, the very greatest is to exercise his brains.

All right, all right.

We know that Suga uses the letter 'to' to represent 'bu', and the letter 'nu' to represent 'ru'. These letters also occur in other circles: the former three times and the latter once.

So, let us proceed.

He picked up a magnifying glass and inspected the circle more closely What are these tiny little lines above the three snakes? Dirt? No, they're written in ink. They look like a *nigori*, the sign for voicing, which changes the syllable 'ka' to 'ga', 'ta' to 'da', 'sa' to 'za'. That fits: 'bu' is a voiced syllable, there ought to be a *nigori*.

Twigs thoughtfully copied out the circle and the two symbols inside it.

Without any encipherment, it would read as a voiced 'to' (in other words 'do'), plus 'nu' or 'n'.

Hang on now, hang on . . .

The doctor rubbed his bald patch in agitation and half-rose out of his chair. But then, just at the crucial moment, the night bell attached to the wall above his desk started growling quietly. It was Lancelot Twigs' own personal invention – he had had electric wires run from the doorbell to his study and bedroom, so that any late-night patients wouldn't wake the girls.

Feeling highly annoyed, he set off towards the door, but stopped in the corridor before he got there. He mustn't! Mr Asagawa had warned him very strictly: no night visitors, no opening the door for anyone.

'Doctor! Is that you?' a voice said outside. 'Dr Twigs? I saw the plate on your door. Help me, for God's sake!'

It was an agitated, almost tearful male voice with a Japanese accent.

'I'm Jonathan Yamada, senior sales clerk at Simon, Evers and Company. In the name of our Lord Jesus Christ, open up!'

'Why, what's happened?' asked Twigs, without the slightest intention of opening up.

'My wife's gone into labour!'

'But I'm not an obstetrician. You need Dr Buckle, he lives on . . .'

'I know, I was taking my wife to Dr Buckle! But the carriage overturned!

378

Just round the corner here! Doctor, I beg you! She's hurt her head, there's blood! She'll die, Doctor!'

Twigs heard low, muffled sobbing.

If it had been anything else, Lancelot Twigs would probably not have opened the door, for he was a man of his word. But he remembered his poor Jenny and his own helplessness and hopeless despair.

'Just a moment . . . just a moment.'

And he opened the door slightly, without taking it off the chain.

He saw a plump Japanese man in a bowler hat and frock coat, with his trembling face streaming with tears. The man immediately went down on his knees and held his hands up to the doctor.

'I beg you! Come quickly!'

There was no one else in the street.

'You know, I'm not well,' Twigs muttered in embarrassment. 'Dr Albertini, an excellent surgeon, lives on Hommura-dori Street. It's only ten minutes away from here . . .'

'While I run there, my wife will bleed to death! Save her!'

'Ah, what is to be done with you!'

Of course, a man should keep his word, but there was also the Hippocratic oath . . .

He sighed and took the door off the chain.

The senior sales clerk Jonathan Yamada sobbed.

'Thank you! Thank you! Allow me to kiss your hand.'

'Nonsense! Come in. I'll just change my shoes and get my instruments. Wait in the hallway, I'll only be a moment.'

The doctor set off quickly towards his study – to get his bag and conceal the secret diagram. Or would it be best to take it with him? No, that probably wasn't a good idea.

Either the sales clerk didn't hear that he was supposed to wait in the hallway, or he was too agitated to think clearly, but he tagged along after the doctor, babbling all the time about kissing his hand.

'At least allow me to shake your noble hand!'

'Oh, be my guest,' said Twigs, holding out his open right hand and taking hold of the door with his left. 'I have to leave you for just a second . . .'

In his emotional fervour Jonathan Yamada squeezed the doctor's hand with all his might.

'Ow!' Twigs exclaimed. 'That hurts!'

He raised his hand to his eyes. A small drop of blood oozed out of the base of his middle finger.

The sales clerk started fussing again.

'For God's sake, forgive me! I have a ring, an old one, a family heirloom. Sometimes it turns round, it's a bit too big. Did I scratch you? Did I scratch you? Oh, oh! I'm so sorry! Let me bandage it, I have a handkerchief, it's clean!'

'Don't bother, it's nothing,' Twigs said with a frown, licking the wound with his tongue. 'I'll only be a moment. Wait.'

He closed the door behind him, walked across to the desk and staggered – everything had suddenly gone dark. He grabbed the top of the desk with both hands.

The sales clerk had apparently not stayed in the corridor after all, he had come into the study too, and now he was coolly rummaging through the doctor's papers.

Twigs, however, was no longer concerned about Jonathan Yamada's strange behaviour, he was feeling very unwell indeed.

He looked at the photograph of Jenny in a silver frame, standing on the small chest of drawers, and couldn't tear his eyes away.

Lancelot's retouched wife gazed back at him with a trusting, affectionate smile.

Everything changes,
Except for the same old face
In an old photo

DONG, DONG

Erast Petrovich did not sleep for very long, he kept glancing at his watch, and at half-past three he quietly got up. O-Yumi was asleep and he looked at her for half a minute, with an exceptionally powerful feeling that he would have found hard to express in words: never before had the world seemed so fragile and at the same time so durable; it could shatter into glassy fragments at the slightest breath of wind, or it could withstand the onslaught of the most violent hurricane.

The titular counsellor put his boots on in the corridor. Masa was sitting on the floor in front of the cupboard, with his head lowered on to his chest. Fandorin touched him on the shoulder and he jumped to his feet.

'Go and sleep,' Fandorin said in a whisper. '*Neru*. I'll keep watch for a while.'

'*Hai*,' Masa said with a yawn, and set off towards his own room.

Erast Petrovich waited until he heard the sound of peaceful snuffling and smacking lips (he did not have to wait for more than a minute), and paid a visit to the prince.

Onokoji seemed to have made himself rather comfortable in his refuge. The shelves holding Masa's supplies and small household items had been concealed by a blanket, there was a lamp, now extinguished, standing on the floor, and the remains of supper were lying on an empty crate. The prince himself was sleeping serenely, with his thin lips set in a subtle smile – His Excellency was apparently reposing in the delightful embrace of sweet dreams. After O-Yumi, to watch anyone else sleeping, especially an individual as distasteful as this one, seemed blasphemous to Erast Petrovich. Moreover, the source of the wondrous nocturnal visions was not in any doubt – there was an empty syringe glinting beside the pillow.

'Get up,' said Fandorin, shaking the witness by the shoulder. 'Sh-sh-sh-sh. It is I, do not be afraid.'

But the idea of being afraid never entered Onokoji's head. He opened his bleary eyes and smiled even more widely, still under the influence of the narcotic.

'Get up. Get dressed. We're going out.'

'For a walk?' The prince giggled. 'With you, my dear friend – to the ends of the earth.'

As he pulled on his trousers and shoes, he jigged and twirled around, jabbering away without a pause – the vice-consul had to tell him to be quiet.

Fandorin led his disorderly companion out of the building by the elbow. To be on the safe side, he kept his other hand in his pocket, on the butt of his Herstal, but he didn't take the gun out, in order not to frighten the prince.

It was drizzling and there was a smell of fog. As the fresh air started bringing Onokoji to his senses, he glanced round at the empty promenade and asked:

'Where are you taking me?'

'To a safer place,' the titular counsellor explained, and Onokoji immediately calmed down.

'I heard a woman's voice in your apartment,' he said in a sly voice. 'And that voice sounded very familiar. Ve-ry, ve-ry familiar.'

'That's none of your business.'

It was a long walk to the thirty-seventh pier, long enough for the effect of the dope to wear off. The witness stopped jabbering and looked around nervously more and more often, but he didn't ask any more questions. He must have been feeling cold – his shoulders were trembling slightly. Or perhaps the trembling was the result of the drug?

This looked like the place. Fandorin saw the number '37' daubed in white paint on a low *godaun*. A long pier stretched out from the shore into the sea, its beginning lit up by a street lamp, and its far end lost in darkness. Set along it were the black silhouettes of boats, with their mooring cables creaking.

The wooden boards rumbled hollowly under their feet and water splashed somewhere down below. The darkness was not completely impenetrable, for the sky had already begun turning grey in anticipation of dawn.

Eventually the end of the pier came into sight. There was a mast jutting up from a large boat, and Inspector Asagawa in his police uniform, sitting on a bollard: they could see his cap and broad cloak with a hood.

Relieved, Erast Petrovich let go of his companion's elbow and waved to the inspector.

Asagawa waved back. They were only about twenty steps away from the boat now.

Strange, the titular counsellor suddenly thought, why didn't he get up to greet us?

'Stop,' Fandorin said to the prince, and he stopped walking himself.

The seated man got up then, and he turned out to be a lot shorter than Asagawa. Has he sent another policeman instead of coming himself? Erast Petrovich wondered, but his hand was already pulling the revolver out of his pocket: God takes care of those who take care of themselves.

What happened next was quite incredible.

The policeman whipped the cap off his head, dropped the cloak – and *he disappeared*. There was no one under the cloak, just blackness!

The prince cried out in a shrill voice, and even Fandorin was seized by mystical horror. But the next moment the darkness stirred and they saw a figure in black, approaching them rapidly.

A ninja!

With a plaintive howl, Onokoji turned and took to his heels, and the vice-consul flung up his Herstal and fired.

The black figure was not running in a straight line, but in zigzags, squatting down or jumping up as it went, and performing all these manoeuvres with unbelievable speed – too fast for Fandorin to follow it with the barrel of his gun.

A second shot, a third, a fourth, fifth, sixth, seventh. Could every shot really have missed the target? The distance was only fifteen, ten, five paces!

When he was at close quarters with Erast Petrovich, the invisible man leapt high into the air and kicked the Herstal (now entirely useless anyway) out of Fandorin's hand. The revolver rattled across the wooden decking and there, right in front of his face, the vice-consul saw two slanting eyes, like two blazing coals, in the slits of a black mask.

Once seen, those eyes could never be forgotten.

It was him! Him! The snake-charmer, the man with no face! He was alive!

The titular counsellor simply couldn't understand how this was possible; in fact he couldn't understand anything at all any more, but he was determined to sell his life dearly.

He assumed a combat pose, just as he had done with Suga and – hoorah! – succeeded in parrying the first kick with his elbow. Now, according to the science of jujitsu, he should build on his success by moving on to the attack. Erast Petrovich lunged (in a way more suited to boxing), but missed his opponent, who ducked under the fist and straightened up again like a spring, and then Fandorin's feet parted company with the pier. The titular counsellor flew, tumbling over and over in the air, and for as long as this flight lasted, he thought of nothing. And he didn't think at all after he struck his head against the edge of the pier: he saw a flash, heard an extremely unpleasant crunch, and that was all.

But the cold water in which the body of the vanquished vice-consul landed with a loud splash brought him round again. And his first thought (even before he surfaced) was: Why didn't he kill me? Bullcox must have ordered me to be killed!

Blood was streaming down his face, and there was a ringing sound in his ears, but Erast Petrovich was determined not to lose consciousness. He grabbed hold of a slippery beam, clutched at a transverse pile, hauled himself up and managed to scramble on to the pier.

A second thought forced its way through the noise and the fiery circles in front of his eyes. What about the prince? Had he managed to escape? He had had enough time. And if he had escaped, where could the titular counsellor search for him now?

But there was no need to search for the prince. Erast Petrovich realised that when he saw a dark heap lying under the only street lamp in the distance – as if someone had dumped a pile of old rags there.

Fandorin staggered along the pier with his fingers over his bleeding wound. He wasn't thinking about the invisible man, because he knew for certain that if the ninja had wanted to kill him, he would have done.

The high-society playboy was lying face down. A glittering steel star had bitten deep into his neck just above the collar. The titular counsellor pulled it out with his finger and thumb, and blood immediately started seeping from the wound. A throwing weapon, the vice-consul guessed, carefully touching the sharpened edges of the small star. And it appeared to be smeared with something.

Once again he was astounded. Why had the invisible man taken the risk of dodging the bullets? All he had to do was fling this thing and it would have been all over.

He leaned down (the sharp movement set everything around him swaying) and turned the dead man over on to his back.

And he saw that Onokoji was still alive.

There was horror dancing in the open eyes and the trembling lips fumbling at the air.

'*Nan jya? Nan jya?*,' the dying man babbled. ('What happened? What happened?')

He must not have realised yet what disaster had overtaken him. He had been running for grim death, at full tilt, he couldn't see anything around him, and suddenly – a blow to the back of his neck . . .

'It was a ninja. Bullcox sent him,' said Fandorin, fighting his dizziness. 'I'll take you to a doctor. To Dr Twigs.'

But it was obvious that no doctor could help the prince now, his eyes were already rolling up and back.

Suddenly he wrinkled up his face, gathered all his strength and said, slowly but clearly:

'Not Bullcox . . . Don . . .'

'What?'

'Don . . . Tsurumaki.'

That was all. His jaw shuddered and dropped open. Only the whites of his eyes were visible under his half-open eyelids.

The name throbbed in the titular counsellor's bruised head, like the rhythm of a tolling bell: Don-Don-Don . . .

> This is how life sounds
> Ding-ding, tingaling, cuckoo,
> Ending with: dong, dong

A HEADACHE

Fandorin thought he had just lain down on the planking for half an hour to wait for the spell of severe dizziness to pass off, but when he opened his eyes again he discovered that he was in his own bedroom, lying on the bed, completely naked under the blanket, with two heads leaning down over him: both had narrow eyes, but one was round, with hair cut in a short, stiff brush, and the other was long and narrow, with a neat parting. It was Masa and Shirota, both gazing at the titular counsellor with expressions of intense anxiety.

'What ... happened ... to me?' asked Erast Petrovich, struggling to force his dry tongue to pronounce the words.

This simple question provoked an entire discussion in Japanese, after which the two men nodded to each other as if they had come to some arrangement, and the secretary began cautiously:

'At dawn Miss O-Yumi shook your servant awake and told him: "The master is in trouble, I can feel it, let's go, quickly". She ran along the seafront towards the cargo wharfs, with Masahiro following her. He says that as she ran, she kept looking at the moorings. At one of the farthest, already in the native town, she found you lying unconscious, covered in blood.'

Fandorin looked at Masa, who narrowed his eyes conspiratorially. Aha, thought Erast Petrovich, they didn't tell Shirota there was a dead body lying beside me. That's good. But how did O-Yumi know that I was in trouble? And how did she guess that she should look for me on the seafront? What an amazing woman. Where is she?

He looked around, but she wasn't in the room.

'Miss O-Yumi did something – apparently she pressed on some vein – and the bleeding stopped. Then she tore a strip off her dress and bandaged you up. She ordered your servant to carry you home, but she did not come back here. She said that an infusion of some mountain plant was needed urgently – Masahiro did not remember the name. She told him that if you did not drink this infusion, the blood in your head would dry up and become a little stone, and after a while his master could die. Your servant carried you as far as the boundary of the Settlement, and there he was fortunate enough to meet an early riksha ... And this morning the consul ran into your apartment and saw you lying here unconscious with a bandage on your head. He shouted at your servant, called me and sent for the doctor. I went to Mr Twigs, knowing that he is your friend ... And the consul left for Tokyo urgently, to go to the embassy ...'

So many things in this story were unclear, but Fandorin was struck most forcibly of all by Vsevolod Vitalievich's strange behaviour.

'He came running in?'

The punctilious Doronin bursting into his assistant's apartment first thing in the morning? Something really extraordinary must have happened for him to do that.

Shirota faltered and did not answer.

'And what did Dr Twigs say?'

The two Japanese exchanged glances again. And once again there was no answer.

Masa said something in an anxious voice and the secretary translated it.

'You need to lie down and change your compress every hour and you must not worry. Dr Albertini says you have a very serious concussion.'

'Why Albertini and n-not Twigs?'

Another animated discussion in Japanese, this time without any translation.

Erast Petrovich's head really was aching terribly, and he felt nauseous, but all this mystery was beginning to get on his nerves.

Damn the doctors and the consul. There was more important business to deal with.

'*Masa, Asagawa-san koko, hayaku!*'* the titular counsellor ordered.

The servant batted his eyelids and gave Shirota a frightened glance. The secretary cleared his throat in warning.

Erast Petrovich's heart started pounding, beating faster and faster with every second. He jerked upright on the bed and bit his lip to stop himself crying out from the pain.

'Masa, I must get dressed!'

Fandorin returned to the consulate after two in the morning, shattered by the scale of the catastrophe. He would probably have been even more shaken if not for the constant dizziness and spasms of pain that repeatedly transfixed his cranium from temple to temple, imparting an air of unreality to everything that happened, as if it were some appalling nightmare. The horror of it all made it too far-fetched to believe. Things like that didn't happen in waking life.

Inspector Asagawa had been killed by hooligans. And, if the Japanese police could be believed, purely by chance, in a pointless, drunken brawl.

Sergeant Lockston had died of a heart attack in his office.

And an autopsy had shown that a blood vessel had burst in Dr Twigs' brain.

All of this was already highly unlikely, but a coincidence of chance events was possible, in theory – if not for that invisible man, who had killed the witness, and the disappearance of the three clues.

The coded diagram had disappeared from the doctor's study. No oaths

---

* 'Masa, get Asagawa here, quickly!' (distorted Japanese)

written in blood had been discovered on the sergeant's body. And the police knew nothing about any file of reports supposedly in the inspector's possession.

As soon as Fandorin tried to fathom the meaning of this monstrous sequence of events, his dizziness intensified and he was swamped by a wave of nausea. And he simply didn't have the strength to digest and extrapolate on the 'Don Tsurumaki' clue.

But the vice-consul was tormented most of all by O-Yumi's disappearance. Where was she? Would she come back? What was this damned business about a mountain herb?

Gibberish. Insane, crazy gibberish.

Just as Fandorin was approaching the consulate, a two-seater *kuruma* drove up from the direction of Main Street, and out got Doronin, with the navy agent Bukhartsev (what the hell was he doing here?). They spotted the vice-consul walking towards them and stared at him dourly.

'Here he is, the hero,' the lieutenant captain said loudly to Vsevolod Vitalievich. 'You told me he was almost at death's door, but now see how chirpy he looks. If I'd only known, I wouldn't have come, I'd have ordered him to report to Tokyo.'

This beginning boded nothing good, but then, how could there possibly be anything good in all this?

Doronin looked hard into his assistant's face, which was as white as if it had been dusted with chalk.

'How are you feeling? Why did you get up?'

'Thank you, I am p-perfectly all right.'

Fandorin shook hands with the consul, but merely exchanged hostile glances with Bukhartsev, who demonstratively hid his hands behind his back. Well, at the end of the day, they worked in different departments, and they were both on the ninth level of the table of ranks, so no insubordination was involved.

But rank was one thing, and position was quite another, and the sailor immediately demonstrated who was in charge here.

In the consul's office, he occupied the incumbent's place at the desk, without bothering to ask permission. Vsevolod Vitalievich had to take a seat on another chair and Fandorin remained standing – not out of diffidence, but because he was afraid that if he sat down, he would not be able to get up again. He leaned against the wall and crossed his arms.

'Secretary! Hey, whatever your name is ...' the lieutenant captain yelled through the open door. 'Stay close, you might be needed!'

'Yes, sir,' said a voice in the corridor.

Doronin frowned vaguely but said nothing. And Fandorin realised that Bukhartsev had said that to intensify the menace of the situation, as if some rigorous trial were about to begin here and now, and sentence would be pronounced, and it would need to be dictated.

'His Excellency and I have not been able to get anything intelligible out of your superior,' Bukhartsev said in an aggressively assertive tone, fixing

Erast Petrovich with a gimlet-eyed stare. 'Vsevolod Vitalievich merely keeps repeating that he bears responsibility for everything, but he can't explain anything in a way that makes sense. So I have been instructed to conduct an inquiry. You, Fandorin, are to consider yourself answerable to the ambassador in my person. Indeed, even more than that, answerable to the state of Russia.'

The titular counsellor paused slightly before making a slight bow. So be it, to the state.

'Well then, the first matter,' the lieutenant captain continued in the style of a public prosecutor. 'The Japanese police of Yokohama have discovered the body of Prince Onokoji, a member of the very highest levels of society and relative of many influential individuals, near some warehouses.'

'Near some warehouses?' Erast Petrovich thought in surprise, and then recalled his servant's conspiratorial grimace. So, before he carried his unconscious master away from the pier, he had had the wits to move the body somewhere else. Well done, Masa.

'On examination of the papers of the head of the foreign police, following his sudden death, it emerged that the aforementioned Prince Onokoji had been kept under arrest in the municipal jail.' Bukhartsev raised his voice, emphasising every single word now. 'And he had been confined there at the insistence of the Russian vice-consul! What does this mean, Fandorin? Why this arbitrary arrest, and of such an important individual? The whole truth, with no dissimulation! That is the only thing that can mitigate in any way the punishment that awaits you!'

'I am not afraid of punishment,' Erast Petrovich said coolly. 'I will expound the facts as I know them, by all means. Although I must state in advance that I acted entirely at my own discretion and risk, without informing the c-consul.'

The agent snorted incredulously, but he didn't interrupt. With all possible brevity, but also without omitting anything of substance, the titular counsellor recited the entire sequence of events, explained the reasons for his actions and concluded with a recital of the terrible outcome to which these actions had led. He did not attempt to justify his own mistakes, he made no excuses. And the only concession he made to his own vanity was to omit the false trail leading from the intendant to Bullcox. Consul Doronin had also not mentioned the Right Honourable, although he was well aware of the 'British intrigue' theory.

'Your servant is smarter than you are,' the naval agent remarked acidly after listening to the whole story. 'He realised he had to drag the prince's body as far away as possible, otherwise, who knows, the Japanese police might have suspected the Russian vice-consul of murder. To hear you talk, Fandorin, anyone might think you were a genuine patriot of your Fatherland, a heroic partisan, a real Denis Davydov. Only why have you omitted to mention the escapade with Bullcox?'

He knows, Fandorin realised. But it makes no difference now.

'Yes, that was my mistake. I allowed myself to be deceived. You see . . .'

He was going to tell Bukhartsev about the intendant's lie just before he died, but the lieutenant captain interrupted him.

'A "mistake", "deceived". You stupid boy! Creating an incident like that! And all because of a skirt – that is, a kimono! A challenge to a duel from Bullcox – a senior governmental adviser! What a nightmare! A diplomatic scandal!'

At this point the titular counsellor stopped understanding absolutely anything at all – he clutched at the stabbing pain in his temple.

'What ch-challenge? What do you mean?'

'Mstislav Nikolaevich is referring to the challenge that was delivered from Bullcox at eight o'clock this morning,' Doronin explained. 'In view of the fact that you were unconscious, I was obliged to accept it. The document is drawn up in due form, the choice of weapons is yours and there is just one condition: only one of the opponents shall remain alive. No sooner had Bullcox's second left than some men arrived from the native police – concerning Prince Onokoji . . . I was obliged to set out immediately for Tokyo, in order to inform His Excellency.'

Fandorin smiled dourly – here was further confirmation that Bullcox was no conspirator, no master villain lurking in the wings who sent assassins to do his bidding, but an English gentleman, willing to respond to an insult by offering up his breast to the bullet or the sword.

'And still he smiles!' Bukhartsev exclaimed furiously. 'He has disgraced the title of a Russian diplomat and he laughs! And for whom? For some flesh-peddling . . .'

'Hold your tongue!' Fandorin shouted at the lieutenant captain. 'One more word, and you and I will fight a duel to the death!'

'Why, he shouldn't be dismissed the service, he should be put in a madhouse, in a straitjacket!' Mstislav Nikolaevich muttered, but without his former hauteur. He obviously did not wish to fight any duel to the death.

'Gentlemen, gentlemen,' the consul intervened. 'We have common cause here, we need to find a way out of an extremely unpleasant situation. Let us not quarrel! Erast Petrovich, you said that before he died the prince named Don Tsurumaki as the leader of the conspiracy?'

'Yes. But why would an entrepreneur, philanthropist and advocate of progress kill the minister? It doesn't make any sense . . .'

It should, perhaps, be noted that at that particular moment the titular counsellor's head was incapable of making sense of anything much at all, the pain was kneading and squeezing it so fiercely.

'Oh, doesn't it?' Vsevolod Vitalievich said slowly, rubbing his chin, 'Why not? . . . It's actually quite logical. Tsurumaki is a constitutionalist, an advocate of parliamentarianism, which opens up unlimited opportunities for a man like him. Okubo was a classic devotee of enlightened absolutism. From the point of view of our Mr Cloud, the minister was an obstacle on the road to social and economic progress – since you have already brought up the subject of progress. There was nothing personal about it. It's just that the "New Japanese" like our mutual friend have got used to solving their problems in the simplest and most effective way. What could possibly be more effective: remove one piece from the board, and the game is won ... And Tsurumaki has more than enough technical means. Firstly, he has retained his own force of guards from the civil war – the so-called Black Jackets, who serve him with fierce devotion.' (Fandorin recalled the invisible servants in the estate at the Bluff.) 'Secondly, the Don effectively owns the entire shadow economy of Yokohama, with all its low dives and dens of fornication. And that means he has close ties with the criminal world, the Yakuza.' (Yes, yes: the Rakuen, the hunchback, Erast Petrovich thought.) 'And finally, ever since that same revolution, the Don has remained in close contact with the Satsuma samurai, who fought with him against the Shogun.'

The consul fell silent, having evidently exhausted his arguments, but under the influence of his words, the titular counsellor's brain finally began to stir, although only feebly.

Tsurumaki had been well aware of the spying activities and unreliability of his indigent noble house guest. And from his telescope he could observe not only the stars, but also his neighbour's house, which Onokuji often visited at night. The Don was also acquainted with Suga ...

And then the lieutenant captain struck the final blow.

'Hmm. And are you aware, gentlemen, that a few days ago the late, lamented Suga won a quite superb estate from Tsurumaki at cards? The Austrian ambassador told me about it – the game took place at his villa. Is this information of any assistance to you?'

It was remarkable how the naval agent's attitude had changed following the mention of a duel. Instead of arrogance, his prevalent tone was now one of statesmanlike concern for the interests of the Fatherland.

Oh yes, the news communicated by Bukhartsev was very significant indeed. Erast Petrovich clutched his head in his hands and groaned.

Asagawa had been going to find out exactly who had 'lost' the estate to the intendant, only the self-appointed sleuths had got too carried away with their game of cops and robbers. And yet the puzzle had really been perfectly simple all along.

How many disastrous, unforgivable errors they had made!

Now there was not a scrap of evidence left. All three clues had been destroyed. The only witness who knew a lot and was willing to talk had been killed.

Intendant Suga would be buried with full honours. His party would remain in power.

And the secret room behind the police chief's office? Its existence would prove nothing. All it contained was a heap of torn scraps of paper. And Asagawa had made sure to tear the compromising documents into such tiny scraps that they could never be glued back together.

'We have only one trump card left,' the vice-consul declared. 'The Don does not know that we know about him.'

'Not a very strong trump,' Vsevolod Vitalievich said with a shrug. 'And how do we play it?'

Erast Petrovich rubbed his temple and said in a low voice:

'There is one way. It is very risky, of course, but I would try it . . .'

'I don't wish to know anything about it!' the lieutenant captain interrupted hastily, even pretending to put his hands over his ears. 'No details. You created this mess – you can sort it out. You really have nothing to lose. All I can do is delay my report for twenty-four hours. But know this, Fandorin: I shall send that document, not to our genial and benign ambassador, but directly to St Petersburg. Well then, *messieurs consuls*, you have exactly twenty-four hours. Either you present me with a scapegoat on to whom we can shift the blame for everything that has happened or . . . don't hold me responsible for the consequences.' Mstislav Nikolaevich paused significantly and addressed Fandorin directly. 'Only remember this: no duels with Bullcox!'

'But how can I refuse? It's d-dishonourable!'

'I can't even tell what would be the greater disaster, with Russo-British relations in their present overheated state: if you kill Bullcox or if he kills you.' Mstislav Nikolaevich pondered for a moment, but then shrugged. 'No, it's out of the question. When what's at stake is the honour of the entire country, Fandorin, one must be willing to sacrifice one's personal honour.'

The titular counsellor glowered at the naval agent.

'Personal honour, Lieutenant Captain, must not be sacrificed for any motives whatever.'

And once again, faced with a rebuff, Bukhartsev softened his tone, abandoning high principle for hearty sincerity.

'Oh, please, drop that, Erast Petrovich. What are all our petty vanities and ambitions in the face of History? And that is precisely what you and I are dealing with here. We stand in the front line of the whole of European culture. Oh, yes, don't be so surprised. I have been thinking about this a lot just recently. The other day I argued with you, Vsevolod Vitalievich, and I laughed at the Japanese military threat. But I had a good think about it afterwards, and I admit that you were right, a hundred times right. Only we need to take a broader view. It's not just a matter of little Japan. Soon a new Genghis Khan will advance against Europe. The giant of China will begin to stir, preparing to awaken. When that yellow wave rises, its crest will reach up to the heavens, drawing all the Koreas and Mongolias after it, and perched high on its foaming peak will be an impudent little island empire with a predatory nobility and an avaricious *nouveau riche bourgeoisie*!' Mstislav Nikolaevich's voice resounded prophetically, his eyes glowed with fire – the lieutenant captain was no doubt already picturing himself pronouncing this speech to the supreme statesmen of the empire. 'The New Mongolism or the Yellow Peril – that is what I shall call it. Millions upon millions of ferocious, yellow-faced Asians with slanty eyes and bandy legs will flood into the peaceful expanses of the Old World in that unstoppable wave. And once again we, the Slavs, will find ourselves in the path of this Chinese giant with a Japanese head . . . That is what you should be thinking about, Erast Petrovich, not your lordly personal honour.'

Having delivered this supremely worthy speech in a superlative tone of comradely reproach, the lieutenant captain left without adding anything more, in order not to spoil the effect. He simply got up, nodded in military style, pronounced a single word ('Gentlemen') and proceeded to the door.

Doronin stood up but didn't move from the spot.

'Shirota will see you out,' he said quietly.

And a little later, when the agent was already outside the gates, he added with feeling:

'Why, the scoundrrrel! And he was lying anyway. He won't wait for any twenty-four hours. He'll scribble out his telltale tittle-tattle right now, in the train. Then he'll send it directly to the ministry, with a copy to the Third Section. And to prevent it looking like any ordinary denunciation, he'll put in all that gibberish about the Yellow Peril that he just rehearsed in front of us. And the most sickening thing of all is that everyone in St Petersburg will be most favourably impressed.' The consul lowered himself wearily into an armchair. 'They'll shove me into retirement, at the very least . . . Well, to hell with my career, I can live without it. But I won't go back to Russia. I'll have myself naturalised and become Japanese, eh? What do you think of that idea?' And he laughed, as if making it clear that he was, of course, joking.

The titular counsellor had no thoughts at all on that count; there were already plenty of other problems for his poor, broken head to puzzle over.

'So the main *akunin* in this business is Don Tsurumaki?' he muttered, as if to himself.

'What did you say? *Akunin*?'

'Why, yes, the villain of the piece. It has been explained to me that Japanese villains are a special kind, unlike any others. That is, of course, they are appalling monsters too, but with p-principles and a certain nobility about them. Or something of that kind.'

Vsevolod Vitalievich chuckled.

'Japan, a country of noble villains? Perhaps. Tsurumaki at least is a classic *akunin*.'

'I'm not so sure . . . you see, I know the man quite well.' Fandorin did not go into the details. 'He . . . he doesn't seem like a sly schemer. And then, should we put so much faith in the testimony of a dying man? I made that mistake once already by believing Suga. And now it's clear that in his final moments of life the only thing on his mind was how to send us off on a false trail.'

'Onokoji is not Suga. The intendant was a strong, resilient individual who was not afraid of death. But your effete Japanese decadent does not fit into the category of *akunin* at all.'

They fell silent, this time both thinking about the same thing.

Unable to come up with any ideas, the consul looked at his assistant, who kept clutching at his temple.

'You said that you saw some risky way of doing something, but what exactly?'

'Proving Don Tsurumaki's cunning villainy to ourselves. Or his innocence.'

'But how do we do that?'

'I have been challenged to a duel. So I shall require a second, shan't I?' Erast Petrovich tried to smile, but instead his face merely contorted in a new spasm of pain.

My most faithful friend,
Back here with me once again,
My own dear headache

A QUIET VOICE

That evening there was another meeting in the same office, with the list of attendees slightly altered. The naval agent was not present, but Vsevolod Vitalievich had invited Shirota instead – no doubt in compensation for his humiliating wait in the corridor.

The Japanese, however, seemed thoughtful, rather than offended, as if his mind was wandering somewhere far, far away. But the remarks that he interpolated from time to time made it clear that he had listened to the vice-consul's story no less attentively than Doronin.

The vice-consul had returned from Don Tsurumaki's, still not having resolved his doubts.

'Since we have no proof of this man's guilt, I have b-based the operation exclusively on psychological factors,' the pale green Erast Petrovich explained rather slowly – either because he was not feeling well, or because he wished to analyse his talk with the suspect once again. 'In brief, I tried to frighten Tsurumaki and at the same time suggest a way for him to avoid the danger.'

Frighten Don Tsurumaki?' the secretary repeated, shaking his head dubiously, as if Fandorin had said something absurd.

'Well, rather, make it clear that he is in danger. To that end, I pretended to be in a state of shock at the news of recent sad events (to be quite honest, I didn't really have to pretend) and spoke to him quite candidly, as a friend.' The vice-consul laughed bitterly. 'He and I are f-friends ... I told him that all this time I had been leading an independent investigation into the assassination of Okubo. That I regarded Bullcox as the prime suspect, as the representative of the power most interested in having the minister removed. Nor did I forget to mention my helpers and our valuable witness, Prince Onokoji, who is well known to the Don. As you can see, all this is quite close to the truth. But beyond that I permitted myself a certain degree of improvisation. In relating the final moments of the dying witness, I modified his final words. I said that what Onokoji whispered as he gave up the ghost was this: "It wasn't Bullcox, I deceived you. It was my ... " – and he died before he could finish. Then I mused out loud at considerable length about who the poor prince could have meant. I asked the Don's opinion – after all, he knew the dead man and his circle of acquaintances very well. My who? Brother? Cousin? Uncle? Tsurumaki responded rather uneasily, he told me: "The Prince didn't have any brothers. But he has any number of cousins once removed and twice removed, and many of them hold important positions. Which one of them did he mean?" He mentioned one, then a second, and a third. And then I launched the following attack. Thinking out loud, I asked: "But what if he didn't mean a relative? My former servant? My friend?" I thought the Don looked wary at that, but I could be mistaken . . . I pretended to drop the subject. I said: "But I haven't come see you just about that." I told him about the challenge to a duel, and said I needed a second. "This is a serious request, and I can only ask a friend . . . " '

Erast Petrovich recalled how Tsurumaki had smiled at those words, as if flattered, but the vice-consul's memory immediately threw up what the millionaire had once said about Bullcox: 'Surely you know, my dear Fandorin-san, that one of the greatest pleasures is the feeling of secret superiority over someone who thinks he is better than you'.

'The time had come to show some emotion – nobody really expects that from such a reserved individual as yours truly. Which only makes the impression all the stronger. "I have no one else I can turn to," I said mournfully. "The consul won't do, because I have been forbidden to fight a duel by our superiors. And all my friends – Dr Twigs, Sergeant Lockston and Inspector Asagawa – have been treacherously murdered. Yes, yes, murdered, I am absolutely certain of it! It was those accursed ninja who did it! But they are only the agents of the man Onokoji tried to tell me about. I swear I shall find him, no matter what it may cost me! I'll identify everyone with whom Onokoji had any connections at all! It's someone very c-close to him, otherwise he would not have referred to that person as 'my'!" And I carried on ranting about the same subject for another five minutes, to make sure that Tsurumaki was appropriately impressed. After all, it's so simple – "my benefactor" or "my patron". I may not have thought of it today, but surely I'm certain to think of it tomorrow. If the Don is guilty, he cannot help but be alarmed by that.'

Erast Petrovich thought back, trying to recall the expression with which the millionaire had listened to his ranting. Tsurumaki's bearded face had been intent and serious, his thick brows knitted together. Was that circumspection or merely normal sympathy for a friend? The devil only knew.

'Then I took a grip on myself and started talking more calmly. "You know, my dear friend, if this challenge had arrived yesterday, I would have killed Bullcox with no hesitation – not because of the woman, but for all his supposed atrocities. But now it turns out that I was mistaken and he hasn't committed any particular atrocities at all. Bullcox is merely a party whom I have offended and, in his own way, he is perfectly right. I burst into his house, started a f-fight, abducted the woman he loves . . . No, I don't want to kill him, I have no right to do it. But I don't want to be killed either. I'm young, I'm blessed with love. Why should I die? So, this is the essence of my request. Be my second and help me set the conditions for the duel so that I shall not have to kill or be killed – naturally, without any damage to my honour. I have tried to think of something myself, but my head is not working very well". And that was no lie, gentlemen, of that you can be quite certain.' The titular counsellor pressed his hands against his temples, closed his eyes and allowed himself to pause for a moment. 'As you can see, my ploy is very simple. If the Don is the individual I am looking for, he is certain to seize such a convenient opportunity to use someone else to rid him of an irksome and dangerous investigator. He thought it over for a long time, I waited patiently . . .'

'And what happened?' Doronin blurted out eagerly. 'Is he guilty or not?'

'I think not. But judge for yourselves. Tsurumaki asked: "Are you good with a sword?" I replied: "Middling. As a youth I was enthusiastic and even became the best swordsman in my grammar school, but then I gave it up. I'm a much better shot." He said: "Firearms are far too deadly, better cold steel. If you know how to hold a sword, that is quite enough. I shall go to Bullcox and tell him that the choice has been made. He can't reject it and he can't refuse to fight. But the fact is that quite recently he fell from a horse and broke his wrist. And now that wrist has entirely lost it flexibility". I told him: "No, not for the world! That is base and ignoble!" And the Don replied: "It would be ignoble if you intended to run Bullcox through. But you will simply knock the sword out of his hand, set your blade to his throat and in that advantageous position you will offer your apologies for invading his home – and only for that. I shall take care that the public finds out about the duel, so there will be quite enough witnesses. After you disarm the Englishman in the presence of an audience and then spare him, he won't be able to challenge you again". That is the plan invented by Tsurumaki. It has a certain air of oriental guile about it, but I think it is quite ingenious in its own way. So it would seem that Onokoji lied. The Don is innocent.'

'He is guilty, as guilty as can be!' Vsevolod Vitalievich exclaimed vehemently. 'Bravo, Fandorin, you have succeeded in exposing the Don's true colours! He has deceived you. Firstly, somehow I don't recall Bullcox walking around with his arm in a sling at any time recently. And secondly, he is an excellent swordsman, which your "dear friend" omitted to mention, aware that you have not been in Yokohama very long and could not know about that. I remember that last year at the Atlantic Club there was a competition between European and Japanese swordsmen. The Europeans fought with a blunted sword, a rapier or a spadroon, according to their choice, and the Japanese fought with bamboo swords. Our side suffered a crushing defeat. The only one who came up to the mark was Bullcox. In the final bout he held out against the finest of the native swordsmen. And do you know who that was?'

'Tsurumaki Donjiro,' Shirota whispered. 'Yes, I remember. It was a splendid fight!'

'You have played your part capitally, Erast Petrovich. He believed that you were acting in secret from me, so there was no one from whom you could learn the truth.'

'Then Onokoji wasn't lying. *Quod erat d-demonstrandum*,' the titular counsellor summed up with satisfaction. 'That is, the garnering of evidence still lies ahead of us, but we know the correct answer to the problem in advance.'

'What do you intend to do? Have the time and place for the duel been named?'

'Yes. Tsurumaki went straight from me to Bullcox and came back half an hour later with the message that the duel will take place tomorrow at eight in the morning on Kitamura Hill, above the Bluff.'

'And are you going to walk straight into this trap?'

'Naturally. Don't worry, Vsevolod Vitalievich, this time I have a reserve plan. Perhaps we won't need to gather any evidence after all.'

'But what if he kills you?'

Fandorin twitched one shoulder nonchalantly – as if to say: The plan does not envisage that outcome.

'It will be a very beautiful death,' Shirota said suddenly, blushing bright red for some reason.

It looks as if this occasion will be my chance to become a 'sincere man', thought Erast Petrovich, noticing the secretary's eyes blazing with excitement. Perhaps another portrait would soon be added to those of Marshal Saigo and Alexander Sergeevich Pushkin . . .

'I'm sorry, gentlemen. I'm feeling a bit tired. I'll go and lie d-down for a while . . .'

He walked out, trying not to stagger, but in the corridor he was obliged to lean against the wall, and no sooner had he stepped inside the door of his apartment than he felt the floor turn into something like the deck of a ship. The deck swayed to the right, then heaved to the left, and eventually slipped out from under his feet altogether. Erast Petrovich fell.

He must have lost consciousness for a while, because when he opened his eyes he was lying in bed, and Masa was applying something cold to his forehead. The sensation was inexpressibly pleasant. Fandorin thanked him: 'Arigato' – and tumbled into oblivion again.

Asagawa and Dr Twigs came. Sergeant Lockston was peering over their shoulders, wearing a broad-brimmed hat instead of his uniform cap. They gazed at Fandorin lying there and said nothing, just glanced at each other.

And then they were replaced by another vision, a sweet one – O-Yumi. Her face was not as beautiful as in waking life – it was pale, haggard and sad, and her unkempt hair hung down on to her cheeks, but Fandorin was still absolutely delighted.

'It doesn't matter that you're not very beautiful,' he said. 'Only, please, don't disappear.'

She smiled briefly, just for a moment, and turned serious again.

The pillow on which the sick man's head was resting suddenly rose up all on its own and a cup appeared in front of Fandorin's lips.

'Drink, drink,' a sweet voice murmured and, of course, Erast Petrovich drank.

The potion was bitter and pungent, but he looked at the slim hand holding the cup and that helped.

'That's good, and now sleep.'

The pillow sank back down.

'Where were you?' asked Fandorin, only now realising that he hadn't imagined O-Yumi. 'I wanted to see you so much!'

'A long way away. On the mountain where the magical herb grows. Sleep. Tomorrow your head will hurt even more. That will be the blood vessels purging themselves. You must bear it. And at midday I'll give you another infusion, and then the pain will pass off, and the danger will be over. Go to sleep. Have a good, sound sleep. I won't go away until you wake up . . .'

Then I must not wake up for as long as possible, he thought. What could be better than lying here, listening to that quiet voice?

> Never in the day,
> Only at night do I hear
> Your sweet, quiet voice

A DRAGONFLY'S RAINBOW WINGS

Fandorin woke up soon after dawn, suffering from an agonising migraine. The day before it had been a dull pain, sweeping over him in waves, but now it was as if someone had inserted a large screw into his temple and they kept turning it, turning it. Even though it was already in right up to its head and could go no farther, some implacable force still kept on tightening that screw, and he felt as if his cranium would give way and crack open at any moment.

But even worse was the fact that O-Yumi had disappeared again. When Erast Petrovich opened his eyes, the only person he saw beside the bed was Masa, holding a small basin of ice and a wet towel at the ready. The mistress went away, he explained as best as he could. Before midnight. She put on her cloak and left. She said she would be back and ordered me to prepare ice.

Where had she gone? Why? And would she come back?

His thoughts were agonising. Thanks to them and the icy compresses, he managed to forget about the screw for a while.

His second arrived at half past seven, dressed as befitted the solemn occasion – in a black frock coat, black trousers and a top hat instead of his customary fez. The top hat did not suit the Don's plump-cheeked face.

The titular counsellor had been ready for some time. His agonised face was as white as his shirt, but his tie was knotted neatly, the parting in his hair glinted sleekly and the ends of his moustache were the very model of symmetry.

Not being entirely convinced of his valet's acting ability, Erast Petrovich had not explained to him that Tsurumaki had been identified as the major *akunin*, so Masa greeted the Don with every possible politeness. And the servant was also not aware, thank God, of the purpose of this morning visit, otherwise he would quite certainly have tagged along after his master. He was told to stay at home and wait for O-Yumi to arrive.

They got into a carriage and set off.

'Everything has been done as planned,' the Don informed Fandorin in a conspiratorial voice. 'The rumour has been circulated. It's a convenient spot for people to spy on events. There will be witnesses, have no doubt about that.'

It was depressing to look at the villain's ruddy, smiling face, but the titular counsellor made an effort and forced himself to thank Tsurumaki and talk about the weather, which was simply wonderful for the rainy season: overcast but dry, with a sea breeze.

The carriage drove higher and higher along the main road. The seafront and the prim residences of the Bluff had been left behind now, and on all sides there were hills, bushes and sandy paths for healthy walks.

'They're here already,' said Tsurumaki.

Three black figures were standing off to one side of the road, in a round open space surrounded on three sides by thick undergrowth. One of the men removed his hat to wipe his forehead with a handkerchief – from the red locks, Fandorin recognised Bullcox. The second man was wearing a scarlet uniform with a sword, and holding a long bundle under his arm. The third had a Gladstone bag between his feet. No doubt a doctor.

'Aha, and there is the public.' The Japanese chuckled contentedly. 'We have a full house.'

The spot certainly had been well chosen. Although the bushes might appear to conceal the sparring area from prying eyes, the impression of privacy was deceptive. A cliff rose up right above the open space, its top also overgrown with some kind of vegetation, and protruding from the greenery were top hats and bowler hats, and even a couple of ladies' white umbrellas. If the sun had peeped out from behind the clouds, no doubt there would also have been the glinting of opera glasses.

The public will be disappointed, thought Fandorin, stepping across the grass, which was wet with dew.

Bullcox's second nodded curtly and introduced himself – Major Ruskin. He also named the doctor – Dr Stein.

'I have something important to say to Mr Bullcox,' the titular counsellor said when the major unrolled the piece of silk wrapped around two swords.

The reserve plan was absolutely elementary. Ask Bullcox whether he had broken his wrist recently. Bullcox would say no, he hadn't. Then expose Tsurumaki publicly, in front of witnesses. Starting with the base deception unworthy of a second, then immediately moving on to the most important part – the accusation of conspiring against Okubo. There was no proof, but the treachery shown by Tsurumaki would set the witnesses against the Japanese and make them hear the vice-consul out. Bullcox might be beside himself with jealousy, but he was a state official and would understand quite clearly the significance of the vice-consul's declaration. Tsurumaki had not only organised a political assassination, he had attempted to cast suspicion on Britain and its representative. That which was hidden would be revealed, and Bullcox wouldn't be interested in a duel any more. The audience was in for a disappointment.

If not for his headache and his anxiety about O-Yumi, the titular counsellor would undoubtedly have contrived something more serviceable. The reserve plan, the frail child of a migraine, proved to be no good for anything and crumbled to dust at the very first contact with reality.

'The Right Honourable Algernon Bullcox warned me that you were capable of something like this,' Ruskin replied with a frown. 'No, no. No apologies. The duel will go ahead in any case.'

'I do not intend to apologise,' the vice-consul assured him coldly. 'This is a m-matter of state importance.'

The major's face set in an expression of dull-witted intransigence.

'I have received clear instructions. No negotiations between the two opponents. Would you care to choose a sword?'

'Hey, Ruskin, why are you dragging things out over there?' Bullcox shouted irritably.

'I have been informed that your friend recently suffered a fracture of the right wrist,' Fandorin told the second hastily, starting to feel anxious. 'If that is so, a duel with swords cannot take place. That is actually what I intended . . .'

The Englishman interrupted disdainfully:

'Rubbish. Algernon has never broken his arm. That trick won't work. I'd been told there were not many gentlemen among the Russians, but everything has its limits!'

'After Bullcox, I'll deal with you,' the titular counsellor promised. 'And I'll hammer those words back into your cast-iron head.'

This shameful outburst by Fandorin can only be explained by his annoyance with himself – Erast Petrovich was already beginning to realise that nothing would come of his plan. He only had to look at Tsurumaki, who was making no attempt to conceal his smirk of triumph. Could he have guessed about the plan? And now, of course, he was quite sure that the Russian had lost.

But there was still one hope left – to tell Bullcox everything when they stood face to face. Without looking, the vice-consul took hold of one of the swords by its leather-covered hilt. He dropped his cloak on the ground, leaving himself in just his shirt.

The major drew his sabre.

'Assume your positions. Cross swords. Commence at my blow. The conditions state that fighting continues as long as one of the opponents is capable of holding a weapon. Go!'

He rapped his sabre against the crossed swords with a clang and jumped aside.

'I have something I must tell you.' Fandorin began rapidly in a low voice, so that the seconds would not overhear and interfere.

'Hah!' the Right Honourable gasped instead of answering, and launched a furious barrage of blows at his opponent.

Barely able to defend himself, the vice-consul was obliged to retreat.

There were exclamations above his head, the sound of applause; a woman's voice shouted, 'Bravo!'

'Just wait, will you! We'll have plenty of time to fight! You and I have been the victims of a political intrigue.'

'I'll kill you! I'll kill you! Only not straight away. First I'll neuter you, like a ram,' Bullcox wheezed, then slid his blade along Fandorin's sword and made a thrust straight for his crotch.

By some miracle Erast Petrovich managed to dodge. He fell, jumped to his feet and assumed a defensive stance again.

'You idiot!' he hissed. 'This concerns the honour of Britain.'

But looking into the Right Honourable's bloodshot eyes, he realised that the other man simply couldn't hear him, and just at this moment he couldn't care less for the honour of Britain, or for any matters of state importance. What did Okubo and devious plots have to do with this? This was an event as old as the world itself, a battle between two males over a female, there was nothing in the world more urgent and remorseless than this battle. The clever Don had understood that from the beginning. He knew there was no power capable of placating the bloodlust that seizes the abandoned lover.

And the titular counsellor felt afraid.

From the way Bullcox attacked and the assuredness with which he parried the clumsy thrusts of the former provincial grammar-school champion, the outcome of the duel was clearly a foregone conclusion. The Englishman could have killed his opponent many times over, there was only one thing stopping him: he was absolutely determined to carry out his threat and kept directing all his attacks exclusively at Fandorin's loins. To some degree this simplified the task of his weaker opponent, who only had to concentrate on defending one area of his body, but the resistance could not continue for long. His wrist, unaccustomed to swordplay, turned numb, and parrying blows became harder and harder. Erast Petrovich repeatedly fell, unable to retain his balance, and Bullcox waited for him to get up. Twice he had to beat off a thrust that had pierced his defences with his bare left hand, and once the tip of the blade furrowed his thigh as Fandorin barely managed to wrench himself out of the way.

His shirt was black from dirt and green from grass stains, there were red blotches spreading on his sleeves and blood was flowing down one of his legs.

In his despair the titular counsellor was struck by a comforting idea – since all was lost, why not run over to the Don and slash his fat belly open in farewell?

The vice-consul had long ago abandoned his attempts to bring Bullcox to his senses. He was saving his breath, his eyes fixed on only one point – his opponent's slashing sword. He didn't try to counter-attack, there was no question of that. He could only fend off steel with steel and, if that didn't work, with his arm.

It was becoming clear, however, that the Englishman did not run in circles round the cricket field every morning, or stretch a chest-expander, or raise heavy weights. For all his subtle skill and dexterity, Bullcox was beginning to tire. The sweat was streaming down his crimson face, his fiery curls were glued together, his movements were becoming more economical.

And then he stopped and wiped his sweat away with his sleeve in a most unaristocratic manner. He hissed:

'All right, damn you. Die as a man.'

This was followed by a furious onslaught that drove Erast Petrovich into a corner of the open area, right up against the bushes. A series of lunges was followed by a mighty, slashing blow. This time too, Fandorin managed to jump back in time, but that was what the attacker was counting on; the vice-consul's heel struck a projecting root and he fell flat on his back. The audience on high gasped, seeing that this time the Right Honourable was not going to allow his opponent to get up – the performance had reached its climax.

Bullcox had already pressed Fandorin's right hand down with his foot and raised his sword to pin the Russian to the ground, when he suddenly started pondering, or perhaps even daydreaming; his eyelids closed halfway, while his mouth, on the contrary, fell half open. With this strange expression on his face the Right Honourable swayed to and fro for a second or two, them went limp and collapsed directly on to the panting Erast Petrovich.

A startled dragonfly soared up out of the grass in a flutter of little rainbow wings.

> They are just the same
> As those of angels and elves –
> A dragonfly's wings

A BLUE STAR

How greatly everything had changed compared with the night before! The world had not ceased to be dangerous. On the contrary, it had become even more unpredictable and predatory. From somewhere out there in the gloom – Fandorin knew this for certain – the keen eyes of a man with cold serpent's blood were watching him relentlessly. But even so, life was beautiful.

Erast Petrovich sat in the darkness, with the peak of his uniform cap pulled down over his eyes, waiting for the agreed signal. The tip of his cigar glowed brightly in the dark – it must be visible from any of the roofs nearby.

The titular counsellor was in a state of bliss that flooded body, heart and mind.

His body – because the migraine had passed off and his cuts and bruises were not aching or stinging at all. When the bleeding duellist was brought home, the first to run out to meet him had been O-Yumi. She wouldn't allow Doronin to call a doctor and dealt with the injured man herself. She smeared something smelly on the slashes on his arms and thigh – and the bleeding instantly stopped. Then she gave Erast Petrovich a herbal infusion to drink – and a tight steel band seemed to fall away from round his head. Fandorin shook his head and batted his eyelids and even smacked himself on the temple, but there was no nausea, or pain, or dizziness at all. And what was more, the tiredness had also disappeared. His muscles were supple and taut, rippling with strength, he could have taken up his sword again – and who could tell who would have come off best this time? This magical new-found lightness in all his limbs had not faded during the day; in fact the feeling had grown stronger. And that was very apropos – the night ahead promised to be stormy.

Bliss filled his heart because O-Yumi was sleeping in the next room. And when all was said and done, wasn't that the most important thing?

Bliss filled his mind because once again Erast Petrovich had a plan, and this time a real one, thoroughly thought through and prepared, unlike that recent bastard mongrel of a plan created by a sick brain, which had almost cost him his life. It was simply miraculous that he had survived!

When the victorious Bullcox collapsed on his vanquished foe, none of the spectators could understand what had happened, let alone Fandorin, who had already prepared himself for death. He pushed off the Englishman's heavy carcass and wiped down his forehead (which was streaming with cold sweat) with his hand (which was streaming with hot blood). The Right Honourable lay there face down with his hand flung out, still clutching the hilt of his sword.

The doctor and seconds were already running towards the men on the ground.

'Are you seriously hurt?' shouted Dr Stein, squatting down on his haunches.

Without waiting for an answer, he hastily ran his hands over the vice-consul, waved his hand dismissively at the cuts ('That can wait') and turned to Bullcox.

He took his pulse, raised his eyelid and whistled.

'Apoplexy. A man can't do all this jumping and jigging about with blood as congested as that! Mr Tsurumaki, your carriage is the most spacious. Will you take him home? I'll come with you.'

'Of course I'll take him, he's my neighbour,' said the Don, making a show of taking the Right Honourable under the arms and avoiding looking at Fandorin.

Erast Petrovich was taken to the consulate by Major Ruskin, who was no less pale than the vice-consul. He was courteous and attentive, and apologised for his rudeness, which had been the consequence of a misunderstanding – he was obviously seriously concerned about the safety of his 'cast-iron head'. But the major was the last thing on the titular counsellor's mind. The young man was shaking all over – not in relief and not from overworked nerves. Fandorin was simply overwhelmed by the evident prejudice of fate, which had saved him yet again, come to his assistance in a quite desperate, hopeless situation. He could hardly believe that Bullcox had suffered a stroke at precisely the moment when his vanquished foe had only a second left to live! No doubt the sceptics would find rational explanations for this, say that the vengeful anticipation of the Englishman, who was already panting and short of breath, had sent the blood rushing to his head, and a blood vessel had burst in his brain. But Erast Petrovich himself knew that he had been saved once again by his lucky star, also known as Destiny. But for what purpose? And how long would this go on?

The entire population of the consulate had assembled at the bedside of the bloodied victim: Vsevolod Vitalievich, turned completely yellow in his grief, with Obayasi-san; and Shirota, chewing on his lips; and Sophia Diogenovna, sobbing; and even the servant Natsuko, who actually spent most of the time ogling Masa. It was a touching picture, almost harrowing in fact – an impression facilitated in no small part by the spinster Blagolepova, who appealed to everyone to send for the priest from the frigate *Governor*, 'before it's too late', but O-Yumi performed her magical manipulations and the man pretending to be at death's door returned miraculously to life. He sat up on the bed, then got up and walked round the room. And finally he declared that he felt hungry, dammit.

At this point it emerged that no one in the embassy had taken breakfast yet – everyone had known about the duel and been so worried about Erast

Petrovich that they couldn't eat a single bite. A table was hastily laid, right there in Doronin's office – for a confidential strategic discussion.

They spoke about the duel for a while, and then turned their attention to Don Tsurumaki. The titular counsellor's reawakened reason was eager for rehabilitation. The plan came together instantly, over roast beef and fried eggs.

'He is certain that I am lying flat on my back and will not get up any time soon, so he is not expecting a visit from me. That is one,' said Fandorin, brandishing a fork. 'He doesn't have any guards at the villa, he told me many times that he is not afraid of anyone. That is two. I still have a key to the gates, that is three. The conclusion? Tonight I shall pay him a visit *à l'anglais*,* that is to say, uninvited.'

'The purpose?' asked Doronin, narrowing his eyes.

'We'll have a little friendly chat. I think the Don and I can find a thing or two to talk about.'

The consul shook his head.

'Are you thinking of trying to frighten him? You've had plenty of opportunity to realise that the Japanese *akunin* is not afraid of death. And you're not going to kill him anyway.'

Erast Petrovich wiped his lips with a napkin, sipped his red wine and took a slice of Philippine pineapple. It was a long time, a very long time, since he had eaten with such a good appetite.

'Why should I want to frighten him? He's not some nervous young damsel, and I'm not a g-ghost. No, gentlemen, it will not be like that at all. Shirota, may I count on your assistance?'

The secretary nodded, keeping his eyes fixed on the vice-consul.

'Excellent. Don't be alarmed, you won't have to do anything against the law. Masa and I will enter the house. Your job, starting in the evening, is to sit on the hill that overlooks the estate. It is an excellent observation point, and it can also be seen from here. As soon as the lights go out in the house, you will signal. Can you find a coloured lantern?'

'Yes, there are some left over from the New Year. A green one, a red one and a blue one.'

'Let it be the blue one. Flash three times, several times in succession. Masa will be watching for the signal on the porch.'

'Is that all?' Shirota asked disappointedly. 'Just give the signal when the lights go out in the house?'

'That's all. They put the lights out there when the servants leave. I take responsibility for everything after that.'

Vsevolod Vitalievich was indignant.

'How you love an air of mystery! Well, all right, you get into the house, and then what?'

Erast Petrovich smiled.

'The Don has a secret safe. That is one. I know where it is, in the library,

---

* In the English style (French)

behind the bookshelves. That is two. I also know where to find the key to the safe – hanging round the Don's neck. That is three. I do not intend to frighten Tsurumaki, I shall only borrow his key and take a look at what is in the safe, and in the meantime Masa will keep our hospitable host in his sights.'

'Do you know what he has in the safe?' asked Doronin.

'No, but I can guess. Tsurumaki told me once that he keeps gold bars in it. I'm sure he was lying. No, there is something more valuable than gold in there. For instance, a certain diagram with serpentine symbols. Or there may possibly be even more interesting documents to be found . . .'

At this point the consul did something very strange: he grabbed his blue spectacles off his nose and started blinking at the bright light. His mouth started twitching and twisting, living a life of its own. He sank his teeth into his thin lip.

'Even if you do find something important, you won't be able to read it,' Vsevolod Vitalievich said in a flat voice. 'You don't know Japanese. And your servant won't be much use to you. I tell you what . . .' He faltered, but only for a second, and then went on in a perfectly firm voice. 'I tell you what, I'll go with you. In the interests of the cause. I'm tired of being a spectator. It's a shameful and depressing pastime.'

Erast Petrovich knew that even the slightest show of astonishment would seriously wound the consul's feelings, so he took his time before answering, as if he was thinking over the advisability of the suggestion.

'In the interests of the cause, it would be better if you stayed here. If my little excursion ends badly, than what more can they do to me – a young pup, a duellist and adventurer? The lieutenant captain has already written me off. Things stand differently with you – a pillar of Yokohama society and Consul of the Russian Empire.'

Vsevolod Vitalievich's eyebrows arched up like angry leeches, but at this point Shirota intervened in the conversation.

'I'll go,' he said quickly. 'Or why should I bother at all? Am I just going to give the signal and then sit on the hill? That's rather stupid.'

'If my assistant and my secretary get involved in a scandalous incident, I'm done for anyway!' Doronin fumed. 'So I'd better go myself.'

But Shirota disrespectfully interrupted his superior.

'I do not count. Firstly, I am a hired employee, a native.' He gave a crooked smile. 'And secondly, I shall write a resignation note this very minute and put yesterday's date on it. The letter will say that I no longer wish to serve Russia, because I have become disillusioned with its policy towards Japan, or something of the kind. In that way, if Mr Fandorin and I are involved in a scandalous incident, as you put it, it will be a criminal conspiracy between a young pup and adventurer (I beg your pardon, Erast Petrovich, but that is what you called yourself) and a crazy native who has already been dismissed from his job serving Russia. No more than that.'

This was all said in solemn tones, with restrained dignity, and that was how the discussion ended. They started discussing the details.

*

When he got back to his apartment, Erast Petrovich found O-Yumi lying in the bed barely alive. Her face was pale and bloodless, her feet were bound in rags.

'What's wrong with you?' he cried in horror. 'Are you ill?'

She smiled weakly.

'No, I'm just very, very tired. But it's all right, it will pass.'

'But what's wrong with your feet?'

'I grazed them.'

He went down on his knees, took hold of her hand and said imploringly:

'Tell me the truth. Where were you last night? Where did you go today? What is happening to you? The truth, for God's sake, the truth!'

O-Yumi looked at him affectionately.

'Very well. I will tell you the truth – as far as I can. And you promise me two things: that you won't ask any more questions and that you will tell me the truth too.'

'I promise. But you first. Where were you?'

'In the mountains. The *maso* herb only grows in one place, on the southern slope of Mount Tanzawa, and that is fifteen *ri* from here. I had to make two trips, because the infusion has to be brewed twice, and it must be absolutely fresh. That is all I have to tell. Now you tell me. I can see that you are planning something and I feel alarmed. I have a bad premonition.'

Fifteen *ri* – that's almost sixty versts in each direction, Fandorin calculated. No wonder she's barely alive!

'To ride thirty *ri* in one night!' he exclaimed. 'You must have driven the horses half to death!'

For some reason O-Yumi found his words amusing, and she broke into quiet laughter.

'That's all. No more questions, you promised. Now you tell me.'

And he told her: about the duel, about how Bullcox's fury burst a blood vessel in his brain, about Don Tsurumaki, and about the forthcoming operation. O-Yumi's face became more and more uneasy, sadder and sadder.

'How terrible . . .' she whispered when he finished.

'You mean about your Algie?' Fandorin asked, immediately jealous. 'Then go to him and feed him your infusion!'

'No, I don't mean him. I feel sorry for Algie, but one or the other of you had to come to grief. What you have planned is terrible. Don't go anywhere tonight! It will end badly! I can see that from the shadow on your temple!' she said, reaching out her hand to his head, and when Erast Petrovich smiled, she exclaimed despairingly, 'You don't believe in *ninso!*'

They argued for a long time after that, but Fandorin was adamant, and in the end O-Yumi fell asleep, exhausted. He walked out carefully, afraid of disturbing her sleep with an accidental movement or the creak of a chair.

The remainder of the day passed in preparations. There wasn't a sound from the bedroom – O-Yumi was sleeping soundly.

But late in the evening, when Masa was already sitting on the porch, gazing in the direction of the dark hills above the Bluff, there was a surprise in store for Erast Petrovich.

As he walked past the bedroom yet again, he put his ear to the door. This time he thought he heard a gentle rustling and he cautiously opened the door slightly.

No, O-Yumi was still sleeping – he could her quiet, regular breathing from the bed.

He tiptoed over to the window in order to close it – there was a cold draught coming in. He glanced at the grey silhouette of the house opposite and suddenly froze.

Something had moved over there, up by the chimney. A cat? Then it was a very big one.

His heart started pounding like a wild thing, but Fandorin gave no sign of being alarmed in any way. On the contrary, he stretched lazily, closed the window, locked it with all the latches and slowly walked away.

Out in the corridor, he broke into a run.

It was the roof of the Club Hotel, Erast Petrovich realised, and he could climb up there from the back, using the fire escape ladder.

Hunched over, he ran along the railings to the next building. A minute later he was already up there. Resting one knee on the tiles, which were wet with rain, he pulled his Herstal out of it holster.

He heard rustling steps close by, on the other pitch of the roof.

No longer trying to hide, Fandorin dashed forward, with just one thought in his head – how to avoid slipping.

He reached the ridge of the roof and glanced over it – just in time to glimpse a black figure in a close-fitting black costume over by the edge of the roof. The invisible man again!

The titular counsellor threw up his hand, but it was too late to fire: the ninja jumped down.

Spreading his feet wide, Erast Petrovich slithered head first down the tiles, grabbed hold of the gutter and leaned out.

Where was the ninja?

Had he been killed by the fall, was he still moving?

But no matter how hard he stared, he couldn't make out anyone down below. The invisible man had disappeared.

'Omaeh ikanai. Hitori iku,'* Fandorin told his servant when he got back to the consulate. 'O-Yumi-san mamoru. Wakaru?'†

And Masa understood. He nodded, without taking his eyes off the hill on which sooner or later the little blue light would flash. Erast Petrovich had been lucky with his servant after all.

An hour later, or maybe an hour and a half, the titular counsellor was sitting at the window in a peaked uniform cap, smoking cigars and, as has already been mentioned, his body, heart and mind were flooded with bliss.

---

* 'You're not going. I'm going alone' (distorted Japanese)
† 'To protect O-Yumi. Understand?' (distorted Japanese)

So they were following him? Let them. The motto of tonight's lightning raid was speed and more speed.

During the fourth cigar Masa looked into the room. It was time!

Fandorin left his servant with some simple instructions and walked out on to the porch.

Yes, the signal. Over there above the Bluff (but it looked as if it was at the very edge of the sky) a little blue star flashed on and off several times.

> In the bright blue sky
> Just you try to make it out –
> A small bright blue star

A BRIAR PIPE

He grabbed hold of the tricycle that had been positioned in advance, lowered it off the porch and pushed it along the pathway at a run. Outside the gates he jumped into the saddle and started pressing hard on the pedals. Come on, then, just you try to follow me!

In order to throw any possible spies off the scent, instead of turning to the right, towards the Bluff, he turned left. He hurtled along at top speed, glancing in the mirror every now and then, but he didn't glimpse a single black figure behind him on the brightly lit promenade. Perhaps his simple attempt at cunning had succeeded. Everyone knew that the simplest tricks were the most reliable.

The trick really was childish in its simplicity. Instead of the vice-consul, Masa was now sitting in the vice-consul's window – in a peaked cap, with a cigar in his teeth. If they were lucky, the substitution would not be noticed soon.

Just to make certain of things, without reducing his speed, Erast Petrovich circled round the Settlement and rode into the Bluff from the other side, across the Okagawa river.

The rubber tyres swished through the puddles with a miraculous rustling sound and water splashed out from under the wheels, glinting joyously in the light of the street lamps. Fandorin felt like a hawk soaring above the dark streets of the night. He could see his goal, it was close, and nothing could halt or impede his impetuous attack. Watch out, you *akunin*!

Shirota was waiting at the agreed spot, on the corner of a side street.

'I was watching through binoculars,' the secretary reported. 'The light went out thirty-five minutes ago, everywhere except for one window on the first floor. The servants withdrew to the house that stands at the back of the garden. Fifteen minutes ago the last window also went dark. Then I came down the hill.'

'Did you look at the terrace? I told you that he l-likes to watch the stars.'

'What stars are there today? It's raining.'

Fandorin liked the secretary's attitude. Calm, businesslike, with no sign of nerves. It could well be that Kanji Shirota's true calling was not polishing an office desk with his elbows but a trade that required sangfroid and a love of risk.

Just as long as his courage didn't fail him when it came to the real work.

'Well, will you join me for dinner? The table's all set,' the titular counsellor said jocularly, gesturing towards the gates.

'After you,' Shirota replied in the same tone of voice. He really was holding up very well.

The lock and the hinges were well lubricated, they made their way inside without a single creak or squeak. And they had been exceptionally lucky with the weather: cloudy and dark, with the rain muffling any sound.

'Do you remember the plan?' Fandorin whispered as he walked up the steps. 'We go into the house now. You wait downstairs. I'll go up to . . .'

'I remember everything,' the secretary replied just as quietly. 'Don't waste time on that.'

The door into the house was not locked – a special point of pride for the owner that was also very handy for them. Fandorin ran up the carpeted steps to the first floor without making a sound. The bedroom was at the end of the corridor, beside the way out on to the terrace.

Wouldn't it be fine if he woke up, Erast Petrovich suddenly thought when his left hand touched the door handle (the revolver was grasped in his right hand). Then, regardless of any unworthy desire for revenge, I would be perfectly justified in smacking the villain on the forehead with the butt of my gun.

When Fandorin stole up to the bed he even sighed deliberately, but Don Tsurumaki didn't wake up. He was sleeping sweetly on a soft feather bed. He had a white nightcap with a vulgar pompom on his head instead of a fez. The silk blanket rose and fell peacefully on the millionaire's broad chest. His lush lips were parted slightly.

The gold chain glinted in the opening of his nightshirt.

Now he's sure to wake up, Erast Petrovich thought as he lined up the pliers, and he raised the hand holding the revolver. His heart was beating out a deafening drum-roll of triumph.

There was a metallic click, and the chain slid down the sleeping man's neck. He lowed blissfully and turned over on to his side. The prickly golden rose was lying on Fandorin's palm.

The soundest sleepers are not those who have a clear conscience, but those who never had one to begin with, the vice-consul told himself philosophically.

He walked downstairs, gestured for Shirota to go in the direction of the study-library, where he had once taken Prince Onokoji – may the Japanese God rest his sinful soul – by surprise at the scene of his crime.

He ran the beam of his little torch over the closed curtains, the tall cupboards with the solid doors, the bookshelves. There, that was the one.

'You hold the light.'

He handed the little torch to the secretary, then spent two minutes feeling the spines of the books and the wooden uprights. Finally, when he pressed on a weighty tome of *Sacred Writings* (third from the left on the last shelf but one), something clicked. He pulled the shelves towards himself and they swung open like a door. Behind them in the wall was a small steel door.

'On the keyhole, the keyhole,' said Erast Petrovich, pointing impatiently.

The thorny rose wiggled and jiggled and slipped into the opening like a hand into a glove. Before turning the key, the titular counsellor carefully examined the wall, the floor and the skirting board for any electric alarm wires – and sure enough, he discovered a thick, hard string under the wallpaper. To get caught in the same trap twice would be unseemly, to say the least.

The pliers were called on again. One snip and the alarm was disconnected.

'Open, sesame,' Erast Petrovich whispered, in order to encourage Shirota. The beam of the torch had started wavering a bit – it looked as if the clerical worker's nerves were beginning to find the tension too much.

'What?' the Japanese asked in surprise. 'What did you say?'

Apparently he had never read the *Arabian Nights*.

There was a quiet ringing sound and the little door opened. Fandorin first squeezed his eyes shut, then swore under his breath.

Lying there in the steel box, glittering brilliantly in the electric light, were gold ingots. There were a lot of them; they looked like bricks in a wall.

Erast Petrovich's disappointment knew no bounds. The Don had not lied. He really did keep gold in his safe. What a stupid, nouveau riche thing to do! Had this entire operation really been undertaken in vain?

Still unable to believe in such a crushing fiasco, he pulled out one ingot and glanced into the gap, but there was yellow metal glinting in the second row as well.

'At the scene of the crime,' a loud, mocking voice declared behind him.

The titular counsellor swung round sharply and saw a burly, stocky figure in the doorway. The next moment the chandelier on the ceiling blazed into life and the silhouette acquired colour, volume and texture.

It was the master of the house, still in that idiotic nightcap, with a dressing gown over his nightshirt, but the style of the trousers showing under the dressing gown was anything but pyjama-like.

'Does Mr Diplomat like gold?' Tsurumaki asked with a smile, nodding at the ingot in Fandorin's hand.

The millionaire's face was not sleepy at all. And another remarkable detail was that he was not wearing household slippers on his feet, but shoes, laced up in an extremely neat manner.

A trap, thought Erast Petrovich, turning cold. He was lying in bed dressed, even with his shoes on. He was waiting, he knew!

The Don clapped his hands, and men emerged from everywhere – from behind the curtains, out of doors, even out of the cupboards in the walls, and they were all dressed in identical black jackets and black cotton trousers. The servants – but Shirota had said they had all gone away!

There were at least a dozen servants. Fandorin had seen one of them before – a sinewy, bandy-legged fellow with long arms like a monkey. The vice-consul thought he worked as something like a butler or major-domo.

'What a disgrace for the Russian Empire,' said Tsurumaki, clicking his tongue. 'The vice-consul stealing gold from other people's safes. *Kamata, ju-o toreh.'*

The last phrase, spoken in Japanese, was addressed to the man with long arms. *Ju* was 'weapon', *toro* meant 'take', *Kamata* was his name.

The titular counsellor recovered from his stupor. He flung up his hand and aimed the Herstal at the forehead of the master of the house.

Kamata immediately froze on the spot, as did the other Black Jackets.

'I have nothing to lose,' Fandorin warned Tsurumaki. 'Tell your men to go out. Immediately, otherwise . . .'

The Don wasn't smiling any longer, he was looking at the titular counsellor curiously, as if trying to guess whether he was bluffing or might really fire.

'I'll fire, have no doubt about that,' Fandorin assured him. 'Better death than dishonour. And if I'm going to die anyway, it will be more fun with you. You're such an interesting specimen. Shirota, stand on my left, you're blocking my view of Mr Tsurumaki.'

The secretary obeyed but, evidently out of agitation, he stood on the vice-consul's right instead of the left.

'You know perfectly well that I didn't come here for the gold.'

The Don moved and Erast Petrovich clicked the safety catch. 'Stand still! And get all these men out of here!'

But then something strange happened. Something quite incredible, in fact.

The titular counsellor's faithful comrade-in-arms, the secretary Shirota, flung himself on Fandorin's arm with a guttural cry. A shot rang out and the bullet clipped a long splinter off the oak parquet.

'What are you doing?' Erast Petrovich shouted, trying to shake off the insane Japanese, but Kamata bounded across to the vice-consul and twisted his arm behind his back, and others came darting after him.

A second later Fandorin, disarmed and helpless, was standing flattened against the wall: they were holding him by the arms, the legs and the neck.

But Erast Petrovich was not looking at the black-clad servants, only at the traitor, who picked the revolver up off the floor and handed it to the Don with a bow.

'You Judas!' the titular counsellor shouted hoarsely. 'You coward! You scoundrel!'

Shirota asked the master of the house something in Japanese – apparently he was requesting permission to reply. Tsurumaki nodded.

Then the turncoat turned towards Fandorin: his face was a pale, frozen mask, but his voice was firm and steady.

'I am not a coward or a scoundrel, and even less a traitor. Quite the contrary, I am faithful to my country. I used to think it was possible to serve two countries without any loss of honour. But Mr Lieutenant Captain Bukhartsev opened my eyes. Now I know how Russia regards Japan and what we can expect from the Russians.'

Fandorin couldn't bear it – he turned his eyes away. He remembered how Bukhartsev had pontificated about the 'Yellow Peril' without even thinking it necessary to lower his voice, and Shirota had been standing in the corridor all the time . . .

'That's politics,' Erast Petrovich interrupted. 'It can change. But betraying those who trust you is wrong! You are a member of the Russian consular staff!'

'Not any longer. As you are aware, I handed in my resignation and even wrote exactly why I no longer wish to serve Russia.'

And that was true too!

'Is it really more honourable to serve this murderer?' Fandorin asked, nodding at the Don to emphasise this, his final argument.

'Mr Tsurumaki is a sincere man. He is acting for the good of my Mother-land. And he is also a strong man. If the supreme authority and the law damage the interests of our native land, he changes the authority and corrects the laws. I have decided that I shall help him. I never sat on any hill, I went straight to Mr Tsurumaki and told him about your plan. You could have harmed Japan, and I have stopped you.'

The longer Shirota talked, the more confident his voice became and the more brightly his eyes flashed. The modest, unassuming secretary had wound the smart Fandorin round his little finger; he even dared to be proud of the fact. Erast Petrovich, soundly drubbed on all counts, including even the moral issue, was seized by a spiteful desire to spoil the triumph of this champion of 'sincerity' in at least some small way.

'I thought you loved Sophia Diogenovna. But you have betrayed her. You will never see her again.'

The moment he said it, he repented. It really was rather unworthy.

But Shirota was not perturbed.

'On the contrary. Today I proposed to Sophie and I was accepted. I warned her that if she married me, she would have to become Japanese. She replied: "With you I would live in the jungle."' The hateful face of the Russian Empire's new enemy dissolved into a smile of happiness. 'It is bitter for me to part from you like this. I have profound respect for you. But nothing bad will happen to you, Mr Tsurumaki has promised me that. The safe was specially filled with gold instead of documents that contain state secrets. Thanks to this, you will not be charged with spying. And Mr Tsurumaki will not sue you for attempted robbery. You will remain alive, you will not go to jail. You will simply be expelled from Japan. You cannot be left here, you are far too dynamic, and you are also embittered because of your friends who have been killed.'

He turned to the Don and bowed to indicate that the conversation in Russian was over.

Tsurumaki added in English:

'Shirota-san is a genuine Japanese patriot. A man of honour who knows that duty to the Motherland comes above all other things. Go, my friend. You should not be here when the police arrive.'

With a low bow to his new master and a brief nod to Fandorin, Shirota left the room.

The titular counsellor was still being held as tightly as ever, and that could mean only one thing.

'The police, of course, will arrive t-too late,' Erast said to the master of the house. 'The thief will be killed while attempting to escape or resisting capture. That is why you have sent the idealistic Shirota away. I am such a dynamic individual – not only can I not be left in Japan, I cannot even be left alive, right?'

The smile with which Tsurumaki listened to these words was full of jovial surprise, as if the millionaire had not expected to hear such a subtle and witty comment from his prisoner.

The Don turned the Herstal over in his hand and asked:

'Self-winding? Hammerless?'

'Yes. Simply press the trigger and all seven bullets will be fired, one after another. That is, six, one round has already been spent,' replied Fandorin, inwardly feeling proud of his own cool composure.

Tsurumaki weighed the small revolver in his hand and the titular counsellor readied himself: now it would be very painful, then the pain would become duller, and then it would pass off altogether . . .

But the Herstal was sent flying to the floor. Erast Petrovich was surprised only for a moment. Then he noticed that the Don's pocket was bulging. Of course: it would be strange if the robber were to be shot with his own revolver.

As if to confirm this guess, the master of the house lowered his hand into that pocket. Events were clearly approaching their conclusion.

Suddenly Kamata, who had been keeping his eyes fixed on the titular counsellor, turned his bony face covered with coarse wrinkles towards the door.

There were shouts and crashing sounds coming from somewhere outside.

Had the police arrived? But then why the noise?

Another Black Jacket came running into the room. He bowed to the master and Kamata and jabbered something.

'*Tsurete koi*,'* Tsurumaki ordered, without taking his hand out of his pocket.

The servant ran out, and half a minute later Masa, looking much the worse for wear, was led in by the arms.

When he saw Fandorin, he shouted something in a desperate voice.

Only one word was comprehensible: 'O-Yumi-san'.

'What's he saying? What's he saying?' the vice-consul asked, jerking in the arms of his guards.

To judge from the master's face, he was astounded by the news. He asked Masa something, received an answer and suddenly started thinking very intently. He took no notice of Fandorin's repeated questions and merely

---

* 'Bring him' (Japanese)

scratched at his black beard furiously. Masa kept on trying to bow to Erast Petrovich (which was not easy to do with his arms twisted behind his back) and repeating: 'Moosiwake arimasen! Moosiwake arimasen!'

'What is that he's muttering?' the titular counsellor exclaimed in helpless fury. 'What does it mean?'

'It means: "There can be no forgiveness for me!",' said Tsurumaki, suddenly looking at him keenly. 'Your servant is saying some very interesting things. He says he was sitting at the window and smoking a cigar. That he felt stuffy and he opened one windowpane. That there was a whistling sound, something stung him in the neck, and after that he remembers nothing. He woke up on the floor. There was something like a thorn sticking out of his neck. He dashed into the next room and saw that O-Yumi had disappeared. The bed was empty.'

Erast Petrovich groaned, and the master of the house asked Masa another question. When he received an answer he jerked his chin, and Fandorin's servant was immediately released. Masa reached inside the front of his jacket and took out what looked like a wooden needle.

'What's that?' asked Fandorin.

The Don examined the 'thorn' gloomily.

'A *fukibari*. They smear this piece of rubbish with poison or some other kind of potion – to paralyse someone temporarily, for instance, or put them to sleep – and fire it out of a blowpipe. The ninja's favourite weapon. I'm afraid, Fandorin, that your girlfriend has been abducted by the "Stealthy Ones".'

At that very moment Erast Petrovich, who had fully prepared himself to die, suddenly felt that he wanted terribly not to. Why, one might think, should he care about anything in the world? If there are only a few seconds of life left, do unsolved puzzles, or even the abduction of the woman you love, really have any importance? But he wanted so much to live that when the Don's hand moved in that ominous pocket, Fandorin gritted his teeth tightly – in order not to beg for a respite. They wouldn't grant him a respite in any case, and even if they did, he couldn't possibly ask a murderer for anything.

The vice-consul forced himself to look at the hand as it slowly pulled a black, gleaming object out of the pocket until it emerged completely.

It was a briar pipe.

After I read it –
The Latin word for 'briar' –
I took up a pipe

TWO HANDS TIGHTLY CLASPED

'I like your Shirota,' the Don said thoughtfully, striking a match and puffing out a cloud of smoke. 'A genuine Japanese. All of a piece, intelligent, reliable. I've wanted an assistant like that for a long time already. All these' – he waved his pipe round at his black army – 'are good for fighting and other simple jobs that require no foresight. But Shirota belongs to a different breed, a far more valuable one. And what's more, he has made an excellent study of foreigners, especially Russians. That's very important for my plans.'

The very last thing Fandorin had been expecting was a panegyric on the virtues of the former secretary of the consulate, so he listened cautiously, not sure what Tsurumaki was driving at.

But the millionaire puffed on his pipe and carried on in the same style, as if he were thinking out loud,

'Shirota defined you very precisely: brave, unpredictable and very lucky. That is an extremely dangerous combination, which is why this performance was required.' He nodded at the safe with the magical radiance streaming out of it. 'But now everything is changing. I need you. And I need you here, in Japan. There won't be any police.'

The Don gave an order in Japanese, and suddenly no one was holding Erast Petrovich any longer. The Black Jackets released him, bowed to their master and left the room one by one.

'Shall we have a talk?' asked Tsurumaki, gesturing towards two armchairs by the window. 'Tell your man not to worry. Nothing bad will happen to you.'

Fandorin waved his hand to let Masa know that everything was all right and his servant reluctantly left the room, with a suspicious glance at the master of the house.

'You need me? Why?' asked Fandorin, in no hurry to sit down.

'Because you are brave, unpredictable and very lucky. But you need me even more. You want to save your woman, don't you? Then sit down and listen.'

The vice-consul sat down at that; he didn't need to be asked twice.

'How do I do that?' he asked quickly. 'What do you know?'

The Don scratched his beard and sighed.

'This is going to be a long story. I wasn't intending to make any excuses to you, to deny all the nonsense that you have imagined about me. But since we shall be fighting a common cause, I shall have to. Let's try to restore our former friendship.'

'That won't be easy,' Fandorin remarked ironically, unable to resist.

'I know. But you are an intelligent man and you will realise I am telling the truth ... to begin with, let's clear up the business with Okubo, since that's where everything began.' Tsurumaki looked into the other man's eyes calmly and seriously, as if he had decided to set aside his everyday mask of a jolly bon vivant. 'Yes, I had the minister removed, but that is our own internal Japanese affair, which shouldn't be of any interest to you. I don't know what your view of life is, Fandorin, but for me life is an eternal struggle between Order and Chaos. Order strives to pigeonhole everything, nail it down, render it safe and emasculate it. Chaos demolishes all this neat symmetry, turns society upside down, recognises no laws or rules. In this eternal struggle I am on the side of Chaos, because Chaos is Life, and Order is Death. I know perfectly well that, like all mortals, I am doomed: sooner or later Order will get the better of me, I shall stop floundering about and be transformed into a piece of dead matter. But for as long as I am alive, I wish to live as intensely as I can, so that the earth trembles around me and the symmetry is disrupted. Pardon the philosophy, but I want you to understand correctly how I am made and what I am striving for. Okubo was the absolute incarnation of Order. Nothing but arithmetic and precise accounting. If I had not stopped him, he would have transformed Japan into a second-rate, pseudo-European country, doomed eternally to drag along in the wake of the great powers. Arithmetic is a dead science, because it only takes material things into account. But my Homeland's great strength is in its spirit, which cannot be quantified. It is non-material, it belongs entirely to Chaos. Dictatorship and absolute monarchy are symmetrical and dead. Parliamentarianism is anarchic and full of life. The downfall of Okubo is a small victory for Chaos, a victory for Life over Death. Do you understand what I'm trying to say?'

'No,' replied Fandorin, who was listening intently. 'But do carry on. Only please, m-move from the philosophy to the facts.'

'Very well, let it be the facts. I don't think I need to go into the details of the operation – you already have a good grasp of that. I employed the help of the Satsuman fanatics and several highly placed officials who see the future of Japan in the same way as I do. I feel sorry for Suga. He was an outstanding man and would have gone far. But I bear no grudge against you – you have given me Shirota instead. For the Russians he was a lowly native clerk, but from this seed I shall grow a remarkable sunflower, just you wait and see. And perhaps you and he will make peace with each other yet. Three friends like you, me and him are a great force.'

'Three friends?' Erast Petrovich repeated, clutching the armrests of his chair with his fingers. 'I had three friends. You killed them all.'

The Don was disconcerted by that and his face fell.

'Yes, that was most unfortunate ... I didn't order them to be killed. I only wanted to take back what should not have fallen into the wrong hands. It is my fault, of course. But only in the sense that I didn't *forbid* them to be killed, and as far as the Stealthy Ones are concerned, the less bother, the better. I forbade them to touch you, because you are my friend. That's why they killed the little prince, but not you.'

The titular counsellor shuddered. That sounded like the truth. Tsurumaki had not wanted him dead? But if that was the case, the entire pattern he had figured out was shot to hell!

Erast Petrovich wrinkled up his forehead and immediately restored the sequence of logic:

'Right. You decided to get rid of me later, when I told you what Onokoji said before he died.'

'Nothing of the kind!' Tsurumaki exclaimed resentfully. 'I arranged every-thing in the best possible manner. I made Bullcox give me his word, and he kept his promise, because he is a gentleman. He satisfied his vanity, cut a dash, humiliated you in public, but he didn't maim you or kill you.'

'But surely . . . surely the stroke was not staged?'

'Why, did you think he was struck down by lightning from heaven? Bullcox is an ambitious man. What would he want with the scandal of a killing? But this way he saved his honour and did no damage to his career.'

The pattern had collapsed anyway. No one had intended to kill Erast Petrovich, and his lucky star apparently had nothing to do with anything!

This news made a profound impression on the titular counsellor, but even so he did not allow himself to be put off his stride.

'But how did you find out that my friends and I had evidence that was dangerous for you?'

'Tamba told me.'

'Who t-told you?'

'Tamba,' Tsurumaki explained matter-of-factly. 'The head of the Momochi clan.'

Fandorin was totally bemused now.

'Are you talking about the ninja? But as far as I'm aware, Momochi Tamba lived hundreds of years ago!'

'The present Tamba is his successor. Tamba the Eleventh. Only don't ask me how *he* knew about your plan – I have no idea. Tamba never reveals his secrets.'

'What does this man look like?' Erast Petrovich asked, unable to control a nervous tremor.

'It's hard to describe him, he changes his appearance. But basically Tamba is short, less than five feet tall, but he can make himself taller, they have some kind of cunning devices for that. Old, skinny . . . What else? Ah, yes, the eyes. He has absolutely special eyes that are impossible to hide. When he looks at you, they seem to burn right through you. It's best not to look into them – he'll put a spell on you.'

'Yes, that's him!' Fandorin exclaimed. 'I knew it! Tell me more! Have you been dealing with the ninja for a long time?'

The Don paused, gazing at the other man quizzically.

'Not very long. I was put in contact with them by an old samurai, now deceased. He used to serve the princes Onokoji . . . The Momochi clan is a very valuable ally, they are capable of working genuine miracles. But they are dangerous to deal with. You never know what is on their mind and what to expect from them. Tamba is the only man in the world I'm afraid of. Did you see how many guards I have in the house? But before, if you recall, I was perfectly happy to spend the night here alone.'

'What happened between you? Did you not have enough money to pay him?' Fandorin laughed mistrustfully, glancing at the safe packed with gold ingots.

'That's funny,' Tsurumaki conceded dourly. 'No, I always paid on time. I don't understand what happened, and that's what alarms me most of all. Tamba has started some game of his own, with goals that are not clear to me. And in some strange way that game is connected with you.'

'With me? In what way?'

'I don't know in what way!' the Don cried irritably. 'They want something from you! Otherwise why would they have abducted your lover? That's why I'm not handing you over to the police. You are the key to this plot. I just don't know yet which way to turn you so that the box of secrets will open. And you don't know either, do you?'

The expression on the titular counsellor's face was more eloquent than any reply, and the disciple of Chaos nodded.

'I can see that you don't. Here is my hand, Fandorin. It is the custom for you Europeans to seal a bargain with a handshake, is it not?'

The millionaire's short-fingered hand hung motionless in midair.

'What b-bargain?'

'An alliance. You and I against Tamba. The ninja abducted O-Yumi and killed your friends. I didn't kill them – they did. We shall strike a pre-emptive blow against them. The best form of defence is attack. Come on, give me your hand! We have to trust each other!'

But the vice-consul still did not reach out in response.

'What trust can there be if you are armed and I am not?'

'Oh Lord! Take your little toy, I don't want it.'

Once he had picked his Herstal up off the floor, Erast Petrovich finally believed that all this was not some subtle trap intended to worm something out of him.

'What is this pre-emptive strike?' he asked cautiously.

'Tamba thinks that I don't know where to look for him, but he is mistaken. My men, of course, are not *shinobi*, but they know a thing or two. I have managed to find out where the Momochi clan's lair is located.'

Fandorin jerked up out of his chair.

'Then why are we wasting time? Let's get going straight away.'

'It's not that simple. The lair is hidden in the mountains. My spies know exactly where, but it is hard to reach it . . .'

'Is it far from Yokohama?'

'Not very. On the border of the Sagami and Kai provinces, close to Mount

Oyama. Two days' march from here – if you travel with baggage.'

'What do we need baggage for? We can travel light and be there tomorrow!'

But Tsurumaki shook his head.

'No, the baggage is essential, and quite heavy baggage too. The place is a genuine fortress.'

'A f-fortress? The ninja have built a fortress close to the capital and no one knows about it?'

'That is what our country is like. Densely populated plains along the sea, but move away from the coast, even slightly, and there are remote, uninhabited mountains. And Tamba's fortress is not one that the chance traveller will notice . . .'

Erast Petrovich was sick to death of all these riddles.

'You have many loyal men, these "Black Jackets" of yours. If you order them to, they will storm the place, even at the cost of their own lives, I have no doubt about that. So what do you need me for? Tell me the truth, or there will be no alliance.'

'Yes, I will send Kamata there with a brigade of my best fighting men. They are all my comrades-in-arms from the civil war, I can rely on every one of them. But I myself cannot go with them – I have elections in three prefectures, that's the most important thing for me at the moment. Kamata is an experienced commander, an excellent soldier, but he only knows how to act according to the rules. He's not much use in an unconventional situation. And, let me repeat once again, it is very difficult to get into Tamba's secret village. Impossible in fact. There is no entrance.'

'How can there be no entrance?'

'There simply isn't. That is what my spies have reported to me, and they are not given to fantasising. I need your brains, Fandorin. And your luck. You can be quite sure that is where O-Yumi has been taken, to the mountain fortress. On your own, without me, there is nothing you can do. You need me. But you will be useful to me too. Well then, do I have to hold my hand out in the air for much longer?'

After a second's hesitation, the titular counsellor finally shook the outstretched hand. Two strong hands came together and squeezed each other so tight that the fingers turned white.

Stupid ritual
That refuses to die out:
Two hands tightly clasped

A DEAD TREE

Europe came to an end half an hour after they set out on their way. The spires and towers of the anglicised Bluff first gave way to the factory chimneys and cargo cranes of the river port, then to iron roofs, then to a sea of tiles, then to the thatched straw roofs of peasant huts, and after another mile or so, the buildings disappeared completely, leaving just the road stretching out between the rice fields, and bamboo groves, and the wall of low mountains that closed in the valley on both sides.

The expedition set off before dawn, in order not to attract unwanted attention. Strictly speaking, there was nothing suspicious about the caravan. It looked like a perfectly ordinary construction brigade, like the ones that built bridges and laid roads throughout the Mikado's empire, which was striving eagerly to make the transition from the Middle Ages to the nineteenth century.

The caravan was commanded by a sturdily built man with a coarse, wrinkled face. He stared around with the tenacious gaze of a bandit, which actually differs very little from the gaze of a construction foreman or master builder. His outfit – straw hat, black jacket, narrow trousers – was exactly the same as the workers wore, it was just that the commander rode and his thirty-two subordinates travelled on foot. Many of them were leading mules, loaded with heavy crates of equipment, by the bridle. Even the fact that the brigade was accompanied by a foreigner with his Japanese servant was unlikely to seem strange to anyone – there were many European and American engineers working on the immense building site that the Land of the Rising Sun had now become. If travellers coming the other way and peasants scrabbling in the meagre dirt watched the foreigner as he rode by, it was only because of the outlandish self-propelled *kuruma* on which he was riding.

Fandorin already regretted that he had not listened to the consul, who had advised him to hire a mule – the animals were slow and rather unattractive, but far more reliable than Japanese horses. However, Erast Petrovich had not wished to appear unattractive as he set out to save the woman he loved. He had taken a mule, but not to ride, only for his baggage, and had entrusted it to Masa's care.

His servant tramped along behind him, leading the solid-hoofed creature on a rein and every now and then shouting at it: '*Get arong*'. The mule was walking along on its own in any case, but Masa had specially asked his master for the Russian words for urging on animals, in order to show off to the Black Jackets.

In everything apart from his choice of a means of transport, the titular counsellor had taken the advice of the experienced Vsevolod Vitalievich. His baggage consisted of a mosquito net (the mosquitoes in the Japanese mountains were genuine vampires); a rubber bath (skin diseases were widespread among the local inhabitants, so washing in the hotel bathrooms was a no-no); an inflatable pillow (the Japanese used wooden ones); baskets of food and lots of other essential items for a journey.

Communication with the commander of the brigade, Kamata, was established with some difficulty. He knew quite a lot of English words, but he had no concept of grammar, so without the habit of deductive reasoning, Fandorin probably would not have been able to understand him.

For instance, Kamata would say:

'Hia furomu ibuningu tsu gou, naito hoteru supendo. Tsumorou mauntin entah.'

To start with, bearing in mind the peculiarities of the Japanese accent, Erast Petrovich restored the fragments of this gibberish to their original state. This gave him: 'Here from evening to go, night hotel spend, tomorrow mountain enter'. After that, the meaning became clear: 'We move on from here until the evening, spend the night in a hotel and tomorrow we enter the mountains'.

To reply he had to perform the reverse procedure: dismember the English sentence into its separate words and distort them in the Japanese style.

'Mauntin, hau fah?' the vice-consul asked. 'Ninja bireju, hau fah?'

And Kamata understood perfectly. He thought for a moment and scratched his chin.

'Smuuzu irebun ri. Mauntin faibu ri?'

It was eleven ri across the plain (about forty versts), and five ri through the mountains, Fandorin understood. So generally, although it wasn't easy, they managed to make themselves understood to each other, and by midday the two of them had achieved such a close fit that they could even talk about complicated matters. For instance, about parliamentary democracy, of which Kamata was terribly fond. The empire had only just adopted a law on local government; elections for prefecture assemblies, mayors and village elders were taking place everywhere; and the Black Jackets were playing a very lively part in all this activity: they defended some candidates and also, as this advocate of parliamentarianism put it, 'smorru furaiten' others, that is, they frightened them a little. For Japan, all this was new, even revolutionary. And Don Tsurumaki seemed to be the first influential politician who had realised the full importance of the little provincial governments, which were regarded ironically in the capital as a useless decoration.

'Ten eas, Tokyo nasingu,' Kamata prophesied, swaying in the saddle. 'Provinsu rearu pawa. Tsurumaki-dono rearu pawa. Nippon nou Tokyo, Nippon *probinsu.*'* But Fandorin thought: The provinces are all very well, but by that time the Don will probably have control of the capital as well. And that will be the triumph of democracy.

The commander of the Black Jackets turned out to be quite a considerable chatterbox. As they moved along the valley, squeezed in tighter and tighter by the hills on both sides, he talked about the glorious days when he and the Don crushed the competition in the fight for lucrative contracts, and then came even jollier times – it was a period of revolt, and they fought and feasted '*furu beri*', that is, with a full belly.

It was clear that the old bandit was in seventh heaven. Fighting was far better than working as a major-domo, he avowed. And a little later he added that it was even better than building a democratic Japan.

He really was a fine commander too. Every half-hour he rode round the caravan, checking to see whether the mules had gone lame or the baggage had come loose, joking with the fighting men, and the column immediately started moving more cheerfully and energetically.

To Fandorin's surprise, they pressed on without a halt. He pushed his pedals economically, matching his speed to the men on foot, but after twenty versts he was starting to tire, while the Black Jackets were not showing any signs of fatigue.

Lunch lasted a quarter of an hour. Everyone, including Kamata, swallowed two rice balls, drank some water and then got back in formation. Erast Petrovich barely even had time to lay out the sandwiches prepared by the thoughtful Obayasi-san, and was obliged to chew them on the move, as he caught up with the brigade. Masa muttered as he dragged his Rosinante along behind.

Between four and five in the afternoon, having covered about thirty versts, they turned off the main road on to a narrow track. This was a completely wild area; at least, no European had ever set foot here before. Fandorin's eye could not discern any signs of Western civilisation in the small, squalid villages. Little children and adults with their mouths hanging open stared, not only at the tricycle, but also at the round-eyed man in outlandish clothes who was riding it. And this was only a few hours' journey away from Yokohama! Only now did the titular counsellor start to realise how thin was the lacquer of civilisation with which the rulers had hastily coated the façade of the ancient empire.

Several times they came across cows – wearing colourful aprons with pictures of dragons on them and straw shoes over their hoofs. The villagers used these imposingly attired cud-chewers as pack and draught animals. The titular counsellor asked Kamata about this, and he confirmed his suspicion that the stupid peasants did not eat meat or drink milk, because they were still completely savage here, but never mind, democracy would come to them soon.

---

* 'In ten years, Tokyo is nothing. Real power is the provinces. Real power is Mr Tsurumaki. Japan is not Tokyo. Japan is the provinces' (distorted English)

They stopped for the night in a rather large village at the very end of the valley, just before the mountains began. The village elder accommodated the 'construction brigade' in the communal house – 'workers' in the yard, 'masters' and 'engineers' inside. A straw-mat floor, no furniture, paper walls with holes in them. So this was the '*hoteru*' Kamatu had mentioned that morning. The only other guest was an itinerant monk with a staff and a shoulder bag for alms, but he remained apart from their group and kept turning away – he didn't want to defile his gaze with the sight of the 'hairy barbarian'.

Fandorin got the idea of taking a stroll round the village, but the villagers behaved no better than the *bonze* – the children shouted and ran away, the women squealed, the dogs barked hysterically – and so he had to go back. The embarrassed elder came, bowed many times in apology and asked the *gaijin*-san not to go anywhere.

'*Furu pazanto nevah see uait man,*' Kamata translated. '*Yu sakasu manki, sinku.*'

He dangled his long arms and swayed as he hobbled round the room, laughing at the top of his voice. It took Erast Petrovich some time to understand what was wrong. It turned out that they had never seen any white people in the village before, but one of the locals had been in the city many years ago and seen an ugly trained monkey that was also dressed in a curious manner. Fandorin's eyes were so big and blue that the ignoramuses had taken fright.

Kamata took pleasure in telling Fandorin at length what fools the peasants were. The Japanese had a saying: 'A family never remains rich or poor for longer than three generations', and it was true that in the city life was arranged so that in three generations rich men declined into poverty and poor men fought their way up – such was the law of God's justice. But the boneheads living in the villages had not been able to break out of their poverty for a thousand years. When parents got decrepit and were unable to work, their own children took the old folk into the mountains and left them there to die – in order not to waste food on them. The peasants didn't wish to learn anything new, they didn't want to serve in the army. He couldn't understand how it was possible to build a great Japan with this rabble, but if Tsurumaki-dono took the contract, they'd build it, they'd have to.

Eventually, weary of deciphering his companion's chatter, the titular counsellor went off to sleep. He cleaned his teeth with 'Brilliant' powder and washed himself in his travelling bath, which was most convenient, except that the water smelled strongly of rubber. Meanwhile Masa set out his camp bed, hung the green net over it and inflated the pillow, working furiously with his cheeks.

'Tomorrow,' Fandorin said to himself and fell asleep.

The last five *ri* were a match for the previous day's eleven. The road immediately started rising steeply and looping between the hills, which reached up higher and higher towards the sky. Fandorin had to dismount from his tricycle and push it by the handlebars, and the young man regretted not having left it in the village.

Well after midday Kamata pointed to a mountain with a snowy peak.

'Oyama. Now right-right.'

Four thousand feet, thought Fandorin, throwing his head back and gauging it by eye. Not Kazbek, of course, and not Mont Blanc, but a serious elevation, no doubt about it.

The place we are going to is a little off to one side, explained the commander, who was thoughtful and taciturn today. We stretch the line out into single file and keep quiet.

They walked on for about another two hours. Before they entered a narrow but short ravine, Kamata dismounted and divided the brigade into two parts. He ordered the larger group to cover their heads with leaves and crawl through the bottleneck on their stomachs. About ten men remained behind with the pack animals and baggage.

'Tower. Look,' he explained curtly to Erast Petrovich, jabbing one finger upwards.

Obviously the enemy had an observation point somewhere close by.

The titular counsellor travelled the two hundred *sazhens* of the ravine in the same manner as the others. His outfit did not suffer at all, though: specially designed for outings in the mountains, it was equipped with magnificent knee-pads and elbow-pads of black leather. Masa panted along behind him, having refused point blank to stay behind with the mule and the tricycle.

Having passed this dangerous place they moved on, standing erect now, but sticking to the undergrowth and avoiding open areas. Kamata clearly knew the road – either he had been given precise instructions, or he had been here before.

They scrambled up the wooded slope and along a stony stream for at least an hour.

At the top the commander waved his hand and the Black Jackets slumped to the ground, worn out. Kamata gestured for Fandorin to come over to him.

The two of them moved away about a hundred paces to a naked boulder overgrown with moss, from which there was a panoramic view of the mountain peaks around them and the valley stretching out below.

'The village of the *shinobi* is there,' said Kamata, pointing to the next mountain.

It was about the same height, and also overgrown with forest, but it had one intriguing and distinctive feature. A section of the summit had split away from the massif (probably as a result of an earthquake) and twisted down, separated from the rest of the mountain by a deep crack. On the side facing them, the separated block ended in a precipice, where the slope had crumbled away, unable to retain the layer of earth on its inclined surface. It was a quite fantastic site: a crooked slice of mountain suspended over an abyss.

Erast Petrovich pressed his binoculars to his eyes. He could not make out any signs of human habitation at first, only the pine trees crowding close together and flocks of birds flying in zigzags. The only structure was clinging to the very edge of the precipice. Adjusting the focus with the little wheel, Fandorin saw a wooden house that was certainly of considerable size. It had something like a little bridge or jetty protruding from the wall that ran down into nowhere. But who could moor at that berth, at a height of two hundred *sazhens*?

'Momochi Tamba,' said Kamata in his distinctive English. 'His house. The other houses can't be seen from below.'

The titular counsellor felt his heart leap. O-Yumi was near! But how could he reach her?

He ran the binoculars over the entire mountain again, slowly.

'I don't understand how they g-get up there . . .'

'That's the wrong question,' said the commander of the Black Jackets, looking at Erast Petrovich, not the mountain. His gaze was at once searching and mistrustful. 'The right question is how do *we* get up there? I don't know. Tsurumaki-dono said the *gaijin* will think of something. Think. I'll wait.'

'We have to move closer,' said Fandorin.

They moved closer. To do that they had to climb to the peak of the split mountain – and then the separated block was very close. They didn't walk, but crawled to the fissure that separated it off, trying not to show themselves above the grass, although on that side they couldn't see a living soul.

The titular counsellor estimated the size of the crack. Deep, with a sheer vertical wall – impossible to scramble up. But not very wide. At the narrowest spot, where a dead, charred tree stuck up on the other side, it was hardly more than ten *sazhens*. The *shinobi* probably used a flying bridge or something of the sort to get across.

'Well then?' Kamata asked impatiently. 'Can we get across there?'

'No.'

The commander swore in a Japanese whisper, but the sense of his exclamation was clear enough: I knew a damned *gaijin* wouldn't be any use to us.

'We can't get across there,' Fandorin repeated, crawling away from the cliff edge. 'But we can do something to make them come out.'

'What?'

The vice-consul expounded his plan on the way back.

'Secretly position men on the mountain, beside the crack. Wait for the wind to blow in that direction. We need a strong wind. But that's not unusual in the mountains. Set fire to the forest. When the *shinobi* see that the flames could spread to their island, they'll throw a bridge across and come to this side to put them out. First we'll kill the ones who come running to put out the fire, then we'll make our way into their village across their bridge.'

With numerous repetitions, checks and gesticulations, the explanation of the plan occupied the entire journey back to the camp.

It was already dark and the paths could not be seen, but Kamata walked confidently and didn't go astray once.

When he had finally clarified the essential points of the proposed action, he pondered them for a long time.

He said:

'A good plan. But not for *shinobi*. *Shinobi* are cunning. If the forest simply catches fire all of a sudden, they'll suspect that something's not right.'

'Why just all of a sudden?' asked Fandorin, pointing up at the sky, completely covered with black clouds. 'The season of the plum rain. There are frequent thunderstorms. A lightning strike – a tree catches fire, the wind spreads the flames. Very simple.'

'There will be a storm,' the commander agreed. 'But who knows when? How long will we wait? One day, two, a week?'

'One day, two, a week,' the titular counsellor said, and shrugged, thinking: And the longer the better. You and I, my friend, have different interests. I want to save O-Yumi, you want to kill the Stealthy Ones, and if she dies together with them, there's no sorrow in that for you. I need time to prepare.

'A good plan,' Kamata repeated. 'But no good for me. I won't wait a week. I won't even wait two days. I also have a plan. Better than the *gaijin's*.'

'I wonder what it is.' The titular counsellor chuckled, certain that the old war-dog was bragging.

They heard muffled braying and the jingling of harness. It was the caravan moving up, after passing through the ravine under cover of darkness.

The Black Jackets quickly unloaded the bundles and crates off the mules. Wooden boards cracked and the barrels of Winchester rifles, still glossy with the factory grease, glinted in the light of dark lanterns.

'About the forest fire – that's good, that's right,' Kamata said in a satisfied voice as he watched four large crates being unloaded.

Their contents proved to be a Krupps mountain gun, two-and-a-half-inch calibre, the latest model – Erast Petrovich had seen guns like that among the trophies seized by the Turks during the recent war.

'Shoot from the cannon. The pines will catch fire. The *shinobi* will run. Where to? I'll put marksmen on the bottom of the crack. On the other side, where the precipice is, too. Let them climb down on ropes – we'll shoot all of them.'

Kamata lovingly stroked the barrel of the gun.

Fandorin felt a chilly tremor run down his spine. Exactly what he was afraid of! It wouldn't be a carefully planned operation to rescue a prisoner, but a bloodbath, in which there would be no survivors.

It was pointless trying to argue with the old bandit – he wouldn't listen.

'Perhaps your plan really is simpler,' said the vice-consul, pretending to stifle a yawn. 'When do we begin?'

'An hour after dawn.'

'Then we need to get a good night's sleep. My servant and I will bed down by the stream. It's a bit cooler there.'

Kamata mumbled something without turning round. He seemed to have lost all interest in the *gaijin*.

'The dead tree, the dead tree' – the words hammered away inside the titular counsellor's head.

To be beautiful
After death is a great skill
That only trees have

THE GLOWING COALS

It was not difficult to get to the next mountain in the dark – Fandorin had memorised the way.

They clambered up to the top by guesswork – just keep going up and when there's nowhere higher left to go, that's the summit.

But determining the direction in which the split-away section of the mountain lay proved to be quite difficult.

Erast Petrovich and his servant tried going right and left, and once they almost fell over the edge of a cliff, and the cliff turned out not to be the one they needed – there was a river murmuring down at its bottom, but there was no river at the bottom of the crack.

Who can tell how much more time they would have wasted on the search, but fortunately the sky was gradually growing lighter: the dark clouds crept away to the east, the stars shone ever more brightly, and soon the moon came out. After the pitch darkness, it was as if a thousand-candle chandelier had lit up above the world – you could have read a book.

Kamata would have had to wait a long time for a thunderstorm, Erast Petrovich thought as he led Masa towards the fissure. Somewhere not far away an eagle owl hooted: not 'wuhu, wuhu' as in Russia, but 'wufu, wufu'. That is its native accent, because there is no syllable 'hu' in the Japanese alphabet, thought Erast Petrovich.

There it was, the same place, with the charred pine on the far side, the one that the titular counsellor had noticed earlier. The dead tree was his only hope now.

'Nawa,'* the vice-consul whispered to his servant.

Masa unwound the long rope from his waist and handed it to him.

The art of lasso-throwing, a souvenir of his time in Turkish captivity, would come in handy yet again. Fandorin tied a wide noose and weighted it with a travelling kettle of stainless steel. He stood at the edge of the black abyss and started swinging the noose in wide, whistling circles above his head. The kettle struck the tree with a mournful clang and clattered across the stones. Missed!

He had to pull back the lasso, coil it up and throw again.

The loop caught on the trunk only at the fourth attempt.

The vice-consul wound the other end of the rope round a tree stump and

---

* 'Rope' (Japanese)

checked to make sure it held. He set off towards the fissure, but Masa decisively shoved his master aside and went first.

He lay on his back, wrapped his short legs round the rope and set off, placing one hand in front of the other and crawling very quickly. The lasso swayed, the stump creaked, but the fearless Japanese didn't stop for an instant. In five minutes he was already on the other side. He grabbed hold of the rope and pulled on it – so that Erast Petrovich would not sway as much. So the titular counsellor completed his journey through the blackness with every possible comfort, except that he skinned one hand slightly.

That was the first half of the job done. His watch showed three minutes after eleven.

'Well, God speed,' Fandorin said quietly, taking the Herstal out of its holster.

Masa pulled a short sword out from under his belt and checked to make sure that the blade slipped easily out of the scabbard.

Erast Petrovich had estimated that the hanging island was approximately a hundred *sazhens* across, from the fissure to the precipice. At a stroll, that was two minutes. But they walked slowly, so that no branch would crack and the fallen pines needles wouldn't rustle. Occasionally they froze and listened. Nothing – no voices, no knocking, only the usual sounds of a forest at night.

The house loomed up out of the darkness unexpectedly. Erast Petrovich almost blundered into the planks of the wall, which were pressed right up against two pine trees. To look at, it was an ordinary peasant hut, like many that they had seen during their journey across the plain. Wooden lattices instead of windows, a thatched straw roof, a sliding door. Only one thing was strange – the area around the hut had not been cleared, the trees ran right up to it on all sides, and their branches met above its roof.

The house was absolutely still and silent, and Fandorin signalled to his servant – let's move on.

After about fifty paces they came across a second house, also concealed in a thicket – one of the pine trees protruded straight out of the middle of the roof; probably it was used as a column. Not a sound or a glimmer of light here either.

Bewilderment and anxiety forced the titular counsellor to be doubly cautious. Before approaching Tamba's house – the one hovering at the edge of the precipice – he had to know for certain what he was leaving behind him. So before they reached the precipice, they turned back.

They covered the entire island in zigzags. They found another house exactly like the first two. Nothing else.

And so the entire 'fortress' consisted of four wooden structures, and there was no garrison to be seen at all.

What if the *shinobi* had left their lair and O-Yumi wasn't here? The idea made Fandorin feel genuinely afraid for the first time.

'*Iko!*'* he said to Masa, and set off, no longer weaving about, straight towards the grey emptiness that could be seen through the pines.

The house of Tamba the Eleventh was the only one surrounded by clear grassy space on three sides. On the fourth side, as Fandorin already knew, there was a gaping precipice.

He could still hope that the inhabitants of this sinister village had gathered for a meeting at the house of their leader (Twigs had said he was called the *jonin*).

Pressing himself against a rough tree trunk, Erast Petrovich surveyed the building, which differed from the others only in its dimensions. There was nothing noteworthy about the residence of the leader of the Stealthy Ones. Fandorin felt something rather like disappointment. But the worst thing of all was that this house also seemed to be empty.

Had it really all been in vain?

The vice-consul darted across the open space and up the steps on to the narrow veranda that ran along the walls. Masa was right behind him every step of way.

Seeing his servant remove his footwear, Erast Petrovich followed his example – not out of Japanese politeness, but in order to make less noise.

The door was open slightly and Fandorin shone his little torch inside. He saw a long, unlit corridor covered with rice straw mats.

Masa wasted no time. He poured a few drops of oil from a little jug into the groove and the door slid back without creaking.

Yes, a corridor. Quite long. Seven sliding doors just like the first one: three on the left, three on the right and one at the end.

Removing the safety catch of his revolver, Erast Petrovich opened the first door on the right slowly and smoothly. Empty. No household items, just mats on the floor.

He opened the opposite door slightly more quickly. Again nothing. A bare room, with a transverse beam running across the far wall.

'Damn!' the titular counsellor muttered.

He moved on quickly, without any more precautions. He jerked open a door on the right and glanced in. A niche in the wall, some kind of scroll in it.

The second door on the left: a floor made of polished wooden boards, not covered with straw, otherwise nothing remarkable.

The third on the right: apparently a chapel for prayer – a Buddhist altar in the corner, statuettes of some kind, an unlit candle.

The third on the left: nothing, bare walls.

No one, absolutely no one! Empty space!

But someone had been here, and very recently – the smell of Japanese pipe tobacco still lingered in the air.

Masa looked round the room that had a wooden floor instead of mats.

---

* 'Let's go!' (Japanese)

433

He squatted down and rubbed the smooth wood. Something caught his interest and he stepped inside.

The vice-consul was about to follow him, but just at that moment he heard a rustling from behind the seventh door, the one closing off the end of the corridor, and he started. Aha! There's someone there!

It was a strange sound, something like sleepy breathing, the breath expelled not by a man, but a giant or some kind of huge monster, it was so powerful and deep.

Let it be a giant or a monster – it was all the same to Erast Petrovich now. Anything but emptiness, anything but deathly silence!

The titular counsellor waited for an endlessly long out-breath to come to an end, flung the door aside with a crash and dashed forward.

Fandorin only just managed to grab hold of the railings, right on the very edge of the little wooden bridge suspended above the precipice. He was surrounded on all sides by Nothing – the night, the sky, a yawning gulf.

He heard the out-breath of the invisible colossus again – it was the boundless ether sighing, stirred by a light breeze.

There was nothing but blackness below the vice-consul's feet, stars above his head; all around him were the peaks of mountains illuminated by the moon, and in the distance, between two slopes, the lights of the distant plain.

Erast Petrovich shuddered and backed into the corridor.

He slammed the door into Nowhere and called out:

'Masa!'

No answer.

He glanced into the room with the wooden floor. His servant was not there.

'Masa!' Erast Petrovich shouted irritably.

Had he gone outside? If he was in the house, he would have answered.

Yes, he had gone out. The entrance door, which the titular counsellor had left open, was now closed.

Fandorin walked up to it and tugged on the handle. The door didn't move. What the hell?

He tugged as hard as he could – the door didn't budge at all. Was it stuck? That was no great problem. It wasn't hard to make a hole in a Japanese partition.

Swinging his fist back, the vice-consul punched the straw surface – and cried out in pain. It felt as if he had slammed his hand into iron.

Erast Petrovich heard a grating sound behind him. Swinging round, he saw another partition sliding out of the wall to enclose him in a cramped square between two rooms, the doors of which (as he noticed only now) were also closed.

'A trap!' – the realisation flashed through Fandorin's mind.

He jerked at the door on the left, with no result, and the same with the door on the right.

They had him locked in, like an animal in a cage.

But this animal had fangs. Fandorin pulled out his seven-round Herstal and started swinging round his own axis, hoping that one of the four doors would open now and there would be an enemy behind it – in a close-fitting black costume with a mask that covered all his face, so that only the eyes could be seen.

And in fact he did see a black man without a face, but not where he was expecting to see him. As he gazed round on all sides, the titular counsellor raised his head – and froze. Directly above Fandorin, there was a ninja lying (yes, yes, *lying*, in defiance of all the laws of nature!) on the ceiling, spreadeagled against it like a spider. The two glinting eyes in the slit between the headscarf and the mask were staring straight at the vice-consul.

Erast Petrovich threw up the hand with the revolver, but the bullet hit the boards of the ceiling – the *shinobi* grabbed the barrel of the diplomat's gun with an incredibly fast movement and turned it away. The spider-man had a grip of iron.

Suddenly the floor under Fandorin's feet caved in and the titular counsellor went hurtling downwards with his eyes closed. Meanwhile the Herstal remained in the ninja's hand.

Erast Petrovich landed softly, on what felt like cushions. He opened his eyes, expecting to find himself in darkness, but there was a lamp burning in the basement.

The stunned Fandorin was facing a lean little old man sitting with his legs crossed and smoking a pipe with a tiny bowl at the end of a long stem.

He blew out a cloud of bluish smoke and spoke in English:

'I wait and you come.'

The narrowed eyes opened wider and glinted with a fierce flame, like two glowing coals.

The wood and the fire,
The coal, the time, the diamond
And the chariot

THE DEATH OF AN ENEMY

Unlike the rooms that Fandorin had seen upstairs, the basement looked lived in and even cosy after a fashion. There really were cushions scattered across the floor, a cup of tea was steaming on a lacquered table, and behind the frightening old man there was a picture hanging on the wall – a portrait of a warrior in a horned helmet, with a bow in his hands, an arrow in his teeth and his glittering eyes glaring menacingly up at the sky.

Erast Petrovich recalled the legend of how the great Momochi Tamba shot the false moon, but the titular counsellor was in no mood for ancient fables just at the moment.

It was pointless to throw himself at his enemy – Fandorin remembered his two previous skirmishes with the *jonin* only too well, and the humiliating way in which they had ended. When an opponent is a hundred times stronger, an individual of dignity has only one weapon – his presence of mind.

'Why did you abduct O-Yumi?' Erast Petrovich asked, trying with all his might to impart a dispassionate expression to his face (after the shock he had just suffered this was difficult). He sat down clumsily on the floor and rubbed his bruised fist. The hatch through which Fandorin had tumbled had already slammed shut – now there was a ceiling of yellow planks above his head.

'I did not abduct her,' the old man replied calmly in his broken but perfectly understandable English.

'You lie!'

Tamba did not take offence or grow angry – he half-closed his eyelids sleepily.

'Lies are my trade, but now I am telling the truth.'

Erast Petrovich was unable to maintain his dispassionate expression: driven by a sudden paroxysm of fury, he lunged forward, grabbed the little old man by the neck and shook him, forgetting that the *jonin* could paralyse him with a single touch of his finger.

'What have you done with Yumi? Where is she?'

Tamba offered no resistance, and his head bobbed about on his skinny shoulders.

'Here. She is here,' Fandorin heard, and jerked his hands away.

'Where is "here"?'

'At home. Midori is expecting you.'

'Who the hell is Midori?' the titular counsellor asked, wrinkling up his forehead. 'Where's my Yumi?'

Behaving as if everything was perfectly normal, the old man glanced into his pipe, saw that the tobacco had been shaken out and packed in a new pinch. He kindled the flame first, puffing out his cheeks, and then spoke.

'Her real name is Midori. She is my daughter. And I did not abduct her. I'd like to see anyone abduct a girl like her ...'

'Eh?' was all that the astounded Fandorin could find to say.

'She makes her own mind up about everything. She has a terribly bad character. And I'm a soft father, she does as she likes with me. The real Tamba would have killed a daughter like that.'

'What do you mean, "the real Tamba"?' the vice-consul asked, desperately rubbing his forehead as he tried to gather his thoughts. 'Then who are you?'

'I am his successor in the eleventh generation,' said the *jonin*, pointing with his pipe at the portrait of the warrior in the horned helmet. 'I am an ordinary, weak man, not like my great predecessor.'

'D-damn the genealogy!' Erast Petrovich exclaimed. 'Where's my Yumi?'

'Midori,' the eleventh Tamba corrected him again. 'She was right in what she said about you. You are half-sighted, short-winged, half-blind. Your sight is keen, but it does not penetrate far. Your flight is impetuous, but not always precise. Your mind is sharp, but not deep. However, I see you have a *kagebikaru* shadow under your left cheekbone, which tells me that you are still at the very beginning of your Path and can change for the better.'

'Where is she?' Fandorin cried, jumping to his feet: he did not wish to listen to this nonsense. And when he jumped up, he banged his head against wood the ceiling was too low for his height.

Bells started chiming in the crown of the vice-consul's head and circles started spinning in front of his eyes, but the old man who called himself O-Yumi's father did not stop talking for a moment.

'If I had noticed the *inuoka* bumps at the sides of your forehead in time, I would not have set the adder on you. Dogs do not bite people like you, snakes leave you alone, wasps do not sting you. Things and animals love you. You are a man of a very rare breed. That is why I assigned my daughter to you.'

Erast Petrovich did not interrupt him any more. O-Yumi had mentioned that her father was an unsurpassed master of *ninso*! Could what he was saying really be true?

'Midori took a look at you and said yes, you were special. It would be a shame to kill someone like that. Properly employed, you could be very helpful.'

'Where is she?' Fandorin asked in a dejected voice. 'I must see her ...'

At that Tamba reached out one hand to the wall, pressed something, and the wall slid sideways.

O-Yumi was sitting in the next room, wearing a white and red kimono, with her hair in a tall style. Completely motionless, her face absolutely still, she looked like a beautiful doll. Erast Petrovich was no more than five steps away from her.

He shot forward towards her, but O-Yumi didn't stir and he didn't dare to embrace her.

'She's drugged!' – the thought flashed through his mind; but her gaze was perfectly clear and calm. This was a strange, incomprehensible O-Yumi sitting in front of him, close enough for him to reach out and touch her, but that distance seemed quite insurmountable. It was not this woman he loved, but another, who, as it turned out, had never existed . . .

'What? Why? What for?' poor Fandorin babbled incoherently. 'Are you a ninja?'

'The very best in the Momochi clan,' Tamba declared proudly. 'She can do almost everything that I can do. But in addition, she has mastered arts that are inaccessible to me.'

'I know,' the titular counsellor said with a bitter laugh. 'For instance, *jojutsu*. You sent her to a brothel to study that wisdom.'

'Yes. I sent her to Yokohama to study. Here in the mountains no one would have taught her to be a woman. And Midori had to study the foreign barbarians, because Japan needs them.'

'Did he order you to study me too?' Erast Petrovich asked the woman of stone.

Tamba answered again.

'Yes. I will tell you how it happened. I received a commission to protect the samurai who were pursuing Minister Okubo. My men could easily have killed him themselves, but it had to be done by the samurai. Then the killing would have a meaning that was clear to everyone and no one would suspect my client.'

'Don Tsurumaki?'

'Yes. The Momochi clan has been receiving commissions from him for several years. A serious man, he pays promptly. When one of the client's men told me that an old foreigner was sitting in the Rakuen gambling house and telling everybody about the group led by Ikemura with the withered arm, the tattler's mouth had to be stopped. The job was done very neatly, but then you turned up, most inappropriately. Ikemura and his men had to hide. And I also found out that you had taken as your servant a man who had seen me and could identify me.'

'How did you find that out?' Fandorin asked, turning towards the *jonin* for the first time since the partition had slid aside.

'From the client. And he got his information from police chief Suga.'

For whom the efficient Asagawa wrote his reports, the titular counsellor added to himself. Events that had seemed mysterious, even inexplicable, began arranging themselves in a logical sequence, and this process was so fascinating that the vice-consul forgot about his broken heart for a while.

'I had to kill your servant. Everything would have fitted nicely – the bite of the *mamusi* would have rid me of the witness. But then you showed up again. At first I almost made a mistake, I almost killed you. But the snake proved cleverer. It did not wish to bite you. Of course, I could easily have killed you myself, but the *mamusi's* strange behaviour forced me to take a closer look at you. I saw that you were an unusual man and it would be a shame to kill someone like that. And in any case, the death of a foreign diplomat would have created too much commotion. You had seen me – that was bad, but you would not be able to find me. That was how I reasoned.' The old man finished smoking his pipe and shook out the ash. 'And then I made another mistake, which happens to me very, very rarely. The client informed me that I had left a clue. An unheard-of kind of clue – the print of a finger, and I had done it twice. It turned out that European science can find a man from such a small thing as that. Very interesting. I instructed one of my *genins* to find out more about fingerprints, it could be useful to us. Another *genin* broke into the police station and destroyed the clues. He was a good *shinobi*, one of my cousins. He didn't manage to escape his pursuers, but he died like a genuine ninja, without leaving his face to his enemies . . .'

All this was extraordinarily interesting, but one strange thing was bothering Erast Petrovich. Why was the *jonin* taking so much trouble to enlighten his prisoner, why did he think it necessary to offer any explanations? This was a riddle!

'By that time Midori had already started working with you,' Tamba went on. 'I found you more and more interesting. How artfully you tracked down Ikemura's group! If not for Suga, who corrected the situation, my client could have had serious problems. But Suga was not cautious enough, and you exposed him. You acquired new clues, even more dangerous than the previous ones. The client ordered me to finish you off, once and for all. To kill Prince Onokoji, who had caused him too much trouble, to kill you all: the head of the foreign police, Asagawa, the bald doctor. And you.'

'Me too?' Fandorin asked with a start. 'You say the Don ordered me to be killed too?'

'Especially you.'

'Why didn't you do it? There on the pier?'

The old man heaved a sigh and shifted his gaze to his daughter.

'Why, why . . . And why am I wasting time on you, instead of wringing your neck?'

The titular counsellor, who was very much concerned about this question, held his breath.

'I have already told you. I am a poor, weak *jonin*. My daughter does as she likes with me. She forbade me to kill you, and I deceived the client. How shameful . . .'

Tamba lowered his head on to his chest and sighed even more bitterly. Fandorin turned round towards O-Yumi, who was really called something else.

'B-but why?' he asked with just his lips.

'The *shinobi* are degenerating,' Tamba said mournfully. 'In former times a ninja girl, the daughter of a *jonin*, would never have fallen in love with an outsider, and a barbarian.'

'What!' Erast Petrovich gasped, and suddenly saw a blush appear on Midori's doll-like cheeks.

439

'I did not kill you, I gave part of the money back to the Don and said you had been saved by a miracle. But my shame was not enough for her, she decided to destroy me. When you fought the Englishman with swords, Midori concealed herself in the bushes. She fired a sleeping dart into the red-headed man from a *fukubari*. It was a terribly stupid thing to do. When Tsurumaki was taking the Englishman home, he discovered the dart sticking out of his throat and realised that this was the work of *shinobi*. The Don imagined that I was playing a double game. He took precautions, crammed his house full of guards – he was afraid that I would come to kill him. And you, not knowing anything, walked straight into the den of the tiger . . .'

'And you didn't say anything to me?' Fandorin said to Midori.

She moved for the first time – lowering her eyes.

'Would you want her to betray her father? To tell an outsider about the Momochi clan?' Tamba asked menacingly. 'No, she chose to act differently. My daughter is a lovesick fool, but she is a very cunning fool. She thought of a way to save you. Midori knew that Tsurumaki was afraid of me, not you. He does not understand why I started obstructing him and so he is very worried. If the Don learned that the ninja had stolen your lover, he would not kill you. Midori put your servant to sleep – not for long, only a few minutes, and hurried here to me. She said Tsurumaki would definitely bring you, since he had to work out what the connection was between you and the *jonin* of the Momochi clan . . .' The old man smiled dourly. 'If he only knew the truth, he would lose all respect for me . . . Tamba the First had no weaknesses. He did not hesitate to abandon his sons to die in the besieged temple at Hijiyama. But I am weak. My weakness is my daughter. And my daughter's weakness is you. That is why you are still alive and why I am talking to you.'

Erast Petrovich said nothing, dumbstruck. The isolated facts had come together to form a single picture, the unsolvable riddles had been solved. But even so he asked – not the *jonin*, but his daughter:

'Is this true?'

Without raising her head, she nodded. She mouthed some short phrase soundlessly.

'I love you,' Fandorin read from her lips, and felt a hot pulse pound in his temples. Never before, not even in the most tender of moments, had she spoken those words. Or was this the accursed *jojutsu* again?

'I am not your enemy,' said Tamba, interrupting the lengthy pause. 'I cannot be the enemy of the man my daughter loves.'

But the titular counsellor, stung by the very thought of *jojutsu*, exclaimed intransigently:

'No, you are my enemy! You killed my friends! What have you done with Masa?'

'He is alive and well,' the old man said with a gentle smile. 'He simply walked into a room with a revolving floor and landed in a pit. My nephew Jingoro squeezed your servant's neck, to make him fall asleep. You will wake him yourself soon.'

But the vice-consul had a long account to settle with the Momochi clan.

'You killed my friends! Asagawa, Lockston, Twigs! Did you really think I would forget about them?'

Tamba shrugged at that and said sadly:

'I hoped you would understand. My *genins* were doing their job. They did not kill your friends out of hate, but because it was their duty. Each one of them was killed quickly, respectfully and without suffering. But if you wish to take revenge for them, that is your right. Tamba does nothing by halves.'

He thrust his hand under the low table, pressed something, and a dark square opened up in the ceiling above Fandorin's head.

The *jonin* gave a brief order and the vice-consul's Herstal dropped on to the rice mats in front of him with a dull thud.

'Take your revenge on me,' said the *shinobi*. 'But do not hold any grievance against Midori. She is not guilty of offending you in any way.'

Erast Petrovich slowly picked up the weapon and flicked open the cylinder. He saw one spent cartridge and six fresh ones. Could the old man really be serious?

He raised the revolver and aimed it at Tamba's forehead. The old man didn't look away, he merely closed his eyelids. 'He could probably mesmerise me, or hypnotise me, or whatever they call it, but he doesn't want to,' Fandorin realised.

Midori looked at him briefly, and he thought he saw entreaty in her eyes. Or did he imagine it? A woman like that wouldn't plead with anyone for anything, not even to save her father.

As if in confirmation of this thought, she lowered her head again.

The titular counsellor forced himself to remember the faces of his dead friends; Lockston, as true and dependable as steel; Asagawa, the knight of justice; Dr Twigs, the father of two girls with a heart defect.

It is impossible to shoot at a man who is not trying to protect himself, but the pain that had welled up in Fandorin's soul demanded an outlet – he had cramp in his finger from the irresistible desire to press the trigger

There are things that cannot be forgiven, or the balance of the world will be shattered, Erast Petrovich told himself.

He jerked his wrist slightly to one side and fired.

The thunderous crash deafened him.

Midori threw her hands up to her temples, but she didn't raise her face.

Tamba himself didn't move a single muscle. There was a crimson stripe burned across his temple.

'There now,' he said peaceably. 'Your enemy Tamba is dead. Only your friend Tamba is left.'

Today we rejoice,
Our enemies are destroyed.
Such great loneliness!

THE LOVE OF TWO MOLES

There was a dull rumbling sound from somewhere above them.

Erast Petrovich raised his head. A thunderstorm?

Another peal, but this time the rumbling was accompanied by a crackling sound.

'What is it?' asked Fandorin, jumping to his feet.

'It is Kamata starting to fire his cannon,' said Tamba, also getting up, but without hurrying. 'He didn't wait until dawn. He must have realised that you and your servant are here with us.'

So the *jonin* knew all about Kamata's plan!

'You know everything? How?'

'These are my mountains. Every tree has ears and every blade of grass has eyes. Let us go, before these stupid people hit one of the houses by accident.'

Tamba stood under the hatch, squatted down on his haunches and then sprang up into the air – so high that he landed sitting on the edge of the opening. There was a flash of white socks and the old man was already upstairs.

Fandorin looked round for Midori and started – the next room was empty. When had she managed to disappear?

Tamba leaned down out of the opening in the ceiling.

'Give me your hand!'

But the titular counsellor didn't give him his hand – it would have been humiliating. He pulled himself up clumsily, banging his elbow against a plank in the process. The *jonin* was wearing black trousers and a loose black shirt. Darting out on to the veranda, he put on black leather stockings, pulled a mask over his face, and became almost invisible. In the darkness a pillar of fire soared up into the air and stones and clods of earth went flying in all directions.

Tamba was no longer anywhere close, he had dissolved into the darkness. A black shadow jumped down from somewhere (was it off the roof?), touched the ground silently with its feet, performed a forward roll, tumbled aside, got up weightlessly and a second later disappeared. The titular counsellor noticed the air trembling in several other places as well and caught a few brief glimpses of dark silhouettes.

Shells were exploding as often as if an entire artillery battery was bombarding the forest. The rapid-firing Krupps gun had a rate of three shots a minute, recalled Fandorin, a veteran of the Turkish War. Judging from the sound, the Black Jackets must have taken up a position on the summit of the mountain. Watching the intervals closely, the vice-consul understood Kamata's tactics. His gunner was laying down the shells in a chessboard pattern, at intervals of two or three *sazhens*. He obviously intended to plough up the entire forest island. Sooner or later he would hit the houses too. And one of the pines had already caught fire – a bright crimson flower blossomed in the darkness.

What should he do, where should he run?

One of the shadows stopped beside the titular counsellor, grabbed his hand and dragged him after it.

They had already run to the middle of the wood when a shell struck a tree close by. The trunk gave a crack, splinters went flying and they both fell to the ground. Following the pattern, the next explosion tore up the ground ten steps away, and the eyes in the ninja's black face flared up – long and moist, full of light.

It was her!

Midori half-rose and took Erast Petrovich's hand again, in order to run on, but he didn't yield – he pulled her back to him.

The next explosion roared on the other side of them and Fandorin saw her eyes again, very close – so beautiful and full of life.

'Do you really love me?' he asked.

A thunderous rush drowned out his words.

'Do you love me?' Erast Petrovich roared.

Instead of answering, she pulled off her mask, took his face between her hands and kissed him.

And he forgot about the rapid-firing cannon, about death's whistling and rumbling, about everything in the world.

The pine tree blazed brighter and brighter, red shadows flickered across the trunks of trees and the ground. Panting, the titular counsellor tore the clothes from his beloved's shoulders and her body changed from black to white.

Midori made no attempt at all to stop him. Her breathing was as fast as his, her hands were tearing off his shirt.

Around them the flames blazed, the earth split open, the trees groaned and Fandorin felt as if Night itself, wild and hot, were making love to him.

Pine needles pricked his back and his elbows by turns – the grappling lovers were rolling across the ground. Once a piece of shrapnel buried itself in the earth where their bodies had been just a second earlier, but neither of them noticed it.

It all ended suddenly. Midori pushed her beloved off with a jerk and darted in the opposite direction.

'What are you doing?' he exclaimed indignantly – and saw a burning branch falling between them, showering out sparks.

Only then did Erast Petrovich come to his senses.

There was no more artillery fire, just blazing trees crackling in two or three places.

'What is this called in your *jojutsu*?' he asked hoarsely, gesturing round at the forest.

Midori was tying her tangled hair in a knot.

'There's never been anything like this in *jojutsu*. But there will be now. I'll call it "Fire and Thunder".'

She was already pulling on her black costume, turning from white to black.

'Where is everybody?' asked Fandorin, hastily putting his own clothing in order. 'Why is it quiet?'

'Let's go!' she called, and ran on in front.

Half a minute later they were at the fissure – in the very spot where the vice-consul and his servant had thrown the lasso across. The dead tree was still there, but Erast Petrovich couldn't see any sign of the rope.

'Where to now?' he shouted

She pointed across to the other side, then went down on all fours and suddenly disappeared over the edge of the cliff. Fandorin dashed after her and saw a cable woven from dry plant stems hanging down. It was thick and strong enough to hold any weight, so the young man followed Midori without hesitation.

She moved on a long way ahead of him, slithering down easily and confidently. But he found the descent difficult.

'Quickly, quickly, we'll be late!' Midori urged him on from down below.

Erast Petrovich tried his very best, but she still had to wait for quite a long time.

The moment he jumped down on to the grass-covered ground, his guide dragged him on into dense, prickly undergrowth.

There, between two boulders, he saw a black crevice in the sheer wall. The titular counsellor squeezed into it with great difficulty, but after that the passage widened out.

'Please, please, quickly!' he heard Midori's voice pleading out of the darkness.

He dashed towards her – and almost fell when he stumbled over a root or a rock. There was a strong draught blowing from somewhere above him.

'I can't see a thing!'

A glowing thread appeared in the darkness, emittting a weak, trembling glow.

'What's that?' asked Fandorin, enchanted.

'A *yoshitsune*,' Midori replied impatiently. 'A falcon's feather, it has mercury in it. It doesn't go out in the rain and wind. Come on! I'll die of shame if I'm late!'

Now, with the light, it became clear that the underground passage had been equipped very thoroughly: the ceiling and walls were reinforced with bamboo, and there were wooden steps underfoot.

Struggling to keep up with Midori, Erast Petrovich barely looked around at all, but he did notice that every now and then there were branches running off the passage in both directions. It was an entire labyrinth. His guide ran on, turning several corners without slowing down for a moment. The titular counsellor was starting to feel exhausted from the long, steep uphill climb, but the slim figure ahead of him seemed incapable of tiring.

Eventually the steps came to an end and the passage narrowed again. The light went out, something creaked in the darkness and a grey rectangle opened up ahead, admitting the damp, fresh breath of the dawn.

Midori jumped down on to the ground. Following her example, Erast Petrovich discovered that he was clambering out of the trunk of an old, gnarled oak tree.

The secret door closed, and the vice-consul saw that it was absolutely impossible to make out its edges on the rough, moss-covered bark.

'I'm too late!' Midori exclaimed despairingly. 'It's all your fault!'

She darted forward into an open meadow where black silhouettes were moving about slowly. There was a smell of gunpowder and blood. Something long glinted in the morning twilight.

The barrel of the gun, Fandorin realised, looking more closely and then turning his head in all directions.

The underground passage led to the summit of the mountain. The ideal spot for a bombardment – Kamata must have chosen it in advance.

The skirmish was already over. And from the looks of things, it hadn't lasted long. Pouring out of the passage, the *shinobi* had taken the Black Jackets by surprise, from behind.

Tamba was sitting on a stump in the middle of the clearing, smoking his pipe. The other ninja were bringing the dead to him. It was an eerie sight, like something out of the afterlife: silent shadows gliding in pairs above the mist that was creeping across the ground, lifting up the dead men (also black, but with white faces) by their arms and legs and laying them out in rows in front of their leader.

The titular counsellor counted: four rows with eight bodies in each, and another body started moving, this time a little one – no doubt the old bandit Kamata. Not one had escaped. Don Tsurumaki would never know what had happened to his brigade . . .

Shaken by this grim picture, Fandorin didn't notice that Midori had come back to him. Her husky voice whispered right in his ear.

'I was late anyway, and we hadn't finished.'

A lithe arm slipped round his waist and pulled him back towards the entrance of the underground passage.

'I shall go down in the history of *jojutsu* as a great pioneer,' Midori whispered, pushing the titular counsellor into the hollow of the tree. 'I've just had an idea for a very interesting composition. I shall call it "The Love of Two Moles".'

Even lovelier
Than two flamingos' loving –
The love of two moles.

THE NOCTURNAL MELDING OF
THE WORLD

Tamba said:

'I know a lot about you, you know little about me. From this there arises mistrust, mistrust produces misunderstanding, misunderstanding leads to mistakes. Ask me everything you wish to know, and I will answer.'

The two of them were sitting in the open clearing in front of the house and watching the sun rising from behind the plain, filling the world with a rosy glow. Tamba was smoking his little pipe, every now and then stuffing it with a new pinch of tobacco. Fandorin would gladly have smoked a cigar with him, but the box of excellent manilas had been left behind with the baggage, on the side of the crevice that divided the *shinobi* village from the rest of the world.

'How many of you are there?' the titular counsellor asked. 'Only eleven?'

He had seen eleven people at the site of the massacre. When the earth-stained lovers crawled out of their underground burrow, the *shinobi* had already concluded their sombre task. The dead had been counted, tipped into a pit and covered over with rocks. Tamba's people took off their masks and Fandorin saw ordinary Japanese faces – seven male and four female.

'There are four children too. And Satoko, Gohei's wife. She wasn't in the battle, because she is due to give birth soon. And three young people, out in the big wide world.'

'Spying for someone?' asked Erast Petrovich. If the *jonin* wanted a straight-talking conversation, then to hell with ceremony.

'Studying. One in Tokyo University, studying to be a doctor. One in America, studying to be a mechanical engineer. One in London, studying to be an electrical engineer. We can't get by without European science nowadays. The great Tamba said: "Be ahead of everyone else, know more than everyone else". We have been following that precept for three hundred years. And he also said: "The ninja of the Land of Iga are dead, now they are immortal".'

'But surely Tamba the First was killed together with the others? I was told that their enemies wiped them out to the l-last man.'

'No, Tamba got away, and he took his best pupils with him. He had sons, but he didn't take them, and they were killed, because Tamba was truly great, his heart was as hard as diamond. The final *jonin* of the land of Iga chose the worthiest, so that they could revive the Momochi clan.'

'How did they manage to escape from the besieged temple?'

'When the shrine of the goddess Kannon was already burning, the last of the ninja wanted to take their own lives, but Tamba ordered them to hold out until dawn. The day before, one of his eyes had been put out by an arrow and all his men were also covered in wounds, but such is the power of the *jonin* that the *shinobi* did not dare to disobey. At dawn Tamba released three black ravens into the sky and left through an underground passage with his two chosen companions. But the others took their own lives, cutting off their faces at the last moment.'

'If there was an underground passage, then why didn't they all leave?'

'Because then Nobunaga's warriors would have pursued them.'

'And why was it absolutely necessary to wait until dawn?'

'So that the enemy would see the three ravens.'

Erast Petrovich shook his head, totally bamboozled by this exotic oriental reasoning.

'What have the three ravens got to do with it? What were they n-needed for?'

'Their enemies knew how many warriors were ensconced in the temple – seventy-eight men. Afterwards they would be certain to count the corpses. If three were missing, Nobunaga would have guessed that Tamba had got away and ordered a search for him throughout the empire. But this way the samurai decided that Tamba and two of his deputies had turned into ravens. The besieging forces were prepared for every kind of magic, they brought with them dogs, trained to kill rodents, lizards and snakes. They had hunting falcons with them as well. The falcons pecked the ravens to death. One raven had a wound instead of its right eye and so the ninjas' enemies, knowing of Tamba's wound, stopped worrying. The dead raven was displayed at a point where eight roads met and a sign was nailed up: "The Wizard Momochi Tamba, defeated by the Ruler of the West and the East, Protector of the Imperial Throne, Prince Nobunaga". Less than a year later, Nobunaga was killed, but no one ever discovered that it was Tamba who did it. The Momochi clan was transformed into a ghost, that is, it became invisible. For three hundred years we have preserved and developed the art of *ninjutsu*. Tamba the First would be pleased with us.'

'And none of the three lines has been interrupted?'

'No, because the head of the family is obliged to select a successor in good time.'

'What does "select" mean?'

'Choose. And not necessarily his own son. The boy must have the necessary abilities.'

'Wait,' Fandorin exclaimed in disappointment. 'So you are not a direct descendant of Tamba the First?'

The old man was surprised.

'By blood? Of course not. What difference does that make? Here in Japan, kinship and succession are based on the spirit. A man's son is the one into whom his soul has migrated. I, for instance, have no sons, only a daughter. I do have nephews, though, and cousins, once removed and twice removed.

But the spirit of the great Tamba does not dwell in them, it dwells in eight-year-old Yaichi. I chose him five years ago, in a village of untouchables. In his grubby little face I saw signs that I thought looked promising. And it seems that I was not mistaken. If Yaichi continues to make the same kind of progress, after me he will become Tamba the Twelfth.'

Erast Petrovich decided to wait a little with the other questions – his head was already spinning as it was.

Their second conversation took place in the evening, at the same spot, only this time the two of them sat facing the opposite direction. Watching the sun slipping down on to the summit of the next mountain.

Tamba sucked on his eternal pipe, but now Fandorin was also smoking a cigar. The selfless Masa, who was suffering morally because he had slept right through the night battle, had spent half the day supplying all of his master's needs by bringing his baggage from the ravaged camp through the underground passage, as well as using a cable hoist (it turned out that there was one of those too). The only thing left on the other side was the untransportable Royal Crescent Tricycle, and there was nowhere to ride that in the village in any case. The mule, set free, wandered through the meadows, dazed and delighted by the luscious mountain grass.

'I have a request for you,' said Erast Petrovich. 'Teach me your art. I will be a zealous student.'

He had spent most of the day observing the *shinobi* training and had seen things that left his face frozen in an expression of dumb bewilderment entirely alien to him in normal life.

First Fandorin had watched the children playing. A little six-year-old had demonstrated quite incredible patience in training a mouse – teaching it to run to a saucer and come back again. Every time the mouse coped with its mission successfully, he moved the saucer a bit farther away.

'In a few months' time the mouse will learn to cover distances of four hundred or even five hundred yards. Then it can be used for delivering secret notes,' explained the ninja called Rakuda, who had been attached to the vice-consul.

'Rakuda' meant 'camel', but the ninja was nothing at all like a camel. He was a middle-aged man with a plump, extremely good-natured face, the kind of man that people say 'wouldn't hurt a fly'. He spoke excellent English – which was why he had been assigned to accompany Erast Petrovich. He suggested that the titular counsellor call him 'Jonathan', but Fandorin liked the resounding 'Rakuda' better.

Two little girls were playing at funerals. They dug a little pit, one of them lay down in it and the other covered her with earth.

'Won't she suffocate?' Fandorin asked in alarm.

Rakuda laughed and pointed to a reed protruding from the 'grave'.

'No, she's learning to breathe with a quarter of her chest, it's very useful.'

But of course, the young man was interested most of all in eight-year-old Yaichi, whom Tamba had designated as his successor.

The skinny little boy – nothing exceptional to look at – was clambering up the wall of a house. He fell off, scraping himself so that he bled, and climbed back on the wall again.

It was incredible! The wall was made of wooden planks, there was absolutely nothing to cling to, but Yaichi dug his nails into the wood and pulled himself up, and in the end he climbed on to the roof. He sat there, dangled his legs and stuck his tongue out at Fandorin.

'It's some kind of witchcraft!' the vice-consul exclaimed.

'No, it's not witchcraft. It's *kakeume*,' said Rakuda, beckoning to the boy, who simply jumped straight down from a height of two *sazhens*. He showed them his hands and Erast Petrovich saw iron thimbles with curved talons on his fingers. He himself tried using them to climb a wall, but he couldn't. What strength the fingertips must have to support the weight of the body!

'Come on, come on,' Rakuda called to him. 'Etsuko is going to kill the *daijin*.'

'Who is the *daijin*?' asked Fandorin, following his guide into one of the houses.

There were four people there in a large empty room: two men, a girl with broad cheekbones and someone wearing a tunic and cap, sitting over by the wall at one side. When he looked more closely, Fandorin saw it was a life-sized doll with a painted face and luxurious moustache.

'"*Daijin*" means "big man",' Rakuda explained in a whisper. 'Etsuko has to kill him, and Gohei and Tanshin are his bodyguards. It's a kind of test that she has to pass before she can move on to the next level of training. Etsuko has already tried twice and failed.'

'A sort of exam, right?' the titular counsellor asked curiously as he observed what was happening.

Pock-faced Gohei and sullen, red-faced Tanshin searched the girl thoroughly – she was obviously playing the part of a petitioner who had come for an audience with the 'big man'.

The search was so scrupulous that Erast Petrovich blushed furiously. Not only was the 'petitioner' stripped naked, all the cavities of her body were explored. Young Etsuko played her part diligently – bowing abjectly, giggling timidly, turning this way and that. The 'bodyguards' felt the clothing she had taken off, her sandals, her wide belt. They extracted a tobacco pipe from a sleeve and confiscated it. In her belt they found a small cloth bag with *hashi* – wooden sticks for eating – and a jade charm. They gave back the sticks, but turned the charm this way and that and then kept it, just in case. They made the girl let down her hair and took out two sharp hairpins. Only then did they allow her to get dressed and go through to the *daijin*. But they wouldn't let her get really close – they stood between her and the doll: one on the right, one on the left.

Etsuko bowed low to the seated doll, folding her hands together on her stomach. And when she straightened up there was a wooden *hashi* in her hand. The 'petitioner' made a lightning-swift movement and the stick sank straight into the *daijin*'s painted eye.

'Ah, well done,' Rakuda said approvingly. 'She carved the *hashi* out of hard wood, sharpened the end and smeared it with poison. She has passed the test.'

'But they wouldn't have allowed her to get away! The bodyguards would have killed her on the spot!'

'What difference does that make? The commission has been carried out.'

Then Erast Petrovich saw training in unarmed combat, and this, perhaps, made the strongest impression of all on him. He had never imagined that the human body was capable of such things.

By this time Masa had finished carrying things about and he joined his master. He observed the acrobatic tricks of the Stealthy Ones with a sour face and seemed thoroughly envious.

The training was supervised by Tamba himself. There were three students. One of them, the youngest, was not very interesting to watch: he kept getting up and falling, getting up and falling – backwards, face down, sideways, somersaulting over his head. The second one – the pock-faced Gohei, who was one of the *gaijin*'s 'bodyguards' – hacked at the *jonin* with a sword. He attacked with extremely subtle and cunning thrusts, swung from above and below, and at the legs, but the blade always sliced through the empty air. And Tamba didn't make a simple superfluous movement, he just leaned slightly to the side, squatted down or jumped up. This entertainment was frightening to watch. The third student, a fidgety fellow of about thirty (Rakuda said his name was Okami), fought with his eyes blindfolded. Tamba held a bamboo board in front of him, changing its position all the time, and Okami struck it with unerringly accurate blows from his hands and feet.

'He has intuition,' Rakuda said respectfully. 'Like a bat.'

In the end Masa could no longer bear the expressions of admiration that Fandorin uttered from time to time. With a determined sniff, he walked over to the *jonin*, bowed abruptly and made a request of some kind.

'He wishes to fight with one of the pupils,' Erast Petrovich's guide translated.

Tamba cast a sceptical eye over the former Yakuza's sturdy figure and shouted:

'Neko-chan!'

A wizened little old woman emerged from the hut near by, wiping flour off her hands with her apron. The *jonin* pointed at Masa and gave a brief order. The old woman smiled broadly, opening a mouth that had only one yellow tooth, and took off her apron.

It was clear from Masa's face just how terribly insulted he felt. However, Fandorin's faithful vassal demonstrated his self-control by walking up politely to the matron and asking her about something. Instead of answering, she slapped him on the forehead with her hand – it looked like a joke, but Masa squealed in pain. His flour-dusted forehead turned white and his face turned red. Fandorin's servant tried to grab the insolent hag by the scruff of her neck, but she took hold of his wrist, twisted it slightly – and the master of jujitsu and connoisseur of the Okinawa style of combat went tumbling head over heels to the ground. The amazing old woman didn't give him time to get up. She skipped towards the defeated man, pressed him down against the ground with her knee and squeezed his throat with her bony hand – he gave a strangulated wheeze and slapped his palm on the ground in a sign of surrender.

Neko-chan immediately opened her fingers. She bowed to the *jonin*, picked up her apron and went back to her duties in the kitchen.

And that was the moment, as Fandorin looked at the dejected Masa, who didn't dare raise his own eyes to look at his master, that the titular counsellor decided he had to learn the secrets of *ninjutsu*.

When Tamba heard the request, he was not surprised, but he said:

'It is hard to gain insight into the secrets of *ninjutsu*, a man must devote his entire life to it, from the day he is born. But you are too old, you will not achieve complete mastery. To master a few skills is all that you can hope for.'

'Let it be a f-few skills. I accept that.'

The *jonin* cast a quizzical glance at the stubborn jut of the titular counsellor's jaw and shrugged.

'All right, let's try.'

Erast Petrovich beamed joyfully, immediately stubbed out his cigar and jumped to his feet.

'Shall I take my jacket off?'

Tamba breathed out a thin stream of smoke.

'No. First you will sit, listen and try to understand.'

'All right.'

Fandorin obediently sat down, took a notebook out of his pocket and prepared to take notes.

'*Ninjutsu* consists of three main arts: *monjutsu*, the art of secrecy, *taijutsu*, the art of controlling the body, and *bujutsu*, the art of controlling a weapon . . .'

The pencil started scraping nimbly across the paper, but Tamba laughed, making it clear that he was imitating the manner of a typical lecturer only in fun.

'But we shall not get to all that for a long, long time. For now, you must make yourself like a newborn child who is discovering the world and studying the abilities of his own body. You must learn to breathe, drink, eat, control the functioning of your inner organs, move your arms and legs, crawl, stand, walk, fall. We teach our children from the cradle. We stretch their joints and muscles. We rock the cradle roughly and rapidly, so that the little child quickly learns to shift its centre of gravity. We encourage what ordinary children are punished for: imitating the calls of animals and birds, throwing stones, climbing trees. You will never be like someone raised in a *shinobi* family. But do not let that frighten you. Flexible limbs and stamina are not the most important things.'

'Then what is most important, sensei?' asked Erast Petrovich, using the most respectful Japanese form of address.

'You must know how to formulate a question correctly. That is half of the task. And the second half is being able to hear the answer.'

'I d-don't understand . . .'

'A man consists of questions, and life and the world around him consist of answers to these questions. Determine the sequence of the questions that concern you, starting with the most important. Then attune yourself to receive the answers. They are everywhere, in every event, in every object.'

'Really in every one?'

'Yes. For every object is a particle of the Divine Body of the Buddha. Take this stone here . . .' Tamba picked up a piece of basalt from the ground and showed it to his pupil. 'Take it. Look at it very carefully, forgetting about everything except your question. See what an interesting surface the stone has; all these hollows and bumps, the pieces of dirt adhering to it, the flecks of other substances in it. Imagine that your entire life depends on the structure and appearance of this stone. Study this object for a very long time, until you feel that you know everything about it. And then ask it your question.'

'Which one, for instance?' asked Erast Petrovich, examining the piece of basalt curiously.

'Any. If you should do something or not. If you are living your life correctly. If you should be or not be.'

'To be or not to be?' the titular counsellor repeated, not entirely sure whether the *jonin* had quoted Shakespeare or whether it was merely a coincidence. 'But how can a stone answer?'

'The answer will definitely be there, in its contours and patterns, in the forms that they make up. The man who is attuned to understanding will see it or hear it. It might not be a stone, but any uneven surface, or something that occurs purely by chance: a cloud of smoke, the pattern of tea leaves in the bottom of a cup, or even the remains of the coffee that you *gaijins* are so fond of drinking.'

'Mmm, I see,' the titular counsellor drawled. 'I've heard about that in Russia. It's called "reading the coffee grounds".'

At night he and she were together. In Tamba's house, where the upper rooms existed only to deceive and real life was concentrated in the basement, they were given a room with no windows.

Following lingering delights that were not like either 'Fire and Thunder' or 'The Love of Two Moles', as he looked at her motionless face and lowered eyelashes, he said:

'I never know what you're feeling, what you're thinking about. Even now.'

She said nothing, and he thought there was not going to be any answer.

But then sparks glinted under those eyelashes and those scarlet lips stirred:

'I can't tell you what I'm thinking about. But if you want, I'll show you what I'm feeling.'

'Yes, I do want, very much!'

She lowered her eyelashes again.

'Go upstairs, into the corridor. It's dark there, but close your eyes as well, so you can't even see the shadows. Touch the wall on the right. Walk forward until you find yourself in front of a door. Open it and take three big steps forward. Then open your eyes.'

That was all she said.

He got up and was about to put on his shirt.

'No, you must not have any clothes on.'

He walked up the stairway attached to the wall. He didn't open his eyes.

He walked slowly along the corridor and bumped into a door.

He opened it – and the cold of the night scalded his skin.

It's the door with the precipice behind it, he realised.

Three big steps? How big? How long was the little bridge? About a *sazhen*, no longer.

He took one step, and then another, trying not to keep them short. He hesitated before the third. What if the third step took his foot into the void?

The precipice was here, right beside him, he could feel its fathomless breathing.

With an effort of will he took a step – exactly as long as the first ones. His toes felt a ribbed edge. Just one more inch and . . .

He opened his eyes – and he saw nothing.

No moon, no stars, no lights down below.

The world had melded into a single whole, in which there was no heaven and no earth, no top and no bottom, There was only a point around which creation was arranged.

The point was located in Fandorin's chest and it was sending out a signal full of life and mystery: lub-dub, lub-dub, lub-dub.

Sunlight parts all things,
Darkness unites everything.
The night world is one

SPILLED SAKE

Tamba said:

'You must fall as a pine needle falls to the ground – smoothly and silently. But you topple like a felled tree. *Mo ikkai.*'*

Erast Petrovich pictured a pine tree, its branches covered with needles, then one of them broke away and went swirling downwards, settling gently on the grass. He jumped up, flipped over in the air and thudded flat out into the ground.

'*Mo ikkai.*'

The pine needles fluttered down one at a time, the imaginary branch was entirely bare now and he had to start on the next one, but after every fall he heard the same thing:

'*Mo ikkai.*'

Erast Petrovich obediently pounded himself black and blue, but what he wanted most of all was to learn how to fight – if not like Tamba, then at least like the unforgettable Neko-chan. But the *jonin* was in no hurry to get to that stage; so far he had limited himself to the theory. He had said that first it was necessary to study each of the three principles of combat separately: *nagare* – fluidity, *henkan* – mutability, and the most complex of all, *rinki-ohen* – the ability to improvise according to the opponent's manner.

In the titular counsellor's opinion, the most useful part was the information about blows to vitally important points. In this area, it was quite possible to make do with the skills of English boxing and French savate while one was still struggling to grasp the unpronounceable and inexplicable principles of *ninjutsu*.

The pages of his cherished notebook were filled with sketches of parts of the human body with arrows of various thicknesses, according to the strength of the blow, and mysterious comments such as: 'Soda (sxth. vert.) – temp. parls.; not hard! – or inst. Death'. Or: '*Wanshun* (tric.) – temp. parls arm; not hard! – or fracture'.

Surprisingly, the hardest thing proved to be the breathing exercises. Tamba bound his pupil's waist tightly with a belt and Fandorin had to inhale two thousand times in a row, deeply enough to inflate the lower section of his abdomen. This apparently simple exercise made his muscles ache so badly

---

* 'Again' (Japanese)

that on the first evening Fandorin crawled back to his room hunched over and very much afraid that he couldn't make love to Midori.

But he could.

She rubbed his bruises and grazes with a healing ointment and then showed him how to banish the pain and fatigue with *ketsuin* – the magical coupling of the fingers. Under guidance Erast Petrovich spent a quarter of an hour twisting his fingers out of joint to form them into incredibly complicated shapes, after which the absolute exhaustion disappeared as if by magic and his body felt strong and filled with energy.

The lovers did not see each other during the day – Fandorin strove to comprehend the mysteries of falling and correct breathing and Midori was occupied with some business of her own, but the nights belonged entirely to them.

The titular counsellor learned to manage with two hours of rest. It turned out that if one mastered the art of correct sleeping, that was quite sufficient to restore one's strength.

In accordance with the wise science of *jojutsu*, each new night was unlike the one before and had its own name: 'The cry of the heron', 'The little gold chain', 'The fox and the badger' – Midori said that sameness was fatal for passion.

Erast Petrovich's previous life had been coloured primarily in white, the colour of the day. But now that his sleeping time had been reduced so drastically, his existence was dichromatic – white and black. Night was transformed from a mere backdrop to the stage of life into an integral part of it, and the universe as a whole benefited greatly as a result.

The space extending from sunset to dawn included a great many things: rest, passion, quiet conversation and even rowdy horseplay – after all, they were both so young.

For instance, once they argued over who was faster: Midori running or Fandorin on his tricycle.

They didn't think twice about crossing to the other side of the crevice, where the Royal Crescent was waiting for its master, then going down to the foot of the mountain and holding a cross-country race along the path.

At first Erast Petrovich shot out in front, but after half an hour, tired from turning the pedals, he starting moving more slowly, and Midori started gaining on him. She ran lightly and steadily, without increasing her rate of breathing at all. After almost ten versts she overtook the tricyclist and her lead gradually increased.

That was when Fandorin realised how Midori had managed to deliver the healing *maso* herb from the southern slope of Mount Tanzawa in a single night. She had simply run fifteen *ri* in one direction and then the same distance back again! So that was why she laughed when he pitied the over-worked horse . . .

Once he tried to strike up a conversation about the future, but the answer he received was:

'In the Japanese language there is no future tense, only the past and the present.'

'But something will happen to us, to you and me,' Erast Petrovich insisted stubbornly.

'Yes,' she replied seriously, 'but I haven't decided exactly what yet: "The autumn leaf" or "The sweet tear". Both endings have their advantages.'

He went numb. They didn't talk about the future any more.

On the evening of the fourth day Midori said:

'We won't touch each other today. We're going to drink wine and talk about the Beautiful.'

'How do you mean, not touch each other?' Erast Petrovich asked in alarm. 'You promised me "The silver cobweb"!'

'"The silver cobweb" is a night spent in exquisite, sensitive conversation that binds two souls together with invisible threads. The stronger this cobweb is, the longer it will hold the moth of love.'

Fandorin tried to rebel.

'I don't want this "cobweb", the moth isn't going anywhere in any case! Let's do "The fox and the badger" again, like yesterday!'

'Passion does not tolerate repetition and it requires a breathing space,' Midori said in a didactic tone.

'Mine doesn't require one!'

She stamped her foot.

'Which of us is the teacher of *jojutsu* – you or me?'

'Nothing but teachers everywhere. No life of my own at all,' muttered Erast Patrovich, capitulating. 'Well, all right, then, exactly what is "the Beautiful" that we are going to talk about all night long?'

'Poetry, for instance. What work of poetry is your favourite?'

While the vice-consul pondered, Midori set a little jug of sake on the table and sat down cross-legged.

'Well, I don't know . . .' he said slowly. 'I like "Eugene Onegin". A work by the Russian poet P-Pushkin.'

'Recite it to me! And translate it.'

She rested her elbows on her knees and prepared to listen.

'But I don't remember it off by heart. It's thousands of lines long.'

'How can you love a poem that has thousands of lines? And why so many? When a poet writes a lot, it means he has nothing to say.'

Offended for the great genius of Russian poetry, Fandorin asked ironically:

'And how many lines are there in your favourite poem?'

'Three,' she replied seriously. 'I like haiku, three-line poems, best of all. They say so little and at the same time so much. Every word in its place, and not a single superfluous one. I'm sure bodhisattvas talk to each other only in haiku.'

'Recite it,' said Erast Petrovich, intrigued. 'Please, recite it.'

Half-closing her eyes, she half-declaimed, half-chanted:

'Dragonfly-catcher,
Oh, how far ahead of me
Your feet ran today . . .'

'It's beautiful,' Fandorin admitted. 'Only I didn't understand anything. What dragonfly-catcher? Where has he run off to? And what for?'

Midori opened her eyes and she repeated wistfully in Japanese:

'*Doko madeh itta yara* . . . How lovely! To understand a haiku completely, you must have a special sensitivity or secret knowledge. If you knew that the great poetess Chiyo wrote this verse on the death of her little son, you would not look at me so condescendingly, would you?'

He said nothing, astounded by the profundity and power of feeling suddenly revealed in those three simple, mundane lines.

'A haiku is like the casing of flesh in which the invisible, elusive soul is confined. The secret is concealed in the narrow space between the five syllables of the first line (it is called *kami-no-ku*) and the seven syllables of the second line (it is called *naka-no-ku*), and then between the seven syllables of the *naka-no-ku* and the five syllables of the third and final line (it is called *shimo-no-ku*). How can I explain so that you will understand?' Midori's face lit up in a crafty smile. 'Let me try this. A good haiku is like the silhouette of a beautiful woman or an artfully exposed part of her body. The outline and the single detail are far more exciting than the whole thing.'

'But I prefer the whole thing,' Fandorin declared, putting his hand on her knee.

'That's because you are a little urchin and a barbarian.' Her fan smacked him painfully across the fingers. 'It is enough for a sophisticated individual merely to glimpse the edge of Beauty, and in an instant his imagination will fill in all the rest, and even improve it many times over.'

'That, by the way, is from Pushkin,' the titular counsellor growled, blowing on his bruised fingers. 'And your favourite poem may be beautiful, but it is very sad.'

'Genuine beauty is always sad.'

Erast Petrovich was astonished.

'Surely not!'

'There are two kinds of beauty: the beauty of joy and the beauty of sadness. You people of the West prefer the former, we prefer the latter. Because the beauty of joy is as short-lived as the flight of a butterfly. But the beauty of sadness is stronger than stone. Who recalls the millions of happy people in love who have quietly lived their lives, grown old and died? But plays are written about tragic love, and they live for centuries. Let's drink, and then we shall talk about the Beautiful.'

But they were not fated to discuss the Beautiful.

Erast Petrovich raised his little cup and said: 'I drink to the beauty of joy.'

'And I drink to the beauty of sadness,' Midori replied, and drank, but before he could do likewise, the night was split asunder by a frenzied bellow: 'TSUME-E-E!'* The response was a roar that issued from an entire multitude of throats.

Fandorin's hand shook and the sake spilled out on to the tatami.

As his hand trembled,
Wine spilled on to the table.
An evil omen

---

* 'Attack!' (Japanese)

A BIG FIRE

Not that it happened often, but sometimes he did come across a woman who was stronger than him. And then the thing to do was not thrust his chest out and put on airs, but quite the opposite – pretend to be weak and defenceless. That made the strong women melt. And then they handled everything themselves; all he had to do was not get under their feet.

In the village of the accursed *shinobis* there was only one object of any interest to a connoisseur of female charm – seventeen-year-old Etsuko. She was no beauty, of course, but, as the saying went, in a swamp even a toad is a princess. Apart from her, the female population of the village of Kaku-simura* (Masa had invented the name himself, because the *shinobi* didn't call the village anything) consisted of the old witch Neko-chan (what a lovely little pussy-cat!),† pock-faced Gohei's pregnant wife, one-eyed Sae, and fifteen-year-old Nampopo. And two snot-nosed little girls of nine and eleven who didn't even count.

Masa didn't try to approach his chosen prey on the first day – he watched her from a distance, drawing up a plan of action. She was a fine girl, with qualities that made her interesting. Hard working, nimble, a singer. And it was interesting to wonder how the *kunoichi* – ninja women – were made down there. If she could do a jump with a triple somersault or run up a wall on to the roof (he'd seen that for himself), then what sort of tricks did she get up to in moments of passion? That would be something to remember and tell people about.

At first, of course, he had to find out whether she belonged to any of the men. The last thing he needed was to draw down the wrath of one of these devils.

Masa sat in Little Cat's kitchen for an hour, praised her rice balls and found out everything he needed to know. There was a fiancé, his name was Ryuzo, a very nice boy, but he had been studying abroad for a year already.

So let him carry on studying.

Now Masa could get down to work.

He spent a couple of days getting friendly with the object. No languorous glances, no hints – Buddha forbid! She was pining without her fiancé, and

---

* Hidden village (Japanese)
† In Japanese *neko-chan* means 'little cat'

he was far from home, among strangers, they were about the same age, so surely they had things to talk about?

He told her a lot of things about the wonders of Yokohama (fortunately, Etsuko had never been to the *gaijin* city). He lied a bit, of course, but only to make it more interesting. Gradually he worked his way round to the exotic bedroom habits of the *gaijins*. The girl's eyes glinted and her little mouth opened halfway. Aha! She might be a *shinobi*, but she had real blood in her veins!

That finally convinced him that he would be successful and he moved on to the last stage but one – he started asking whether it was true that *kunoichi* women really had the right to do as they wished with their own bodies and the idea of being unfaithful to a husband or a fiancé did not even exist for them.

'How can some little hole in your body be unfaithful? Only the soul can be unfaithful, and our souls are true,' Etsuko answered proudly – the clever girl.

Masa had no interest at all in her soul. The little hole was quite enough for him. He whined a bit about never having hugged a girl – he was so very shy and unsure of himself.

'All right, then, come to the crevice at midnight,' Etsuko whispered. 'And I'll give you a hug.'

'That would be very charitable of you,' he said meekly, and start blinking very, very fast – he was so touched.

The place chosen for the rendezvous was absolutely perfect, all credit to the girl for that. At night there wasn't a soul here, and it was a good hundred paces to the nearest house. They didn't post sentries in Kakusimura – what for? On the other side of the crevices there were 'singing boards' under the earth: if anyone stepped on one, it started hooting like an eagle owl and it could be heard from very far away. That time when he and the master had climbed across the rope they'd had no idea that the village was ready to receive visitors.

With Etsuko everything happened quickly, even too quickly. There was no need to act like an inexperienced boy in order to inflame her passions more strongly – she came dashing out of the bushes so fast she knocked him off his feet, and a minute later she was already gasping, panting and scree-ching as she bounced up and down on Masa, like a cat scraping at a dog with its claws.

There wasn't anything special about the *kunoichi*, she was just a girl like any other. Except that her thighs were as hard as stone – she squeezed him so hard, he would probably have bruises left on his hips. But she wasn't inventive at all. Even Natsuko was more interesting.

Etsuko babbled something in a happy voice, stroked Masa's stiff, short-trimmed hair and made sweet talk, but he couldn't hide his disappointment.

'Didn't you like it?' she asked in a crestfallen voice. 'I know I never studied it . . . The *jonin* told me: "You don't need to". Ah, but do you know how good I am at climbing trees? Like a real monkey. Shall I show you?'

'Go on, then,' Masa agreed feebly.

Etsuko jumped up, ran across to the dead pine tree and clambered up the charred trunk, moving her hands and feet with incredible speed.

Masa was struck by a poetic idea: living white on dead black. He even wondered whether he ought to compose a haiku about a naked girl on a charred pine. He had the first two lines all ready – five syllables and seven:

> The old black pine tree,
> Trembling like a butterfly . . .

What next? 'With a girl on it?' Too blunt and direct. 'See love soaring upwards'? That was six syllables, but it should be five.

In search of inspiration he rolled closer to the pine tree – he couldn't be bothered to get up.

Suddenly Masa heard a strange champing sound above him. Etsuko dropped out of the tree with a groan and fell on to the ground two steps away from him. He froze in horror at the sight of a thick, feathered arrow-shaft sticking out of her white back below her left shoulder-blade.

He wanted to go dashing to her, to see whether she was alive.

Etsuko was alive. Without turning over or moving her head, she kicked Masa, so that he went rolling away.

'Run . . .' he heard her say in a muffled whisper.

But Masa didn't run – his legs were trembling so badly, they probably wouldn't have held up the weight of his body.

The night was suddenly full of rustling sounds. Dark spots appeared at the edge of the crevice – one, two, three. Black men climbed up on to the edge of the cliff at the point where the *shinobi* had their secret hoist. There were many of them, very many. Masa lay in the tall grass, looking at them, horror-struck, and he couldn't move.

One of the black men walked over to where Etsuko was lying face down and turned her over on to her back with his foot. He leaned down, and a blade glinted in his hand.

Suddenly the girl sat up, there was a wheeze, and he was lying, but Etsuko was standing with a sword in her hand, surrounded on all sides by the mysterious newcomers. White among the black, Masa thought fleetingly.

The clash of metal, howls, and then the white figure disappeared, and the men in black were furiously hacking at something lying on the ground that crunched as they hit it.

Masa clearly heard a girl's voice shout out:

'*Kongojyo!*'

One of the killers came very close. He tore up a bunch of grass and started cleaning off his sword. Masa heard loud, sporadic breathing.

The pale light of the moon seeped through a thin cloud for a moment and Masa saw a hood with holes instead of eyes, a cartridge belt over a shoulder, a black jacket.

Don Tsurumaki's men, that was who they were! They'd followed the *shinobi's* example and covered their faces so that they wouldn't show white in the darkness!

How had they managed to get past the 'singing boards'? Surely they couldn't have come through the underground passage? Who could have showed it to them?

Masa crawled on all fours into the undergrowth, jumped to his feet and ran.

The Black Jackets didn't waste any time. He heard a muffled command behind him, and fallen pine needles started crunching under rapid footsteps.

He had to get to the houses quickly, to raise the alarm! The Don's men wouldn't bother to find out who was a *shinobi* and who wasn't, they'd finish off everybody regardless.

When he had only twenty paces left to go to the first hut, Masa was unlucky – in the darkness he ran into a branch, tore his cheek and – worst of all – he couldn't stop himself crying out.

The men behind him heard and realised they had been discovered.

'TSUME-E-E!' roared a commanding bass voice.

The response was a roar from many voices.

'An attack! An attack!' Masa roared as well, but shut his mouth almost immediately, realising that he was only exposing himself to unnecessary danger.

The attackers were roaring and tramping so loudly that the inhabitants of Kakusimura couldn't help but hear them.

Now, if he wanted to live, he had to think very quickly. So Masa didn't run towards the houses, he hid behind a tree.

Less than half a minute later a crowd of Black Jackets went rushing past, spreading out and forming into a half-moon in order to take in the whole width of the island.

Torches blazed into life, thrust into the ground along a line at intervals of five paces. The chain of fire cut across the entire forest, from one edge to the other.

'Fire!'

Rapid, crackling salvoes of carbine fire. Masa could hear the bullets thudding into the wooden walls and the squeal of splinters flying out.

Ah, what a disaster! How could he save his master from this hell? The Black Jackets would riddle the first three houses with bullets now, and then they would set about Tamba's home.

Masa dashed about between the pines in despair and saw that he couldn't possibly slip through the brightly lit zone and the cordon.

A crunch of branches. A man running with a limp from the direction of the crevice. Black jacket, black hood – he must have fallen behind the others. Masa attacked him from the side, knocked him down with a single blow and then, to make sure, squeezed the fallen man's neck with his knee and waited for it to crunch. He didn't have to worry about the noise – all the shooting that was going on was deafening.

He pulled the trousers and jacket off the corpse and put them on. He covered his face with the hood – it was very helpful that the Don's men had decided to wear such a useful item.

While he was still fiddling about, the shooting stopped. The wooden walls that had been riddled with bullets were covered in black dots, like the poppy-seed bun that Masa had given Netsuko as a treat. It was almost as bright as day, there were so many torches all around.

One by one the gunmen entered the houses, holding their carbines at the ready. Then they came back out – in twos, dragging dead bodies that they laid out on the ground. The commander leaned down, looking into the dead faces.

Masa counted nine big bodies and four little ones. There were two adults missing.

'Tamba's not here,' the commander said loudly. 'And the *gaijin*'s not here either. They're in the house on the edge of the precipice.'

And he walked away, but not far, only a few steps.

Suddenly one of the bodies came to life. The man (Masa recognised affable, talkative Rakuda) arched up like a cat and jumped on to the commander's back. A knife blade glinted, but the leader of the Black Jackets proved to be very adroit – he jerked his head to dodge the blow, threw himself backwards and started rolling about on the grass. Men dashed to help him from all sides, and a shapeless black octopus with arms and legs sticking out in all directions started writhing on the ground.

Taking advantage of the commotion, another body started moving, this time a little one. It was eight-year-old Yaichi. He rose halfway to his feet, staggered and then shook himself. Two Black Jackets tried to grab the boy, but he wriggled between their outstretched arms and scrambled up a tree in an instant.

'Catch him! Catch him!' his pursuers shouted. There was a rumble of shots.

Yaichi flew across to the next tree, and then the one after that. The branch he was holding broke off, smashed by a bullet, but he grabbed another one.

Meanwhile they had finished off Rakuda. Two Black Jackets were left lying on the ground. The others dragged the dead *shinobi* away and helped their commander to get up. He pushed their willing hands away angrily and pulled the hood off his head. A revolver glinted as he aimed the barrel at the boy skipping though the trees. The barrel described a short arc, spat out a gobbet of flame – and Yaichi came tumbling down like a stone.

Masa froze open-mouthed, astonished by the gunman's accuracy and the gleam of his smoothly shaved head. He had seen this man before, only a few days earlier! The itinerant monk who had spent the night at the village hotel with Kamata's 'construction brigade', that was who it was!

And everything was finally clear.

Don Tsurumaki was a prudent man. He hadn't relied on the faithful but dull-witted Kamata. He had attached a spy to the brigade, a man who had watched everything and sniffed everything out without making himself known. He had seen the massacre on the mountain, noted where the entrance to the underground passage was, and the hoist . . . Neat work, no two ways about it!

The Monk (that was what Masa called the Black Jackets' commander now) was obviously afraid that another dead ninja would come back to life. He pulled a short sword out of its scabbard and set to work. The blade rose thirteen times and fell thirteen times and a pyramid of severed heads rose up by the wall of the house. The Monk handled the sword deftly, he clearly had a lot of experience.

Before moving on to the concluding stage of the storm, the commander ordered his unit to form up in a line.

'Our losses are small,' said the Monk, walking along the line with a springy step. 'The naked girl killed two, the dead man who came to life killed two more, one was hurt when he fell off the hoist. But the greatest danger lies ahead. We shall proceed strictly according to the plan drawn up by Mr Shirota. It's a good plan, you've seen it. Mr Shirota assumes that the house of the werewolves' leader is full of traps. And therefore – extreme caution. Not a single step without orders, is that clear?' Suddenly he stopped, peering into the darkness. 'Who's that there? You, Ryuhei?'

Realising he had been spotted, Masa slowly stepped forward. What should he do? Walk over or take to his heels?

'So you got up after all? Didn't break any bones? Good man. Get back in line.'

Most of the Black Jackets had followed their commander's example and taken off the hoods, but a few, Buddha be praised, had left their faces covered, and so no one suspected Masa; only the man next to him in the line squinted at him and nudged him in the side with his elbow – but he thought that must be a kind of greeting.

'Twenty men cordon off the clearing,' the Monk ordered. 'Hold your carbines at the ready, stay awake. If one of the *shinobi* tries to break through, drop him on the spot. The others come with me, into the house. No crowding, in line, two by two.'

Masa didn't want to join the cordon. He attached himself to the men who would go into the house, but he couldn't get into the first row, only the third.

The plan of the storm had clearly been worked out in detail.

The long double column trotted to the clearing with the *jonin*'s wooden plank house standing on its edge. The twenty-man cordon took up position round the edge of the clearing and stuck torches into the ground.

The others stretched out into a long dark snake and moved forward.

'Carbines on the ground!' the commander ordered, keeping his eyes fixed on the house, which was maintaining a sinister silence. 'Draw your daggers!'

He dropped back a little bit from the men in front and stopped, as if feeling uncertain.

He doesn't want to stick his own neck out, Masa realised. And he's right too. Rakuda (whose heroic death had probably raised him to the next level in the cycle of rebirth) had said that when there was danger, Tamba's house became like a prickly hedgehog – there were some secret levers that had to be pressed for that. The inhabitants of the house had had plenty of time, so there would be lots of surprises in store for the Black Jackets. Masa remembered with a shudder how the floor had tilted under him that night and he had gone tumbling down into darkness.

The Monk was a cautious man, and there was no point in pushing forward too fast.

And then immediately, as if to confirm this idea, it started.

When one of the two men at the front was just a step away from the porch, he disappeared, as if the ground had opened and swallowed him up.

Or rather, there was no 'as if' about it – it did swallow him up. Masa had walked across that spot a hundred times, and he had no idea that there was a pit hidden under it.

There was a spine-chilling howl. The Black Jackets first shied away from the gaping hole, then swarmed round it. Masa stood on tiptoe and looked over someone's shoulder. He saw a body pierced through by sharp stakes, still jerking about.

'I only just stopped myself, right on the very edge!' the survivor from the first row said in a trembling voice. 'The amulet saved me. The goddess Kannon's amulet!'

The others remained morosely silent.

'Line up!' the commander barked.

Skirting round the terrible pit, from which groans were still emerging, they started walking up on to the porch. The owner of the miraculous amulet held one hand out ahead of him, clutching a dagger, and pulled his head down into his shoulders. He passed the first step, the second, the third. Then he stepped timidly on to the terrace, and at that very instant a heavy section fell out of the thick beam framing the canopy. It smacked the man standing below across the the top of his head with a dull thud and he collapsed face down without even crying out. His hand opened and the amulet in its tiny brocade bag fell out.

The goddess Kannon is good for women and for peaceful occupations, thought Masa. For the affairs of men the god Fudo's amulet is more appropriate.

'Well, why have you stopped?' shouted the Monk. 'Forward!'

He ran fearlessly up on to the terrace, but stopped there and beckoned with his hand.

'Come on, come on, don't be such cowards.'

'Who's a coward?' boomed a great husky fellow, pushing his way forward. Masa stepped aside to let the brave man past. 'Right, now, let me through!'

He jerked the door open. Masa winced painfully, but nothing terrible happened.

'Good man, Saburo,' the commander said to the daredevil. 'No need to take your shoes off, this isn't a social call.'

The familiar corridor opened up in front of Masa: three doors on the right, three doors on the left, and one more at the end – with the little bridge into emptiness beyond it.

The hulking brute Saburo stamped his foot on the floor – again nothing happened. He stepped across the threshold, stopped and scratched the back of his head.

'Where to first?'

'Try the one on the right,' ordered the Monk, also entering the corridor. The others followed, crowding together.

Before going in, Masa looked round. A long queue of Black Jackets was lined up on the porch, with their naked swords glittering in the crimson light of the torches. A snake with its head stuck into a tiger's jaws, Fandorin's servant thought with a shudder. Of course, he was for the tiger, heart and soul, but he himself was a scale on the body of the snake . . .

'Go on!' said the commander, nudging the valiant (or perhaps simply stupid) Saburo.

The hulk opened the first door on the right and stepped inside. Turning his head this way and that, he took one step, then another. When his foot touched the second tatami, something twanged in the wall. From the corridor Masa couldn't see what had happened, but Saburo grunted in surprise, clutched at his chest and doubled over.

'An arrow,' he gasped in a hoarse voice, turning round.

And there it was, a rod of metal protruding from the centre of his chest.

The Monk aimed his revolver at the wall, but didn't fire.

'Mechanical,' he murmured. 'A spring under the floor . . .'

Saburo nodded, as if he was completely satisfied by this explanation, sobbed like a child and tumbled over on to his side.

Stepping over the dying man, the commander rapidly sounded out the walls with the handle of his gun, but didn't find anything.

'Move on!' he shouted. 'Hey, you! Yes, yes, you! Go!'

The soldier in a hood at whom the Monk was pointing hesitated only for a second before walking up to the next door. Muffled muttering could be heard from under the mask.

'I entrust myself to the Buddha Amida, I entrust myself to the Buddha Amida . . .' Masa heard – it was the invocation used by those who believed in the Way of the Pure Land.

It was a good prayer, just right for a sinful soul thirsting for forgiveness and salvation. But it was really astonishing that in the room which the follower of the Buddha Amida would have to enter there was a scroll hanging on the wall, with a maxim by the great Shinran:* 'Even a good man can be resurrected in the Pure Land, even more so a bad man'. What a remarkable coincidence! Perhaps the scroll would recognise one of its own and save him?

It didn't.

The praying man crossed the room without incident. He read the maxim and bowed respectfully. But then the Monk told him:

---

* Shinran (1173–1263), the founder of the Jodo sect of the school of the Way of the Pure Land

'Take down the scroll! Look to see if there's some kind of lever hidden behind it!'

There was no lever behind the scroll, but as he fumbled at the wall with his hand, the unfortunate man scratched himself on an invisible nail. He cried out, licked his bleeding palm and a minute later he was writhing on the floor – the nail had been smeared with poison.

Behind the third door was the prayer room. Right, now – what treat would it have in store for visitors? Not staying too close to the Monk (so that he wouldn't call on him), but not too far away either (otherwise he wouldn't see anything), Masa craned his neck.

'Well, who's next?' the commander called and, without waiting for volunteers, he grabbed by the scruff of the neck the first man he could reach and pushed him forward. 'Boldly now!'

Trembling all over, the soldier opened the door. Seeing an altar with a lighted candle, he bowed. He didn't dare go in wearing his shoes – that would have been blasphemy. He kicked off his straw *jori*, stepped forward – and started hopping about on one leg, clutching his other foot in both hands.

'Spikes!' the Monk gasped.

He burst into the room (he was wearing stout *gaijin* boots) and dragged the wounded man out into the corridor, but the man was already wheezing and rolling his eyes up into their lids. The commander sounded out the walls in the prayer room himself. He didn't find any levers or secret springs.

Back out in the corridor he shouted:

'There are only four more doors! One of them will lead us to Tamba! Perhaps it's that one!' He pointed to the door that closed off the end of the corridor. 'Tsurumaki-dono promised a reward to the first man to enter the old wolf's den! Who wants to earn the rank of sergeant and a thousand yen into the bargain?'

There was no one who wanted to. An invisible boundary seemed to run across the corridor: in the section farther on there was plenty of space – the commander was standing there all on his lonesome; but in the first section there was a whole crowd of about fifteen men crammed close together, and more were piling in from the porch.

'Ah, you chicken-hearts! I'll manage without you!'

The Monk pushed the door aside and held out his hand with the pistol in it. Seeing the blackness, he started back, but immediately took a grip on himself.

He laughed.

'Look at what you were afraid of! Emptiness! Well, there are only three doors left! Does anyone want to try his luck? No? All right . . .'

He opened the farthest door on the left. But he didn't hurry inside; first he squatted down and waved his hand for them to bring him a lamp. He examined the floor. He struck the tatami with his fist and only then stepped on to it. Then he took another step in the same way.

'A stick!'

Someone handed him a bamboo pole.

The Monk prodded at the ceiling and the wall. When a board in the corner gave out a hollow sound, he immediately opened fire – one, two, three shots roared out.

Three holes appeared in the light yellow surface. At first it seemed to Masa that the commander was being too cautious, but suddenly there was a creak, the wall swayed open and a man in the black costume of a ninja fell out face first.

There was a dark hollow in the wall – a secret cupboard.

Without wasting a second, the Monk switched the revolver to his left hand, pulled out his sword and hacked at the fallen man's neck. He pulled off the mask and picked up the head by its pigtail.

Gohei's pockmarked face glared at his killer with furious bulging eyes. Tossing the trophy into the corridor, right at Masa's feet, the commander wiped a trickle of blood off his elbow and glanced cautiously into the cavity.

'Aha, there's something here!' he announced eagerly.

He gestured impatiently to call over one of the soldiers who had just removed his hood.

'Shinjo, come here! Take a look at what's in there. Climb up!'

He folded his hands into a stirrup. Shinjo stepped on them with one foot and the upper half of his torso disappeared from view.

They heard a muffled howl: 'A-a-a-a!'

The Monk quickly jumped aside and Shinjo came tumbling down like a sack. A steel star with sharpened edges was lodged in the bridge of his nose.

'Excellent!' said the commander. 'They're in the attic! You, you and you, come here! Guard the entrance. Don't stick your noses in the hole any more, or else they'll throw another *shuriken*. The important thing is not to let any *shinobi* get out this way. The rest of you, follow me! There has to be a way into the basement somewhere here as well.'

Masa knew how to get into the basement. The next room, the second on the right, had a cunning floor – you ended up in the basement before you could even sneeze. Now the man with the shaved head would finally get what he deserved.

But the Monk didn't blunder here either. He didn't barge straight in, like Masa, but squatted down again and examined the wooden boards for a long time. He prodded them with his pole, suddenly realised something and gave a grunt of satisfaction. Then he pressed down hard with his fist – and the floor swayed.

'And there's the basement!' The commander chuckled. 'Three of you stand at the door, and keep your eyes on this!'

The Black Jackets swarmed thickly round the last door. They slid it open and gazed expectantly at their cunning commander.

'Ri-ight,' he drawled, running a keen gaze across the bare walls. 'What do we have here? Aha. I don't like the look of that projection over there in the corner. What's it needed for? It's suspicious. Come on, then.' Without looking, the Monk reached his hand backwards and grabbed Masa by the sleeve. 'Go and sound it out.'

Oh, he really didn't want to go and sound out that suspicious projection! But how could he disobey? And the Monk was egging him on too!

'What are you hanging about for? Get a move on! Who are you? Ryuhei? Take that hood off, you don't need it here, it just stops you looking at things properly.'

I'm done for anyway, thought Masa, and pulled off the hood – he was standing with his back to the Black Jackets and their commander.

He prayed silently: Tamba-sensei, if you're looking through some cunning little crack right now, don't think I'm a traitor. I came to save my master. Just in case, he winked at the suspicious wall, as if to say: It's me, I'm one of you.

'That's not Ryuhei,' he heard someone say behind him. 'Ryuhei doesn't have a haircut like that, does he?'

'Hey, who are you? Right, turn round!' the Monk ordered.

Masa took two rapid steps forward. He couldn't take a third – the tatami closest to the suspicious projection was false: just straw, with nothing underneath it. With a howl of despair, Masa tumbled through the floor.

A strip of metal glinted right in front of him, but no blow followed.

'Masa!' a familiar voice whispered. Then some Russian words: 'Ya chut ne ubil tebya!'

The master! Alive! Pale, with his forehead contracted into a frown. A dagger in one hand and a little revolver in the other.

Midori-san was beside him – in black battle costume, only without a mask.

'We can't stay here any longer. Let's leave!' the mistress said, then adding something in the *gaijin* language, and all three of them dashed away from the rectangular hole with gentle yellow light pouring down through it.

In the very corner of the basement there was a black shape that looked like some kind of chute, and Masa made out two jute ropes in it – that must have been the projection that had seemed suspicious to the Monk.

The master took hold of one of the ropes and went flying upwards as if by magic.

'Now you!' Midori-san told him.

Masa grabbed the rough jute and it pulled him up towards the ceiling. It was absolutely dark and a little cramped, but the ascent was over in just half a minute.

First Masa saw a wooden floor, then the rope pulled him through a hatch up to his waist and after that he scrambled out by himself.

He looked round and realised he had ended up in the attic. He saw the sloping pitches of the roof on both sides of him, with pale light seeping in through the wooden grilles of the windows.

After blinking so that he could see better in the semi-darkness, Masa made out three figures: one tall (that was the master), one short (Tamba) and one middle-sized (the red-faced ninja Tanshin, who was like the sensei's senior deputy). Midori soared up out of the hatch and the wooden lid slammed shut.

Apparently all the surviving inhabitants of the village of Kakusimura were gathered here.

The first thing to do was look to see what was happening outside. Masa moved over to the window with glimmers of scarlet light dancing in it and pressed his face to it.

A fiery border of torches ran round the house in a half-circle, from cliff-edge to cliff-edge. Loitering between the tongues of flame were dark silhouettes with guns held at the ready. There was no point in sticking their noses out that way, that was clear.

Masa ran across to the other window, but that way was really bad – there was just the black yawning abyss.

So where did that leave them? A precipice on one side and guns on the other. The sky up above and down below . . . In the far corner of the attic there was a yellow square of light in the floor – the hatch discovered by the Monk in the third room on the left. There were Black Jackets in there with naked daggers. So they couldn't go down there either.

But what about all the way down, into the basement?

Masa ran over to the lifting device and opened the hatch slightly – the one he had clambered out of only a couple of minutes earlier.

Down below he could hear the tramping of feet and a buzz of voices – the enemy was already getting up to his tricks in the basement.

That meant they would soon reach the attic too.

It was all over. It was impossible to save the master.

Well then, it was a vassal's duty to die with him. But first to render his master a final service: help him leave this life with dignity. In a hopeless situation, when a man was surrounded on all sides by enemies, the only thing left was to deprive the enemies of the pleasure of seeing your death agony. Let them have nothing but the indifferent corpse, and your dead face gazing at them with superior contempt.

What method could he suggest to his master? If he was Japanese, it would be quite clear. He had a dagger, and there was more than enough time for a decent seppuku. Tanshin had a short, straight sword hanging at his side, so the master would not be left writhing in agony. As soon as he touched his stomach with the dagger, faithful Masa would cut his head off.

But *gaijins* didn't commit seppuku. They liked to die from gunpowder.

So that would be it.

Wasting no time, Masa went over to the *jonin*, who was whispering about something with his daughter, while at the same time doing something quite incomprehensible: inserting sticks of bamboo one into the other.

After apologising politely for interrupting the family conversation, Masa said:

'Sensei, it is time for my master to leave this life. I wish to help him. I have been told that for some reason the Christian religion forbids suicide. Please translate for my master that I would consider it an honour to shoot him in the heart or the side of the head, whichever he desires.'

Then the master himself came across to him. He waved his revolver and said something. The master's face was sombre and resolute. He must have had the same idea.

'Explain to him that he shouldn't open fire,' Tamba told his daughter, speaking rapidly in Japanese. 'He has only seven cartridges. Even if he doesn't miss once and shoots seven Black Jackets, it won't change anything. They'll take fright, stop the search and fire the house. They haven't done that so far because they want to present the Don with my body and they're hoping to find some secret caches. But if they're badly scared, they'll set the house on fire. Tell him I asked you to translate because my English is too slow. Take him to one side, distract him. I need another minute. Then act according to our agreement.'

What agreement was that? What did Tamba need a minute for?

While Midori-san was translating what Tamba had said to the master, Masa kept his eyes fixed on the *jonin*, who finished fiddling with the bamboo sticks and starting shoving them into a narrow kind of case with a large piece of black cloth attached to it.

What weird sort of device was this?

A flag, it's a flag, Masa guessed, and suddenly everything was clear.

The leader of the *shinobi* wanted to leave this life in beautiful style, with the flag of his clan unfurled. That was why he was spinning things out.

'Is that the Momochi banner?' Masa whispered to Tanshin, who was standing close by.

Tanshin shook his head.

'Then what is it?'

The rude *shinobi* left the question unanswered.

Tamba picked up the cloth with the bamboo sticks inserted in it, threw it across his shoulders and belted it on, and it became clear that it wasn't a flag at all, but something like a wide cloak.

Then the *jonin* held out his hand without speaking and Tanshin put the naked sword in it.

'Farewell,' said the *jonin*.

The *shinobi* answered with a word that Masa had heard once before that night.

'*Kongojyo*.' And he bowed solemnly.

Then Tamba walked out into the middle of the attic, pulled a string on his neckband, and the strange cloak folded up, fitting close around his body.

'What does the sensei intend to do?' Masa asked Tanshin.

'Look down there,' Tanshin muttered gruffly, then went down on all fours and pressed his face to the floor.

So Masa had to do the same.

The floor turned out to have observation slits in it, through which it was possible to observe the corridor and all the rooms.

There were Black Jackets scurrying about everywhere, and the Monk's head was gleaming in the centre of the corridor.

'Haven't you found anything?' he roared, leaning down towards a hole in

471

the floor. 'Sound out every *siaku!** There must be hiding places!'

Lifting his head up from the slit, Masa glanced at Tamba – and just in time.

The *jonin* pressed some kind of lever with his foot and yet another hatch opened, located above the corridor. The old man jumped down, as straight as a spear.

Masa stuck his nose against the floor again, in order not to miss anything.

Ah, what a sight it was!

The *jonin* landed between the Monk and two Black Jackets. They just gaped open-mouthed, but the tricky man with the shaved head jerked to one side and pulled his revolver out of his belt. Ah, but what could he do against Tamba! A short, easy stroke of the sword and the glittering head went tumbling across the floor, and blood spurted out of the severed neck. Without turning round, the old *shinobi* flung his left hand out backwards and gently touched the nose of one of the soldiers: the soldier fell woodenly, without bending, and crashed to the floor. The second man squatted down and covered his head with his hands, and Tamba didn't touch him.

He leaned forward slightly and then ran, slowly at first, but picking up speed all the time, towards the wide-open door with the precipice beyond it. A whole crowd of pursuers dashed after him, shouting and yelling.

Masa was in ecstasy. What a fine idea! To take a final stand on the little bridge above that abyss. First, no one would attack from behind and, secondly, it was so beautiful! And then these Black Jackets didn't have any guns, they had been left outside. Oh, old Tamba would really pulverise them right at the end!

He heard a rustling sound beside him. It was Tanshin jumping to his feet and dashing to the window. He wants to see his master's final battle, Masa realised, and dashed after him as fast as he could.

The little bridge was clearly visible through the wooden grille. The moon peeped out, and the wooden planking turned silver against the black precipice.

There was the *jonin*, running out on to the little bridge at a furious pace, the sides of his cloak jutting out like the wings of a bat. Still running, Tamba pushed off hard with his foot and jumped into the precipice.

But what about the final battle? Masa almost cried out.

He could have killed a dozen or two enemies and then dropped over the edge of the abyss like a stone.

But Tamba didn't fall like a stone!

The Black Jackets crowding on the little bridge howled in horror, and fine drops of cold sweat stood out on Masa's forehead too. And for good reason . . .

The leader of the Momochi clan had turned into a bird!

The huge black hawk soared above the valley, cutting through the moonlight and slowly descending.

---

* A unit of area (0.033 m³)

Masa was brought round by a slap on his shoulder.

'Now we have to act quickly,' said Tanshin. 'Before they can recover their wits.'

Midori-san and the master were already clambering through a hatch on to the roof. He had to catch up with them.

Tiles grated under his feet and a fresh wind blew into his face. Masa turned towards the precipice for another glimpse of the magical bird, but it wasn't there any more – it had flown away.

They crawled the last few steps on their stomachs so that the Black Jackets in the cordon wouldn't see them.

They needn't have been so cautious – the torches were burning in the clearing, but the sentries had disappeared.

'Where are they?' Masa asked in a whisper.

He guessed the answer himself: they had all gone dashing into the house. But of course! The commander had been killed, the head ninja had turned into a hawk. If he hadn't seen it with his own eyes, he would never have believed it.

There was no cordon, but what good was that to them? If they jumped down, they'd break their legs, it was four *ken** here. But Midori-san waved her hand just before the ridge of the roof and a gentle ringing sound filled the emptiness. A thin, transparent cable was stretched from the house out into the darkness. Midori-san took off her belt and threw it over the cable, tied a knot and showed the master how to put his elbows through it. But she herself managed without a strap – she just took hold with her hands, pushed off and soared over the clearing in a single sweep. The master didn't waste any time either: he took a firm hold of the belt and flew off, setting the air rustling.

It was Masa's turn. Tanshin prepared the strap for him in a second and pushed him in the back.

Rushing through space above the brightly lit clearing and the blazing flames was scary but enjoyable. Masa barely managed to stop himself whooping in delight.

The flight could have ended better, though. The trunk of a pine tree came flying towards him out of the darkness and if the master hadn't grabbed his servant by the arms, Masa would have been flattened. As it was, he hit his forehead hard enough to set sparks flying.

There was a small wooden platform attached to the tree, and he had to climb down from it by feeling for branches with his foot.

As soon as he jumped down on to the ground, Masa saw that Tanshin had stayed on the roof – from here, on the other side of the clearing, his black silhouette was clearly visible.

There was a glint of steel, and something rustled in the air. Midori-san picked up the transparent rope and pulled it towards herself.

'Why did he cut the cable?' Masa exclaimed.

---

* A unit of length (1.81m)

'They'll climb up on the roof, see the cable and guess everything,' the mistress replied briefly. 'And Tanshin will jump down.'

As soon as she said it, men climbed out to the roof from below, a lot of men. They saw the *shinobi* poised on the very edge, started clamouring and ran towards him.

But Tanshin huddled down, jumped up, turned over in the air, and a moment later he was down below. He rolled across the ground like a ball and jumped to his feet.

But they were already running towards him out of the house.

'Quickly! Quickly!' Masa whispered, squeezing his fists tight.

The ninja reached the middle of the clearing in a few bounds, but he didn't run into the forest – he stopped.

He doesn't want to lead his pursuers to us, Masa guessed.

Tanshin pulled a torch out of the ground, then another, and rushed at his enemies. The Black Jackets first recoiled from the two furiously swirling tongues of flame, but then immediately closed back round the *shinobi*.

Someone's clothing burst into flames and someone else ran off howling, trying to beat the flames off their burning hair. The fire swirled about above the crowd, stinging, scattering sparks.

They had to get away from there as quickly as possible, but Masa was still watching the beautiful way Tanshin was dying. A fiery death framed in glittering sword blades – could anything possibly be more beautiful?

The master pulled Midori-san into the thicket and pointed in the direction of the crevice – he must be pointing towards the hoist.

Masa had to explain to the bird-man's daughter that they couldn't get away through the underground passage. The Monk must have left sentries at the bottom of the crevice: they wouldn't let anyone get down – they'd shoot them.

'Better to sit it out here, in the forest,' Masa concluded.

But Midori-san didn't agree with him.

'No. The Black Jackets have let my father get away, and now they have to find your master at any cost. They won't dare report to the Don without his head. When they finish searching the house, they'll start combing the forest again.'

'What can we do?'

The mistress was going to answer, but then the master butted into this important conversation at just the wrong moment.

He pulled Masa aside and said in his broken Japanese:

'Lead away, Midori-san. You. Trust. I here.'

Oh no! Masa didn't even listen. He objected gruffly:

'How can I lead her away? I'm not Tamba, I can't fly through the sky.'

He flapped his arms like wings to demonstrate but the master, of course, didn't understand. How could Masa possibly explain anything to him when he had no language?

The Black Jackets flocked round Tanshin's body, arguing about something in loud voices. Many of them had been killed, including the commander, but there were even more left. Thirty men? Forty?

Masa had always been good at mental arithmetic, and he started counting.

The master had seven bullets in his little revolver. Masa could kill three. Or four – if he was lucky. Midori-san was a ninja – she'd probably polish off ten.

How many did that make?

Midori-san prevented him from finishing his calculation.

'Wait here,' she said. 'My father will come back for you.'

'Are you really going away, mistress?'

She didn't answer and turned to the master.

He also asked something in a tense, halting voice.

She didn't answer him either. At least, not in words.

She stroked his cheek, then his neck. A fine time she'd chosen for lovey-doving! A woman was always a woman after all, even if she was a ninja.

Midori-san's hand slipped round to the back of the master's head, the white fingers suddenly closed firmly together – and his round *gaijin* eyes turned even rounder in amazement. The master sat down on the ground, slumping back against a tree trunk.

She had killed him. The accursed witch had killed him.

With a fierce growl, Masa aimed the fatal *kubiori* blow at the traitor: it should have ripped her scurvy throat out, but a strong hand seized his wrist.

'He's alive,' the *shinobi* woman said quickly. 'He simply can't move.'

'But why?' hissed Masa, wincing in pain. What a grip!

'He wouldn't have let me do what must be done.'

'And what is that?'

She let go of him, realising that he would hear her out.

'Go into the house. Go down into the basement. There's a barrel of gunpowder there in a secret place. The charge is calculated to make the house collapse inwards, crushing everyone in it.'

Masa thought for a moment.

'But how will you get into the house?'

'His strength will return in an hour,' Midori-san said instead of answering. 'Stay with him.'

Then she leaned down to the master and whispered something in his ear in *gaijin* language.

And that was all – she went out into the clearing and walked towards the house with a light stride.

They didn't notice her straight away, but when they spotted the figure in the black, close-fitting ninja costume, they were startled.

Midori-san raised her empty hands and shouted.

'Mr Tsurumaki knows me! I am Tamba's daughter! I will show you his secret hiding place!'

The Black Jackets swarmed round her and started searching her. Then the entire crowd moved towards the porch and went into the house. Not a single soul was left outside.

The distance was only about thirty paces, Masa suddenly realised. If there was an explosion, wreckage would come showering down. He had to drag the master farther away.

He put his arms round the motionless body and dragged it across the ground.

But he hadn't carried him very far, only a few steps, when the earth shook and his ears were deafened.

Masa turned round.

Momochi Tamba's house collapsed neatly, as if it had gone down on its knees. First the walls caved in, then the roof swayed and came crashing down and broke in half, sending dust flying in all directions. It was suddenly completely light all around and a blast of hot air hit him in the face.

The servant leaned over to protect the body of his master and saw tears flowing out of the wide-open eyes.

The woman had deceived him. The master did not come round in an hour, or even in two.

Masa went to look at the heap of rubble several times. He dug up an arm in a black sleeve, a leg in a black trouser leg, and also a close-cropped head without a lower jaw. He didn't find a single person alive.

He came back several times and shook the master to make him wake up. The master wasn't actually unconscious, but he just lay there without moving, looking at the sky. At first the tears kept running down his face, then they stopped.

And not long before dawn Tamba appeared – he simply came through the forest from the direction of the crevice, as if everything was perfectly normal.

He said he had been on the other side and killed the sentries. There were only six of them.

'But why didn't you fly here through the sky, sensei?' Masa asked.

'I'm not a bird, to go flying through the sky. I flew down off the cliff on wings made of cloth, a man can learn to do that,' the cunning old man explained, but, of course, Masa didn't believe him.

'What happened here?' asked the sensei, looking at the master lying on the ground and the ruins of the house. 'Where's my daughter?'

Masa told him what had happened and where his daughter was.

The *jonin* knitted his grey eyebrows together but, of course, he didn't cry – he was a ninja.

He said nothing for a long time, then he said:

'I'll get her out myself.'

Masa also said nothing for a while – for as long as was required by consideration for a father's feelings – and then he expressed concern about his master's strange condition. He enquired cautiously whether Midori-san could possibly have tried too hard and whether the master would now be paralysed for ever.

'He can move,' Tamba replied after taking another look at the man on

the ground. 'He just doesn't want to. Let him stay like that for a while. Don't
touch him. I'll go and rake through the rubble. And you cut some firewood
and build a funeral pyre. A big one.'

> I could sit watching,
> Watch it till the break of dawn –
> The flame of the fire

HE DIDN'T ANSWER

Fandorin lay on the ground and looked at the sky. At first it was almost black, lit up by the moon. Then the highlighting disappeared and the sky turned completely black, but seemingly not for long. Its colour kept changing: it became greyish, acquired a reddish glaze and started turning blue.

While Midori's final words were still ringing in his ears ('Farewell, my love. Remember me without sadness') – and that echo lingered for a long, long time – tears flowed unceasingly from benumbed Erast Petrovich's eyes. Gradually, however, the echo faded away and the tears dried up. The titular counsellor simply lay on his back, not thinking about anything, observing the behaviour of the sky.

When grey clouds crept across it, crowding out the blue, Tamba's face leaned down over the man on the ground. Perhaps the old *jonin* had appeared earlier, Fandorin wasn't entirely sure about that. But in any case, until this moment Tamba had not attempted to shut out the sky.

'That's enough,' he said. 'Now get up.'

Erast Petrovich got up. Why not?

'Let's go.'

He went.

He didn't ask the old man any questions – he couldn't care less about anything. But Tamba starting talking anyway. He said he had sent Masa to Tokyo. Masa had been very reluctant to leave his master, but it was necessary to summon Tamba's nephew, a student in the faculty of medicine. Dan was the only one left, if you didn't count the two who were studying abroad. They would come too, although not soon, of course. The Momochi clan had suffered grievous losses, it would have to be restored. And before that Tamba had to settle accounts with Don Tsurumaki.

The titular counsellor listened indifferently. None of this interested him.

In the clearing beside the ruined house a huge stack of firewood had been piled up, with another, smaller stack beside it. On the first stack there were bodies wrapped in black rags packed close together in three rows. Something white and narrow was lying on the second one.

Fandorin didn't really look very closely. When you're standing up it's awkward to tilt your head back to look at the sky, so now he was mostly just examining the grass at his feet.

'Your servant spent several hours chopping and stacking the wood,' said

Tamba. 'And we carried the dead together. They are all here. Most of them have no heads, but that is not important.'

He walked up to the first stack of wood, bent over in a low bow and did not straighten up for a long, long time. Then he lit a torch and touched it to the wood, which flared up immediately – it must have been sprayed with some kind of combustible liquid.

Watching the fire was better than watching the grass. It kept changing its colour all the time, like the sky, and it moved, but still stayed in the same place. Fandorin looked at the flames until the bodies started moving. One dead man squirmed as if he had decided to try sitting up. That was unpleasant. And there was a smell of scorched flesh.

The titular counsellor first turned away, then walked off to the side.

The fire hissed and crackled. But Erast Petrovich stood with his back to it and didn't turn round.

After some time Tamba came over to him.

'Don't keep silent,' he said. 'Say something. Otherwise the *ki* will find no exit and a lump will form in your heart. You could die like that.'

Fandorin didn't know what *ki* was and he wasn't afraid of dying, but he did as the old man asked – why not? He said:

'It's hot. When the wind blows this way, it's hot.'

The *jonin* nodded approvingly.

'Good. Now your heart won't burst. But it is encrusted with ice, and that is also dangerous. I know a very good way to melt ice that shackles the heart. It is vengeance. You and I have the same enemy. You know who.'

Don Tsurumaki, the titular counsellor said in his head, and listened to his own voice – nothing inside him stirred.

'That won't change anything,' he said out loud.

Tamba nodded again.

Neither of them spoke for a while.

'You know, I found her,' the old man said quietly a minute later, or perhaps it was an hour. 'I had to rake through the beams and the planks, but I found her. She's there, look.'

And he pointed to the second pyre.

That was when Erast Petrovich realised what it was lying there, covered with white material. He started shaking. It was impossible to stop the shuddering, it got stronger and stronger with every second.

'She's my daughter. I decided to bury her separately. Come, you can say goodbye.'

But the titular counsellor didn't move from the spot – he just shook his head desperately.

'Don't be afraid. Her body is shattered, but I have covered it. And half of her face survived. Only don't go close.'

Tamba didn't wait, but set off towards the pyre first. He threw back the corner of the cover and Fandorin saw Midori's profile. White, slim, calm – and as beautiful as in life.

Erast Petrovich dashed towards her, but the *jonin* blocked his way.

'No closer!'

Why not? Why not?

The titular counsellor tossed Tamba aside like a dry twig, but the old man grabbed him at a slant round the waist.

'Don't! She wouldn't have wanted it!'

The damned old man was tenacious and Erast Petrovich couldn't move another step farther forward. He went up on tiptoe to see more than just the profile.

And he saw.

The other half of her face was black and charred, like some terrible African mask.

Fandorin recoiled in horror and Tamba shouted angrily:

'Why do you shrink away? Dead ninjas have no faces, but she still has half of one. Because Midori had become only a half-ninja – and that's because of you!' The *jonin*'s voice shook. He lit another torch. 'But never mind. Fire purges everything. Watch. Her body will bend and unbend in the tongues of purifying flame and then crumble into ash.'

But Erast Petrovich didn't want to watch her poor body writhing. He strode off towards the forest, gulping in air with his mouth.

Something had happened to his lungs. The air didn't fill his chest. The small, convulsive breaths were excruciating.

Why, oh why had he not listened to Tamba! Why had he gone up close to the pyre? She had wanted to part beautifully, following all the rules, so that her tender face and her words of farewell would remain in her beloved's memory. But now – and he knew this for certain – everything would be overshadowed by a black-and-white mask: one half indescribably beautiful, the other half the very incarnation of horror and death.

But what was this that had happened to his lungs? His breaths had become short and jerky. And it wasn't that he couldn't breathe in – on the contrary, he couldn't breathe out. The poisoned air of this accursed morning had stuck in his chest and absolutely refused to come back out.

'Your skin is blue,' said Tamba, coming up to him.

The old man's face was calm, even sleepy somehow.

'I can't breathe,' Fandorin explained abruptly.

The *jonin* looked into his eyes and shook his head.

'And you won't be able to. You need to let the bad energy out. Otherwise it will suffocate you. You have to shatter the ice that has gripped your heart so tightly.'

He's talking about the Don again, Erast Petrovich realised.

'All right. I'll go with you. It's not very likely to warm my heart, but perhaps I'll be able to breathe again.'

Behind the titular counsellor's back the flames raged and roared, but he didn't look round.

'I have no weaknesses any more,' said the *jonin*. 'Now I shall become a genuine Tamba. You will also become stronger. You are young. There are very many good women in the world, far more than there are good men. Women will love you, and you will love them.'

Erast Petrovich explained to him:

'I mustn't love anybody. My love brings disaster. I cannot love. I cannot love.'

Tamba didn't answer.

> Nothing is worse than
> When someone knows everything
> But will not answer

A POSTMAN

They set out for Yokohama at night, Fandorin on his tricycle, Tamba running. The tricyclist turned his pedals smoothly and powerfully, but soon fell behind – the ninja moved faster, and he didn't have to stop to tauten a chain or negotiate a stony patch. They hadn't actually arranged to travel together, merely agreed a meeting place: in the Bluff, on the hill that overlooked Don Tsurumaki's house.

Erast Petrovich immersed himself completely in the rhythm of travelling, thinking of nothing but breathing correctly. Breathing was still as difficult as ever for him, but otherwise the titular counsellor felt a lot better than he had during the day. The movement helped. It was as if he had been transformed from a man into a chain-transmission and ball-bearing mechanism. His soul was filled, not so much with peace, as with a certain blessed emptiness, without any thoughts or feelings. If he could have had his way, he would have carried on like this through the sleeping valley until the end of his life, never feeling tired.

There really was no tiredness. Before setting out, Tamba had made Fandorin swallow *kikatsu-maru*, an ancient food that ninjas took with them as rations for long journeys. It was a small, almost tasteless ball moulded out of powder: grated carrot, buckwheat flour, yam and some cunning root or other. The mixture was supposed to be aged for three years, until all the moisture evaporated. According to Tamba, two or three of these little balls were enough to prevent a grown man feeling any hunger or fatigue all day long. And instead of a bottle of water, Erast Petrovich had been given a supply of *suikatsu-maru* – three tiny pellets of sugar, malt and the flesh of marinated plums.

And there was one other present, which was obviously supposed to inflame the thirst for vengeance in Fandorin's indifferent breast: a formal photograph of Midori. The photo seemed to have been taken at the time when she was working in a brothel. Looking out at the titular counsellor from the clumsily coloured portrait was a china doll in a kimono, with a tall hairstyle. He stared at this image for a long time, but didn't recognise Midori in it. And her beauty had disappeared somehow as well. Erast Petrovich thought abstractedly that genuine beauty was impossible to capture with the camera lens: it was too vital, too anomalous and mercurial. Or perhaps the problem was that genuine beauty was not perceived with the eyes, but in some other way.

The journey from Yokohama to the mountains had taken two days. But Erast Petrovich trundled back in five hours. He didn't take a single break, but he wasn't tired at all – no doubt owing to the magical *maru*.

To get into the Bluff, Fandorin needed to go straight on towards the racecourse, but instead of that he steered his vehicle to the left, towards the river, beyond which lay the crowded roofs of the trading quarter, wreathed in the morning mist.

The titular counsellor raced across the Nisinobasi bridge into the straight streets of the Settlement, and found himself, not on the hill where Tamba was no doubt already tired of waiting for him, but on the promenade, in front of a building with the Russian tricolour flying over it.

Erast Petrovich had not changed his route out of any absentmindedness resulting from the shock that he had suffered. There was no absent-mindedness at all. On the contrary, the consequence of the frozen state of his feelings and the hours of mechanical movements was that the titular counsellor's brain had started to function with the direct, linear precision of an adding machine. Wheels whirled, levers clicked and out popped the answer. In his normal condition Fandorin might possibly have over-intellectualised and produced some fancy construction with bells on, but now, while the non-participation of his emotions was absolute, his plan came out amazingly simple and clear.

Erast Petrovich had called round to the consulate or, rather, to his own apartment, on a matter relating directly to his arithmetically precise plan.

As he walked past the bedroom, he averted his gaze (the instinct of self-preservation prompted him to do that), turned on the light in the study and started rummaging through the books. Methodically picking up a volume, leafing through it and dropping it on the floor.

While doing this he muttered unintelligibly under his breath:

'Edgar Allan Poe? Nerval? Schopenhauer?'

He was so absorbed by this mysterious activity that he didn't hear the quiet footsteps behind him.

Suddenly a strident, nervous voice shouted:

'Don't move or I'll shoot!'

Consul Doronin was standing in the doorway of the study, wearing a Japanese dressing gown and holding a revolver in his hand.

'It is I, Fandorin,' the titular counsellor said calmly, glancing round for no more than a second before continuing to rustle the pages. 'Hello, Vsevolod Vitalievich.'

'You!' gasped the consul, without lowering his weapon (owing to surprise, one must assume). 'I saw a light in your windows and the door standing wide open. I thought it was thieves, or something worse . . . Oh Lord, you're alive! Where on earth did you get to? You've been gone for a whole week! I already . . . But where's your Japanese servant?'

'In Tokyo,' Fandorin replied briefly, dropping a work by Proudhon and taking up a novel by Disraeli.

'And. . . . and Miss O-Yumi?'

The titular counsellor froze with the book in his hands, totally overwhelmed by this simple question.

Yes indeed, where was she now? After all, it was impossible for her not to be anywhere at all. Had she migrated to other flesh, in accordance with the Buddhist teachings? Or gone to heaven, where there was a place waiting for all that was truly beautiful? Or gone to hell, which was the right place for sinners?

'. . . I don't know,' he replied after a long pause, at a loss.

The tone of voice in which this was said was enough to prevent Vsevolod Vitalievich from asking his assistant any more about his lover. If Erast Petrovich had been in his normal condition, he would have noticed that the consul himself looked rather strange: he didn't have his habitual spectacles, his eyes were blazing excitedly and his hair was dishevelled.

'What of your expedition to the mountains? Did you discover Tamba's lair?' Doronin asked, but without seeming particularly interested.

'Yes.'

Another book went flying on to the heap.

'And what then?'

The question was left unanswered, and once again the consul did not persist. He finally lowered his weapon.

'What are you looking for?'

'It's just that I put something away and I c-can't remember where,' Fandorin said in annoyance. 'Perhaps in Bulwer-Lytton?'

'Do you know what an incredible stunt Bukhartsev pulled while you were away?' the consul asked with a brief laugh. 'That brute wrote a complaint about you, and he actually sent it to the Third Section. The day before yesterday a coded telegram arrived, with the signature of the chief of gendarmes himself, Adjutant General Mizinov: "Let Fandorin act as he considers necessary". Bukhartsev is totally annihilated. You're the cock of the walk now, as far as the ambassador is concerned. The poor baron was so frightened, he even proposed you for a decoration.'

But this joyful news entirely failed to engage the titular counsellor's interest; in fact he was beginning to demonstrate increasing signs of impatience.

It was a most singular conversation, with the two men hardly even listening to each other: each was preoccupied with his own thoughts.

'I'm so very glad that you have come back!' Vsevolod Vitalievich exclaimed. 'And today of all days! Now that is a genuine sign of destiny!'

At that point the titular counsellor finally tore himself away from his search, looked at the consul a little more closely and realised that he was obviously not his usual self.

'What has happened t-to you. Your cheeks are flushed.'

'Flushed? Really?' exclaimed Doronin, clutching at one cheek in embarrassment. 'Ah, Fandorin, a miracle has happened. My Obayasi is expecting a child! The doctor told us today – there's no doubt about it! I resigned myself long ago to the idea of never being a father, and suddenly . . .'

'Congratulations,' said Erast Petrovich, and wondered what else he might say, but couldn't think of anything and solemnly shook the consul by the hand. 'And why is my return a sign of d-destiny?'

'Why, because I'm resigning! I've already written my letter. My child can't be born illegitimate. I'm getting married. But I won't go back to Russia. People would look askance at a Japanese woman there. Better let them look askance at me instead. I'll register as a Japanese subject and take my wife's family name. I can't have my child called "Dirty Man". A letter of resignation is all very fine of course, but there was no one for me to hand the job over to. You disappeared, Shirota resigned. I was prepared for a lengthy wait. But here you are! What a happy day! You're alive, so now I have someone I can pass things on to.'

Happiness is hard of hearing, and it never even occurred to Vsevolod Vitalievich that his final phrase might sound rather insulting to his assistant, but, in any case, Fandorin did not take offence – unhappiness is not distinguished by keenness of hearing either.

'I remember. Epicurus!' the vice-consul exclaimed, pulling down a book with gilt on the edges of its pages. 'Yes! There it is!'

'What is?' asked the future father.

But the titular counsellor only muttered: 'Later, later, no time just now,' and blundered towards the door.

He never reached the agreed meeting place. On Yatobasi Bridge, beyond which the Bluff proper began, the tricyclist was hailed by a young Japanese man dressed in European style.

Politely raising his straw hat, he said:

'Mr Fandorin, would you care to take some tea?' And he pointed to a sign: 'English and Japanese Tea Parlour'.

Drinking tea had not entered into Erast Petrovich's plans, but being addressed by name like this produced the right impression on the vice-consul.

After surveying the young Japanese youth's short but well-proportioned figure and taking especial note of his calm, exceptionally serious gaze – of a kind not very commonly found among young people – Fandorin asked:

'Are you Dan? The medical student?'

'At your service.'

The 'tea parlour' proved to be one of the hybrid establishments that were quite common in Yokohama: tables and chairs in one section, straw mats and pillows in the other.

At this early hour the English half was almost empty; there was no one but a pastor with his wife and five daughters taking tea with milk at one of the tables.

The titular counsellor's guide led him farther on, slid open a paper partition, and Erast Petrovich saw that there were even fewer customers in the Japanese half – only one, in fact: a lean little old man in a faded kimono.

'Why here? Why not on the hill?' Erast Petrovich asked as he sat down. 'The Black Jackets are up there, are they?'

The *jonin*'s eyes rested inquisitively on the titular counsellor's stony face.

'Yes. How did you know?'

'Not having received a report, the Don realised that his second brigade had also been destroyed. He is expecting vengeance, he has prepared for a siege. And Shirota told him about the hill that has a c-clear view of the whole house. But why don't you tell me how you guessed that I would ride into the Bluff from this side?'

'I didn't. Your servant is waiting on the road that leads from the race-course. He would have brought you here too.'

'So there's no way to g-get into the house.'

'I sat in a tree for a long time, looking through a *gaijin* spyglass. It is very bad. Tsurumaki does not come outside. There are sentries right along the fence. Vengeance will have to be postponed. Possibly for a week, or months, or even years. Never mind, vengeance is a dish that will not go stale.' Tamba lit his little pipe slowly and deliberately. 'I shall tell you how my great-grandfather, Tamba the Eighth, took his revenge on someone who did him wrong. A certain client, a powerful *daimyo*, decided not to pay for work that had been carried out and killed the *shinobi* who came to him to collect the money. It was a great deal of money, and the *daimyo* was greedy. He decided never to leave the confines of his castle again – indeed he never left his own chambers, nor did he allow anyone else into them. Then Tamba the Eighth ordered his son, a boy of nine, to get a job in the kitchen of the castle. The boy was diligent and he was gradually promoted. First he swept the yard, then the back rooms. Then he became the servants' scullion. Then an apprentice to the prince's chef. He spent a long time learning how to grate paste from a shark's bladder – that requires especial skill. Finally, by the time he was nineteen, he had attained such a degree of perfection that he was allowed to prepare a difficult meal for the prince. That was the last day of the *daimyo*'s life. Retribution had taken ten years.'

Fandorin listened to this colourful story and thought: Live ten years with cramped lungs? No thank you.

But to be honest, another thought also occurred to him: What if vengeance doesn't help?

This question went unanswered. Erast Petrovich asked a different one out loud.

'Did you see Shirota in your spyglass?'

'Yes, many times. Both outside and in a window of the house.'

'And a white woman? Tall, with yellow hair woven into a long plait?'

'There are no women in the house. There are only men.' The *jonin* was looking at Fandorin with ever greater interest.

'Just as I thought. In planning the defence, Shirota sent his fiancée to some s-safe place ...' Erast Petrovich said with a nod of satisfaction. 'We don't have to wait for ten years. And a shark's bladder will not be required either.'

'And what will we require?' Tamba asked in a very, very quiet voice, as if afraid of frightening away the prey.

His nephew leaned forward eagerly, with his eyes fixed on the *gaijin*. But Fandorin turned away and looked out at the street through the open window. His attention seemed to have been caught by a blue box hanging on a pillar. There were two crossed post horns on it.

His answer consisted of only two words:

'A postman.'

Uncle and nephew exchanged glances.

'A man who delivers letters?' the *jonin* asked, to make quite certain.

'Yes, a man who d-delivers letters.'

> Letter-bag brimful
> Of love and joy and sorrow –
> Here comes a postman

THE REAL AKUNIN

The municipal express post, one of the greatest conveniences produced by the nineteenth century, had made its appearance in the Settlement only recently, and therefore the local inhabitants had recourse to its services more frequently than genuine necessity required. The postmen delivered not only official letters addressed, say, from a trading firm on Main Street to the customs office on the Bund, but also invitations to five o'clock tea, advertisement leaflets, intimate missives and even notes from a wife to a husband, informing him that it was time to go to lunch.

After Fandorin dropped the envelope with the five-cent 'lightning' stamp on it into the slit above the crossed post horns, less than half an hour went by before a fine young fellow in a dandified blue uniform rode up on a pony, checked the contents of the box and went clopping off over the cobblestones up the slope – to deliver the correspondence to the addressee at Number 130, the Bluff.

'What is in the envelope?' Tamba asked for the fourth time.

The first three attempts had produced no response. Fandorin's feverish agitation as he addressed the envelope had given way to apathy. The *gaijin* didn't hear any questions that he was asked – he sat there, gazing blankly at the street, every now and then beginning to gulp in air through his mouth and rub his chest, as if his waistcoat was too tight for him.

But old Tamba was patient. He waited and waited – and then asked again. And then again.

Eventually he got an answer.

'Eh?' Erast Petrovich asked with a start. 'In the envelope? A poem. The moment Shirota reads it, he'll lose control and come running. And he'll pass along this street, over the b-bridge. Alone.'

Tamba didn't understand about the poem, but he didn't ask any questions – it wasn't important.

'Alone? Very good. We'll grab him, it won't be hard.'

He leaned across to Dan and started speaking rapidly in Japanese. The nephew kept nodding and repeating:

'*Hai, hai, hai . . .*'

'There's no need to grab him,' said Fandorin, interrupting their planning. 'It will be enough if you simply bring him here. Can you do that?'

Shirota appeared very soon – Tamba had barely finished his preparations.

There was the sound of rapid hoof beats and a horseman in a panama hat and a light, sandy-coloured suit came riding round the bend. The former secretary was unrecognisable, so elegant, indeed dashing, did he look. He had the black brush of a moustache sprouting under his flattish nose, and instead of the little steel-rimmed spectacles, his face was adorned with a brand new gold pince-nez.

The native gentleman's flushed features and the furious gait of his mount suggested that Shirota was in a terrible hurry, but he was obliged to pull back on the reins just before the bridge, when a hunchbacked beggar in a dusty kimono threw himself across the horseman's path.

He grabbed hold of the bridle and started begging in a repulsive, plaintively false descant whine.

Restraining his overheated horse, Shirota abused the mendicant furiously and jerked on the reins, but the tramp had clutched them in a grip of iron.

Erast Petrovich observed this little incident from the window of the tea parlour, trying to stay in the shadow. Two or three passers-by, attracted for a brief moment by the shouting, had already turned away from such an uninteresting scene and gone about their business.

For half a minute the horseman tried in vain to free himself. Then, at last, he realised there was a quicker way. Muttering curses, he rummaged in his pocket, fished out a coin and tossed it to the old man.

And it worked – the beggar immediately let go of the reins. In a sudden impulse of gratitude, he seized his benefactor's hand and pressed his lips against it (he must have seen *gaijins* doing that somewhere). Then he jumped back, gave a low bow and scurried away.

Amazingly enough, though, Shirota seemed to have forgotten that he was in a hurry; he shook his head, then rubbed his temple, as if he were trying to remember something. Then suddenly he swayed drunkenly and slumped sideways.

He would quite certainly have fallen, and probably bruised himself cruelly on the cobblestones, if a young native man of a most respectable appearance had not been walking by. The youth managed to catch the fainting horseman in his arms and the proprietor of the tea parlour came running out to help, together with the pastor, who had abandoned his numerous family.

'Drunk?' shouted the proprietor.

'Dead?' shouted the pastor.

The young man felt Shirota's pulse and said:

'Fainted. I'm a doctor . . . That is, I soon will be a doctor.' He turned to the proprietor. 'If you would allow us to carry this man into your establishment, I could help him.'

The three of them lugged the insensible body into the tea parlour and, since there was nowhere to put the sick man down in the English half, they carried him through into the Japanese half with its tatami – to the very spot where Erast Petrovich was finishing his tea.

It took a few minutes to get rid of the proprietor, and especially the pastor, who was very keen to comfort the martyr in his final minutes. The medical student explained that it was an ordinary fainting fit, there was no danger and the patient merely needed to lie down for a little while.

Soon Tamba came back. It was impossible to recognise this respectable-looking, clean old man as the repulsive beggar from the bridge. The *jonin* waited for the outsiders to go, then he leaned over Shirota, squeezed his temples with his fingers and sat down to one side.

The renegade came round immediately.

He batted his eyelids, studying the ceiling quizzically. He raised his head – and met the titular counsellor's cold, blue-eyed gaze. He jerked upright and noticed the two Japanese near by. He barely glanced at young Dan, but stared at the quiet little old man as if he had never seen a more terrifying sight.

Shirota turned terribly pale and drops of sweat stood out on his forehead.

'Is that Tamba?' he asked Fandorin. 'Yes, I recognised him from the description . . . This is what I was afraid of! That they had kidnapped Sophie. How can you, a civilised man, be in league with those ghouls?'

But when he glanced once again at his former colleague's stony face, his features drooped and he murmured:

'Yes, yes, of course . . . You had no choice . . . I understand. But I know you are a noble man. You will not allow the *shinobi* to do her any harm! Erast Petrovich, Mr Fandorin, you also love, you will understand me!'

'No, I will not,' the vice-consul replied indifferently. 'The woman I loved is dead. Thanks to your efforts. Tamba said that you drew up the plan of the operation. Well then, the Don is fortunate in his choice of d-deputy.'

Shirota looked at Erast Petrovich in terror, frightened less by the meaning of the words than the lifeless tone in which they were spoken.

He whispered fervently:

'I . . . I'll do whatever they want, only let her go! She doesn't know anything, she doesn't understand anything about my business. She must not be held as a hostage! She is an angel!'

'It never even entered my head to t-take Sophia Diogenovna hostage,' Fandorin replied in the same dull, strangled voice. 'What scurrilous nonsense you talk.'

'That's not true! I have received a note from her. This is Sophie's hand!' Shirota extracted the small sheet of pink paper from the torn envelope and read out: '"My poor heart can bear this no more. Oh come quickly to help me now! And if you do not come, you know I shall lose my life for you". Tamba guessed where I had hidden Sophie and kidnapped her!'

The fiancé of the 'captain's daughter' was a pitiful sight: lips trembling, pince-nez dangling on its lace, fingers intertwined imploringly.

But Erast Petrovich was not moved by this selfless love. The vice-consul rubbed his chest (those cursed lungs!) and simply said:

'It's not a note. It's a poem.'

'A poem?' Shirota exclaimed in amazement. 'Oh, come now! I know what Russian poems are like. There's no rhyme here: "more" and "know" is not a rhyme. You can have no rhymes in blank verse, but that has rhythm. For instance, Pushkin: "I visited once more that corner of the earth where I spent two forgotten years in exile". But this has no rhythm.'

'But even so, it is a poem.'

'Ah, perhaps it is a poem in prose,' Shirota exclaimed with a flash of insight. 'Like Turgenev! "I fancied then that I was somewhere in the Russian backwoods, in a simple village house".'

'Perhaps,' said Erast Petrovich, who did not wish to argue. 'But in any case, Sophia Diogenovna is not in any danger, I have n-no idea where you have hidden her.'

'So you . . . You simply wanted to lure me out!' Shirota flushed bright red. 'Well then, you have succeeded. But I won't tell you anything! Not even if your *shinobi* torture me.' At those words he turned pale again. 'I'd rather bite my tongue off.'

Erast Petrovich winced slightly.

'No one is intending to torture you. You will get up in a moment and leave. I have met you here to ask you one single question. And you do not even have to answer it.'

Totally confused now, Shirota muttered:

'You will let me go? Even if I don't answer?'

'Yes.'

'I don't somehow . . . Oh, very well, very well, ask.'

Looking him in the eye, Fandorin said slowly:

'I remember you used to call me a friend. And you said that you were in my debt for ever. Then you betrayed me, although I trusted you. Tell me, sincere man and admirer of Pushkin, does serving the Fatherland really justify absolutely any kind of villainy?'

Shirota frowned tensely, expecting a continuation. But none came.

'That's all. The question has been asked. You can choose not to answer it. And g-goodbye.'

The admirer of Pushkin turned red again. Seeing Fandorin getting up, he exclaimed:

'Wait, Erast Petrovich!'

'Let's go,' said Fandorin, beckoning wearily to Tamba and his nephew.

'I did not betray you!' Shirota said hastily. 'I set the Don a condition – that you must remain alive.'

'After which his men attempted to kill me several times . . . The woman who was dearer to me than anything else in the world was killed. Killed because of you. Goodbye, sincere man.'

'Where are you going?' Shirota shouted after him.

'To your patron. I have a score to settle with him.'

'But he will kill you!'

'How so?' asked the titular counsellor, turning round. 'He promised you to let me live, did he not?'

Shirota dashed up to him and grabbed hold of his shoulder.

'Erast Petrovich, what am I to do? If I help you, I shall betray my Fatherland! If I help my Fatherland I shall destroy you, and then I am a low scoundrel, and the only thing left for me to do will be kill to myself!' His eyes blazed with fire. 'Yes, yes, that is a solution. If Don Tsurumaki kills you, I shall kill myself!'

A faint semblance of feeling stirred in Fandorin's frozen soul – it was spite. Fanning this feeble spark in the hope that it would grow into a salutary flame, the titular counsellor hissed:

'Why, at the slightest little moral difficulty, do you Japanese immediately do away with yourselves? As if that will turn a villainous deed into a noble act! It won't! And the good of the Fatherland has nothing to do with it! I wish no harm to your precious Fatherland, I wish harm to the *akunin* by the name of Don Tsurumaki! Are you eternally in his debt too?'

'No, but I believe this man is capable of leading Japan on to the path of progress and civilisation. I help him because I am a patriot!'

'What would you do with the man who killed Sophia Diogenovna? Ah, now see how your eyes blaze! Help me take revenge for my love and then serve your Fatherland, who's stopping you? Get yourselves a constitution, build up the army and the navy, put the foreign powers in their place. Are p-progress and civilisation impossible without the bandit Tsurumaki? Then they're not worth a bent kopeck. And another thing. You say you are a patriot. But how can a man really be a patriot if he knows that he is a scoundrel?'

'I need to think,' Shirota whispered. He hung his head and made for the door.

Dan waited for him to leave the room and then started after him without a sound, but Tamba stopped his nephew.

'What a pity that I don't know Russian,' said the *jonin*. 'I don't know what you said to him, but I have never seen the zone of self-satisfaction below the left cheekbone change its form and colour so irrevocably in five minutes.'

'Don't be too quick to celebrate,' said Erast Petrovich, anguished to feel that the flame of wrath had not taken hold – the little spark had shrivelled away to nothing, and once again it was difficult to breathe. 'He has to think.'

'Shirota has already decided everything, he simply hasn't realised it yet. Now it will all be very simple.'

Naturally, the master of *ninso* was not mistaken.

Indeed, the operation looked so simple that Tamba wanted to take only Dan with him, but Erast Petrovich insisted on taking part. He knew he would be a burden to the Stealthy Ones, but he was afraid that if he did not exterminate Tsurumaki with his own hands, the tight ring constricting his chest would never open again.

In a secluded spot on the high seashore, they changed into black and covered their faces with masks.

'A genuine *shinobi*,' said Tamba, shaking his head as he examined the titular counsellor. 'Only very lanky . . .'

Masa was ordered to stay and guard the clothes, and when Fandorin's servant tried to rebel, Tamba took him gently by the neck and pressed – and the rebel closed his eyes, lay down on the ground and started snuffling sweetly.

They didn't head straight for the gates – there were always sentries on duty there. They went through the garden of the Right Honourable Algernon Bullcox. The ferocious mastiffs were pacified by Dan; he blew into a little pipe three times, and the terrifying monsters sank into a peaceful sleep, just like Masa.

As they walked past the familiar house with the dark windows, Erast Petrovich kept looking up at the first floor and waiting for something to stir in his soul. Nothing stirred.

They stopped at the small gate that led out of the garden into the neighbouring estate. Dan took out some kind of slide-whistle and trilled like a cicada.

The gate swung open without a sound, not even the spring jangled – Shirota had taken care of that by lubricating the gate earlier.

'That way,' said Fandorin, pointing towards the pond and the dark silhouette of the pavilion.

Everything was set to end where it had begun. In a detailed note, Shirota had informed them that Tsurumaki did not spend the night in the house. One of his men went to bed in his room and the master of the house went off to sleep in the pavilion. No one else in the house knew about this, apart from Shirota and two bodyguards.

That was why Tamba regarded the operation as not very complicated.

As they approached the pavilion where he had spent so many happy hours, Erast listened to his heart again – would it start pounding or not? No, it didn't.

The *jonin* put his hand on Fandorin's shoulder and gestured for him to lie down on the ground. Only the *shinobi* went on from there. They didn't crawl, they didn't freeze on the spot – they simply walked, but in such an amazing way that Fandorin could hardly see them.

The shadows of the night clouds slid across the grass and the paths, and Tamba and his nephew managed to stay in the dark patches all the time, not getting caught even once in a brightly lit patch.

When the sentry on duty between them and the pool suddenly turned his head and listened, they both froze absolutely still. It seemed to Erast Petrovich that the bodyguard was looking straight at the Stealthy Ones, who were separated from him by a distance of no more than ten paces. But the sentry yawned and started gazing at the glimmering surface of the water again.

There was a very faint sound, like a light exhalation. The sentry tumbled over gently on to his side, dropping his carbine. Dan had fired a dart from his blowpipe. The sleeping drug took effect instantly. The man would wake up in fifteen minutes' time, and think he had just dozed off a second ago. The young ninja ran straight over to the wall and round the corner. A few moments later he peeped back round and gave a signal: the second bodyguard had also been put to sleep.

Fandorin could get up now.

Tamba was waiting for the titular counsellor by the door. He didn't let Fandorin go ahead, though, but ducked in first himself.

He leaned down over the sleeping man for no more than an instant and then said in a voice that was low, but not a whisper:

'Come in, he's yours.'

The night lamp came on with a flash – the same one that Erast Petrovich had used so many times. Don Tsurumaki was lying on the futon with his eyes closed.

Even the bed was the same one . . .

Tamba shook his head as he looked at the sleeping man.

'I pressed his sleep point, he won't wake up. A good death, with no fear or pain. An *akunin* like this deserves worse.' He held out a little stick with a pointed end. 'Prick him on the chest or the neck. Lightly, so that only one drop of blood seeps out. That will be enough – no one will guess that the Don was killed. The bodyguards will swear that they never closed their eyes. A natural death. His heart stopped in his sleep. It happens with excessively full-blooded individuals.'

Erast Petrovich looked at the ruddy features of his sworn enemy in the grip of a magical stupor. This is no chimerical déjà vu, he told himself. This really has happened once before. I stood over the sleeping Don and listened to his regular breathing. But everything was different then. He wasn't asleep, he was pretending. That is one. I was the prey and not the hunter. That is two. And on that occasion my heart was pounding, but now it is calm.

'I cannot kill a sleeping man,' said Fandorin. 'Wake him.'

Tamba muttered something under his breath – invective, no doubt. But he didn't argue.

'All right. Only be careful. He is cunning and brave.'

The *jonin* touched the fat man's neck and skipped back into the shadow.

Tsurumaki started and opened his eyes, which opened wider at the sight of the black figure with one hand raised.

Erast Petrovich pulled the mask off his face, and the Don's eyes opened wider still.

The most stupid thing that Erast Petrovich could do in this situation was enter into conversation with the condemned man, but how could he strike a man who was unarmed, and without saying anything, like an executioner?

'It's not a dream,' said Fandorin. 'Farewell, *akunin*, and may you be cursed.'

Well, he had said his farewell, but he still hadn't struck the blow.

Who could tell how all this would have ended – but the titular counsellor was lucky. Don Tsurumaki, a man with strong nerves, snatched a revolver out from under his pillow, and then, with a feeling of relief, Erast Petrovich prodded the villain on the collarbone.

The Don made a strange, snoring sound, dropped the gun, twitched several times and lay still. The whites of his upturned eyes glinted between the half-closed eyelids.

Fandorin tried to breathe with his full chest, but he couldn't!

What was this? The death of his enemy had not brought him relief? Perhaps because it had happened too quickly and simply?

He swung his hand back to strike another blow, but Tamba interfered and grabbed his wrist.

'Enough! It will leave marks.'

'I still can't get my breath.'

'That's all right, it will pass off now,' said the *jonin*, slapping the vice-consul on the back. 'The death of an enemy is the very best medicine.'

Incredibly enough, at those words Fandorin suddenly felt better. It was as if some kind of spring unwound inside him. He breathed in cautiously – and the air flowed easily into his chest, filling it right up. The sensation was so delightful that it set Erast Petrovich's head spinning.

So it hadn't all been in vain!

While the titular counsellor was relishing his new-found freedom of breath, Tamba hid the revolver under the pillow again, laid the dead man out more naturally, opened his mouth slightly, sprayed something into it, and bubbles of foam sprang out on to the lips. Then he lowered the collar of the nightshirt and wiped away the solitary drop of blood.

'That's it, let us go! Let us not cause trouble for our friend Shirota. Well, what's wrong with you?'

Fandorin's clarity of thought had returned to him together with his breathing. He looked at Tamba, and seemed to see him properly for the first time – see all of him, just as he was, right through.

'*Our friend?*' Erast Petrovich repeated slowly. 'Why, of course, this whole business is about Shirota. That's what you needed me for. You could have avenged yourself on the Don without me. But that's not enough for you, you want to restore your alliance with the powerful organisation that Tsurumaki created. You calculated that once the Don was gone, Shirota, his right-hand man, would take over the organisation. Especially if you helped him to do it. But you didn't know how to approach Shirota. And then you decided to use me. Right?'

The *jonin* didn't answer. The eyes in the slit of his mask blazed with a furious fire. But, swept on by the irrepressible flood of liberated mental energy, Fandorin continued:

'I couldn't breathe! Now I remember how it began. Beside the funeral pyre, when you pretended to restrain me, you squeezed my chest very hard! I thought I couldn't breathe because of the shock, but it was all your tricks. With my lungs half paralysed, my soul frozen and my rational mind numbed, I was like wax in your hands. And the reason why it has passed off just now is nothing to do with the death of my enemy – it's because you slapped me on the back! But now I've played my part, and my usefulness is exhausted. You're going to kill me. The Don was a villain, but the blood in all his veins was alive and hot. He wasn't the real *akunin*, you are – with your cold heart, devoid of all love and nobility. You didn't even love your daughter at all. Poor Midori! At her funeral all you were thinking about was how to make the most advantageous use of her death!'

Evidently Erast Petrovich's mental clarity had not returned to him in full. Otherwise he would not have shouted his accusations out loud, he would not have shown that he had seen through the old *shinobi*'s game.

There was only one way to correct this fatal error. The titular counsellor lunged, aiming the poisoned stick at the schemer's chest. But Tamba was prepared for an attack. He dodged and struck Fandorin gently on the wrist, leaving the hand dangling limply. The *jonin* immediately took the wooden weapon.

Erast Petrovich was not in the right state of mind to clutch at life. Holding his numbed hand, he turned his chest towards Tamba and waited for the blow.

'Your conclusions are only half right,' said the *jonin*, putting the small stick away. 'Yes, I am a real *akunin*. But I won't kill you. Let us get out of here. The guards will wake up any minute now. This is not the time or the place for explanations. Especially since they will be long. Let us go. And I'll tell you about the Diamond Chariot and a real *akunin*.'

A real *akunin* –
Husky laugh, knife in his teeth
And wild, crazy eyes

THUS SPAKE TAMBA

Tamba said:

'The sun will rise soon. Let's go up on to the cliff, watch the dawn and talk.'

They went back to the spot where Masa was waiting, surly and offended. They changed their clothes.

Erast Petrovich had already realised why the old ninja didn't kill him in the pavilion. It would have contradicted the story of the Don's supposed natural death and cause problems for Shirota in taking the dead man's place.

There was only one thing he could do now: try to save Masa.

Calling his servant off to one side, the titular counsellor handed him a note and told him to run to Doronin at the consulate as fast as his legs would carry him.

Tamba observed this scene impassively – he was obviously certain that Masa would not escape from him anyway.

Probably that was it. But the note said: 'Send my servant to the embassy immediately, his life is in danger'. Doronin was an intelligent and reliable man – he would do it. Tamba probably wouldn't bother to break into a foreign embassy in order to kill a witness who was not really all that much of a threat. And in the final analysis, the *jonin* had only one assistant now.

So that Masa would not suspect anything was amiss, Erast Petrovich smiled at him cheerily.

His servant stopped sulking straight away, replied with a beaming smile of his own and exclaimed something in a joyful voice.

'He is happy that his master is smiling,' Dan translated. 'He says that vengeance has done his master good. He is very sorry for Midori-san, of course, but there will be other women.'

Then Masa ran off to carry out his errand, and they let Dan go too.

The two of them were left alone.

'There is a good view from over there,' said the *jonin*, pointing to a high cliff with white breakers foaming at its foot.

They started walking up a narrow path: the *shinobi* in front, the titular counsellor behind.

Erast Petrovich was almost half as tall again as him, he had his trusty Herstal lying in its holster and his adversary was even standing with his back to him, but Fandorin knew that against this lean little old man he was as helpless as a baby. The *jonin* could kill him at any moment.

Well, let him, thought Erast Petrovich. Death didn't frighten him. Or even interest him very much.

They sat side by side on the edge of the cliff, with their legs dangling.

'Of course, watching the dawn on the edge of the precipice was much better.' Tamba sighed, no doubt remembering his ruined house. 'But here there is the sea.'

Just then the sun peeped over the edge of the world, transforming the watery plain into a steppe blazing with wildfire.

Despite himself, the titular counsellor felt something like gratitude – he was going to be killed beautifully. No doubt about it, the Japanese were connoisseurs when it came to death.

'There's just one thing I don't understand,' he said, without looking at his companion. 'Why am I still alive?'

Tamba said:

'She had two requests. The first was for me not to kill you.'

'And the second?'

'To teach you the Way. If you wanted me to. I have kept my first promise, and I will keep the second. Even though I know that our Way is not for you.'

'I don't want your Way, thank you very much,' Fandorin said with a sideways glance at the *jonin*, not sure whether he could trust him. What if this was just another Jesuitical trick? A simple movement of his elbow, and the vice-consul would go flying down on to the sharp rocks below. 'A fine Way it is, built on villainy and deception.'

Tamba said:

'I brought you here so that you could see the departure of darkness and the arrival of light. But I should have brought you at sunset, when the opposite happens. Tell me, which is better, sunrise or sunset?'

'A strange question,' Fandorin said with a shrug. 'They are both natural events, essential phenomena of nature.'

'Precisely. The world consists of Light and Darkness. Of Good and Evil. The man who adheres to Good alone is unfree, he is restricted, like a traveller who only dares to travel by the bright light of day, or a ship that can only sail with a fair wind. The man who is truly strong and free is the one who is not afraid to wander through a dark thicket at night. That dark thicket is the world in all its completeness, it is the human soul with all its contradictions. Do you know about Mahayana and Hinayana Buddhism?'

'Yes, I have heard about that. The Hinayana, or Lesser Vehicle, is when a man seeks to save himself through self-improvement. The Mahayana, or Greater Vehicle, is when you seek to save the whole of m-mankind, or something of the sort.'

Tamba said:

'In reality these two vehicles are the same. They both call on men to live only by the laws of Good. They are intended for ordinary, weak people – in other words they are one-sided, incomplete. A strong man has no need to restrict himself to the Good, he does not need to squeeze one eye tight shut to avoid accidentally seeing something terrible.'

Tamba said:

'There is a third vehicle, and the privilege of mounting it is granted only to a small number of the elect. It is called *Kongojyo*, the Diamond Chariot, because it is as strong as diamond. We Stealthy Ones are riders in the Diamond Chariot. To ride in it means to live by the rules of the entire creation, including Evil. And that is the same as living without rules and contrary to the rules: the Way of the Diamond Chariot is the Way to truth through comprehension of the laws of Evil. It is a secret teaching for the initiated, who are willing to make any sacrifices in order to discover themselves.'

Tamba said:

'The Way of the Diamond Chariot teaches that the Greater World, which is the world of a man's soul, is incomparably more important than the Lesser World, which is the world of human relations. In actual fact, sacrificing yourself for the sake of others is the worst possible crime in the eyes of the Buddha. A man is born, lives and dies face to face with God alone. Everything else is merely visions created by a Higher Power in order to subject a man to tests. The great religious teacher Shinran stated: "Reflecting profoundly on the will of the Buddha Amida, I shall find that the whole of creation was conceived for me alone".'

Tamba said:

'Ordinary people are torn between the illusory world of human relations and the real world of the free soul, and constantly betray the latter in the name of the former. We Stealthy Ones are able to distinguish diamond from coal. All things exalted by ordinary morality are mere empty words to us. Killing is not a sin, deception is not a sin, cruelty is not a sin, if they are necessary in order to race on along the appointed Way in the Diamond Chariot. To riders in the Diamond Chariot, the crimes for which riders in the Greater and Lesser Chariots are cast down into hell are merely the means to attaining Buddha nature.'

The titular counsellor had to protest at that:

'If human relations are nothing for you diamond riders and deception is no sin, why keep your word to someone who is no longer among the living? What does it matter if you did promise your daughter? Treachery is a virtue for you, is it not? Kill me, and it's all over and done with. Why waste time on me, reading me sermons?'

Tamba said:

'You are right and wrong at the same time. Right, because to break the promise given to my dead daughter would be to act correctly, it would raise me to a higher level of freedom. And wrong because Midori was more than a daughter to me. She was an Initiate, my companion in the Diamond Chariot. This chariot is cramped, those who ride in it must follow certain rules – but only in relation to each other. Otherwise we will start jostling each other with our elbows, and the Chariot will overturn. That is the only law by which we abide. It is much stricter than the ten commandments that the Buddha proclaimed for ordinary weak people. Our rules say: If a companion in the Chariot has asked you to die, then do it; even if he has asked you to jump out of the Chariot, do it – otherwise you will not reach the Destination to which you aspire. What is Midori's little whim in comparison with this?'

'I am a little whim,' Erast Petrovich muttered.

Tamba said:

'It is not important what you believe in and what you dedicate your life to. That does not matter to the Buddha. What is important is to be faithful to your calling – that is the essential thing, because then you are faithful to yourself, which means you are also faithful to the Buddha. We *shinobi* serve a client for money and, if necessary, we willingly give our lives – but not for the sake of money, and even less for the sake of the client, whom we often despise. We are faithful to Fidelity and we serve Service. Everyone around us is warm or hot, we alone are always cold, but our icy chill scorches more powerfully than fire.'

Tamba said:

'I will tell you a true legend about something said by Buddha, one which is known only to a few initiates. The Supreme One once appeared to the bodhisattvas and told them: "If you kill living things, excel in falsehood, consume excrement and wash it down with urine – only then will you become Buddha. If you fornicate with your mother, sister and daughter and commit a thousand other atrocities, there is an exalted place in store for you in the kingdom of the Buddha". The virtuous bodhisattvas were horrified by these words, they trembled and fell to the ground.'

'And they did right!' Fandorin observed.

'No. They did not understand what the Supreme One was talking about.'

'Well, what was he talking about?'

'About the fact that Good and Evil do not really exist. The first commandment in both your religion and ours is: Do not kill. Tell me, is it good or bad to kill?'

'Bad.'

'And to kill a tigress that has attacked a child, is that good or bad?'

'Good.'

'Good for whom? For the child, or for the tigress and her cubs? This is what the Buddha was expounding to the holy beings. Surely, under a certain set of circumstances, the actions that He listed, which seemed so vile to the bodhisattvas, can be an expression of supreme nobility or self-sacrifice? Think before you answer.'

The titular counsellor thought.

'Probably they can . . .'

Tamba said:

'And if this is so, of what great value is a commandment that restrains Evil? There must be someone to possess complete mastery of the art of Evil, so that it will be transformed from a fearsome enemy into an obedient slave.'

Tamba said:

'The Diamond Chariot is the Way for those who live by murder, theft and all the other mortal sins, but still do not lose hope of attaining Nirvana. There cannot be many of us, but *we must exist and we always do*. The world needs us, and the Buddha does not forget us. We are as much His servants as all the others. We are the knife with which He cuts the umbilical cord, and the nail with which He tears the scab off the body.'

'No!' Erast Petrovich exclaimed. 'I don't agree with you! You have chosen the way of Evil, because that is what you wanted for yourself. It is not what God wants!'

Tamba said:

'I did not promise to persuade you, I promised to explain. I told my daughter: He is not one of the chosen. You will not attain the Greater knowledge, you will be confined to the Lesser. I shall do what I promised Midori. You will come to me and I shall teach you, little by little, all that you are capable of mastering. That will be enough for you to pass for a strong man in the world of people of the West. Are you willing to learn?'

'The Lesser Knowledge, yes. But I do not want your Greater Knowledge.'

'Well then, so be it ... To begin with, forget everything you have ever learned. Including what I have taught you before. We are only starting our real studies now. Let us start with the great art of *kiai*: how to focus and direct the spiritual energy of *ki* while maintaining the quiescence of the *shin*, which Western people call the soul. Look into my eyes and listen.'

Forget your reading.
Learn to read all things anew.
Thus spake the *sensei*

PS. THE LETTER WRITTEN AND BURNED BY THE PRISONER KNOWN AS THE ACROBAT
27 MAY 1905

Father,

It feels strange to call you that, for since I was a boy I have been used to addressing someone else, the man in whose house I grew up, as 'father'.

Today I looked at you and recalled what I had been told about you by my grandfather, my mother and my adopted relatives.

My journey has reached its end. I have been faithful to my Way and walked it as I was taught, trying not to succumb to doubts. It is all the same to me how this war ends. I have not fought against your country. I have fought to overcome the obstacles which malicious Fate has raised up on the Path of my Chariot in order to test me. The most difficult test of all was the one at which the heart softens, but I have overcome even that.

I am not writing this letter out of sentimentality, but to fulfil a request from my late mother.

She once said to me: 'In the world of Buddha there are many wonders, and it may happen that someday you will meet your father. Tell him that I wished to part from him beautifully, but your grandfather was adamant; "If you wish your *gaijin* to live, then do my bidding. He must see you dead and mutilated. Only then will he do what I require". I did as he ordered, and it has tormented me for the rest of my life'.

I know this story, I have heard it many times – how my mother sheltered from the blast in a secret hiding place, how my grandfather dragged her out from under the rubble, how she lay on the funeral pyre with black clay daubed over half her face.

The only thing I do not know is the meaning of the phrase that my mother asked me to relay to you if a miracle were to happen and we should meet.

That phrase is this: YOU CAN LOVE.